"THE HEART DID SPEAK TO ME . . ."

"What did it say?" Margret's words were gruff.

"I . . . I'm not certain."

"What do you mean, not certain? Riddles? Prophecy?"

"Your pardon, Matriarch. I meant simply that while the Heart speaks, it speaks in a language I do not understand. I think that you should hear what it says."

Margaret gestured. The wagon rose out of the tunnel. "Not yet," she said. "Not so close to the ground that the words can be heard.

"Here," Margaret said when they'd climbed high above the Arkosan camp. "Here we can talk. What did the Heart say?"

As Diora began to speak—her voice retrieving the sounds of an old tongue—she watched Margret's face, and she knew, the moment she saw the changing shape of the older woman's mouth, that she should have come in haste. "Matriarch!" Diora said. "What is it saying?"

"Zahar Serpensan."

"What is that?"

"Serpent's tears," Margret said hoarsely. She was almost immobile. "Wake them, help me wake them!" But if Margaret was immobile, her voice was not; it shook like plates of earth.

She was terrified. . . .

The Finest in Fantasy from
MICHELLE WEST:

THE SUN SWORD:
THE BROKEN CROWN (Book One)
THE UNCROWNED KING (Book Two)
THE SHINING COURT (Book Three)
SEA OF SORROWS (Book Four)

THE SACRED HUNT:
HUNTER'S OATH (Book One)
HUNTER'S DEATH (Book Two)

Sea of Sorrows

The Sun Sword: Book Four

Michelle West

DAW BOOKS, INC.
DONALD A. WOLLHEIM, FOUNDER
375 Hudson Street, New York, NY 10014
ELIZABETH R. WOLLHEIM
SHEILA E. GILBERT
PUBLISHERS
www.dawbooks.com

Cover art by Paul Youll.
Map by Michael Gilbert.

DAW Book Collectors No. 1184.

First Printing, May 2001
1 2 3 4 5 6 7 8 9

This is for Kristen, who, having married into an unusual extended family, has borne all oddities with (gentle) humor and grace, and who—much to my deep gratitude—has never once mentioned that she did, over dinner at my mother's very crowded table, come up with the title for *The Shining Court*, a fact I completely forgot when I wrote the acknowledgments to that book.

I'm always too scattered and too underorganized (I like this word because it's so much kinder than the ones that are more accurate) to say thank you properly, so:

Thank you for understanding that family has as much to do with time and commitment as it does to do with genetics, and welcome aboard.

ACKNOWLEDGMENTS

I want to say up front that the delay between *The Shining Court* and *Sea of Sorrows* was entirely mine, from start to finish. My publishers and my editor are entirely blameless in all of this; they've been patient and understanding. I apologize for the delay between these two books, and I will do my best to make sure it doesn't happen again. I only hope that the novel itself was worth the long wait.

Sheila Gilbert managed to come through for me when she was dealing with circumstances that would have shut me—and almost anyone else I know—down entirely.

Debra Euler held the fort, and my hand, on more than one occasion, mixing pragmatism with a very down-to-earth sense of humor. She also really came through for me when I'd hit a big, messy brick wall—and I'm certainly not the only author either of them has to deal with.

My husband and my son's godfather covered for me when I slipped into writer-land here, and my parents provided safe haven for my two sons.

I know that other writers manage to juggle their lives with a lot less help and a lot more competence, but I'll be eternally grateful that I haven't had to.

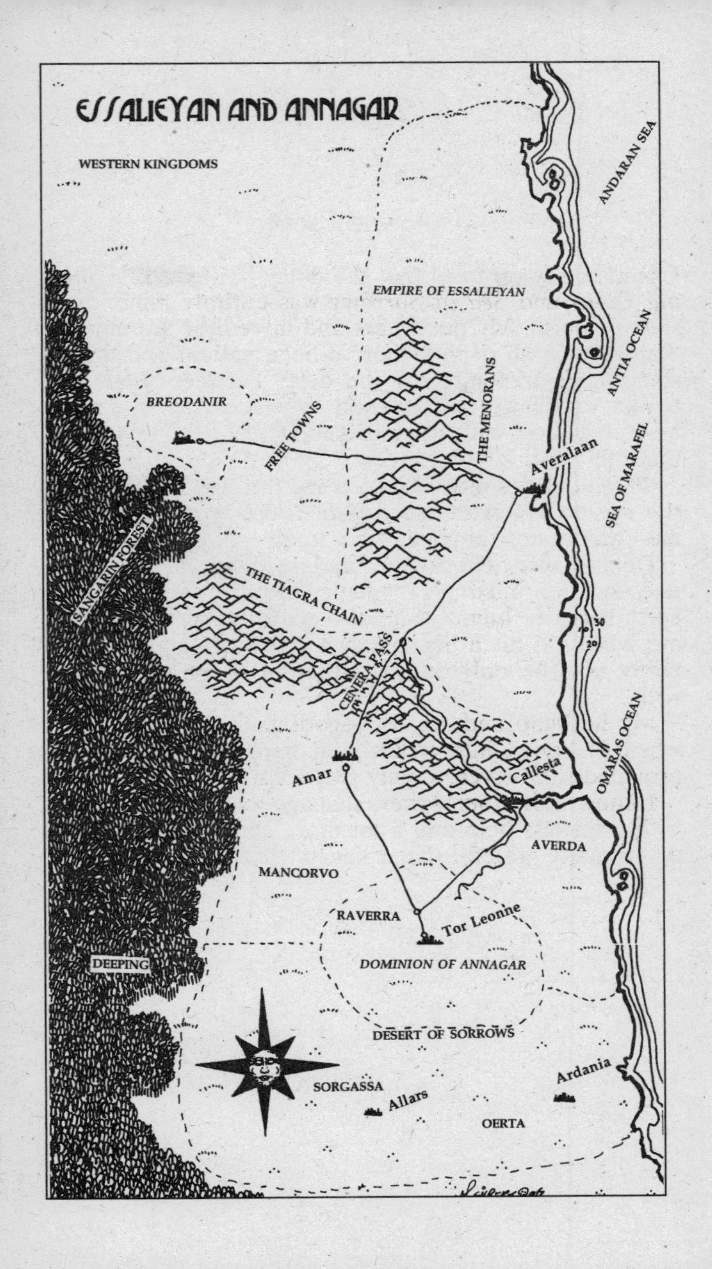
ESSALIEYAN AND ANNAGAR
WESTERN KINGDOMS
ANDARAN SEA
EMPIRE OF ESSALIEYAN
ANTIA OCEAN
THE MENORANS
BREODANIR
FREE TOWNS
Averalaan
SEA OF MARAFEL
SANGARIN FOREST
THE TIAGRA CHAIN
CENERA PASS
30
20
OMARAS OCEAN
Amar
Callesta
AVERDA
MANCORVO
RAVERRA
Tor Leonne
DEEPING
DOMINION OF ANNAGAR
DESERT OF SORROWS
Ardania
SORGASSA
Allars
OERTA

Annagarian Ranks

Tyr'agar	Ruler of the Dominion
Tyr'agnate	Ruler of one of the five Terreans of the Dominion
Tyr	The *Tyr'agar* or one of the four *Tyr'agnate*
Tyran	Personal bodyguard (oathguard) of a *Tyr*
Tor'agar	A noble in service to a *Tyr*
Tor'agnate	A noble in service to a *Tor'agar*; least of noble ranks
Tor	A *Tor'agar* or *Tor'agnate*
Toran	Personal bodyguard (oathguard) of a *Tor*
Ser	A clansman
Serra	The primary wife and legitimate daughters of a clansman
kai	The holder or first in line to the clan title
par	The brother of the first in line; the direct son of the title holder

The Voyani

In the Voyani clans, the men will often use their name and their clan's name as identifiers (i.e. Nicu would be Nicu of the Arkosan Voyani or Nicu Arkosa.)

ARKOSA

Evallen of the Arkosa Voyani—The woman who ruled the Voyani clan. She is/was seerborn. Dark-haired, dark-eyed; died at Diora's hand, a mercy killing.

Margret of the Arkosa Voyani—The new, untested Matriarch of the Arkosan Voyani. Dark-haired and dark-eyed like her mother; she is not seerborn.

Adam—Evallen's boy, the light of her life, and much indulged. Charming, easily charmed, he is *also* very perceptive, very sharp of wit; he keeps it to himself, for the most part.

Nicu—Bearded, broad-shouldered; cousin in his early twenties. Son of Evallen's cousin. Looks older.

Carmello—Darker in coloring than Nicu, dark-haired, dark-eyed, one year his senior. They're friends, sword-mates.

Andreas—Shorter than either Nicu or Carmello, but dark as the Voyani are dark; stocky and barrel-chested; one of Carmello's and Nicu's supporters.

Donatella—Nicu's mother. Evallen's cousin once removed; Margret (and Elena's) second cousin.

Stavos—Margret's uncle, much loved and crusty; gray beard, broad belly, laughs like a bear.

Tatia—Stavos' wife. Wide as well, but hardened by the sun and wind. Hair gray and long, eyes cutting and dark.

Elena—Margret's cousin; the heir to the Matriarchy should Margret perish without a daughter. They are both close and rivals, Margret and Elena, and it is Elena that Nicu loves. Elena is a firebrand in most senses of the word; her hair is auburn-red, her skin sun-bronzed, her eyes brown with green highlights.

Tamara—Margret's aunt. Bent at the back, older in appearance than her older (and now dead) sister, she is

Margret's support and strength, although she nags rather a lot. Closer than kin. She is Elena's mother.

HAVALLA

Yollana of the Havalla Voyani—Peppered, dark curls, almost black eyes. She is in her forties, healthy, wiry.

CORRONA

Elsarre of the Corrona Voyani—Long, straight hair, dark with streaks of white. She was, until the death of Evallen, the youngest of the matriarchs at the age of 36.

Dani—Slender, of medium height. His hair is long, thick and is always pulled back in a single braid. His beard is small, his face long, his eyes (as most Voyani eyes) are dark. He is Elsarre's Shadow; Elsarre has no brothers, and no cousins she chooses to trust with her life.

LYSERRA

Maria of the Lyserra Voyani—Hair white as northern snow, eyes blue as Lord's sky, she is slender and silent much of the time. She has the grace of gesture Serra Teresa possesses, and for this reason is less trrusted than the other Matriarchs. Her husband is the kai of the clan Jedera; *Ser Tallos kai di'Jedera*. They have four children:

Mika—Mika is broad-shouldered, dark-haired, dark-eyed as all clansmen; clean-shaven, as the Voyani are not.

Jonni—Jonni is quiet; large-eyed, clear-skinned; he wears a beard.

Aviana—The Matriarch's heir; she shelters with, and lives with her mother's kin in preparation for her eventual role. She loves her brothers fiercely, even if they are of the clans.

Lorra—The family baby. Beautiful, but fair-skinned, she lives with her sister, and her mother's people.

PROLOGUE

I.

6th of Scaral, 427 AA
Averalaan Aramarelas, the Common

They were gone.

He had lost them.

His memory was perfect, precise; it was his comprehension that was flawed. He had seen them, standing beneath the splintered bower of fallen trees, framed on one side by the shattered street, and on the other by the buildings that, thin as dry wood, had failed to stand against the least direct of the magical attacks the *Kialli* brought to bear. Behind them lay bodies; ahead, bodies as well. None of the fallen were *Kialli*.

He had seen the expression transform the Warlord's face as the pathetic demeanor of mortality fell away; had experienced the sharp anticipation that comes before battle. He had even seen the signature of ancient power as it cut across the pale insignificance of unadorned day—the mark of the Warlord's magic.

What had happened?

Between that moment and this, the Warlord had glanced at the only mortal left standing in the square—an insignificant mortal woman—and then, between the falling of a stall and the rising of the earth, he had vanished.

The Warlord did not flee battle. He left the field—if he so chose—when he had broken the forces of his enemies; when they fled, or fell. He left the field when the field had no suitable challenge to offer; when, among the fallen, the bodies of the *Kialli* could be counted before they were claimed by the elements. Or, on one or two occasions, he left the field when he destroyed it.

But he *had* fled.

A power such as his could not be concealed with ease if there were witnesses. Verdazan was not a seeker. Seekers were like mortal dogs—with the single exception of Lord Ishavriel, a lord Verdazan neither served nor crossed. But there was a seeker present. Verdazan growled his name, and he appeared, hands red with blood, eyes glistening.

"What have you been doing, you fool?"

"Hunting," the creature replied, all ability to dissemble gone.

"Hunt later. There is work for you to do."

"Hunt *later.*" Black eyes were clear as day as Verdazan met them; the words were a hiss, like water spread thinly over an unbanked flame. "When would that *later* be? The Lord has forbidden us all hunting; he has forbidden us all reaving. It is only when he feeds himself that we are permitted to *see* what we cannot touch."

"And do you intend to live here, hunting? You will not live long. Either they will kill you—"

"These?"

"Or the Lord will."

But the light in *Kialli* eyes was there to stay. Verdazan knew that there was only one way to quench the flame. "Where is the Warlord?"

"The Warlord?"

"**Sargathan**," the *Kialli* lord growled, as another of the kin swept the roof off a quaint, fragile building.

Sargathan froze. His hands came up, curled into slender, slick fists. "L-lord." Dry word. Dry sound. He struggled against the binding of his name. Had he not been necessary, Verdazan would have killed him instantly for the insult.

And yet . . .

And yet, beyond them both, roof having been peeled from a nearby insubstantial building, the occupants were riven from their illusion of safety, and then from the illusion of life in all its brief and fierce vibrancy. Their screams were short and sweet. Too short. And too sweet by far. Had it been that long?

No. Surely not. They had lived in the Hells for millennia; they had lived on the surface of the world for mere decades. The world could not exert so strong an influence that the *Kialli* themselves could be driven like hungry, lumbering beasts to feed at random, to feed in the heart of their enemies' stronghold.

"Where is the Warlord?"

Sargathan's lips pulled back slowly, as if the skin were being shed, to reveal teeth the length of his hands. Battle, like storm, was building in the air; in the crackle of electricity gathered but not yet released. He wanted it.

He wanted what the others wanted.

Instead he forced himself to listen to Sargathan's reply. "The Warlord is . . . gone."

"Gone? Gone *where*?"

Sargathan's laugh was bitter, but the madness had momentarily left it. "Where does the Warlord go when he tires of battle? If any of the seekers in the history of our Lord's War could have answered that question, he would be ours now. Or dead."

"The legends say he cannot be killed."

"Yes. And when his god existed, perhaps they were even true." The teeth and lips blended in smile. "Verdazan . . ."

A request. There were too many mortals here; too many *Kialli*. And no battle; no battle to sustain them.

"Our enemies will come."

"Yes."

"But your presence here has already been noted. Yes. Go."

The wild music was in the air. The smell of blood, the sharp tang of old wood that, when snapped, released the hidden scent of its pale center. Stone, dust, the fruits of the mortal market. And the trees, towering, ancient.

The trees.

He smiled. Gave himself to the fight, or to the fight he thought might follow. There were so few mortals with power, and to that handful, word would travel slowly.

6th of Scaral, 427 AA
Averalaan Aramarelas, Order of Knowledge

The city was burning.

Across the narrow stretch of bay, broken only by slender bridge, booth, and the guards chosen by the Kings' deputies, black smoke scudded like angry cloud through a flawless sky. Averalaan in winter.

Light glinted off his silvered hair; he stood in the stillness above water and wave, a living statue, pale and clothed in the drab colors of the Order. He almost turned away from what he saw, but he found that he could not; the tower that contained him had a balcony of stone, and the stone rails had become attached to his hand in such a way that he was forced to bear witness.

He heard the screaming.

Meralonne APhaniel, member of the Order of Knowledge, had heard so many screams in his life they did not affect him as they did others; they were but some of many sounds, and each told its own story. But when the first of the ancient trees fell, motion returned to the tower.

Sigurne Mellifas stood in the parting of door and frame, her pale hair drawn back in a way that made her face reveal the truth that few accepted: she was aged, polite, politic—and ruthless in pursuit of her chosen goals. Her principles were among those valued goals. Were they not, many men would lie dead who might present a danger to her. He was keenly aware that he was one. The awareness made him prize her more highly, not less, and he wondered, as he often did, why beauty was defined as youth in the eyes of so many. She was beautiful, scarred as she was by experience.

She was also angry.

His hand left the rail. He bowed, aware of the mollifying effect of manners.

"Did you think I wouldn't find out before you departed?"

He raised a brow. Then he turned briefly to the cloudless sky. She did not look at the fire that burned in the heart of the Common.

"No, Sigurne. You would never disappoint me in such a fashion."

"When you offer flattery in that grave a voice, I know I won't be happy with what you intend. You have summoned—your students."

"Yes."

She was silent.

"Understand that they share two traits. For the mageborn, they are young."

"And powerful," she said softly. Only Sigurne could make those words an accusation.

"We face old enemies, and we are older ourselves; we must train the next generation," he said, surprising himself by the softness of his tone. "And while we have never spoken openly of it, you know better than any what the extent of that danger is; what the cost of failure will be."

"I know better than any save yourself."

"Save perhaps myself; I am less certain that it is your knowledge that is the inferior. But we speak of the city, Sigurne."

"Yes."

"And if we are to prove our ability to wage this war, if we are indeed to stand against the *Kialli,* and the return of even worse danger, we must be prepared to wield power. We were not always so weak a people. The power is there if we are willing to use it." An old, old argument. No matter what their intent, they returned to it; it lay at the heart both of who they had once been and what it had made them.

"And at what cost? Were it not for the ambition of 'men of power,' I am almost certain we would not need to train the young to death and death's arts."

"It is not to death's art that I train them," he said softly. "Men were the only mortal creatures who stood unbowed in the face of the gods, when they walked these lands. We have forgotten," he added quietly, "but the potential still resides within us."

"You will turn them into weapons."

"I will turn them into men who are *capable* of wielding true weapons. It is not the same."

"And when we stood against the gods in these lands, when we stood shoulder to shoulder with the wild and ancient powers, what were we, Meralonne?" Her eyes were wide, unblinking, but the shadows cast by the door's frame robbed them of color. "Did the Twin Kings stand as well? Did they demand justice for those too weak, or too insignificant, to be counted among the great?"

His smile was brittle. He did not answer.

"I would not see them turned from the path the Twin Kings have carved for the Empire. I will not see them judge worth by power alone. They *have* power, but I do not wish them to become that power, and nothing more."

"Then make a spell, Sigurne Mellifas, that will somehow ascertain ambition at birth and kill all those who possess it."

She did not move or flinch at the heat of his tone, and the anger deserted him. He was left with the knowledge that truth, like an oily merchant, had two faces, two edges. "But understand that some ambitions are born of fire." The streets were now burning with the fire of which he spoke. "What is forged in that fire will endure in a way that youthful intention seldom does. These men are not boys, Sigurne. They are not born of the streets; they have never struggled for their own survival above all else. That much you have taught them. And I . . ." His smile was odd, almost devoid of amusement. "Against my better judgment, I have chosen to uphold what *you* value."

"What I value, Member APhaniel? Surely you mean what *we* value."

"Indeed."

Her gaze broke. "I would not have chosen this life."

He understood exactly what she meant. "No one chooses the course of their life. You have risen from painful obscurity to the mastery of the First Circle of the Magi, yet I believe that if you had more faith in the competence of the Council of the Magi, you would return to obscurity. That is the miracle of you. Yet you have lived the life that you did not choose well, regardless." He raised his head to look beyond her shoulder. "They come."

She listened for the sound of footsteps; they were both distant and heavy. There was no mistaking their direction. "Have you ever questioned the value of what you've built?"

"I rarely question my decisions, once made."

She said, "They will die."

"Not all of them."

The first of the warrior-adepts came through the open arch. He marched past Sigurne Mellifas, hesitation marring the timing of his very military step. It was clear that he knew who she was; clear also that he knew that paying the respect due her station would compromise the efficiency of the unit's arrival; the tower was not designed for the comfortable gathering of large numbers of men. It had been one of the qualities Meralonne valued in a residence, and he was certain, circumstance aside, that it was a quality that he would continue to value.

The fledgling group of warrior-adepts assembled on this balcony would be winnowed; some would survive this first flight, and some would falter and perish.

In minutes.

Another tree fell.

"I have summoned you here," Meralonne said, into a calm he forced from the wind, "to fulfill your oath. Your sworn duty is to use the gifts granted you by the gods in defense of those less privileged. Across the bay, in the old city proper, the enemy waits, unaware of your existence. They destroy with ease those they feel cannot fight back.

"You have practiced and trained for this day; prove them wrong."

He turned his back, his simply robed back, upon them and lifted his arms. The men he had called students were silent, but one breath, short and sharp, was drawn; he did not look back; he knew whose. The elbows of his sleeves rippled; the edges of his cloak skittered above the stones. His hair was braided, but strands framed his face and rose, as if he had summoned lightning, and waited merely for its strike.

No lightning came.

Instead, infinitely more subtle, more dangerous, the elemental air, the wild wind.

"We cannot walk," he said, and added dryly, "and there are no horses within the Order's grounds that would carry us into that danger."

The few who had come from patrician homes chuckled. He let that noise ease those who had not before he spoke again.

"I have been your master and your teacher; I know your measure. I trust it. Now, I must ask a single question. You will know how to answer it.

"Do you trust me?" Without looking back, Meralonne APhaniel stepped up, onto the balcony's railing. The wind swept him off.

Now he heard their voices, the words muted and merged into a single noise. As they understood what they saw, the current driving those murmurs changed. Meralonne APhaniel stood, buffeted and untouched, a hundred feet—more—above the ground.

"Join me," he said.

They paused.

A hundred years ago, a thousand, in lands held by different men, that hesitation would have been their death. But he expected it; he waited, refusing to turn toward them; refusing to see their indecision. He was not so kind a teacher that it would not have angered him or insulted him; the words were not, and could not be construed as, request.

Gyrrick reached the rail first. The wind carried the familiar sound of his step, coveting the momentary silence of drawn and held breath that was particular to Gyrrick. He was the boldest of the students, but also the man who best understood consequences: seldom did such an alliance of traits sit so easily in a person. His hair was short; Meralonne suffered no man the foolish grace of lengthy hair save himself. His shoulders, though slender, were strong, and his jaw was not weak; he was attractive in the way that men who wield power as if it were breath so often are; naturally, without artifice.

He stepped into air, and the air held him.

There were two approaches to training men such as these; the first was to break their natural leader and replace him; the second, to co-opt that leader, to become that leader's lord. He had chosen the latter course, the former being almost certain to draw Sigurne's wrath, but he was surprised at how well it had worked. It took more patience than the first option; it left one vulnerable.

After Gyrrick, they followed. He counted them by the scrambling uncertainty of their steps.

Twenty-four.

Twenty-four men.

He turned only when the balcony was as it should be: occupied by one. He knelt, although the wind was howling in outrage at the burden he had placed upon it. "Magi," he said. "We are at your disposal."

What the students had not granted, the master did, in their full view: respect for the authority Sigurne Mellifas had chosen to accept; acknowledgment that she was the guild's ruler, inasmuch as an Order made of quirky men and women could have one.

She surveyed them all, the bowed man and his students. Then she nodded, grimly, accepting what he offered—both halves, the adepts and his respect—as the necessities they were. "Save our city," she said, her voice carrying without interference over the wind's current. "Only you can."

The words carried them, and they rose, the wind gathering behind and beneath them like a wild horse that would only—barely—tolerate what had been set upon its back.

Look, look there— the magi told it, and the wind, in fury, did as bid.

The wind saw *fire*.

Everything has its natural enemy.

Fire, earth, water, and air. Burn the world, bury it, drown it, tear it to pieces; each, in its natural dominion.

The common wisdom—in this tame world where wilderness was a dream's dream, buried so far beneath mortal knowledge it never came to light—pitted fire against water, and earth against air. But it was not so: they were, each of the four, powers, and in any world, only one power could claim dominance.

Torn between rage at the indignity of being a beast of burden and rage at the indignity of the presence of its natural enemy, the wind balanced a moment before turning, like a great dragon, to make its way toward the Common where the hearts of trees were cracking.

Gyrrick could not speak; he could barely breathe. But the difficulty of gasping for breath did not bother him in any visible fashion. Following his first step into the insubstantial air from the height of a tower he might one day hope to occupy, he readied himself for his second. Meralonne expected no less . . . but he was old enough now that the fulfillment of expectation was its own peculiar joy. The mage rode the wind, inches above the ground; the students tumbled into the streets like flotsam carried by unnatural tide. They would right themselves, or they would not.

It had become immaterial.

The last thing the mage was peripherally aware of before

he drew his blade and spoke its name to the wind was Gyrrick's long shadow across the broken ground.

That and the enemies who turned, as a single creature, to face blue fire and elemental air.

"They told us," one said, rising as if ground were illusion, "that you were here." Red fire seeped out of his fingertips in lazy circles, becoming brighter and darker as Meralonne approached. "But I hardly credited the reports as truth. I did call your name when I arrived, but perhaps you failed to hear it."

"Perhaps I considered it inconsequential."

"Judge, then," the creature replied, its lips spreading in a smile that split its slender face.

"You did not come here for me."

"No. You are considered less of a concern than the Warlord." Fire became sword; sword became the symbol of all battles, past and present. This battle would become one of many to the victor. The loser would become memory.

But he wanted the experience that would form that memory, be it insignificant or not. Because this creature was a creature he understood. He asked for no quarter; he offered none. He had spent his existence fighting for survival and supremacy, and clearer proof of his success could not be found than this: his sword was his own. Red light and fire, grace and death.

The clarity of combat was a joy Meralonne APhaniel had dutifully ordered his students to be wary of seeking. Proof, if needed, that observation was a substitute for personal experience in the classroom—and only there.

Sigurne's face wore the shadows well. She took comfort in them.

The city was burning.

She watched in silence as the light and the fire of Meralonne's students burned themselves into the unblinking field of her vision. The men who lay dead in the Common had done the demons no harm.

She wondered how many of her own would join them.

The demons were fast.

The mages expected speed. They had not been given leave to summon demons in order to hone their craft—

Sigurne would have had them all killed had they attempted it, and if rumors were true, slowly—and what they had been left to study did no justice to the truth of this first meeting.

But Meralonne had taught them. No summoned enemy? It mattered little. Their lack of knowledge was matched only by their pathetic skill. Had Sigurne taken sudden leave of her senses—or come into them, depending on who one asked—and allowed them the use of demonology, they would all be dead. Sigurne aside, they would all be dead when they eventually encountered the enemy in something other than song, story, or faded, crumbling book, and *that* would be an embarrassment that he would not tolerate; it had been costly to gain the Council's permission to create their small division within the Order's more peaceful fold.

Therefore, they would *learn*. And as there were no demons, they would have to content themselves with facing something superior: the master himself. Meralonne APhaniel made it clear that he would stop short of killing them. They discovered that he didn't differentiate between "short" and "just short"; the healers grew fat the first year.

Gyrrick had learned the hard way—they all had, and Meralonne was not a kind master—not to close with the magi. He bore three scars, one of which earned Meralonne the dubious distinction of being the first member of the Council of the Magi to be suspended in over a century.

But more important, that scar had taught them clearly—what Gyrrick learned, the rest learned—that to close with the master was death. Their reflexes always paled in comparison. They needed a stretch of ground—or air—in which to react to his power; to diminish that distance in any way led to injury. In the classroom.

Here, it was death.

And when will we be good enough? When can we stand and fight?

Not in this decade, Gyrrick.

And the Kialli?

You are skilled enough now that you should know on sight who presents a threat . . . and who is certain death. I am not Magi Mellifas; it is not my intent to rob you of the battles you can win. But my tenure within the Order depends on your ability to gauge danger and survive it. If I had discovered you as a child . . .

Gyrrick's hands trembled as he raised them.

The demons were closing, and not all of them were bound—as Gyrrick and his men were—to earth.

He barked out orders, reminding his men that distance was—for the moment—their best defense. But it was only that: defense. All of the stories that he had studied became fodder for children. He gazed upon the enemy, upon their numbers, upon the damage they had casually done to the Common, and he knew that what the master had taught—what had *never* been tested—would either save or damn them.

But his hands were shaking.

Hold any other weapon, he heard the master say, *and you will perish if you close with the enemy. Do you understand? You do not have the fire, cold or hot, to best the* Kialli *in direct conflict. But in your long history—much of it forgotten—you had the* power. *And you still have it, if you are willing to take the risk of using it.*

What risk?

Here, the sound of demons keening like rabid dogs, their language high and sharp and piercing as they rushed in like air filling vacuum, the master's answer returned.

Of death, of course.

Gyrrick had fought demons before. But not many, and not *Kialli.* The master had said he would know the difference, and as always, he had been correct. They were closing.

He could not afford to let them close unhindered.

Why do you not teach us all this?

Because, idiot, not all of you are capable of learning. You may not have noticed, but I abhor wasting my time.

Gyrrick's compatriots knew almost as well as he did that to let the *Kialli* close meant death. Plumes of fire—of human fire—and lightning were coaxed from air and sky; walls of coruscating orange light—if one had the gift and knew how to look—sprang into shimmering life at the command of will and a few hasty words of focus. Meralonne would have failed them in their exercise had he heard those hasty words, because he loathed foci as much as he loathed stupidity. Possibly more. He considered them crutches, not necessities, and he reserved his harshest words for those who could not let go of the security of their use, for they telegraphed much to an enemy. It didn't matter; there was no classroom now; no reprimand to fear.

There was only death.

He shouted out orders; the words were short and harsh. If he hadn't felt the vibration of his throat, he wouldn't have known they were his. But his men knew, and they responded entirely by reflex, doing as they were ordered. No consensus, not here. No committees.

Just his judgment, forced into words as reflexive as his compatriots' response, while they could hear it.

Meralonne had given them that. Had humiliated them, time and again when they failed to respond as quickly as he wanted (which seemed—which *had been*—impossible), or with the precision he desired. He would not, Gyrrick thought, be satisfied with them now.

But now . . .

The fires cut through the lines of their defense as if orange light and enchantment were spider's gossamer. He saw three men bisected by something that looked like red light. And he heard the enemy laugh. Distorted as it was by long fangs and impossible, slender jaws, by lips that seemed things of leather or steel or jade, he knew contempt when he heard it.

In the air, in the sky above, there was no laughter; Meralonne had drawn sword, and his enemy had replied in kind—which was as much attention as Gyrrick could spare them. But in that brief glimpse, he understood that Meralonne was no object of contempt; he had somehow proved himself a danger, a worthy foe, in a way the enemy could understand.

Two more men died. The others scattered, retreating carefully, defensively. None of the demons had even been singed, although Alain—he thought it was Alain's signature—had killed lesser demons with his fire-strike before.

Gyrrick spoke to his men across the distance; they heard his words, acted on them, following a command that he had beaten, one way or another, into their subconscious.

The creatures looked up. One of them, tall and slender, with wings as supple as fine hide, said, "I will take the . . . leader." Gyrrick would remember the sneer for as long as he lived. However long that might be.

He summoned, not fire, because fire was not his element, but earth; sent a benediction, torturous and slow, as the enemy's fire lapped holes in the pathetic defenses Meralonne APhaniel had taught them to erect before they drew breath. The earth replied, ponderous, weighty.

The stones above it snapped in jagged, cobbled lines, throwing the creature off its feet.

Or it should have; the cost to Gyrrick was enormous, given the speed of the earth's breaking, the change of its shape. But the creature rose to air; smiled red fire, cast it with contempt and ease. Gyrrick's defenses were second only to Meralonne's. The creature's eyes widened slightly in surprise—even at this distance, surprise was evident—when they held.

Gyrrick struck again; lightning, something forced from the folds of the sky. The bolt passed by the creature, veering at the last moment as it lost shape and structure, as a liquid might. It struck something behind the creature's tall back; wall—brick or stone or clay or wood; something that shattered easily with the force of the blow. Gyrrick heard screaming, and something twisted inside him; not fear of his own death, but fear of the deaths the use of that much magic had just caused.

The cure, he could hear Sigurne say, *must not be worse than the disease. There is no justification for our existence if the damage we do is as great as the damage we prevent.*

It almost cost him his life.

But he was *fast*, and other voices crowded in on him as the cobbled stones hit his cheeks and the broken dirt provided a momentary cover against needles of sharp flame. When those needles struck, they struck hair, cut flesh, searing wound with heat and pain. Only Meralonne APhaniel was fast enough to wear armor without paying a price for its encumbrance.

The creature was grinning.

You have a weapon. Not fire, and not ice; it is not elemental, and not, in the end, magical, although it is through your mage-born talent that you will reach it. It is human. Manifest it.

Manifest it? How?

Summon it. Summon it from the same place you summon

the earth; bespeak the darkness and shadow that you carry within you.

And?

Must I spoon-feed you, Gyrrick? Tobacco, glowing like fire-touched wood, leaves crackling in memory and in reality: perfect harmony. *I cannot tell you how to call upon your talent; it is the first lesson all magi learn. Assuming, of course, that you* have *learned it.*

Yes, Master.

Power is *power, and the cost of its expenditure is always the same. But the summoning? Unique. No two men will find their power in the same way. No two ever have, in all of your history.*

But I—

Within you, the weapon resides, waiting. The master's sword met sword in the air; the clash of steel, of something that was more than steel, rang out across the broken landscape.

Gyrrick dodged again, easily now, at home in the fissure his power had made; at home in the earth.

Burial was a thing that most men feared; not Gyrrick; cremation was his: that in the end, not even ashes remain. Let him be given to earth, instead.

The creature growled.

And when I find this weapon, if I can?

Take care. If it breaks, it is broken, but not as your arm, or your leg might be; it will not heal. *To fix it requires an ability to forge that has not been seen in centuries, and if it is broken, every skill you now possess will be diminished.*

Then why? Why risk it? This seems to be power made emblem, and emblem exposed.

Indeed. It is when we are exposed in our entirety that we have truly set aside all fear. The fearless are fools, but they have ruled this world throughout the millennia.

I'd rather be cautious. He had weathered the glare of Meralonne's contempt for many, many years. It stung, but it did not deter.

Fire did. The shields that Meralonne had spent years forcing upon him—upon them all—through tiresome, demanding exercise dissolved; he faced death, hands lifted and shaking. But the earth rose in response to something beneath the surface of his fear, and against the *earth*, fire had to work for its victim.

He felt, rather than saw, the buildings shattering like glass; heard screams that started—and worse, stopped, cut off from the air that fueled them. Here, in the trench, these things were muted. Earth. Defense. Meralonne would have scoffed, pipe in the crook made of lips dependent on its stem.

There is no weapon as effective against the Kialli*—or any other immortal—as a weapon of this type.*

And what will it cost?

His answer had been the making itself. No other. And that answer had nearly killed him, and nearly killed Meralonne when Sigurne Mellifas had—as she always did—discovered what had transpired between them.

He had been unable to face the master for three weeks while he convalesced. And he refused to draw what had been made by earth and blood and magic and will again.

Oh, he had dared the darkness. He had thought of fire. Of pain. Of sacrifice. He had been willing to die the noble death in a heroic attempt to do the right thing. Younger. He had been much younger.

But he had discovered that his darkness was a quiet, strong shadow, buried someplace between two things: Earth. Magic. He understood why the art of fashioning weapons such as this had died; most men who had tried it had probably taken their own lives shortly afterward. There were things about oneself that one should never have to face, but in order to reach the weapon, the killing force, one not only had to face them.

One had to become them.

Slumbering in a metaphysical shadow, beside the thing he defined as his power and the thing he defined as himself—until that day—he had discovered things that he would have killed men for accusing him of. Sadism, desire, fascination with things too ugly to be human. But not too ugly to be *Kialli.*

Of course not; if he wished to fight the *Kialli*, could he fight them without becoming them, measure for measure? He had been naïve, and the master delighted, coldly, in the destruction of naïveté. Why wouldn't he? He *had* his own weapon. And he never hesitated to call the sword. It sang in his hands; scored the field of vision if one was careless and watched it at play for too long. Meralonne APhaniel had faced his own demons.

But a man that arrogant probably thought anything demonic about himself was a matter of fact. A man that arrogant could not possibly be stopped by self-loathing, doubt, fear of—for the first time—one's own power. A man like the master was at home with his demons.

Gyrrick did not wish to wake his.

And today, he would have no choice. He *knew* as clearly as his body knew how to breathe, and just as consciously, that to be bereft of weapon here was death. The shattered bodies of trees lay just beyond his feet, pale, broken splinters, sharp enough to draw hearts' blood; the foremost of the creatures they faced picked up a splinter that was half Gyrrick's width and twice his length. With ease, he used it to break the magical defenses behind which a full quarter of the magi hid, preparing their enchantments in a grim silence.

"Come out, come out, little mortals. Come and *play*. We've been bored, killing trees and the squealing, pathetic creatures that can't lift a hand in their own defense."

He had to go back. He had to go back.

Where does this weapon come from, Master?

That is something you will answer for yourself. For a moment, there was something akin to empathy in the cool, calm face of the Council's strangest mage. It didn't linger long.

Anger.

He did not close his eyes; he could not afford to. But he lifted his chin; put his hands up, over his shoulder. Gripped the air behind him as if it had a shape he could feel.

Desire.

The first of his men was pierced by the front of that splinter; riven in two as if his body offered no more resistance to wood than water would have. His blood was dark and bright against the dust and rubble; startlingly wet and new. The sky above him was deep and endless, blue. Perfect. The fires were burning low.

Power.

It came to hand, slender, bent; it came to hand strung, although he knew enough about bows now to know that a bow of value and quality was never carried that way for any length of time. The second of his men was screaming as fire took him—took him slowly; the others were retreating. Not a rout, not that, but they had fallen into a silence that spoke of fear.

Hunger.

And is that all?

No. But that is all I can tell you; we find our own reasons for what we create, and once created, we do not forget them.

He reached into air, and out of it, pulled arrow. He reached into air, and out of it, pulled bow. Both came as if the heart itself was pulled beating from his chest. He *felt* the drawing of string as if it were a muscle that someone had reached into his open chest cavity to pull.

And the moment the weapon was in his hands, he understood.

He could finally see.

The trees were luminescent as they lay across the broken ground; the earth more so, the dirt itself a rich and layered brown. The cobbled stones above it were so pale, if he hadn't known they were there, they would have faded from sight.

As would most of his compatriots. One or two burned as the earth did, warmly. But for the most part they were like walking shadows, ghosts of themselves, things that didn't matter because in the end they weren't truly alive.

He *saw* the enemy.

Five on the ground, two in the air. Tall, these creatures, and defined not by their shapes—for their shapes varied greatly, although in the end they each had two arms and two legs—but by something that he had really only heard of when he was a child and his mother's lap was still a refuge open to him.

Names.

Demon names.

They were not . . . clear. They were not written, the way Weston is, in a script that comes easily to eye and from there to tongue. They were not, in fact, written at all, but he recognized them instantly for what they were. Just as a child might see a hand and know it for a hand, or a foot and know it as such; or better, might note the absence of a foot or a hand and ask embarrassing questions about it because he has not learned the guile called tact. He knew what he saw in a way that defied explanation, and he accepted the lack of explanation in a way that no honest member of the Order of Knowledge otherwise would.

He joined combat.

"VERDAZAN!" he cried, and the creature who had killed two of his men with contempt and ease looked up.

Gyrrick was not a killer by birth; not a killer by avocation. But he wanted the moment to stretch on and on, for the creature's eyes grew wide and round; shock melting into surprise, surprise giving way to something like respect. Every moment that passed was measured in human life, and Gyrrick forced himself to value that life.

It was a struggle.

The life wasn't his.

The arrow flew; he felt it travel through air, felt it strike the ridge of bone between the demon's wide eyes as if it were still attached to him; as if it were an extension of his hands, the sensitive tips of his fingers.

Bone shattered, just as human building had done; he recognized the sensation although he had never shattered bone with his hand before. Wondered what it would feel like to shatter rock with the weapon. Had no question at all that he could.

One of the *Kialli* roared, and Gyrrick understood the language embedded in the thunder; understood it without capturing the sound in imperfect memory and dissecting it, painful syllable by syllable, under the disapproving eye of Sigurne Mellifas, who was always present for post-battle debriefings.

"Illaraphaniel! What have you done, you fool!"

And his master's voice, punctuated by the clash of blade that was not quite steel. *"What have I done?"* Laughter, carried by the wind as if it were sand in a desert storm.

"I have ushered in the End of Days."

The creature who had first spoken snarled, and Gyrrick found, for the first time, that there was a rough musicality to demonic voices that made each voice easily recognizable.

"The End of Days was ushered in long ago, and by better than you. Do you think that teaching your pathetic pets a dangerous trick will harm us?"

"Pets? They are hardly my pets, Lornanan, although I don't expect you to recognize the distinction between pet and mortal.

You've never been perceptive. Not that it matters; you'll be ash and dust and the winds will write your epitaph."

All this time, they fought, their voices as loud as their swords, their words far less graceful.

Gyrrick found another arrow in his hand.

He fired.

Flesh parted, absorbing the arrow; denying it.

"These creatures are not a threat to us!"

"You have forgotten our history, without even the pathos of mortality as excuse. Remember: the Cities of Man were not destroyed; they were only barely humbled.

"On second thought, don't; remember other things instead. The wind in the abyss. The texture of the suffering of those you Chose to guard. You will not last out a single mortal day unless you retreat, and your last moments should be pleasant ones."

"And yours?" the creature countered. "*Will you think of failure among the squalor and be content?"*

"No. I shall think of your destruction and be content."

He could not speak their language.

He hoped he could not speak it. His throat closed over the attempt to make words, and his hands clutched arrows convulsively. He wondered, if they closed, what he would do; he had no sword, and he knew that a sword would not give him the preternatural speed the *Kialli* possessed.

Or at least, he *had* known it.

But now, he knew nothing; he was reborn in the world of man, and it was *not* the world he had left.

Faint as leaves' rustle, he heard the voices of his own: his men, his friends, his compatriots in the Order of Knowledge. They were shadows here, they were among the fallen.

Illaraphaniel.

The Cities of Man.

II.

23rd of Scaral, 427 AA
The Terrean of Raverra, the Sea of Sorrows

She's the most beautiful woman I've ever seen. She's sixteen, seventeen—and her eyes are filled with fire; she kneels as if she's supplicant, but she's wearing a thin crown, and a bloodied sword is staining the silks she wears.

She tells me that I cannot turn back.

The Chosen are scattered. I can only find Torvan; the rest are blind or deaf. He says, "Why did you have to leave?" . . . and he drags me to The Terafin's Chambers.

She's dead. There are three knives in her body and she lies across the council table. There is fighting, of course. The war for succession.

The Terafin sits up. Her eyes are dead eyes. Her wounds don't bleed. And her voice—it's not her voice. She says, "Another lesson. The hardest. There will always be blood on your hands. Glory in it or weep at it as you choose, but when you choose who must die, choose wisely."

Jewel ATerafin woke.

In the heat of midday, at what the Voyani called desert's lee for reasons that were not obvious to her, sun cast shade that was more felt than seen. She wore a wide-brimmed hat, tied down beneath her chin by a thick silk; she wore something like a blanket, but with a lot more cloth. Avandar made certain—as if he were a domicis, even here, or worse, a seraf—that her skin was covered.

"I'm not fair-skinned," she snapped, hating the fussing that no other person in the caravan was subject to.

His smile was unpleasant. "What you call dark is no proof against even this much sun. You will do, in this, as I tell you."

He readjusted her sash and straightened her hat, tucking her hair back beneath its brim and her ears. Only when his fingers actually brushed her earlobe did she shy away. But his expression was utterly impassive; she realized it was the neutral touch she had ignored for a decade, no more.

Everything with Avandar had become awkward, and she hated awkwardness.

"ATerafin?"

In her early years in House Terafin, she had quickly realized that a first meeting with anyone was often the most important meeting she would have, and she had allowed Avandar to choose clothing appropriate to the function she was to attend. That had been her first mistake.

Because it never ended with the clothing; he was determined to teach her the subtleties of interaction with the powerful, and lectured her endlessly. Much of these lectures involved the House ring, for she had come early into its possession by the standards of Terafin. He had made it clear when she was to wear the council ring openly by placing her hand in a certain position on the table, and when to let it fall into her lap, beneath view. He had decided when she would wear something drab to allow another member to stand out—usually to the detriment of that other member. He had carefully chosen her dresses in order to cultivate age, and therefore experience; conversely, he had also decided when she was to play on youth. He never asked her to simper; there were limits to the advice she was willing to follow.

He had notably never attempted to have her play on her beauty.

For some reason, that bothered her. She wasn't sure why, but she had a feeling she would be, and she didn't particularly like it.

"I don't see why you're fussing," she said, standing to put some distance between them. "It's not as if anyone else here is dressed any differently."

He raised a brow, but did not join that particular conversation; it had never been one of his favorites.

"We're leaving soon anyway."

"ATerafin—"

"Don't start. We avoided what—what would have happened. We averted a slaughter in the Tor Leonne. We *did* what the visions said we had to do."

"ATerafin."

"What?"

"Are you so certain that we have finished—that *you* have finished—playing a role in the South?"

"Yes."

His smile was thin. "You really should learn how to lie. It would make such transparent attempts less insulting."

When it became clear that her silence was to be her only reply, he relented. Inasmuch as Avandar had ever relented.

"Your den will survive," he said gently. "Carver and Angel are no fools, and if they think they are protecting your interests in your absence, they will do well."

Her silence continued.

"ATerafin."

"I'm sorry. I had a dream last night. I wanted to talk to Teller. He wasn't here." It made her sound like a child, and she was so far past childhood that she knew she had no excuse.

"If I guess correctly, you will know for certain if you are free to leave before three days pass."

"Three days?"

His smile was cool. "You have not been listening to the Voyani speak, have you?"

"Some."

"Very well. They plan to leave this place. I believe they will travel into the Sea of Sorrows."

"When?"

"Obviously within three days."

"Good. Three days." But she was thinking: *Home.*

And because of that, her first meeting with the most beautiful woman in the world—at a close guess, and leaving out anyone of nonmortal origin—was a deeply disappointing affair.

The sun was an hour or two above the horizon when Kallandras of Senniel College came to find her. It wasn't hard; she was seated on a fallen log that had come dangerously close to collapsing under her weight, and watching the children.

They were engaged in a rough and tumble game of capture the flag, although Jewel thought the objective had been lost to the immediate imperative of running and shrieking, and she had found it easier to watch them, fights and all, than it was to while away the hours in useless worry.

"ATerafin." He bowed.

She should have known that he was about to deliver bad news; he was only this formal when formality counted.

She rose quickly, hand falling to her dagger. "What's wrong?"

His smile was slight, but it was genuine. "Insofar as hiding from the armies of the Tyr'agar at the desert's edge can be said to be normal, nothing is wrong. But I would like to introduce you to two women who are new to the camp. And the Voyani."

"Why?"

He turned, and she hesitated for just a minute before she followed; she had to jog to keep up with his long stride.

The fire was being built, but it would not be lit, not yet. Food was being prepared by the women, although Stavos wandered among them, heckling them and getting his arms and chest slapped for his trouble.

Everything seemed all right.

Until she saw the three strangers who stood by the Matriarch's wagon. She stopped. Kallandras slowed.

"ATerafin?"

Jewel ATerafin knew in that moment there was no easy way back home.

"May I introduce you to the Serra Teresa di'Marano and her niece, the Serra Diora di'Marano?"

Jewel bowed, always her first reaction when polite words failed her.

The Serra Teresa was at ease in the garb of the Voyani; she might have been a man if not for the delicate line of her chin. The men did not shave, not often. And they seldom had skin so pale, faces so unscarred. The Serra's hair was dark, but it was drawn back above her face, lending the line of her forehead severity.

"Serra Teresa, this is Jewel ATerafin."

"Ah." The Serra nodded. "You wear one of the council rings."

"You know about these?"

"I spent many years in the Tor Leonne," the Serra said quietly. Her expression softened for a moment, and hardened again. "There were, at one time, members from each of the Ten Houses within the Tor."

Jewel looked away. They both maintained their silence.

Kallandras skillfully broke it.

Jewel would have been happier if he hadn't.

"ATerafin, this is the Serra Diora. Serra Diora, this is Jewel ATerafin; she is the youngest member of the governing council of House Terafin."

The Serra Diora's face was as beautiful, as flawless, as Jewel remembered.

Even though she had seen it only once.

The Serra bowed gracefully. Bowed demurely. She did not offer words.

Jewel stared at the woman. She wore a simple sari, but

if Jewel was any judge of fabric, it had been a costly one. She wore a cloak above that, one that skirted the dry growth beneath their feet without quite gathering loose twigs and leaves. And in her arms she carried something that had been carefully wrapped in a blanket.

It was a sword. Jewel knew it was a sword.

Her gaze traveled between the weapon and the woman who was a symbol, for a moment, of all the fate and destiny that she had let control her life. And she swallowed.

At last, she said, "I'm—I'm pleased to meet you." It was awkward, it was gawky, it was all the things that she suddenly felt in the presence of the younger woman.

The Serra did not even condescend to notice. Her smile was delicate; everything about her seemed to be. "I hope that we will have a chance to converse as we travel. I have much interest in the North."

"Serra," Kallandras broke in quietly, "the Matriarch will expect you soon."

The Serra nodded. "Forgive me, ATerafin."

"Of course."

The Serra Diora walked—if walk was the word for something so light and so graceful—between the walls the wagons made.

She was gone. The Serra Teresa followed, and behind her, like a faithful shadow, the seraf no one had named. Jewel hated that. No name.

"I want you to go home."

"We have had this discussion, or a variant of it, before, Jewel."

"I take it that's a no."

"It is, as surmised, a refusal."

"Well, then, I want you to send a message."

He laughed. "I am not a bard, and there is not a bard born—nor has there been one—who could speak across so great a distance. What would you say?"

"I don't know."

"You said your good-byes. Would you add to them?"

"I don't know. But I know that—I know that it's possible to use magic to deliver something *to* someplace. A letter. Anything."

"You know too little, or too much, for your own comfort.

Yes, it is possible, but there are reasons that such acts are carried out in specific places at specific times. I will not explain them; you are not mage-born, and you haven't the patience to sit through the entire lesson."

"Could you not just go and say—"

"Could I squander power in order to say nothing at all that will be of value?"

She turned, angry, and stared toward the North.

And after a moment, she felt his hands—both of his hands—upon the ridges of her collarbone. She froze. He froze.

Awkward. She hated that.

Because for just a minute . . .

"My apologies, Matriarch. You have done so much, saved so many lives. But I cannot grant your request at this time."

"It's *not a request.*"

The young woman—the beautiful, almost flawless young woman who by appearance alone made Margret feel old, wind-worn, sunburned, and distinctly unattractive—bowed her head. Her hair was tied back in an almost careless knot, but its perfect, raven's wing black caught the firelight and held it as if it were a dark, dark diamond. Her skin was white and unblemished; Margret knew it was childish, but she looked forward to the effect of wind and sun on that pampered, oiled, powdered skin.

Because there wasn't any way that the Serra was going to return to the life she'd just left. How could she?

And what did it matter?

The clansmen could politic to death; all Margret wanted—all she had ever wanted—from them was now hanging on a slender chain around this woman's throat.

The Heart of Arkosa.

"Did you hear me?"

"Margret, don't!" Elena's voice. Elena's words. They were just a little too far away. Margret crossed the circle, circumventing the fire that protected them all, and grabbed the Serra by the shoulders, shaking her.

"Yes," the Serra replied evenly, the steel hidden in velvet. "I heard you, Matriarch."

"It would be impossible not to," Yollana snapped.

"Heartfire's protection or no, *Matriarch*, it's nothing short of a miracle that the whole family isn't listening."

"And making bets, if I know the Arkosans," Elsarre added. But her criticism was muted. Of the four Matriarchs, she had taken the sharpest dislike to the Serra Diora, and while she was willing to snipe in general, she was careful not to do it in a way that would aid the Serra. To Margret's embarrassment, it was Elsarre's dislike that made her treat the Serra with anything approaching courtesy; it was the safest way to slap Elsarre in the figurative face for free.

Slapping her in the face in any other way would just rekindle the wars that—with the luck of the Lady—had been put to rest by the Night's work and the presence of their ancient enemy. The Corronans and the Arkosans were not friendly. Of course, with a Matriarch like Elsarre—all pretense of beauty and importance, all sharp-edged arrogance and casual cruelty—it would be hard for the Corronans to *make* friends. Unfortunately, killing one's own Matriarch was a precedent that a woman with a tenuous hold over her own title couldn't quite support. And sadly, if Margret wanted to do her in, the Corronans were likely to express their gratitude for being rid of such a blight in only one way: war.

But at least it would be a fight that Margret understood. Unlike this one, with this Serra, this so-called Flower of the damn Dominion.

It was hard to have an argument with stone.

Slapping stone also had its consequences, and they were obvious enough that Margret, in fury, managed to hold her hand, although her fingers were curled into fists that trembled with her effort. But she couldn't contain movement, and within the guarded circle of heartfire and Voyani magics, she paced the thin grass off the earth. Grinding her heels into the packed dirt made her feel slightly better.

"We *saved* you, you ungrateful—"

"Margret!" Yollana made her name a harsh bark.

But the Serra-Diora-damned-di'Marano said nothing at all. Strands of her hair had fallen loose with the shaking, and now trailed down the side of her delicate face; disheveled she looked . . . beautiful. Margret hated her. And was fascinated by her, in a furious way. There she knelt, hands in lap, on an unrolled mat that the Serra Teresa had brought into the circle for her when Margret made it perfectly clear that her seraf was *not* welcome to enter. Her precious knees never once touched dirt. She had spoken only a sentence or two—but she was like all clanswomen; as speech was so often denied them, they'd learned to hone words until they were like the thin edge of a dagger in their effect.

On the other hand, no one knew how to wield a dagger better than a Voyani Matriarch. No one.

The Serra Diora bowed low, her head touching her perfect, protected knees. "Yes," she said softly. "Although I do not understand how it was possible, I have some understanding of what you faced, and what you defeated; I understand my debt to you. I do not know if I will be able to pay it, and I regret . . . that I must refuse your request." She sat in that submissive posture, and Margret understood, again, the subterfuge of posture.

Because there was *nothing* submissive about this woman. Oh, she was good. If Margret didn't keep an eye on her, she'd probably have the caravan wrapped around her little finger without speaking more than a dozen demure words.

It wasn't a request! Margret wanted to shout. But Yollana's expression had passed from forbidding to actively threatening, and Elsarre looked a bit too eager for a fight. Maria? Silent, silent, silent. But her gaze lingered a moment over Diora's bent back, and she straightened her shoulders, compressed her lips.

Enough. The only winner in this confrontation was likely to be Diora, and Margret wasn't about to hand her her victory; let her work for it. It certainly didn't look like she'd ever had to work for anything else.

"When, then?" Margret said, terse now because it was bloody hard not to say what she was thinking.

In answer, Diora unfolded until her back was straight and her chin parallel with the ground. The Serra had, Margret thought, the most beautiful eyes she had ever seen. Not cold, like Maria's almost Northern eyes, but dark as Lady's night and Lady's shadow. Mystery, there. She didn't want to be beguiled. She didn't want to seem intimidated; she met those eyes and held them.

And then she said, in a voice that she knew was hers because of the sensation of speech, the movement of air across lips, the intake of breath and the sharp punctuation of the same breath when she was done. "Tell me about Evallen of the Arkosa Voyani."

"Have a care, Matriarch," Yollana said. Margret almost ordered her out of the circle.

And *that* would be the act of a fool.

"Did she give you your—burden—when she was dying?"

She expected the Serra to look away, as Serras so often did. She expected some pretty hesitation; the Serras were so often fluttery, delicate things, who moved with enviable grace and spoke in soft, fluting voices, and never wrinkled their faces with anything as common as a *frown*.

But this Serra, while she did not frown, did not flinch.

The eyes, Margret thought. For a minute, they were the dark of the Lady's Night—the Lady's desert Night; the terrible oblivion of cold. *What have you done, Serra? What have you seen?* She didn't ask. And not only because she knew better than to expose ignorance in front of an enemy or a rival.

Part of her didn't want to know what the answer was.

But as Diora didn't have the decency to look away, neither could Margret.

"Evallen of the Arkosa Voyani came to me in the company of the Radann kai el'Sol."

"Impossible."

"I would have thought so, and perhaps it was; but she had a unique voice."

The Serra Teresa reached out gently and touched the Serra Diora's shoulder, and although she was dressed as a slender clansman, the movement made it clear that they were of the same blood. Family. It made Diora seem less cold.

Which was no doubt what they both intended. Margret didn't trust them at all.

"And?"

"She gave me the pendant."

Silence.

"Matriarch," Yollana said, her voice the cracked, dry voice of age withered by sun and wind—the perfect foil for the Serra Diora's voice. "The Arkosan Matriarch made her decision."

But the bitch knew that she was going to die; she knew, and she gave the Heart to—to her!

They watched, and Elena touched Margret's shoulder, her grip harder and more obvious than the Serra Teresa's grip upon the Serra Diora. A small mirror. Margret shrugged Elena's hand off; Diora failed to notice Serra Teresa's.

"How did she die?"

"You know how she died, Margret." Yollana, again.

"Were you there?" Margret said, deliberately ignoring Yollana—which would no doubt have repercussions later—because, Lady's blood, the wound was open, the pain raw in a way that spoke of all kinds of loss.

Diora froze for a moment, although, until she did, Margret would have said that she had not moved at all. There was some subtle difference between her economy of motion and its complete lack; it was as if the cold had spread in a flash, like fire, from her eyes to the rest of her. The Serra Teresa seemed to be speaking, but there was no sound, no words. Then the young woman—whose gaze had never left Margret's—said, "Yes."

They all turned to stare at her. Until then their gaze had been bouncing, like a child's toy, between the Serra and the leader of the Arkosan Voyani.

"You—you were witness?"

"More," she said quietly.

The Serra Teresa's hand tightened perceptibly. The younger Serra raised her own and touched it, capturing it, or perhaps easing its grip.

"More?"

"I killed her."

Before Elena could stop her—before she could stop herself—Margret slapped the young woman who sat, her perfect knees bent on a rolled mat before the fire. That brought noise back into the circle.

Elena caught Margret's wrist in a grip that said, clearly, do-that-again-and-I'll-break-it, and Yollana shouted her name in a tone reserved for Havallan curses. The Serra Maria, the Matriarch Maria, ever on the fence between the two worlds she had chosen, spoke.

"Serra Diora," she said flatly, "that was unnecessary."

Her hair disheveled, the bruise coming to her cheek, the

Serra Diora di'Marano turned to look—at last—at her accuser. The grim stare was as much a struggle as Margret's attempt to free her wrist from Elena's grip.

But in the end, Elena won.

Serra Diora di'Marano bowed her head, bowed now as a clanswoman did in the company not of women, but of men. Or of enemies. "She was being questioned by the Sword's Edge, another man, and a servant of the Lord of Night.

"I do not know what you know of the Sword's Edge—"

"We know enough," Yollana replied, grim now, her voice as flat and cold as Diora's. It was as frightening a transition as Margret had seen in the old woman.

"—but she was not afraid of him; it was the demon. The demon was destroying her."

"This was done in public?"

"It was done at midnight."

"And you just conveniently happened to *be there*?"

"No."

"Why were you there?"

"Her punishment for the crime of daring to wear the robes of a Radann was that she be put on public display for the remainder of the Festival and killed at its height."

"And?"

"I could not free her; it was not within my power. But I—"

The understanding did not ease Margret at all. It came, like a flash of storm-light, blinding, terrible. "You went to kill her."

The Serra did not flinch. Did not bow or scrape. Did not offer the submissive noises that made it clear that she understood the full consequences of her crime. Instead, as if they were equals here—*here*—she answered. "Yes."

If she could have, Margret would have slapped her again, or worse. But she knew her cousin; Elena *would* break her wrist. That much was clear by the white edges around lips pressed into as thin a line as Margret had ever seen.

"She knew everything," Diora said softly, lifting her head again. "She knew *everything*. Understand that what is at stake is too important to let knowledge slip into enemy hands without even the attempt to preserve our secrecy. I have lived the secret life," she added, her voice showing a hint—a trace—of emotion that vanished before Margret could name it. "I understand the need for secrecy."

Yollana's voice, unexpectedly gentle; Margret *hated* it. "She would have expected no less from you, Serra. She would have done the same, or worse, were your positions reversed."

The Serra nodded. "She gave me one other thing."

"What?"

"A dagger. The dagger is long and slender; it is not jeweled or adorned in any obvious way. But she named it—"

"*Lumina Arden,*" Margret could not keep the incredulity out of her voice. She had never had to. The cool of this . . . this . . . woman galled her, enraged her. "She *gave* you *that* knife?" But not so much as the fact that her mother's last act of significance had been to gift this stranger, this unblooded clansman, with the responsibilities that Margret herself had sought approval for for an entire lifetime.

She had never hated anyone so much in her life—or rather, had never hated any two people. She wasn't certain whom she hated more: the stranger or her mother.

"Yes. A gift, she said, free of geas." She bowed her head for another moment. "I kept both. I had both with me when I went to . . . to find your mother before the first full day of her ordeal had started. I did find her. But she was not alone."

"Not alone."

"She was being . . . questioned. I arrived too late."

Now, three breaths were drawn, held: Yollana's, the Serra Maria's, Elsarre's. Margret's, already held in an attempt to keep her bitter, sharp words where they couldn't do any further damage to her reputation among the Matriarchs, didn't change. But the Serra was staring at a point beyond them, into night sky, dark night. Memory called, and to judge by the expression on her face, she was an audience and Memory was the stage, the ever-unfolding play; she was captivated.

"Your mother saw me. I do not understand the gift she gave—and I wish no understanding; in my experience a true understanding of things Voyani is often a precursor to a death; death guards secrets far better than life, and I have much to do before I keep secrets in such a fashion."

Margret realized that the Serra was actually speaking.

Since she'd arrived she had done nothing but defer or demurely shunt aside all questions, pointed or gentle; this was as much speech as Margret had heard. And the words were soft and sweet; not too high and not brought low by age. The voice was *perfect.*

Even in capitulation, it was perfect.

"I do not know if it was the pendant or the knife that brought me to your mother. She called me, and I came; I had to come to her side." She paused and looked away for the first time, seeking the faces of the three Matriarchs who had not built fire with heart's work and blood. They had faces of wood or stone; faces of earth. Everything was beneath the surface. She turned back to Margret, to Margret who struggled so ineffectually to keep rage and pain from her voice and face.

"I walked among her enemies and they did not see me, but she did. She asked me—she asked me for death.

"She was dying. She was dying and she was—I think—stronger than most men would have been. She told me she had told them nothing. I . . . am skilled in some of the Lady's arts. Very few of the living can offer me a lie that I will accept; she offered only truth. But she also said—and, forgive me, Matriarch, but I did not and still do not understand this—if I did not kill her, the servant of the Lord of Night would bind her for three days."

"*The* Three Days," Yollana said quietly.

"Yes."

The oldest of the Matriarchs closed her eyes then, turning her head to one side to protect the brunt of her involuntary expression.

"And you killed her? You're telling us that you—" Elena's hand, like a steadying, constant presence, piercing the flesh around collarbone in an attempt to shake the words loose in a way that wouldn't diminish them.

"She wasn't *there*, Margret; *think*. What was she wearing? What did she bear? Evallen was alive; wearing it or no, she was still the source of its power; it was hers to command. The girl had no choice; she has never been schooled in our arts. Had Evallen commanded you or I that way, we would have had some ability to refuse. Although our ability and hers would be tested at that moment.

"The Heart carried her spirit to Evallen; there is some

mercy in the forces that drive us, inexplicable and beyond our ability to invoke, but present in its fashion." Again, Yollana's voice, for all the harshness of the words, was gentle. It was more than Margret could bear, but she was Matriarch; she bore it. "The knife?"

"The knife? I—ah. Yes, Matriarch. You are wise. I carried the dagger, *Lumina Arden.* I have carried it in any sari I wear since it passed into my hands; it is . . . light and . . . easily hidden."

"It is."

"It was the only weapon I had with me that night."

The old woman bowed her head. "I will make my offerings to the Lady," she said, "before dawn. Had you carried any other knife, we would not, I think, be here tonight. But I'm old, and I am easily distracted. Tell us the rest, and I will smoke in silence."

True to her word, she fumbled in her vest a moment and pulled out a short, squat pipe, something that seemed a lot like her: ancient, practical, and as enduring as the seasons. Margret had never taken comfort from the pipe. Or from drink, although the latter was more attractive. She wished she had one now, and that it was both warm and strong. The night was cold.

"I pulled it out of my robe that night. I pulled it. She asked me to kill her." Her eyes fell to her hands, to her perfect, unblemished, undarkened hands—and she stared at them as if they were anathema; as if they were offensive to her in a way that only memory provided the key for.

It made her seem human, for just a moment. It eased—only slightly—the terrible bitterness that Margret could not contain. It was almost as if—but, no, that was impossible. A woman like this one had killed before, would kill again. Could probably do it without crying or weeping, or shouting or smiling—without surrendering any part of herself to the act.

"And he looked *at* me."

"He?" All gentleness was gone from Yollana's voice, from Yollana's expression.

"Yes. The servant of the Lord. He knew I was there." She was silent; the silence had the quality of indecision.

Had it been Margret, Yollana would have snapped like

a rabid dog; it was the Serra; she held her tongue and waited. Margret was almost beside herself with bitter fury.

"He saw me."

"He saw you." The oldest of the Matriarchs had a voice dry as desert dust—the kind the wind sweeps away without effort. Her lids fell; she sat a moment in a bleak, stiff silence that spoke of death or mourning. Yollana had a touch of the seer's blood in her. They all did, but in Yollana, it ran true. The silence held until she chose to open her eyes and speak. "And?"

"He could not stop me. I drew the dagger from my robes, and I killed Evallen of the Arkosa Voyani. Or I should have; the blow was fatal. But he would not let her die. He held her somehow."

"She died?" The words were cutting.

Diora was silent a moment. "The dagger," she said at last. "I cut him with the dagger."

"Interesting. And he bled?"

"Yes."

"Then we understand," Yollana said quietly, "why Evallen gifted you with *Lumina Arden*. We can only guess why she did not ask you to return it with . . . other burdens. There is much about the ancient weapons that we understand only by story and myth, and there are reasons why we have each come to pray that our understanding is never improved. You did what you had to do. And if we are, as clansmen, taken by wind, there is a voice in the storm that blesses you, Serra."

Diora was silent. When she spoke, the words were hesitant; it was clear that if such a blessing were offered, it was lost to wind; it did not reach her ears. "He came to me, later."

"He?"

"The . . . demon. The one that almost bound Evallen. The one that saw me, when the others couldn't," she replied quietly. "He came to me, as seraf."

"As *seraf*?"

She nodded.

"What did he say, when he came to you?"

"That he was curious," she replied, her face once again so smooth it might have been a mask. Margret had seen enough of masks in this lifetime to wonder what it cost to wear this one. She didn't ask.

Yollana was silent a moment; the moment stretched. "What about?"

"He wanted to see the woman who had angered the Sword of Knowledge."

"And survived it?"

"He did not say as much plainly."

"But you inferred it?"

Her lips curved slightly, just slightly, but the momentary warmth it brought to her expression was astonishing. "While I acknowledge the difference between the clans of the Dominion and the Voyani families, I must say in defense of the clans that rumors of our demonic nature are exaggerated. I would hesitate to ascribe motive to a creature so much beyond my ken."

Yollana's response was almost as astonishing: She smiled in reply. "Well played, Serra. Well played. In you, the Serra Teresa's blood runs true."

But the Serra Diora looked up, her cheek red and slightly swollen, to the daughter, the Matriarch's daughter. Margret, who was determined to fall to no charm, no beauty, no clannish wiles. "She asked me to protect the pendant; she said it was of immeasurable value to the Arkosans. She asked me, in time, to give it to you. And Matriarch, that is my intent."

"In time."

"In time."

The Serra Teresa lifted a hand from her niece's shoulder. "Tell them," she said, her voice as cool as Diora's expression. "Tell them, or I will."

"Ona Teresa," Serra Diora replied, the words somewhere in the uncharted territory between plea and command. "Does it matter? In the end, prudence dictates that I follow this course of action."

"It matters."

The younger Serra was silent for a long time; Margret wondered if she would accede to what was, in the end, a command, or if she would, with grace and skill, slide out from beneath what was clearly a threat.

But it appeared that the Serra Teresa had as much influence with the Serra Diora as she had had with Evallen of the Arkosa Voyani—and would never, never have, Margret vowed in quiet fury, with the new Arkosan Matriarch—for the younger Serra bowed her head to ground a moment—or rather, to knees kept above the commonality of dirt the rest of the women shared. "I cannot remove the pendant."

Whatever she had expected, it was not this. Margret, shook herself free from her cousin's grip. "*What*?"

"I cannot remove it. I have tried." Her face, like the moon's, was a pale light in the growing night sky. "I thought, perhaps, there was some Arkosan ceremony, some Voyani ritual, that came with the end of an obligation such as this."

"And you didn't ask us?"

As the answer was obvious, it was clear the Serra was not going to condescend to give it. She offered a different one in its stead, one which was less pleasing. "As I intended to follow the course I am now taking, I did not see that it was relevant. Let me be blunt," she added, and Margret snorted.

"You wouldn't understand the word."

"I would not have your understanding of it, no. But I believe that my version of blunt will serve even here."

"Na'dio."

"Ona Teresa." She turned for a moment, exposing profile as if it were dagger's edge. Then, in the ensuing silence, she turned back. "It is clear that you disdain the clans; clear that you have no desire to be involved in a fight that involves them—regardless of whether or not it serves your interest in the long term.

"And that is, perhaps, as it should be; I cannot say. Women are not given whole families to rule among the clans."

Margret, seeing them, aunt and niece, Serra and Serra, snorted.

"It is true; the power we gain, we gain by subtlety, and we are aware, always, that it is given and sustained by the intricacies of our art, our ability to cajole. Limited by the illusion of our beauty. You clearly do not labor under the same . . . restriction."

Elsarre laughed. "The little girl has fangs."

"The 'little girl,' " the Serra Maria—the Matriarch Maria—

said quietly, "is not a serpent; she is a warrior of the Lady's heart."

"I would expect you to support her; you are from the same place."

"A place that understands courtesy? Hospitality? Yes. Perhaps you would do well to visit it yourself, Matriarch, although that is the topic for another—fruitless—conversation."

And you have them fighting over you, now; you know they hate each other—or that Elsarre hates everyone—and you've already started to turn it to your advantage. I'm watching *you, Serra.*

"If I could remove the pendant, I would not return it to you yet; not here in the heart of my enemies' territory."

"And where would you deign to return what is Arkosan to Arkosa?"

"In Mancorvo," she replied quietly. "Or Averda, if you choose it. The Arkosans hold the Averdan passages for most of the year, although I believe they were contested bitterly two years ago."

"They were." Margret frowned. "Your information is good. But a warning: we do not discuss such contests when the Matriarchs gather."

"Pardon me for my clumsiness, Matriarch."

As if, Margret thought, *you didn't know that.* The woman was clever; beauty had not robbed her of cunning. "A question, Serra."

"Ask."

"If you cannot remove the pendant now, how do you know it will come to hand so easily when you arrive at the destination you have chosen?"

Without so much as a change of expression, the Serra replied. "I don't."

Margret snorted. She hated it; she knew that it made her seem ungainly, intemperate. But she *was* those things. "I would make a poor Matriarch," she said softly, "if I did not question the worth of that bargain. I am to take you—with my family—into the heart of Averda. You know the clans will come; you know that by doing so, I will have chosen a side in a war between clans."

For a moment, the clanswoman's expression sharpened; there was, Margret thought, a very real anger that, like desert night, waited to descend upon the unwary. But she held it, shaped it with words into something that defied the rawness of emotion. "If you choose to abdicate your responsibilities by calling this a war of clansmen, so be it. I am not familiar with the ways of Arkosa; perhaps this is acceptable.

"But you know that the man who wears the crown is not the enemy I face; the Lord who stands behind him is. Should you choose to ignore that, that is, of course, your prerogative; hide then, in shadows, as Voyani do—and pray to the Lady that the shadows are safe.

"But do not attempt to deter me in my fight. Do not take from me the weapons I require."

Elena's hiss of drawn breath was almost exactly like the sound of metal against metal. She stepped forward, red hair catching the fire's reflection and holding it.

But she left the talking to Margret. "And if I choose to take back what is mine, how will you stop me?"

"I won't," Diora replied evenly. "If my understanding of these things is correct, the pendant itself will."

"Impossible."

"Is it? Try, then, Margret of the Arkosan Voyani. Try, if that is what you wish. Satisfy your curiosity and then decide what you will do with me. I must make my decisions based on yours and the only thing we have in common at the moment is the necessity of haste."

Yollana of the Havalla Voyani rose. She rose so smoothly and so swiftly it was easy to forget that her legs were injured, that she required canes to walk with. "*Enough,*" she said, and the heartfire flickered with the force of her word.

"Serra, I understand your vow; in my fashion, I respect it. Margret, I understand yours. But this bickering is pointless. You can hate each other on your own time.

"Serra, I must ask you what Evallen of the Arkosa Voyani said when she gave you your duty to Arkosa."

"She asked me to carry what I wear to Margret of the Arkosa Voyani."

"No more?"

"No."

"And yet you cannot remove the—what was given."

"No."

"Try, please."

Diora's expression shifted slightly. For a moment, Margret thought she would refuse. But the fire lit Yollana's harsh features from beneath, and there was nothing in them that brooked refusal. Kneeling, the Serra Diora lifted both of her hands to her collarbone, to something that lay against it.

Margret stopped breathing when she realized that she couldn't even *see* the Heart. She stumbled forward; Elena caught her.

It was clear from the way the Serra's hands and fingers moved, from the way her palm curled protectively in the night air, that she handled something. But . . . it did not call Margret at all. *We've made a mistake*, she thought. *She doesn't have the Heart.*

But that doubt did not touch the Serra, if any doubt did. She lifted the pendant, pulled it over her head. Or tried. A bright, white light encircled her neck in a flash as her hands rose above the line of her perfect chin.

Denial.

More.

Much, much more.

The Serra's breath was sharp; it was lost, almost lost, to the cries of the other women: Elsarre, Maria, Elena, and, yes, Yollana. Only the Serra Teresa was completely silent, but her hands now rested one on either side of her niece's shoulders.

Before them, robbed of color, robbed of flesh, stood a woman they recognized.

Mother.

Margret, she said, lips moving in absolute silence. No wind would carry these words; spells existed that could breach the heartfire, but Margret *knew*, in a way she seldom knew anything, that no spell existed that could gather the words this apparition would say.

When you take the Heart, you will know how I died. You will know exactly *how. I leave that; this is not the time, not the place.*

Serra Diora, she continued, and the woman on her knees looked up, face as white as the light that her mother's spirit was made of. *I am sorry. In order to protect the Heart from our enemy's detection, I made you, in blood, Arkosan.*

"Mother!"

"In blood?"

It was not a simple task; not an easy one. But if you can hear me now, it means that you stand in the circle of a fire made by the Matriarch of Arkosa. Forgive me. Forgive me, Margret. The Tor contained within it creatures of such darkness that our ancestors might not have been able to stand against them. They knew what we are, and what they were looking for; had I worn the Heart, they would have found it.

And had the Heart been given, by accident and fate, to another, they would already own it; it would already be destroyed.

The Serra Diora offered blood to the Heart stone.

Yollana's gaze broke away from the dead. "Is this true?" she demanded, sharp now, the words fired like quarrels.

Serra Diora started to speak; she started to offer her denial . . . and then she raised her hands. Her perfect, unblemished, uncallused hands. She stared at the lines of her palms; at the rise of flesh that gave way to thumb. And she said, softly, "Not knowingly, Matriarch. But the Heart of Arkosa is hard and its edges are all sharp. I—" She looked away. Looked back. "I bled while the Heart was in my hands.

"But if it—if it were that easy—"

"It is *not* that easy," the oldest Matriarch replied. The lines of her face sank, as if with gravity and weight, with age and knowledge. "What she has done to you, Serra, is a poor thanks for the risk that you took, and the service you did by freeing her. Poor thanks, indeed." Her voice was grim. "This Evallen will not answer my questions. See? She has words for her daughter alone."

Diora nodded, looking through the back of the ghost of Evallen as if through a glass or a lens; Margret's face had become unguarded; her emotion as obvious as a child's.

"My hands bled, but I was not aware that they were bleeding."

"When?"

"I . . . am not sure. I was aware of the damage only after it had occurred. But—I am certain my hands were bleeding when I killed her."

"Then the bond had already been made. Serra . . . there were men in the past who would have killed for what you were unknowingly granted." She smiled, and her smile was chilling. "And that is because they are fools. You have been cursed, and you will pay for whatever aid Evallen of the Arkosan Voyani gave you."

She is of Arkosa. She was blooded, by sacrifice; bound, by Heart and the power of the dagger. She is *a daughter of the Heart, and as daughter, she, as you, must make the pilgrimage. You will be watched; possibly followed. Be prepared for war, Margret; be prepared for the End of Days. Our ancient vows bind us, not because we are fools or sentimentalists, but because, having seen our enemy, I understood that those vows define who we chose to become when we chose to walk the long* Voyanne.

The Serra Diora is blood of our blood; a daughter in binding, if not by birth. In order to retrieve the Heart from where it now rests, you will either have to kill her—and in so doing, overcome the Heart's protections—or accompany her. And if you kill her . . .

I will never wear the Heart of Arkosa.

"Mother . . ."

Silence.

Silence and anger and something else. Margret's cheeks were wet.

"Mother . . ."

I won't waste time. Arkosa does not have it. But you will know, when you complete your trial, what I feel and what I desire. You will be—if you control your temper and your bitterness—a better Matriarch than any family has seen in our history since the founding. But if you cannot control these things, then Arkosa, like the other lines of Man, will perish.

Having said that, Margret, her mother continued, looking calmly into her daughter's eyes, *I will say one other thing. Be harsh when you must, and when you are asked to judge, when you are asked to judge at the appointed place and at the appointed time, leave mercy to the Lady and the Lady's whim; offer none. Do you understand?*

Arkosa was never a kind master, and it knows no kindness. As you will discover. I am . . . sorry. For a moment, it seemed that she was; her expression was almost—almost—gentle. But it changed. As it had always done, the gentleness gave way to the edge of Evallen's duty: Arkosa. Everything for Arkosa.

Go, Margret.

Go to Arkosa.

25th of Scaral, 427 AA
Raverra

Jewel ATerafin sat, knees tucked beneath her chin, blankets around her shoulders, looking distinctly less powerful than rank and natural ability dictated. The only thing that would have set her apart in a crowd—the signet that had been given her by The Terafin—looked remarkably dull in the fading light.

"Is it me," she said out loud, "or is it cold? Because I'm freezing."

In response to the words, spoken more to break silence than because they were true—although they *were* true—the great stag appeared from between trees that circled the clearing; he made his way to where she sat, and then, when she gazed up—and up, for he was tall—nudged her very, very gently with the tines of his antlers.

She knew a *move over* when she didn't hear it, and she moved, exposing her back to the tips of antlers that had already pierced skin once. The stag slid between her and the tree she had chosen to lean against, and then nudged her again. When she sat down, her back touched his flank; there was something about the muscle and the sleek sheen of his coat that felt . . . wrong. She was afraid to relax.

But he was warm, very warm; he radiated heat in a way that the distant fire, surrounded by what she was certain were angry women, did not. "You're not mine," she said, whispering the words. "I don't own you. If you think I do, you don't understand what our argument—hers and mine—was about."

His nose touched the skin of her cheek. She met his eyes, large eyes, dark and round; she swallowed and looked away. She could *see* what lay beneath the facade of animal face, animal form. Little things like this made the talent of sight a burden. And she knew with certainty that she would understand just how much of a burden it was in the months to follow. His skin brushed her skin as if he were touching her; she looked back. *Oh, I heard your argument,* the stag said, in a voice so deep she felt it as a sensation rather than a sound. *And while I benefited from its outcome, I do not entirely understand it.*

"Why?"

Because by right of victory, she ruled. By right of victory, you rule. The world has always been thus. The strong and the weak clash, and the weak give way. If they are pleasing, they are kept; if they are displeasing, they are discarded.

"You sound like Avandar," Jewel snorted, uncomfortable.

"You speak with her mount," Lord Celleriant said.

She did not reply. Nor did she look at the disgraced lordling of the Winter Court; he was beautiful in a way that reminded her of his Queen. She had seen women—and men—attempt to use beauty as a weapon before, but she had never been scarred in that particular battle.

She was now. Kalliaris had chosen to smile; the scars were invisible. But the Winter Queen lingered like both dream and nightmare when she closed her eyes.

She had told no one because she felt foolish doing it, but she had spent three days weaving the long strands of the Queen's hair into a bracelet; she wore it around her left wrist. She had seen such keepsakes before; they were usually fastened to gold or silver clasps because hair wasn't very good at staying in place. They were also usually taken from the dead.

Although she had developed an appreciation for finer metals—in her duties as merchant, among other things—she had no skill at working them, and besides, lacked the necessary tools. But the hair thus braided and twined clung as if made of links of chain, circling her wrist three times before ending in a rough knot.

She had a feeling that nothing would remove it; that the knots she had tied were true knots. Jewel ATerafin was seer-born. She trusted her feelings. So there was no reason whatever to sit in the dark, fingering the handmade bracelet as if to make sure it hadn't somehow vanished into the strange and perfect darkness that had swallowed the Winter Queen.

But she did. Her fingers stroked the texture of pale, pale

braid as if she couldn't believe it was there, as if somehow touch could stop things from vanishing.

As if. Hadn't she learned better? She could feel, for just a moment, aged skin beneath her fingers; could see the wide-open, unblinking stare that was the end of all stories, the end of all shelter. Her Oma's death. She could hear her father's steps, wide, as he took the stairs two at a time in an effort to spare her this: death, the knowledge of what death looked like, felt like, smelt like.

And she could see the story of death, like moving, cursive script, as it traveled the length of his face, altering his expression. He struggled to be calm and accepting for her sake, but he grieved for his own. Her Oma was his mother, and Jewel had come to understand, as she had gotten older and had the time and leisure to observe people, that the death of a mother—to a person who remembered having one clearly—always struck some hidden place in the heart, no matter how old the person was when the loss happened.

Her den, most of it, had lost mothers so long ago that the loss was just a natural part of their lives, like heartbeat or breath. It wasn't something they talked about.

Funny, that the bracelet could invoke that, here.

She pulled her hand away from her wrist.

"Wise," Avandar said softly. His first word that evening. Well, no, realistically it was his tenth.

"Why?"

"Because you've done willingly what no man would have done when the Winter Queen was free to wander these lands as she pleased."

"Oh?"

"You've marked yourself," he said softly, and when she did not immediately acknowledge his words, stared pointedly at her wrist. The Queen's hair caught light as if it were platinum in fact, and not just poetic fancy.

Jewel frowned. "And you've marked me. Am I to suppose that what I willingly wear is more dangerous than what I didn't ask for?"

He fell silent again, and Jewel was almost instantly sorry; he was never a particularly talkative man—unless she'd done something "wrong"—but she could count on one hand—on half a hand—the number of words he'd spoken in the last day and a half.

"Avandar—"

"As you say."

He retreated.

She pulled the blankets more tightly across her shoulders, and the stag's flank rippled at her back as he curled his neck around until his face was almost touching her shoulder.

"You have a friend, I think, Jewel of Terafin."

The most famous bard that Senniel College had ever produced walked into the clearing as if it were a tavern. A *crowded* tavern.

"Are they almost finished?" Jewel said.

"I don't know."

"You don't?"

"I cannot hear what they say. The fire that they have spent so much time and effort building protects their words from any listeners."

"Avandar?"

"If I could breach the barrier of Voyani heartfire, do you think I would be foolish enough to mention that ability within their encampment?"

She couldn't keep the smile off her face.

"I've amused you."

"Twenty-four," she said, the smile broadening.

His eyes narrowed, and then his brows rose dismissively. "Twenty-four?" For a moment, he was genuinely confused, and that made her smile wider.

"I believe, Avandar," Kallandras said with mock gravity, "that your lord is referring to the number of words she has heard you speak today. You've been remarkably . . . taciturn, even for you."

"You will never be a leader, ATerafin, if you persist in these trivial games."

"Thirty-nine." She laughed because she saw the frown deepening as he turned away. "Of course, most of them were critical, so I suppose I should be grateful that you've been quiet."

"I cannot recall, in my long service," and the word long was stretched in a way that implied centuries, not years, "any display of gratitude on your part."

"Which probably says more about your service than it does about—"

The comfortable warmth at her back was gone. The stag leaped up, over her, hooves tearing dirt as he reared. Tines cut air; she could have sworn, although she wouldn't have bet something as substantial as, say, money or life, that she saw the air move, like whirlpools, around them as he tossed his head wildly.

"What is it?" she shouted, as both Avandar and Lord Celleriant threw themselves out of the stag's way.

The exiled lord of the Arianni looked up at the stag that had been the Winter Queen's mount. "Apparently," the tone of his voice made the evening air seem warm, "the heart-fire, as Viandaran called it, is not proof against the Queen's stag."

She turned to the stag. "What?" she asked softly. "What is it?"

We go to the Cities of Man.

"The Cities of—"

"ATerafin, **be silent***."*

The words froze in mid-syllable; she choked on them, as if they were physical objects. It was a shock; her neck snapped round as she turned, wide-eyed, to Kallandras of Senniel. Her lips formed the word "why?"—but even that one couldn't follow the ones he'd stopped.

Instead, in the clearing that they had chosen to occupy, she heard something worse: the sound of metal against metal. The drawing of blade.

Lord Celleriant.

Before his sword had been raised—and he did raise it—Kallandras of Senniel College had armed himself as well; two blades, to the single long sword.

"You do not mean to challenge me?" Contempt failed to rob Celleriant's face of beauty. Standing with a sword in his hand, he seemed to illuminate killing in a way that hallowed it, and Jewel ATerafin was suddenly glad that she had witnessed no supernatural hunt, no death.

What grace, after all, could be retained in the pathos of terror and mortality?

Kallandras replied softly, so softly the wind didn't carry the word to Jewel's waiting ear. She started forward, and the stag, silent, and as beautiful in his way as the Arianni lord, was suddenly in her path, tines gently pressed against throat and forehead like a caress.

No, Serra.

She could hear his voice.

Just as she had heard Avandar's—in a place where words had never reached, weren't meant to reach.

But Avandar's words—when he spoke them—made her arm throb, her stomach twist, her mind catch fire with the peculiar heat of fear. The stag's voice . . .

No one calls me Serra, she said. *I'm called three things I answer to: ATerafin, Jewel and . . .*

And?

Two things. Two things. What are you doing?

There are three here who have the gift of the voice.

The gift of— She was silent because she had to be; the silence didn't rob her of words. Only privacy. *Kallandras.*

Yes. And two others. His is the strongest talent that I have heard in a long time, although I grant I have heard little in the way of human speech these many years.

He's a bard.

He is much more than that; he is bound to a god, and he derives some power from the kill. I am . . . surprised. . . .

Jewel's eyes left the stag's; she gave him a get-out-of-the-way shove that would have sent anyone but Arann half-flying. She might as well have tried to fell one of the many trees that defined the clearing with her bare hands. *Surprised? What do you mean, surprised?*

He is a killer; his scent is death's.

I told you, he's a bard.

With those weapons?

She was silent. When had she first met Kallandras of Senniel College? He was so much a part of her conscious life she could not objectively say. But the memory that was at the root of all things was as old as her association with Terafin, and she did not willingly go there. Not there.

He's not a killer, she said firmly. But willing or not, she remembered the screams of the dying beneath a wall of earth so magicked and so deep that there was nothing anyone could do to save the people whose voices had become her most visceral memory. Her most visceral, most avoided memory. It came back, in this faraway clearing.

Because of all the songs that had been sung that day, she remembered his.

"You're dangerous," she said, forcing the words to leave

her lips. Surprised that she could, now. She needed the distance.

Yes. I always was.

"Get out of my way."

He used his power against you. Will you allow this?

"What does it look like? Get-out-of-my-way."

The stag bowed. *I am in your service, ATerafin. I will do as you command. But I warn you—*

She was past warning. "The man Lord Celleriant knows as the Warlord *is* my chosen servant. If I were in any danger at all, he would protect me; he has never failed. But I made it clear years ago that crimes against my dignity were not capital crimes. If they were, I'd be responsible for more deaths than *he* has been by now. Let it be."

As you wish.

Swords clashed.

She turned and bounced off the chest of the man who had been domicis, and who was something now that she didn't want to think about. That was the problem; she knew that a false step was death, and she was so damn tired she was willing to take *no* steps, to stand in stillness until the motion of life passed her by.

"ATerafin?"

Almost. "Don't bother." She pushed past him in a way that she had not been allowed to push past the stag, and was surprised at how much the familiarity of the action comforted her. But she was also aware, as she hadn't been before, that Avandar allowed her this act of familiarity; that he, in fact, had more in common with stag and Arianni lord than he had ever had with her, her den, and the House that she loved.

Why did he serve? Why did he serve her?

No, that wasn't the real question. And she wasn't going to ask the real question right now.

Lord Celleriant and Kallandras of Senniel had participated in a single conversation, all by the edge of blades; they now circled each other warily. Something about that wary preparation for combat was wrong, but she was tired; it was a minute before Jewel realized what it was. There was no sound.

Well, fine. She'd make some.

"Lord Celleriant."

She thought he would ignore her. He seemed consumed by the pattern of the circle made over fallen leaves, dying grass, waning light. His shadow was as long and slender as he when it came to rest.

"Kallandras."

The bard sheathed his weapons. "My pardon, ATerafin."

"Why? I was obviously about to say something stupid."

He was silent.

"And someday you can tell me what it was."

He smiled slightly. "Some day." The smile, as always, was beautiful, and as always, brief. "Although I think you will understand what it is better than I do now by the end of our journey."

"Our?"

"I think we're fated to travel together for some distance." He turned to the Arianni lord. "You are in mortal lands."

"I have been in mortal lands before." His smile put Kallandras' to shame, but it was thing of ice and death.

"Indeed. But you will find they are very different when you are forbidden to kill those who dwell within them. My apologies. You will not find a worthier lord than Jewel Markess ATerafin, but she is . . . spontaneous in all reactions."

"This means I speak without thinking."

"Indeed."

Lord Celleriant turned to face her. "You allow this?"

"This?"

"This . . . easy contempt."

Jewel closed her eyes. Opened them. The Arianni lord was still there. *Kalliaris*, she thought. *Smile.*

"You have a lot to learn," she told him. "And I'm sorry you have to learn it."

That evoked a response. "I desire none of your *pity.*" Wasn't the one she wanted, but she'd had worse in her time.

"Don't earn it, then."

Take care, a warm voice said. She saw the stag's shadow join hers. Felt his fur beneath her hands and realized she had raised her hand to touch him automatically.

"ATerafin?" Kallandras had exchanged the swords for the harp.

"Yes?"

"Have a care, now. What you built once, you built in desperate circumstances, but you chose the materials well, and you have been rewarded. Here, you have been given no choice." He bowed. "We will enter the desert soon, and it has only one face; Lord's or Lady's. They already speak of you, ATerafin, in the encampment."

"Great," she said, in a tone that implied anything but. "What are they saying?"

"That you faced the Winter Queen and won."

She snorted.

"That you have a mount that not even the clansmen could claim."

She snorted again.

"And that you are served by one of the Lady's warriors. You are becoming legend."

"Legend is old and musty," she snapped. Then, after a moment, she added, "Help me."

"I will do what I am able. But my influence extends only so far. If you cannot take the wonder out of the companions fate has chosen for you . . . your story will travel across the Dominion like brushfire."

"Thanks."

"I will withdraw now, to prepare." He smiled again, and his smile was the smile he offered the Queen Marieyan when he flirted as openly as any unmarried man dared with the Queen of the wisdom-born King. She had seen him, swords in hand; had seen the expression on his face—or rather, the lack of expression—as he joined silent battle with an Arianni lord. Kallandras was many, many people—and the tricky part was that in some measure, *all* of them were genuine. **"Have faith in your own ability, ATerafin."**

She laughed. Looked around the clearing. What, Lady, what did she have to work with?

A lord who had tried to kill her.

A stag that could speak to her, and whose tines, she knew, were more than decorative mating tools.

A man that the Winter Queen called Viandaran; that the Oracle had called the Warlord, who had—until he had marked her in a fortress beneath mountains—been a grudgingly trusted domicis.

She could make a den out of these?

The silence was long. And into it, mixed with doubt, was a very real homesickness.

Angel. Arann. Carver. Finch. Jester. Daine. Kiriel. Teller.

What are you doing?

CHAPTER ONE

7th of Scaral, 427 AA
Averalaan Aramarelas, House Terafin

Home was where his mother brought her clients.

He learned—well before conscious memory started—that those clients were important men. And that many of them didn't want to know that she had a child.

During those nights, he would hide in the closet, or sometimes in the kitchen if the lights were low, and he would hoard his words, his inexplicable child noises; it was part of hiding. Afterward, his mother would come to him and take him quietly into her bed. He never asked her about the men; she never spoke of them. But sometimes she would go out with him the next day, and buy him something special, fruits or white bread from the bakers.

He learned to love the day. And to hate the night.

She was often angry. He remembered that clearly. He learned to fear her anger more than he feared hunger or cold, but he found that silence was the best way to avoid it, and silence became a rule of life, a comfortable law.

Sometimes she would talk about her childhood. He loved those times. She spoke about her birthday, her mother, always her mother. She never spoke about her father, but that seemed natural to him; he had no father of his own. They lived like that, mother and son, their days a prelude to her evenings, his silence.

As he grew older, it was harder; harder to hide.

As he grew older, and she grew older, her youth fading beneath the glare of sun, heat, hunger, her back bent by the poverty that he understood as part of his life, she would sometimes leave for the evening.

She would tuck him into bed, and tell him that she would

return in the morning, and he would stay awake in the still of the night, staring at the low ceiling, until sleep snuck up on him. But he promised her that he would help her. That one day, she would live in a better place, and she would never have to spend time in the company of her men again.

He started thieving when he was six.

He was small for his age, waiflike; he could get close to people because they ignored him. Because he was quiet.

She was angry about the theft. The first time he had given her money, she went all gray, and instead of being proud of him, as she so seldom was, her anger came up instead, like sunrise. He knew she was angry. But she didn't hit him, and she didn't shout at him.

Instead, she left their two-room home, while the light of the sun was high.

She returned before sunset, to change into the gaudy clothing she wore at night, her lips a thin line, the corners of her mouth deep with age.

"You don't have no call to go thieving," she told him, her words as tight and angry as her expression.

"But it's money, Mom."

"It ain't *our* money, boy."

"But—but—it's better than the money you get from those men. I can get us money, Mom. You don't have to see them no more."

She caught him by the shoulders, her fingers sharp as knives. "That's *my* job, boy."

"But Peg says you're just selling yourself."

"And what if I am? I'm selling what's *mine*. I'm not selling what belongs to anyone else. You understand? It's honest work. I do it because it's all I can do, but I ain't selling anything that belongs to anyone else. Where'd that money come from?"

He was smart enough not to shrug. "Some man."

"Some man? And what if that man has a little boy, like you? What if he has a bunch, eh? What if you just stole the food off their plates?"

He was silent. It had never occurred to him to wonder.

"I want you to be bigger, to be stronger. I want you to be *better* than that. You grow up, you can join the Kings' army. You can make an honest living. But they don't take no thieves, and I don't want no thieves in my house. You want to stay with me? You don't steal." She spit. "You can beg, if you want. You can sit in the streets with your hands out. But you take what they give you, you understand?"

He nodded, because nodding was safe.

And she looked as if she was going to cry. "You're the only thing in my life I've done right," she told him, touching his hair and his face with her shaking hands. "The only one. Don't break my heart. Don't make a lie out of all the work I done."

But it wasn't, in the end, his choice; it wasn't in the end, hers. That was the lie.

"Teller?"

He looked up. The surface of the kitchen table was as clean and polished as the counters. They were never this clean. It was a bad sign. Where was the inkwell, the messy blotters, the quills that, time and again, Jewel ATerafin destroyed?

She had packed them away. Had cleaned house. Had left. That was the plan.

She'd done everything she could to make them a home in House Terafin. They had jobs now. They had more money than he had ever dreamed of having. They had responsibilities that they could be—that they were—proud of. Jewel's little den of thieves. Jay's misfits.

Because of her.

Where was she?

He didn't want to talk to Finch. He didn't want to talk to anyone. But he looked up and nodded when she called his name again.

Didn't much like what he saw there. Hadn't really expected to. "What—what's the news?"

She was so pale, so gray; he had learned to hate those colors when they resided beneath the soft peach tones of skin.

"Half the Common's been destroyed."

"We knew that."

Finch swallowed. She started to speak, but the door banged the wall behind her, and they both looked up. Angel was in the door, hands on either side of the frame as if—as if he were trying to shore up his own weight. His hair was in full spiral, his one conceit.

Finch gave conversational ground as easily as Teller did. "Angel?"

"She wants us."

For a moment, Teller felt a wild hope, but he killed it quickly.

"Who wants us?"

"The Terafin." He turned to look at the frame six inches above his hand. "Jay was in that market, as far as anyone's been able to tell. We've got her movements down just that far."

Teller ATerafin lowered his head to the surface of the kitchen table and let it rest there, against the cool wood.

"We're supposed to help her," Angel continued. "Word's out for Arann as well. Carver's already left with Jester."

The gates of the Terafin Manse passed by him like a dream. He had seen them for half of his life, but every so often he would pause in front of them, to the amusement or the consternation of the House Guard, and touch their polished rails. Nothing encroached upon that brass patina, that endless shine; whole days were spent tending to their appearance, as if they were the House armor.

Whole days, and more money than he and his mother would see in a month, when they had lived in the twenty-third holding, in the hundred, in the old city.

He tried not to steal. He really did try.

But there were nights when his mother came home empty-handed, and her face was sallow with exhaustion and fear, her voice hoarse. He hated that fear. She would go to bed, and he would join her, and they would wake hungry and go to bed hungry until she left again.

When he was seven, those nights came more frequently. She said it was because of her teeth, because she had lost two. It was true. Her teeth, her lack of teeth, changed the way she looked. But she was his mother, and he loved her fiercely, and with a child's terror.

Those days, he would go to the streets himself—never at night, never then. And he would spend the day begging, and if that didn't go well, he would try his hand at worse. He always lied to her, though. He always told her that he had come by the money honestly.

He thought she believed him, because she didn't beat

him. He would take her out to the market. He would give her the money. She would choose the food they ate, as she always did, and they would go home.

"One day," she would tell him, "you'll laugh at all this. You'll be the Kings' best man, mark my words. You'll make me so proud of you."

If she could see him now. If she could see him—if he could walk up to her and tell her that his name was Teller *ATerafin*—she would be more than proud. But she was wrong about one thing: He never did learn to laugh about their life together.

Finch tried to keep an eye on Angel. Arann was fine; quiet, worried, but very much the House Guard he had become. Carver and Jester were already gone, and Kalliaris knew, maybe they were even being useful. But Angel was . . . Angel. The only one of the den who had refused to take the name ATerafin when it was offered. Jewel had been pissed. But Angel had been Angel. *I'm your man, not* hers. *You become The Terafin, I'll take the name. But not until then.*

Teller had been almost embarrassed at how readily he'd accepted The Terafin's offer, but it had been too late to back down; he didn't want to look as if he were following Angel's lead. None of them did. And what difference did it make? They *were* all hers.

Until now.

"Look, if the two of you can't keep up, you can meet us there, all right?"

Teller was quiet. Finch looked pained. But after another city block had passed, they let him go. Let him go. They had miles to cover.

When Teller was eight and a bit, his mother went out for the evening, as she often did. He hated that she went out at nights, because more and more often she came home exhausted and angry and frightened. Just two days previous, he had tried to convince her to let him do what he could. Beg, he'd said. Let him beg. Maybe she knew. Maybe she just didn't trust him. Maybe so many things, all incomprehensible, their lives were now so different. She had gone out, as she always did.

But by morning, she hadn't returned. Morning.

He woke and he was alone. They only had one bed. He thought, for a moment, she might be in the kitchen. But she wasn't there, and that was worse. He waited for an hour, trudging in an endless circle between the two rooms, bed and table. It felt like a day.

Footsteps came and went, but he knew the sound of hers, and hers were absent.

When the sun was high in the sky, when all trace of dawn had vanished, he left the apartment and headed through the warrens to the Mother's small church. The priests and priestesses there sometimes offered a hand to those who were sick or injured—when it wasn't too crowded. When it wasn't winter, and the lines didn't twist round the building like a cat's tail, twitching to and fro.

He recognized the frail old woman who answered the door; she had that weary smile that all of the Mother's children had.

"My mother didn't come home last night. Did she come here?"

The woman's eyes widened slightly. And then they came down at the brow, not narrowing exactly, but changing in every other way. "Why don't you come in and check?" She said.

And he knew that she wasn't there. He backed away from the old woman, turned and ran.

Because he didn't know where she was. He only knew where she was supposed to be. At home. With him.

His mother had always told him to stay close to home, where people knew her. Where people knew him. She had made him promise, time and again, to be careful.

But at eight years old, all he knew that day was that his mother was gone, that she was somewhere else, and that he needed to find her. He needed to find her.

7th of Scaral, 427 AA
Averalaan, the Common

The Common. Teller had always counted the trees in the Common as he passed beneath their ancient bowers, had let his gaze drift up and up until his chin was almost a continuous line with his neck. He'd loved them, and Jay had loved them, although neither could quite say why.

He noticed their loss first. At a distance.

"Teller?"

No one had ever asked him about his life. Not even Jay. He had never asked Finch about hers. It came to him that he did not know who any of them were outside of their life together. But some things came from that life, that outside life.

"Mother's blood," Finch whispered.

He looked. The Merchant Authority, grand old building that was a city block unto itself, had been staved in on the east side; great stone walls were crumpled like the thinnest of thatch. Men toiled in the rubble, like an army of workmen, their shadows short compared to the shadow cast by the destruction.

He did not want to go there.

He did not want to search the streets of the city—any city—again. Not like this. Not this way.

It's not the same, he told himself this as his steps grew smaller and smaller. *I'm not a child. This is not the twenty-fifth holding.*

But he had been a child.

And he had run, from the twenty-third to the twenty-fifth, with no clear idea of when he had crossed two boundaries. He had asked questions, endless questions, talking more in those hours than he had in months. Have you seen my mother? Have you seen my mother?

On that day, he had discovered that he was an orphan. He had looked death in the face, and he had sat by its side, crying in bewildered terror. He still woke sometimes, sweating, the cold, gray flesh of his mother's cheek beneath his hands. He had shaken her. He had shaken her body and when she hadn't responded, he'd hit her. To try to wake her, although he had never seen sleep like this. He had tried to drag her body home. He remembered that as well, because it was on the way home that he understood how helpless he was.

And it was on his way home that he had been saved by an angry angel, a stranger who inexplicably showed the kindness not even his mother had shown.

Had he been suspicious? Gods, yes.

But there was something about her narrowed eyes, her hunched shoulders, her liberal cursing, and the hair—which hadn't changed at all, even if she'd smoothed the rough edges off everything else—hanging in her eyes no matter how often she shoved it aside, that made her seem less auspicious than a miracle.

There was also something about the people she gave orders to that was less than angelic. He remembered Lefty best of all because it was Lefty who held the dagger. Duster hadn't come yet, although Jay'd found Arann and Carver by then. In just a few more months she would have almost all of the men and women who were Teller's family in everything but the flimsy tie of blood.

Lefty hadn't made it out of the twenty-fifth holding. Teller was certain, that day, that he probably wouldn't either—but anything was better than dying alone in an alley of starvation or worse.

And Jewel had offered to help him take his mother home. She made Arann do most of the heavy lifting because he was the biggest, even then, and while Teller cried, they'd followed his steps, had lifted his mother's body, had carried her into the building that had been his home for as long as he could remember.

They put her in the bed. Teller tucked her in. And then he'd fallen over, hugging her, terrified. Hugging her. She never hugged him back; that had been the last time.

Jay'd waited for him, outside. And when it had been long enough, she'd come back to get him. And he'd let her take him away.

Now, now he would have insisted on burying his mother.

Over time he had learned that Jewel *was* magic, and her magic took two forms, both of them equally precious, both intangible but unshakable. One: she could sometimes *see* the future. It hit her in dreams, in nightmares, in moments of sudden spasm as she walked at the heart of the den—protected on all sides by Angel, Arann, Carver, and Duster—through the city streets. And two, more precious: she was loyal. She chose her den for reasons no one ever questioned out loud, and she would *never* desert them.

Not while she lived.

He had been so terrified, that first year, and the second,

that she would die like his mother had. That had been his nightmare, before he had become the keeper of hers: of wandering in terror through the city streets, searching for her the morning after she hadn't come home on time. Searching, and afraid—gods, paralyzed now—of what would end that search.

When had he gotten so complacent? When had he let go of that fear until it wasn't even a distant nightmare?

He should have known better.

He felt the tears start down his cheeks, and he was so numb with dread he didn't realize what they were until Finch touched them gently and wiped them away.

"Teller. Finch." The Terafin was dressed in the plainest of robes; those robes were lined with dust and splinters. She was comfortable on horseback; she had been here for the better part of an hour, searching as if she were the least of the members of House Terafin, and not its Lord.

But Teller understood it the moment he saw her face. She needed to do something.

"Angel and Arann are to the west. Carver and Jester are just up ahead, near the permanent stalls. Near where they stood. Bodies are being brought to the west end of the Merchant Authority; there are healers there in number. Morretz is there. Daine is with him. So far no one has unearthed Jewel. Join Daine if you like. Join the others if you feel that you're better used in the search.

"And if you discover anything—let me know immediately. That's all."

"Terafin," they said, speaking—and bowing—in unison.

There were *so many* bodies.

To his left, men and women were grunting under the weight of stone and wood. Fabric, stretched between poles, awaited whatever it was they could retrieve from beneath that burden. They didn't judge the condition of whatever it was they found. They left that to the healers.

But in some cases, it was impossible not to know death.

He looked across what had been the beginning of the Common's circle. The ground was broken now, like dry, old loaves.

At a distance, across the fissures made by split earth and

ruptured stone, he could see the royal blue of the highest ranking Kings' Swords. He could not tell what their relative ranks were, but years ago, rank would have meant nothing: they served the Kings. Their job, he thought bitterly, being to protect the people who had money and means from those who didn't.

The momentary resentment surprised him; it was so old, he had thought it buried by the present. Destroyed.

The rubble. The wood. The bodies.

But so many things were coming back to him. The feel of stones like this beneath his feet, the harsh, painful dryness that grew in the walls of his throat, the unseasonal, bitter cold. Even then he had had the wits to take what little of value his mother owned; a dagger, a knife, a small handful of coins. He had never intended to desert the room he had shared with his mother.

Death changed all plans.

Jay.

The Kings' Swords were not here on their own; they did not venture out of *Avantari* in these numbers and these uniforms unless they accompanied a member of the royal family. From where he stood, he could not see which member, but he was fairly certain it would be the Princess of the blood, Mirialyn ACormaris. The Kings themselves rarely left the Isle; the Queens only slightly more often, and usually for functions that involved the powerful guilds or the churches. Ah, yes. There she was. She wore armor, although the day was warm; her visor was up, her face exposed. The horse beneath her moved carefully over the rubble of broken street, upturned cobblestone, soft dirt. He had never much liked horses.

"Carver, *shut up*." He was brought back to himself by the sharp crack of Finch's high voice.

Here and there, Arann, Angel, or Carver stopped to lend arm and back to the lifting of heavy stone; they worked in silence at the side of the magisterial guards, as if they were part of the Terafin House Guard. Once, they would have run from them, and with reason; the magisterial guards were not paid to smile cheerfully at hungry thieves.

The other Houses had sent small contingents to represent their interests—or their concerns, if one was not being cynical—but only one House had lost one of its governing council in the inexplicable attack on the market.

Years ago, fifteen or more, on a Henden as dark as any story could make it, demons had dwelled beneath the city of Averalaan, in the tangled web of tunnels and ancient passages at the heart of the old city. The fear their presence evoked had nearly broken the city's spirit. Then, he thought, the princess had ridden, in the Queen's party; so had Commander Sivari. They had drawn swords; they had taken arms; they had spoken against an enemy that could be seen by no one, and felt by all. Songs were still sung of that ride, fiercely, passionately, tearfully. Teller sang them. How could he not? He had been alive in that Henden; he had heard the demonic voices. He had *seen* the demons in the flesh.

Princess Mirialyn ACormaris presided, as she had then, over ruins. The city had seen its demons, and it knew, it knew now, that they had returned. He wondered, idly, if the magi were clever enough to make political use of the fear. The old woman who ruled the Order was, to listen to Jay talk.

Jay.

He did not run. He felt no need to run. He knew that whatever there was to be found would be found here. And he wasn't alone here; he was a man of means, surrounded by his den, with a House name to back him up. But, as if he had run the same frenzied run as he had the day he became an orphan, his throat was constricted and dry; breath came with difficulty.

The men led by Mirialyn ACormaris pulled a body from beneath the fallen slats of what had been a permanent stall in the Common. Stalls such as these were handed down from parent to child; they were rare and highly prized, although from the wreckage it would not be clear why to a casual observer. Wood had splintered, cloth had torn, both acts revealing color the sun seldom saw: pale, unstained wood grain, unfaded burgundy.

Other things caught and held his attention. Not the stall itself, but the flagpole that had made its presence known from a distance: metal, not wood, the pole looked as if it had been crumpled, like so much cloth or paper.

He turned again, this time to the center of the Common.

Men and women worked there who wore the robes and the emblems of the Order of Knowledge. He did not choose to approach them closely enough to see if they were mage-born; where the magi were concerned, sanity, and therefore safety, was always in question—and besides, they were busy. They stood, some dozen or so—fourteen, he thought, as he counted more precisely—in a loose circle. They did not touch each other, but they were clearly connected in purpose.

And that purpose: a tree.

Funny, that so many people lay dead or broken, and yet the magi were consumed by this: Giants had fallen.

Teller watched, as he always did, struggling to find words that made sense. Jewel had named him because he spoke so rarely. He could not explain why, and if he understood it now—at two decades remove—the knowledge served little purpose. It had become his habit to think before speaking, and he could not be hurried through either thought or speech, but when he did speak, his words were always measured, always calm, and always to a purpose. He did not curse or swear, did not vent rage or frustration in useless arguments or fights. He had learned that at his size it was worse than pointless. Instead, he observed, hidden, as unseen as he could make himself, and he bound his thoughts with words, when words would come. Sometimes they came quickly. Today, they would be a long time in arriving.

Those trees had stood in the heart of the Common since before the founding of Averalaan.

"Angel, for the Mother's sake, can't you be more careful!"

Angel's reply, half grunt, half spoken word, would have earned him a swat to the head, but Finch didn't have Jay's temper. She frowned. "I *know* it's heavy, but you're supposed to be helping the victims, not adding to them!"

Like Teller, she was slight of build and slender; they didn't expect her to be of much help. So she fluttered; he watched; they bore witness in their own way.

"Teller?"

He lifted his head, and as he did, strands of brown hair parted like a curtain. He did not, in principle, like long hair—but during his convalescence, it had grown, and Finch had been too busy to nag him to have it cut. So had Jay.

Jay.

"Teller?"

Turning, he saw that one of the Terafin Chosen was navigating broken ground; here, the damage had been concentrated in the earth. He nodded at one of the two captains who between them commanded The Terafin's Chosen. Wondered briefly if his face was as expressionless as Torvan's. He doubted it. "I've come from the west," he said quietly.

Teller waited.

"There's no sign of her."

He exhaled. Spoke a safer name. "Avandar?"

"None." The Captain of the Chosen turned away, hiding his expression by exposing his profile. Not a look that Teller liked, it was so unusual.

"What happened?"

"You know as much as we do. There were a number of demons present in the Common itself; they attacked a large group of people and destroyed just over a third of the market in the process. There is some evidence of struggle; some evidence that resistance occurred before the magi were summoned. But that resistance . . . crumpled. The attackers were eventually destroyed by the Council of the Magi."

"But Jay—"

Torvan turned to face him. "Yes."

"Yes?"

"She was here."

"But—"

"There are a lot of dead, Teller. We've . . . questioned the magisterial guards; guards were apparently in the Common during the battle."

"And?"

"There were no survivors in either the first or the second group to arrive here."

Not hard to believe. Not hard at all.

"Witnesses outside of the Common place her close to the center of . . . the attack."

"You think they were trying to kill her."

"We know they've tried before."

But never like this.

And the last time, he thought, they had sent only one creature. One creature, and Angel and Jay had ended up in the infirmary, bleeding to death while The Terafin and Alowan argued about which of the two was worth saving. He looked away.

"We'd like your help," Torvan said quietly.

"Help?"

"There are other witnesses."

"Yes, yes, sir," the young boy said, obviously flushed with excitement at the importance of his story, but just as obviously intimidated by the arms, armor, and size of those who questioned. "There was fire."

"Fire?"

"In the sky."

"And the—"

"They were demons. My grandma said so. Demons."

"There were many?"

He held up his right hand, extending his fingers. Then he held up his left hand. Teller knew the boy couldn't count, but that didn't mean he was stupid.

"What were they doing?"

"I don't know. They killed all the magisterians, though."

The old woman with her hands on his shoulders frowned; the boy winced as her nails bit into his collarbone. "Uh, the magisterial guards."

"How?"

"I think," the old woman said, her face frozen into a harsh series of lines that could not be mistaken for permission, "that that can be best determined by the magi."

The House Guard started to speak, and the old woman added, "They're still looking for his mother. My daughter." Her voice made ice seem warm.

Teller very deliberately stepped on the man's foot.

"How did the demons die?" He asked the boy, while the House Guard reined in the frayed temper of a long day without answers.

"The magi came," the boy replied. "On the wind." And he looked up, up again, as if between sun and cloud, between cloud and ground, they flew there still, circling the city.

One mage did.

It had been a risk that he had not wished to publicly acknowledge to summon the wind. To ride it, to summon the air and to give it commands that it followed was more than a skill; it was an act of seduction; it required a delicate balance, an intuitive understanding of the bargaining done by men of power that could not be separated from the elemental ability itself. He could cajole the wind with the whisper of its own voice; could stand at the edge of its storm before he earned a place in its eye, watching as it destroyed at its leisure. He could promise it many, many things—but making such a promise to a wild element was not a matter of words and contract, not a matter of human law with its labyrinthine clauses, its ifs and ands, its laughable penalties. The price was written in blood, paid in blood. Old laws.

Aiee, one considered the cost carefully when one summoned the past. Carefully. Delicately.

The wind's voice was a roar; he could literally hear nothing else.

To summon the wind as if it were a kept, tame creature—to demand that it carry not only himself, but the cadre of the elite who had been trained to fight, and to fight creatures such as the kin—was entirely different. It required not bargain, but force.

He was powerful enough that he could force the element to his bidding, but not so powerful that he could escape its wrath. Costly. Costly, these acts of desperation. Beneath his feet, blind to his flight, the beneficiaries of that desperation crawled across the broken surface of earth, excavating by slow degree the bodies of their dead. He was not a master of the intricacies of life; had he been, he would never have survived the great wars of his youth. But he knew enough to know that the men and women who toiled would find little worth their time and their worry beneath the bodies of the great trees and small buildings that lay broken.

He felt the loss of the trees keenly. Men passed on to some majestic hall and some hidden destiny at the whim of Mandaros when they died. But the trees that had existed for millennia—the last of their kind, although only the Order of Knowledge seemed to have a deeper appreciation of this fact—had been reduced to mere sap and wood; they represented a true loss, a profound loss.

Still, the arrival of his mages had been timely. Over half

of the trees had been untroubled by the battle that had raged across the less contested grounds; of the fallen, there was some hope that the knowledge of the magi might save or heal some few. The Common would be scarred by the loss, its voice stilled. But in time, the fallen would be forgotten.

In time. He stopped the wind from doing anything more harmful than tearing at the wide hand-shaped leaves.

As he brushed the edge of branches, as he cajoled the angry wind, he felt a change in the composition of the men and woman who toiled below; he looked down.

Sigurne Mellifas, leader of the Council of the Magi, had set foot upon the Common's ground. She rarely deigned to display her power, and when she did, it was so often offered as an act of mercy, not an act of war. She was frail, but not fragile; she played upon the weaknesses that age had given her, making them cunningly disguised strengths. He knew the games she played, but he was not above being bound by them. Although the person did not exist for whom Meralonne would give his life, he acknowledged with a grimace that he would give much to protect hers.

Just as there was not much she would not give to protect what she had chosen to dedicate her life to. It was complicated. At first, he had thought her like other magi, but colder. Of the magi, she faced death, even painful and violent death, with a calm unperturbed by human pain or suffering. Just as he himself might. But they were not kindred spirits. She accepted what she could not change; she made plans to change what she could; she wasted no energy—none at all—on the gray area between the two that tormented lesser people.

Yet she did not give her heart to the magi. He knew—although she had never said as much, and he doubted she would, even when questioned by Mandaros himself—that she had taken the helm of the Council of the Magi to guide and control them, not to protect them.

It was these, these broken and helpless mortals, these talentless, visionless men and women, that she had made her life's responsibility.

She had never approved of his warriors. She had never approved of the tactics he had used to train them. She had nearly disbanded them three times when injuries had been, in her word, *unacceptable*. As if they played boys' games.

She was right, of course; they were games. His own students could not see it; he did not choose to enlighten them. Instead he filled their heads with glorious nonsense, all the more powerful for the truth it contained: that they were the men who would stand between the *Kialli* and the city when the *Kialli* at last showed themselves; that their lives were the lives that would shield and protect what the Twin Kings, over the centuries, had struggled to build.

A just society.

A free society.

His laughter was taken by wind. Sigurne, watching, had said nothing at all. But she had, in the end, given him leave to let his students prove their worth in the only way that mattered: against the enemy they had been trained, since a dark Henden many years ago, to fight.

Being old put him at a disadvantage.

There was a bitter, fierce joy that lingered at the edges of his awareness; he had met his chosen enemy, had named him, had defeated him. As promised, that name was committed perfectly to memory, as was the struggle itself.

But into the enjoyment of the battle had entered something that he had never thought would hamper him.

He had watched these callow, and often useless, students make mistakes and die for them, and he felt their deaths as if they were the physical blow his enemy had tried, unsuccessfully, to land. It came, a rawness and a regret that had never marred his composure on the field of battle. The wind sensed weakness, of course; he would have, in his youth, when all he understood was power.

Sigurne, he thought, with a bitter envy, *what life shaped you, that you can be so cold in your failing years*?

He could not afford to land while any of that weakness governed him, or the damage done by demons and magelings would pale in comparison to the damage done by the wind.

But he *wanted* to land. He wanted to go to the fallen, *his* fallen, and honor them. He wanted to see their faces, and commit them to the same memory that now held the details of his combat and his victory.

* * *

The Terafin was absolutely silent.

One step from her side, close enough at any time that he could reach out and touch her, could—had she been a different woman—offer her physical comfort, was her domicis, Morretz. He carried one thing for her; a simple, heavy cloak, proof against the sea wind and the inclement weather.

She almost never wore it; it had a value that only history could give an item. She would ask for it soon. The lights that mages had cast were dimming; the lamps that guards carried, flickering. The noises in the Common were night noises. Many weaknesses were forgiven in the darkness. He had thought in his youth that he had found a woman without weakness; he had learned with the passage of time that the ability to reveal weakness—for a woman of Amarais' stature—took a different form of strength. She understood the demands of her rank. She waited; he waited, watching in protective silence.

From a bitterly cold sunrise—surprisingly cold, given the geography—to a cool, star-broken nightfall, The Terafin watched her Chosen work at the side of Jewel's den. Noting the difference in armor, in arms, in the deference they were trained to give: The Chosen were perfect, and the den, handpicked in no less careful a way given the circumstances in which it had formed, far less polished. But she saw the potential in them. They were terrified. They worked through it, hid it. Served.

He knew what she observed by her expression. She knew, for instance, that when Captain Torvan ATerafin approached her and knelt beneath the rising face of the narrow moon, he would report failure. She knew that the Council of the Magi, represented by Sigurne Mellifas, would likewise offer no comfort, but she offered words to the woman who wore the quartered moon. To her Chosen she had offered a grim silence, no more.

"Were they hunting your girl?"

"I had hoped that the Council of the Magi would offer an answer to that question."

"We are not all-seeing, Terafin. We labor under an understanding of the demon kin that is very little improved since the last time we were forced to deal with their presence in the streets of Averalaan."

"A motion was made, or so rumor would have it, that the forbidden arts be once again a subject of study within the Order. It was defeated by a narrow and forceful margin."

"You have, as always, impeccable sources, Terafin. Enough so that you will refrain from insulting my intelligence; you know the vote carried, and the head of Council exercised her right of refusal."

"You credit me with better sources than I have," The Terafin said quietly. "I was not aware of the rule in Council that allowed the head of council such a veto."

Sigurne Mellifas was frail; her skin was the color of light on water. Hard to imagine a woman such as this could successfully veto the decision of the most powerful members of the Order of Knowledge. Until she smiled, the amusement mixed with momentary appraisal. "We are both too blunt, Terafin."

"Indeed. Perhaps because we can be."

"You haven't the excuse of age and ill temper."

"Nor have you, although as any ruler does, you choose the excuse that's expedient."

"The excuse, yes, but not the veto, it seems."

The Terafin was silent. At last, she said, "I would know when to trust my own and when to have them watched. But I am not a mage; my sense of the expedient, where magical study is concerned, would be tempered by ignorance."

Morretz's brow rose a fraction; fell again before either woman could notice the ripple of expression. *You trust this woman, Amarais.*

Silence. "I don't know whether or not they were hunting, as you call her, my girl," The Terafin said quietly. "But I would have to guess, without further investigation, that hunting or no, they found her."

"Oh?"

"Terafin has ways of contacting its ranking members during a crisis." As was proper, she offered no further comment.

"I see. I will, if you desire his aid, offer Member APhaniel the choice of service to your House. I believe he has already served your House in some capacity." She knew, of course, what capacity he had served in, and when; the only detail she was unlikely to know was the amount of money that had exchanged hands, although Morretz would not have been surprised if she did.

"I believe that Meralonne APhaniel has pledged service to the Crowns in the South."

"True. And you think that the two—your girl and the South—are unconnected?"

"A good point."

"Would you know if she was dead?"

"I am considering the purchase price of such an enchantment in future, but understand me; I would not waste your time with questions if I already knew their answers. We have too much to do to waste each other's time with such tests of knowledge or power."

Sigurne smiled. "You chastise me, and I accept it; you have no idea how envious most members of the Order would be." The smile vanished. "I have trusted my instinct for all of my adult life. I do not think Jewel ATerafin is dead."

"No?"

"No.

The Terafin was silent a moment, and then she offered the unexpected: a smile.

"Let me clarify that. I do not believe that she died *here*."

The smile froze and then vanished, like northern ice sublimating. "Please explain," she said softly, in a tone of voice that belied the possibility that the two terse words were a request.

"You are familiar with translocation?" Sigurne unexpectedly turned and began to walk to the west. The Terafin fell in step by her side; Morretz fell in behind them.

"I am unfamiliar with most of the magi's arts, but if you mean the passage from one place to another as if nothing existed between the two points, yes. I am also aware that perhaps a handful of the mage-born will ever attain the power necessary to cast this spell; the attempt would kill them."

"Indeed. I am not one with that power. Meralonne, as I suspect you know, is. Your Jewel ATerafin was with someone who cast the spell."

"You know this?"

"We deduce it. Power is always a personal trait. How it is used is also personal. You are not The Terafin your predecessor was, and your heir—should one ever be chosen—will not be the woman you are. Power makes its mark.

"Here, Terafin, power has left its mark."

Morretz came to stand beside the woman whose service had become his life's work. The slight narrowing of her eyes told him all he needed to know—but he was certain that Sigurne knew it as well; she was frustrated with the superficiality of her knowledge. "I see nothing."

"No. I doubt that even Jewel would see it, and her natural sight is unrivaled. But a spell was cast here of power sufficient to move two men.

"And we do not recognize its signature."

Clearly this was a significant statement. To save his lord from the appearance of ignorance, Morretz spoke. "Is this unusual?"

Sigurne's gaze brushed his face. "That we cannot identify with ease a mage of that power? I should leave that for you to deduce, young man. But think on this: Why have there been no sorcerer kings, no blood barons, in the last three centuries? It is certainly not because the magi have become pure and untainted over the course of time.

"You have spent time within the Order's walls; you are bound by the laws that bind us. You know that the paradigm of each mage's magic is unique.

"So, too, is evidence of its use. Those who understand people enough to want a particular type of power *also* have a clear understanding of cause and effect. If they wish to misuse power, or to seek it by the unfortunate . . . losses . . . of others, they must do it by conventional methods." Her expression clouded a moment. "There are, of course, many conventional ways of gaining power—but the use of one's own power in the commission of a crime is only done by the young or the foolish."

"Or the desperate," The Terafin said softly.

"Or the desperate."

"We believe that Jewel ATerafin left here injured, but we don't believe that she left dead."

Injured.

"Many of my mages have been trained to deal with minutiae. There is blood on the ground, here and here."

"There's blood everywhere."

"Yes, but within the circle of the power's signature there appears to be only one person's. There were no people here; or rather, there were no bodies."

"Inconclusive."

"Yes. But hopeful. We will pursue this, Terafin, to the best of our abilities."

"You have my gratitude."

The older woman caught the younger woman's hands; spoke three words, all of which were empty of resonant sound.

Morretz could not hear what was being said. Not that this magically induced inability bothered him. The domicis were trained to notice everything, and something as simple as the absence of sound did not hamper their observation.

Sigurne said simply, "I want more than your gratitude. I think it's obvious now what you intended for her; you are present."

The Terafin said nothing.

"If this was an assassination attempt, it is clear that someone has a vested interest in having a . . . different ruler for Terafin in future."

Again, The Terafin said nothing; Morretz had to stop himself from speaking by force of habit. There were many things spoken about in the presence of The Terafin, but one of them was not, by implication, her death. Not unless she broached the subject first, and she did not do this with strangers.

But . . . he was not supposed to hear the words, and an interruption of that nature would be awkward. Amarais did not forgive that type of awkwardness easily. As long as he did not break the illusion of deafness, she ignored the fact that all information accrued to him; he stepped around her so that he might also be privy to her response.

"It is not advantageous for the leader of a House such as mine to be obvious," The Terafin replied.

"Understood, Terafin, although I fear that your intent is already understood; you are hampered both by the fact that you cannot tolerate stupidity and that you believe cunning serves the interests of your House well." She raised a frail hand. "It has served your House well."

The Terafin said nothing.

"If it is possible, we will find your girl. I believe that she is of interest to the Crowns as well."

"Oh?"

"Well, if I'm not mistaken, that would be the Lord of the Compact."

The Terafin's eyes narrowed slightly.

Sigurne bowed politely. "And it would be best not to continue this conversation in silence. That very rude young man has a sensitivity to the use of magic that extends for miles."

"Indeed."

The older woman did not so much as lift a hand. But they turned to face Duvari, and stood shoulder to shoulder while he walked with a cool purpose toward them: The lord of House Terafin and the leader of the Order of Knowledge.

Morretz, on the other hand, looked for the Kings. Duvari seldom left the grounds of *Avantari*; when he did, it was as the Lord of the Compact, and he traveled in the company of Kings, in the shadows they cast, the most feared of their protectors. With justification.

Mages served the Kings. The Swords did. The Ten did.

But there was about Duvari the certain sense that he would, without blinking, slowly torture his own children in order to fulfill that obligation. He would certainly torture anyone else's.

If the laws did not bind him.

Another King, another set of Kings . . .

But that was idle speculation; there were two Kings. While the Empire stood, there would always be two kings. There was comfort to be found in that thought until the Lord of the Compact stopped—for just a moment—his attention caught not by The Terafin or the woman who ruled the Order of Knowledge, but by the splinters of trees that had stood since the Empire's founding.

Funny; they were only trees, but the effect of their fall had been profound. Duvari did not condescend to notice the bodies that were being recovered and carried away around him.

Perhaps Morretz did because he was afraid that one of those bodies would belong to Terafin; that it would belong to Jewel ATerafin. When news of the attack in the Common had reached Amarais, she had stiffened slightly, her face falling into lines that could not be mistaken for a smile by a man who knew her. But when other reports filtered back, even the smile faltered.

No, Morretz, Jewel had said, *I have no idea how I'm getting there. I don't have any real idea of where I'm* going. *But to be practical, there are a few things we'll need on the way there. Or that I'll need, anyway. Avandar can take care of himself.*

And you'll find these?

Don't be so suspicious. She'd laughed. *We'll be going to the Common.*

For what passes for food, no doubt, Avandar had added dryly.

The past was between the two domicis, would always be between them. But he had watched Avandar serve this girl for ten years and understood that the asset Amarais considered most precious to the House was in his keeping.

Somewhere.

"Terafin," the Lord of the Compact said. He bowed, his form perfect. She countered with a nod of the head.

"AMellifas." Sigurne tendered a bow. She understood that the game of rank was just that: a game.

His hands slid behind his back—a position that no one was comfortable with. "The search goes poorly."

Not a question. Sometimes, when he was feeling politic, he couched his phrases as questions; sometimes—as now—he chose not to. No one who had any experience with the Lord of the Compact mistook any question he chose to ask as a request for information; it was an act of manners, at best. A test, at worst.

"It depends," The Terafin replied, condescending to play the game. "We haven't found the wrong body."

"Good."

He surprised them. Morretz saw the curve of The Terafin's brow ripple slightly. Saw her eyes narrow. "You show an . . . uncharacteristic interest in the affairs of one of the Houses."

His smile was knife-edge thin; his shrug was brief. "It is a . . . significant House."

"It has always been significant."

"Indeed." He looked past the two women, deliberately scanning a horizon broken by fires, damaged buildings, the trunks of splintered trees. He continued to scan the horizon as he spoke; his words were soft and Morretz had the feeling that they traveled a very short distance. "It appears that you have both chosen and lost at least one successor in the past few months."

She said nothing.

"It is not of concern. Or it was not. Within the Houses, the more difficult elements are often . . . eliminated . . . in such a fashion. But your presence here implies that you have chosen another successor. Your prerogative, of course. The result . . . the result, Terafin, if this is indeed connected to that choice . . . *is* my concern." He turned.

The Terafin's expression was set, bleak. "Understood, Lord of the Compact. In this investigation, you will, of course, have my full cooperation, and the full disclosure of all pertinent information."

"The decision of what is pertinent—"

"To remain mine of course, although if you desire, the option to petition the Crowns for a Royal writ of seizure or invasive use of magic is your prerogative."

"I . . . see. Member Mellifas?"

"You know my feelings on rogue magery, forbidden magic, and demons," Sigurne's reply was quiet. Her words were hard to catch, and the expression on her face was hard to look at; it was shorn of both the austerity and fragility of age. For a moment, she reminded Morretz of Duvari. It was not a comfortable thought.

Less comfortable was the implication made by the head of the Astari.

"May I remind the Lord of the Compact that this is not the first attempt on the life of Jewel ATerafin; that the first attempt occurred not because of House politics, but rather the affairs of state between the Empire and the Dominion?"

"No, Morretz," The Terafin said quietly. "You may not."

He fell silent.

"We are aware of that," Duvari replied. "We are aware

that the interest in the younger ATerafin maybe be entirely because of her duties to the army that is to travel South before winter. But, as always, all options must be studied, and all information gathered.

"Terafin."

"Lord of the Compact."

He turned quietly, having offered the only warning he was likely to offer.

Sigurne Mellifas watched his back, and when it had vanished in the distance of sparse crowd and coming evening, said simply, "I trust him."

And given that the Order of Knowledge was the one institution that Duvari was more suspicious of, and less friendly toward, than The Ten, that said much.

"Morretz," The Terafin said, her voice like the Northern ocean wind, "gather her den. I think we've found everything we're going to find here."

He bowed.

Evening, 7th of Scaral, 427 AA
Order of Knowledge

The knock was firm.

She did not wish to deal with it.

In the privacy of the largest set of personal rooms in the Order, Sigurne Mellifas could acknowledge the frailties that drove her—but only here. She was tired; the sea made her bones ache; her feet hurt from a day spent standing or walking without break. But these were minor considerations. Major: that she was *angry*; that she was tired; that she could still sense the aura of demonic names imprinted over the Common. So many.

So much for the promises made in the darkest of years. Failure did not sit well with her.

She had seldom had to deal with it. The table beneath her hands was as fine as any table The Ten might possess; the carpets as fine; the windows were made not by Makers, although much else in the room was, but by Artisans, a gift of the mad to the mad in the Order's early years. They were not the only thing about the room that was special, but they were the only thing about it that was unique. And only the man—or woman—who had the right to these rooms by their position on the Council and in the First Circle could invoke the magics placed upon that glass hundreds upon hundreds of years past.

It was not well known.

But she had known of it. In the quiet of servitude, in the silence that the poor or the weak adopt in the presence of unchecked power, she had learned what she needed to know.

It had brought her here.

Sigurne did not rule the Order of Knowledge so much as shepherd it; an Order of such diverse—and often antisocial—men and women was an organization that responded best to coaxing and cajoling, to flattery, and to embarrassment. Orders in the Council fell flat for the most part, and that was as it should be.

But outside of the Council, among the junior mages—as she thought of the men and women who had not yet reached the height of their potential—the desire for the mysterious power and austerity granted by the title, *Magi*, was a temptation. She had been such a mage once.

A temptation such as that could be manipulated; upon such thin foundations, a man—or several—could build factions of which they were, de facto, rulers.

Most of the men and women who played these games had been born into the patriciate. But not all; she herself had spent the earliest years of her life in a village far, far to the West. For a moment she felt an ache that had nothing to do with age. She set the memory aside.

The knock at the door broke the silence. Again.

Bitter now, she pressed her hands against the flawless flat of ancient table and levered her weight from her least comfortable chair. Messages could be sent with the use of magery; indeed, simple requests often were. But if privacy was desired, old-fashioned methods were best, for the use of containing magics could be detected if one knew how to look and was willing to expend the energy and time doing so. As the first member of the Magi, Sigurne knew, with that same bitterness, that she was worth that time and energy. But she disliked the private because too much could be inferred from its use.

She almost ignored it.

But the windows had opened into a deep, charcoal sky, storm held in the folds of something too harsh and dark to be called clouds. There were days when she loathed the position she had risen to; days when she wished there were another mage—any other mage—that she trusted enough to relinquish that position to.

She seldom wasted this much of her time in futile thought and daydream, but it had been a long day.

The door opened upon a man in very fine robes, the hue an indigo that was costly and fashionable, the fabric a stonebeaten silk, edged in something more durable. She recognized his face, although the lines of it had softened from angularity to a sullen roundness with the passage of time. He was a middling mage, although had he dedication and focus, he might have been Second Circle.

She wondered, idly, how long he had stood outside of her doors composing himself; the journey up the great stairs was a test of endurance for even the healthiest of the Order. Only Sigurne, or those granted permission by her, might enter these chambers in a way that did not involve the complication of flights and flights of tower stairs.

Sigurne loved the members of the Order of Knowledge who did, in fact, come seeking knowledge. But the talent born were just that: born. No quirk of nature or fate had given them the desire for knowledge or truth—although some did, indeed, possess it. She dreamed of the separation of the two: the magi from the seekers.

Especially when one of the more politically minded of the mage-born stood at her door.

"Your pardon, Member Mellifas," the younger man said, his bow perfect. "Member ATerafin sent me. He has information, from the House, which he has suggested would be best relayed directly."

"Relay it, then."

His brows lifted slightly, and then his cheeks paled. The man was nonplussed, and therefore blessedly silent, for a full minute. In the distance, unnatural thunder underscored that silence. Not that he could hear it.

No one could be entirely stupid and still be a member of the Order, although many members tested that idiom to its outer limit.

"My apologies, First Member."

What civility she could manage was sorely, *sorely*, tested. Although the title was technically correct, it was a title she loathed, and she did not use it by choice. Not even among the highborn and the powerful.

"Accepted."

"I've offended you."

"I'm not offended," she replied, forcing a gentleness into the words, smoothing the edges from them. That it was so much effort spoke of the weariness brought on by the day.

"Thank you. Please, let me try this again. Magi ATerafin has requested your presence. He has information—and possibly artifacts—taken from the Common shortly after you left, that he feels are of import to both the Order and his House."

"And he did not choose to bring them here?"

"He has seldom been an errand runner," the man replied, the carefully modularity of his words giving way to a momentary sneer. It made him ugly. He worked to contain that ugliness, but it remained like a shadow across features exposed to scant light. "It would be suspicious for him to travel here."

"But not for his aide."

"No."

"Then he is fortunate indeed to have as aide a man who does not mind being known as an errand runner." She wanted to dismiss him; it was well within her rights. And it had been a long day, too long a day to end in such a way.

But there were some things which had to be done; best do them, then relax. That had been her mother's—her long dead, oft forgotten mother's—motto. And Sigurne had spent a lifetime struggling to live up to it. She had never yet reached that blessed point where she might relax.

And perhaps, just perhaps, she was wrong. Perhaps all was as it seemed.

"Will we—"

"We'll take the stairs," she said firmly. It was easiest. The stairs were always such a temptation.

He held the door open, and as she passed him, she smiled sadly. "It is so seldom that young mages remember anything as common as courtesy. I remember the day you arrived."

"You do?"

"Oh, yes." She walked through the open door, pausing a moment in front of him. He said nothing, and she continued on, brushing the door's frame with the tips of her fingers. He waited until she had passed him before he released the door.

It slammed shut as if closing were a rejection.

Sigurne did not look back. She looked down, into a darkness that was alleviated by scant window light and the magestones that graced the Order's walls and brackets in place of torches.

The young man walked quickly, quietly, efficiently, substituting grace for awkwardness, silence for bluster, purpose for purpose. Without misstep, he centered his hands behind her back and pushed her as she made her slow descent down stairs which wound, against wall, into shadow.

And cried out in surprise when his hands passed through her bent form, the full force of his weight behind them. It had not been a gentle nudge.

She watched from the open door as panic cost him the only chance he had at halting his descent. Then, as he began to strike stair after stair on his long way down, she reached out with her signature skill and took from him the information she required: that somewhere within the Order someone had expended the power necessary to watch her death through his servant's eyes. She hoped he now had an intimate acquaintance with the flat stone steps. Whoever he was. The signature of his power was not familiar enough that she recognized it. She knew the ATerafin's signature well; it was too much to hope that the hand behind the assassin could be implicated so easily.

She turned back to the windows in her rooms, wondering why it was that the old were assumed to have left wit behind with youth.

The tower grew silent.

She made her way to the windows again, caught in the tangle of old arguments, old politics. Numbers brushed by: three. Three men had died in the last year attempting to take her life. Possibly four if this one didn't survive his fall down the stairs. No names now came to the faces that had made themselves remarkable solely by their attempts.

But Meralonne had felled two almost as casually as he lit his pipe. She smiled grimly; his dignity was such an odd thing. He could walk into a crowd of dignitaries half naked; could begin to eat when the Kings themselves had deigned to join the magi at their feast—before either of the Crowns had blessed the meal. He could lose himself in research or study; could, in the middle of a meeting of the greater governing body, spend four hours staring at a plant. But the moment he was required to *fight* he became all edge, all steel.

As cold in his way as Sigurne herself had become because of her youth, but much, much more obvious in his ice.

Meralonne APhaniel was by nature the most aggressive of her mages; the least trusting. She had long suspected that if not for a minimal respect for the laws that governed the country, he would have trapped his door in such a way that an unwelcome visitor never troubled him—or anyone else—again.

Although she would never admit it, and further, knew it would never even be suspected, she had the same urge herself.

Four.

Four men, and she knew it had only begun.

Perhaps here was a reason that these finely appointed rooms boasted banks of windows, but no doors into the outer world, no balcony—such as Meralonne possessed—upon which one might experience sea breeze and the momentary illusion of freedom beneath the open sky.

CHAPTER TWO

17th of Scaral, 427 AA
Avantari, Arannan Halls

"He's just a stupid kid." Alexis' glare was about as cold as anything could get at midday in Averalaan; it glanced off the side of Duarte's face as if it were the flat of a dagger that had sheltered in the shadows of a cellar. Captain Duarte AKalakar, her superior officer.

Whatever that meant to an Osprey.

The heat of the midday sun often provided an excuse—and in dealing with Ser Anton and his young Tyr, excuses were in short supply—for rest and momentary relaxation. If the word "alert" and the word "relax" could be somehow forged into a single thing and still have some meaning.

There was, about these recesses—as about all else with Ser Anton di'Guivera—a sense of ritual. The old man would signal a recess. Swords would stop, almost in midmotion if the two students had actually closed; be lowered warily if they had not and their feet were contained by the circle, and he would allow the Tyr to withdraw to secure quarters. There, a smaller number of personal guards was required, and the rest could . . . be less nervous.

The Arannan Halls, with their courtyards and fountains, their multiple rooms and the serafs—ah, servants—handpicked by the Lambertan hostages, had become, at the largesse of the Kings, the property of the young Tyr'agar. Duarte's hand had delivered the decree; paper, headed by the symbols of the Twin Kings, and sealed by wax the color of blood, so ubiquitous in the North and so absent in the South.

"What does it say?" General Baredan di'Navarre had demanded, once the seals were broken and the wax had fallen, in thick shards, against the surface of perfectly smooth wood. That desk, old and dark, was as fine as any The Kalakar owned. Or rather, Duarte thought with a grimace, any The Kalakar owned that the Ospreys had ever seen. They were not among her closest advisers.

"It is . . . an extension of their offer of hospitality, General."

The General's frown was nonexistent, but it was there if you knew him well enough. His shoulders rose a fraction of an inch; his chin came up slightly.

"Satisfy the curiosity of a loyal liege," Ramiro di'Callesta had said dryly. "Tell me what hospitality has been extended."

Although he could have handed either the General or the Tyr the parchment and let them read it themselves, he adhered to proper form. "The Kings have gifted me," the boy who was not a man, the man who had not been tested, said quietly, "with the Arannan Halls. They are to be in all ways my personal quarters. My laws reign here."

"A generous offer." All three men understood that the offer changed very little about the daily life of Valedan kai di'Leonne; they also understood that in spite of this, the lack of change was significant.

"And one which I will, of course, accept," Valedan had replied, equally dry. "I . . . need time to compose a reply."

They understood a dismissal when they heard it. They bowed, Southern style. That room, its large windows designed to give light and cast shadow, had quieted as their steps echoed into stillness.

Only after the stillness was complete did Valedan choose to break it; he rose. At his shoulder, Ser Anton stood, as impassive as the walls, as merciless, in his fashion, as the sun through the open window. "Well?" he said softly.

Ser Andaro di'Corsarro frowned. "The words—you closed the scroll too quickly. I couldn't read them, Tyr'agar."

"Here." He offered the scroll to the only man he had taken as Tyran. Ser Andaro di'Corsarro had sworn his life, his life's blood, and his honor in Valedan's service, and the vow, simple and crude though it had been, was a vow that death would end. Nothing else.

It surprised Duarte slightly to know that Valedan took that vow as seriously as Ser Andaro had; that he took what was offered in pain and anger, in respect and in emptiness, and extended it, strengthened it, made it in truth what it had been in promise. For it was only to Andaro that he handed the missive of Kings.

He read slowly, his eyes struggling over the loops and curves of an unfamiliar script. His spoken Weston was exotic but flawless, his written Weston little better than Aidan's. At last, his brows rose, changing the lines of his intent, even handsome, face. "But—but why did you not tell the General of this offer?"

It was Ser Anton who replied. "Because he does not choose to accept it."

Ser Andaro's expression chilled. There was, between the old man and the young, a very bitter death. Duarte wondered if the corpse would ever be buried, or if it would stand there as wall and accusation for the duration of Ser Anton's life.

"Tyr'agar?"

"As usual," Valedan said, carefully failing to notice the moment's chill, "Ser Anton is correct."

"May I ask why?"

"You are Tyran, Andaro. Not cerdan, not simply guard. You may ask me anything, and if it is in my power to answer it, I will answer it. Your fate and mine are not separate. Come," he said. "Stand here." He called for pen, and for paper; something far too fine to be demeaned by such a term was delivered into his hands. He dipped quill into ink, touched it to blotter.

These halls, he wrote, *have been my home. It was in these halls, for no reason that any man of power in the Dominion would understand, that the ACormaris chose to school me in the art of the Sword and in the art of the Bow. It was in these halls, so starkly and simply designed by a nameless Maker, that I have been confronted, in every moment of peace, by the truth of our concept of Justice.*

That Maker who carved the statue in the courtyard understood the South; perhaps he understood the North as well; I cannot say. But I have grown to understand all that I have been offered.

Names have power. I pray—to Cormaris in the North, to the Lady in the South—that the experience of these halls never deserts me; that I continue to draw strength and wisdom from a past that has been defined by Your hospitality.

In future, I hope to achieve something which will merit the honor of your regard. If I am successful, I hope you will consider what I have—perhaps unwisely—said. Leave these halls as they have been, in my memory.

For when I take, at last, to the field, I wish to know that some small part of the world remains as it was, and when I speak of home, I wish the name Arannan *to invoke in perpetuity what it invokes in me now.*

He labored, did Ser Andaro, with each word. But at last, he nodded. "I am not sure," he said softly, "that the Leonne Halls would not be the more appropriate name."

Ser Anton stiffened.

"I know," Valedan said, carefully rolling the words he had written into something that resembled a tube. He stood, walked to the window, and stared out of it at the open courtyard a story below. There, in the waters that were life in the South, and decoration in the North, the boy stood waiting in a smooth basin, his blindfold a thing of stone and artistry, inseparable from his perfect, delicate features.

Valedan had stood observing that boy until Alexis—Alexis of all people—had deftly separated him from his message with a quiet promise to have it delivered.

Which was how Duarte knew its contents, of course. Ospreys were Ospreys, and the Tyr had no official Northern seal; none was needed; in the South all words were carried by slaves, and all vows were made by the named blade.

Duarte's gaze scanned the perimeter of that courtyard now. It was open to observation from the heights of the grandest buildings in all of the Empire, old or new—the towers and the balconies of *Àvantari*, the palace of Kings. He had become used to spectators, although spectators were not something that the worst dress unit in all of Kalakar derived any pleasure from. He had even come, in the course of this unexpected, this unpredictable duty, to recognize the spectators although the distance that separated them was, of necessity, great. In particular, two women would stand in the breezes that graced the heights: The Serra Alina di'Lamberto—a woman as dangerous, in her cold, graceful beauty as Alexis was in her fire—and Mirialyn ACormaris.

Neither woman was present for this brief pause; he was glad of it. There were things one tried not to do in front of witnesses.

Like, perhaps, have an argument with the woman that you are trying to remember you love. Alexis had an unusual idea of "recreational activity."

"Alexis, the Tyr—" he began, seeing in that steady, dark gaze something that was familiar enough that he wanted to walk away from it. He glanced to the wall and back; the well worn spot that had become shelter from midday sun was conspicuously empty. Which was a good thing. The "stupid kid" that Alexis AKalakar felt she was defending was old enough to take umbrage at the words she had chosen as a means of that defense; Aidan was not quite a child but certainly not an adult. A difficult age.

"He almost died at the Challenge, the little fool. You'd think he might have learned *something*. It's a mistake to have him there." She jerked her head, hard, to the left; her hair came free in strands and wavered a moment in the still air like a dark, moving frame.

Cliché, Duarte thought, was what it was for a reason: it embodied a truth so common it was, in the minds of those not intimately involved with its resonance, boring. But . . . she had always been beautiful when she was angry. And dangerous. And infuriating.

"Alexis, the Tyr—"

"He doesn't know any better," she continued, as if she hadn't heard him. Unlikely. She was probably ignoring him, as she often did when she was, in fact, beautiful in just this fashion. "He's under the mistaken impression that we're real House Guards."

"He's not here for us." Duarte's voice was soft. The softness—forced, implacable—was wasted on Alexis; she heard the edge in it as if that was all there was. And there was more.

"No, of course not. He's here for the old man and the Tyr."

Take care, Duarte. Care. "I'm pleased," the Captain of the Black Ospreys said, in a tone that was unfortunately anything but, "we agree."

She shrugged. "It doesn't mean it's any safer for him. We've taken what—two? Three?—would-be assassins in the last three weeks. He was *there*."

"And you've suddenly become the guardian of naïve young men?"

"He's not a man. He's a boy." Her hands found the way to her slender hips and perched there, an inch away from the hilt of a simple dagger. He wondered if it was meant as a threat; Alexis was usually straightforward when it came to matters of life and death.

But she wasn't above slitting your throat if your back was turned and you'd crossed a line that only she understood clearly. Or at least she hadn't been.

For a moment the memories of the younger woman overlapped and overwhelmed his memories of the older one; he was not certain whether time's changes had ever taken root, grown deep. The older woman, he loved. The younger woman he had loved as well, but he'd been forced into an intimate understanding of the price of any weakness she could sense.

"He's no younger than you were when you killed your first man."

She was rigid for a minute. Duarte took a half step toward her.

"Alexis—"

She lifted a hand, turning away from him. Duarte could see the side of her face, and for a moment, that was all he wanted to see; she was like stone, and would remain so, unless he caught sight of her eyes. She shrugged. "Yeah. That's me. Born killer. No, don't bother," she snapped, as he took another step. "You're right. Why should I give a shit? No one watched out for *me*."

She turned and walked away, her heels tapping out a precise retreat.

Duarte watched her leave. She had set the rules of the encounter; always a mistake, to allow her that much freedom. To allow himself that much. Because every loss, with Alexis, was costly. And every victory as well. He knew that when he was a younger man, he might *just* have been stupid enough to mistake her agreement for some kind of victory, and for a moment, he missed the naïveté of that younger self.

* * *

The boy was allowed to watch.

There was a risk in it, and that risk, enumerated for both his benefit and the benefit of the students who—under the heat of the sun and the salty humidity of the sea-laden air—attempted to gain, if not the skills Ser Anton possessed, than at least some sign of his approval, had been accepted for what it was: truth.

But the boy, in Ser Anton's opinion, had proved himself worthy of being allowed to make his own choice—although he knew that the choice was really no choice at all, merely permission—by saving the life of the Tyr'agar.

And so, Aidan, born the son of a wheelwright, watched the play of light and steel he best loved: swords beneath an open sky. It was just such a sound that had drawn him, like the siren call of sea creatures in a sailor's dark stories, to the side of the older man; it was just such a desire to bear witness that had almost cost him his life.

So much for learning by experience.

The Ospreys had become used to him; he had grown used to them. In many ways, he and they had more in common than the men they now watched, and the man they now served. Aidan was more careful with his words than they were, but it was almost entirely due to size; he'd learned the hard way that being too bold with words ended—if he was very lucky—in bruises.

As always, Ser Anton di'Guivera remained a quiet man. It was as if he went out of his way to avoid any word that might flatter, any gesture beyond the occasional nod that might give a student a dangerous confidence.

The first time that Aidan had seen him, he had had twelve students; he now had two. He had excused himself from the duties he held to the men who had traveled North for the Kings' Challenge. Aidan wondered, briefly, how the Southern students must have felt. He knew he would have been crushed.

And yet . . . having seen the two students that remained, he wasn't certain that some part of him wouldn't have been relieved as well.

Because Valedan kai di'Leonne and Andaro di'Corsarro were *so* much better than any of the rest of them. Only Carlo had been close, and Aidan learned quickly that you didn't mention Carlo di'Jevre's name anywhere where Andaro or Ser Anton could hear it. Andaro would go cold as deep seawater, and Ser Anton would stiffen; they would stand there, *not* looking at each other, until Valedan stepped in, leading them either back to the drill, or away from it entirely.

Valedan was always present when Andaro and Ser Anton were together. He often stood between them, if they were forced to stand together, although no harsh word was ever exchanged between the men as far as Aidan could tell.

He wasn't used to silence as a container for anger; certainly his father's silences were reserved for other emotions: loss, joy, terror. Anger was quickly and easily wrapped in words and thrown at the nearest person—although the anger was greatly lessened as his father found work that demanded care and sobriety.

But although he had come late to silence, he had grown to understand some of its textures; Ser Anton was patient in all things, and if he chose to explain little, he was willing to allow Aidan to absorb knowledge, whole, from experience. Many young boys of Aidan's acquaintance would have cheerfully killed to be where he was.

But that, Ser Anton said, the words now engraved as if by a jeweler's pick in the gold, false and real, of memory, *is not the question. The question is: How many would die just as easily for the same privilege?*

All of them, Aidan had said.

Ser Anton's smile was quiet, a quiet that meant thought, memory, and the disturbing collision between them. *Perhaps,* he said at last. *And perhaps that was a foolish question, given how very many of them might die anyway.* He had risen to join Andaro and Valedan.

And Aidan, the quiet student, understood that he had seen one of Ser Anton's very few retreats.

"What will you do, Tyr'agar?"

Valedan stiffened slightly. To come from the breadth of a circle in which Ser Anton was undisputed master, and he student, and oft-bruised student at that, to this courtyard in the Arannan Halls, in which a fountain stood in solemn expectation, was often a difficult transition.

He wanted advice. He wanted, in truth, the same near

wordless but effective counsel that Ser Anton granted him when he held a naked sword beneath the Lord's gaze. Things were clean, there; stark and easily realized.

Outside of the circle, he was, again, the uncrowned Tyr; the man who had claimed a throne and a sword that he had seen only a handful of times in his life—all of them before he had reached his eighth year; a sword he had never held. A man who intended to lead a Northern army into lands in which the North was hated and despised, and to somehow shed little blood and come out, as the Ospreys said, on top.

He had no idea how to achieve this.

And to be asked was . . . awkward.

The water trickled in the wordless pause between question and answer. Valedan, as Tyr, was not obligated *to* answer, but here Ser Anton's position held sway. Ser Anton had fallen into a dangerous shadow, and having survived it, having learned from it all that he needed to know about his basest of impulses, had stepped into the light again a changed man; a man Valedan had accepted, without question, as swordmaster.

To the swordmaster to the man who wielded—or would—the Sun Sword by right of birth was an honor, an honorable position.

Made so, in fact if not by custom, by Ser Anton di'Guivera.

"I don't know," Valedan said at last, when the silence dwarfed the words.

"What have I taught you, Tyr'agar?"

The young Tyr's hand fell to the hilt of his sword and rested there, as if he derived strength and comfort from the connection with his weapon. He didn't, not now, but it was an important posture.

"That it is better to make the wrong choice and deal with the consequences than to make no choice."

Ser Anton's nod was almost genial.

"Every action, every decision, every movement that takes me closer to the South, involves *wrong* choices. I was hoping that, with the passage of time and the . . . education . . . that I've received from both yourself and indirectly, the ACormaris, a right choice would present itself."

Ser Anton said nothing, but he was still. The water spoke

for both of them until Valedan at last turned to fully face this man, his master and his most famous vassal.

"There are no right choices."

Ser Anton's smile was slight, but it was present. "You are learning, Valedan. And you are correct." He bowed, slightly, toward the kai Leonne. But beyond the man who had undertaken the rule of the Dominion, the statue that bore such a difficult name also received the meager depth of his bow: Southern Justice. That statue, of a young seraf, blindfolded and in chains, was accusation and truth, neither of which was easily accessible to men born and bred in the North.

"There is no right choice. Make one of the wrong choices instead, and make it decisively. Against Alesso di'Marente, in the end, you must be decisive."

"I will have the Commanders."

"Yes."

"They have bested the General in battle before."

"Ah." Ser Anton slid his hands behind his back; a bad sign. Then he turned to face Valedan, his dark eyes somehow darker, although the alcove contained little shadow at the height of day unless one deliberately sought the shade. "Let me make this perfectly clear: They bested the General in battle because he was hampered by the dictates of a weak and foolish Tyr.

"Commander Allen was only slightly compromised by the orders of his Kings; the field was his to lose, and he is not a man who is accustomed to giving away *any* advantage. He will not have the luxury of a weak Tyr when he meets Alesso di'Marente again: Alesso takes his orders from no man save himself."

"But—but—"

"Yes?"

"Is he not beholden to the allies he has made?" Neither man spoke of the *Kialli* by name; it was unnecessary, even if their silence seemed a tacit acceptance of the suspicion that names, once acknowledged, give power.

Ser Anton's smile was brief, fierce; it was the smile of a man who appreciates a work for its superb artistry even when the subject matter might otherwise weaken him. "Trust me in this, if in nothing else.

"Understand what I say now, kai Leonne, and you will

understand the man far better than the allies that we shun mention of. *This*, this is the test of a man; this is the test that Alesso di'Marente was born to pass or to fail. When the General takes to the field of battle, he will be beholden to no one."

"You think—you think he might win this?"

"You ask me what I think? Let me answer, but let me also remind you that you must never ask me this question where anyone other than Ser Andaro can hear it. I think that we must allow for that possibility, yes—but if it happens, it will not matter. The Lord will judge our corpses."

19th of Scaral, 427 AA
Avantari, Hall of Wise Counsel

"No."

The word, said as it was in a unison that was almost unheard of, echoed in the curves of stone architecture that had stood for longer than the men and the woman beneath it had lived. Cumulatively.

The Berriliya did not flinch, or waver, or in fact deign to notice the odd harmony the single word produced. His profile, hawkish, did not change at all; he might have been chiseled from the same stone that had trapped the single word. Or from ice, although ice rarely formed this far from the North.

The Kalakar's pale brow rose, however, and she turned, her gaze glancing off the face of the man who was both Commander and House ruler like an ineffectual blow. She was, in every possible way, his equal—and certain proof that equality and uniformity were two very different concepts. The Berriliya chose to encase his disapproval in Northern chill, The Kalakar, in the motion of fingers against the perfect sheen of well-kept tabletop.

"The boy cannot travel to Annagar with the army."

Commander Bruce Allen had wondered, briefly, if she would rescind her refusal in the wake of The Berriliya's, but it was idle curiosity of a type that is born—and dies—in the awkward silence between a single inconvenient word and any reaction to it. In truth, the man known to the vast majority of the Kings' armies as the Eagle felt a great deal of sympathy for the position The Berriliya and The Kalakar had chosen to take.

He rose, however, forsaking the comfort of chair and gaining the authority of height and motion. Neither the Hawk nor the Kestrel chose to join him in flight; they watched him, as they always had, for some sign of weakness.

"It can't have escaped your notice," he said dryly, speaking to them both but looking toward Devran, whose glacial stare was the more aggressively displayed hostility, "that the boy is the only legitimate reason we have to take the armies South."

Devran didn't shrug; Ellora did, her lips twisting a moment in a wry grimace. "Tell the Kings' spies to find a different reason, then; that's what they're paid for."

If possible, Devran's expression grew distinctly more chilly.

"But one way or the other, Bruce, we won't expose the army to the risk of taking the boy."

"The boy—"

"If *we* succeed, the boy will rule in the South. There is an advantage to having, as the Dominion's ruler, a man who has lived in a land where power, strictly speaking, is not the only law."

"Careful," Bruce said quietly. "We each have old habits, born of earlier wars, that it would be unwise to indulge. Yes. Of course there is an advantage to having Valedan kai di'Leonne as ruler."

"But the advantage," The Berriliya said coldly, "is merely a weapon, like any other; what we can use from a distance with difficulty, our enemies can use, at his side, with ease."

"They don't understand the North well enough to make use of him," Ellora snapped, more comfortable in disagreement with Devran than in agreement. They wore their rivalry with the same intimacy that most wore friendship that had been tested—successfully—in every possible circumstance.

"It is not in the North that he will rule," Devran snapped back. "But in the South, and *because* of that, he will need the advice of men who have managed to retain their hold on power."

They turned to the Eagle, because once again they had reached the heart of the argument. "Callesta," The Kalakar said, as if the word were profanity. "And Navarre."

Commander Allen nodded, the movement an almost imperceptible tilt of chin. "Understand," he said at last, "that our role here is advisory." His smile was grim and brief, but it was genuine. "And that the Kings themselves are locked at the moment in dispute over the question we address now."

"There should be no question," Devran said. "The boy himself, shorn of those two allies, is less of a threat, but if he can answer the inevitable questions Ramiro di'Callesta will put to him, it will lay our logistic system open for Callestan inspection. The Tyr'agnate can travel in safety to the South; tell the boy that our armies will meet up with the Callestan army when we cross the border."

"I'm afraid," the Eagle said softly, "that it's not that simple."

Duarte AKalakar's gaze was like the Lord's as he met Valedan's unblinking stare. They were separated by more years than Valedan kai di'Leonne had lived, and by vastly more experience, but in the end it was Duarte who looked away. Here, in the privacy of the chambers that served as Valedan's only palace until the campaign in the South was won—or lost—he could afford to do so.

But the Ospreys were restless, and some, driven by memories of the Southern valleys and the slaughter of the compatriots that Duarte himself had chosen—*don't go there, not now, not in front of the kai*—had already begun to circle. There was an intensity to the practice field that spoke—movement for movement, word for word, silence for silence—of death, of killing.

The Ospreys had never been a force comfortable with peace. They were waking now.

And in a place they would never have woken, had they a choice, although it was not as uncomfortable as they feared it might be: as guards for, guardians of, a *Southern* noble.

Duarte AKalakar could no longer afford any sign of weakness. Not only must he expunge all gestures that might make him *appear* weak, he must also expunge the weakness that led to the gesture.

"There are other guards you might choose," he said at last, uncomfortable in the silence. "Certainly," he added, with a touch of grim humor, "more tractable or obedient guards; guards with an understanding of the gravity of your situation—and of your station."

"True," Valedan said, in the tone of voice that indicates conversational placeholder rather than agreement. It was a mannerism of the South, to give the appearance of agreement, rather than its substance. Duarte wondered when Valedan had adopted it.

"But if you choose to retain the Ospreys in the role appointed for them, there is no safe way for us to cross the border without the army."

"The Callestan—"

"Kai Leonne," he said softly, "with all due respect, I must say that you have not spoken with the Tyr'agnate if you can even suggest that we might follow you ahead of the army into *that* territory."

"The Tyr'agnate has control of his forces, surely?"

"Of his forces, yes. And anyone who disobeys his orders will die. But so will my men. And in numbers. We are not . . . well-loved . . . in the South. Our colors are known."

"And you would have me accept Callestan Tyran in your place?"

"With all due respect," Duarte said, in a way that might make another man wonder exactly how much respect *was* due, "it's been a long time since you lived in the South. You know how well the Ospreys fare during dress inspection or dress maneuvers. Imagine that your rank and your standing depend on our ability to be perfect."

Valedan's expression shifted; it was a barely perceptible motion.

"If you choose to—"

The doors—the heavy, Northern doors which would be so out of place in the heart of the South—flew open.

Or so it appeared—but instead of spinning on hinges, they *continued* into the room, driven as they were by the force of a very large object.

Two swords were drawn by the time that object gained height and shape, unfurling obsidian limbs—legs and arms that gave it reach, hands whose fingers extended into gleaming, and familiar, blades.

Duarte cursed in a way completely inappropriate to Valedan's station; Valedan, however, did not move.

Something outside in the hall was cursing with the easy inventiveness of someone who does little else. "Gods curse you, Kiriel! *Wait for me!*"

Kiriel di'Ashaf, blade drawn, leaped into the breach of the now doorless entry as if she hadn't heard the words. Judging by the ferocity of her intent, it was a good bet she hadn't.

"Tyr'agar," Duarte said, sliding into the formality that came with so much difficulty to the rest of the Ospreys, "I suggest you stand behind me." He gestured, his hands moving with less grace and less force than Kiriel's sword, as the demon pulled back its arm and let something fly.

Whatever it was, it glanced off the air, skittered groundward, scudding off soft carpet and clattering into stillness against the cool stone.

"A good suggestion," Valedan replied, his words lost to the creature's frustrated roar.

Kiriel di'Ashaf had changed. The first time Duarte had been introduced to her, he had had to battle the urge to look over his shoulder any time he was forced to turn his back, and in truth, he had done all in his power to ensure that it was seldom necessary. But something had happened to her; something that she would not speak of. He was uncertain that she understood it herself.

She had lost some of her speed, some of her edge, all of the sense of menace that could make a man's hair stand on edge when she did nothing at all.

But what she was left with had become, over the course of three months, good enough.

Good enough, at any rate, that she had beaten Auralis through the open door carrying a sword that was heavier than his when he outweighed her by, at best guess, more than half. She charged toward the demon—just as Auralis himself would have done—as if she still possessed all of the terrible strength which none of the Ospreys had forgotten—and all of the Ospreys would have liked to.

But she pulled up at the last minute, her headlong rush trailing into a circling pattern that seemed only slightly slower. Auralis, still cursing, joined her, weaving in the other direction, matching her speed until he came to face her; only then did he shift to match her chosen circle—counterclockwise—his steps short and quick, his sword jumping from hand to hand.

Through the open door, footsteps were caught by the high ceiling and their sound deepened; Duarte was used to this effect and guessed—correctly—that the next person to tumble lightly through the door would be Alexis AKalakar. She came up with a dagger, but she came up near the wall, using the flat expanse of stone surface to guard her back. Sanderton joined the circle that Auralis and Kiriel traced, by step alone, in the carpet; Cook gave him just enough room to safely follow his drawn sword. They were sweating.

Kiriel, Duarte mused, had lost much of her ability, or so she claimed. He did not actually believe it, although he believed that *she* did; her instincts were far, far too good. She had led them; they had followed. And, as usual, she was both right and in time.

The creature was of a type that they had seen before. It roared its fury at Kiriel. She did not roar back. She might have, once, but the single time she had tried it since she had lost some of her strength, the sound had been high and weak. It had had the effect of astonishing the creature—which the Ospreys took immediate advantage of. They weren't proud; they took what they could, when they could, being fond of life. But she had made no other sound during the combat and afterward she had disappeared. Auralis, after cleaning the blood off his sword, disappeared as well, and when he returned, she walked in a grim silence by his side.

Thereafter, when she chose to speak in combat, she used words.

Or, Duarte thought, her sword.

There was, between Kiriel and Auralis, a very odd friendship. Based on instability, fear, and a hatred of the kin, it was bolstered by a competitive streak that had caused the deaths of lesser—and younger—men. Well, men younger than Auralis.

The two understood that the kin were deadly; they understood that the kin were *fast*. They also wanted to land two blows: the first one, and the one that killed the creature. It was a game, but a desperate game, a game that drove them both to dance on a very fine, very sharp edge.

Duarte was amazed that one, or the other, had not yet been killed or maimed, a sure sign that Kalliaris still favored the mad.

Auralis landed the first blow. He often did, to Kiriel's great annoyance. The kin focused on her when she was in the room; it was almost as if they could not conceive of the danger any other mortal represented. If they were capable of mounting a strong offense, she bore the brunt of it; if they were capable of solid, impassable defense, they turned it in her direction. It was a wonder that Auralis was not farther ahead in their contest.

But . . . to Auralis' great annoyance, it was almost always Kiriel who landed the killing blow, and in this case it happened almost on the heels of Auralis' victory; the creature, circled now by four swords, and watched by Alexis and Duarte, either of whom could offer less obvious means of damage, roared at the bite of the blade. The injury itself was minor.

The mistake of allowing it to be a distraction was not. The creature's attention wavered from Kiriel's blade.

If Kiriel had lost the darkness that had given her a quiet and natural menace, her sword had not; there was something about the blade itself that made any other death seem welcome. There was a tendency to take a step back when the blade was drawn, even if you happened to be engaged in combat at the time it left its sheath.

The only person who seemed immune to the subtlety of its menace was Auralis; twice now, the two Ospreys had crossed swords—without demanding a subsequent trial by combat. Which was good; he was certain that one of them wouldn't survive it, no matter what rules of conduct were laid down before its start.

The blade seemed to lead Kiriel's hands as it bisected the creature from the crook of its neck on the right to the pit of its arm on the left.

Auralis' cursing could be heard *over* the creature's brief scream. It continued as the upper shoulder, arm, and head toppled to the carpet. The circling Ospreys jumped back to avoid the splash of its blood. Something else they'd learned the hard way.

Duarte waited; the body did *not* vanish. His glance met Alexis', briefly. She nodded.

He turned back to the kai Leonne, who was waiting patiently, his hand nowhere near the hilt of his plain but fine sword.

"Tell me again," Valedan said calmly, surveying the fallen, the standing—and the ruined carpet which lay beneath them both—with a calm that Duarte found slightly unnerving, "why you believe anyone else would make a suitable personal guard for my particular circumstance."

Ramiro di'Callesta was impatient.

Had Valedan been any other Tyr, the Callestan Tyr'agnate would have been far away, in the heart of Averda, gathering his men, planning their routes; deciding which of his villages he could afford to sacrifice, and which he was likely to lose regardless. He would have taken his par with him; would have left surrounded by the Tyran that were the most trusted men in the Dominion of Annagar; his blood, his brothers.

But Valedan was Valedan, raised in the Northern Court and therefore surrounded by Northern advisers with their superficial understanding of the South. The only adviser of note that the kai Leonne had was the Serra Alina di'Lamberto—a woman Ramiro felt disinclined to trust, if one ever trusted a woman one did not own or father.

"Tyr'agnate," a man said, and the Callestan Tyr waited the count of three full breaths before he turned to face the General Baredan di'Navarre. At the General's back, sunlight glinted off seawater. Averda was bounded on one side by the vastness of oceans, and the Callestan Tyr, as all Tyrs before him, professed no great love of the sea; men of power in the South were bred by the desert of sand and wind and sun; their endurance was strengthened by heat, their lives were scoured of weakness by the grit of sandstorm, their resolve tested by the screaming howl of the wind, and by the sudden, inexplicable chill of the night, the Lady's cold reception for men who truly served the Lord.

No Tyr would profess any knowledge of, any desire for, the sea; Ramiro understood this well.

And yet he found himself by the seawall often, his men at a remove, both physically and intellectually. Here, he might stare out into the bay, where at any point vessels scudded gently over the lap of waves as they came to harbor, or left it, at the whim of men too foolish to understand the true value of land.

He had made it a point to gain all possible information about these vessels, and he had discovered that the Northerners guarded nothing as jealously as they did their ships. Whole nations, he felt, were almost beside the point to the men who sailed the grandest of these vessels; and upon the water, no matter who their allegiance might in theory be to, they ruled as little kings if they owned small fleets.

He wondered at the word: fleet. It implied speed, and certainly, watching the ships recede, it seemed an appropriate word. Hands behind his back, he would watch the great sails come down, billowing in wind that was the only thing over which these captains could not exert immediate control.

It had not escaped his notice that the number of ships coming into, and leaving, the port city had increased as the time to move the armies South drew near.

Nor had it escaped Baredan's.

No Southerners of their rank had ever been this far North this close to the beginning of a campaign. Curiosity was a poor word for the avid interest he felt but did not openly display; years from now, a better understanding of the movement of armies might give him an advantage that no Southerner had ever had when faced with Imperials at war.

"It is," Baredan said softly, reaching into the folds of his robes and drawing out a scroll, "as expected."

"Indeed."

The General handed the scroll to the Callestan Tyr; Ramiro unfurled it. There, in perfect Torra, was a graceful, even elegantly worded letter. Had it not, in fact, *been* a letter, had it not been committed to words and paper rather than sun and wind, it might have been the work of a Southerner, so exact was the phrasing, so perfect the choice of words. It invited the General to go to the South—where, it conceded, with both grace and economy, his true knowledge and therefore his greatest strength lay, to better prepare the land for the coming of the kai Leonne, and the kai's claim. It further beseeched the General—in terms that a man might use, and not a *true* supplicant—to prove that Valedan was capable of traveling without the Northern army by *introducing* him to the South in the company of his compatriots, and his compatriots *only*.

Ramiro nodded. The letter he had received had been different in only one way: it had been written in Weston, not Torra. Idly, he wondered why; the choice of the language—as the choice of so many things Northern—was no doubt deliberate.

"It is," Baredan said, "well done. We understand each other," he added, as Ramiro handed back the scroll. "Everything Commander Allen has stated here is the truth. To arrive at the head of a Northern army is, in fact, worse than arriving alone. To arrive at my side, or at yours, is already a risk—but the kai Leonne has proved himself capable of withstanding any comparison with his allies."

Ramiro's smile was brief, like a glint of sunlight over the moving surface of the sea. "Indeed," he said softly. "The kai Leonne is young, but he is capable of presenting himself as a leader, rather than a puppet." The Callestan Tyr folded his hands behind his back and turned his face to the salt-laden breeze. The salt was the only thing he disliked, although it had become such a constant presence he wondered if, when it was absent again, he might not miss it.

"And there is a problem."

"Indeed," Baredan said, in a tone of voice that meant serious, rather than logistic, difficulties.

The ships, laden, were low to the water; the poles of great oars broke its surface again and again, gathering sunlight and shedding it, over and over, little rivulets of broken light.

"Have you noticed," he said quietly, "how many of the new ships seemed to be manned by soldiers?"

He could sense Baredan's momentary frown; he did not turn to dignify it with a glance. Had he been Callestan, the General would have understood this minor censure. He was not. "What is the problem?"

"The kai Leonne will not leave the capital without the Ospreys."

The words might have been in a completely foreign tongue, they made so little sense. Ramiro di'Callesta turned and met the General's unblinking gaze, and any suspicion that Baredan had developed a Northern sense of humor during his stay in Essalieyan was destroyed by that meeting of eyes.

Shock, like the eddies beneath the constant lap of waves, moved the Tyr to raise a brow, no more. And then he smiled, and was chagrined to note that in fact, if any man could be accused of the contamination of Northern triviality, it was not the General. "I fear, kai Navarre, that this is no longer our problem."

"Pardon?"

"The Eagle," he said, using the title by which the Commander was known throughout the North and the South, "has no desire to take the kai Leonne with the armies. No doubt, in the future, he fears that the kai Leonne will be an enemy, and not an ally; an enemy and not a pawn. He has no desire to have the . . . impressive logistics of his army revealed for the inspection of such a man.

"We have offered a sound strategy to further the Eagle's desire. It has been refused by the man who will be our . . . lawful . . . liege lord. Therefore, it would seem to me that we are about to see a test of both will and diplomatic skill on the part of the Eagle."

"You find this amusing."

"Yes."

"May I ask why, Tyr'agnate?"

"Because it is clear to me that we are about to find out what Valedan's role at the head of armies *will* be. The Eagle does not wish his presence along the Northern route, and the Eagle's word, in matters of the army, is law. But the Ospreys cannot be detached from the army without their destruction. And the kai Leonne's, in all probability. They are remembered in the South."

"If the kai Leonne desires to travel with the army, he will either be rebuffed or he will be accepted."

"They could withdraw the Ospreys or replace them."

"They could, yes. But I doubt they will."

"You are saying—"

"Yes. Let us see what the Kings decide. It will tell us much about how the Crowns regard Valedan kai di'Leonne's role."

Baredan was silent a moment, and then he, too, turned

to look out at the sea. "I hate this land," he said, his voice mild.

"Indeed."

The Princess Mirialyn ACormaris had been summoned to the chambers her father occupied when he was not in session. They were very, very fine; ceilings were carved in stone reliefs around bordered edges of wood that rose from the floor, dark and gleaming with the oils that had protected it from the worst of time's passage. In stone, the divine eagle, its rod elongated and detailed, its ring, overlarge, both clutched in fine, fine claws, stood watch in its frozen flight above the great windows that admitted light into the chamber.

The symbol of Cormaris, Lord of Wisdom.

Her grandfather.

Her father was capable of being informal. She had seen it in her life, although in truth, were it not for the sharpness of her memory, she might have doubted such informality existed; she had seen very, very little of it in the last fifteen years.

"ACormaris," he said, as the Astari who shadowed every door of his hall moved to allow her entry.

She bowed, her form perfect. When she rose, she said, "Your Majesty."

"We find ourselves in a most delicate situation." For just a moment, the corners of his lips twitched slightly. "It seems, as you suggested, that the Tyr'agar does not wish to travel without the protection of the army."

She waited, her hands at her sides—where, in fact, the Astari who now stood at her back could see them clearly.

"Commander Allen does not, for reasons that are obvious, desire the Tyr'agar to accompany the army."

She continued to wait. "But for equally obvious reasons, the Tyr'agar cannot be the lone Southerner to do so, should he indeed do so."

She was silent.

"You understand what is at stake, ACormaris."

"Your Majesty."

"The Tyr'agar was once one of your students; I wish you to speak with him."

She bowed.

Knowing, as perhaps her father knew, that there was one other she would speak with first.

The rooms that had once welcomed her with their combination of understated wealth and Southern austerity were now simply austere. The fine hangings that had adorned both wall and door were nowhere in evidence, and Mirialyn ACormaris, the only Princess of royal blood to be born in generations, wondered if they would ever be seen again. Certainly not in the North. And in the South?

What use did the South have for a woman like Alina?

As if she had heard the question—and she was a master of hearing the nuance of all silences—she appeared, as austere in her fashion as the rooms she was deserting by slow degrees.

"ACormaris," she said softly, as she said all things. Desert night, Northern ice; hard to say which was colder. Her expression was almost nonexistent as she turned her slender face, the severer lines of her hawkish profile diminished by the movement. She was so very graceful, so very perfect.

"You will travel."

"Yes. But we have discussed this."

"Yes." There was a silence she chose not to fill with words. Into that silence, the Serra Alina brought stillness; they waited for a long moment, glances brushing the contours of each other's face, as if seeking familiarity. As if unsurprised to find so little of it.

"Your pardon, Serra Alina," Mirialyn said at last. She offered a perfect Northern bow. "I have to come to ask you to intercede on behalf of . . . wisdom."

"I assume you refer to the influence you feel I have with the Tyr'agar."

"As always, the Serra Alina is astute." Mirialyn was silent for a full minute, and then she said, "Alina."

The Serra said nothing.

"It is your choice, to leave the North."

"It is your choice, ACormaris, to stay."

"We each have our duties."

"Valedan depended on your advice no less than mine. You will send him to the battle that will decide his fate, should he survive it, in the company of *men*."

"There are women—"

"The Kalakar is a *soldier*."

Mirialyn said quietly, "There is you. No matter how we view our decisions, or each other's, in the end, he takes his most valuable adviser with him."

The Serra Alina di'Lamberto was immune to flattery; as all Southern women before her, she had learned its value as a tool, and cared little for its use. But she understood that in the North, flattery had different faces and spoke in different tongues, and none of these were Mirialyn's. "What would you have me do?"

"I would have you follow your head," was Mirialyn's quiet reply.

A bitter smile swallowed the words, leaving, as always, silence. "Oh?"

"I am not born of, or to, the South. But I recognize the damage that marching at the head of the Northern army will cause. Having our armies cross the border at all in his cause is danger enough; it will damage him, but that damage is unavoidable."

"Yes."

"He must . . . separate himself in every other possible fashion from the North. If he arrives, the lone Leonne, at the side of the Tyr'agnate of the richest Terrean in the Dominion, and served by the only General canny enough to survive the slaughter, it will serve his cause far better than arriving at the side of the Northern army."

Alina's brow arched; it was the equivalent of a shrug. "If he has no army at all, he will be accorded the respect of men who are not in a position to be of use, no more."

"He has an army," Mirialyn replied. "He has Ser Anton, and Ser Anton's name is *known*. Even here, in the North, it is known."

Alina nodded quietly. "Yes. Known."

"And the fact that Ser Anton chooses to serve him might balance itself against the use of the Northern armies—but not if he comes with them. He will be seen as a puppet, no more; I must assume, as he wishes to pursue this course, that he cannot see the cost clearly."

The smile twisted slightly, and then it was gone. Serra Alina turned away from the open door, both exposing her back and retreating into the rooms she occupied; rooms that were, in their stark and elegant way, the place where battles were devised and discarded. "It is not a wise assumption, but a fair one. I believe that he knows, as you say in the North, *here,*" she said, raising a hand to her forehead, "but the reality of what this will mean to him has not made its way *here*." She shrugged; silk rippled and fell, bright shadows cast by the motion. "It is a delicate balance. The *Kialli* come in no predictable fashion. The . . . Ospreys . . . have been the most effective force in dealing with their presence." She frowned. "The second most effective force, but I do not believe the Kings would agree to send the Astari South."

For a moment, the Princess of the blood smiled. "There are many noble Houses that would owe a vast debt of gratitude to the young Tyr should he merit such a command on the part of the Kings—but you've met Duvari, no doubt. Even were such an ordered issue, I don't believe he would follow it, or allow it to be followed."

"Indeed. May I offer you water or wine?"

She didn't answer, and that was an answer in itself. Instead, she followed Alina into the central chamber, the meeting room. There, a low, flat table that was perfectly round occupied the room's heart, and upon it, the perfect Southern vessel; delicate clay, worked in a pale blue, and fired by sun's heat. Sunlight cast that slender vessel's shadow against inlay. It rose and fell in the perfect Serra's hands, as it had done countless times in the past. In a different country, in a country where two women of vastly different cultures, unfettered by the responsibility and the complicated joy of children or husbands, might change all rules of etiquette that had bound them to their previous lives, shedding them slowly and shyly at first, as one might shed clothing when in desire of, and terror of, not sex, but intimacy.

She met Alina's gaze, held it a moment, thinking her unkind. Watched her face until she turned back to the task at hand, making an art of service.

"We have argued," she said, over the slow trickle of the wine that Mirialyn seldom drank.

"The Tyr'agar?"

"And I, yes. You are right, of course; I understand exactly what the cost will be. He is . . . impatient. In that fashion, he is like so many of the Southerners. Were he

Ser Kyro's age, his impatience would be . . . an embarrassment; a liability. He is not—but in youth, lack of malleability shows itself in such a fashion. As the army travels South, he disdains the subterfuge—and the lack of safety—in traveling apart from it."

"There is no subterfuge. If we are to travel, you know as well as I that we must be seen to travel at *his* request; at his behest. If that is to happen, he must meet the Tyr's people, and he must—if at all possible—be seen by the men and women in the Terrean of Averda as a man who rules."

"And of Mancorvo?" the Serra said, her voice as smooth as a dagger's flat.

"That war is yours to fight," the Princess answered softly. "But, yes, he needs Mancorvo. He needs the *Lambertans*, and their approval, if he is to have any chance of holding what we hope to win. You know what the reputation of the Lambertans is among the clans. Even among the Callestans, whose enmity is so bitter, there is a grudging respect for your brothers."

"Yes. Among the Callestans of little account and little power. The Lambertan men are not known for their canniness."

"Honesty and a lack of canniness do not go hand in glove, Serra; if the Lambertans were truly without guile, they would never have held Mancorvo. I know it; you know it. It is enough.

"But that is beside the point; it is the men of little account and little power who will, like grains of sand, be the storm upon which Valedan will ride. You know as well as I that it is those hearts and minds he must capture."

"And you know as well as I that he must survive to do so."

"Alina—"

Yes, I know. No words now, just a momentary grimace; a ripple that crossed the line between amusement and anger, wavering, or perhaps touching either side in equal measure. She let that ambivalence be seen because, in the end, they had been as open with each other as two women of power could be. "It is not the army," she said at last, "that draws him, although he is very curious about the logistics."

"Logistics?"

"He has never traveled with a large body of armed men

before. He has not had to see to their needs; to see that they're fed; to see what price their passage demands of the countryside."

"In this case, very little."

Alina raised a dark brow. "In this case, perhaps. But he will, he is certain, command armies in his time—and he wishes to learn from the men who have bested us."

"Let him learn, then, when learning will do him good; let him learn when they engage."

"He could be convinced of that," she said at last, reluctantly. "If the Ospreys were to be detached from the body of the army and accompany him to the South."

"And that is the only circumstance under which he will detach himself from the army?"

"It is," Alina said softly. "And to my great surprise, ACormaris, the Kings have acceded to his wishes. Should he desire to travel at the head of the Northern army, he will so travel."

Mirialyn was completely silent. Rigid. "That means the Kings have given him command of the armies."

"Your pardon?"

"Commander Allen, Commander Kalakar, Commander Berriliya. They have all but refused his request. If Valedan is to accompany the army in spite of this, it means that the Kings have ordered the Generals to report to Valedan if it comes to that, and not merely to . . . facilitate his capture of the Tor Leonne."

"But that—"

"It is not impossible," the Eagle said, his voice completely devoid of emotion. "Politically, the stated reason for our entry into the Southern war *is* the kai Leonne."

"The kai Leonne is barely adult and has no experience with, and *no training for* war. The Kings cannot possibly—"

His expression as constant as the rocks above and below them, Commander Bruce Allen produced a large, ornate silvered tube that bore at either end the sign of the crown, and was decorated on either side by the sword and the rod. Crossed swords, crossed rods, in opposition; crossed rod and sword, crossed rod and sword, between. An expert eye could make out the faint outline of wings; the curved talons of the Eagle; could perhaps see the noble line of a wolf's jaw. No doubt, when the tube had first been made, those faint lines had been stronger.

The tube's presence silenced The Kalakar. She watched, as impassive now as her rival, Devran, as the tube was twisted, the lines of its pattern broken a moment, and the scroll within removed.

Commander Allen had already perused the contents; he had done so precisely once. More was unnecessary. But he felt the hand of King Reymalyn in every word, although the signatures, scrawled in both splendor and at leisure, were signatures he recognized. At precisely the end of a such a document, several times in his career—once at the death of the man who had been both his mentor and, in privacy where honesty could be its most grim, his inferior—he had seen these orders, bearing these signatures; the memories were engraved in some place that time touched slowly, if at all. He knew their truth on a level that was much more visceral than simple intellect, even passionate intellect; they were not forged.

Had he wished proof, it was simple enough to check for authenticity. It would also be the act of an angry fool, and in the end, if he was one, he was not the other. He was not above letting The Kalakar speak, after she had read the document from top to bottom, her eyes slowing down over the sparsely—but precisely—chosen words it contained before they raced up to the top and began again.

"Is this authentic?" She was hunched slightly over the table, as if, even seated, she found herself in the center of the circle.

The Berriliya's momentary glance was heavy with contempt. It had the effect of silencing Commander Kalakar.

"Why?" she asked at last.

"I believe," the Eagle said, sitting back in his chair with the scroll, heavy enough in weight that it did not immediately roll into a tubelike curl, "that King Reymalyn's words carried weight in this matter."

"But the boy—"

"Ellora, I know. But admit it: the boy has become more than any of us first envisioned. He is not a fool; he is not, at least not at first, second, or even tenth glance, a pawn. He serves himself, and his complicated sense of rulership and responsibility has impressed the Kings—and possibly the Queens—enough that he has been given the final say in what occurs in the country he claims as his own."

Devran's gaze was cutting as it swept up the slightly stiff line of the Eagle's jaw.

"He has no experience on the battlefield."

The Eagle rose. "No. But he has—in our brief experience—the propensity for taking advice from those he believes have the experience he lacks."

"A fine thing to risk our armies on."

"Ellora, enough."

Silence.

"The kai Leonne is no fool. He understands why it is imperative that he travel South ahead of the army. But he maintains—and with cause, if the reports of the Astari are to be believed—that the Ospreys constitute his best chance of survival against . . . the assassins our enemies have chosen to deploy against him. He has chosen to travel with the army because he believes it is only with the army that the Ospreys are guaranteed safety against the less supernatural exploits of their past in the Dominion."

"He needs the Ospreys; the Ospreys need the army."

Commander Allen nodded. "Yes. Is it true?"

"Which part?"

"Both."

She was silent, turning the words over. Rejection and acceptance fought, like any of the other seasoned warriors under her command, in the private circle of unvoiced thoughts. Her expression, rather than a window into that conflict, was sort of like an arrow slit; a man could look, but only at the right angle.

Devran's smile was a weapon; he used it briefly to inflict a cut, not a wound.

"They did what had to be done," she said, without rancor, although the look she gave Devran promised there would be, later. "They fought a war the South could understand, and better than the Southerners could fight it. But the Annies—"

"Commander, may I remind you who has command of the armies?"

"The Annagarians, then. The Southerners. They expected us to play by Northern rules while they played by none." She shrugged.

"So instead, you chose a group of your personal men and told them to play outside of the rules as well. And we paid the price for their lack of discipline."

Old arguments had a consistency and a strength that came out of surviving the harshest of emotional climes intact. All of the arguments that so visibly divided Commander Kalakar and Commander Berriliya were old ones; even the new ones that occurred from time to time relied heavily on the foundation of their history in old wars and skirmishes. She did not—because Commander Allen was present—allow the discussion to slide into the minutiae of the discipline problems that had plagued the Kings' armies during their sojourn in the South. But those deaths were there between them.

Although if she were honest, if it weren't those deaths, it would have been something else. Everything about their approach to command was different, and in a way guaranteed to cause conflict.

The Ospreys were not the only example of that conflict, but they were the most glaring. And yet.

And yet, out of the broken, the half-mad, the men—and women—who would have otherwise made their way to the gallows or the sword, Duarte AKalakar had fashioned a unit that, playing by its own rules, had far exceeded her expectations. Possibly even his; hard to say. The early days had been difficult, and he had been forced to his own brand of justice, while they looked the other way. She had wondered what it would be like, to take the Ospreys into battle, rather than to forge them out of its fires.

But she was no longer certain that that curiosity would ever be satisfied. She rose.

"Very well," she said coolly.

Commander Allen rose as well.

He could have thanked her. He spared her that. Instead, he remained standing until she left the Hall of Wise Counsel.

CHAPTER THREE

20th of Scaral, 427 AA
Averalaan Aramarelas, Kalakar Manse

Sunrise behind cloud.

Warm, although the darkness was also warm, even here, at season's ebb. The harbor city that was the heart of the Empire rarely understood the cold. It flirted with such understanding in the drizzle of rain, when the clouds were thick and heavy and the sunlight momentarily denied its people, but it was a passing fancy; the city knew the warmth would return and merely found cover while the shadows passed. Boats sat like great, fat fowl, sails, like wings, tucked in, at the edge the city exposed to the sea.

You could only see those boats from a particular angle when your home was *Averalaan Aramarelas*. The Kalakar Manse was not particularly tall, but it did boast towers of a sort—wide, squat squares set firmly one on top of another until they ended in parapets. The man who had designed that tower had been pragmatic to the core, something The Kalakar admired, and very few others did. Her Council had, during the decades—as had the Council of her predecessor—attempted to have them removed as an eyesore; to have them remade or replaced with structures that better suited their position on the isle. It pleased Ellora—and said much about her—to leave the tower as it was, not so much to save the enormous sums of money that would go into destroying it and putting something else in its place, although it would undoubtedly do that, but as a gesture of stubborn solidarity with the past. If you understood that about her, you understood something fundamental about her character.

Duarte understood that. Admired it, in some small fashion. And as an officer—even an officer whose strict duties took him out of the Kalakar fold—he had access to the heights.

He rarely took advantage of that access. But today, this morning, he had felt the restless urge that drove him up to where he might gaze out on the bay. As if he were an Osprey in fact, not name, and now perched on the highest peak in his small dominion.

The sea breeze was strong. He tasted salt in the air, and wondered at it; salt was a part of his daily life, and he rarely noticed it as keenly as he did this morning. It reminded him of the fact that he had not spent his entire life in Averalaan; that at some point in the distant past, the taste of salt had been an unpleasant reminder of things left behind.

A reminder that all things end.

Endings.

He had been summoned to House Kalakar specifically for this interview. That in itself was unusual; he was accustomed to offering The Kalakar a report on the activities of the Ospreys—and their charge—four times a week. Any procedural irregularity that came up was dealt with during those frequent meetings, as were all bureaucratic details. Most of those details usually involved complaints laid against one or another of the Ospreys—usually Auralis, although his drunken binges and the resultant claims of damage had lessened dramatically of late. Enough so that he had become the butt of betting that, by Kalakar rules, was strictly forbidden to all soldiers, and overlooked in the Ospreys.

But this particular meeting was signaled not by routine but rather, the presence of a Kalakar Verrus. Any request that came from a Verrus had the weight of emergency behind it. Worse still, Verrus Vernon Loris—the man known as The Kalakar's harbinger of bad news—was not the set of quartered circles that crossed the threshold of the Arannan Halls. The man who had arrived bearing the sealed scroll was Verrus Korama. Duarte had long suspected that of all the men who served Ellora, it was Korama that she would save if she could only save one. He had often wondered if they were lovers.

He could not imagine the pragmatic Commander and the

quiet Verrus together, and shook his head to clear it of the image.

"What is it?" Alexis had said, coming from behind as always, her slender form catching the corner of his eye and demanding his attention. Time had changed the line of her hair; had sharpened the point of her chin, dulled the glint of eyes that had once, round or no, had the sharpest edge he had ever seen on anything not flat and steel.

"A . . . summons."

"What for?"

"I don't know." He had handed her the scroll, his eyes never leaving the place it had resided; the palm of his hands retained the memory of paper's weight, his mind, the words.

"Duarte—"

"I don't know," he said, with less force, the space between each word precise and measured in the quiet.

She shut up. He thanked *Kalliaris* for that, the gift of her silence. There had been others in the room. The only man he was aware of, when he had at last looked up from the lined surface of sun-worn palms was, oddly enough, Valedan kai di'Leonne.

Their eyes met, brown and brown. Whose gaze held whose, he couldn't say, but at last, it ended; unanchored he turned to Verrus Korama AKalakar.

"Thank you," he said quietly. "I will accompany you shortly."

The Iron Hand, as Vernon Loris was known, was the grim face of The Kalakar; the face that exacted no sympathy and delivered no mercy. He was the law, such as it was, when The Kalakar herself was not present. When Korama was sent, it was . . . worse. Vernon Loris was sent to deliver complaints filed against the Ospreys for their unfortunately frequent drunken bouts in the old city; Korama was sent to tell them that one of their own had unexpectedly died, and that The Kalakar wished their help or advice in locating family, if they existed. Not that many of the Ospreys had ever had family they were willing to claim as their own.

Since the Ospreys had become Valedan's personal guard, they had managed—after they had lost two members to the first demon they encountered before any warning could be sounded—to keep out of the tawdry brawls that *always* attracted the magisterial guards. And as far as he knew, no one else had died.

Perhaps someone was going to.

Sea breeze.

Squawk of gulls on thermals.

Verrus Korama, like shadow—or shroud—appeared at his side on the battlements. Duarte wondered, briefly, how the Verrus had known exactly where to find him; he almost never came to the parapets. But he didn't ask, and the Verrus, subdued and oddly respectful, didn't volunteer the information.

"The Kalakar," he said softly, as softly as he walked, "will see you now."

She had her back to the door when he walked through it. Bad sign.

Her first words were, "Verrus Korama, that will be all."

Verrus Korama nodded, the movement as precise as the salute that protocol forbid between people of their rank. He bowed, slightly, to Duarte AKalakar, gaze glancing off his face.

Duarte heard the door shut behind him and wondered what a corpse would hear when a coffin lid was dropped. Her words, he thought, as they came, were the patter of dirt.

She did not immediately turn to face him. Sunlight made a shadow of her back; a shadow with slightly stooped shoulders, and a head that was bowed toward the ground beyond his vision.

"Captain Duarte," she said. The shadows darkened her pale hair; they were not as strong as shadows cast by full sunlight, but they were there, if one knew how to look. Duarte had spend his life looking into the shadows. "You've never been given the easy duties."

He said nothing, but his body fell into rigid lines; feet firmly planted against the grain of old wood, hands behind his back, chin up, face forward.

"And when you perform the duties that are required of you, you perform them in shadow; you perform them as if you were a step above criminal. I have always thought that a crime." She turned, now, her expression so many things, its chaos was unreadable. Her pale hair had been pulled back from her face in a severe knot; he saw the lines around her eyes, the lines etched in her forehead; time's gift and judgment. They seemed deeper.

He knew.

He knew then. But he waited.

"You have always done the impossible. You—you *personally*—made the Ospreys, culling them from the gallows in ones and twos. You took the risk and the responsibility of . . . correcting your errors in judgment. You gave the South something to remember, and gave the North the clean hands and breathing space *we* needed.

"That has never been acknowledged by anyone who is not Kalakar. Not even the Kings themselves have been moved to commend you in a fashion that you—and your own—deserve."

He was profoundly weary. But discipline held him.

"Nor, to my profound shame, can I." She started to turn, and then her feet became as rigidly planted as his own; no coward, Ellora. Only a leader, and at that, a leader to follow and die for.

"Why did you summon me?"

Her expression shifted slightly. The silence was pointed, but she did not extend it.

"You will not understand this," she replied, in a tone of voice that might be mistaken as conversational by a casual listener—if there could be such a thing, in a room like this, in these circumstances. "You will not understand it, and I'm old enough, and powerful enough, not to beg you to make the attempt.

"You are not a stupid man, Duarte. If you were, you would never have been accepted by the Order of Knowledge; if you were, you would never have retired from its vast and useless walls. You don't have the look of a killer about you, but if you hadn't the heart of one, you would never have survived the Ospreys, and the Ospreys would never have survived the war."

"They almost didn't."

"No," she said, the single word displaying a ferocity that he realized she had kept from the conversation so far by force of a will that was legendary. It eased him, somehow, to know that she hurt.

His own pain was building.

"Yes," she said evenly, forcing that quiet into her voice again, "they almost didn't."

"They wouldn't have, Commander, had you not personally interceded."

She winced. She had the grace to wince. "You are a dangerous man," she said, when she at last chose to speak. "To remind me of that, here."

"It was not said as a political gesture," he replied, staring now at the surface of an uncluttered desk, an uncluttered room. "But as fact. We know what it cost you. We know that Commander Allen all but forbid it. But you chose your men from among the House Guard, and you led them personally into the trap that killed two thirds of our number.

"They were willing—even eager—to lose us. But not you, not Ellora AKalakar."

"No," she replied, ferocity returning as his words pricked restless memory, "the House Guard was not eager to lose you. You were always a part of the House."

"The House Guard," he said, "was not, technically, yours at that time. Not yours to risk."

"No. But mine to lead."

"Yes."

She looked away. "And they are still mine to lead." She swallowed. "But the Ospreys are *yours,* Duarte. Tell them."

"Tell them?"

"That if they desire it, there is still room for them within the House Guard."

The enormity of the words took a moment to sink in. "Still room?" he said at last, reduced to mimicry, his voice almost too quiet to be heard.

"No matter what decision they make, they will be AKalakar until they commit a crime too great for the House to overlook. They've been under your peacetime care for over a decade; I can well believe that they are capable of retaining the honor their role in war purchased."

She closed her eyes. Opened them, as if unsheathing a flawless steel that had been carefully guarded until that moment. "I am retiring the colors of the company," she told him, each word flat and without inflection. "The Black Ospreys—as they were—do not have the numbers necessary to form a unit in the army, and because we will be traveling through largely friendly terrain in the South, it is believed that the Annagarian cerdan will be up to the task of fulfilling the role they once held."

He was speechless.

She expected this. She started to speak. Stopped. Started again. Protocol was something she understood well; how could she not? She was *The* Kalakar; ruler of one of The Ten, a political force to be reckoned with among the most elevated of the patriciate.

But she was more than that. Much more.

"Duarte," she said, voice low, "understand that I have no choice in this."

"Just as," he said sharply, "you had no choice in the Averdan valleys?"

"*Just* as," she spit back, as if slapped. "Figure it out for yourself. Or do you want me to say it?"

He didn't answer.

"Very well. *You* were the single force responsible for the Southern fear of the Northern armies. And with cause. I am not ashamed of the role you played. I would not have had that responsibility in any other hands. You did better than any of us could have foreseen.

"But if you travel with the army, the Tyr'agar and his retinue travel with the army. You know the politics of the South. You know that this is not the last war we will have. Either this generation, or the next, will come back to the borders with something to prove."

He nodded.

"I can withdraw you from the service of the Tyr. That was my first choice."

He bowed his head then.

"You know why I can't."

"I would prefer that to this."

"I know. You lived and you died for those colors; they're a part of everything you've achieved. To retire them in battle—at the end of the war—may have been the wisest decision. But I thought to leave you what you had achieved. I did not intend to—

"It doesn't matter. The colors will be retired. If you wish it, you will be absorbed into the House Guards, and with honor."

"They won't do it," he said.

She didn't insult him by asking who. Instead, she leaned across the desk. "You have never disappointed me. Not in any way that matters. You know why I did not withdraw you from service to the Tyr'agar."

"Because you're afraid he'll die."

"Because I *know* that anyone else will fail," she said quietly. "I will deny this, and you know full well why, but no other unit could have achieved what you have in the months that we've been preparing for this war. The boy is *alive*. And alive is how we need him.

"But not even the Ospreys are good enough to travel in Averda with that flag flying in their gods-cursed winds. Not without the rest of the army. You're a legend there," she added, with a trace of bitter pride. "The Berriliya would be happy to see you make the attempt if he was not also certain it would cost us the life of the boy."

Duarte AKalakar—no longer captain—was silent for a long, long time. "What happens after the war?"

"You will always be AKalakar," she said. "You will always have a home in the House."

"And the colors?"

"What has been retired," she replied evenly, "can be honored again by men and women who have proved their worth—and their loyalty—to the House."

"And what if they would rather stay with the House?"

She snorted. "You serve me," she said softly. "But they serve *you*. They always have."

"Kalakar—"

"I need you there."

"And is that an order?"

"I have a suspicion that the moment you leave this room, I will no longer have the legal right to give you a military order; I can't as much as inspect your uniform."

"Probably a good thing."

She smiled. Gallows humor. "I have the legal right of the head of a House, and that is murky and easily contested."

He nodded. It was true.

So much about her was true. If he closed his eyes, he could see her face in the harsh and unforgiving sunlight of the Averdan valleys, blood streaming from a grazed forehead, like the proverbial river; he could trace its flow down the creases of her face as it met with the blood from a badly wounded shoulder. He remembered the shock of it; the one wound and the other; it was as if a statue was bleeding, no, worse, as if a *House* was.

She spoke, her lips moved, the sound came to him over so many sounds it was hard to distinguish the words; but because they were her words, and she was inexplicably there, and bleeding, he had struggled to do so. Light glinted off mail and glove; light off sword, as if her sword were somehow burning. She was the Lord's Lady, on this field, and at her back, grim-faced and feral, stood the House Guards of Kalakar. *Did you think we would leave you behind? I'm on the field, Captain. You're* mine. It was foolish, but at that moment, surrounded by arrow and magefire and the broken bodies of the men he had forged into weapons, and worse—gods, so much worse—into friends, he had felt . . . safe. She had come to bring them all home.

Strange, that he should recognize the feeling, when he had never experienced it before in his life, either in youth or in adulthood.

Safety.

Home.

And he had known, then, although he had suspected it before that moment, that he would willingly follow this woman for the rest of his life, no matter how long or how short that might be.

"Duarte," she said quietly.

He frowned and then realized that he had been staring at her, searching for the old scar of that particular battle. Like a map, he thought, the scar would lead him. But to where?

She met his gaze, and he stared at her face for a full minute, understanding what she asked of him. Understanding what she promised: that she would cross the valleys for him—and his—again.

If he did this; if he followed yet another set of orders that it was not within her legal power to give, and not within her power to acknowledge directly.

He found himself smiling, although his mind was already twisting and turning around the explanation he would have to give his Ospreys—his, regardless of the flag that flew above their heads. "One question, Kalakar."

"Ask it."
"Who's going to pay us?"

It had been so long since Auralis had blushed that he would have bet money—his own even—that he was no longer capable of it. Luckily, it wasn't a bet that anyone with half a brain would have taken, even after a night of heavy drinking, so his money, what little of it there was, remained safe.

"Auralis?"

By way of reply he kicked a stone. Unfortunately, that stone was part of a road that was actually in very good repair, given the section of town they were in. You could always count on the roads to be whatever it was you didn't want. He cursed.

Kiriel frowned. "You tripped over the *road*?"

"It happens."

"Oh." She paused, her gaze half glare, half question. Since the night that she had lost most of whatever it was that had made her so deadly, she had also lost the preternatural ability to pick out a lie from a truth, or vice versa. She had what everyone else had: instinct. She also had very little raw ability to use it. But she was Kiriel. Anything that had an offensive application, she learned *quickly*.

"Did you hear my question?"

She also defined the word dogged when it sat in front of the word determination; once she started in on something she simply refused to let go. He had seen mastiffs who were easier to shake off.

In a fight, it was a trait Auralis admired. She approached each combat as if the possibility of dying was so foreign a concept her language didn't contain a word for death, except in as it related to *other people's*. Unfortunately, she approached everything else the same way.

"Kiriel, that's not a question you can just come out and ask a man."

"Why not?"

"Because you ask that of the wrong man, and you won't like the answer."

She snorted, an unattractive habit she'd picked up from either Alexis or Fiara. "At least I'd *get* an answer." She paused a moment, and then smiled.

For just that stretch of lip and teeth, he felt the hair on the back of his neck go up. He no longer faltered in stride or reached for a weapon when this happened in Kiriel's presence, but the upper and lower halves of his jaw met in a tight grinding of teeth.

"Besides, if I didn't like the answer, he'd never give it again."

"True enough," Auralis said, forcing himself to shrug. It wasn't hard; by nature his movements were quick and graceful. Even caution couldn't force stiffness into them. "And then every magisterian in the city would be after your head. I've *seen* your idea of 'never.' " As he rounded the buildings that formed a tall and narrow corner of the intersection, he reached up and smacked a heavy sign that hung from two twisted chains. The words were lost to darkness—or dirt—but he knew what they said. This was Smacker's place. Neither he nor Kiriel had ever started a fight in it, and consequently it was one of a handful of places where they didn't have to circumnavigate a large man with a sword to get in.

"We're here."

"But you haven't answered the question."

The door was open. The sound of a full house drifted lazily out into the cool night air. He hung back; he did not want to have this particular conversation in any place that could be remotely considered public.

But he did want a drink.

"Kiriel," he said, staring into a welcome haze of smoke and light, "just because you ask the question doesn't mean I have to answer it."

He didn't much like the look he got in response. She was such a mystery to him. There wasn't anyone else he'd choose to have at his side—or back—in a fight. First, because of all the Ospreys she was the only one who was consistently—to his great chagrin—faster than he was, both on the draw and to the actual battle. Second, the Ospreys had an informal contest that had started up at about the same time as they met their first demon. It was a friendly competition, or about as friendly as any competition among Ospreys ever got; a head count. They'd started an Annie head count in the war twelve years past—one that was strictly speaking forbidden by the Crowns. That had been easier to win.

The demons never arrived in great numbers. But at the moment, the kills racked up by himself and Kiriel counted as joint efforts, putting the informal team where Auralis best liked to be: at the head of the pack, rather than in the middle. He didn't allow for the possibility of being anywhere near the back. No way he could be, and still be fighting side by side with her.

But outside of a fight . . .

She was young enough to be his daughter, much as it pained him to admit it. In and of itself, this wasn't a problem; he'd certainly had any number of girls that were scarcely older.

But he was no longer a young fool; he understood that entanglements of any sort had their price, and he paid it grudgingly. Better to cleanly offer coin and take only what was wanted, when it was wanted, than to pay in other ways.

"You find me attractive." It wasn't a question.

"A corpse would find you attractive." He smiled; the smile was politely refused by the stiff lines of her—yes, very beautiful—face. "But I don't sleep with Ospreys."

"You've slept with Alexis."

This was not he first time he had a strong desire to kill Alexis; if he somehow failed to do it, it probably wouldn't be the last.

"Did she happen to tell you how long ago that was?"

"When she was almost as young as I am," Kiriel said, through clenched teeth. "She says you don't like 'em old."

Strike that. This time, he *was* going to kill the bitch. He wondered if she were somewhere in the bar, listening with what little mage-talent she had, and laughing. The slightly condescending and unpleasant expression that passed for a smile on Alexis' face often made everything about her seem sharper and harder.

It was only with Duarte that she really let her guard down. Of course, it was only with Duarte that she *really* stuck the knife in and twisted.

"Okay, let's try this a different way." He really wanted the drink on the other side of the door frame. Almost as much as he wanted to kill Alexis. He thought about both of these things with a forced intensity; it was better than actually thinking of Kiriel.

Because she was beautiful; she was attractive. She had every bit of allure that walking death always does for the right kind of man—and Auralis knew that he *defined* that type. He also knew death when he saw it. Not the risk of death, but death.

He didn't love life, but he had a few things he wanted to do before it ended.

He had experience in letting people down. Bitter experience. He had learned the patina of letting them down gently when given the opportunity; was not above cruelty in the right circumstance. Was certainly not above a gentle lie.

But she was Osprey. She would kill for him. He suspected that in the right circumstances, she would die for him. Somehow, the outsider had come in, when he wasn't looking.

He owed her honesty. He considered honesty to be highly overrated. He put his left hand, half flat, against the wall; there was nothing he could do to stop the right one from curling into a fist with suspiciously white knuckles. Long experience made him give up after a minute of trying. He took a step away from the door to let people in and out. The sign above them swung, creaking when the winds came tunneling into the still streets; they didn't stay long.

"Kiriel, I don't sleep with virgins. Too complicated."

She was silent for what seemed hours. "Alexis told me," she said at last, "that you would say no."

"Alexis," he said, "is smart. She's a bitch, but she's not a stupid bitch." He started toward the door, exposing his back. Stopped in the frame, when no echo of armor or footstep fell in behind him. He could feel his jaw clamping tight, and worked to loosen it.

"Kiriel," he said, turning.

She was still as stone, and about as colorful.

"You are going to be my life and death when we leave this city. You're already unofficially considered my partner, the other half—the better half—of a team. I can't—I will *never* be able—to be a real lover, a half-husband like Duarte is to Alexis, like most men are to the women they love. All I can offer is a good time, and I can't even guarantee that. I can't do that with you. *You* have to mean more to me than just a quick—" The door hit him, hard.

The person pushing it made it clear that he thought people who got in his way were lucky to get hit in the back by a door traveling at high speed, and not something more fatal. Auralis, already not in the best of moods, thanked Kalliaris briefly for the interruption, and drove his conveniently preclenched fist into the man's gut, hard.

Which was fine, but unfortunately, the three men behind *him* weren't all that impressed when he went over and started retching in the street.

There was some chance, given the situation, that everyone's ruffled feathers could be calmed by a judicious display of apology for unfortunate reflexes, but Auralis, sometime Decarus of the Black Ospreys, wasn't about to let an opportunity slip away.

20th of Scaral 427 AA
Terafin Manse

"What is it about men and fighting?" Finch ATerafin did not have Jay's unruly hair, but she had—over years of exposure—picked up some of her gestures; she shoved straight hair back out of her eyes, giving it a frustrated tug over the forehead.

Teller, so aware of the value of words that he used them seldom, shrugged.

Carver's right eye was swollen shut; Angel's nose was broken. Finch considered it a small miracle that neither of them had lost any teeth—at least none that were visible. She didn't bother to ask them why they hadn't gone to the healerie. Unless it was likely to be fatal, neither the aged Alowan nor his young apprentice, Daine, were willing to offer their aid in relieving the pain of a self-inflicted wound.

Or several.

"Well?"

They were silent, but Carver's eyes flickered to the side of Angel's impenetrable expression. Which meant that Angel had started the fight, and Carver had come to his aid. Again. Angel had chosen not to take the ATerafin name; he could not be accused of being a disgrace to the

House. Carver didn't have that much leeway. He had already been called in, quietly, to speak with Gabriel, The Terafin's right-kin; the man she trusted to deal with potential embarrassments to the House name.

Do you know *what you're doing to him?* She wanted to shout at Angel. Wanted to add to the bruises that were already discoloring his once perfect, pale skin. But what was the point? Carver had taken the House name, but at heart he was what he had always been: part of Jay's den, and willing to die to defend it when he wasn't scared witless by whatever it was that it needed defending from.

The kitchen was absolutely silent. Finch was certain the reflection that stared back at her from the rounded sides of carefully cleaned pots had actual *gray* hair. On the other hand, she had walked into the job with her eyes open; she had always covered for Jay during Jay's merchant voyages.

But those voyages, undertaken at the behest of The Terafin, were different from this one. Because on regular Terafin business, Jay always took Angel and Carver with her; she often took Teller. Jester, she left behind to man the kitchen with Finch. Finch had traveled with her once, by boat, and left Teller in the kitchen. She learned from that experience that she did not enjoy boats, and that she enjoyed the Northern cold and the Northern barbarians—a word she had to struggle not to use—even less, and she had commandeered the reading and writing work for every absence that followed.

She would have gone with Jay this time, given half a chance. Might have even had to fight with Teller for the opportunity.

But she would have given it up if she could have sent Angel in her place. If they could only send one person, it would, by unspoken agreement, be Angel.

"What was it about this time?"

"Same as usual," Carver replied.

"Which means nothing."

"Pretty much." His shrug was economical, a Carver gesture pared down to its bare minimum. "You haven't heard anything, have you?"

Which meant, of course, anything from Jay.

"No."

Silence. The silence was grim. It was getting tiresome.

And Finch was bloody tired.

"She's fine," she heard herself say.

"And you know that how?" Angel snapped, speaking for the first time in about two days.

"We've been over this before. They found no bodies."

Silence.

"Look, if someone as important as Jay was killed, we'd know."

"We'd be the last to know. *She's* the important one, don't you get it? Without her, they don't give a shit about the rest of us."

"Angel, she can't be killed. It's not like they've—"

"They've already come damn close."

More silence. Heavy, uncomfortable silence. Finch was good at arguing; hells, everyone in the den could hold their own in a verbal free-for-all, although Teller almost always turned silent as stone and Jester, earning his name, usually tried to divert hostility with humor.

Jay, send word.

To Angel, she said wearily, "Damn close is as close as 'they' get. And it's a lot farther away than she'll get if she hears about this."

He tensed a moment, and then relaxed, lifting his hands to his face. Quite a bruise there, across his eyes and the bridge of his nose, but then again, he'd always been a bit too pretty for Finch's taste.

Not that anyone really noticed who was pretty anymore within the den, although some people couldn't keep their eyes from wandering all over the place outside of it.

"Did you call us because of the . . . fight?"

"The brawl? No. Not even because of this," she said, picking up a piece of paper with a very uneven but perfectly legible—and long—itemized statement of Financial Grievance. She handed it to Teller, who had been summarily deputized into passing all such matters to Gabriel. Teller was a hard person to lecture.

"Then why?"

"The damn Council's been sniffing around." That got their attention.

"The council?"

"Rymark. Elonne. Marrick." She turned her face to the side and spit toward the hearth. "Haerrad, the bastard."

"You told him we work for her," Angel said. Not a question.

"Yeah."

"And?"

"He told me we were *all* ATerafin."

"Shit." Carver's voice was low, the single word a stretch of tension that was palpable.

"Not all of us," Angel said.

"Not all of us, and I expected you to bring that up. Satisfied?"

"Not particularly."

"Too bad. It'll have to do."

"What are they asking for?"

"God knows. Not money. They want our support."

"*Ours*?"

"Sure." Finch put both hands against the tabletop and pushed her negligible weight out of the chair. She glanced at Teller, who set aside the lamp—which wasn't lit, given the time of day—and rose with her. He had become a nonpresence; he took no notes, kept no record that was not internal. But if he was a nonpresence, it was in the way that air was; you missed it like anything when it was gone. "They know Jay values us; they know that we work for Jay. They know that we have some pull with her."

Jester laughed out loud. "They need better sources."

The corners of her lips tugged up; response to Jester was a part of her that was so old she didn't remember the first time she'd laughed at something he'd said. "Yeah, well.

"Teller?"

"I know. But we can dance."

"Jay said no the last time, and it—"

"I *know* what happened. It was me that ended up in the healerie with broken bones. But Jay handled it wrong. She barreled through. She should have said yes, and played her hand carefully."

"She sucks at cards," Angel said grudgingly.

"She does," Carver concurred, shoving a lock of hair out of his eye and grinning. "I've got the money—and bruises—to prove it." His smile was brief and perfect.

"*We've* never been that straight. Not without her. Think about what we do. We can agree to whatever it is they're asking us for, but cautiously. Carefully. They won't trust us, unless we can be properly greedy, and we won't trust them, and they'll know it, but they all want power and if we 'want' it, too, they'll believe it. We can dance this dance."

Finch stared at Teller for a long stretch. Aside from the fact that he'd spoken more at this meeting than he had all week, he'd also broken a rule that was never put into words. You could criticize Jay for many things. Her temper. Her language. Her clothing. Her eating habits, or lack thereof.

But you just didn't criticize her for a *real* decision. She'd brought them from the streets of the twenty-fifth holding, a band of petty thieves headed for starvation—or worse—to the most powerful House in the Empire. She'd given them a name—well, all except Angel. A real future.

And a war.

"Haerrad isn't asking for a dance. He's asking us to juggle big, sharp knives."

"They're *all* asking us to juggle big, sharp knives. I think Haerrad is the most obvious, and therefore the least dangerous, of the four."

"But he could have killed you!"

"Finch," he said quietly—as quietly as he ever spoke to Jay, and more gravely, "they could all kill me. Or you. Or Carver. Or Angel. Jester. Arann."

"What are you suggesting?"

His shrug was, like everything else about him, economical. "They've spoken with me. With you. With Arann."

"They haven't talked to us," Carver said.

"Gosh," Finch replied brightly, thinking about the grave they'd be digging—well, the survivors, anyway—if sarcasm could actually kill, "I guess it's because you've both been so *busy*."

Angel's face was set in ivory, but Carver had the grace to flush. Which was too damn bad, because she would bet every crown she had—and she was a spender—that Angel was the cause of most of the expensive conflicts.

They'd built a lot here, with Jay. She looked at the Financial Grievance, tallied the numbers that she'd so painstakingly learned to deal with, the archaic, funny squiggles that had a significance and a power that rivaled magic. Jay would kill them if they lost it all.

And they'd never been as close as this. God, the years

were melting. They were young and in older bodies, and more was expected of them because the rough edges had been shined to a careful polish. By Jay.

They were afraid.

They could not afford to be afraid. What had she said? *I need you here.*

"You know what?" Finch said quietly.

"What?"

"We need help."

"The last time you said that, we ended up with curtains the head of Household nearly used as shrouds. For us."

The wince was genuine. He was right. But Finch had A Plan. And the plan pleased her and worried her.

"I have to talk with Morretz," she said quietly.

"Morretz? Why?"

Morretz could not be easily pried from the woman whose service was his life. He could, however, occasionally be distracted when the opportunity arose. When, for instance, the Terafin was surrounded by her Chosen and he could become a shadow in the background. Or when The Terafin chose, as she did often of late, to visit the Terafin Shrine. He did not approve of these outings inasmuch as she insisted he remain at a distance, but the habit had had years to form.

Finch could see this clearly only because she had overheard so many arguments between Jay and Avandar on exactly the same subject, and seen their subsequent outcome. She was not comfortable around Avandar; there was something about him that made her want to keep her back to a wall, and, conversely, something that on a deeper level made her realize that, surveillance or no, if he wanted her dead, she *was* dead, no chance of escape.

But Jay, who could see clearer, farther, *truer*, than anyone, ever, could argue with him and win.

She *had* to be alive. Had to.

Wrong thing to think about, and she knew it. Think about something else.

The one thing they all knew how to do was blend in with the servants and watch. The dirt from the streets clung to them, and in many ways the servants were far more refined than the den, but they were indulgent in their fashion because the den had become over the years not so much outsiders—whom everyone often disdains—but black sheep, the ragged bunch of kids-made-good that so many of them secretly cheered for.

Word came in from Carver: The Chosen had assembled and had escorted The Terafin to the grounds on which the shrines sat. Finch left immediately, traversing the great hall with care to avoid being seen. Unless one were looking for her, it was easy; she dressed more like a servant than a member of the merchant services.

It was easier than asking for money to spend on clothing. Easier to stand behind Jay, and let Jay absorb the harsh glare of light and the intense scrutiny that came with it. Jay.

Think. Shrines. Morretz.

She could see him as she stepped carefully along the path that any House member was allowed to follow, and that so few did. The unspoken conventions were at least as strong as the spoken laws; one flouted them only when one had good reason. And she'd talked herself into believing that she did.

Morretz was waiting. Not for her, although he was aware of her as she approached; but for his Lord. The Lord, Finch thought, that one way or the other they all served.

Yet he nodded when she did reach his side.

"The Terafin will be a while yet, ATerafin," he said, choosing the formal tone as if it were the only tone he could adopt. It probably was.

Finch shoved her hands in pockets that were deep and comfortably empty. "Well, good."

At that, he raised a brow that moonlight had muted—or perhaps aged; hard to say. "Good?"

"It's you I want to talk to."

"Me?" His expression didn't change at all, but his tone shifted over the length of the single syllable.

She swallowed slightly, remembering that Jay liked this humorless man, this perfect servant. She couldn't imagine why. In the moonlight of the garden, with the carved hedges turned to ebony statues and the lamps muted so that the path was a gold-tinged gray, he looked as if he were a statue, some tribute carved in fleshlike stone by Maker hands to guard the way to the heart of Terafin: The Terafin Shrine.

"I want to know what it would cost us to hire a domicis."

He raised a brow. He was a bit like Teller in that he didn't speak a lot. A lot less like Teller in that his expression didn't offer much either. "Us?"

"The den."

He turned his gaze back to the temple in the distance. Finch squinted; the lamps at the temple were either low or guttered, save for one. She could not clearly see The Terafin there, although there was no doubt she was; Morretz would stand guard at the foot of that path for no other reason.

For a moment Finch wondered what it would be like to be that woman, to be served by this man. By any man, really. Then she took a breath and smiled ruefully; the darkness would hide the expression, and besides, he wasn't looking.

She thought she would have to repeat the question, but found that the silence seemed to demand the tribute of silence in return.

"I don't know," the domicis said at last. "Your situation is not Jewel ATerafin's situation, and it is only in such a situation, and with a person of such obvious value to the House—and possible danger to a rival House—that such expense would be condoned by the House."

"I know. That's why I'm asking what it would cost *us*."

He turned to face her fully, the ruler of the House momentarily consigned to the shrine that was her refuge. "More than you want to pay," he replied softly. "But I understand what you are asking, ATerafin, and my answer is yes."

"Yes?"

"I will plead your case."

CHAPTER FOUR

21st of Scaral 427 AA
Guild of the Domicis

Morretz stood on the wide, flat steps that led to the three doors through which one could enter the Guild of the Domicis. Men and women moved around him like a thin river, winding past him to the right or the left. Very few entered the middle door.

Deliberately forbidding, it was twice the height of the two that flanked it as it reached for the elaborately carved architrave on which impudent birds now preened and slept. Above their rounded bodies, heads recessed into fluff until they looked comfortably old and fat, the words *A Life Of Quiet Service* had been carved in a language that was no longer honored by the simple expedience of speech. Morretz could read and write old Weston; it was one of the few subjects that he had approached with interest and affection while learning at another Order, under a different teacher.

All of his lessons had led here.

But only when he stood before these doors was the whole of his life summed up so neatly; only here were the events of a decade past, of two, of three, as immediate as yesterday. Perhaps more so; they were sharp; they had the power to cut him, although he had long since learned to ruthlessly hide pain.

The first day that he had arrived here, he had come in the robes of an apprentice to a magi in the Order of Knowledge, that being the only clothing he owned. His hair had been braided, rather than cut; his hood adorned his shoulders, the cowl uncomfortably hot in the summer weather. He had had little in the way of possessions, but they came with him, slung over his shoulder, just as they had been a decade prior, when homeless and desperate, he had approached a different manor. This time, he was not fleeing for his life, and he had choice in how little he carried.

He could not say, now, what had drawn him to the Guild of the Domicis. He had discovered that he was unsuited to the life of the magi, and had also discovered that once taught, one was marked forever. The fear of rogue mages was strong.

He was therefore still a member of the Order of Knowledge. That would never change. He was bound by their rules, both arcane and simple, and if he happened to transgress them in a way that drew the attention of the Council of the Magi, he would pay with his life. There was only one justice for a rogue mage; not even the laws of the Kings superseded the responsibility of the magi. If, indeed, one lived in a town that was close enough to the Council that they could intervene *in time*.

In time.

Time was always an enemy.

He was surprised—although he shouldn't have been—at how bitterly he still resented the magi for their terrible failure, although he acknowledged, with the force of a quiet intellect that was still powerless in the face of a young man's rage and sorrow, that his life would have amounted to so much less had they fulfilled their duty *in time*.

He would never have made his way, ragged with both fear and poverty, to this city of cities; would never have crossed the threshold of the Order of Knowledge; would never had discovered that the power he had lacked as a young man would give him no rest from the guilt of surviving when so many had not.

And he would never have met Amarais Handernesse ATerafin, because he would never have come to the Guild of the Domicis.

The door stood out. It had drawn his attention then, although for a different reason; it was so very plain compared to the entrance the magi had designed and paid for. It did not suggest power; it did not suggest grandeur.

But although it was not any of the things he had come to expect from a guild or an order, he paused on the steps. The door had opened as he stared at it doubtfully, hesitating on the flat of the same steps he stood on now. At almost the same distance.

An older man had walked out of that door, pausing to hold it open as he looked Morretz up and down.

"Have you come," he had said, "seeking a domicis?" He was polite. It would be obvious, of course, that Morretz had not ventured to the guild for that reason; he was poorly dressed, and obviously not maintained by a member of the patriciate.

"No, I'm afraid I couldn't afford one."

"Not all of the domicis are interested in gold, although I will admit," the man added, with a small smile, "that it keeps the roof in good repair." He held out a hand, and without hesitation, Morretz offered his own in return. "I am an instructor here."

"Instructor?"

"Yes. You may be accustomed to the term master, as it is the more common appellation among other guilds or orders—but I am an instructor; the men and women who become students of the guild will take a master when it is appropriate."

"I . . . see."

"If you did not come to request the contract of a domicis, might I ask why you did?"

"Did?"

"Come to these doors?"

"I—I came seeking employment."

The peppered brows that would become familiar as the years progressed rose and then plunged. "You're terribly unaccomplished as a liar; I suggest you refrain from attempting to dissemble until you've gained some polish."

Morretz was too old to blush. He grimaced instead.

"Let me ask a different question," the older man said, after giving the younger man a chance to feel the awkwardness of silence. "Why did you not enter these doors?" His hand rapped the center of the door he had come through as he spoke.

"I—I don't know."

"They are not so fine a set of doors as—if I judge your apparel correctly—you must be accustomed to entering."

"No."

"And yet?"

Morretz frowned. "I don't know," he said with a shrug. "They did not seem the correct doors to enter."

"Astute." The instructor surprised him. "Very astute. There may be some hope for you."

"Hope?"

"If you will follow me, the correct doors to enter by—and to leave by—will be the doors on your right as you face them."

"Correct doors?"

"Yes. To the left are the doors used by those who work for the guild in various positions. In the center, those who seek to contract the service of a domicis. And to the right, those who serve. Those who would serve." The older man turned away, and then turned back; his expression was serious, but there was some play in the lines around his eyes that suggested a smile.

"Not, of course, that we do not excuse newcomers their ignorance. But it is an auspicious sign in a newcomer to be so sensitive to nuance.

"I will leave you to make your decision."

"My . . . decision?"

"Yes. You have not yet answered my first question. Not honestly. And perhaps that is because you have no honest answer to give." The old man bowed. "My name, should you enter and have cause to seek me out, is Ellerson."

He had returned to the guild several times as the domicis of Amarais Handernesse ATerafin. He wore finer clothing than he had as a failure of a mage's apprentice; certainly better shoes. He spoke, when he spoke at all, with the guildmaster, Akalia, a woman now so old one's natural instinct was not to breathe in her direction for fear it might knock her over. Her mind, however, was sharp, and her tongue a match for it.

It was not to Akalia that he went now.

Not to Akalia that his thoughts turned.

He almost walked away. His hand found the stone railing that had been replaced three times in the history of the guild—the last, years before Morretz' birth in a distant, border village—and he steadied himself. He had agreed to help Finch ATerafin, and she had been grateful.

But he had not expected the arrival of Teller ATerafin.

Teller had not waited by the Terafin Shrine, as Finch had done; his visit had been an act of indiscretion that Morretz was certain Finch would not have condoned.

The domicis had been summoned to the doors of The Terafin's library by one of The Chosen. Possibly the last person he expected to see when he opened those doors—from a safe distance, with the expedient use of cautionary magic—was a slightly winded Teller. His build, a product of a very underprivileged youth, had changed little over the years, and he maintained that peculiar hesitancy in speech that one associates with shyness—itself a youthful trait; both beguiled.

But he was not young, not in the way that Morretz had been before he had lost his earlier life. Not in the way he had been afterward either, unable to sleep or eat or speak without rage and fear dogging every physical gesture. Teller's peculiar quiet seemed undisturbed by the wrongs done him; unperturbed enough that he failed, when he achieved a position of power, to do those wrongs to others in the name of justice. Yet he was scarred.

These were the wounded that Jewel had gathered. Of all the things about her besides the obvious—the gift she was born and cursed with—they were proof of a singular talent: the ability to find the very little gold buried beneath the rubble. Her den were like the gemstones found in the dark and intricate maze of stone tunnels.

And they did not come to *him.*

"The Terafin is currently involved in study for negotiations of the merchant Crown route through the Western Menorans. Even those who have been granted permission to risk visiting the library without an appointment have not been granted leave to disturb her today." It was meant as a rebuke; it was something that anyone who worked for Jewel should have been aware of.

But Teller nodded slowly. "I have very little to add to her studies," he said. "But I need to speak with you."

"ATerafin," he replied, "my role here—"

"Finch asked you for help."

"I see. Yes."

"You said you would. Help."

"Indeed."

"It has to be now."

"ATerafin—"

Teller shook his head, his eyes wide, the expression on his face unguarded. Hard to look at.

"We don't have time."

It was always a matter of time.

"And if we wait too long, it'll be too late. They don't know," he said at last. After a moment, "they" resolved itself in Morretz' mind as "the den"; Finch, Carver, Angel, Arann, and Jester. "And I wouldn't tell you if I didn't think you needed to hear it—but I do. Jay left."

"There is not a member of this House that is not aware of that," Morretz replied, cool and dry.

Teller took that, swallowed it, found strength in the distance. "Jay accepted what wasn't much of a choice, and she left. She said her good-byes. No," he raised a hand as if it were a weapon or a shield. Teller, who never interrupted and rarely spoke. "Let me finish," he said, into Morretz's muted surprise. And he did the worst thing possible; he met the domicis' pale eyes, and he looked away.

There are men who look away when they lie; their eyes glance slightly off the cheek or the forehead, evading the pinning grace of sight. Morretz had learned, quickly, to understand this shorthand of expression. But there are men who glance away to spare you their knowledge of your reaction when they speak—or are about to speak—a truth that they know will cause pain.

Very, very little in Morretz's life could cause him pain. But not nothing; he was alive, after all. Still alive. He might have told the younger man that his concern was baseless. But he didn't believe it.

Years of training made him graceful. He let Teller ATerafin speak.

Aware that he would never let a man approach him with a knife, never let him strike the certain blow, with such bitter equanimity, although the knife's cut would be far, far less terrible. He *knew* what he would hear.

"The Terafin's going to die while Jay is gone."

Morretz was not surprised.

He should have been. No one had ever said that of The Terafin, except during the House War that had made them—domicis and lord—what they had become. But those words were separated from these, for these were true.

He knew they were true. His honesty was of the type that made him acknowledge The Terafin's particular silence, the barriers she had erected against his knowledge, as if ignorance would lessen pain. He had never spoken of it, because he waited for her, always for her, although the knowledge had lingered like a baleful ghost from the moment The Terafin had made clear her desire to select an heir.

"How?" he asked softly. Coldly.

Teller met his eyes again. Held them, this time. "We don't know. Not even Jay knew for certain. But—"

"But?"

His gaze dropped again. "People—in power, like her—they have to trust people." His lips thinned. Twisted. "Sometimes it doesn't pay out."

"Someone she trusts is going to betray her?"

Teller shrugged. "I don't know. Jay didn't know. The Terafin is one of the smartest people I know; hard to imagine anyone else *could* kill her. But . . . Jay saw it."

"Teller—"

"Jay has never been wrong. She misses things. Things happen that she doesn't see beforehand. But what she *does* see . . ." He had the grace, again, to look away. "The Terafin is important to us. Not because we know her—we don't. Because she's the House. She's never lied to us; she's never screwed us over. She—she *deserves* to wear the Terafin sword.

"But, Morretz—she knows."

"She?"

"The Terafin. She knows. She knows she's going to die; she doesn't know how. If she knew how—but it doesn't matter; what matters is she *knows*. She knows Jay, she knows seers, she knows there's no point in spending the time trying to prevent her death when she can—"

The flow of words stopped as he caught up with them.

Silence. Silence was comfortable.

"They're alike, Morretz. That's why she chose Jay. And Jay left *us* behind to guard the House." Teller looked suddenly far younger than his years. Miserable. Terrified. "Because *she* trusts *us*. But we always let her do the shark-walking, and now when we need to, *we* don't know how. We fail, we fail her. And more.

"If you don't go to the Guild of the Domicis now, I'm not sure we'll survive when—when The Terafin goes down. And if we don't survive, neither does anything she's spent her life as lord here building."

"ATerafin."

Something in Morretz's voice surprised them both.

Teller stilled; the obvious panic slowly submerged itself beneath the surface of nondescript eyes.

"You are talking about the death of my lord."

Teller bowed his head. He turned without another word and walked away, but when he reached the end of the hall, he turned back to where Morretz stood guard, against all truth, and he offered the domicis a bow.

Morretz returned nothing.

But the following morning, with strict instructions to the Chosen who guarded her, Morretz left The Terafin to make an early report to Akalia, the woman in whose hands the Guild of the Domicis had been so carefully nurtured for decades.

And he paused, in front of a door that had been the start of his life; gripped an old stone railing, and left some of his skin on its porous surface before he chose to enter the building.

Just as, exactly as, he had chosen years before.

He walked, for a moment, not into the horrible necessity of the present, but the uncertainty of the past:

The man was old.

The building that contained him—as most buildings fortunate enough to be situated on the poverty-free political stronghold that was the Isle—had changed little over the length of both of their lives, and Morretz knew that, should he be granted some brief recess from Mandaros' Halls long after his death—and should he choose that recess to come here—the building, like the institution itself, would be fundamentally unchanged—a monument that defied fashion, that embraced tradition. It was not overtly fine, but the details were there if one knew how to look. The foundations were solid, and no less enduring was the framework, from joists below the floor to the broad ceiling beams beneath which students, in varying degrees of discomfort, learned the limitations of the life they hoped to someday lead.

Less than a handful would live up to that hope; as the illusions were pared away, so, too, was the desire.

Some came to this guild who were too passive, who confused service with the abrogation of responsibility, men and women so crippled by the fear of decision that they wanted a life in which all choices were made for them—as if that were ever possible, as if anyone could truly escape the responsibility of their lives.

They learned.

Had he been one of those men? The domicis were never required to examine their past, searching for answers to their voyage here amidst the emotional debris. But required or no, there was about the debris of one's own life both attraction and repulsion; enough so that he visited it with morbid fascination as the unchanging halls that housed the domicis brought him into momentary contact with his youth.

This had not been the first place in which he labored as an apprentice. But something in his tenure here had provoked more than simple intellect, no matter how passionate that intellect might be; it had touched something deeper, something so carefully buried beneath the horror of memory that he had assumed it safely dead.

Belief.

"You have all learned—and I see it in all of you so don't waste your breath or my time denying it," no one doubted which of the two was the more valued, "that there is no justice in the world. Power rules."

He had learned something equally valuable: You could only be hurt if you cared. Care nothing, care for nothing, and the world passes above you, beneath you, around you.

Silence.

Ellerson's silences were akin to another's punctuation; break them at the wrong place and you not only courted obvious disapproval, which was usually given anyway, but you committed the greater crime of breaking the stream of thought that led to the words themselves. And they had learned to value the words, so they waited.

Of course, he was a temperamental man, and often inserted a silence as a form of question.

The difference between punctuation and question was length and a certain chill if silence lasted too long.

Into the chill, a younger voice said, "Power rules. Did we spend three years studying just to come back to such basic truth? We've chosen to serve," the younger man added, "and most of us have chosen to serve people of power."

"Indeed. You have all chosen to serve people of power."

"Not all."

"Not all of you have chosen to serve people whose power is purely political or financial, but you have chosen the avenue of power that best represents your own interests."

Silence.

"You," he said, pointing at one of the older men, "have chosen to serve the maker-born. And you, their distant cousins: the painters who rule the academy on the Isle. You have chosen to serve the magi, and although they do not rule the Isle, they are unarguably among the most powerful men and women upon it.

"The only men and women you will never serve are the Kings and Queens; all others might come, if not now, then in a decade or two, through the doors of the guild itself, seeking service and not merely suitable people to employ.

"You have chosen to serve them. To place yourself in the path of their power; to accompany its rise or its fall, and to prevent that fall where at all possible. We have seldom spoken of ethics, of morality; we have spoken of the oaths and the service itself, as if those oaths and that service are blind in their binding."

No one but a fool would have spoken then. No one.

Morretz had never thought of himself as a fool. "If we had come seeking power, we could have stayed where we were. Not a man among us has not set foot on that path."

The piercing glare of Ellerson of the domicis made him feel—on that day—as if he were alone in the room, a supplicant, a student from the streets who thought only of a roof over his head and a permanent home. "And yet you choose to serve it."

"Yes."

"What does that acknowledge, Morretz?"

The room collectively exhaled. The man who was teacher and distant friend had not chosen to descend to the cool mockery that was often his trademark when, from a distance of wisdom and experience, he looked down upon his students.

"Acknowledge?"

"Yes. You of all people have reason to distrust the powerful."

He was silent, but not for long. To speak of power was in all ways to speak of things personal, but having begun, he had chosen to take that risk. "I cannot speak for the others," he said at last. "I am not as subtle as they; I choose to serve the politically powerful and in my time, if the gods are willing, I will serve one of The Ten.

"But speaking for myself, I can say that I would not serve just any of The Ten. I would not give my service and my life's work to a lord whose desire for power did not in some ways mesh with my own desires, my own goals."

"And you value your goals so highly? Is not your chosen life to *serve*? Is it not the goals of the lord you choose to serve that should be paramount?"

"The lord I have chosen to serve is the guild," Morretz replied evenly.

Ellerson snorted. "Evasion."

"Yes. Evasion. You ask a simple question, and you've spent years telling us that there are no simple answers. I will not demean your teaching by attempting to provide them."

The old man's brow rose into his hairline, and then he did something that Morretz had never seen him do in this room: he laughed. The sound carried to the heights of stone and wooden beam, the echo of his mirth remarkable for its resonance, the richness of its changing tones. It deprived him of years and dignity.

"You were always too clever by half," he said, the smile still lingering in the corners of a mouth that was usually caught in a thin line or a frown. "But let me turn it around. I have spent years waiting for you to resolve the complexities of a difficult answer."

Morretz nodded. "I have."

Expressions defined a man; Ellerson's, brow and lip lifted in something akin to mockery, was proof, if it were needed, of that truth. Time had gentled it, the way salt and storms will take the sharpest lines from harbor statues which possess no magical blessing, but it remained, a blending of skepticism, reproval, and a vague hint that approval could still, with Cartanian dedication, be won. It sometimes was. "That, in the end, is all that is required. Would you share that resolution with us?"

The class was silent. The stiffness of tables and chairs had given way over the years—when the students had proved their knowledge of the many idiosyncrasies the guild considered law—to an environment that was, in theory, less formal.

It was certainly more threatening.

"Understand," Ellerson added softly, "that that was a genuine request; I will not compel you to divulge what is private."

"But you asked."

"Yes. I am an old man." It hadn't been true, not then, but it was one of the many phrases he wore, masklike, in conversation. "I'm curious to know what it is you feel you have learned."

"If it was simple curiosity, you would have asked me in private."

"Perhaps," Ellerson had replied gravely, "your reaction to the nature of the request in the presence of your peers will tell me more about what you've gleaned from our lessons than the answer itself."

Morretz, sitting in the Great Hall as a visitor, as a man who had passed all the tests it was possible to pass, remembered that moment clearly.

He had reached for a cut crystal goblet; water sluiced up its side as he lifted it. The sun that filtered in through long narrow windows, cut by lead and colored by glass, was nonetheless bright enough to cut across the surface of the water in a sharp, bright spray of color, the glimmering of a deity seen through merely mortal eyes.

He took a breath and set the water down, seeing, as the glass passed into the shadows cast by his shoulders, some glimmer of his own reflection. He knew then that he would speak. After all, what he would say out loud in this room, in front of these men, would never be said again, although he would return to it, like a pilgrim, as the years tested his resolve with experiences, some very bitter. How could he speak of his own goals in such a direct fashion where his lord might hear them, without becoming akin to peer, rather than remaining a domicis?

And what, in the end, *was* a domicis, and was it—like parenthood was reputed to be—a thing that a man could only understand when he finally became one? Or was it something he made of himself? Was it something that was defined individually, between a lord and a domicis, in a privacy much like a marriage? None of the answers were as clear to him as he had always desired they be . . . but one thing was.

Commitment.

For a moment, in that hall, beneath the weight of questions that had plagued him for three years, he felt it, like a whisper of foreknowledge: *this* was what he would do with his life, and his life *would count.* Not by any accident of fate—for Kalliaris had been brutally unkind to him, and he did not trust her whim—but by his own determination; by the decision not to be deterred or distracted.

And what better way to confirm it than to speak it aloud to the only peers he would have, no matter how far they scattered in the isolation of their service? He was not without pride; he understood that to speak of one's goals in public was to risk humiliation if one failed.

But not to speak was to hide, a hedge against failure, a nod to that sense of possible shame; it served neither his goal nor his growing sense of what he would make of himself.

"I understand that the goals of any adult shift with time and circumstance. That the man or woman I choose to serve now may walk a path, a decade from now, that *without my service* would be reprehensible to me. But I'm arrogant enough to believe that with my service that path might never be walked."

"Oh? And you believe you will have that influence?"

"Yes. Why else would I spend three years of my life slaving as your student?"

Others in the room chuckled, their mirth little eddies in the undertow of his words.

"If you've learned to have that much influence in three

years, you might consider replacing me at the front of the class," Ellerson replied dryly.

He heard another rush of chuckles, like wind in the leaves; he was the tree. Here, above stone floor, within stone walls, beneath beams cut from trees long dead, he was at the center of the life he had never thought, as a terrified and grief-driven young boy, to live. The screams of the dead were mercifully absent.

"I will serve a lord I admire. My years here have taught me that those men and women do exist in positions of power, although I would not have believed it in my youth."

On the steps of the guild, his hand on one of three doors, Morretz accepted the fact that he would never escape his youth; that it had fashioned him, in the way the maker-born fashion stone and wood—a simple statement of life, arresting in its detail, no matter how much pain went into the making. He wondered if the ability to capture *life*, and not its pallid fancy, was the real reason that Artisans—the most powerful of the maker-born—always went mad.

He accepted his past. No, he accepted the slaughter of his family, his friends, the burning of the farms in the township. He accepted the circumstances which had made an uneasy, a terrible, ally of the man he had sworn he would one day destroy.

Accepted it, then shied away from it.

He opened the door. Walked into the Hall of the Domicis.

An easy life would not have led him to the guild; a simple life would never have led him, in the end, to Amarais Handernesse ATerafin.

Amarais.

"I will find such a patris. And such a man or woman will understand that admiration is a burden, a geas they accept when they accept *my* services. Service such as we have been trained to perform is not a simple, one-way affair, not a simple exchange of money for goods."

For the first time, Ellerson spoke, not breaking the monologue, but adding to it, a harmony to the melody. "There is a reason the guild interviews those who choose to inquire about the services of a domicis; a reason why more than half of the men and women who come are ultimately disappointed. Go on. Go on, Morretz, of no family and no House save this one."

"I am not interested in *making* history." He rose, as if height gave strength to the words. Or as if it would give him strength to finish them. "But I *am* interested in history." He turned to the shadow; to the youth that had scarred him, had decided which path he would take and which he would reject.

"I am interested in a history that does not repeat itself for me, for mine, for those who, helpless, were like us, and are like us now."

He bowed his head. "There exist men and women—besides the Kings—who have at heart that goal; who understand the life I lived and the lives I lost; who will work against such a loss with a skill I do not possess." There. Spoken. Out loud. *A skill I do not possess.* "And when I find that person, I will make them strong; I will be shield if they choose battle, and I will be healer if they are injured by it. I will give my life to their life so they can give their life to their cause."

Ellerson bowed his head a moment; it shocked Morretz into silence.

But when his teacher raised that familiar face, his smile was a shallow curve of lips. "There *is* one problem, of course."

"Sir?"

"By strict guild rules, it is the guildmaster who will choose the lords you may serve."

Morretz's smile was shallow for a different reason, although the expressions, young and old, were similar. "Of course. But by guild law, the right of refusal is mine."

"Indeed. And you may say no to Guildmaster Akalia—but I will warn you in advance that *I* never have."

Days later—maybe weeks, as at this remove the passage of time had become a stream rather than a discrete measure—the guildmaster had summoned him.

Akalia was not a pretty woman; not a patrician woman. But she was a power in her own right, and only a fool could have failed to accord her the respect she was due.

He had been foolish at times as a student, but had never been a fool.

He had been offered the service of three members of the patriciate, all born to power, and all within the ranks of The Ten; none at their head. He had refused two by the simple expedient of asking Akalia for her assessment of their goals.

But the third . . .

The third had been so intriguing. She came and interviewed *him*, and then adjourned, saying that she wished—with the permission of the guildmaster—to conduct the remainder of the interview at the heart of her small home. That had been humor, although he had failed to note it at the time. She had tested him, showing, by such a test, that she understood that if she offered, and he accepted, her contract, it would be binding; permanent.

Service. Loyalty. Duty.

He made his way not through the halls in which he had lived and studied, but to the halls in which he might meet the men and women who had passed whatever tests were set them by their inscrutable or irascible instructors.

There, he took a seat, staring into the knots and dyes of a tapestry that told the story of someone else's life.

He rose from the comfort of soft leather, his hand raised in greeting, as the older—almost old enough to *be* old—man approached. At some point in his life he had become the unthinkable: this man's peer. In a classroom a lifetime away, the thought that they would be peers had never occurred to Morretz, although with the simple application of reason and logic, it should have seemed inevitable. Which brought him quietly to this conclusion: nothing in life was simple; all answers were arrived at the way Morretz himself had learned to arrive at any conclusion: in the grace of uncertainty, in the balance, intricate and unending, between the experiences of the past and the changing goals of the future.

Unending? As the older man drew close Morretz, domicis to Amarais, The Terafin, realized that even that was inaccurate.

"Morretz," Ellerson said quietly. "I received your message."

"You are looking well."

The man considered by most to be the future head of the guild frowned. "Your manners are impeccable. Either that or your eyesight leaves something to be desired, a certain sign that you've finally begun to approach the age of reason. I had occasionally despaired of that possibility."

Morretz smiled. It had been years since he had offered anyone this particular smile; too many. The Terafin's life did not lend itself to such ordinary affection.

The smile dimmed.

"You know I've retired."

"You've retired before."

"I'm not currently teaching."

He started to say something light and clever; the words didn't even reach his lips. Everything on which a lifetime was founded had shifted, and not to his liking. "Not teaching? May I ask why?"

"No."

He expected this answer; in truth, he had asked the question only to buy himself time. "You know why I'm here."

"No, although I assume you want to waste my time with a request I'm going to turn down. People seldom visit just to be social."

"You would have them hanged for wasting your time."

It was the old man's turn to laugh. "I've almost missed you, Morretz. Our brightest always seem to choose a contract more binding than marriage."

"You never did."

"I was never considered among the brightest," was the dry reply. "But I have found satisfaction in the people I have served, and I have learned much."

"Enough satisfaction that you might be willing to do so again?"

"Serve? Perhaps you're not as bright as I thought. Does the expression 'retire' or the infinitive 'to retire' mean nothing to the young?" His eyes narrowed. "Is that why you've come?"

"Yes. But you knew that."

Ellerson shrugged. "Perhaps. But my stated intent—retirement—should be treated with a modicum of respect. Who do you feel merits such service?"

"Someone you may or may not remember." If he ever

forgot anything. "Not a person of power. Not a leader; not technically a person at all."

For the first time since he'd sat so heavily at Morretz's side, Ellerson lifted a brow. "Not a person?"

"No."

"I see. . . . You are a guild member. You are aware of the rules that govern the organization. Not a person?"

Morretz nodded.

"Although there are no rules against accepting the contract of something nonhuman, I must assume, given your current involvement in Terafin, that you are not asking me to serve something demonic—and anything else, if it exists outside of children's story—does not require service. Therefore I must assume that you are asking me to serve an institution."

Morretz shook his head. "I may have foolishly decided to go beyond these walls decades ago, but I did not entirely take leave of my senses. I do not ask you to serve a House, except as I have done: as it serves the interests of those you serve.

"I ask you to consider serving a . . . family."

"Morretz."

"I would ask another but I am bound by two considerations. First, the family in question is difficult. The last stranger that was thrust upon them from the outside took five years to gain their trust. If they are to—to prosper, they will not have that time."

"Second?"

"You are the only man who would consider accepting this task. I asked them to choose from among themselves an individual whom I could present to the guild as a possible candidate for the service of a domicis. Their response was unanimous: No. They have a leader who has already been accepted, and they will do nothing to supersede her."

Ellerson was not a stupid man.

"She's gone."

Morretz had so many questions to ask; he asked none. "Yes."

"And . . . her domicis?"

"From all reports, they disappeared together."

The older man looked, for a moment, old. "They were in the Common." It was not a question.

"From the scant information we've been able to gather, yes. But their bodies were not among the fallen." *And you know this*. Morretz had personally delivered The Terafin's report to Akalia. She had taken it without comment; no reply had been requested.

For a moment, Avandar's name hung between them, an accusation that had never been given voice. It was Ellerson who looked away, looked down at his hands as if he had been asked to complete a surgeon's most delicate work long after the steadiness of youth had deserted him.

"I will think on it, Morretz."

"Ellerson."

"I said—"

Morretz lifted a hand. "Years ago, I answered your question."

"Which question?"

"You asked me why."

"Why?"

"Hide behind your age with someone who has time and less wit."

"Ah." Ellerson's smile was sharp, brief. "That question. You're wrong, of course. You didn't answer *my* question; you answered your own."

"You asked it."

"Did I?"

"Yes."

"Memory," the old man said softly, "is tricky. I have learned two things from it. One: that without meaningful memories, there is no life. Two: that we are desperate for our lives to make sense, to have meaning—and at a great enough remove, all memory is malleable.

"Perhaps I asked you a question. Perhaps I asked you the question you remember so clearly.

"But perhaps I ask that question every year, day in and day out, looking over the rolls of students who I know, from the moment they enter those doors," he inclined his head toward not the right or the left, but the center, and his lips curved slightly when his gaze returned to Morretz of the Guild of the Domicis, "will fail. Perhaps I ask it, and every student answers it, and that answer has meaning and purpose to them, and them alone.

"Or perhaps to their peers as well. I have taught so

many, my memory blurs the boundaries of students from year to year." He began to rise.

And to Morretz' surprise, a hand prevented him from leaving the long chair. His own. His skin was pale; protected, as The Terafin was protected, from the vagaries of sun and wind. It looked odd against the deep, brown-green of Ellerson's attire. He had seen those robes year in and out, but he had never touched them before.

You don't remember? He felt, for a moment, that part of his life was unraveling, like a tapestry whose story has become merely long, faded thread. He had defined himself in some ways by that moment. "What of you, Ellerson? Why have you chosen to serve?"

A darker hand covered his; lifted the fingers from cloth that should have remained untouched. "I answered that question in my own time, for my own teacher," the older man said sternly. "And there is a reason that I told you, when you chose to answer publicly, that the answer was yours, to give or to conceal."

He rose, unhindered. "You showed courage; I have always been impressed by either your stupidity or your commitment. Perhaps both. Wait here, Morretz, if you can. Wait an hour."

"But I—"

"Wait."

22nd of Scaral 427 AA
Terafin Manse

Finch worked in the kitchen. She worked at the table, the lamp burning, the papers stacked neatly in a row of escalating urgency. The ink blotter was almost unmarked, the quill unsavaged by a too heavy hand, the desk unstained by the spill of a hundred different bottles. In every possible way it was the opposite of Jay's desk.

But it was the only space in the wing that reminded her of Jay; the only place in which Finch felt her presence. If she could have summoned that familiarity from the comfort of her own rooms, she would have; she had chosen, four years ago, a desk that she loved when a carpenter's rich client had declined it because he didn't quite care for the stain he had chosen. This craftsman's masterpiece had places for paper, for quill, for ink; it had three small locked drawers in which she might keep sensitive information; it had a shelf, built with a ridged lip, upon which the few volumes Finch now owned might be carefully placed. Arann and Angel had almost broken their backs carrying the desk into her room; the workmen had offered their help, but she didn't feel comfortable having strangers in the wing. Old habits; she was half afraid they would steal something.

Kalliaris knew that she would have, more than a decade ago.

But it didn't matter; that desk, which was her pride, was in her room, and this table, the table that had always been the center of the war room—the kitchen—was where she had chosen to take up pen; to read agreements, to attempt, in as much as it was even possible, to *be* Jewel ATerafin's aide, not Jay's little urchin.

And Jewel ATerafin's aide sat looking at a lovely invitation from Elonne ATerafin. It had not yet been placed in a pile; it sat in the space between hands placed palm down on the wooden tabletop in an attempt to still their shaking. Elonne's handwriting was so perfect it might have been an act of enchantment and not pen and ink; her paper was fine and smooth, her seal exact. It was almost impossible to believe the seal was the same as the one Finch was entitled to use—*did* use—it was so perfectly proportioned when it rested in blue wax.

Elonne was one of the House Council. Finch was one of Jay's den. They never talked, except in passing, and there hadn't been much of that; Elonne handled a different part of the House affairs, and she and Jay were about as different as two people could be and still have anything in common. The House. Gender.

You can't say no, Teller had said.

You can't say yes, Carver countered. *You know Haerrad's been watching us all like a hawk. He only needs an excuse.*

He didn't need much to have me run down.

Yeah, well, he didn't have you killed. Jay was here. He wouldn't have dared.

They wouldn't be asking any of us for anything *if Jay were here.*

They want you to sell her, Angel said at last, a part of the discussion because he was as much a part of the den as Jay herself, but apart *from* it because he'd chosen not to be ATerafin, and he could afford to ignore the politics.

They'd looked at her. She'd wished, then, that she wasn't sitting in Jay's chair. Promised herself she'd never do it again. It was hard to fill that damn chair, and the chair itself was hard on the butt.

She hadn't answered.

They, cowards all, left the decision hanging.

And it still was, the perfect words of the invitation an accusation of either cowardice, incompetence, or both.

"Jay," she said, out loud. "Jay, damn you, damn you damn you. Tell me what to do. I don't know this woman, and she might rule the damn House if we can't be careful enough. If you don't come back. Jay, help me."

"Might I suggest that it would be more constructive if you asked for help from someone who was actually present? Absentee leaders, like gods, rarely offer advice of use."

No, Finch thought, as she lifted her head. *You're wrong.* The movement was slow, not because her head was particularly heavy, but because she *recognized* that voice; had thought she would never hear it again, and had—just as Jay had done, although Jay would've killed anyone who said it—missed it. A lot. And she didn't want to break the spell of familiarity by seeing who had actually spoken.

But whoever it was, he was in her kitchen—in *Jay's* kitchen—and he wasn't allowed in without permission. She took a deep breath, snapped to attention.

And met the eyes of Ellerson, the domicis.

She had never been a particularly quiet person; that was Teller's job. But she knew when to keep her mouth shut until the words had settled into something intelligible.

"*Ellerson*?"

He raised a brow, his features as stiff and formal as a perfect suit. "Indeed," he said. His hair was grayer; the lines of his face deeper. But his posture was so perfect she felt like a dull slouch, and she found herself lifting her shoulders into what she hoped was a better line.

"Sometimes the gods do listen."

His smile was shallow, but it was there. "You had best hope that that is not the case; the gods are known to exact a steep price for their intervention, and it is my intent to teach you how to avoid the inevitable results of such poor negotiations."

"Good." She lifted her hands and found that they were, sadly, still shaking. Clutching the invitation in them, she said, "Start with this, okay?"

He stepped to the desk, bowed slightly, and then took what she offered.

"You—why are you—did you talk to Morretz? Did he tell you what—"

"I did, indeed, speak with Morretz."

"What did he say? Did he tell you—"

"He is not your domicis. He is not my servant. Guild law, however, requires that he speak on your behalf should you choose, for some reason, to appoint an agent rather than venturing into the guild itself. He let me know how things have changed in the last sixteen years. And yes, Finch," he added, in a voice that was at once gentle and formal, "I know full well who Elonne ATerafin is.

"You will forgive me," he said at last, "if I choose to see this as an opportunity?"

"Only if you're going instead of me."

The smile deepened and then vanished.

"No. It would be unspeakably rude to send me in your place, an insult. There may be a time in the future in which you wish to offer such an insult—but when doing so, you must offer that insult *deliberately*, you must offer an insult you can survive, and you must make certain that it is the vanguard of a larger political action."

Just that. As if he had never been gone.

And as if he had never been gone, his expression wrinkled into lines of distaste—ones which he reserved for the privacy of quarters, and never offered in public. She remembered that clearly. "Your clothing," he said at last. "I hope that Avandar sees that Jewel does not attire herself in such a . . . fashion."

She stood, carefully pushing the chair away from the kitchen table. She wanted to hug this man, but she knew she couldn't. Instead, she rushed past him, containing the urge; she burst out into the hall, the kitchen doors swinging wildly, the names of her den-mates passing from her lips in an increasingly loud demand for attention.

Behind the wildly swinging doors, Ellerson of the domicis looked down at the uncreased invitation in his hand, his expression unreadable.

Then he looked up at the sound of the names: Teller, Jester, Carver, Angel, Arann.

He stood alone, in the kitchen, before a table that was both familiar and foreign, while the slanted light of the afternoon grazed his legs.

CHAPTER FIVE

22nd of Scaral 427 AA
House Kalakar grounds

Colors were a funny thing.

The analytical part of Duarte's mind, the part that had misled him in his youth into believing that the magi were his calling, looked at the unit he had built out of men and women considered gallows fodder. They had seen the slaughter of two thirds of their number without tears, although the wounds they had taken there had never healed.

That was what this new war had been about for the older Ospreys. Time had not gentled them. It had, at most, rounded the edges of corners, as if they were blocks of new-cut stone, stained with salt and the ill use of weather. Not a single one of them, with the exception of Sanderton, had a family they cared to name; they had given their lives to the Ospreys. The Ospreys *defined* them. And The Kalakar, curse her, curse her, curse her, *knew*. But in spite of this, or perhaps because of it, she had chosen to absent herself from address, an absentee patrician. Duarte had never considered her a coward.

He was not entirely certain that her decision had been an act of cowardice now; she understood her soldiers—even the ones under Duarte. Even the Ospreys.

"You have been offered the choice of remaining with the House Guard. Each and every one of you has distinguished yourself with honorable service; the House acknowledges this. No, The Kalakar acknowledges this."

"By retiring our colors?" Fiara shouted, her voice stained with a rage that he was certain also stained her cheeks. Hard to tell; the sky itself was pink and deepening into the purple that would become blue-black; his favorite color. He had chosen the early evening as the time to give the address; the bars and taverns would be open, and the window between knowledge and action for his Ospreys—or whatever it was they would become—as small as possible. He could not therefore see her face clearly without the aid of magical enhancement to his vision.

Ah, and perhaps he had chosen the early evening as the appropriate time for reasons of his own.

"We are a third of our former number," he said, angry at anyone who made this job more difficult than it already was, no matter—no matter—how justified their own anger. "We are, and have been since the war, below the minimum number necessary to maintain a unit within the House Guard."

"She never let us recruit!"

"*Fiara—*"

Rescue came from an unlooked for place.

"You know why she's doing this." Alexis stood forward, on the raised platform that had been erected in a hurry in the Osprey's training ground.

Duarte would have preferred a medium in which he could control the passage of sound; he expected that things would be said about The Kalakar in this meeting that would not bear repeating. But the trees, tall and tended, lent the soldiery a sweep of shadow; the grass or what remained of it after the singeing of fire and magery that had always been a part of their exercises, gave them a battlefield on which to stand. As Ospreys, one last time.

Silence.

"You know," Alexis said, her voice knife sharp, "you don't have any choice. She gave us our colors and our unit *because* we'd won the war for them, and they could keep their hands spit and polish and shiny while we bled and we died. They paid us what we were *due*.

"But that was during peacetime. This is war. We're *soldiers*. That's what we're paid for. You've been given your orders. Quit *whining*."

"We're *Ospreys*, damn you!" Fiara countered. Fiara, stupid, fierce, beautiful in defiance in a way that she otherwise never was.

Yes, the trees shadowed them, but there was no shelter there; Duarte had provided that for as long as he could, and now the scales were off their eyes. *This* was the reality they had always known: the swift boot. The kick in the teeth.

The flag was flying. Black bird of prey against a background of House colors mercifully muted by the fall of dusk. They were right: the Osprey was what had always counted.

Soon, Duarte thought, the music would start. Cook would play. There would be no singing, but the notes, dirgelike, would be song enough by which to lay colors to rest. He was surprised at how much pain the reality could cause; he had thought—more fool he—that he had made his peace with it in The Kalakar's quarters, when she had given him her oblique orders, made her oblique offer.

"You're *all* AKalakar," Alexis continued, doing for him what he had become accustomed to in war: fulfilling the role of adjutant; speaking when he could not, for a moment, speak, and the words needed saying.

He would pay for it; that was the nature of her gifts. She would turn on him later, tongue sharp as her steel, eyes flashing with contempt and anger and the pain that she held back in order to soothe theirs. All of it had to go somewhere; he knew who the target would be. But here, now, he would marvel at the gift for what it was.

"AKalakar. She didn't take that from you, and she could have. She would have no choice if she could hear half of what you're saying now. Less. She *knows* what we did for her. You think you're dirt? There are people out there now who are less," her hands swung, now wildly, but precisely, to the gates at her back. "We all know 'em. People who would have sold *us* into slavery to get what we *earned*. The Kalakar's name behind us."

"Well, what if we don't give a shit about the name?"

"Then you're as much a fool as everyone always said you were!"

Saying what he could not say because he was their captain, and she was . . . family.

Kiriel turned quietly to Auralis. She touched him, gently, on the arm between elbow and shoulder. It was a signal of sorts. Jewel called it shorthand because she knew how to write. She said it was like the signals that had been used by the den—ones that Kiriel had learned in days, and would never forget.

Kiriel had learned how to read; Isladar had pressed that upon her as if it were a weapon. But her writing had never become the equal of her reading, and both lagged behind the skill that had defined her early years: the sword. So she understood the concept of shorthand poorly. Not as poorly as she understood the concept of friendship; it was like ally, except there was trust beneath it, and trust . . .

But she was capable of learning this, this language that wasn't language. She touched his arm.

He failed to notice.

She wasn't sure what this meant, and after a moment, Fiara's angry voice the only sound worthy of note, she touched him again. Spoke his name, like an enchantment, to call him back from the place he had gone to.

He looked down at her. "What?"

"I don't understand."

"What don't you understand?"

"They are . . . retiring . . . the colors?"

He didn't answer.

Hard to know whether to speak or to leave things be; she spoke after a moment, the desire to understand greater than the desire to be . . . politic.

Politic was a word Duarte had taught her.

She'd learned it because he was lord here; she could not understand how it was that so many of the Ospreys failed to do the same.

"How will you ever be powerful if you can't learn from those who have power?"

"If someone big attacks me with a sword right now, what happens to them?"

Kiriel shrugged. She had learned, with time, that Auralis' pointless questions served their purpose and had learned not to interrupt him. It was a lesson she had never been required to learn with Alexis. She had never interrupted the woman who claimed Duarte. If she thought about it for a moment, she realized that she'd never interrupted Fiara; on the rare occasion that Mirialyn ACormaris had had cause to address them, she had likewise known that it would be unwise to break the flow of her words.

She regularly interrupted the men and wondered if this was significant.

"They die."

"So?" She had also learned that arguing the validity of the finer points of his torturously slow explanations—for instance pointing out that his outcome did not take into account the relative power of said attacker—only served to lengthen the time until her enlightenment, such as it was, and besides, older instincts prevailed. One did not question another's claim to competence unless one was willing to prove how little it was worth. And she was strangely unwilling to kill this man.

"Kiriel?"

"Yes?"

"Did you even hear what I said?"

"No."

"I said yes. They're retiring the colors."

She frowned. "What does this mean?"

He closed his eyes. "To you? Nothing. Nothing."

"But it does."

"If it meant anything at all to you, you wouldn't have asked. You wouldn't have needed to."

"But it does," she said, touching him for emphasis.

"Kiriel—please. Not now."

"Why?"

His expression paused the way it did when he was between anger and vulnerability. She felt it: a sharp, terrible sweetness that passed so quickly she forgot about his pain. No; she forgot that it was his; forgot that it was anything other than a way to satisfy a hunger. The sensation was like pain. The pain was exquisite.

She cried out when the ring took it away, replacing it with a fire that was far more mundane.

"Kiriel?"

She did not look at him; she could not. Not yet, not when he had almost been . . . Food.

"You're right," she said, her voice sliding uncomfortably over the syllables as she struggled to master the first, the most important lesson: show no weakness. "It's not important to me."

He watched her for a moment and the lovely expression that had arrested all thought dissipated.

It was replaced by an expression that she understood better, one that she could easily associate with this man's face. "Then why did you say it was?"

"Because," she replied, clutching her hand as he somehow failed to notice the smell of singed flesh, "it's important to you."

"And that's important? Why?"

"I . . . don't know. Maybe because whenever you're angry you fight poorly."

His expression soured. She was always surprised when she found it could get worse. "I don't fight any worse."

"You do."

"I don't."

"You do. Your swing," she said, pointing to his sheathed sword, "goes wild. You only think of attack; you open up your lower left side; you extend yourself too far. If you paid attention, you'd fight a bit more conservatively, but . . . you don't pay attention to your own pain."

"Oh, and you do?" He laughed. "You of all people?" His smile turned, as hers had often done, onto an edge that was thin and dark. It was why she was comfortable with Auralis. With many of the Ospreys. This was what she was used to.

And used to ignoring, when it suited her.

"Yes. I do. I don't let it control me. I don't show it. But I feel pain. And I pay attention to what I feel; pain exists for a reason."

Pain exists for a reason, little Kiriel. Your own pain serves as a warning, and it is a warning that you must not *share with others. But heed it. When I cut you, and you bleed, there is a shock that pierces skin . . . here. Here. The bleeding is not heavy; the wound will not kill. But if I cut you deeply, if you are foolish enough to remain where I* might *cut you deeply—and you are not—the pain would be exquisite, and the blood would tell the brief story of your life.*

It is interesting in those moments. Some people understand what the end of that story will be; some don't. Some fear that end, even if it is not the story being told by the fall of their blood, the depth of their wound. I have watched humans die countless times, and it is often fascinating; even the weakest will surprise you in the fashion with which they choose to acknowledge the truth of their death.

And the Kialli? She had asked him.

The Kialli? His stare was cool. *You change the subject, little one.*

Do I? Hand on blade, hers; she could remember the feel of the supple leather in the curve of her palm even at the remove of years. There are some things that cannot be taken away, cannot be given away.

We are not mortal, Kiriel. You are. I speak of the death of mortals.

But you are not eternal, she had answered. *You live, somehow, and you die.*

You are developing a dragon's smile. Be certain, little one, that when you use it, you have the breath behind it to give it strength; it will almost certainly be necessary, for in the Shining Court, where everyone knows of the weakness of your birth, the taint of your mortality, false bravado is certain to attract challengers.

He had not answered her, not directly. But she had been persistent then, as she was now.

Do the Kialli *feel no pain*?

He had laughed. Lord Isladar. The sound of his laughter, like the edge of his momentary claws or the matte feel of leather against palm, was hers to keep even in his absence.

All *we feel is pain. Why else would we have chosen to be the reavers of the mortal dead?*

And he had ended the lesson.

But the lesson itself had taken root in the darkness of thought and memory, and like all of his lessons, flowered unexpectedly in difficult places.

Her eyes were stranger's eyes. He had seen the look before. Not often, and not recently, but a different man could spend the rest of a life trying to forget a glimpse of that expression; could wake up wrapped in the knowledge of it, nightmare's grip so visceral he couldn't hear over heartbeat and labored breath.

They didn't speak of her past. Here, all pasts were insignificant; it was the present and the future that counted. *Ospreys*, he thought bitterly. *We were Ospreys before we were whatever the past made of us. We could leave it all behind.*

The flag was flying. Or it should have been. But it was a hot, still day, and the colors, just like any common fabric, clung to the pole as if afraid to fall.

She was right. It was just cloth.

As long as they paid him, he served under it, but it was all the same to him.

Something caught his eye. Something hurt his throat. He wondered idly if the summer sickness had managed to find him. But although he was good at lying to himself, Auralis AKalakar was not a miracle worker.

The *bitch* was retiring the colors they had laid across every gods-cursed coffin and *every* gods-cursed Osprey grave in the Southern valleys. Two thirds of their number, butchered, screaming or silent as they took their sweet time getting to Mandaros' Hall. Men who had died at his back, had lived up to the oaths that real battle *should have* destroyed, taking the swords that were meant for him. She was destroying what they had built without having the courage to face them.

And maybe that was wise.

He heard the rumbling anger of Cook, a man who would never have made it to the Ospreys had it not been for the unexpected savagery of his hidden temper. He was speaking, and Auralis, having somehow made Decarus again, knew he should be paying attention. Even Fiara had fallen silent.

It should have been easy. Cook was saying what they *all* felt. All of them but her.

"Kiriel?"

She turned as if he hadn't spoken and left the grounds. It wasn't hard to do; she was never comfortable in crowds and when forced to join them, stayed on their edges. One place where edges didn't cut.

"Kiriel!"

He realized he was in danger of interrupting Cook, and hesitated a minute on the edge of the crowd that he had chosen to stand apart from as well.

Then, cursing quietly, he followed.

Isladar was everywhere. There was no place in which his memory did not exert power. The streets of Essalieyan were almost literally alive; the stone broken by weeds and the roots of great trees which would have found no purchase in the dominion of her father. And around those trees, odd creatures: cats and dogs; spindly-legged red-furred things that seemed a cross between the two; birds of all manner that in the poorer quarter were still hunted for food. On a bad day she enjoyed killing them, but she was beyond bad now; no simple death would serve.

There were places in Essalieyan that were dangerous. It had taken time to discover them, and once she had, she hoarded the knowledge. Although it pained her to admit it, the magisterial guards were more efficient than *Kialli* at weeding out the men and women who posed the danger she craved.

Simple things.

The fight for survival.

She thought of the succubi. Considered the weakest of the *Kialli* who could still remember their ancient choice, all of their power resided in their ability to beguile, to convince their victims to surrender, through desire, what nothing else might convince them to relinquish. In the Hells it was their only option; they could not take by force what they required from the kin.

She pitied all but a handful of them; they did not seek the glory of simplicity because they were not certain they could survive it.

Cowards.

They are not cowards. Coward is a simple word, and the subtlety required of a succubus is complex. They understand the limitations they labor under and they use the guise of helplessness in order to achieve their goal.

But—

They no longer care if they are seen as weak, if they ever did. They have risen above the need to swing sword and display the momentary corpses of their enemies.

Although his tone was quiet—as it always was—she had been unable to ignore the criticism in the words. *You told me that I could never afford to be seen as weak!*

She could still see the color of his eyes as he condescended to look at his unsatisfactory—his sole—pupil. *That is because what is seen, in your case, would be truth. You have learned to lie the way a mortal learns to wield a great ax—as a blunt and convenient weapon. It is far more than that. Yes, there can be a particular beauty in the starkness of simplicity, but your use of the art succeeds only because you choose enemies of little intellect.*

Assarak and Etridian are not—

They chose you. *There is a difference. No student of mine would make the mistake of choosing the Generals of the Lord's Fist as enemies. Not yet. And not until they had mastered the art and the artifice of subtlety.*

His tone clearly implied that he thought her incapable of such mastery.

Her hands closed around the hilt of her sheathed sword; her steps were quick and light and loud as the streets became both narrower and emptier. He haunted her, and he wasn't dead.

And he would be. He would be. Dead as Ashaf was dead.

Around her neck, the stone that had been Ashaf's parting gift, in a fashion, made the chain heavy. She felt a flash and a warmth against skin, in the hollow between her breasts. Against the building rage came another pressure.

He is dangerous, Kiriel. I know that he cares for you in his fashion, although I would never have thought it possible—but he is Kialli.

And you're not.

Meaning that I can't understand what Kialli *are? I have eyes, and ears; I know how to think. I observe them.* Her smile had been a bitter twist of lips, there and gone as she met the face of her almost-daughter in the cold, clear light. That's what Ashaf had called her. Almost-daughter. And Kiriel had called her Ashaf.

But in the shadows where night was darkest and the tower was empty of everything save the old woman's breathing, she had called her mother.

The sword was heavy, the pendant burned, the day was bright as it hovered on the welcome edge of night. She could not think of Isladar and Ashaf together; the thoughts overlapped and burned; they made her mad with the frenzied desire to grab memory—as if it were solid, as if it were an enemy—and rip it out, challenge it with sword and shield, and butcher it slowly, slowly, slowly. . . .

Ashaf.

I never thought you were stupid.

But it was a lie, and Kiriel—as Isladar had often pointed

out—was not a master of artifice. She *had* thought the old woman stupid.

He will change you. He has *changed you. He is not interested in what makes you human; he is interested in what makes you . . .*

Yes?

Kiriel . . .

But that's what I am, Ashaf. Can't you understand that? How can you tell me that you love me *and not understand that? You can't separate me from me. Isladar—at least he knows.*

Does he?

Yes.

The silence was heavy. The old woman had turned away, as Isladar often did, but with a very different expression. *Perhaps,* she had said, *you are right. After all, it was Lord Isladar who chose me to raise you.*

And without him, you would raise me as if I were merely mortal.

Yes. Yes, because that's all I am, and I've willingly given you everything I am, Kiriel. She had bowed her head, and—gods, no—Kiriel felt it: that rush of pleasure, that warmth for which words were a pale expression, that came with pain. Even Ashaf's. Especially Ashaf's.

But he wants everything for me.

Ashaf had turned back, her expression concealing nothing although it was now smooth as the tower walls. *There were always evil men, Kiriel. And in the end, if you walk Lord Isladar's path, that is what you will be: an evil mortal. Not more. Not less.*

I'll be much *more. You have no idea what kind of power I* do *have if you can say that!*

Does it matter? Does it matter if you kill a man by riding him down with a sword and a small contingent of bored young clansmen, or if you kill him by shadow and darkness? In the end, he belongs to the wind either way. Does it matter if you can consume a whole village by your own hand, where the clansmen might need tens, when in the end, the villagers are still dead?

You are just a different kind of weapon. That's all. But in the history of the darkness, how many have served their own beliefs and their own cause?

Kiriel's anger destroyed her pleasure in the old woman's pain, and she clung to it. She remembered that clearly: clinging to anger as if it were her only salvation. *We all serve our own cause. How can you tell me that you're paying attention to the Court if you can't see that?*

You serve his cause.

My father—

Lord Isladar's.

Silence. And then, *you mean I serve his cause instead of yours. I have no cause, Ashaf. I survive. I enjoy surviving when my enemies don't. Sometimes I feel like a bone that the two of you are struggling over. Except that the struggle is all yours; he asks nothing except that I survive.*

There is more to life than survival.

What more?

And she had turned to the tower's window; the window past which the wind's voice was a continual howl and shriek. Here, she had once said, her voice drowsy with sleep and heavy with fear, the damned wailed hardest, and the sun was cold. She now said, *I hated the sun in my youth; I hated the heat. But having spent fourteen years in the North, Kiriel, I'm not sure that death by fire is any worse than this.* She had looked down at her hands as they touched the sill that would outlast her. Outlast them both. God's work.

She had a strange dignity that Kiriel found beautiful only *now*, now that it was lost.

And it had been lost.

No matter what their intentions were, no matter how brave they thought they could be, pain destroyed a person completely. Pain. Fear.

Kiriel was burning, now. Burning. The pain was terrible.

Your pain makes you foolish, Kiriel.

You told me to pay attention to it.

To listen to it, yes, but never *to give in to it. Only the weak do that, and they lie a moment at your feet before they become ash and dust at the whim of the mortal world. Listen. Take care. Pain tells you where your weakness is.*

And, Kiriel, child, I do not have to say this, but I will, again and again, because you must learn it. Never reveal that pain.

She had learned every lesson that he had cared to teach. But she had not been the perfect student of his desire; she had been marred by the mortal need for comfort, and she had sought it, again and again, in the lap and the arms of an old, weak woman that even an imp could have killed with impunity.

The only woman now alive to whom Kiriel had gone for comfort had disappeared in the streets of Averalaan, under attack by *Kialli*. Kiriel, less than half a city away, had not even sensed their coming. The den had called her, and called her late, as an afterthought, a grudging duty; she had walked through the rubble and the roots of upturned trees; the cracked, great branches like the broken limbs of ancient guardians that have finally fallen in the act of fulfilling their duty.

The demons, of course, were gone. She could sense their shadows lingering in the small fires that the magi struggled to recapture and return to the elemental plane. Duarte AKalakar, terse and pale, had walked by her side, and directly in front of her—in a position that only one other would have dared to occupy less than a year ago, Verrus Korama.

Once or twice, the magi glanced up.

One stopped at once.

"AKalakar," he said, bowing to Duarte. It took her by surprise; Duarte was called many things, few of them polite. "AKalakar." And then he turned his steel-gray eyes to her and bowed again, just as formally. "Kiriel."

She did not return the bow. There was something about this mage that she would never like. Circumstance might force them to be allies. But circumstance was capricious; she looked forward to the day when it forced him to raise sword and test himself against her in the only way that mattered.

He offered her no challenge. Instead, he quietly said, "It is my belief that Jewel ATerafin survived this attack."

As if he *knew* that she was weak enough to care, to need the answer.

She was. She was.

She ran; the streets were too narrow, the buildings too small, the people in them too soft, too weak, too many. She held her sword; she couldn't remember drawing it, but it didn't matter. It was not technically illegal, but she had learned quickly that that law did not prevent fear or timidity in the people it was designed to protect.

They made as wide a path for her as the streets themselves allowed.

He understands who I am.

But, ring on her hand now dull in the dying light, the truth was different.

The truth had always been different. Ashaf had hated the cruelty and aggression that was essential to her nature; her father's gift; the power of his blood. Lord Isladar had, in protecting her from her weakness, denied her the other half—but with subtlety.

For her own good.

And it was for

Ashaf

Her own good; she was weak

Jay

And she had always been weak

Falloran

And weakness was the single unforgivable sin; there *were* no others

Father

She knew it now. She was sweating in the heat, and the comfort of a simple thing like breath eluded her. Her lungs would not fill with this salty, humid air. And she needed it, although she hated the sea and swore that she would see it evaporated when she ruled the—when she—

She was running. She forgot why; struggled with memory and found an answer, any answer. There were fights to be fought. Men to kill. Yes.

Lie, Kiriel. Lie.

No. She was driven by ghosts. By the dead. By the living she'd sworn to kill. By her failure to even consider any vulnerability but her own. The word 'protection' hadn't even been a part of the singular vocabulary that had been built for her by her sole teacher. And had she not understood what it meant?

Yes: the thing you must get around if you desire to kill something that has sworn service to a creature more powerful than itself.

She had been so *good* at that.

She had been taught by a master.

No. *No*. Why was she thinking about this now? All she wanted—all she needed—was a real fight. All she wanted was a fight.

But all they wanted was a fight as well, the Ospreys. They feared her. Some desired her. All accepted her, in spite of who they thought she might be—when they bothered to think at all. And they were raging, shouting, or silently weeping because of a *flag*. And she wanted—she wanted for herself what they exposed themselves by giving to a piece of handworked cloth. She wanted the weakness.

Roaring filled her ears: she knew the sound even though it had been so long since she'd last heard it. Her voice. Her true voice.

Her hand was burning. She ignored it; it was painful, but it was a type of pain she understood. It was the type of pain she had been nurtured by when she was growing up in the Hells.

Better, better by far, than this new, this other, pain.

Auralis knew the sound.

Recognized all the sounds that followed it, inevitable as water after thunderclap and lightning. Voices made pale and thin by the contrast with the richness of hers, full of wordless fear. Footsteps; boots and flat sandals against the cobbled and pocked roads. *Send for the magisterians. Send for the magi.* Some clear heads among the lot.

A demon was loose in Averalaan. No one was close enough to stop it. And the damage done in the Common made clear what that meant to a normal person. The fact that the demons were destroyed by the magi didn't bring back the dead.

But this was different.

He knew whose face the demon wore. And he had to admit that the grandeur of her voice made the thin screams of everyone else sound pathetic. Faceless. Dead, or as close to it as made no difference.

Dammit, Kiriel, were in the Hells are you?

She knew the rules of the City. The human laws. The first thing she'd learned. No magic. No killing.

If the only thing you learn is how to kill, the only thing you'll be is a killer. Ashaf's voice. Pendant at her neck warmer than the ring around her finger, but without the resulting pain, the searing of flesh.

But in the Shining Court, that had been enough. More than enough. *I am learning other things. I am learning about power, Ashaf, about politics. About the human court.*

To what end?

To rule.

Silence.

In the world my father builds, she had continued, the words leaving her lips in the past mirrored by a similar movement of lips now, the action a bridge between past and present. *In the world my father builds, what I learn will be more than enough. What else do I need? What else do I need to know? I kill them before they kill me. I grow powerful enough that they don't waste their lives even trying.*

What else do I need?

All the lies. All the lies she had been allowed to believe.

She roared now, because now she had her answer.

Because she had had her answer the day—the night—that she had, convulsed with pleasure, discovered what it was.

Ashaf.

And there was no place for Ashaf in any world her father would build.

It had been eight years since Ashaf had carried her. Years. Ten years, more, since she had comfortably fit beneath the sagging curve of the older woman's chin; years since the burden of her weight had not been so great that the older woman could no longer bear it. But she remembered it. In dreams, she was wrapped in warmth, and in dreams, the woman whose voice was balm and sweetness and sustenance—all weakness, all of it—came back to haunt her, like the dead woman herself.

The sun has gone down, has gone down, my child, Na'kiri, Na'kiri dear . . .

"ASHAF!"

Auralis heard it. He was not the closest, but unlike the woman who stood in shadows, he did not hesitate, did not freeze. He lifted his head, his eyes widening, his mouth opening in surprise and something akin to fear. It didn't last. He had run from the moment he had first heard her voice; now he sprinted, throwing his head and shoulders forward, bending into his knees, lengthening his stride.

Awkward as hell to do that with a sword that long strapped across your back.

She knew it; in her youth, she had tried.

Youth was long gone. What remained, implacable as ever, was duty. She turned to her companion. His perfect profile was motionless as he watched a man who wore Kalakar colors and armor break through a crowd that was already becoming sparse.

"Well?" she said quietly.

Pale hair, longer than Evayne's had ever been, had been braided and fell in a straight line down his back, bisecting the fall of emerald-green robes. "You ask me to judge?" he replied at last, aware of her scrutiny. "Any insight I have is inferior to the talent you've developed over the years. You have walked the Oracle's path." He turned to face her then, his slate-gray eyes slightly narrowed. "You did not summon me from my Tower in the Order to ask me for my opinion."

"No."

"Good. I have been . . . restless of late."

"Maybe you need another student."

"The last one was more than enough." His lips thinned as he spoke; his eyes narrowed. The humor in the words was sharp and cold. "Why did you call me?"

"I don't know. You used to counsel patience, and you have so little of it."

"Little enough that I resent the waste of—"

They heard it: Wind, and within its folds, a name.

Evayne had heard people die in less pain, with less anger, with less fear.

"You also used to tell me to be careful what *I* wished for, Master."

He was already in motion. She followed, shunting the crowds aside not by the force of her momentum, but rather by the artifice of magical suggestion. If Meralonne APhaniel, member of the Order of Knowledge and special adviser to Kings, thought poorly of this illegal use of magery, he did not condescend to note it. But he did not use it either; he wore the official medallion by which the magi were known, and it served to clear a path in magic's stead.

He moved in silence for half a city block, and then he said, without looking at her, "I do not think Myrddion truly saw the depth and range of this child's power. If he understood her nature at all."

She lifted a hand, shunting aside the curiosity of eavesdroppers in the same way as she had the men and women in the crowd she had passed through. "He must have; the ring went to her. The rings know their masters."

"Masters?" His laugh was unkind. "An amusing word, and an inappropriate one. This—this should not have happened."

"What?"

Silver brows rose; gray eyes narrowed. He did not express contempt with words because it wasn't necessary. "Listen to her voice, Evayne."

Just like that.

"The ring—"

"If its sole purpose was containment, it is already failing."

Her fingers, adorned by three rings now, curled into fists. All of her life came down to that ring, this girl. Earth and air, fire and water—these she understood. She had seen the workings of one of the elemental rings intimately. She had never clearly seen the purpose behind the simple, unadorned band, the ring that Myrddion had considered the most powerful of the five.

But she understood this. What she heard in Kiriel's voice, in this city, on this street—it was death.

Meralonne knew well why she had summoned him. He was discreet, for reasons of his own.

And he was her equal in magery, should it come to battle.

She didn't look human.

She didn't look demonic.

She looked—like a dream of Death, like an angel of judgment, like something that had never known mortality.

Or had caused a lot of others to become intimately acquainted with their own.

Auralis grabbed two men by the shoulders and threw himself forward using their weight as a brace.

She had drawn her sword.

Damn, damn, damn.

She had drawn her sword, and her eyes when she turned to face him were the color of her blade.

His hand was on the hilt of the sword he wore across his back, but it froze there. It froze, although he had to fight every instinct he had ever honed in combat—and had proved by survival—in order to keep it there. He wanted to *run*.

It had been a long, long time since flight had been an option. Since fear had hit him in the gut, visceral as a heavy kick, had taken his breath, had made his hands weak and slick with sweat.

"*Kiriel!*"

"Stay your hand," Evayne said, lifting hers. Around her wrist, as if caught in howling winds, the sleeves of her robe twisted and gathered.

Meralonne did not choose to obey. He lifted his hands, crossing them. She was afraid that he was going to summon the elemental air, but a pale, orange glow gathered and grew in his upturned palms, and the voice of the wind was silent. He held the spell in abeyance.

Together, they watched.

But she thought it interesting; orange was protection's light; hearth light. It was only in her youth that she had been naive enough to believe that Meralonne APhaniel would willingly spend his power and his carefully hoarded knowledge on something as simple as the public good.

She might not have believed it now, but she recognized the signature of the spell. He had taught it to her, the last of many spells, at a time when she had not realized how difficult defense was to master, and although the intervening years had embroidered it with her bitter experience, giving the spell a signature that was unique, the spells were kin. The magi-historians would be able to trace the one back to the other with effort and time.

The magic would create a circle around Kiriel, should she lose control—or rather, lose more of it—separating her from the crowd. And, more relevant, the crowd from her.

For as long, Evayne thought quietly, as it lasted.

What had gone wrong? What was the ring doing?

Why had the path she had chosen to walk led her here? She was weary.

Evayne, who had lost the habit of prayer, given the closeness of her relationship with the gods, cursed instead. She was old, now; powerful in a way that she had not been in her youth. She had seen so *much* death; had witnessed the failure of so many plans.

But the failure of this, a plan that she barely—no, that she honestly had never—understood, would be profound.

Hard, to have given your entire life to a cause that depended on so many fragile people. Blood filled the crescents in palms where fingernails bit deep.

It took a moment.

Auralis hated fear more than he hated Annies. More—almost—than he hated demons. Especially when it was his own. He drew his sword. People who were smarter ran screaming if they could spare breath for sound.

Shit, he thought, *if we survive this, The Kalakar will have our heads, never mind our names.*

And then he had other things to worry about.

Like keeping his head for long enough that it could be presented to her.

Kiriel swung.

She was slow. Her hand was on fire. But her vision was clear. For the first time since the ring had shorn her of strength, she could *see.*

Auralis was no longer a simple mask and a shell of flesh; entwined in these things was a light and a shadow that she had always thought lay beneath the flesh, trapped by it. But now she could see it for what it was; a part of the living body, inseparable from it.

No, not inseparable.

She had seen the division of the two. If she paused for just a moment, she could clearly recall each time it had happened.

But that would take her to the final time, and the final time was not an event she wished to revisit; not in memory, not in nightmare. Not in the Hells, when and if she arrived there, although she was certain that was what was waiting: an eternity of Ashaf's death.

And Kiriel's failure to prevent it.

She cried out, and her voice was the dragon's voice; her

voice was death. Any demon who heard it—when it was used in the Shining Palace—would have fled unless he was foolish enough to think himself a match for the Lord's daughter. The humans were fleeing, too. All of them but one, this one.

There was really only one way to learn a lesson in the Hells: from someone else's mistake. Mistakes were so seldom survived.

But Kiriel had become, under Isladar's tutelage, an excellent teacher.

The sword, her sword, was singing; she could hear its keening, could feel it as if it were an extension of both her hand and her shadow. She was *alive.*

She swung.

Auralis was the only Osprey who had thrown himself, time and again, into the circle with Kiriel. She had beaten him every time. He didn't fight fairly; he had learned to really fight in the South, where anything that *worked* meant survival, and questions of what was "fair" became so academic they were treated with scorn and derision by the rank and file.

He knew how to cheat in the circle.

She hadn't even noticed.

And he knew, as he rolled out of the way, that his reflexes and instincts were either going to save his life or get him killed in the next two minutes—because he realized, seeing the compelling darkness of her eyes and the shadows that pooled across the flat of a sword that should have reflected sunlight, that he had never fought Kiriel. He had sparred with her; had played some game that she struggled to understand the rules of, but he had never fought *Kiriel.*

"Well?"

Meralonne's voice.

Evayne frowned. "Not yet."

She heard the friction between hair and cloth; a shrug.

Auralis lied. A lot.

But there were a couple of truths that defined him: He knew when to run. And he hated running.

He had gotten used to self-loathing; this was a good time

to hate himself. But he brought his blade around in a parry, deflecting the blow's force and rolling out of its way. He'd learned that his size and his strength weren't a match for hers; everything about her was deceptive. All those lost bets in the training circle had been good for something after all.

But she was better at cheating than he was.

If she was thinking at all.

She could *see*. She could *hear*. Everything in the street was alive with the color of eternity. She wanted to weep with joy at it; at the light, at the gray, and the growing shadows. It was as if she had been drowning in mortality, and for the first time in months she had managed to take a real breath.

She did not want to exhale. But the ring was burning; it slowed her down.

"Kiriel!"

The frail, mortal darkness was calling her.

"Kiriel, snap out of it! They've already gone for the magi!"

She had meant to shake him off; he parried the blow.

Very few of the mortals—or the imps that were their closest cousins in the Hells—could parry her sword; when she was intent on the combat, she could slice through steel.

She looked up, and saw a darkness she was familiar with. Sensed, in the air between herself and that shadow, a wonderful fear.

Was surprised when the man chose to destroy the fragility of that moment by striking her—with the *flat* of his blade.

It wasn't the smart opening move. Then again, against Kiriel there were no smart opening moves—and the closing moves were, sadly, all hers.

But it had the single advantage of being a move he had never tried before, and it was—

Completely incomprehensible. Not even in the pathetic games the Ospreys called training had anyone treated her with this much condescension; certainly not Auralis, driven by the desire to win at any cost.

She was confused enough to let him land a glancing blow. Not confused enough to let him land a second. She returned the attack almost casually.

Old habits died hard. Auralis stopped himself from screaming because he'd felt similar pain before. Familiar pain was never as terrifying as unknown pain. Even when it was magical in nature.

The damn sword had sliced through metal and padding; he'd felt it cut.

There was no blood. And there should have been. A lot.

Shit.

First time for everything, he thought, shifting his grip on his sword and circling Kiriel at the outer edge of her reach.

Who would have thought he'd ever be unhappy at the lack of his own blood?

Evayne shed hood in the dusk. The street had emptied but would fill again, and she had no intention of allowing Kiriel this kill in front of the people who would fill it. But she was surprised that she still had the opportunity to intervene.

Meralonne reached out. Touched her. Risky, that; the cloak that had been her father's only useful gift was more . . . independent . . . than other forms of armor. But it allowed the contact.

Meralonne did not speak.

He was still alive.

Kiriel frowned; her hand hurt; the sword burned her palm. Pain was something to appreciate at a distance; she did not savor or enjoy her own. She looked at the hilt reluctantly; it was made of gold and shadow, and limned in an ugly light that had never been there before.

An early lesson—never let go of this sword. She had learned it quickly, although when she had reached the age of fourteen, she had insisted on learning to fight with other weapons as well. It was a simple precaution, and one Lord Isladar had shown pride in, for the sword was obviously enchanted, and it was an enchantment that, having been placed there by another, could never be fully trusted.

The sword itself had been that most suspicious of things:

a gift. Isladar had offered it to her while its maker looked on, as if observing a ritual.

"This has never been done by our line," the strange *Kialli* lord had said.

"Nor will it be again. I fear the time for your art has passed."

"Will you take this risk, mortal?" He turned to face her for the first time, his eyes unblinking and devoid of everything but a bleak, bleak curiosity. She remembered it clearly, could label it only now. As a child, she had thought him sad.

Sad.

She looked to Isladar for guidance; his face was impassive. It was enough. She nodded.

"You are capable, in my estimation, of summoning a cruder weapon with no ties to any other maker's hands."

Lord Isladar frowned. "Enough."

But the stranger was not deterred.

"If I could do that, why wouldn't I, instead of accepting something another lord made?"

"Because the shape and the form of that weapon will not be of *your* choosing, and you might find it one not to your liking. It is created by will, but it is not easily molded."

She frowned.

Lord Isladar's voice was cool and distant. "You might invoke dagger, with no reach. You might invoke spear or bow. Any weapon you created in such a fashion you would be forced to wield as a true weapon."

She absorbed this, the newness of the knowledge, Isladar's annoyance, and the stranger's quiet patience. At last she nodded.

"The sword will kill you, or it will become a part of you. But first, you must feed it."

She took the sword. It was the heaviest thing she had ever lifted on her own. She wanted to ask him how to feed a sword—but Isladar's eyes had narrowed to edges. He was not angry; she had only rarely seen him angry. But he would be, if she continued. Cold and distant, like the mountain peaks. She had hated that, as a child.

She looked up. Saw the man. Recognized him.

"*Auralis*?"

"Kiriel. I think it's time to go back."

His gaze was wary; he did not stop circling. As if that motion, this close, was preparation for any attack she might launch.

She was surprised when her sword failed to skewer him. But not surprised enough that his countering strike connected. She saw the glint of steel six inches from her feet and smiled; it was the edge of his blade that had hit the dirt between the cobbled stones.

What she had not realized, when she had lifted this cumbersome, great sword, was that she would not be allowed to let it *go* until she had offered it whatever it was it required. She would not be allowed to *ask*. Until she could figure it out for herself, she was trapped by its weight.

"Do you like the sword, little one?" the stranger asked.

"I'm not sure," she said, too absorbed by the sheen of the naked blade to be cautious. "I don't think it likes me."

She saw his smile—his perfect smile—as a reflection in the blade's flat. He was beautiful, then. She would have turned to look at him, but she couldn't imagine that the smile could be better than the smile's reflection across new steel.

"Isladar," she said, forgetting his title.

"Kiriel?"

"Why is he smiling?"

"Is he, Kiriel?"

There was no anger in his voice, but whenever he asked a question it demanded more than an answer: he wanted her to think about what she had just said before she answered anything. If she answered at all. But what had she said?

Why is he smiling.

What was Isladar doing? She turned, sword still heavy in her hands, to see his expressionless face. Turned back to the sword. Something was wrong, but it took a moment before she realized that she *could not* see Lord Isladar's reflection in the shining steel. At all. She turned then, to see the other *Kialli* lord. His face was as cold as . . . as steel.

But the steel . . . the steel still held his smile.

The stranger's brows rose. And then his lips curved in a

pale echo of the smile she had seen. "You do not know what you have found here, Lord Isladar."

"Do I not?"

The tall man walked past Lord Isladar as if he was no longer of interest. That got her attention; no one did that to Isladar. Yet Isladar waited in silence. "I have . . . misjudged you, young one," he said, touching her; taking her chin in the palm of his hand. His hand was callused and rough. But although Lord Isladar had always cautioned her against the gentle touch of any other *Kialli*, she raised her chin until she could meet his gaze with her own. "I was not a lord when I dwelled upon the mortal plane," he said quietly. "That was not my art. But this . . . this was." His lips thinned; his beauty was lost a moment to the edge of something bitter. But when the creases in his lips and around his eyes unfolded, he was beautiful. As beautiful as the sword he had crafted.

"Feed the sword, and it will serve you."

She nodded.

"What happens if the sword isn't fed?"

"I believe you already know the answer to that."

"But I—" She did. "If I feed it?"

"You will be a warrior without parallel. You will fight as men fought when the Cities stood."

"Enough," Lord Isladar said quietly. "She is young, and her curiosity might lead her to ask questions in the Court of humans who would be interested in that bitter history."

She frowned. "I don't want to be the best warrior *just* because of a sword."

He smiled as if she had said something very clever. But he removed his hand from her chin as Lord Isladar approached. "I thought the mortals were happy to win at any price? Why would you refuse such an offer?"

"May I remind you, Anduvin, that she is our Lord's daughter. His plans are—"

"Don't be tiresome, Isladar. I expect it of the pompous and graceless Fist, but I expect better of you."

"But I am of the Lord's Fist."

"Ah . . . I had forgotten."

"Then perhaps I erred in requesting a sword from your forge; what weapon of value could possibly come from a . . . lord of such diminished memory?"

For the first time, Kiriel saw a *Kialli* lord draw sword against Isladar. He brought his free hand to the sword's hilt and raised the blade, turning it on edge so that it was a gleaming line of fire that divided his face. He called no shield. She had seen the *Kialli* draw swords before; Ashaf, fanciful, had called them tongues of flame—weapons of Hells.

But this blade was different.

She forgot to breathe, fascinated. She had seen the kin fight—and kill—and she had seen the *Kialli* challenge. Of the challenges, elemental was the most enviable. It was a power she would never possess, although Isladar assured her that she would have the power to destroy the kinlord who attempted to humiliate her by offering her a challenge that she could not accept.

But she had never seen a lord challenge Isladar.

"Be certain you wish to continue," Lord Isladar said mildly. "You know my blade. You forged it."

"Perhaps." Lord Anduvin lowered his blade. "But I have not seen you draw it since you traveled the divide. Much was lost in the first transition. Much has been lost in the second."

"Your own blade—"

"I am the master; I am the Swordsmith."

"There were others."

"There were no others!" He lifted his perfect sword. The Southern humans in the Shining Court often discussed the edge of the blade; the temper; the mix of metals that had gone into its birthing. They argued about sheaths, and the style of sheaths; about human conceits. She found any discussion about armaments interesting. But she would never find mortal discussion as interesting again.

Anduvin's sword . . .

Air had been its sheath; Kiriel had not known, until the hilt was in his hand, that he had carried a weapon at all—although the lack of a weapon meant less for the *Kialli* than it did for the mortals.

"Will you draw your blade, Lord Isladar?"

"If I draw it, I will pay its price."

"I would see that."

"It would be the last thing you saw." His words were mild; he folded his arms across his chest, but he did not otherwise move. "If I have offered insult, it was merely parry; if you seek to die for it—*Kialli* have died for less."

"Or killed for less."

"Yes."

But she knew, when he spoke, that the fires in Anduvin's words had been banked.

"Lord Anduvin?"

"Hush, mortal."

She was silent for the full count of ten seconds. But before she could speak—and she was young then and would have, he turned to her. "Now ask your question."

"Your blade."

"Yes?"

"It is not like other *Kialli* swords."

He became as still as the ice on the mountains outside her favorite window. "How is it different, child?"

"It looks like any other *Kialli* sword," she said, with the ease of youth, "but it . . . is not of the fire."

"Not of the fire? But it is—can you not see the flames that surround it?"

She nodded, quietly. "But the swords of the others—the others who draw swords at all—have hearts of fire. Flame surrounds your sword, but its heart is steel."

His eyes widened. "This child," he said to Isladar, momentary animosity forgotten, "will be a marvel."

"Or a doom."

"Or indeed a doom. You see truly, child. The red flames are camouflage; they are not the blade's heart. I am Anduvin the Swordsmith. In the Hells. Or here." He bowed. "Once, ages past, I made swords for mortals and for the living children of the gods. This is the first such blade that I have made since—for a long time. And I believe it will be the last.

"It will kill you today if you do not understand its nature."

The blade burned her now; between the one hand and the other, she wondered idly if opposing magicks would cripple her.

She wondered why the blade of her sword was slick with a red, wet sheen.

CHAPTER SIX

"Where did you get that sword?"

Ashaf's voice.

Ashaf's unwelcome voice, sharp with disapproval. Years later, Kiriel would understand that it was no less a weapon than a sword, a claw, a fang—but she would deflect it less effectively, for all her understanding. She did not understand why, but she did not like to see Ashaf unhappy, and if she was the source of that unwelcome emotion, it was worse.

Isladar and Anduvin had left Kiriel in the relative safety of the courtyard at the base of her Tower. Twilight had come to the wastes, and it lingered. When the long night fell, the old woman would return to the safety of walls that Lord Isladar had enchanted to protect them both while they slept.

But until the darkness came, Ashaf felt at ease at the Tower's base. And ill at ease with the weapon.

Kiriel had been alone with it for two hours now, examining the intricacies of its surface, the subtleties of its maker's craft. She had examined Southern swords before—and they were considered to be the finest swords that mortals could now produce. Although there were hints among the kin and the *Kialli* that this had not always been the case, the kin now felt that the Swords of Annagar were little more than sharpened utensils, best used for eating things that were already dead and would therefore offer no resistance.

Two hours, and she did not feel sick, or unwell; she did not feel fevers; she did not feel bespelled. And yet she had heard Anduvin's words, and she knew that he spoke the truth: the blade would kill her if she did not figure out what to feed it.

"Lord Anduvin made it," Kiriel told her, ill at ease as

well, but determined not to disgrace herself by showing it—and resenting the old woman's reminder. She wanted to add "for me" but was aware—as if truth in that childhood place was as stark as the weather of the Hells—that this was not precise.

"And why did Lord Anduvin give the sword to you?"

"I need a weapon. And Lord Isladar asked him to make it for me."

"Why? Kiriel, have you blooded the blade?"

She did not lie to Ashaf. She did not need to. "No."

"Good." Pale, wrinkled hands, veined in emerald and sapphire beneath delicate skin, reached for the hilt.

Kiriel cried out; a visceral anger and an equally visceral terror took hold of her, both too strong for words. She struck her nursemaid, shunting her to one side with the full force of a slender shoulder. The old woman struck the wall and crumpled, winded.

She hadn't been hit very hard.

For the first time, Kiriel wondered if she would end up like this: Bowed by age; weak and helpless in the face of the slightest of blows. It was a terrifying thought: mortality.

Almost as terrifying as the disgust she felt staring across at this soft, useless woman, this waiting victim. The sword, untouched by any hand but hers, now hung at her side, its tip trailing flagstone as she turned, slowly, toward the gate.

Lord Isladar's words joined her as she stood, sword in hand in the courtyard before Ashaf's bowed head; the rest of him did not follow. A reminder that he watched, always.

Feed the sword, Kiriel. Feed it, and it will serve you.

She understood, then. The disgust receded. She saw not weakness, not victim, but Ashaf. The only woman—the only person—with whom she could share the desperate desire to be both comforted and loved.

No.

You accepted what was forged, Kiriel. The sword is not a child's weapon. It was created by the Swordsmith; he is Kialli *in a way that defies your experience. His Art has survived the passage to, and from, the Hells. This is the first blade he has created since the* Kialli *were appointed the stewards of those who have Chosen. Do you understand? Millennia of deprivation have ended with this blade. It is powerful; more powerful than we intended.*

Fail to feed it, and you will die.

No.

The sword is an extension of you. An extension of us. It reflects our basest truths. The woman is old and frail. She cuts herself on shards of simple stone; she has no defense against something as simple as air; the weather can kill her. A single imp would be her death—her slow death. Do you not understand her purpose?

She was brought here to take care of me!

Yes. Until such a day as this. You have been given your weapon—you no longer need to be treated like the human young.

No!

He came then.

She had only rarely seen him robed in Shadow; had only rarely been forced to acknowledge the power that he kept—against all demonic protocol—concealed. At his side, eyes the color and sheen of new steel, Lord Anduvin.

"I would not, if I were you," the Swordsmith said, speaking not to Kiriel but to her master.

Lord Isladar did not move. "Do not offer advice when you are not well acquainted with the particulars of the situation."

"I am acquainted with the particulars of the weapon; it is one of mine, and inasmuch as a creator can understand the complexities of a living work, I understand it. You cannot force her to give what is required."

"I have never forced her hand," Lord Isladar replied, his eyes on his student. "I have always allowed her both choice and its consequences. At most I have made certain she understands the consequences of her decision."

Kiriel met his eyes and looked away, the motion almost continuous. But her gaze was not a random attempt to avoid his glare; there was purpose in the movement. The old woman, winded by the force of a blow meant to save her life, was stirring. It was clear, as she lifted her head, that she was struggling for breath. And struggling with pain. Could something so simple have broken her ribs?

She saw Ashaf clearly: weak, soft, old. So close to death it might be a mercy to end the life that bound them.

And they were bound.

She reached out with her free hand to help her nursemaid to her feet, and she found herself turning to both Anduvin and Isladar, subtly interposing herself between them and the old woman.

Even though she was disgusted. Even then.

"She is mine," her words said; her voice told a different story.

"Is she worth your life?" Isladar spoke, for the first time that day, in Torra.

Kiriel answered him in the language of the *Kialli*. She lifted the sword and swung it in a slow, steady arc, until it came to rest point first, in a straight line that joined them.

She was young, but she wasn't stupid.

Lord Isladar's eyes narrowed. "You are not my equal, Kiriel."

"I've seen you use more of your power than anyone."

"She has fangs, Isladar. Even if they are too small to be of real danger, she attempts their use. How like a . . . young one." His eyes narrowed as he spoke the last two words.

Kiriel's curiosity and her muted anger struggled for a minute. It wasn't a contest. This *Kialli* lord was like no *Kialli* she had ever met—and she had met a lot of them. "Did you have children?"

"*Kiriel.*" Isladar's word was a whip's snap. Anger appeared in the brief break of syllables; he concealed it by the time the last had died into silence.

Lord Anduvin said nothing at all, his gaze intent. She did not like him . . . but she did not instantly *dislike* him, as she did the other kinlords.

"Kiriel?" Ashaf's voice was surprisingly steady as she pulled her hand free and stood without aid. Kiriel felt the sudden freedom as a shock of cold against her empty palm.

She said nothing.

"Kiriel, what did he mean when he asked if I was worth your life?"

"Nothing."

"But he—"

"He wants me to kill you."

"That isn't what he said. He said—"

"I heard him," Kiriel snarled. "But he never speaks in Torra—to me—without a reason. I'm not going to do what he wants, so he's trying to get you to—to help him."

"Why is he speaking of your death?"

"Because," she said slowly, as if Ashaf were the child, and Kiriel the mother, "if I'm not willing to kill you, he thinks you might be stupid enough to kill yourself to save me."

Isladar lifted his hands and clapped, slowly. "Very good," he said, still speaking in Torra. "But, Kiriel, I have no need to lie. I am telling her the truth."

"I want you to go upstairs," Kiriel continued, speaking to Ashaf as if Isladar had not interrupted her. Ashaf didn't move; Kiriel glanced over her shoulder and saw the old woman's face. The lines there had been etched by sun and wind long before Kiriel's birth, but Kiriel had always found them beautiful.

The strangest thing in this long afternoon was finding that she still did, "Ashaf?" She reached out with her cold, empty hand. The older woman relented, and took it. "I need you to go upstairs. Please. You know he wants something. You know he's never let me be killed. But if you're in danger, I can't *think*. You know what happens to *Kialli* who can't think."

The expression on the older face softened visibly as she looked down at her charge.

Deliberately, because she knew a public act of contrition would anger Lord Isladar, Kiriel added, "I'm sorry I hit you so hard. But the sword—you can't touch it."

"Why not?"

Lord Anduvin said, unexpectedly and quietly, "It will kill you. Heed your mistress. This is a *Kialli* matter, and it would best be solved by your absence."

Ashaf turned to the stranger. Isladar seldom allowed the *Kialli*—or the lesser kin for that matter—into the Tower courtyard. "Is Kiriel's life in danger?"

"Oh, yes," he said, smiling at the way her face lost color. "But your presence here is no longer a factor in her survival." Ashaf hesitated another minute, and the Swordsmith said, "There are things that are best faced in private."

His voice was gentle. He looked at Ashaf for a long while, and then added, "I would give much to know what he offered you to come to the wastes to raise this child, for I see that you are not bespelled, and you are not ignorant. You must know that you will never leave the Shining

Palace, and that your death, when it comes, will be . . . unpleasant."

"She's not going to die!" The sword, which had been heavy, lost weight as she swung it, wordless, a second time.

"Hush, child. There are more imminent deaths with which to concern yourself." But again his voice was gentle.

"Do you still search, Anduvin?" Lord Isladar was as quiet as Anduvin had been. "I fear that you search, as always, in vain."

"So you said, in a different age, in a different world."

"Indeed."

"And you were . . . not wrong."

"Indeed."

"Search?" Kiriel asked, although it was hard to speak while he was staring at her.

"Oh, yes."

"For what?"

"The perfect sheath."

The sword burned. The ring burned. Between them, flesh. Mortality. Ashaf had been mortal.

Something was caught in Kiriel's throat: a scream. She struggled to suppress the sound, but it was choking her; she managed, barely, to turn it on its edge, to make a roar of it.

It was a wild, terrible sound.

"Kiriel!"

Kiriel.

She recognized the voice.

"Auralis?"

The sword, she realized, was burning her because she had cut him; she recognized the scent of his blood on the blade.

For a moment she was herself. But it lasted for as long as it took her to realize she didn't know what that meant.

She killed. She killed imps. She killed kin summoned and controlled by lords who had tried unsuccessfully for years to kill her. It occupied the dark, clear evening.

Like shadows, the Swordsmith and the lord who taught her everything she knew about survival trailed behind her, watching in silence. Waiting for her to admit what she already knew, these minor deaths did nothing to feed the sword.

But the sword took the blood she offered; there was no need to wipe the blade clean.

It also seemed to lose weight or substance as the evening drew to its natural close. What had been a struggle to lift became less and less of a burden until, by night's end, it felt as natural as her hands. It was certainly more efficient.

But she had no answer.

"The sword," Meralonne said.

"It is the sword Kiriel has always wielded," Evayne replied.

"It cannot be. I would have recognized the maker's mark."

"From this distance," the woman who had once been his student said, "I see Shadow and the blood of a brave—or stupid—man. If there is a mark—"

"You have always been so powerful it is easy to forget that there are some gifts time and experience will not grant. We must stop her, Evayne."

"She may be able to contain herself: Look."

Auralis bent at the knee as he parried the clumsy overhead blow—a movement too brutish and crude to be identified with Kiriel's regular fighting style. It left her open.

Whatever held her in its grip, whatever possessed her now, she was fighting it. In the only way she knew how. Sadly, there was only one way to take advantage of what she offered. They had at least this much in common: they had learned to fight in a place where death was the most common reward for making a mistake. They did not know how—not safely—to lessen the force of their blows.

And he didn't want to kill her.

But he wasn't willing to die.

Come on, damn you.

"That's not what I meant," Meralonne said.

Dawn.

Ashaf rose with the sun, as much a part of daybreak as the wash of rising color across the northern peaks. No doubt she would be waiting now, rice dust under her fingernails, a fire in the grate, mats laid out on either side of the low table.

She would wear the heavy formless robes that she said kept the cold at bay. Kiriel had never really felt the cold. Proof, if more were needed, that Ashaf was weak.

And the weak died. That was the Law of the Hells.

"Kiriel," Isladar said.

"How will it kill me?" she said, speaking to the Swordsmith.

He frowned. "In my youth, I made a blade for the Queen of the Winter Court. It was the finest weapon I had ever crafted."

Kiriel's confusion was clear, but it was not Anduvin who chose to ease it.

"She was our Lord's greatest rival. We were not always what we are now, Kiriel. Nor was the Winter Queen."

"But if she was—"

"Is."

"—is our greatest enemy, why did he give her his best sword?"

"Do you not understand?" He smiled. "Do not feel your lack of understanding too keenly. Very, very few of the *Kialli* could answer that question."

"Lord Anduvin?"

He did not look at her. His eyes were the color of Winter sky seen through storm's mask. "Understand that a weapon is not a trophy; not a badge of rank, not a sign of power. It is a weapon, no more, no less.

"Among my . . . kin were those who failed to understand this basic truth. They traded in magicks and drew their swords as a matter of quaint ritual. They had their power. My swords were a trifle."

"An exaggeration, Anduvin."

Anduvin's shrug was graceful. He stepped forward. Isladar raised a hand.

"Isladar," Kiriel said quietly, "If I'm old enough to have this sword, I'm old enough to defend myself."

"Your fitness to wield the blade has not yet been established." But he lowered his hand.

Kiriel was staring at Anduvin intently. "The Winter Queen used her sword."

"Oh, yes, little one."

"But she used it against the kin. Against the servants of our Lord."

He laughed. "And who did you wield your sword against this eve? Who will you wield your blade against in the months to follow? No enemy of the Lord's will ever be as much a threat to you as his strongest servants already are. She was—"

"Have a care, Anduvin."

Anduvin nodded.

"Why did you give her the sword?"

"Because she was the most powerful of the Firstborn. And I wanted a sword of mine to be wed to her name and her glory."

Kiriel frowned. What he said made sense . . . but there was more.

He raised an ice-white brow. "You don't believe me?" There was no anger in the question, which was very unusual. The kin made an art of lying, but if accused of its practice, reacted with slightly less anger than they would have had you accused them of weakness.

"I do. But . . . there's something else you haven't said."

"There is much I have not said. I do not regret my decision. I do not regret my offering—or her acceptance."

"You . . . liked her."

"Kiriel, have a care," Isladar said.

But the *Kialli* lord ignored the interruption. "Yes, little one. I owe her a debt," he added, gazing beyond Kiriel into the past he spoke of. For a moment he seemed very human to her. She understood why Lord Isladar allowed him entry to her Tower.

"In her Court I honed my craft." He paused. "Let me explain something briefly. The Southern sword is a single edged blade. It is designed to cut, and the slight curve of the blade maximizes the presentation of the cutting edge. The Winter Queen—as she is most often called—is a single-edged blade. But," he added, his fingers dancing quietly along sword hilt, "I traveled with the Court of the Arianni for two seasons. Winter . . . and Summer."

Kiriel waited for him to continue, but the silence stretched.

"Lord Anduvin?"

"My blades exact their price. But—they cut both ways."

"What do you mean?"

Anduvin did not answer. Isladar did.

"She used his sword."

"But—"

"—as the Summer Queen."

Auralis was bleeding.

She was surprised at the contrast of red and white, because his bronzed skin—as Alexis mockingly called it—had paled into something pasty and unpleasant: the complexion of fear. Without effort, she had pierced armor. She could smell blood and metal.

"Why don't you *run*?"

Her own voice shocked her into silence. She heard it as he must have heard it: as a foreign sound, a mixture of menace and grating roar that hinted at the bestial.

He laughed. Or he tried to; the sound was uneven, a forced expulsion of breath. "I'm damn tired of running."

"You never run," she said, nonplussed. Herself.

The line of his shoulders straightened, as if he heard the change in her voice as clearly as she did.

"Don't—" she cried out.

He *moved*.

The sword moved with him.

She wasn't sure whether or not she had spoken to the sword or the man.

"You are mortal. You are living. You are not yet what you will be."

"I'm not a child."

"So all children say." He smiled, a *Kialli* lord. "Peace. If you raise sword against me, you will die. Do not offer a challenge you do not understand."

She frowned, stung to be corrected in front of the silent Isladar. "And what if I don't want your stupid sword?"

"You have already accepted the responsibility of the blade: You have killed with it. But I think you are too young to make the sword your own."

"What do you mean?"

"The *Kialli* call their blades, little one. They summon their shields. Have you not seen this?"

She nodded.

"Would you not like such a blade? It can never be stolen,

and it can never be broken outside of combat. It is safe until you require it."

"How does it work?"

"The blade becomes a part of you; as much a part of you as heart or spirit. Or will."

She did not say yes. Instead she said, "But you made this blade."

He raised a brow. "Yes, of course."

"And I wouldn't be able to remake it."

"You would change it, in effect; you would alter its substance. But no; the blade is forged as it is forged, and you will destroy it should you attempt to reforge it."

She snorted, then, a young child. "I wouldn't trust anything another person made inside of me."

He laughed. "If you of all *Kialli*—you who sleep while the lord least understood by all watches over you—are not willing to take that risk, so be it. It is strange, and it surprises me. But understand that the sword will never be yours; it will be something you wield, no more. Understand that to own something is to be owned by it."

"You want me to kill Ashaf."

"No, little one. Who you keep as pet is not my concern. But had you chosen to sacrifice what you obviously valued, it would have satisfied the Covenant between yourself and the blade."

She was quiet.

"The blade, I think, will wait. Of course, I may be mistaken—but I believe you will give the blade the minimum that it requires in order to secure your own safety." He bowed. "You are not what I expected. I will watch with interest.

"But do not forget, Kiriel."

She was so tired of being weak. She was so tired of struggling to figure out what right, and worse, wrong, meant in this city.

And she was so angry that tears she could not shed—had never been allowed to shed—because of the risk such a statement posed to her life, could be shed over something as trivial as a flag. Even now, the pain became rage by some alchemy of a spirit her only teacher had not possessed and had not claimed to understand. Alchemy. Purification.

She hated it. She hated it because Ashaf would have hated it; only Ashaf had ever understood how to peel back layers and layers of anger to expose what lay beneath.

But worse—she was afraid. Because the debt she had almost forgotten she owed was coming due and she did not want to pay it.

After Anduvin had left, there was a coolness between Kiriel and Lord Isladar that was unmatched by the voice of the Northern Wastes. She had, of course, failed him, and he tolerated failure only slightly better than the other *Kialli*, the proof being her continued existence.

"You wanted me to kill her."

"I wanted you to be more powerful."

"But by killing Ashaf."

Isladar shrugged.

"I want you to protect her, not destroy her!"

"She is not my concern. She is your weakness."

Kiriel's hands curled and uncurled around the hilt of her very fine sword. There were only three things she loved in the depth and breadth of the Shining City, and she was tempted to challenge one of them *right now* and have it over. Give him to the sword, and protect Ashaf, who could not—it was perfectly clear now, would remain clear forever—protect herself.

But he turned a look upon her that froze her in place. And she discovered, in that remote wilderness—or perhaps rediscovered, as Lord Isladar disparaged her ability to remember anything well—that she did not want to die.

He was ill-pleased.

She forgot her own anger, or rather, her own anger was dwarfed by his, and although her grip on the sword hilt did not change, the reason for it shifted.

"Why are *you* angry at *me*?"

"You do not understand what passed there."

"He gave me a sword."

"Yes."

"And he told me that the sword would kill me if I didn't figure out how to feed it."

Isladar's smile was cold and grim. "Yes. And then he . . . withdrew . . . that threat."

"He didn't. He said—"

"You have never seen him gift a weapon before. You failed, Kiriel, and yet he chose to let you keep the sword. You failed to give him what he requires of the *Kialli*, but he made it as clear as it could be made that his sword—and until you feed the sword, it *is his sword*—will serve you and your interests."

"What do you mean, his sword?"

"He is its maker, Kiriel. Until you forge a bond with the blade that is more intimate than the bond it has with its maker, it belongs to him. It was always . . . a tricky proposition. To ask the Swordsmith for a blade was to put yourself at risk." He turned away from her, his anger guttered by words, as it often was.

"You have been given a gift."

She was still. "*Kialli* gifts are never without cost."

His smile was slight, but it was present. "No, never."

"Not even yours."

"Especially not mine." His smile broadened. "In the end, I am *Kialli*. But you have proved a most interesting charge. Very few of the *Kialli* have chosen to raise a child. And none a God's child."

"What do you think he wants?"

"The Swordsmith? Or your father?"

"The Swordsmith." She was not, had never been, comfortable with the word "father." It drew his attention whenever it was spoken. The shadows took edge, carrying all words—and all thoughts, she was certain—to the most powerful of the gods. She feared him. He was the only creature in the world that she feared.

"I do not know. But you have attracted his interest. He is interested in so very little."

"The sword?"

"It is the most powerful blade he has ever crafted—but it is a wild element now, a thing unknown. There is not another *Kialli* lord who could do what he has done. There are others."

"Others?"

"The Arianni. Among them, there are those who have a skill that is almost the equal of the Swordsmith's. They are not, however, amenable to the request of a mere *Kialli* lord, unless it involves combat and death.

"You have been given a gift from one of the few who truly *remember*."

"Remembers?" She had fallen so easily into the familiar, shedding resentment, shedding anger. She had wanted to be his student—if that was the word for what she had been—forever. Why?

Why?

"Yes. Memory defines things that know life. Everything we are is shaped by everything we were. What do you think the word *Kialli* means?"

"Lord?"

He laughed. "Not that, Kiriel. Never that." He bowed his head a moment in the direction of her father's Tower. Knelt into the flagstones, as if penitent. It was some moments before he rose, and when he did, the winds were quiet.

"No. It is—it was—our word for the memory that scars." He smiled. She had learned not to trust that smile, but she had never learned to fear it. "What did you have for breakfast last week?"

"Last week when?"

"All of it. Any day."

She was silent. After a moment, she said, "Sianti." It was a Southern mix of brown rice and herbs, a warm, thick gruel that sustained the men and women who toiled in the fields.

"You forget; we ate with the Court in the morning. An intelligent guess. But . . ."

She waited.

"That is not *Kiallinan*."

"What about the day you brought me Falloran?"

"No, although that was significant." He nodded gravely, offering the approval she craved. "You learn quickly in almost all things. Let us forget Ashaf for now, Kiriel. I will not ask you to take her life again; that decision has been made, and it is behind us. Do you understand?"

She had nodded. She had *smiled.*

"*Kiallinan* is neither the trivial nor the significant memory. These memories—of food or the beginning of friendship—are not memories of passion. They do not burn. They cannot scar. They cannot move you to acts of great destruction.

"But I promise, Kiriel, that you will one day understand *Kiallinan*. And on that day you will better understand the kin. Because you will have to choose."

"Choose?"

"Whether or not you have the strength and the will to remember."

"Why will it take strength? You remember or you don't."

He laughed. He laughed and she had been both wise enough to take a step back, and wise enough not to run. "Ask them, Kiriel. But only when you are powerful enough to survive their greatest wrath."

"Ask?"

"The *Kialli*."

"And if I asked you?"

"What did I give as a condition?" he responded, but gently, so gently there was no threat in the words. She should have known then.

Instead, she had nodded.

She *screamed*.

She forced her blade to strike stone, scarring the earth as the road beneath her feet shattered.

She understood *Kiallinan* now in a way that words defied; she could not speak of it. She could not bear to be trapped by it. It was, she thought, what mortals suffer who have at last chosen to reside in the care of demons, in the Dominion of her father.

Ashaf was dead.

And Isladar—Isladar—

She had left herself open a moment in rage and pain; the memories, had they struck her this way in the Court, would have been certain death.

Auralis struck her again, and again, it was with the wide flat of solid steel.

The only other person who had ever deliberately struck her with the flat of his blade was Lord Isladar.

But Isladar had had the power to destroy her; he had chosen—had *condescended*—not to display it. Auralis had nothing. Nothing at all.

But he stayed, in the street of this terrible, mortal city,

this crowded, hot, smelly place, bleeding from a dozen different wounds, holding his hand. Turning his blade.

"Why won't you fight me?" she said, or thought she said.

"Kiriel," he answered. "Kiriel, *come back*. Stop this. We don't have much time."

"Why don't you *fight*?"

He stopped for a minute. Then, to her surprise, he smiled. "Same reason I won't sleep with you."

And for a minute—just a minute—the shadows were still.

"Evayne, there *is* a risk."

"Yes, I know."

"Do you? Your knowledge of the Arianni was always superficial."

"It was—when I was your student. I learned much in your absence."

They watched Kiriel stiffen.

"She will kill him," Meralonne said softly. "Shall we intervene?"

"Not yet."

She put her blade up.

"Do you want to?"

"Kill you?" His frame rose and fell; hair had fallen into his eyes, and he brushed it aside with the back of his hand, taking care to never once obscure his line of sight. He didn't trust her. And yet he stayed.

"Sleep with me."

"I think we had that discussion already."

"I think you had it." She shrugged. "But if it's the same . . . all right. Do you want to?"

"To kill you?"

"To kill me."

"No. If you think I fight the impulse to kill when it's not a matter of my life or death, you haven't known me long enough. But you will."

"Why are you doing this?"

"Don't know. Don't know why *you're* doing this either. But—to me it's just another life-and-death battle, and in the end you're an Osprey."

"There are *no more* Ospreys," she said. Deliberate now, watching the pain arc like fire through the shadows that surrounded him. Seeing it, truly, viscerally, for the first time in far, far too long.

It left a bitter taste in her mouth.

It had never done that before.

He stiffened. Straightened out to his full height, which even among the *Kialli* would have been significant. "There's no more colors," he said. "No flag. But the Ospreys are still the Ospreys as long as Duarte leads us. And while he leads us, while we exist, you're one of us. I don't know what battle you're fighting. And I know damn well that Alexis or Fiara wouldn't understand it. But if I walk away, we lose you."

"You walk away," she said, the grip on the sword shifting, "and you save yourself. And maybe," she added, as the blade came up in a way that sent light in a spray across the buildings and the shattered ground, "you'll leave me something to come back to."

The shadows came back.

He didn't understand what had parted them. But he did understand—because only a fool would have missed it—that she was gone again. And the Kiriel that remained wasn't even the killer that had been introduced to the Ospreys by a reluctant Verrus; she was worse.

She would kill him.

He turned his sword from flat to edge.

And then he smiled. Laughed.

The sound brought her back. Because it was his reckless laugh. It was the laugh he used when he tried to get himself killed; when he tried—because he was *stupid*—to take a kill from her. They were partners within the Ospreys, but they were also fiercely competitive when it came to the actual kill.

The sword froze.

Froze above her head, casting its slender shadow, even among the unnatural shadows that she herself had cast, and was casting.

But she saw no blade's outline against the ground that had broken before the sword's edge.

She recognized the profile of a slender, tall, *Kialli* lord. And she spoke his name.

"*Anduvin.*"

The shadow turned. The sword spoke.

"Kiriel."

"Now," Evayne said quietly.

"Now?"

"The young man, the one who has been fighting a half-goddess with the flat of an admittedly fine sword."

"He's not young, Evayne. You are almost at the height of your power, but so, too, is he."

She frowned. "Split hairs if it satisfies you. He has served his purpose. She has—inasmuch as she can—won the battle. Leave him here now, and she will lose the war."

"I have a feeling that he's not going to want to leave."

"No."

He swore in one of the several long dead languages he had spent a lifetime studying. Then he paused. "And why are you here, Evayne?"

"For the same reason you are, Illaraphaniel. Look: he comes."

"He?" And then he was utterly silent; completely still. Not even wind moved a single strand of his ivory hair.

"Do you recognize him?" she asked softly, because she looked to the man who stood between the rise of buildings in the narrow streets as if they were a forested wilderness, and not at the man who had once been her master in the Order of Knowledge.

"The Swordsmith," he replied, his voice flat. "I do not know what you have planned here, Evayne, but if it involves the Smith, it is poor planning."

"Perhaps. But our time is now, Meralonne. Will you stand in the shadows?" She gestured, and the hood that framed her face fell from it in folds; she was, in her master's estimation, almost as old as she had ever been when she had come to him. But she had none of the frailty of Sigurne about her; nor, he was certain, would she ever.

Without a word, he followed her into the street.

He bowed.

To her.

She snarled.

He rose at once from the gesture that obviously displeased her, his face devoid of something as common as expression. "Perhaps I misunderstand," he said, voice smooth as glass, but as opaque as the steel he had worked for her at Isladar's request.

"Misunderstand?"

"Is it not for fealty that you accepted the Lord's gift? Was it not to enforce the obedience of the *Kialli* lords that you accepted your title?"

"Do not," she said coldly.

"Do not?"

"Do not speak of that here. I am not in the Hells. It is *not* my title."

"You are not, indeed, in the Hells. And a number of the lesser kin have been dispatched to seek you."

"You are not one of them."

"I? No. I have the advantage of always knowing, of always having known, where you reside."

She started to speak; stopped. Looked down at the blade in her hand.

"Indeed," he said, again softly. "I do not, however, serve another lord, and it did not suit my interests to reveal that information."

"Does he know?"

"Lord Isladar?"

She swallowed.

His smile was infinitely cruel. "Of course."

"Did he send you?"

A very real ice in the flash of gray eyes. "I am not his keep, to be sent at his whim."

"You came at your own?"

"The sword," he said coldly. "I came because the owner of the sword has changed, and not with my permission. I travel . . . less quickly than Lord Isladar. It has taken me time to arrive here, in safety."

She froze, as cool in stance as he was in expression. The terrible heat of the urge to kill, the *need* to kill, dissipated a moment; her hand was no longer on fire. For the first time since she had fled Kalakar, she was not in pain.

"Do you want it back?"

"That is not the way it works, youngling, and you knew that when you accepted the blade."

"Maybe." She advanced a step. "But we could test it,

now. I was a child. I couldn't offer you a challenge I had any hope of winning."

He laughed, not unkindly. "You are *still* a child. You cannot offer me such a challenge. I am bound to you through the blade. I know how you fight. It would be no contest."

"You said I was not the same."

He frowned. "I see why Lord Isladar valued you as a student. You are quick. Yes, you are not what you were; the blade knows. And you have killed so very little the steel has grown restless."

"And that's brought you here? These are not your lands."

"Yes," he replied, ignoring the second half of her comment. "That is what drew me here."

He turned, drawing her attention to where Auralis stood. "In the Hells, there were always deaths. There was always combat. Every creature with any memory at all was intent on your destruction. You could not rest except under Lord Isladar's care—and of that, I will not speak further. Here, you live fettered by mortal law and mortal command. I would not have thought it possible. I do not understand it now.

"But I understand this: The Covenant that you made in ignorance is binding. The blade needs what you have ceased to offer it, and you know this.

"You fight him; but you fight the blade as well. It has tasted his blood; finish him. Let the sword have what it desires."

"And that will end it?"

He favored her with an intent stare. And silence.

But she pressed him. "If I give you now what I refused you then, will the sword be mine? Will all connection between us be severed?"

His voice was surprisingly gentle when he replied; it put her on her guard instantly. "You did not refuse me, Kiriel. You refused the sword. Ultimately, it is the sword that must be satiated."

He gestured.

Auralis rose six inches off the ground, cursing roundly as he struggled against a force he could not see. Kiriel could; clearly. She lifted her blade to sever the power from the hand that controlled it.

And the blade swerved in her hand, and her hand burned, and Auralis grunted.

But again, the wound she caused was not substantial. Her arms and shoulders ached with the effort of that slight a cut; she looked up and she met Auralis' eyes. His face was almost never expressionless, certainly not when he was fighting, and only barely when he was gambling—which was his word for losing money, according to Alexis. But it was expressionless now. No anger there. No resignation.

But she knew that he knew he was going to die.

She cried out in Torra. In Torra, her mother tongue, if she could be said to have one. It was prayer and plea and curse in a language formed in a land whose gods were at best indifferent.

But it was said in the North, where the gods were something else.

She saw the orange light fade into summer gold; saw shadow struggle against it and fail; saw Auralis drop to the ground, grunt, and fall to one knee. He lurched to his feet, swaying there a moment before he planted himself firmly against the edges of the crater she had made in the road. They were going to pay for this later, if they survived. Perhaps they would pay for it now. It didn't matter. The Empire had no concept of suffering.

She wanted to approach Auralis; to ascertain that he was all right. But she knew that she couldn't. She couldn't go near him.

"Hello, Kiriel."

That voice. She almost forgot Auralis as she turned to look at the woman in midnight blue. "You."

"I know not who you are," Anduvin said coolly. "But clearly, Lady, you are a mortal force. Therefore, let me tell you that your interference here will likely cost the girl her life."

"In the old days," Meralonne APhaniel said, speaking for the first time since his spell had forced the release of the Osprey whom Kiriel clearly, and inexplicably, valued, "that would have been certain.

"But this blade was not forged when you had ties—legitimate ties—with this world."

The Swordsmith lost the steel of his expression to winter ice, and to something too intense to be simple cold. "*You.*"

"Destiny works in strange ways," Meralonne replied. "But you are here, and I am here. And between us, one god-born child and one bleeding mortal."

"Thank you, APhaniel," Evayne said wryly. It passed unnoticed.

Kiriel lifted a hand. The hand that burned. "Hold. Evayne. APhaniel. Hold. I am in your debt. Take Auralis away. Take him anywhere safe."

"Kiriel—"

"*Please.*"

Evayne lifted a hand. Let it fall. Bowed. "As you ask." She turned to the man.

He grimaced, his expression twisted with recognition. "And if I ask you to leave me be?"

Her smile was bitter. "I am always caught between two voices, two powers. At another time, Auralis AKalakar, I might choose to listen to yours."

"You'll pardon me if I pray to whatever joke of a god governs my life that there never be another time."

"Gods don't govern mortal lives. But pray, if you like. It's never done me any good."

He spit.

She said nothing, but raised both hands as Kiriel's blade also rose, moving in time with her movement, a silent harmony; a quick one. Orange fire fell upon him like a warm, summer rain. He didn't even bother to flinch. It didn't burn.

He did flinch when the blade struck.

And then he laughed.

For the first time in his life, he saw surprise, open surprise, in the widening of her eyes, the lifting of her brows. Her hood rose at once, to protect her expression, but the naked shock stayed with him.

The mage, motionless until her failure, stepped forward. "It is not defense," he said calmly, "that you require. It is Summer, Evayne."

And he, too, cast.

The Swordsmith smiled.

"You will have as much success," he said. "I traveled with the Queen in both of her seasons."

"There are more than two seasons," Meralonne said quietly. "We know well the ways of Summer and Winter, but the mortals are creatures of the spring and fall. They may surprise you. But if they don't," the mage shrugged. "There are other ways.

"Kiriel di'Ashaf." Meralonne APhaniel turned to her, bowing. "Is there anything else you wish to say to the AKalakar?"

"Yes."

"And that?"

"Why?"

The bleeding man said nothing.

"Auralis, why? Why are you doing this? Why didn't you run?"

"They'll call the magi," he said. "They'll kill you."

"But I—"

"You're either a demon or a rogue mage. Ask him," he added, pointing to Meralonne with a toss of the head, his gaze never leaving her face—but never meeting her eyes.

"And does it matter?"

"Kiriel, this is not the place."

"I don't know if there will be another place."

"Then I'm not leaving."

She laughed. Her laugh was not quite as sharp as her blade. "You've never been very smart. But—you've always been the worst of the Ospreys. I saw it in you the first day I met you; the shadows are cold and hard. Alexis, Duarte, Fiara—the others are different. You're like—you're very like—the lords of the South, the men of the Court."

He shrugged. "Can't argue that. Can't see it."

"Why did you stay?"

"Too stupid to run."

"Auralis—" She grimaced. Smoke, black and greasy, rose in a fine plume from her hand. The sword rose with it.

"You don't understand," he said quietly, as he stared at the blade through a sheet of twined orange and gold. "You never have. I don't give a shit if I die. I've got nothing to lose."

And before she could speak or strike again, he was gone. So was Meralonne APhaniel.

"Very clever," Anduvin said, looking at the woman in robes, speaking to the woman with the sword. "But the blade will find him if you so choose."

"I don't."

"But you do, little one. You don't want to die. You are fighting yourself in this. You are *only* fighting yourself. And you are losing. You are your father's child: survival is everything, and the only certainty of survival is rulership, absolute authority. Absolute power."

"I am more than that."

"You are not."

"I *am.*"

"You are less; you are mortal. You will know age—and death."

She was silent for a while, struggling; she had never been good with words when they hadn't been used instinctively to wound.

It was Evayne who came to her rescue. "What knows age and death knows change, Swordsmith. What knows change will always retain the ability to surprise, to shock, even to delight something as jaded as a *Kialli* lord."

He was silent as he studied Kiriel.

And then he bowed, as he had done when he had first appeared. "Your . . . companion . . . has acute vision. There is much about you that is of interest. And it has become more interesting in such a short, short time. I did not expect you to flee the Shining City. The Lord was . . . angry."

Kiriel's sword hand was shaking. The sheen of the blade reflected no light.

"I did not expect you to be here, of all places, in the stronghold of the Lord's enemies. I did, however, find some amusement in your frustration—and subsequent humiliation—of Etridian.

"However, I do not lie. I had hoped for a different resolution to the problem I posed you when I gifted you with this blade. Take that mortal's life, and it will suffice, and you will own the sword; you will be ruler, and not ruled.

"It is not what I desired."

"And if I don't?"

"You ask me that? The blade has a voice, Kiriel, even if you cannot hear it. It has a will that simple steel should not have been able to contain. I had not the skill to forge such a weapon before the Sundering. No Swordsmith did. There are Makers who might have created such a . . . thing . . . by summoning and by trapping one of the kin within its casing—but a sword of that nature would never be accepted as a true weapon by anyone of rank or power.

"I had the skill to exact a price for the blade; no more. But it was a bitter price."

"But you—"

"I understand the nature of the sword; I crafted it. I saw, in you, in the sword, in the single evening in which you strove to conquer it—a futile gesture—a symbiosis. You evaded the choice that had been laid before you; it piqued my curiosity. And more." He shook his head. "I will not speak of that.

"In the Shining City, you killed. And you killed. You had no choice. There is a beauty that comes with simplicity; the rules were simple. Were you there now, they would be simple still. Regardless, you fed the blade; the blade was satisfied. Had I known that Lord Isladar would kill the old woman—"

She swung the sword that hung in midair in the direction of his words. It was not an accident.

"I mean no challenge," he said softly.

She said nothing at all, and the silence was eloquent.

He watched her carefully for a time before speaking, and when he did, he said simply, "The Lord was displeased by your departure."

She nodded.

"I would not have known to look for you here, had you not carried the sword. But I know where the sword is, Kiriel. Until you bind it with your own offering, some part of it is mine. I had hoped for a different resolution," he added again. "But who would have imagined that you, of all the god-born, would end up in the only remaining mortal City our Lord has cause to fear? Who could have foreseen that you would walk its streets—its busy, crowded streets, where every moving creature's soul has a color and a texture just waiting to be explored—and abide by its *laws* and its *rules*?

"You have not killed. You *must* kill."

"I've killed demons."

"Three," he said quietly, "over too long a time."

"And how do I know you're telling me the truth?"

He raised a pale brow, but his expression did not otherwise change.

"How do you ever know a *Kialli* lord speaks truth?"

"I don't."

"Indeed. But nor do we, without blood-binding, and there are few whose words are worth listening to who can be so bound."

"How will I die?"

His brows rose. After a moment he said, "You are truly surprising. How? I do not know. I have never seen it happen in all of the time I have crafted such swords."

"Never?"

"Think of who they were made for." He paused. "You are not in any way what you seemed to be while you occupied a Tower in the Shining City. But I have my own reasons for wishing this resolved in a fashion that does not end with your death."

"Can you remove the compulsion?"

"No. It is . . . not as simple as that."

"Then," the god-born girl said, hands shaking with the effort of holding the blade still, "Not even you survived the transition to, and from, the Hells intact."

She heard two things simultaneously: Evayne's sharp intake of breath, and Lord Anduvin's utter silence. He became a thing of ice; the mountains she had seen from her windows every morning were not as cold and still as this. But he chose to break that stillness with a smile.

She was well-trained; she did not take a step back. But it was a near thing.

"If you were *Kialli*, child," he said quietly, "I would kill you for that."

"Why? Because it's true?"

"No," he replied. He lifted his hand, palm out, and she saw for the second time, the Swordsmith's blade as it coalesced out of air at his whim. "Because it is an attack, a challenge, and there *is* only one answer to such a challenge between the kin."

"I was raised among the *Kialli*," she said coldly. "I'm not a human child; I know what I've chosen to do."

"The fact that you could be raised at all—"

"And I understand *Kiallinan*," she added, and her hands shook for the first time. "I understand it all."

His brows, pale and perfect, rose. And fell. He bowed his head a moment. "Your master," he said quietly, "gave you a gift that you cannot comprehend, if you both understand that at his hands, and live; he has taken a risk that no other among us would have taken. Not even I."

His eyes narrowed. "Do you think to offer the blade my life in the stead of the mortal's?"

"Yes."

He laughed. It was a lovely, wild sound, arresting because it was so powerful, so vibrant. So unlike the *Kialli.* "Well then, why not? Why *not*?" He lifted his left hand, and she saw, for the first time, his shield. It was unlike any shield she had ever seen; it ran the length of his body from knee to shoulder, and spanned his width, although he was slender. It shone brightly with reflected light, and the sun traced the contours of worked metal that formed the head of . . . a dragon.

The dragon *roared.*

Had she been another person, that roar would have cost her her life. But she had been trained by Lord Isladar; every possible use of illusion, every inverted use of magic, every lie—*every lie*—that could possibly be used against her had been so used. Whether or not the dragon was real, contained by the Smith's craft, or illusion, was immaterial.

This was a combat.

This was something she understood.

Clarity.

Death.

He waited for her; she waited for him. They stood in the stillness of the summer heat a long time. Evayne's shadow fell between them, and it grew taller as the minutes passed.

"You offered the challenge," he said, a gentle rebuke. "Will you wait upon my attack?"

"I offered the challenge," she replied, "to a lord, not mere kin. I don't know what you call me, any of you, but I am no *Kialli* lord."

He raised a brow. "You are different from what I expected. You have held your own against the machinations of the Lord's Fist; I expected you to be a more easily controlled weapon. But you are so very mortal."

She swallowed air. "And you are so very immortal. But

immortal and eternal aren't the same: you die, just the way any mortal does on failing in combat."

"Is this a challenge, Kiriel? Or is this a challenge of the sword?"

"I don't care which. The sword is my weapon; I'll use it."

"But you *do* care, little one." A different voice. A voice from above.

They both turned, slowly, unwilling to let their opponent out of the field of their vision, but equally unwilling to ignore the threat from the air.

Lord Isladar of the *Kialli* stood on the edge of the closest building, looking down.

CHAPTER SEVEN

"You!"

"Kiriel," Evayne snapped. "Remember his teachings; they have value, even if he no longer does. *Remember* them!"

"I remember *everything*."

"Do not let anger guide you, then."

She turned her back on Evayne. On the woman who had taken her away from the mountains that had been her only home; had brought her here; had given her to the Ospreys. Had given her the treacherous ring that singed her hand.

"Lord Anduvin," Lord Isladar said, bowing. "I must respectfully request that you decline the challenge that she has not—quite—put into foolish words."

Lord Anduvin lifted his blade; he held it, edge on side, before his face. The *Kialli* ready stance. "And can you make her kill what you could not force her to kill when the sword was first gifted?"

"Hardly."

"She has not offered challenge idly."

"No. So I understand from my tenure upon the rooftop." He took a step from the edge of the short half wall upon which he'd been standing and hovered a moment in the air before descending.

Kiriel was paralyzed as she watched him land.

Paralyzed as she watched him do what he had never done for her: he summoned his blade. She had wondered, every time he took up wooden sword, or later, simple metal, if he truly had one; he had not chosen to reveal it where she could experience the momentary wonder of a sword that came at call, like a servant, like a blood-bound demon. He had relied instead on magic, on magery, on deception and threat.

She had seen him fight with sword once.

To save *her*.

Bitter, bitter truth.

Her eyes stung, and she *hated* it. Hated him. Hated the memory of Ashaf that was tainted in all ways by the memory of Isladar.

The screaming . . .

She cried out suddenly, her breath an enemy's advantage, her viscera clenching in a terrible, inexplicable pain. She *would not* think about that. That *could not* be her final memory.

And Lord Isladar of the *Kialli* looked upon her as if he could—as he had always done—use every nuance of her expression to invade the privacy of her thoughts.

"You understand only the seeds of *Kiallinan*, Kiriel. You have not decided to accept what it has become for the *Kialli*."

"What is there to accept?" she shouted—and was ashamed of the lack of control that stripped her voice of ice and quiet.

"She's dead," he said quietly.

"I know that!"

"I killed her. I enjoyed it."

She raised the sword, twisting away from the Swordsmith as if Isladar had pulled strings. She lunged at the lord who had taught her everything she knew, wild now; the roar that broke the silence of the city was a dragon's roar, a sound that she should never have been able to make.

She *had* to stop him. She had to make him stop.

He evaded her thrust, stepping fluidly to the side and parrying; she had left her side open, and he cut her as momentum forced her to travel past.

He cut her, but he did not kill her, and he could have.

And it wouldn't have mattered. Just for this one second, just for this moment, it was not the sword's need that drove her; not the shadow's need. It was the need of the child who had lost an old woman's lap—and everything that lap represented—and was fighting in a frenzy to preserve what remained of that comfort: memory.

But memory is not inviolable.

She staggered at the force of the blow. Turned, placing her feet more carefully upon the road; shattered stone surrounded the pit she had made with her sword, and on either side of it, they stood: master and student.

Some of the wildness left her with her blood. Like a slap in the face, the wound brought a moment's clarity. She didn't bother to look at her side; she knew it was bleeding.

"You do not need to face him," Evayne said.

She would have been furious at the interruption once. But she answered, without looking away from her opponent. "I do."

"You don't, Kiriel."

"If for no other reason than that the sword needs to be fed, I do."

"Killing him will change nothing."

Kiriel laughed. It was an ugly sound, and she cursed herself silently the moment it left her. She couldn't contain it. She was all things ugly. That was her truth. "You understand nothing," she snarled. "Nothing at all."

"Kiriel, you are what you are. You will *always* be darkness born. You will always feel other people's pain in a way that dwarfs what the kin themselves are capable of feeling. It's—"

The words broke as Isladar gestured; the ground broke as well, as the earth around Evayne a'Nolan swallowed her whole.

Rock flew; earth flew; the air was a haze of painful, flying things. Kiriel summoned shadow, and the shadow failed to answer; she ducked to ground, protecting her face from the worst of the debris with her mailed arms. Her hand was cool. The ring was dormant.

They're never going to let us get away with this, Kiriel thought, and realized that the thought itself made no sense.

"I will brook no interruptions," Lord Isladar said, as the winds died. "Rise, Kiriel."

She had been his only student. When he commanded her, she rose, pushing herself from the earth with the flat of one palm, while the other gripped—had never let go of—the sword. Against the hand splayed across the ground, a single band caught the light. A ring.

A ring.

"You should have paid the sword's price when you were given the opportunity," Isladar said gravely.

Said it in a tone of voice with which she was intimately

familiar. She had failed him; she had paid. He had always made certain that she understood the high price for failure, while making certain that she survived it.

She had refused Ashaf a near painless death.

A death far kinder than the one she had met.

"You are not my match, Kiriel."

She said nothing.

But she raised the sword. "You have a blade Lord Anduvin crafted before the Sundering. I have the only blade he crafted after it.

"You said the *Kialli* are made by *Kiallinan*. That might make my sword stronger. It might make it weaker."

"The strength of the sword," he replied softly, "is defined by the one who wields it. No more, no less. You offered a challenge."

Her hands were shaking. She hated that they shook. But she stared across a pit that had been shorn of detritus by the force and howl of wind, and her lips formed the word *why*, but her voice had lost all strength to utter it.

Perhaps because it would have sounded too much like a plea, and he had never been particularly gentle with anything that sounded like weakness.

"You are not going to kill me, Kiriel," he said quietly. "But you have taken a step away; you have asserted an independence that has yet to be . . . tested."

He gestured.

She lifted a hand to ward his spell, and fire struck her, lambent in its warmth. His expression, if it were possible, became even icier in its disapproval.

It underwent an infinitesimal thaw as the ring again caught light. "What is that that you wear, Kiriel?"

"A ring."

"I see . . . I suggest you remove it before we begin."

She wondered, then, if he knew how trapped, how diminished, she was by the ring's presence. True to his teachings, she did not choose to enlighten him.

When he struck, he was faster than she had ever seen him; she was slower than she had been since he had first begun to teach her.

The edge of the blade cut four of her fingers to the bone; the ring was unscathed, although the sound of the metals meeting—sword and ring—echoed unnaturally.

She lifted her blade. The anger she had felt, the anger he had evoked—it had drained with the blood of the two wounds. She fell into a stance that he had taught her, one of many; she felt the heat of the summer sun across her dark hair, her pale skin—although the sun was waning, had waned, and provided heat only by its echo; felt the weight of his gaze, felt the tendrils of her father's legacy in the darkness that pooled at her feet.

She felt—almost—at home.

No.

She had no home with Isladar. He had destroyed it.

How? An insistent and ugly voice asked. *By killing a weak old woman? Haven't you done the same?*

No.

By taking the pleasure that comes only from pain?

No!

She stood in the street, and the sword began to burn her hand with a darkness that had always been a part of the blade—and a fire that had *never* been. The ring no longer reflected the sun's light; it *was* light.

"Interesting," Isladar said. Just that. His own blade, his own perfect, slightly curved blade, was rimmed in red and orange, white and pale blue; the subtle dance of heat.

"You really don't understand, do you?"

Silence.

"She had so tainted you, Kiriel, that you were not the child your father desired. You were not even the equal of the *Kialli* lords, although I grant you that when he chose to elevate you, he gave you the gifts you required to become almost that." He stepped into the shallow crater, walking toward her, his gaze unwavering, his eyes reflecting fire.

She waited.

"You did not understand what made your enemies; you failed to even guess what motivates them now. I have endeavored—as I have always done—to teach you to better understand the *Kialli*. You now have the memory, Kiriel, the memory that burns. You live in the Hells."

Before she could reply, he stepped swiftly into a stroke that would have easily bisected her sword arm at the shoulder had she not leaped and rolled; the blade she held clanged a moment against the ground, grating as if straining to return, as if flight—even this dodging of death—was anathema.

Feed the blade, Kiriel, a voice said. *Feed it, and you will own the sword.*

She rose.

"But even though you have the memory, you haven't the *will*. You do not accept that memory for the truth that it is, however bitter. You do not plan, you do not design, you do not *live for* a way to put that memory to rest. You rage like the child you once were.

"But there is no one now, Kiriel, who will pick you up. No one who will either comfort or discipline you. You will stand, or you will die, on your own. You will always be alone."

She shook. Standing, both feet placed slightly apart, knees bent, the pain was hideous.

"Have you not sworn to kill me?"

She said nothing.

He took a step toward her again, his sword in flames, his eyes a color that she had never seen. The shadow he cast against the ground did not mirror his action; it was no artifact of sun and light.

"What do you think we were faced with, Kiriel? We *ruled* the lands we owned at the side of our chosen Lord. We spoke to the elements, and the elements answered; we built cities, created art that you cannot dream of now in these impoverished, gray times.

"You have seen the Hells from a distance, but you are only beginning to understand some part of what it means to reside there. And you have never had what we had when we dwelled here.

"What do you think has made the *Kialli* what we are? Why did we not all become the worthless, the stupid, the merely ugly and hungry, as did most of our kin?"

Silence; she wanted to speak, and at the same time, she wanted never to speak again.

"Memory, Kiriel. *Kiallinan*.

"You can turn your back on the memory now, as you have struggled to do—as you have *succeeded* in doing, to my great surprise. I would have thought the old woman meant more to you. Or you can become something more."

Burning. The flames and the shadows had somehow descended; they were devouring her whole, from the inside. And she wanted them to. She wanted them to finish.

She staggered.

"How do you think the imps became imps, too stupid and weak to lift talon or claw? How do you think the kin became kin, no matter how physically strong their eventual form? They are the shadows of what they were when they walked this world in Glory—and they could have been *more*."

She drew breath. Salty, humid air filled her lungs. She hated it. She longed for the crisp, clean comfort of ice and clarity. She missed her home.

She had missed it, in intervals, when she chose not to think of what it had become; chose to ignore why she had fled.

"But they failed to *remember*. They failed to hold on to the memory of what they had, and what they were. Why?" For just a moment, scorn touched his expression, sharpened his voice—Isladar, who had always been so neutral. "Because it *hurt* them to remember. Because it was *easier* to forget; to become diminished; to fulfill their role in the Hells. Easier to trade pain for pleasure; to trade duty for duty.

"Do you think an existence like yours can ever be easy? You were born to cause pain, Kiriel; it is the essence of your nature: mortality and darkness; loss and death.

"And you will become less than the least of the kin if you choose their path." He stopped speaking a moment. Closed his eyes. "You have what you require, now. You must make the correct choice."

She could hear the screaming.

She hadn't heard the screaming since the ring had taken away the power that had protected her in the Hells, and for the first time, she was truly grateful for the presence of the ring. Frightened at the sudden lack of power on its part.

She could hear it all. She had thought she would recognize that voice in any circumstance. She had been wrong. Ashaf.

Ashaf.

"The memory is painful in two ways. Because of the loss," he said, measuring each word, his voice uninflected, his expression devoid of anything resembling triumph or enjoyment, "and because of what it tells you about yourself.

"Accept both. You *cannot* flee from your own truths."

She cried out in anger. She raised the sword. She started toward him, walking in time with his measured step, but with less grace and more raw force.

"And what truths does a *Kialli* lord know," a familiar voice said, and Kiriel looked up. Where Isladar had stood on the rooftop, there now stood a woman in robes the color of a clear, moonlit midnight. "There is no truth that is absolute. Not even yours. There are goals, yes—but memory is a funny thing. Any ten people can view the same battle; they can watch events unfold around them without taking their eyes from whatever it is that occurs. But question them later, and they will give you ten different versions of the fight; they have watched, but selectively, and their memory has hoarded and embellished those details of import."

Without looking up, Isladar said coldly, "I tire of you. I am not . . . accustomed to interruption."

"I am," Evayne a'Nolan replied, with the strangest of smiles. "Kiriel, death is death; you cannot change what has happened. But—in the South of Ashaf's birth, there is a saying. *Only the living can give meaning to death.*"

"What do you mean?"

"If you accept as the sole truth all that Lord Isladar has said, you accept his vision of meaning. But if Ashaf were alive now, if she stood at my side, she would tell you a different story; she would ask you for a different ending to the story that your birth began."

Isladar's eyes were completely black as he lifted his head and turned toward the woman on the rooftop. He gestured.

She gestured. Fire and light met in the emptiness between them. When it cleared, Evayne was gone.

But Kiriel had no sense whatever that she was dead.

Nor did Isladar. His frown lingered as he faced her once again. "Do you know that woman?"

She said nothing.

"I see that you do. She is . . . dangerous."

Kiriel surprised them both by laughing; the laugh was bitter. "She is the only person I've ever met who says less and knows more than you."

He raised a brow. "I . . . see."

Kiriel lifted the sword—not her sword—with effort; it was heavier now than it had been. But the pain was different. The sun was almost gone from the sky; the streets were dark. Had they been fighting so very long?

"The sword is burning you, Kiriel. The sword is killing you. You were safe while you dwelled within the Shining City . . . but I do not think you will find a home there until you choose to become *Kialli*, with all that implies."

"I am not *Kialli*," Kiriel said, fighting to maintain control of her voice. "I was meant to be more than that."

He smiled for the first time. "Perhaps you were. But if you cannot even attain *that*, you will never be more. And, little one—"

"Don't call me that!"

"—if you cannot feed the sword, then all suffering, all loss, means nothing."

"Don't talk to me! Don't *teach* me anything else! I'm not your student anymore, I'll *never* be your student again!"

He looked at her, his expression remote. "You will never," he told her quietly—so quietly, she should not have heard him—"be anything else.

"And some lessons are more urgent than others. Come, Kiriel. Let us finish this."

He moved.

She moved.

She barely saw him coming, but she felt again the edge of his blade. She had been struck by *Kialli* blades before. But never his. Never.

Isladar was the only person who had ever deliberately struck her with the flat of his blade. No, the only other person.

He did not choose the flat now.

She leaped up, to avoid the next strike, and found that she was inconveniently bound by gravity, by the city, by the mortality that the ring had conferred upon her with such force. She struck broken rock, stumbling into the center of the pit.

On the periphery of her vision, Lord Isladar circled. She tried to summon shadow; felt her hand burn; saw light where shadow should have been. She had always thought light beautiful.

But the darkness was beautiful as well, and he embodied it. He bowed; changed stance; raised sword. She realized that, although he had not asked it, and she had not granted it, he was obeying the rules of the Challenge of the Sword.

Ashaf, she thought. *Forgive me.*

She couldn't see. For a moment, she couldn't see.

He struck, of course. Circling, breaking circle, moving in as if flight were denied to only one of them.

It was. He wounded her.

He struck to wound, as if he were playing a game; as if she had graduated from the flat of his blade to the edge of it, but had not yet crossed the divide between that edge and death.

Kiriel, she heard him say, from the remove of a memory that defined terror and death, *you are safe. I will protect you.*

She felt the ghost of his arms, the tip of his chin grazing the top of her hair; she felt that child's terror subside as she sank into those arms. He was *Kialli*; his lap and his arms did not have the warmth or the pliancy of Ashaf's.

But he had done what Ashaf would have failed to do had she been present: he had saved her life.

It struck her with a peculiar, a terrible, pain: memory. She was now bleeding from a dozen wounds. He had failed to say a single word; to punctuate his blows—as he had often done—with the lesson that he intended her to learn.

The sword was burning her; the ring was burning her, and the pain that had come from either of these quarters for the entire eternity of the afternoon was nothing compared to the memories.

I will protect you, Kiriel.

But you told me, she had said, quiet, shaking, *never to trust you.*

Yes.

Can I trust you?

She could not see his face; she found the comfort of his arms too unique an experience to want to withdraw just to look at an expression that almost never changed anyway.

No.

But why not?

Silence. And then, *Because I am Kialli. You forget that, Kiriel. You forget too much.*

But you just said you would protect me.

Yes, but that act has nothing to do with trust.

And yet. She felt safe. She felt safe, and that had been enough. . . .

She roared now.

She roared; the pain was terrible. But she understood why the kin were kin. Was that the point? Was that truly the reason he had killed Ashaf? To make her understand what a terrible thing a memory could be?

When he circled again, her pain had become a frenzied anger; she used it; she parried. The force of the parry drove him back; forced him to acknowledge gravity for a moment.

He spoke. "Better."

He circled.

And it occurred to her, as she watched the changing light and shadow of that movement, that the pit made in stone from the force of the sword's blow was not so very unlike the circles drawn in pigment against the Kalakar grounds; places in which to train; places in which the rules of a combat that did not involve death reigned.

And that made no sense.

"Why are you doing this?"

He could have feigned ignorance; when he had trained her as a younger girl, he often had.

Instead, he put up his sword, in the style of the *Kialli*, and stilled. As if he were unprepared to offer the comfort of familiarity, of any familiarity.

"Do you really not know?"

She could not see him clearly. She thought he had summoned his power, but the power itself felt unfamiliar, and she knew shadow better than anyone who dwelled within it save perhaps the god who defined it.

She raised a hand to her eyes; lowered it instead of rubbing. It was getting darker.

And her hand was cold. The sword that had seared her flesh now chilled it; her arm was becoming numb. She had never felt the cold in her life; she felt it now, but not with terrible panic, although she understood what it must mean. Whatever price the sword demanded was going to be met by her death.

Why, she thought, as she failed to lift her arm, *didn't I kill Auralis*? She would have happily destroyed half the human Court if it would have purchased an extra hour of life. Why not Auralis?

But she thought it without panic, without rancor; just such idle thoughts had kept her awake as a child, while Ashaf dozed in darkness—or light—and she lay against her, listening to the insistent, the persistent, beat of her heart.

She had not fled the North to avoid the consequences of her actions. She had not fled to avoid any possible retribution for the deaths of the *Kialli* lords who served her father, and there had been many. She had not fled Isladar, although in the end . . . in the end perhaps that was her only lie.

It didn't matter.

It didn't matter here, now; it was cold, and dark, and she understood the cold and the dark in a way that she had never understood the warmth, the sunlight, the people that gathered in it.

"I believe," she heard, at a great remove, "that you are . . . late . . . Lord Isladar."

She had almost forgotten the Swordsmith.

"Do not interfere."

"I do not have that capability. Had I, I would have . . . but this is more . . . enlightening."

She turned in the direction of his voice; turned in the direction of Isladar's footsteps.

"She is strong," the Swordsmith said softly.

After a pause, Lord Isladar's voice, closer now, cooler, "You have changed, Swordsmith, if you define as strength the weakness that allows your blade to kill her without a fight."

The Swordsmith's silence was brief. "I have always defined mortals by their ability to endure; so few can, and live. And you are wrong, Isladar. She has fought—and beat—the blade; she did not kill the mortal, and the blade should have given her no choice.

"She has not chosen *Kialli* battles, but she knows how to fight the battles she does choose."

It was odd, to hear the words and see nothing.

"Perhaps," the single word was even colder.

"She is mortal," the Swordsmith continued. "Our Lord's child, or no, she will die in such a brief period of time; does it matter if it is sooner rather than late?"

"Anduvin, you are beginning to bore me."

Silence, followed at last by wild, wild laughter. "You were never so dangerous, brother, as when you were bored."

Footsteps.

Kiriel rose, and only when her knees unbent did she realize that she had been crouching against the ground. She could see stone, and ice, and shadow.

The Swordsmith said softly, "I do not know what you intended for her, but I can see your hand in her now. Look; she stands."

She lifted the sword.

Isladar said something in a language that she did not understand. Spoke forcefully, the smoothness of his voice breaking over syllables with some emotion that she could not identify because he had shown her so little by which she could judge.

Can I trust you?

No.

As his footsteps grew louder, he fell silent, but the shadows parted; she could see, if not Isladar, than the sword he carried.

"You killed her," Kiriel said softly.

"Yes."

"And you enjoyed it."

"Yes."

Her cheeks were hot. She was used to this, had become used to it in the months during which she had labored under the bane of ring and heat and Osprey training.

"But I loved her."

Silence.

"And if I betrayed her then, somehow, it doesn't mean that I have to keep doing it. There was only one thing she wanted from me while she was alive."

"And would you have given it to her, while she was alive?"

"Does it matter? She's *not* alive now. And—" her cheeks were *so* hot. "That's all that really matters."

She lifted the sword, and she realized her cheeks were wet as well. Wet and hot. She knew, then, that she looked pathetic, pitiable, weak.

And she didn't care.

She was too tired to care.

She had never been so tired.

He saw his sword. She waited. And then he lowered it, slowly, and she saw his eyes through the odd mist that had taken the world away. "Kiriel," he said. He walked toward her. She did not lower her sword.

"I have miscalculated," he said, in a voice that was so familiar she might have been a child in the Shining Palace again. "I did not realize how young you would be, at this age, at this time. You are not like we were, when we had life and a form born of this plane, and not wrenched from it. Your age is reflected in your appearance."

The sword began to shake; her arms were not strong enough to hold it. But strong enough or no, they did.

"Come," he said. "If you have made your decision, abide by it. But remember that you are mortal, and that all things mortal know both growth and change; that no decision is forever fixed."

He continued to advance, and as he did, his sword's light guttered and vanished. Shadow, the *Kialli* version of sheath, took it.

She thought he would stop then.

But he kept walking.

"*Isladar, no!*" Anduvin's voice, so changed in pitch and tone it was almost unrecognizable. His footsteps started at a distance, but grew closer very quickly.

She felt the cold begin to dissipate; felt the oppressive weight of light's absence ease. Neither of these—cold or dark—had ever troubled her in this way before. She didn't like the sensation.

The sun was in the sky, swathed in a glorious magenta. It had been growing dark; it would be dark soon. But she saw the color of the evening sky and for the first time realized that something as trivial as color could be . . . beautiful. The sea breeze was still salty. The heat was still oppressive. But they were like a blanket now, that covered everything, that lay above and beneath all sensation. The ring . . .

The ring no longer burned.

With the return of light came vision. The edges of the city's streets came first, color bleeding into a lifeless gray, although the streets were otherwise still. The buildings on either side of the cobbled road then cast shadows, but the shadows muted color rather than destroying it, dipping with the contours of the road, traveling the edge of broken and shattered stone, rising and falling along the mounds of unsettled earth.

Where shadows weren't cast, the colors were brighter, arcing from the distance to where she stood like the beginning swell of a wave.

She had seen the ocean; the waves could kill.

The footsteps were close; she looked to them, because it was easier. She saw Lord Anduvin, and realized that the only time she had *ever* seen a *Kialli* lord run was the single time she had appeared in the Shattered Hall, sword in hand, feet upon the table. But they had been running away. Lord Anduvin was running toward her.

"Isladar!"

She looked up, then. Not right or left, as she had done, and not above to clear sky, nor to ground, but directly in front of her. It was hard. She flinched before she could see, for the shadows that the dusk dispelled in all other corners of the city seemed to have retreated to this single spot, to regroup, retrench. If she lied to herself, she could pretend they could not yet be pierced.

But she had never learned—as Lord Isladar had said—the subtle use of the craft; she was a poor liar. The shadows were strongest; she could sense their struggle here, but they, too, were diminishing. They gave way to simple vision, to simple color, to simple fact.

She could follow the stretch of her arm from elbow to hand, which still clutched the sword by the hilt; from hilt to steel; from steel, inexplicably, to flesh.

And from the place in the expanse of a remarkably still chest, where steel and flesh were joined, she could lift her gaze, could raise the sudden weight of her head, until she could look into the impassive eyes of the only *Kialli* lord she had ever obeyed.

CHAPTER EIGHT

The sword shivered in her hands as if it were alive. Isladar grimaced.

"I had hoped that this would be less . . . obvious."

She could see that the shadows were lessening, lessening. But she had thought they were her shadows. Now she understood what she saw. What she wanted to see. What she had dreaded seeing.

She cried out, the sound so raw it contained too many emotions to be simple: anger, grief, triumph, denial. She pulled the sword free—

Or tried—

And it would not budge.

Anduvin came. She could see his hands on Isladar's shoulders, could see his perfect skin cast in the alabaster that the *Kialli* almost never know: fear.

"It won't—it won't come free!"

"You fool," Anduvin said, and his voice was wild. But he did not speak to her. "Do you know what you've done?"

"I . . . have suspicions."

"*Why*?"

"Because, Brother, I have plans. Obligations."

"You have—"

"I made my oath," he said.

"You did not bind yourself to it."

"Spoken like the *kin*."

The shadows were diminishing. She thought if they spoke a few moments longer the shadows would be, in their entirety, gone.

And with it, Lord Isladar of the *Kialli*; the man she had sworn to kill.

"Do you think I remember nothing of honor?"

"Our honor never involved the sacrifice of our own for the . . ."

Silence.

She cried out, again, "The sword *won't come out*!"

And this time, they both looked at her, Isladar with the resignation that often touched his features when a particularly difficult lesson had failed to take, and Anduvin with incredulity.

"She doesn't understand what you've done—she can't comprehend what *you've done*!"

"Anduvin, you are making a fool of yourself."

"Does it matter? The only witness of value is you, and you will be gone."

"Anduvin—"

"She is your student, not I. What is weakness, if none are there to witness it? What is strength?"

She had never heard a *Kialli* lord speak so wildly. It seemed that she must have succumbed to the sword after all; that she must be caught by delirium.

The blade, she thought, as she looked away from them. He had—he had walked—he had walked *onto* the sword.

The fear came upon her like a frenzy and she understood not Isladar, but Anduvin.

The sword was feeding. He had . . . he had done this. He had freed her.

She was afraid. She was terrified. She would not name the fear.

But she would not sit idly by while it consumed her. She removed her glove. Looked at the sword's edge as it caught magenta. "This is your own fault," she told him softly, although she doubted he was listening. "You should never have asked for this sword."

And steeling herself against pain, she grabbed the blade by its edge and forced her palm up, until steel split skin.

And then, and then she pulled, straining.

She had strained like this as a child; Ashaf had suggested that she take the old, thick rope that was used for the flag on the Tower, and give one end to Falloran; she had, and Ashaf had directed her to take the other. Then she had said, simply, "Pull." It had seemed a stupid game, to start.

But Falloran was strong, and in the end—it was a game they could play that did not involve the death of one or the other. There were few games in the Hells, all of them deadly. Falloran had thought it strange—she could tell this, although he had no words, no voice. But she had loved it, because as she had grown, she had become strong enough to move him.

And that was the strength she used now.

She *pulled.*

The blade moved. But not enough.

"Kiriel," Isladar said—and unless her imagination was unusually active, his voice was weaker, softer, "that was foolish. A blade must know its master, and the taste of its master's blood is not the way in which to teach it that lesson."

"Why?" she said, ignoring him, forcing her bone to meet steel, feeding that steel her blood in some desperate attempt to distract it.

"Give anything that you desire to serve you a taste of power or weakness, and it will rule."

"That's not what I meant."

"I know."

She was sweating. She felt water slide along the contours of brow and cheek, tuck in beneath the underside of her chin.

This was a better death than he had given Ashaf. A cleaner death. She had meant to kill him. She had vowed to kill him.

She pulled. The blade moved.

Lord Isladar flinched. It might have been winter, and she a mortal; she froze, chilled.

And then a hand touched the back of hers. She looked down; the hand was slender, fair, unblemished. Unmailed. Lord Anduvin of the *Kialli* bowed. She had not even seen him move.

Her life depended on her ability to be aware—*always*—of the movement of the *Kialli.* She had not seen his hands leave Isladar's shoulders.

"This is like Isladar," he said softly. "The Isladar of *my* youth. He was impulsive, and he was wild, and he was willing—always—to risk everything playing games that no one of us could understand."

"You—you called him—brother."

"It does not have the same meaning among the *Kialli*

that it does among the mortals." He turned away a moment. "But it is not without significance.

"I do not understand the events of this day, Kiriel, and I dislike them. I have never interfered in the games that the Lords play."

"Neither has Isladar."

He laughed, and the laughter was rich and sweet, a terrible sound in the darkening streets.

"That is *all* he has ever done, but he is infinitely subtle.

"But . . . he is also the only one who truly remembers. The only other one." The Swordsmith lifted a hand. Hesitated a moment, glancing at Kiriel's open fear, and at Isladar's impassive face. "Did you plan this, Brother?"

"I? It would be a foolish plan indeed that put me in this position." His smile was cool. "A foolish plan that depended upon the generosity of the *Kialli*."

"W–what are you doing?"

"You do not have the necessary strength to do what you are doing, child," he said softly. He rose—and only then did she realize that he had bent to one knee so that their faces were level. He walked past her. Walked around her. She saw his arms come to either side—*he's behind me!*— and her first instinct was to spin, to drop the sword, to stop him.

But her second instinct was truer: She knew that she could not let go of the sword. Not yet.

His arms paralleled her arms. The top of her head barely came to his shoulders; she felt the presence of his chin hovering above her hair; felt it dip, touch, settle. In just such a way, Ashaf had often hugged her when she was an older, recalcitrant child. But his reach was longer; the span of his hand wider. His hand traveled the length of both her arm and the sword he had crafted until it had passed the place where both blood and grip marked it.

He then said, quietly, "No matter what we do, you will never recover from this."

He was not speaking to her.

Isladar said nothing. But he watched as Lord Anduvin of the *Kialli* drew the inside of his palm along the sword's edge until it rested just above Kiriel's.

He grunted as he cut himself. His fingers curled, as Kiriel's had done, around the flawless steel.

"Now," he told her softly. "Pull."

She was confused. His back and his arms enveloped her; she was small enough to feel like the child she had sworn she would never be again. Tired enough to obey, to time her strength to follow his. To *pull* with everything she had.

It wasn't much.

"The sword," he said, through gritted teeth, his voice reverberating in her ear until her spine tingled, "is yours. It is not just effort that will move it."

"But—"

"Do you not understand what has been offered you? Take it. Command the blade."

No, she wanted to tell him, *I don't understand.*

But she did; the facts were facts, even if the motivations had been pared away.

She had never owned a *Kialli* blade before. Understood that, in a strange way, she did not own one now. A sword had been given to her when she was—she could say this now, at the remove of years—a child; it had been fed when she was a child; it had been forged when she was a child.

That was gone, with childhood; what remained was complex, complicated, and painfully simple.

She willed the blade to *go away.*

And it refused.

Not in words, of course; it was not that type of sword.

As if he could feel its refusal—and he probably could, as he had forged it—Lord Anduvin cursed. He looked up, his brow creased, his lips thinned by effort and by things unsaid. "Is this the end you desired, Brother?"

"I desired, in truth, no end," Isladar's reply was mild.

Kiriel couldn't see his expression clearly, and she knew why; her eyes were filmed with water. If she cried, he would be worse than angry: he would be contemptuous.

She ordered the blade to go away, and again, it refused. It had not, she knew, finished feeding.

Wasn't this what you wanted? she asked herself.

She hated the answer so much she couldn't acknowledge it. Instead, she turned the anger and the confusion on the blade.

And was not surprised when she failed to move it.

Her hand stung. Her hand did not bleed.

Or rather, it did, but the blade absorbed that blood, just

as it had Auralis'. What had Lord Isladar said? *A blade must know its master, and the taste of its master's blood is not the way in which to teach it that lesson.*

But he was wrong.

She looked up at him, looked up at Lord Anduvin, and said, without thinking, "But blood binds."

"Indeed," Lord Isladar said, his voice fading. His lips curved in the thin, cold expression that had always been his signal of approval.

Anduvin looked up. Looked down to the place where steel and flesh intersected; the steel he had tempered; the flesh he now wore.

"A gamble," he said softly. And then he laughed, and his laughter . . . was painful and beautiful, a sound unlike any Kiriel had ever heard from the *Kialli.* It was almost mortal. "You were always impulsive, but I do not believe you were ever this reckless."

"I was always this reckless," Isladar replied. "Kiriel."

She was staring at him.

"This path is a path of your choosing. I am not without mercy, although it is a mercy that you are not perhaps ready to understand. I would have spared you this, had you been less headstrong. Remember that."

"But—"

He placed his own hands upon the sword's edge.

When he touched it, all light fled; the darkness that came from his hands seeped down the length of the blade, to be joined as it flowed by Lord Anduvin's shadow. And her own.

She cried out; the ring on her hand flared and the light from it traveled like lightning's fork. It struck them all; before searing white enveloped her entire field of vision, she could clearly see two tall, slender men with pale, falling hair and faces unlike any that she had seen within the Shining Court.

Do you have a soul? she had once asked Isladar.

No, little one.

Do I?

Oh, yes.

She had had no reason to disbelieve him.

But the men she had seen in vision were not the men she saw in life. For the first time, she wondered what a soul was, what its value was, and how it could be weighed, judged, found wanting.

And when she could see again, she stood in the street, her hand on a sword's hilt, the tip of the sword resting against the upturned earth. She dropped to one knee, forgot to breathe, felt her chest constrict.

Felt a hand on her shoulder.

It was not Lord Isladar's hand.

"He is . . . not dead." The Swordsmith said, before she could speak, if she had intended to speak at all.

She did not reply. Instead, she lifted the sword, raised it slowly until the flat of the blade was before her eyes. With a deliberate slow twist of the wrist, she turned the blade; she faced its edge.

The blade did not vanish.

"You cannot simply gesture it away," The Swordsmith continued. "It is a matter of will and intent; a certain knowledge of complete ownership."

She lowered the blade slowly. After a long moment, she chose to sheath it—within the scabbard she had carried since the day the Swordsmith had come to visit.

"Kiriel. That is not the way to sheathe that sword. Not now."

She didn't look at him. Not directly. Did not even ask him why he was there, why he had stayed. The street, broken only by the blow she had struck in the cobbled stone, stretched out in peaceful isolation, and she began to follow it.

It didn't really matter where it led.

But he fell in behind her. She knew this not so much because of his footsteps—she couldn't honestly say she heard any—but because of sheer presence.

"Master APhaniel, should we act?" Gyrrick spoke quietly as he watched Kiriel di'Ashaf walk down the empty streets with her tall, slender companion.

The magi lifted a hand; the mage bowed instantly and retreated, passing the unspoken command to the others in a whisper that traveled like a dry breeze. Sigurne would have been displeased indeed by such a sobering display of obedience.

And at another time, he would have been pleased by it in equal measure.

But he was lost in momentary wonder at the complexity of what he had just witnessed. He had almost been forced to miss it; the darkness-born child's companion had been both energetic and disobliging. The threat of sending the bill for property damage—in addition to the extensive use of magic pursuant to saving the life of a member of the Kalakar Household who may or may not have been involved in questionable magical activity—failed to have the desired effect, and in the end, Meralonne had been forced to call upon Member Mellifas to deal with the situation as she saw fit. A certain privilege of rank. His smile was momentarily unpleasant. Power, in the Empire, was fraught with the dangerous need for diplomacy, tact, and the ability to offer a threat in a benign and gentle fashion.

For that reason, among many, he had refrained from actively seeking it. But . . . even with such restraint, he could not simply disappear into anonymity; he was of the magi, and the Council of the Magi; he was of the echelons in the Order that could boast both knowledge and the power to use it.

"Master?"

"The danger has passed, Gyrrick. Congratulate your men on their timing and their silence, and then instruct them to return to the Order. Return with them and deliver your report to Member Mellifas—and only that member."

"Master." He bowed again. Hesitated. "You will not be returning with us?"

Meralonne refrained from what would have been the obvious lecture in a different situation. These men were what passed for militia within the Order, but they would never quite be a military order unto themselves, and they would never have that perfect discipline—or, more significantly, obedience—that came with years of dedicated training.

"No, Gyrrick. There are one or two things that I must attend to here before I return."

"They are not dangerous?"

There was obedience and then there was obedience. The mage raised a silver brow. "Gyrrick, I have taught you everything that you currently know about martial arts. Believe for a moment that I am capable of actually using what I have taught."

He expected the mage to bow or kneel. The mage surprised him. "Master," he said, although it was technically not a title that the Order used, "you are currently the *only* member of the Order who could teach what you have taught us. We are all inclined toward the more . . . obvious . . . arts; none of us are men obsessed or consumed by the simple desire for knowledge."

"That desire is never simple. Continue."

"If anything happens to you, that knowledge is lost. We have discussed it among ourselves, and we have come to realize—"

" 'Among ourselves'?"

"Myself and my fellow students."

"I see. Continue."

"We have come to realize that as a ward against future necessity it is of utmost import that your life be preserved."

"I . . . see."

"Therefore—"

"You understand that in my culture what you have just said would constitute deliberate and possibly dangerous insult?"

Gyrrick's expression was implacability itself. He did not answer.

But he did not, Meralonne noted, back down either. This was the result of the Empire and Imperial custom; it had given the City men of power who did not understand the meaning of either being a soldier or going to war.

"If I foresaw danger, Gyrrick, I would not send you back to the Order to make your report." He lifted a hand to forestall the obvious reply, and the gesture worked. "I will take what you have said under advisement for the moment. Return to the Order, assure Sigurne Mellifas that all is well within the Old City. I shall follow shortly.

"Ignore this at your peril; I am unused to having my orders questioned when they are stated this baldly."

Gyrrick struggled with silence and won; the words—whatever they were—remained unsaid. He bowed.

And Meralonne returned the bow with a nod.

These warriors were not what he would have fashioned for his own use when he was a younger man, but they were, in some ways, more rewarding for the challenge they represented.

He waited until he was certain they were gone, and then he stepped into the street and began a leisurely walk, the medallion of the Order tucked deliberately into the folds of his tunic.

"Where are you going?" she asked him, although the curiosity in her voice, if any, was muted. She felt oddly detached from herself, very light-headed. No, that wasn't it, not precisely. She felt as if she were *not* herself; as if she observed the streets of Averalaan through borrowed vision, walked them in borrowed form.

"I? I do not know. Does it matter?"

"Yes. No. I'm not sure." She stopped in the street, and the peaceful night was damp and cool, and her lips tasted of the salt that was a perpetual presence. She was very, very tired.

"I know," the Swordsmith said softly. But the tone of his words was strange. Hesitant.

She continued to walk, as if the presence of a *Kialli* lord by her side was an everyday occurrence. It had been, once. But never here, never where the mortals lived, in their crowded, hot city, with its myriad sounds and scents, its nooks and crannies carved not by wind and god, but by simple people.

By mortals.

She was one; she understood that now in a way that she had never understood it. She would age, as they aged; she would die—if she were lucky—as they died, taken by Mandaros or his servants to answer for her life, and to choose.

And she would regret the loss of what she loved so bitterly that an eternity of living with that regret made mortality seem . . . welcome. Because there would be an end.

For the first time, she wondered if she had lived before. What she had been if she had. What she would be if she was not consigned to the Hells for her failures in this life; they were profound.

"What happens to you when you die?"

"Happens?"

"Happens. Mortals go to Mandaros, and come back, go

and come back. To forget," she added softly. Ashamed of the words, of the fate.

"Until they choose."

"How can we choose if we don't remember?"

Lord Anduvin raised a winter brow. "I am *Kialli,*" he said quietly. "You can ask me many questions, and almost all of them will be more relevant than that one. I do not know how mortal memory works; it is fragile; it is whimsical; it changes with time."

Her memory. She should have been insulted. But anger had to come from somewhere, and she felt . . . empty. Too empty to sustain such a raw emotion. "What happens to the *Kialli*? What happens to the kin?"

The Swordsmith frowned a moment, and then offered an elegant, graceful shrug. "Does it matter?"

"Yes."

"Then ask the gods, little one, when you die and meet them. Ask them who the Makers were, if there were indeed any, ask them what the plans of those Makers might have been, if such a thing as a plan existed. The world was a wild, wild place when the *Kialli* were at the height of their power and the peak of their youth."

She nodded, hearing the words but failing to absorb their meaning. "Why?" she questioned softly, looking toward the North. He seemed to expect this, and changed course as easily as a small river might when flowing around a rock.

"No one understands Lord Isladar. I have often wondered if Isladar himself does."

"No," she said quietly. "I didn't mean Isladar. I meant you."

He raised a brow. "Among mortals," he replied, his voice even softer than hers, although with different reason, "it would be considered rude to ask personal questions of relative strangers."

"How do you know?"

"I have observed mortals in my time. There were—among them—one or two who might, in their brief lives, have been considered my peers." His smile was cutting. "I would not have condescended to acknowledge that fact while they lived. Much has changed since then. These lands are impoverished. There are only a handful of named blades that exist in this world, and they slumber now, unaware of their Makers' intent. But the human smiths knew who I was; I knew who they were.

"I digress. What I understand of mortal behavior, I learned when the mortal cities were truly great, and the men who ruled them, mages almost without peer. I observed them then." His smile sharpened. "Enough, certainly, to understand what caused offense, humiliation, or pain."

"Was that personal?"

"The observation?"

"My question."

His smile thinned. "The discussion—the voluntary discussion—of any act of weakness is always personal."

"Is it weakness if you do something that you don't understand?"

He laughed. "Especially then. The less of ourselves we understand the more prone we are to manipulation by others who understand us better."

She was silent for a moment, her face absorbing the gentle glow of the magelights scattered about the city at regular intervals for no other reason than that they provided light to people without the personal power to summon light on their own behalf. "You mean like Isladar."

"I do, indeed, refer to Lord Isladar." He looked at her face, studied it as if he could see the gradual march of time across skin momentarily unfettered by wrinkles. "I was away in the South when you were brought to the Shining Court. I do not know why he agreed to teach you. If, that is, it was not somehow his suggestion.

"I did not come until I was summoned."

"Summoned?"

"Do you not remember? You were young by mortal standards. But you rode the great beast, at the side of the Lord, and all of the *Kialli* were called to bear witness."

She lifted a hand. "Enough. I remember."

He walked by her side while she struggled a moment with memory and silence, clearly waiting. "She did not attend."

"She?"

"Your companion."

"My companion? You mean Anya?"

"Ishavriel's willful mage? No—I mean the old woman."

She started to snap out a name, and then closed her lips over the first syllable, hoarding it. "No. She never went."

"And the Lord allowed it? Attendance was mandatory for all of the Shining Court."

"She was not a member of any Court but mine."

"Yes."

She stopped in the street, weary. "You know that this hurts me. It will always hurt me."

He stopped, surprised. "Yes."

She felt it, his surprise, although none of it showed on his face.

"Then leave it. I will not fight you, not . . . this eve. But I will not let you use her that way."

"Will you let her memory fade?"

"What do you think?"

"I think that you have the choice: You will let her memory cause you pain, or you will let her memory fade."

"And there's nothing in between those? Not all memories of Ashaf cause me pain."

"No, but they point, in the end, to the only thing that can: her death. If you follow them to their inevitable end, it doesn't matter where you begin the thread of the reminiscence."

"Is this your truth as well?"

He laughed. "Yes. But the difference is simple: You do not know what *my* memories are."

"Or what Isladar's are."

"Or what his are. But what his are, no one knows." He bowed. "If you would allow it, Kiriel di'Ashaf, I would travel with you."

"Why?"

"Because I no longer know what your sword will become, and I am curious."

She accepted this as truth because it was—but there was something else there, nestled between the cracks of his words; something that flickered like shadow.

She looked up to see his eyes, wide now, intent; met them. "You aren't telling me all of the truth."

Those eyes widened slightly. "No." He did not deny it. He had not denied anything. But his gaze dropped to the wound across his hand. The bloodless wound.

Hers had already begun to heal.

"No."

"No?"

"I don't want you to travel with me."

"Perhaps I ask as a matter of courtesy."

"Or perhaps you ask because you know that I'm traveling with mortals who hunt demons."

He smiled thinly. "Perhaps."

"And perhaps he asks because he has no choice, and he seeks to save face."

Kiriel turned.

Meralonne APhaniel stood in the street, alone.

"Perhaps," the Swordsmith said again, turning more slowly to gaze at their visitor. "Illaraphaniel."

"Anduvin."

"Have you come to test Summer magic against the Winter? Winter is almost at its height."

"No," the mage replied quietly. "Can you not feel it? The Winter has passed. The Summer—so very long in coming—has arrived." And then he smiled. "I forget my ancient history. Of course you can feel it. Of course you know."

"Know what?" Kiriel snapped, weariness giving way to a slightly peevish whine that she instantly despised.

Lord Anduvin had become completely still. "You can tell her," the mage said quietly.

"Or I could kill you and prevent it from being known?"

"Or you could make that attempt, yes."

The Swordsmith was rigid; his skin was the color of fire's reflection across melting snow. But he smiled.

"Meralonne." Kiriel forced peevishness out of her voice—which left it sounding curiously hollow. "Either tell me what you need to tell me, or go away."

He bowed; sarcasm and grace combined in a way that should not have been possible. "I have, in my keeping, your companion. Without supervision, the Order of Knowledge will not release him. And without supervision *soon*, they will choose the form of supervision under which he leaves the Order." He frowned. "Perhaps you are indeed too exhausted; be cautious for the next few days. If you had some hidden reserve of power, it is empty."

"Why are you telling me this? Why are you even here? Wasn't it you who counseled the Kings to kill me?"

"It was indeed." He rose from his bow and shrugged. "But it has been many years since I have been accused of the crime of perfection, and I am willing to entertain the possibility that I was in error."

"And if I were to somehow remove the ring?"

"I do not believe that you will ever be able to remove the ring. I could be wrong. But it is not to discuss such difficulties that I have returned."

He turned to the Swordsmith.

Kiriel did not.

"Go, Swordsmith. Go until she has need of your presence and your skills."

"I cannot leave until she releases me."

Meralonne turned again to Kiriel, and Kiriel stared blankly at them both. Exhaustion made the lids of her eyes heavy, and the desire to sleep was almost overpowering.

Almost.

Sleep had always been the worst of her vulnerabilities. She knew it. Had always known it. It was during her hours of sleep that Lord Isladar—*Isladar*—had proved her most constant companion, for he required none, and he could watch over her, to guard against the dangers that his magicks had not foreseen.

Isladar.

Ashaf.

Isladar had walked onto a sword to save her life. Isladar, who had taken from her the only other thing she had ever valued in the Shining City.

What had she said, when she had looked at him, impaled upon that blade; when she had taken what the Swordsmith had offered?

Blood binds.

Her eyes widened in surprise. She looked again at her hand, and then raised her face to Lord Anduvin.

"I—I release you," she whispered.

His eyes narrowed. But he bowed. "I will never be far from you," he told her quietly.

Meralonne interrupted with his usual curt grace.

"Kiriel di'Ashaf—or Kiriel AKalakar, if you prefer—if you do not come with me to collect Auralis AKalakar from the Order of Knowledge, you will be forced to collect him from a more extended visit in the magisterial jails."

CHAPTER NINE

23rd of Scaral, 427 AA
Averalaan Aramarelas, Avantari

They met in *Avantari*.

Baredan di'Navarre noticed the change in the Ospreys immediately; his brows curved down a moment, and then rose, joining across the bridge of his nose before his expression fell into the stiff neutrality of concern. That shift in his expression was enough to catch the attention of the young man who stood, hands behind his back, studying a map that had been pinned to the table in literally a hundred different places. It was more than enough to catch the attention of the man who stood beside him, inserting another flagged pin into the surface of textured paper.

"General?"

The General looked across the table at the sound of the young Tyr's voice. "I believe that there has been a change in circumstance," he said quietly.

Ramiro di'Callesta frowned and straightened, leaving pin and map in his shadow. He turned as Valedan did, toward the room's main entrance.

Standing in the doorway, arms folded, legs planted against finely polished wood, were a handful of men and women. Ospreys.

"General?" he said quietly.

The General said nothing.

The Tyr'agnate said simply, "They have made their choice." His voice was very cool, but he nodded before he rounded the table to join Baredan at the map's west edge. At this late date, he still did not turn his back upon the Ospreys if he had the choice.

What choice?

Duarte AKalakar moved from the center of the Ospreys to their front, detaching himself. He stopped walking about ten feet away from Valedan.

The hall had never seemed quite so long, although Valedan conceded a certain familiarity with it, having spent the better part of every waking day for two weeks within its confines.

"Captain." Valedan nodded as Duarte bowed crisply and then rose into the fist to shoulder salute that was so uncommon in the South.

"Reporting for duty."

"Captain, may we speak?"

"Tyr'agar."

Valedan took him aside. "What has happened?"

"Kai di'Leonne?"

"Did you suffer a casualty? Was there some conflict beyond the grounds we currently occupy that was not brought to our attention?"

"No."

"You're . . ." He almost said *lying*. Turned the word aside with ease, surprised that it had almost been spoken. "You are not being entirely truthful. Let me ask you instead the relevant question. Will it affect your ability to lead the Ospreys? Will it affect their ability to perform as my guard?"

Captain Duarte AKalakar said nothing. Valedan looked beyond him to where the rest of the on-duty Ospreys now stood.

Auralis was thin-lipped and narrow-eyed; Kiriel was absolutely still. Both of them were pale and bruised, and Valedan saw the fiery red of scratches and cuts across both of their faces. Beyond them, Cook looked angry, and Sanderton looked fatigued. Fiara, who was in theory on shift, was nowhere to be seen. Alexis was subdued.

It was not their finest hour. Valedan kai di'Leonne had the strong suspicion that they would not comport themselves as befit *his* rank until they had crossed the thin divide between the North and the South.

He looked back to Duarte.

The Captain of the Ospreys wore a variant of the uniform the Ospreys had, until yesterday, worn with pride. Something was missing, and Valedan was almost embarrassed when he realized what it was. The symbol of their company. The bird in flight.

What remained was the uniform of the Kalakar House Guard, with the quarter circles that denoted the rank of the man who led this particular unit. Valedan had never understood the individuation of units within a larger army until he saw the effect of its removal.

"Captain?"

Duarte AKalakar had some mercy. He waited, in silence, until things became clear. And they did; Valedan was no fool. He hesitated a moment, and then he bowed to Duarte AKalakar.

He did not, however, speak. Some things lost strength or power when put into words because the words that contained them were inadequate.

"How will this alter your duties?"

"We report to you; we are responsible to you."

"You do not travel as part of the Kings' army?"

"No. We are not a part of the Kings' army. We have been relieved of that duty for the duration of this war. We have been given permission to travel to the South, with the clear freedom and understanding that binds any nonmilitary member of House Kalakar."

"But your duties will be military in nature."

"That is not the concern of either the House or The Kalakar. As long as we aren't breaking any of the laws that govern the Empire, The Kalakar has no active say in our decisions."

"The Kalakar will be coming South; we will arrive before her, but both she and The Berriliya will travel with Commander Allen into Raverra."

Captain Duarte shrugged. "Do you see yourself in conflict with the Generals? If you do, our loyalty will be the least of your concerns."

"Loyalty in the South is rare—and it is therefore never the least of my concerns."

Duarte met his gaze quietly; Valedan did not blink or look away. In the end, it was the veteran who smiled slightly, the veteran who bowed. "It's easy to value something in theory."

"Is it?" Only when Duarte looked away did Valedan relax.

"Perhaps. You are not what I expected, Valedan kai di'-Leonne; you are not what any of the Ospreys expected."

Valedan nodded quietly. "I hope to be as much of a disappointment to my enemies."

Duarte's smile was quick and clean.

"If the Kalakar uniform is not to your liking, choose another. But, Captain—do not be late again."

The captain nodded quietly. "Not until the end of the war, I think."

"Good. Position your men and join me."

It was Duarte AKalakar's turn to pause. The pause was fleeting. *Boy*, he thought, the respect in the word profound, *you will be a shock to allies and enemies alike when you take to the field. And if the Ospreys—no, if* we *have any say in it, you'll get there.*

He followed Valedan, took the place the Tyr'agar indicated at his side. General Baredan di'Navarre was silent as stone—mausoleum stone—and just as cheerful. But the Tyr'agnate Ramiro di'Callesta looked up at the Tyr'agar.

And then at the man who stood beside him. Men fell into trenches narrower and shallower than his pause. But when he spoke, he said only, "You are familiar with the terrain of Averda."

"With the terrain of a decade ago, yes."

"This . . . is a map . . . of the territories that are likely to be threatened by the pretender's army."

He offered no warning; Duarte needed none. But he understood why the room was shorn of the Empire's finest Generals.

Valedan, he thought, *do you know what you've done here?*

"The blue markers?"

"Belong to Mancorvo. As you are aware, the Mancorvans and the Averdans are . . . not friendly. But of the Tyrs, Mareo di'Lamberto is the man most likely to be swayed by the honorable cause.

"If he perceives that cause to be owned by anyone other than the Callestans," Duarte responded.

"Indeed, AKalakar. You are perceptive."

Duarte started at the map for a long while, absorbing

the information; seeing in this map, in these men, in this gathering, the true harbinger of war.

"What is he doing?" Alexis said under her breath to no one in particular. Many of the Ospreys spoke out loud for no reason; Kiriel had ceased to find it disconcerting—but she still had difficulty separating the rhetorical from the conversational.

"I think," she replied, when no one rushed in to answer, "he is looking at the maps."

Alexis snorted. "We've been guarding that boy for months now, and he's never invited Duarte to stand guard over the tabletop."

"No," Kiriel said quietly.

Alexis' narrowed glance came in from the side; Kiriel ignored it. She had learned this from Auralis, who received a similar glance and handled it the same way. Only an idiot could fail to notice their bruises, cuts, and scrapes. But only another Osprey would know that beneath newer armor, and newer clothing, the wounds were deeper.

"You two are up to duty?"

They both nodded.

As if she'd expected a different answer. She shrugged; their funeral, if they were stupid enough to want one.

23rd of Scaral, 427 AA
The Terafin Manse

Elonne ATerafin was striking. She was not, Finch decided, classically beautiful, but her eyes caught one's attention from half a room away, and they didn't let go easily. Or at all. She had chosen—as had all of the members of the House Council—to keep a coterie of House Guards by her side, but they were few: four in total, two at the doors to the sitting chamber she had picked for this meeting.

Her rooms were finely appointed. Very finely. But they were not overdone. Finch wondered if she had chosen the decor herself.

"ATerafin," Elonne said, inclining her head. "I am pleased that you could make the time to accept my invitation."

I bet. Finch remembered to smile. The clothing she wore was less elegant than Elonne's; less daring. Elonne wore deep blue and deep green in a flowing trail from her left shoulder to the floor. Ellerson had chosen, for Finch, muted colors; a pale cream edged in simple gold. Not for her the single-shouldered dress; hers was more practical. And, if she were honest, more youthful. Ellerson had stressed that.

You are small for your age. And you are younger than Elonne by a good ten years. She should not expect much from you. Give her what she expects, or perhaps less.

"I'm honored to have been invited," Finch said at last. Elonne gestured to a chair, and Finch took it, trying to keep her back and shoulders straight. She had spent the better part of three days listening to Ellerson's disparaging comments, and she knew that slouching was not acceptable.

That was easier to remember than she'd thought; there was nothing comfortable about this room, this woman, those House Guards.

A servant came in through the double doors that led to the sitting room. He carried a tray with the stiff perfection of bearing that the best of servants displayed. His steps were light, his movements deliberate, his silence perfect.

Elonne gestured when he had set the tray down, and he made his retreat.

For the first time in a few years, Finch wished she was a servant.

Elonne's smile was about as friendly as a smile on such a patrician face could be. It did not immediately set Finch's teeth on edge.

What should I do if she offers me something to eat?

Eat it.

But what if—

Finch, this is House Terafin. *Elonne ATerafin would no more poison you in her own quarters than Jewel would.*

But what if—

This is simply a meeting, no more. If you choose to refuse her hospitality, do so. But be aware that she will note that refusal, and understand exactly what you mean by it.

What would Jay do?

Jewel is a person who has always accepted a challenge.

Finch dearly wished that she were more like Jewel. As if he could hear what she hadn't said—and she'd said it enough since he'd arrived that that wasn't hard—he offered her his formal smile. *You are not Jewel ATerafin. You are Finch ATerafin. But think: Jewel chose you because she trusts you. I do not think that you—that any of you—understand how much she relied on you.*

Short of spitting in the face of Elonne ATerafin and storming out—which is something Jewel would be more likely to do—there is nothing you can do that is fatal here.

Can't you come, too?

Not yet. It would be hard to explain my presence to Elonne, and if you said I was your domicis, she would merely think that the den is of value to The Terafin in and of itself, and the pressure she applied would be more extreme.

"I imagine that you're wondering why I've asked you here."

Finch nodded, and then forced herself to speak. "Well, yes, a little."

Elonne's smile deepened. She reached for an empty glass, and lifted the carafe from the tray. "Will you join me?"

Finch nodded again.

Elonne poured. Over her bare shoulder, the armor of House Guards caught light, drawing the eye.

"I imagine you have relatively few of the House Guard in your wing."

"Almost none. Unless The Terafin comes."

"Truly? And who attends Jewel ATerafin?"

"Her domicis."

Elonne's smile stiffened for a moment. She finished pouring a second glass in silence. "That would be Avandar Gallais?"

"I think so."

"You think so?"

"I can't remember his family name. We never use it."

Elonne's fingers brushed Finch's as she handed her the glass. Her eyes never left Finch's face. "You don't seem comfortable speaking of the domicis. Do you dislike him?"

Finch shrugged. And then, realizing that this would be an "etiquette mistake," she added, "I don't know him well enough to like or dislike him."

"Well said. Very well. You might consider asking The

Terafin to extend the use of the House Guards to the wing."

"Oh, we've always had the right to call the House Guards, but we don't use them."

"Oh?"

Finch almost said something, but remembered that Elonne had House Guards in *this* room.

"We've never needed them," she said instead, and knew it was lame.

She put the glass down on the table, because it had started to shake. She knew that Elonne would notice it; she had the feeling that she noticed everything. Sort of like The Terafin, which made sense, since that's what she wanted to be.

"Have you had any word from Jewel since her departure?"

Finch said nothing.

Elonne lifted her glass to her lips. "Finch," she said, when she lowered it, "I am concerned for you and your friends."

"W-why?"

"It did not escape my notice that Teller ATerafin recently had an unfortunate accident. I believe he has recovered, but it must have been a shock."

When Finch didn't speak, Elonne frowned slightly. The expression added years to her face, stripping it of the semblance of amiability.

"I will be blunt, then. I know that Haerrad ATerafin had a hand in that injury."

"He d-did?"

"Can it be that Jewel has not seen fit to tell you of this?"

Think, dammit, think. "She—she said that—that it might be because of someone in the House, but she didn't say w-who. We don't, we don't deal with the Council directly. This is the first time I've met anyone on it, outside of Gabriel."

"And Jewel, of course."

"Well, yes, and Ja—Jewel."

"It may be, in the absence of the younger ATerafin, that you will be called upon to 'deal,' as you so quaintly put it, with other members of the House Council. Perhaps Haerrad will leave you be; he is not a subtle man, and may decide that without Jewel ATerafin to guide you, you are no more than glorified servants." Elonne smiled at Finch's snort. "But I believe that the ATerafin is far too intelligent to gather fools about her. She obviously values your skills and your knowledge."

"T-thank you."

"If Jewel ATerafin does not return, and you must concede, given the place of her departure, that this is a likelihood, I would be pleased to offer you my protection, and a place in my service."

Everything Ellerson said flew out of her mind, as if on the wings of the bird after which she'd been named.

"Jewel is going to return."

"Oh?"

"She's not dead. She's on a mission of—she's gone." Stupid, stupid, stupid. And to cover stupidity she did what she often did; she threw more words over the old ones in the hopes that she could bury them. "She can't be killed very easily. People—and a lot damn worse—have tried. She's smart, she's fast, and she's just—just hard to kill. Plus, she has Avandar with her, and anything that wants to kill her has to get through *him* first."

"Yet she ended up in the healerie, and her life was in the balance."

How much did this woman know?

"Anyone else would have been dead. And it doesn't matter if she came close, does it? She's still alive. She's coming back."

"And you think her talent so singularly strong that it guarantees a safe return?"

Finch's tongue tripped over her words again. "Her—her talent?"

"Finch, *I* am a member of the House Council. Jewel's ability, and therefore her value to the House, are well known to those who serve The Terafin closely."

It was meant to be a rebuke; it was. But Finch felt more comfortable with it than she had with the honeyed overture of friendship.

Finch shrugged. "Then, yes. Yes, her talent will keep her alive. It always has. *Always*."

Elonne smiled. "Good. Because she *is* of value to the House. I do not think, were I to make the decision, that I would squander her ability, or needlessly risk her life, by sending her so far away from Terafin, so frequently."

Most of the Terafin family that's died this year has died here, Finch almost said. She bit her tongue, hard.

"But I thank you for confirming a suspicion. Let me restate my offer, then. I would be more than honored to take you under my protection for the duration of Jewel ATerafin's absence. You would, of course, remain within Jewel's wing, but you would be more heavily guarded, and more closely watched; I would guarantee no other undue interference in your affairs.

"No, don't answer me now. I realize that this has come as a surprise to you, but I wish you to think of what it might entail for your friends. I also wish you to think of the alternative. And do not mistake me, Finch; I do not seek to threaten, merely to inform. If you do not accept my protection, you may well be granted another's, and one less to your liking. Haerrad has privately expressed some interest in the merchant offices. This is normal; upon the House Council we frequently oversee less significant portions of the House operations. He has never mentioned you, or your friends, by name, although I am certain he knows them well. He has merely pointed out that some offices have been left, for some time, with less than full supervision, and he has also pointed out that he has the resources, and the prior experience, to be of aid.

"The Terafin has heard his offer, and considers it now.

"But among those offices would be yours."

Finch sat with her forehead against the cool wood of the kitchen table. She hadn't summoned the den; she was alone in the room, with the flicker of lamplight, the flow of candle wax. It was a waste, and she knew it, but she wanted light, and the sun had gone down far too quickly.

The door swung open. She recognized the fall of the step across the threshold and didn't bother to raise her head.

"ATerafin."

She mumbled Ellerson's name.

"The meeting was not to your liking?"

She lifted her face then, frowning slightly where Jewel would have scowled. "No."

"Did it go poorly?"

"Yes."

"How poorly?"

"She—she said—she said that Jay might not come back, and I sort of—" She looked away. "I sort of went on and on. Telling her she was wrong."

"You called her stupid?"

"No!"

"Good. She offered you her protection?"

"Yes. How did you know?"

He smiled. "There is very, very little else that she could offer you, Finch. You are more than you seem to be, but no one with any perception at all could think that you would be less. She has paid you a compliment, of a type. She knows that you—that none of the den—can be bought."

"She probably thinks that's because we're afraid Jay would know."

He laughed. "True enough."

"But she said something else. She said Haerrad has asked to 'help' oversee the merchant offices that have been unsupervised. And one of them is ours."

He smiled. "And so he has."

"How—how do you know?"

"I am afraid, ATerafin, that I am not at liberty to discuss my source. And neither are you." He opened the door, reached for the lamp, drew the light that she wanted away. "You have been awake long enough. Do you think that The Terafin is so careless with people of value? She knows well what Haerrad's offer means; she will spend time considering it, but in the end will decide that such a minute operation is beneath his station; that to use him in such a fashion would be to the detriment of the House. She would not dream of demeaning him in such a fashion."

The tears started out of the corners of her eyes before she could stop them. "Ellerson," she whispered, "I'm—I'm so afraid."

He set the lamp down; let the door swing shut. "ATerafin," he said, his voice stern, his expression gentle.

"No—I *am*. Jay always led us. Jay always told us what to do. Jay could *see*. I can't." She pulled at her hair a moment, and stopped when a small handful obliged her by coming out. "I don't want to die here. I don't want my den to die here. And I don't—I don't know that she's coming back—I don't—"

"It is not my policy to discuss former masters with a new one," he told her gently.

It was more than just policy; it was strictly against the code of the guild; Finch knew it.

"But let me discuss, instead, a member of the den that is my Master. Jewel ATerafin was destined to be a woman of power, and it is not power that I am destined to serve. I . . . was fond of Jewel. I was fond of you all, which is why I agreed to forsake retirement and return."

The tears were running down her cheeks. She smeared them across her face.

"But I chose Avandar Gallais as her domicis."

"You? You did?"

"Yes. I'm afraid it was me. And I did so with misgivings," he added softly, and for a moment his expression was as distant as memory could make it.

"What misgivings?"

"You must promise never to repeat this; it goes against guild law, and I am a proud member of the guild, and in good standing."

She nodded.

"Having understood at an early age that it was not my destiny, not my desire, to serve people who desired power, it became incumbent upon me to recognize such people. Avandar Gallais is perhaps the most powerful man I have ever met.

"B-but—but if he's so powerful—why—"

"I do not know, Finch. But I have observed him, through reports, for many years, and I am satisfied with the choice that I made. I am not certain that a force exists, now, which could bring about his death. But I am certain—very certain—that there are forces which would try. I know that there has been speculation that Jewel ATerafin was the target of the attack in the Common. But I do not believe those speculations."

"You think they were after Avandar."

"Yes. This would not be the first time, in this city, that demons have chosen to challenge him. It would not be the first time that he has accepted that challenge in the heart of the Common. But I believe it is one of the first times that he has chosen to flee. With Jewel. Until the day he brings me her body, I will not believe that she is dead."

The tears still fell, but they were different tears. Better tears. He let her cry for a while, in silence, and then he lifted the lamp again.

"Why hasn't she contacted us?"

His lips twisted a moment in a wry smile. "The truth? It is difficult to remember, in war, that duties other than survival are paramount. Ah, let me say it differently. Jewel is always focused on the task at hand. She said her good-byes. She told you she was leaving. I believe, if I am not mistaken, that she has been busy enough that it has not occurred to her just how worried you are by her absence.

"She feels she has left you in safety."

Finch laughed.

Ellerson did not.

"I'll smack her when I see her," Finch said. "I'll smack her so hard—" She leaped up out of her chair, ran the few feet to the kitchen door, and threw it open.

"TELLER! ANGEL! CARVER! JESTER! ARANN! KITCHEN, NOW!"

He raised a frosted brow.

Finch froze. "Ummm, that bit about never repeating what you just told me—you didn't mean to the den, right?"

He raised the other brow as the doors in the hall began to fly open, dislodging her den-mates into the night.

29th of Scaral, 427 AA
The Terrean of Raverra, the Sea of Sorrows

The city stretched out so far beneath her feet her shadow was lost to other shadows; the fall of buildings, the rise of tents and awnings that colorfully staved off the worst of the blistering midday heat, and the moving wraiths of the memory shades that stood along the demi-walls of the first city.

Jewel ATerafin did not know what memory shades were. Not in this life. But nonetheless, she recognized these monuments to fallen nobles, these created ghosts that haunted those who lived beneath their terrible shadows. She had never lived in this city, but she hated it instantly.

Heights had never appealed to her, but she felt the distance between herself and the ground as certain death. She would have taken a step back, but there was nowhere to step that would not invoke that death.

He spoke her name.

Avandar.

And who was she? Who was she here?

Jewel Markess ATerafin. And she was dreaming. The familiarity of Avandar's voice brought a flicker of peace, but it was a pale flicker, and it died when she turned—carefully—to face him. She knew instantly why the heights were certain death. The domicis had been swallowed by the man, and if there had been any question about how she would feel about the man, it was answered. Sadly, there was no rule that said she had to like the answer.

He did not call her Jewel. He called her by some other woman's name. A dead woman.

"Avandar," she said, looking for a rail—or anything else she could hold—with increasing dread. "Why did you kill this girl?"

"It was nothing personal," he replied quietly. "But she caught the eye of my least obedient son, and she was an unsuitable object of affection."

"Why didn't you tell him to stay away from her?"

He chuckled. She *hated* the sound.

"I did, my dear. But he had much of me in him, and he chose not to regard what was, in the end, the only warning I was willing to waste time offering."

"You killed her because you didn't approve of her?"

"No." He frowned as if her stupidity was unusually severe. "I killed her to make a point to my willful son."

"And did it work?"

The mage frowned. Shrugged. "He was young and destined for weakness."

"He died."

"Yes."

"You killed him."

"Yes."

"Gods, I hate you."

"No doubt."

She knew she had run out of time an instant before he gestured and the ground beneath her feet dissolved. But she woke up with a terrible rawness in the back of her throat that reminded her—if a reminder were necessary—that foreknowledge never obviated fear.

The music was there, although the dawn wasn't. The night air left her breath's ghost hanging above her as she forced her fingers to relinquish the shape and texture of fist. The lute provided comfort and distance, drawing her away from the dream the moment her eyes opened to the perfect clarity of Southern sky. Strange stars looked down on her, waking or asleep. Curled beside her, the stag that had once been a man kept the worst of the night's chill at bay.

Kallandras had told her that the cold here would be matched and deepened when they at last entered the Sea of Sorrows.

"Do you ever sleep?"

"Yes." The music continued to cushion her fall.

"When?"

"When necessary, ATerafin." But his smile tempered the distance in the words.

"I think I owe you one."

"And on the road we take it is likely that you will have a chance to rid yourself of that debt." The bard stilled the strings of his famous lute. "Sleep well for what remains of the evening."

She nodded quietly.

"But ATerafin?"

"What?"

"I think that you must speak with your domicis. It is clear that you cannot continue in this fashion."

"W-what do you mean?"

"Look at your arm."

She knew what she would see the minute the words left his lips, wrapped in the privacy which was the gift of bards. But as if he had used *the* voice to compel, she lifted her arm anyway. To her eye, clear as starlight and just as bright, the sign of the serpent—stylized S bisected by two small vee's—was glowing with a silver blue aurora.

She cursed under her breath in both of the languages she knew. The stag nudged her forehead with his nose. She met his eyes.

"Don't you start, too."

But the stag replied by touching the skin of her wrist very lightly with the tine of his lowest antler.

She woke at dawn before the night had given way to the harsh exposure of sunlight. In this time, as at dusk, a man could speak freely should he choose. The Lord and the Lady paid no heed to that which they did not rule unless it threatened their Dominion.

A lone woman who would never return home was not such a threat. She passed beneath them.

There were propitiations to make; she carried a flask of wine in one hand, a flask of water in the other. She also carried a small silver spade, tucked safely away in the little pouch that rested between sash and skin. It had value that was both sentimental and monetary, and the latter always posed a threat on the open road. So she had been taught as a sheltered, young girl, sitting by her grandfather's side. Basking in his warmth, as if it were the sun's warmth.

And it had been. Just as harsh, as unmerciful, as blinding. Just as necessary.

But she was no child, and would never be again. She was no longer certain who she was, although she had been the Serra Teresa di'Marano, one of the most powerful women in the Dominion, where a woman had power the way a spider does; by spinning the incredibly fine web and hoping that it went unseen. Now, she wore the clothing of the Voyani women, and she did their work; she spoke little and attempted to mime the clumsiness of their gestures. She failed, and it was a profound disappointment, this failure. But she had not come to think of failure, and if she dawdled doing so, she would lose the only thing she had: time.

She found her place and knelt against dirt that was hard with water's lack. But it still held moisture; the Arkosan caravan had not yet reached desert's edge. Taking great care to disturb none of the sparse vegetation that clung to this crusted soil, she turned a small spadeful of earth to one side—the left side—revealing a darker brown. Earth would give way to sand soon.

But not yet; not yet. She lifted her flask and very carefully trickled a thin, burgundy line across the wound she had made in the earth's surface. She spoke quietly, and in a voice that no other person listening—be they bard-born or no—would hear. She set the flask down, and bowed her head. Waited a moment, and then repeated her careful actions, but with water instead of wine.

Lady, please, hear me. Protect my niece. Guide her. We fight your true enemy. Give her a home among the wanderers who have never forgotten your laws or your ways. Please hear me. Please hear me. She did not speak the words. Not even the Lady liked the way pleading stretched an otherwise melodious voice thin.

When she was finished, she rose.

Diora. She bowed her head.

Margret heard the Serra's name, again and again, in a dozen different voices. Each time she heard it, she felt a little prickle across the back of her neck. It was tied to many things: her mother's death. Her mother's choice to trust—to always trust—strangers rather than her own daughter, her own heir.

Had it been only that, she might have left the clanswoman to freeze in the desert night, to burn in the desert heat; they were almost upon either. But Stavos, Uncle Stavos, had taken the girl under wing inasmuch as it was possible to take something that cold and placid under wing, and Tamara—'Lena's mother, and therefore a woman who should *know* better, by Lady's blood and wind—had done likewise. She shooed the gawking men away.

Margret's men.

"Matriarch."

Margret was baleful. "What?"

Nicu stood in silence at her back, waiting for her to fully turn and acknowledge his existence. She had beaten him in public and she had stripped him of some of his duties, but he was still popular among the younger men whose responsibility it was to fight and die protecting the Matriarch's van. Her cousin. After a moment, contemplating what she would see, she turned; she wasn't surprised. Nicu's eyes had taken on a darkness, a haunted exhaustion, that felt like accusation.

When she looked at his face, she saw, imposed upon it like a ghost, the knotted muscles of his back, the blood that flayed skin shed. Her own hand holding the whip. Nothing, nothing at all, was clean anymore.

But at least Nicu, the prettiest of the men by far with the single exception of Margret's baby brother, was not gawking after the Serra; he was constant in his obsessions. He mooned after Elena, and Elena, true to bitter form, did what she could to be anywhere in the encampment that did not contain her cousin.

Margret had once loved Nicu in her fashion. She had once thought him beautiful. "Yes?"

"The men are ready, Matriarch."

"And the others?"

"They are making ready to leave."

She turned back to the desert, the evening sky coloring its sand and cooling its heat. This was the path to Arkosa; she could *feel* it in the sand beneath her feet. She wondered if the Serra could as well. Wondered, bitter, if the Serra could feel it more strongly.

"Good."

"How many?"

"No more than fifteen men, Nicu. Bring no children."

"Adam?"

She laughed. "Leave him behind if he'll stay." And then, on a fierce whim, because she wanted family with her, she added, "No, bring Adam."

"And the others?"

It occurred to her then, as he shuffled slightly from foot to foot before remembering just who he was supposed to be, that he had never made this trek. She herself had only made it once, at her mother's behest. And she had nearly died there, although no one but her dead mother knew it.

"Nicu?"

He shook his head. "Will we take the strangers?"

"The strangers?"

"The pale-haired Northerner; the woman who came from the heartfire; the man who is and is not her seraf; the . . . pale-haired . . ." he swallowed.

"Leave the question of the others to me."

"Matriarch," he said, bowing. He turned, and then turned again. "'Gret?"

She relented because she had always relented. "What?"

"Is it true that at least one man always dies on the trek?"

"Or a woman. Sometimes as many as ten. Our great

great great grandmother came back from the desert path with only her sister; her daughter perished."

He bowed.

The strangers sat in their own circle outside of the caravan, and it was just as well. Although Jewel ATerafin—as she styled herself—had some Voyani blood, it was clear that she was the descendant of traitors who had been too weak to fulfill their promise and follow the *Voyanne* to its rightful end.

And yet she was here. She had been delivered to Arkosa in the hour of their need, coming from the heart of the Lady's fire into the heart of the Arkosan camp. It was, as entrances went, spectacular, and it lingered in Margret's memory the way a violent act will linger across flesh: like a scar.

"ATerafin?" she said, as she approached.

The most beautiful man she had ever seen—and was certain she *would* ever see—placed one slender, perfect hand on the hilt of a sword; he glanced at Jewel ATerafin, and the profuse shake of unruly curls—hair not so very unlike Margret's—caused him to withdraw. There was nothing in him that was friendly. There was nothing in him at all that responded to her.

Even clansmen offered disdain and contempt, mixed with a healthy dose of caution.

She found that she wanted response. And was embarrassed by the desire. Especially when he looked up at exactly the moment desire and guilt met, his eyes cutting in their silence and their perception.

He stepped aside without a word. And she, awkward and ungainly, trudged past him. She stopped at the edge of the clearing that had been made; the night was already chilly.

"My apologies," she said, striving for formality.

"None necessary," Jewel replied. Her smile was open, friendly; she had none of the caution that the clansmen had, and none of the distrust of strangers that the Voyani did. Or rather, if she felt them at all, she hid them. She offered a hand, and after a moment, Margret took it.

"I know that you'll be leaving soon."

"We will."

"If you want us, we'd be happy to accompany you."

Margret hesitated. She did not want to offend this stranger, and she chose her next words with uncharacteristic care. "The trek into the desert is not a trek that is usually undertaken by any but Arkosans."

Jewel nodded, as if she had expected no less. Her smile faded, although her expression was still open, still friendly. "I think . . . that if there is any way for you to stretch that rule, you might want to."

"You've seen something?" Margret struggled to hide the envy in her words. She wasn't sure if she failed or not.

"Not anything specific. But—"

"But?"

This time, the stranger did hesitate. She took a deep breath, and then said, "I left my Northern home because of a vision. I came to the South, seeking two things. The Winter Queen, and a young woman."

Margret knew, then, and she felt a moment of fury, and a moment of bitterness, that were too strong for words.

Jewel ATerafin could not mistake her silence for anything other than what it was, but she continued to speak. "The Serra Diora is that woman, and I fear that my companions and I will be of as much aid in the desert as we were in the Tor Leonne, if you will accept us."

Only years of her mother's harshest lessons prevented Margret from refusing the offer and stalking off.

But it was a near thing.

Everyone was interested in that Courtesan. Everyone.

The Serra Diora di'Marano was silent. In all things, silent. In movement, silent. In sleep, silent. While eating, silent.

Margret wanted to slap her until she said something, even if it was a curse. Especially if that. "Why do they stare at her like that?" she snapped.

She had steadfastly failed to notice that the men in the caravan seemed to either fall silent when Diora passed them, or fall all over themselves to get out of her way, or to offer her shadow or shade when it existed. But it was getting hot, Margret was tired, and the euphoria of the escape from the capital had fallen off sharply. That and it took effort to fail to notice the completely obvious.

Elena laughed, but the laugh had a very, very sharp edge.

"Because she's beautiful, 'Gret. Don't you know what the clansmen call her?"

"No."

"Liar."

"I don't pay attention to clansmen's gossip. No one does."

Elena laughed again. "Adam!" she shouted, wildly waving a hand so that anyone standing across the divide of the fire's circles might see her.

Margret's slender brother, dark hair bobbing as he came charging across the clearing, obeyed the unspoken command of the Matriarch's heir. Pretty much everyone did; Margret was Matriarch and technically the leader—but Elena had the freer temper, and certainly the freer hand. Her hair was now that bright, burnished copper that the sun made of auburn, and it was long and as uncontrolled as Adam's gait.

He stopped about three feet away from her, panting. "Yes?"

She laughed. "What do the clansmen call our guest?"

"Which guest?"

"The Serra."

He beamed—he had a grin that defined the word infectious—because he *knew* this one. "The Flower of the Dominion."

The grin faded into something distinctly more sickly when he saw his sister's expression cloud and sour at the same time. "Where did you hear that?"

"Well, everyone knows it."

"Who is *everyone*?"

He cringed. The shadow of her hand crossed his face and stopped there. "Is everyone talking about her?"

"Well, *you* and 'Lena are," he said defensively.

She spit. "Don't you have something to do?"

He wasn't stupid. He took the hint. Margret wanted to snarl; her lips thinned instead. "She better not think she's a treasured guest," she snapped. "No one else travels the *Voyanne* without doing their share of the work."

Elena shrugged; Margret cast a glance in her direction. Her cousin had always been the untamed beauty of their immediate family; she still was. But she—like any of them—didn't take well to a rival in their own wagon. "With hands like that," 'Lena said, "she can't have done much work in her life."

"And you're the judge of another life now?" A sharp voice said. "You barely live yours in a way that suits a Matriarch's daughter."

Both young women started slightly; only one of them had the grace to flush. "Matriarch," Elena of the Arkosa Voyani said, inclining her head with a respect that she seldom showed.

Yollana of the Havalla Voyani frowned. Her legs were still not fully healed from her ordeal at the hands of the Sword's Edge, and it was privately thought that they would never be healed without the intervention of one born with the Lady's gift.

They were very few, far between, and no Matriarch would trust a healer born outside of her clan under any circumstance; Yollana therefore hobbled on canes, often at the side of an attentive Serra Teresa di'Marano, the Northern bard, or both, although she sometimes allowed the Arkosans to carry her in a makeshift palanquin from one end of the encampment to the other.

At the moment, she had chosen the canes. She had an intense dislike for dependence of any type, and it galled Margret to think that the help of a stranger—the striking but ice-cold bard of the North—was preferable to the help of her own. "Yollana," she said, inclining her chin very slightly. "This *is* the Arkosan van."

"So?"

"Margret—" Elena began, but her cousin lifted a hand so sharply a slap wouldn't have been a surprise. There wasn't one. But there was a bit of night in the dawn.

"The laws of the *Voyanne* have nothing to do with petty jealousy and hampered vision," the older woman continued. "Carry a grudge if you feel you must, but understand it for the ugly thing it is."

"You think I'm jealous of that?"

Yollana frowned. "Don't insult my intelligence, Matriarch. It does us no good. Remember who our enemies are. We can bicker among ourselves later."

As whole Voyani wars were the result of bickering, and the dead that occurred between both sides of particularly vicious disputes were probably too great in number to count—although each family spent time counting anyway, and storing all sense of grievance against that day when reckoning was due—Margret simply shrugged. "Even you," she said after the silence had grown irritating.

"Yes?"

"Even you fall under her spell."

Yollana's bark was almost a cough, although Margret was pretty sure it had been intended as laughter.

Margret felt instantly ashamed of the anger she could not control. "Matriarch," Yollana said, without preamble, "have the preparations been made?"

Margret nodded bitterly.

"Then the Matriarchs will take their leave; they have much to do now that the Tyr has unwisely chosen to give the Sword of Knowledge free reign. Elsarre is called upon by her own; Maria is seeking word on the fate of her husband and sons; they were apparently foolish enough not to trust our ability to defend the city against whatever doom we felt was upon it, and they remained within its walls."

"And you go back to Havalla?"

"It would be the wise choice, although I confess I have little in the way of escort."

"Take the bard and the Northerner with you." Margret frowned. "There is something about her seraf that I *do not* trust."

Yollana was silent. "You have your mother's instinct, if not her talent," she said at last. It was not a compliment, but there was praise in it, if one knew how to look. The Havallan Matriarch paused for a long, long time, and then said, "if you would grant it, Matriarch of Arkosa, if our old alliance still has value, I would ask that you allow me to accompany you."

"Accompany us where?"

Elena nudged her with a toe; it was hard enough that it missed being a kick by a sand grain. She looked at her cousin; her cousin lifted a hand and curled it a moment in a fist over her heart.

Margret—almost never at a loss for words—was nonetheless silent for a full minute as she absorbed what Yollana had just said. She started and stopped twice, remembering that no heartfire burned to protect her words—or the Havallan Matriarch's—from outsiders.

"Had I asked the same . . . favor of the Havallan Matriarch, what would her response have been?"

The old woman said, without preamble, and with no apparent difficulty, "I would have refused, of course."

"And you expect *me* to say yes?"

The old woman's laugh was dry and harsh, the rattle of wind. Margret felt the chill of desert night travel the length of her spine.

"I expect you to do what is in the best interests of Arkosa, Matriarch. Only that." She started to turn, placing the cane against the sand.

She was not particularly surprised when the old woman turned back. "But never less."

CHAPTER TEN

Margret went to her wagon.

Elena, hearing the command that was unspoken, followed, and watched for a handful of time as Margret slammed tin and silver around in the small, cramped quarters, venting a fury that she managed—barely—not to put into words.

And after she had finished, Elena calmly offered her sweet wine; a single glass.

Margret stared at it. The glass was the oldest thing her mother had owned; one of the items that had been passed from Matriarch to Matriarch. It had no partner; no companion piece. Light nestled in the crescents made in its clear, hard surface, and light blended with the contents of the glass until the liquid, in the poor light of the wagon, looked a little like blood.

"So that's it?" Margret said, her throat suddenly swollen, the words thick. She stared at the glass. Stared at the liquid. And then looked up from her place at the flap of a table, and stared at her cousin.

Her cousin's red highlights were lost to the shadows, and the sparkle of her defiance had been guttered—although it wouldn't stay that way—as she stared back.

"I never—I never understood—that glass," 'Lena said, each word distinct.

Margret picked it up. There was nothing delicate about it, although she had no doubt it could be broken with ease. "What didn't you understand?"

'Lena shook her head; her hair came out from beneath her band in little sprays. She answered, but she didn't answer the question. "I envied you.

"When we were younger, I hated the fact that you would get everything, and I would be—if I were lucky—your trusted adviser. I thought—" she laughed, and it was a shaky, weak sound that was completely unfamiliar,"—that you were too timid, too temperamental—"

"Me?"

She laughed again, "and too damn sensitive. I really thought—when I was younger—that *I* would be the better Matriarch."

Margret said bitterly, "Why are you telling me this?"

"Your head is full of sand," Elena snapped back. "I'm *telling* you this because it's my way of apologizing, so don't interrupt me!"

Margret laughed. "I don't need your apology."

"Maybe I need to say it."

"That's not my problem."

They bristled a moment, and then Margret looked down at the glass; at the wine poured for her by her cousin.

"Okay, maybe it is my problem," she said softly. She lifted the glass. "My mother—" Put it down again.

There was only one. There had always been only one.

As if she could hear the thought, 'Lena said, simply, "You're all that stands between me and what I wanted as a child. And I'll do everything in my power to make sure that you stand between me and what I wanted until you make us a Mother's Daughter the proper way."

Margret emptied the glass; the wine would sour if she left it, and there was enough that was sour in her life. "What do we do?"

"We take her."

"And the others?"

Elena spread her hands out in a gesture that mocked helplessness. But her expression was serious. "They came to us in the fires. They came when we needed them."

"And the deserter?"

"The deserter's *descendant*," Elena said, stressing the word. "She—it's said she *stopped* the Hunt. How much of a deserter could she be and still have that much of the Lady's grace?"

"But her seraf—"

"He's no seraf."

"I know."

"I think he'd kill us all before he let us take her anywhere without him."

Margret grimaced. "And Kallandras?"

"Take him. He's pretty."

"I'm being serious."

"You're *always* serious. We can leave him behind; I think if you told him to get lost in a sandstorm, he'd do it. But we have to take the Serra Diora with us." She paused and looked at the dust on her boots. Or at something more interesting than Margret's face in the shadows.

"And?"

"What do you mean, 'and'?"

"What else are you not saying, 'Lena?"

"I want to take the Serra Teresa."

"Why? She's not family."

Elena's silences were uncomfortable because she employed them so seldom. But she did speak because Margret's patience was even less often employed. "She's never going to go home. Wherever she goes, she will always be outcast because of this."

The Arkosan Matriarch snorted. "What crime did she commit that her brother's daughter hasn't? And don't even try to tell me that the Serra Diora has any plans of forsaking the ruling clans."

"The Serra Diora . . . it is said . . . has done all she has done out of loyalty to the memory of her dead husband. The clansmen will admire that, in their fashion, because she has done it in a seemly way."

"And the Serra Teresa?"

"Unmarried. She has betrayed her brothers and her clan. But worse, she has done so in the guise of man. Wherever she goes from here, she will never have what she enjoyed before she made her choice. She's come to the *Voyanne*. And I think the Lady means her to travel it at our side."

Margret dreamed.

She looked into the face of a frightened young woman—a beautiful, slender girl with perfect skin and dark, sleep-wild hair. The girl was clearly a clanswoman; she had a scent that was flower oil and perfume and musky sweat. Fear didn't really have a scent, but had it, she would have embodied it. It was overpowering, demanding, terrifying. She reached for the girl, unsure of whether or not she was offering comfort or asking for it; she was mute.

But the girl pulled away, the whites of her eyes growing around dark irises, dark pupils.

"There's nothing to be afraid of," she said, or tried to say, although she knew with a bitter horror that it was a lie. The words wouldn't come. She felt as if her own words would never come again. In their place, the song of steel, the sharp, harsh crack of lightning's tongue, the cries of the wounded—storm's voice: the language of men, of war.

Promise me, the young woman said, voice growing wilder as the sounds drew nearer to where they sat, trapped, waiting.

Anything, she tried to say. Tried. The voice of the wind was a howl.

You brought our son into the world. You saved him. You birthed him. If it weren't for—if it weren't for what we can't say—

Save him. Save only him. Please.

She wanted to make that promise. She wanted to defend that child with her life because what else was a life *for*?

But the words, damn them—she would hate words forever after—*would not* come. Instead, the screaming. The woman cried out in a voice so raw it would haunt Margret for the rest of her life, and given the sounds of approaching death, she prayed that wouldn't be long.

The woman handed her a baby, a boy, and then grabbed an expensive, large vase, holding it in her hands as if it were an awkward club.

Margret's throat was thick now; her arms were numb, but she forced them to gather the child to her breast, as if holding children were natural, as if nothing in the world were as delicate, or as precious.

As if by pretending hard and long enough she could change the fact that his neck was broken.

She woke in the dark, alone. Sweating, which given the chill of the night, was not good. Blankets were bunched in her hands and her arms were stiff as a corpse's.

Someone was knocking, gently, insistently, at her door. She owed them a favor, whoever they were. She owed them.

But the Voyani hated being in anyone's debt. She

wrapped the blankets around herself once she could force her arms to move, and she stumbled to the door. There she stopped, pressing her head against wood, dragging breath into her lungs, buying time to compose herself. She was crying.

She hated the tears.

She opened the door upon the Serra Teresa di'Marano, backlit by full, bright moon, face lit by orange, dim lamp.

The Serra immediately bowed her head.

"What—is something wrong? Did Yollana send you?"

She shook her head; dark strands brushed her cheeks. Beyond the two men who served as a perpetual guard—and Margret was tired enough that she wasn't sure what the time was, and therefore who the guards should be—there was only one other person: Serra Teresa's seraf.

Wearily, she stepped back into the wagon, offering by action what she was disinclined to offer by word: hospitality. Grudging or no, it was accepted.

She didn't have the energy to be angry, and that was surprising; it was a Matriarch's first emotion, and it was usually a Matriarch's last. But—as her mother had said, when the sting of her open palm was subsiding—there was a world of emotion between the first one and the last one, most of it bitter, all of it necessary.

"What do you want?"

The Serra Teresa, by all accounts one of the most accomplished of the clanswomen, took no offense at the tone or the words—which was unfortunate, as some offense had been intended.

"I don't know."

Whatever she had expected to hear, that wasn't it. She frowned. "Why did you come here?"

The Serra was silent for a moment, and then she lifted her head and met Margret's eyes; they were of a height, although Margret had always assumed that the Serra Teresa was somehow more delicate, more diminutive. "I came," she said quietly, "because the Lady's Moon is strong and I had hoped to . . . convince you . . . to rethink your approach to my niece."

"My—" And the frown changed, sharpening the lines of Margret's face. "Convince me?"

Serra Teresa didn't answer. She didn't need to answer. They stood staring at each other in the wagon. "And you've changed your mind?"

"Yes," the Serra replied.

"Then why did you knock?"

"Because the desert waiting to swallow us is not the only desert; just the obvious one. I do not know what you have lost, Margret, but I suspect it is not much compared to what you *will* lose, and willingly, when you come into your power."

"You're a seer now?"

"No more than anyone who has experienced much." She turned. Turned back. "Ask Yollana, and tell her that if she wishes to speak of me, she has my blessing. But, daughter of a friend, let me offer you a warning. The name that you spoke in your sleep is a name that you would do best never to speak at any other time."

"Name?"

The Serra bowed her head. "Forgive me my intrusion," she said softly. "If you were not aware of the name you spoke . . ." She looked up. "It is not our way, clans or Voyani, Lord or Lady, to show mercy, or to desire it for ourselves."

She walked toward the guards; spoke a few words that were inevitably too soft and too distant to drift back to Margret. Her seraf bowed and fell into perfect, graceful step at her side. As if she wore fine silk saris, gold and the jeweled combs of her upbringing, and not the dusty, dirty, sweaty fabrics the road decreed.

All before Margret realized that the Serra knew who the woman in the dream was, and had somehow escaped without telling her.

Jewel didn't speak when she woke.

She bit her lip, curled up, arms wrapped around her body. She felt the ground beneath her cheek; it was cool. Had she fallen asleep outside?

Tines brushed her hair. The stag. The stag who had once been a man, and at that, a man who had once been the Winter King. She swallowed, tried to compose herself. It wasn't easy. Sleep had a way of stripping her of all defense, and only slowly did she gather it again as wakefulness took hold.

I had, the creature said, and she startled at the strange texture of his completely silent voice, although at the same time . . . at the same time it felt warm and natural, *a daughter once.*

A daughter?

I had several children. I had more than one daughter. Not all were . . . children that you would have approved of, if you indeed approve of anything rational.

She snorted. But his words relaxed the hard curve of her back; she could lift her head from the ground, could sit up.

But I had one daughter very like you.

One daughter?

Yes. It is . . . long ago now . . . and I had almost forgotten. It is not a fond memory.

What happened? Jewel asked, clear proof if it were needed that she could put her foot in her mouth when her mouth wasn't even open. If she could have, she would have taken the question back; left the answer in the darkness.

What happened?

His eyes were not, would never be, human—but that robbed them of none of their ability to wound.

She was very like you. She was very, very weak. She was no fool—but you are no fool if you could force the Winter Queen to surrender anything she valued. I believe you will regret that, although it has been years since I could summon the power necessary to ascertain how.

But I was speaking of the weak.

She was dead. They were all dead, this man's children, but not all of the deaths haunted him.

No, of course not, he said, and the words were as dry as desert sand. *It is always easier to forget the tragedy inherent in the deaths of those who have tried—and failed—to kill you.*

She did not visibly recoil, but it made no difference; none of their conversation had been visible. Tines crossed her cheek in a caress, and she realized, perhaps for the first time, that this creature that she had rescued needed no further rescue; was, in fact, dangerous. Strands of her hair twined a moment around something that looked like ivory as he lifted his head.

It was my own fault, he said. *I . . . indulged . . . the weakness that destroyed her, instead of destroying it. I valued it; she paid.* He lifted his head; the breadth of his antlers lay against the watching night like a cage, not a crown—if there was any difference between the two. *I did not make that mistake again.*

"And instead you raised children who tried to destroy you. Thanks, but I think I'd rather risk loss."

Who said this was a matter of choice? Why do you assume that it was her *pain that I sought to avoid? In the end, she was dust, and I remained, and her memory, and the loss, is everlasting.*

She did not seek to hold him when his hooves compressed sand into the dirt; his trail was quickly lost to the evening.

But she sat a long time, hearing the dead, smelling the dead, and thinking about all the ways in which people of power kill—and had killed—each other.

Here, the sand not thirty yards away, the tent he carried by day a small and flimsy enclosure against the deep chill of night, Kallandras of Senniel College dreamed. It was a night for dreaming; a night in which ghosts and memory were very nearly the same.

But the ghosts were not of the dead; nor were they the brothers that he would never, by the binding of the Lady, forget. Here, he heard the passing howl of wind over barren plains, and in its folds, as it carried sand and debris to sting and rebuke him, were the voices of whole cities, lost to time, or worse, and buried without ceremony.

Death had no way to hold him; the dying had no purchase over him. His training had seen to that.

But the wind's howl and fury spoke of other types of loss, and when it ripped the moorings of his tent free with contempt and ease, he rose in its folds. He looked at his hand; saw no ring, and realized, belatedly, that he was not—quite—awake.

But sleep had different meanings for a man who had sworn his soul to the keeping of a jealous, an angry, god. He went with the wind, and the wind carried him, in the moonlit chill of desert night, to the place where shadows were growing.

Here, it said sibilantly.

He could see a lone tower, like a knife blade, jutting out of the sand.

But the wind whispered, *There are four*.

As it carried him, he could see them, less prominent than the first, but there.

And what is the interest of the air in the four?

The answer: he fell, plummeting as he was given to gravity. The wind caught him before he struck ground—and presumably lost consciousness—and carried him up again, singing in accusation; pulling his hair from his face. The voices the wind carried were voices of those who had once served the wind, and had been served by it, in their fashion. Wild magics.

Wild mages.

How did they die?

They are not dead, the wind said, and the storm came upon them both. *They are sleeping. Wake them.*

He woke instead. He was upright almost before his eyes were open, and when they did open, the first thing he saw was his hand. It was no accident; on his finger, Myrddion's ring was burning with a cold, blue light.

She sat—there was no room to stand—in the corner of the tent closest to escape, waiting, her eyes clear, her face exposed. He spoke, but not even the wind was privy to what he said; the words for Evayne alone.

"Your father is restless."

Her face was smooth as glass, and her eyes glittered. After a moment, he bowed his head. "I . . . assume that the gods are touching the dreaming."

"There are gods touching the dreaming," she said softly, rising. "But not all of them are alive; not all of them are known. You are to travel with the Voyani."

"Yes."

"You have done so once before."

He felt the chill of the night keenly, but he endured it; there were other things to speak of, and pleasantries about weather were lost on Evayne. "I was younger. I was younger and the Matriarch . . . *was* Matriarch." He paused, and then after a moment, he reached for the battered case that contained the single item he valued. He drew his lute out of concealment. The rounded wood of her bowl was old, but it had been magicked; water did not condense in the movement between heat and cold; the wood did not warp with moisture and crack with its lack. The strings, alas, could not be magicked in a like fashion without changing their sound, although he did not clearly understand why this should be so. Maker-born strings, he was told, would endure all, but he had not yet found an Artisan who was both sane enough to approach and musically inclined enough to fashion such things, and although he had seen finer instruments made by Maker hands . . . this one had some hold on his voice.

He placed her curve carefully in his folded lap, and touched her, drawing something like melody out of the random touch of fingers against neck and string. "Why are you here?" he asked, when the music had calmed the voice of the wind and the ring had become just another band of jeweled metal in the darkness.

"Merely to wake you," she replied, and he lifted his head and met the striking violet of her eyes.

"To . . . wake me?"

She nodded and rose. "Be careful, Kallandras. The ring . . . is not proof against the element. Not in the desert. Too much that is buried there is not yet dead."

"I know."

"You did not travel with the Arianni, when last you came. You did not travel in the shadow of the Warlord, you did not walk beside a man who once presided over the greater Councils of Man. Every step of the way will be difficult because you are walking beside a people who do not understand that their way is dead."

"Is it?"

Her own smile was grim, bitter.

He was silent for a long moment as he absorbed her words, their meaning, the things that she did not put into them, and the things that she did. At length, he said, "The Warlord?"

She frowned. "I . . . do not know. I did not foresee him clearly. I do not see him clearly now."

"And Lord Celleriant?"

She looked away. Looked back. "If the Queen bound him to Jewel ATerafin, he will be safe."

"If she did not?"

"Then he will perish when you reach your destination. You may wish to have Jewel leave him behind."

"I think . . . that it is unlikely she will agree. She has not changed much, Evayne."

"Yes, she has," the seer replied, in a very strange tone of voice. "But she has yet to realize how much. I will leave you with a warning; the wind's voice will try to bring sand and storm to the caravan.

"Do not sleep lightly, Kallandras. Do not ignore your dreams. And . . . do not let the young ATerafin ignore hers."

He was so used to accepting both her orders and her disappearance that it felt perfectly natural to watch her rise and vanish between one step and the next.

Last to wake from dream that night, although wake he did, was Nicu of the Arkosan Voyani. The dream itself was fragile, and broken like web or gossamer the moment he struggled up from beneath its cloudy surface—but the feel of it remained, like an ache in a joint or a bone that has been both broken and healed. He stood at the height of a wide, wide stone tower—a tower of a type that could only exist in dreams, for it seemed to him that the base touched the earth below the clouds. In the distance, winging toward him in a lazy spiral, were things that he at first had taken for carrion birds.

But when their great wings caught the light, when they reared and turned the sky into patches of lazy, perfect fire, he felt . . . awe. Desire. Even a little fear, although the tower was said to be proof against the very gods.

A dream, indeed. But there was something about it . . . .

He struggled out of the curved bunk in his mother's wagon. Although he was old enough by now to deserve a wagon—and a wife—of his own, the only woman he desired eluded him.

And now, as Matriarch's heir, he wondered if she would do so forever.

Forget about Elena, Nicu; she is not for you. She is the Lady's wild face, and she will bring you nothing but grief.

How can you say that, when you listen *to what she says? When* you *treat her with such respect?*

She's a woman, his mother had replied. *And she'll live and die for Arkosa. But she won't live and die for a man or a child, and when it comes to men or children . . .*

Maybe she just has to meet the right man!

His mother's scorn emerged for a moment, as she showed true Voyani colors. *She's known you all your life—something has happened that has turned you from the boy she played with to the man for her?*

It stung. Still stung. When the other girls had started to notice him, when Margret and Elena had first played their furtive games, he had thought the world his. Things had changed—his back pained him, and the skin across his shoulder blades would never lose its peculiar tightness—but what could change once, could change again, no?

He did not bother to creep or sneak past his sleeping mother; her snores filled the wagon with a familiar rattle and creak that meant a sandstorm would half-bury the wagon before she'd be roused. But he did leave the wagon, lifting the flap and cursing slightly at the nip of the chill air.

The man was waiting for him.

He looked slimmer than he had the previous two times he had offered Nicu his gifts. Slimmer and taller, lean but not gaunt. The clothing he wore was robbed of color and texture by the Lady's night, but it was obviously fine, especially compared to what Nicu now possessed. Much had been lost—as it always was—to flight.

But the sword lay in the Matriarch's wagon, and the shield, in his mother's, hidden against a day of need. Hidden against the accusation that might follow it. He wasn't a fool; being publicly lashed had taught him something.

The stranger bowed. "It appears," he said quietly, "that your chance to be the savior of the Voyani has not yet come to pass."

Nicu said nothing.

"The encampment did not suffer attack of any nature."

"The fires," Nicu replied, lowering his voice although he had a feeling—a cold, uncomfortable feeling—that his words would not escape to other ears. "The fires the Matriarchs called protected us." He did not glance over his shoulder to see who might be watching them; did not look from side to side. Instead, he brought his arms across his chest and allowed himself to relax into the side of the wagon, between the wheels. The worst thing he could do to attract attention was to appear furtive.

The stranger's smile was as cold as the night air. "Ample protection against an attack that does not come."

"Or an attack that could not come. The Matriarchs summoned simple fire to protect the wagons, but they went in person to defend the Lady's gift."

At that, the smile folded into the darkness of a momentary frown. Nicu, who had found the smile unpleasant, found the frown vastly more chilling. The desert night was contained in the curve of thinning lips.

Even when those lips relaxed, dispelling the frown, memory lingered. He had always known that this man was a danger. But he had deliberately refused to acknowledge that he was an enemy. As he was leaning against the wagon, he did not attempt to retreat.

"You do not know your history," the stranger said softly.

"I know enough."

"Do you? What have the Matriarchs chosen to tell you of the Cities of Man?"

"I know," he said simply, "that they were devoured by sand because of the arrogance of their rulers. I know that their rulers were in league with the Enemy, and for it, perished. Only four lines were spared. Only four, who had not chosen to serve the Lord of Night."

"And you know that the men—"

"Yes, they led us into *this*."

The stranger's gaze was appraising. After a moment, he nodded. "Very well. I will not play that game with you now. But is not the dream of each of the Voyani, no matter of which family, to finally reach the end of the *Voyanne*? To be judged worthy again in the eyes of the Lord and the Lady; to return—and to claim—a homeland? Is this not why so many of your number forsake their vow and head to the safety of the North?"

Nicu did not answer.

After a moment it became clear that he would not.

"I thought you were stronger, Nicu, Donatella's son. Your Matriarch has beaten all spirit out of you. Perhaps it would be best if we did not meet again."

But Nicu looked up at the veiled threat, caught between two desires, one of them survival. "When—when the other came to the caravan, he said—he said he had the keys to Arkosa."

"Did he?"

Nicu's frown deepened. "What did he mean?"

"You would have to ask the Matriarch," the stranger replied. "It is not an answer that I am capable of giving to one who does not understand the power of the Cities."

Nicu was completely silent.

But it didn't last. The sun was creeping up over the horizon. "I . . . will . . . be accompanying the Matriarch," he said at last.

"She is standing on the edge of the desert that we call the Sea of Sorrows."

"Yes."

"Is it possible that she has never made the trek?"

"She's been," he said coldly. He pulled his back away from the wagon's side. "We don't talk about the *Voyanne* with outsiders. We don't talk about the desert."

"But I already know of both. What does that make me?"

Nicu shrugged, and then smiled. "Ask the Matriarch," he said softly.

The stranger surprised him: He laughed. There was something warm in the laugh—but warm the way the desert sun is warm. "You and I will see each other again, Nicu. When you are less ignorant and you understand what it is you have to offer your tribe."

"My family," Nicu snapped.

"Your family, then." He bowed. There was nothing at all subservient or polite in the gesture. "They wake now. I can spend no more time here.

"But I did not lie about the shield, and if you desire the sword—" He held out his hands, palm up, as if in offering.

And Nicu was ashamed. Because he did desire it, even now.

Elena woke early to feed the children.

She stopped at Donatella's wagon to rouse her, and hesitated when she saw Nicu outside of the tenting. It had been hard to meet his eyes since the public flogging; every time she saw his face, she also remembered his back, and she ached for him and wanted to kill him at the same time.

Not a comfortable feeling.

"'Lena?" he said, as she stood, watching him, her expression guarded.

She almost turned and fled; she had, so many times. But they were going to the Sea of Sorrows; they were going *with* Nicu, for he was still in charge of the defense of their diminished caravan. Margret had not kept that away from him, although she had diminished him greatly by the punishment she had chosen to inflict.

"'Lena?" He said again, profoundly hesitant, just as she was.

She ground her teeth a moment, and then she *looked* at him. "Nicu."

"Are you going to—"

"Yes. I'm going to feed the children. Donatella is supposed to help."

"She's sleeping. She's been—she's been tired."

Elena shrugged. "We've all been tired. Doesn't matter; the children still need feeding."

He took a deep breath; she waited for him to spit out whatever it was he was thinking about saying. But when it came, it wasn't what she'd expected. "I'll do it."

The silence lasted about five heartbeats too long, and his expression had already half turned sour before she found an answer. "*You'll* do it?"

"I'm a better cook than either you or Margret, if not as good as my mother."

She raised an auburn brow. "Better than 'Gret maybe, but you're half the cook I am."

"We can ask," he snapped back. "We can ask anyone." He stopped for a moment and then added slyly, "we can ask the children. They won't lie to curry favor."

She stared at him for a moment, and she felt, in the space between night and day, that she might one day have her cousin back.

"You're on," she said, "but if you win, you'll be feeding the children for a long, long time."

He hesitated, and she looked away as he said, "but isn't that one of the most important things? Feeding the children?" And he said it in the hopeful voice of a much, much younger boy.

She looked at him; her eyes stung and watered, and she

hated that. "Yes," she said. And then, before she could change her mind or remember who she was and who he was, and why he wasn't that young boy anymore, she hugged him.

CHAPTER ELEVEN

25th of Scaral, 427 AA
Terrean of Raverra

Cherry blossoms.

The young Serra Diora di'Marano stared at a pale shade of pink and watched as the sun revealed what lay beneath its living surface: minute veins of color that spread its branches from the center of each petal to its delicate edge, an echo of the tree on which it blossomed, year after year. But it was not always easy to see those veins, that color that lay beneath the surface. The blossoms—from her vantage as a small child—were out of reach; it was not until the sun perched at a certain height that such mysteries were exposed.

The sun.

He is not your friend, Na'dio. Remember that.

But the cherry blossoms, she said softly, *never look so beautiful as when the sun touches them. Look, Ona Alana. Look, Ona Teresa.* She lifted a hand, a perfectly smooth, small hand, and pointed to the veins beneath her own skin, the blue-green movement of blood that spoke of life in such an odd way.

They are beautiful, Na'dio, her Ona Teresa had said. *The blossoms are lovely at this time of year.*

Serra Teresa, Alana en'Marano said severely.

The Serra Teresa, from beneath the sun-shelter provided by Ramdan's steady hands, inclined her head slightly, lifting a fan and spreading it before her delicate features. The sun touched only the folds of silk that fell from her knee to the softness of perfectly tended grass—but even in touching that, it added colors the silk itself should not have possessed; pinks and blues and greens, skittering along the surface of something that was in theory white.

Alana en'Marano's expression was as sour as if she'd swallowed wine left standing too long in air and sun. *Your enemies are not your enemies because they are ugly, or worthless, or foolish, or weak. They are your enemies because they seek to damage you, to injure you, to rob you of worth in the eyes of those who have the power to judge you and to shorten or extend your existence based on that judgment. You understand this,* she had added sharply. *You are not a child.*

Diora felt honored by this. She could not clearly remember how old she had been when it was said, but the warmth of feeling adult came with the memory, and if the feeling had been false, the warmth remained nonetheless, an entirely different sensation from the heat of the desert sun.

She could not clearly remember how old she had been when it had been said, but she was absolutely certain that it had been said; the texture of Alana's rough voice, the weight of each syllable, the pause between each phrase for sharp, short breath—these were the things that she did not forget. Memory blurred sight, scent, the sensation of touch and taste. But time did not exist that could chip away at the memory of things heard. Her gift.

Her curse.

She lifted a fan as delicate and perfect as the fan that her Ona had raised that day; raised it and placed it before her face, spreading each segment slowly to reveal the silk across the whole—a delicate unfolding; one that was perfect to the eye, should any eye be watching. Habit.

The heat was fierce.

There were no flowers, no lilies, no falls or brooks, no cherry trees, no Lord's eye, the ubiquitous blue flower with a center of gold that sprang up like weeds in otherwise carefully tended pockets of wilderness. There were no winding brooks, course guided by the careful application of stone and rock; no grass, no soft moss to invite the weary traveler to take refuge.

There was only the sparse and wiry dwarves that might once have had trees as ancestors, and the rounded thick succulents that promised moisture and guarded it with spines and needles—and the sun could not reveal beauty that did not exist.

The sun is not your friend. Stay in the sun like those blossoms and you will suffer their fate.

What is their fate, Ona Alana?

To fall, little one. To fall and be trampled by men too careless to appreciate delicacy or beauty.

But won't that happen anyway, without sun?

Yes, the older woman had answered, pausing a moment to search for her own fan. *But it will happen more quickly. Keep your youth for as long as you can.*

Why, Ona Alana?

Because it is youth and beauty that attracts the attention of men.

But I don't want the attention of men.

Alana's laugh was both amused and slightly bitter, although only examining it at the remove of years could both of these things be understood; Diora had the gift as a child, but not the experience to understand what it revealed.

Men will desire you, and if they desire you, they will value you—if you are a clanswoman of repute, whose family can protect your honor. So long as they desire you, so long as they find you as beautiful in passing as you find the cherry blossoms or the Lord's eyes, or even the Northern roses upon the plateau, you, too, will blossom; you will have water when there is no water to be found; you will have food when the sun has dried and cracked the land that yields it. Should war be necessary to protect you, or your children, you will have war.

But your value—the sun will leach it away, as it leaches color and dye from silks, as it destroys the paintings that come from the Northern merchants.

But . . .

But?

But the sun reveals beauty; it reveals color. It—

Yes. And that is the second lesson you must learn. To reveal something is to make it, in the end, less interesting and less desirable—just as the sun destroys what it sees, so, too, does familiarity.

The sun is not your friend; endure his gaze only when there is no other choice to be had—and if you must endure it, take precautions with your skin, your face, your hands.

Because if you are old, Na'dio, you will not be a flower; you will be like the petals that have fallen from the cherry tree and now lie across the ground waiting to be trampled by careless men.

She stared, from beneath a sun-shelter over a decade removed from those words and that conversation, a fan in her hand, the sky a deep and cloudless blue above her, and in the distance only sand as far as the eye could see. And she looked at her hands; the skin was slightly darker than it had been when she had carried the Sun Sword away from its haven into the darkness of the Lady's Night.

But she understood, now, what she had been unable to conceive of then, as a small child, as a *safe* child. For she could look up, just a fraction of an inch, to where the women worked in their bustle of morning activity, gathering water—what little they spared—and grain, a handful of sugar, a handful of something else that Diora could identify only as a mixture of herbs.

They were old. Older in appearance than Ona Teresa.

And they were young; younger by ten years, younger by twenty, than the Serra. The sun's gaze—the simple truth of the sun's gaze—and the wind's voice had carved lines in flesh, cracking the skin around eyes and lips, the skin across hand and wrist, in a way that could never be recovered from. Sun scars. Wrinkles. Spots.

Her own hands were young, pale, uncallused. And she needed them to remain so.

But she could see, in the eyes of these women, that it would be a costly necessity.

Ramdan attended her.

It was disconcerting to have the steadiness of his presence without the wisdom of her Ona's, and although none of that dissonance marred her expression, it was there, like cloud across clear sky.

She had asked the Serra Teresa—if indeed she was entitled to that title, in this place—to rescind the command that had brought him, like shade or shadow, to her side, but the Serra had quietly refused.

"He understands what the Voyani cannot understand, Na'dio. Your worth, and what your worth rests upon. If the Lady truly values those serafs who have served in honor and obedience, in grace and with a full understanding of duty and responsibility, she will honor Ramdan above all serafs who have been judged worthy to serve her and sit by her feet."

But there are no serafs here, Diora replied, feeling behind the words a surprisingly sharp bitterness which she kept from her face, her posture, her movements. *Not even the Serra Maria brought serafs to the caravans; she attends her own needs. I am . . . ill-loved. I cannot afford to draw more attention to myself. Not in this fashion.*

You will never draw less attention to yourself in this caravan. No matter what you do, you are marked. Ona Teresa paused. Lowered her head, her hair bound by cloth in a fashion that was foreign to the Serra Diora—as it would have been foreign to any Serra. *And perhaps I will ask a boon, Na'dio. Perhaps I will ask a favor. Ramdan is seraf, yes. But he is more than that, to me; he has saved my life in all ways, great and small, and he chose to travel with me when I chose to leave Marano, simply because he serves me.*

But . . . he was trained to serve a Serra. And not a foolish Serra, not a girl who blossoms with youth and beauty that then fades, diminishing her value, but a Serra with mind and vision and ambition; a Serra who can perform the intricate steps of the dance one must *dance when surrounded, always, by the ambitions of powerful men.*

He has served me well. But he will never serve me in that capacity again.

Diora had fallen silent then.

And I would not deny him the ability to practice his art, his craft. Not when there is clearly a worthy successor who requires his service.

She was silent now. The enormity of Serra Teresa's words had been slow to blossom; so much of Diora's intellect had been turned, like weapon and shield, toward surviving both the Voyani and the enemy that lay beyond them.

He will never serve me in that capacity again.

The Serra Teresa—Ona Teresa—was nowhere in sight, although in truth, had she been it would have been hard to spot her. There was noise in everything the Voyani chose to do. Even when they moved without speech, their movements themselves were loud and graceless, their footfalls heavy, their arms flying in all directions, their bodies hunched forward or back as if they spoke with their movements, and graceful posture was an element of an entirely foreign language.

From time to time, they stopped to gape at her. The children pointed as they spoke, the men just stared. The women stared, but the quality of their gaze was different depending upon many things: there was heat in the look that grazed her. Jealousy. Disdain. Curiosity. Even envy. No desire. All of it so simple to read, all of it in the open.

It would pass soon.

She found the mornings easiest because they had a rhythm and a routine that seemed to be missing from all other elements of Voyani life.

First, the children were woken. They came from both wagons and tents, dragged in twos and threes by men and women who were sometimes their parents, and sometimes not. Elena, the Matriarch's heir, her fire-hair windblown and wild, would come with the food that the children would eat, and she and the older women would set about preparing it. They argued, snapped, snarled at each other; they sang; they listened to the arguments that erupted from the children.

Even the arguments were strange. They were like the arguments that lay hidden behind the curtains of harem life, where children could afford to use words and phrases that would displease their elders. But the children of clansmen used such words—as Diora had—when they were too young to know better; too young to know anything except that speaking them in the presence of their father was *strictly* forbidden.

After the children ate, the men and women arrived, and they seemed to come randomly. With the exception of the Matriarch's immediate family, age seemed to define who sat next; the older you were, the more quickly you ate.

So unlike the clans. So unlike.

She felt a pang, and she could not name it, and did not wish to try.

Instead she turned her face up, beneath the bower of a large, ivory sunshade, to see the solemn face of the quiet, steady man who held it.

These loud and boisterous people surrounded her as she sat in her isolation. They spoke without apparent thought;

without grace or control or modulation. She who had always been able to hear the emotion that lay beneath the spoken word found that to listen for it was one thing; to be confronted by it at all times, quite another.

"Serra," Ramdan said, bowing low to preface a possibly unwelcome interruption.

Her gaze traced the underside of his chin; her attention, pulled by a gift that was far too sensitive had wandered. "Ramdan?"

When she turned to, or from, him, she moved deliberately and slowly. When she raised her fan, or lowered it, each gesture was as soft, as graceful, as she could make it. Like the lilies upon the waters of the Lady's Lake, she seemed to float above the cacophony of the Voyani caravan. For the first time, she wondered where the roots of such flowers resided, if lilies lay down roots at all.

"At the edge of the desert, it is . . . more peaceful." He bent and placed by her side a small, rounded cup made of delicate clay. Into it, although its maker had intended it for other liquid, he poured water. Sweet water.

She said nothing at all for a long moment, staring at the water that reflected the heart of the desert's heat: sun's face. One of her many enemies.

Then she lifted the cup that had been offered.

Ramdan was old. He would, she thought, serve with grace for another five years, another ten. He had served the Serra Teresa di'Marano for as long as Diora could remember; had been a shadow, a perfect, graceful, resourceful shadow, cast by the Serra's light, or perhaps, cast by her as she stood in the light. They had never been separated.

The desert makes me weak, she thought. *The Tor is so far away, the Voyani so close, I forget who I am.*

But forget or no, she looked up, the water untouched, as if to drink it was significant. "Ramdan?"

He nodded to indicate that he paid attention; he met her eyes. But he did not speak.

"Please," she said, modulating her voice until it carried to his ears, and his alone. "Speak as you would, if you would."

He nodded again, but this time he did not look at her; his hands strayed to the wooden grip by which he held the sunshade.

"You have served the Serra Teresa di'Marano for all of

my life. You have served her in everything she has chosen to do, in silence; there is not another man—not a clansman, not a seraf, not anything in between—that she has valued or prized so highly."

He said nothing. To praise of that nature, there was nothing to say.

"Would you not—do you not—miss her?"

Silence.

"Can you leave the service to which you have dedicated your life in order to serve another? Or do you serve me because it is another service she demands of you?"

Silence, broken by the cacophony of the Arkosans.

But not by Ramdan. He held the sunshade.

"She will never go back to the Court," Diora said quietly.

"No," he replied. She looked up from the cup in her hands to his face; if she followed the direction of his intent stare, she thought she might find her Ona. She was no longer certain that she wanted to.

What will become of you, Ona Teresa?

Does it matter?

No. Of course, no. What other answer could there be?

"Ramdan?"

He was silent again.

"Have you ever desired freedom?"

With infinite care, he turned to where she sat, protecting her from the sun's grace with one hand while he offered her liquid with the other. It was the only answer he would ever give to that question.

It was the only time she would ever have the temerity to ask it.

Music filled the still, dry air.

Clans' music, mournful, slow, stately—deprived, as they were deprived, of useful things that would allow anyone else to participate in its making: words. Harmonies.

Elena rose a moment as it started, and then bowed, her forehead creased, her eyes narrow. It was not a music she liked—but if she were honest, it was not a music she could ignore. The notes that filled the air were cool, slow, stately—much like the woman who made them. But they were cool in the way river water was in the North; they wound toward something, gathering speed and strength as they moved.

She had once seen waterfalls that could kill a man who was careless. They had gone on forever, clear liquid becoming white foam, trickle becoming a roar over which only shouting could be heard.

Margret shouted, or rather, she cursed.

To make a point.

There was work to be done. Elena and Margret did much of it, or rather, Margret did; she cut the heartwood that they would take to the desert. She held her mother's ax, as she had done a dozen times now, and with each fallen limb of tree, each chip of dead wood from fallen trunk, her mother's memory receded until only two things remained: the ax and the duty that drove Margret to wield it.

Elena gathered herbs, and spent her time at her own mother's side, brewing them into the thick and heavy potions that might also be required. She had peeled bark off the trees that could survive so close to the desert, but they were few, and her wandering had taken her closer to Raverra than she would have liked. She searched in the shade and shadow of tall, old trunks for the mosses that sometimes grew in the North; they were absent.

But she found skyflowers almost everywhere, their tiny blossoms and spider-thin stems a tribute to the Lady's design. She found no nightshade, which was unfortunate, but as she had found skyflowers in abundance, she gathered these by some unnamed impulse, sweeping them into the ever-growing roundness of her satchel.

She had not had much time to speak to anyone, save during the mornings when she clung to the duty of feeding the children as if it were sanity—and in truth, it was. Elena had never liked make-work; if she was to be kept busy, she wanted to be doing something that *mattered*, something that was necessary. This gathering of random herbs and flowers had, perhaps, some use—but the use was murky and poorly defined, full of "maybes" and "ifs".

But she took poorly to isolation; she always had. She knew this because the words she didn't normally speak to herself came out the minute she saw her family—as if her closed lips were simply a dam.

With Margret, the silence was different; like a canker,

not an act of momentary denial. The Matriarch—and it was hard seeing her cousin bent beneath the weight of wood and stained with the sweat of sun, her lips compressed into a thin line, her expression as sour as standing wine, to think of her as anything else—crossed the threshold of the caravan as if the caravan itself was somehow responsible for the private task that she performed, day in and day out.

And it was.

This was the end of the second day of such work. It was, if the gathering went well, the last day they would be forced to toil in such thin forests, such poor grasslands, looking for the things that were required for their passage into the Sea of Sorrows.

Margret dumped the heavy sack she carried at the foot of her own wagon and snarled at the first guard to approach it. Luckily, that guard was Adam, used to her moods and the particular tenor of foulness that permeated them whenever she was forced to complete a task that would have been her mother's duty. He did not touch what she had laid aside, but he did not take offense, and did not leap out of her way as if stung or worried that she might do something worse than simply bark.

Instead, he followed her, at a discreet distance, leaving room between his steps and her shadow—which in the evening was long enough to guarantee safety from the outstretched reach of her open palm or closed fist—to where she walked with deliberate purpose.

Elena saw where she was going and started to follow, but she, too, kept her distance, albeit for reasons other than Adam's.

Others came; Nicu, Stavos, Donatella, even Tamara. There were one or two children, but they were babes in arms, and if there was violence done here, it would pass them by without leaving the shadow of memory.

Margret of the Arkosan Voyani came to stand at the feet of the intruder who sat—who had continued to sit—in the shade provided by a seraf since she had arrived at the caravan. Who wore simple sari, but sari nonetheless; whose hair was bound in combs, whose skin was pale as light on water, whose every movement was so graceful and perfect it was *wrong* . . . and made every other woman in the encampment feel ungainly, ugly, old.

The Serra Diora had come to them with little, and much of it had been procured by the Serra Teresa, who herself forbore to wear outlandish clothing, to play outlandish instruments, within the encampment. It was the Serra Teresa who gave her niece both fans and combs; the Serra Teresa who brought, from her own satchel, the creams and powders of the High Clans; it was the seraf who carried the samisen that she now played. Not even the Matriarch Maria dared to come, and stay, as a Serra among the Arkosans, although they were all well aware that she lived half her life in that guise.

The mournful strains of samisen music underlined rather than broke the stillness of the cooling dusk. The instrument lay in her folded lap, and her fingers, her perfect, graceful, supple fingers, ran up and down its length, pausing to let a note rise and fall as the vibrations of the strings sustained it.

It hadn't therefore been particularly hard to find the intruder—the woman who kept the Heart of Arkosa away from its rightful owner. No, Elena thought, watching from an angry distance, that wasn't fair. That had been Evallen's choice, not this Serra's.

But everything else about the Serra *was* her own choice. What did she do? She ate little, slept little, and did not lift a finger to help the Voyani in any of their duties.

And would her help be accepted?

Shut up, she told her conscience. Even if it wouldn't be accepted, the offer would be appreciated. Elena started toward Margret only when Margret had become a still body, rather than a body in motion. But she was the only person to approach; Adam and the others had taken a step back and now stood in a loose semicircle around the woman who had claim, by blood and birth, to lead them.

Margret had gathered the Arkosans, as if they were burrs and she a fine cloak; they had grown in numbers until those who had not joined them felt their passing in the quiet murmuring that rose in her wake.

Serra Teresa—perhaps just Teresa, as Margret was just Margret and Elena was just Elena—rose from where she had been tending the Havallan Matriarch. She shaded her eyes, for this gathering crowd walked into sunset that had not yet finished with the edge of the sky.

Her expression became smooth as Northern glass; she

listened carefully. Spoke a word into the wind, and waited again.

But it was only when the sound of distant music—a music that eased her in these new and strange duties by being the single reminder of the grace and beauty of her abandoned life—stopped completely that she turned to the old woman at her feet, dropping as she did to her knees in an automatic gesture of subservience.

"Yollana, please, intercede."

The oldest of the Matriarchs frowned. Her hands were cupped under the bowl of an unlit pipe—a habit that the Serra Teresa privately thought distasteful, although she helped gather the weeds and the herbs that Yollana added to the tobacco she burned.

"How?" she asked.

Teresa did not reply; she had fallen into the posture, and she had let her forehead touch the cooling earth while she kept the silence that posture demanded. It was almost comfortable to rest thus, although in truth she had seldom been forced to do so in her later years.

"That damn girl's temper," the Havallan Matriarch said, to sinking sun or night air. "Don't sit there groveling like a pathetic clanswoman, Serra. Help me walk."

Teresa rose at once, the movements as graceful and perfect as those that earned her niece so much contempt. But she wore the wide skirts and shirt that the Voyani women almost always wore when they did not wear pants made for riding, and she no longer had a seraf to tend to her needs. The sun had darkened her skin a shade, and there was evidence that it would continue to do so; if salves and creams had been offered her, they had been offered in a privacy so absolute that no Voyani save the one offering could bear witness.

"Damn her temper," the Havallan Matriarch said again. "And damn my pipe. It never stays lit when I want it." She handed the bowl to Teresa, who took both pipe and the older woman's weight and managed them in silence. "And damn your niece."

"You know why she is forced to choose the actions she chooses."

"Yes. But when you traveled with us, you managed to

blend in without ever losing the elements that made you Serra, and therefore alien."

Serra Teresa said nothing.

"Your niece has that gift, Teresa. She has that ability. The fact that she is feared or despised is therefore her choice."

"It is . . . not . . . simple choice. She has learned too much in too short a time. I am not certain that she is even aware of it," she added, stepping over a large stone so that Yollana could hobble around it, "but I believe that she keeps the others at a distance because of those losses."

"Your niece does not understand. Among the Voyani walls are only meant for one thing: to be brought down. She has built a wall that is thicker and wider than any I've seen; not even the clansmen who approach us when they want a favor—or an ally in one or another of their wars—have approached us with such ice and distance."

"Yollana—"

"Don't talk. Move."

Serra Diora di'Marano looked up as Margret's shadow crossed her. Her hands were still against samisen strings, which had also stilled. But she did not remove them; the contact between string and skin was welcome, familiar. The only contact she desired.

Ramdan stood between the Serra and the Matriarch, but to one side. He was not cerdan; it was not his duty to protect her from anything but thirst or sunlight.

"Go away," the Matriarch said coldly. She glared at the Serra, but it was clear to anyone who stood at her back—and there were not an inconsiderable number of Voyani, backs to sun, arms across chests—that she spoke to the seraf.

The seraf bowed to her, his movements almost as graceful as the Serra's, his dignity somehow less reproachful, less isolating. He turned to the Serra.

She did not speak, but she inclined her head, and he stepped back, behind her. Over her head, over the face that would have been exposed to sunlight were it not for the looming presence of Margret of the Arkosan Voyani, he still held the sunshade.

"She has no right to compel you," Margret snapped. "She's among the Voyani, and we own no serafs, we take no slaves. You're free, do you understand? You're free to do what *you* choose."

The Serra Diora, face now upturned, said quietly, "You take poor clansmen as slaves; you sell them to their own when you find them; you prey on them as much as their own do. If you do not own serafs, Matriarch, you are just as responsible for making them as the clans."

Teresa stilled. Yollana, not expecting this, took a step that nearly overbalanced them both; they teetered as Teresa caught both herself and the old woman. Pipe embers fluttered down to dry dirt and dry, wild scrub, undisturbed by the movement of air. She crushed them with the heel of her traveling boots before she drew another breath.

"*What* is she doing?" Yollana demanded, when they were both on solid footing again—or as solid a footing as two women could be who had two good legs between them.

"She is . . . opening . . . a sally port in the wall."

"What?"

"It is a Northern term," the Serra said softly—and her voice, her pitch, the line of her neck, the remote smoothness of her expression, were suddenly kin to the Serra Diora's in every way. "She is angry."

"That's your idea of anger?"

The Serra Teresa's smile was thin and brief. "Yes."

"It won't mean a damn thing to the Matriarch."

But Yollana was wrong.

Margret's hand snaked out, found the upturned cheek—pale, perfect cheek—of the interloper. The only sound in the flat, quiet space was that contact—the first contact—between them.

Color rushed to white skin—not the red of sun's blister, nor the red of labor and contribution and community; this was the red of anger, and it held the shape of a woman's hand, fingers splayed, palm open. But it would do.

"That's not how you speak to a Matriarch," she snarled.

"The Voyani only pride themselves on truth among their own?"

* * *

"What is she doing?"

"I am sorry, Yollana," Teresa said softly. "I . . . do not know."

Yollana was moving as quickly as she could. Unfortunately, speed was relative; her gait, awkward and broken, was slow. She had lost all care for dignity; speed was the only essential. If she could have left Teresa behind, she probably would have—but she was hampered by injury and dependency, and she was too used to accepting the judgment of the Lord and the Lady to rail against infirmity.

"At least we don't enslave our own."

"No. You kill them when it suits you, which is no different from the clans; you sacrifice your sons instead of your daughters, which is."

"Shut *up*."

But Diora's silence, when it came, was no more welcome to Margret.

Elena came up behind her. Close enough to touch, but not stupid enough. "'Gret," she said, as softly as she could.

Margret held out a hand. It was still a fist. Still shaking. It was also a command. "Don't presume to judge us."

"I do not judge you, Matriarch," the Serra said, sitting, regal, her face red in only one place, her hands across the samisen strings as if they were her only labor. "And I do not particularly care if you judge me."

"You should."

"Perhaps. And perhaps I will care when I no longer have anything that you require. But in that, you are no different from any powerful man who has held my life in his hands."

Yollana was almost there. She elbowed her way past Arkosan Voyani because—for perhaps the first time in Serra Teresa's experience—presence alone did not move them. Their backs were toward her; Margret and Diora held them all.

Na'dio, Teresa thought. She did not speak, although she might have. But the plans her almost-daughter made were, in the end, her plans. The loss that drove them was her loss. Hard, to be defined by loss.

And in this world, beneath this sky, with these gods, impossible to be defined by anything else.

* * *

She *knew* that she could not afford to lose face, not here, not to this interloper, this stranger. She *knew* that this was not a fight she should have started, and having started it, it was not one that she should continue. She was Matriarch of Arkosa.

Bitter, that. *No.*

She wasn't Matriarch because her mother, in secrecy, had decided to go to the clansmen, to die at their hands, and to give the Heart of Arkosa to . . . this . . . this pale, perfect stranger. Even in death, Evallen's plans meant so much more to Arkosa than Margret's.

"Do not compare me to the clansmen," she said, trying to rein in the anger that was driving her tongue.

The Serra inclined her head in a manner that was calculated to look subservient while maintaining the spirit of defiance. She offered silence. Her hands had not moved as they lay against the samisen strings.

Before Margret could stop herself, she lashed out; her boot slammed into the side of the instrument, driving it off silken lap.

It landed on the sparse grass with a dull thud; the strings thrummed in unison, a quiet cacophony that sounded wrong even to Margret's ears. Had the Serra been one of hers, had she been an Arkosan, Margret would have stepped back. She wouldn't have apologized—a Matriarch wouldn't have been expected to—but the retreat would have served the same purpose.

Why does she make you so crazy? Why do you want to spit daggers every time you see her face? Because she's beautiful? Because your stupid cousins and uncles and yes, even your aunts, are captivated by her every time they walk by? Because they think her brave just for condescending to be here *living the life of a* guest *when they all walk the* Voyanne *until they die?*

No.

Evallen. You trusted her.

For a moment—for just a moment—a ripple of expression marred the Serra's perfectly composed face. But it was gone quickly. Her empty hands fell, like weightless, delicate leaves in a dance of breeze and wind, to a now empty lap; she folded them, as if they were two halves of a fan, and waited, the posture as much of an accusation as anything that perfect could be. Margret's shadow had grown longer.

"'Gret," Elena said, her voice harsher, her grip more painful.

"Not *now*, Elena."

The Serra Diora lifted her chin. Met the eyes of the Matriarch. "You think the clansmen—or women—cold-blooded. You think that to strike out in anger, to shout in frustration, to weep in pain, somehow makes the Voyani human." She turned a moment and deliberately looked at the now silent samisen. Although no words accompanied the glance, silence was her weapon.

Margret saw that now, clearly. She could not stop her hands from curving into fists, but they were loose fists now. Kicking the samisen had somehow crossed a line that striking the woman herself had not.

"Matriarch, you are wrong, and you expose yourself to the judgment of others by the fallacy of your judgment. Do you think that the man who sheds no tears at the death of his son is weak? Do you think that it is weakness that prevents the pain from showing?" Her eyes, her perfect eyes, lost some of that large, round beauty as they narrowed. "Then you understand *nothing*."

The Arkosan silence was sudden.

Into it, the Serra continued to speak. "You are angry. You strike. You have perhaps *once in your life* had to hide what you feel; perhaps once had to ignore your impulse to react. Once. Imagine, Matriarch, a lifetime of such perfect control.

"We *choose* what we share, and who we share it with, and like the Voyani, we do not share what we are with outsiders. But to assume that what we are is simply what you are witness to . . . is unwise. What you see is almost never the whole of the truth."

"What *I* see? They say that the Flower of the Dominion sat and watched the slaughter of all of the wives in her harem without raising a cry. I have not seen this for myself, but having seen you, I don't doubt it."

The Serra Diora di'Marano became still as only stone could be. For a moment, breath seemed to elude her.

Silence. Margret felt a vicious, a curious, satisfaction; she also felt something else she had no desire to name.

"And having seen you," the Serra said, speaking so coldly it seemed that she had swallowed desert night and transformed it into words, "I understand why Evallen of Arkosa chose not to trust you to do the necessary and the wise."

Margret *did* pale.

"You want truth, Matriarch? Very well. We all want others to be vulnerable while we protect ourselves from the things that make us flinch. She gave me what I carry without once speaking to you about her intent because she knew that if we could not stand together against the Lord of Night, we would fail separately. But she was afraid that your temper and your prejudice would never allow you to see that, so she enforced it." The Serra turned her hands over, so they were cupped in her lap; she did not otherwise move. "We do each other no kindness here. How much more of the truth must be said?"

Perhaps none. The silence was heavy, the way a storm laden sky is. The Serra looked at the harsh, dry ground in the distance, and her skin deepened in color.

"What do you know of *truth?*" Margret spit back.

"Ruatha, don't—" The Serra froze, the words deserting her as they almost never did. There was no expression on her face; the anger that had been there—and it *had*—was locked away from the eyes of the strangers who bore witness.

Margret's hands were shaking; she could not ease the shape of fists, so she lifted them and sat them on the slight shelf of her hips. "What do any of the clans know as truth? *We* saved the South—and you—"

"*Be silent!*"

Both women stopped. Yollana's voice was unmistakable. The oldest of the four Matriarchs had been, until this moment, cautious, even diplomatic, because she stayed in the caravan of another Matriarch. She was wise, in her fashion, but in age much like the Voyani Matriarchs tended to become: increasingly short of temper. She had never suffered fools gladly, but in Arkosa had managed, with effort, to overcome her natural impulse to smack the ones she came across; they were, after all, Margret's problem.

That the biggest fool was their leader had come as a

surprise. Yollana was of an age and position where surprises were almost never pleasant.

But she was Voyani; she had both temper and a sense of responsibility. There were no betrayals so profound that anger and fear could not conspire to produce them—but there were some that could not be forgiven.

And the Havallan Matriarch did not desire the death of all of the Arkosans who might bear witness to what fell out of Margret's foolish mouth if she were allowed to continue.

But she knew that such interruption could prove costly later. Any display of overt power in the wrong territory often did. The wind made no sound on these plains; it was still. But she heard the echo of its voice in the whispers of Arkosa as the uncles and aunts, the cousins, the brothers and sisters, slowly realized what had happened: She had given an order. The Matriarch of Arkosa had obeyed.

Margret did not move. She had not turned to see who had spoken. She had not offered her acknowledgment in any way save obedience—but obedience was enough.

The stillness stretched.

It was broken not by Margret, not by the Arkosans, not by Yollana of the Havalla Voyani. And if these two could not move, the rest of the Voyani could not, although Elena's hand had once again found its way to the familiar perch of Margret's shoulder.

Only the Serra Diora di'Marano seemed free to move, and she did—with the same grace and delicacy so despised by Margret. She reached to the side. There, from Ramdan's shadow, she retrieved the samisen that Margret had dislodged from its place in her lap.

She cradled it as she lifted it, her fingers carefully inspecting the flat of the surface that rested on her lap for any crack or gouge. She had chosen to leave all instruments behind, but someone had found this; someone had delivered it to her seraf.

Kallandras?

Ona Teresa?

Did it matter? It was here, reminder of the life she had forsaken, and she clung to it in her fashion. The samisen strings thrummed as her fingers passed across them, dancing now, light but certain. She listened and heard only silence; lifted her head and saw, as a response to the music, the face of uncertainty in the men and women who watched.

She had done this. She felt a bitter, bitter shame. Not since she was four years old, not since she was a child in fact, and not merely impulse or desire, had she lost control so completely.

In her adult life she had only argued so boldly with one other woman. Even with her Ona Teresa, her strikes and parries were the acceptable nuances—and edges—of polite words and silences.

Her hands were shaking. The strings echoed the quiver of flesh in a way that she was certain only Ona Teresa or Kallandras himself would catch.

Why? Why now when she had not—

Ruatha.

Her fingers danced like leaves in a strong, strong wind. Music stumbled after them. She had entered the storm. The storm had entered her.

The world had died around her. It had died screaming. It had died whimpering. It had died in the silence of bone being broken at a distance. She had not raised her voice. She had not lifted her head. Nothing she had ever done had prepared her for the death that had awaited her in that room—but everything she had ever done had prepared her to leave it; to leave it, alive and whole, her face as perfectly composed as it had been the day she had arrived as adornment for the kai Leonne.

Every word Margret had spoken was true.

She had been unable to think. But afterward—after, in a stillness of clean silk, the unsightly blood gone at the hands of her father's serafs, along with the sari that had been stained by the carelessness of the Tyran—she had thought it would be the hardest thing that she, that *anyone* would ever face.

But there was worse: memory.

In the face of the Lord, she was impassive, but when the Lady's time began, so did the bitter regret. It was sharp and terrible in its unexpected ferocity.

Her sister-wives had seen her use her gift, and her curse; they understood the strength of the gift that they had never once named. They had died believing that she had betrayed them.

She had.

They would never have cared about vengeance.

Ruatha. Faida. Deirdre. Serafs, all. Serra Diora en'-Leonne was clanswoman. In the harem, there had been so little difference between the two, the most accomplished of the High Court's Serras could believe that difference merely a word and a slight lack of polish. In the harem, with the child she had saved—and for what fate?—in her arms, she could believe that they were family in a way that defied blood, birth, and time.

They were gone.

She remained. She had thought if she were strong enough not to die with them, she could make their killers pay. And she had begun; she had maneuvered the pieces with a skill that General Alesso di'Marente could not match for subtlety and timing. Her hands on the strings faltered again, skipping and losing a beat.

The dead did not return. And in dreams, they granted her no benediction for the victory she had won.

They were serafs. They did not understand that to *win* was everything. In the end, everything. The Lord had no patience for the weak, but he granted his strength to the victor—no matter how long, how subtle, how costly the battle.

And everything was empty.

Her gift caught the stutter and hesitation of shaking hand and made out of it a current, an eddy, some artifact of emotion. She played around it, transforming a flaw into a strength; her strength. Was it not always so?

If she had had the ability to walk across the face of time, to make a track of small and even footprints, delicately spaced in just the way she had been raised to space them, she would have gone back to the harem and the darkness and the fire, and when the Tyran had crossed the boundary from the outside world into *her* world, she would have done everything in her power to stop them.

To buy the time her sister-wives might need to escape, however short a distance their flight would take them. To die trying, because death seemed a comfort now, an ending. She no longer believed that the howl of the wind carried the souls of the dead, because she had listened and listened and listened and she could discern no voice at all in the keening and whistling of night air.

Only memory held their voices.

She had lived while they died, but as an outsider. A—bitter word—clansman.

And in the end, it was as clansman that she sat, in this scorched, dry place, among men and women who defined power and strength by the duty one owed to family. It was as clansman that she stood accused by a graceless, ill-tempered woman. Dark-haired and dark-eyed and quick of tongue—

Ruatha.

She knew why she had lost her temper.

The knowledge did not ease her. Evallen of the Arkosa Voyani had ventured into the heart of the Tor Leonne. She had given into Serra Diora di'Marano's keeping the Heart of Arkosa . . . and it was the Heart of Arkosa that guaranteed the Serra Diora's safe passage. The Arkosan Matriarch had survived neither gift.

And this—this temper, this pain, this pride—was poor payment of the debt that Evallen's death had laid before the Serra's folded lap.

She was no fool; Yollana's shout and Margret's obedience injured Arkosa. Voyani or not, they were still born and bred to the South; they traveled and lived beneath the Lord's sky, the Lady's night. What people were not damaged by the knowledge that their Lord was weak?

She felt a dryness in her throat, a heaviness about her neck where the Heart of Arkosa hung. She did not know what Margret had been about to say. But she did know that if she had no way to ease her own memory—no way that would not weaken her beyond repair or use—she had a way to ease the memories of the watching Arkosans.

It was simple.

Serra Diora di'Marano—Serra Diora en'Leonne—sang. She sang, fitting words around the memories that drove her. She bowed her head because she did not wish to look up; did not wish to see what the Arkosans felt when they understood what she was offering them: a glimpse into the truth, her truth.

She saw a shadow pass before her. Saw it falter briefly.

She could not raise her head to see who had cast it, and it mattered little; it was in the present, and in order to find the song she had begun, she had pushed aside the hangings that were drawn across the past.

Shadows fell across her samisen; the samisen sat across the spill of silk in a still, perfect lap as the Serra leaned over it. Around her face, like a perfect frame, fell hair that was dark and twined in strands. A pearl brushed her cheek.

She sang of Deirdre, Deirdre the gentle, Deirdre the mother of their husband's son. Raven-haired, dark-eyed, lush in the way that women are when they are young and have just borne a child; skin smooth, curves rounded and softened, heart opened to the wonder of and piercing fear for this noisy, helpless miracle.

She sang of Deirdre the hesitant, Deirdre the peacemaker, Deirdre the timid. It hurt to speak of joy; it was infinitely worse to sing of it.

When the words failed her, the voice did not; she skipped across syllables, stretching octaves in a brief display of range and depth. She flew, like a hawk; she soared; she plunged. There was a freedom in the wordless song that was so pure and perfect if she had not been joined in that wild flight by the deeper harmonies of a tenor, she might never have landed.

At another moment she would have been angered.

With the bright clarity of morning sky as witness, she had offered not Deirdre but her own attachment to Deirdre. In penance for her inability to control her own temper—the edge of it so bitter and sudden, so *foreign*—she bound the attention of the Arkosans now. The Flower of the Dominion. The woman whose destiny, beneath the open sky, was to wed the man who could wield the Sun Sword without being consumed—as even the Radann kai el'Sol had been—by the fires it contained.

Kallandras had come, to rob the moment of isolation. But she could not be angry. In the guise of harmony, he offered words, and beneath words, he offered loss. It was profound; profoundly moving. She did not understand why he sang. He had no penance to perform. Nothing at all to prove.

But what he offered *was* genuine; it was a truth, a vulnerability, that she had never heard in his voice before—for his voice was, as hers, perfectly schooled.

A thin film of water colored her vision, distorting his shadow and the slim length of strings beneath her hands.

She did not love him.

She was certain that she would never love anyone again; all the people who had been capable of loving her were gone. Her father, her father's wives, her own wives.

Love or no, she heard herself in the song that he sang: his loss, like hers, stretched from the past into the future with no end in sight, no peace. He did not promise light at the end of the darkness, or darkness at the end of the day; he did not promise hope, or even triumph; his song was devoid of anything that intrusive.

She knew, then, that he understood her completely. She could not remember the first time she had seen him, but she could remember Lissa's excited description of the golden-haired Northerner who had won for himself the privilege of performing for the Tyr'agar.

And she remembered the night of the Festival Moon, when he had come with the voice of the wind and had forced a healer to give Lissa back the life that was bleeding away. She had not thought of that in years, but she heard it now: his voice.

Why, Kallandras? Why did you save her?

But she knew he would never answer the question because she knew she would never ask it. Generosity was its own weakness, and neither of them could afford to be weak.

But when his harmony trailed into silence, when her words once again stood alone, she felt an inexplicable fear of his absence and looked up.

He stood before her. He cast no shadow across her face; the shadows had moved with the light. Only the audience remained where it stood, its silence as perfect as applause, but more telling.

"Serra Diora," the Northern bard said, bowing. He held out both hands, and cupped in his palms with a careless, precise grace, was a single, pink flower.

She stared at it for a long moment and then she reached out, her hands so much smaller and paler than his, to touch the petal of a cherry blossom.

CHAPTER TWELVE

Evening of the 27th of Scaral, 427 AA
Arannan Halls, Avantari

They came upon each other beneath the face of the watchful moon.

Ser Valedan kai di'Leonne had taken his customary place beside the fountain called *Southern Justice*. It was not, in the darkness, an accusation; it was a fountain, with a stone basin, rather than the marble work so often fancied by the Northern craftsmen. In the basin, standing on a pedestal submerged in fallen water, a young boy. The perfect lines of the boy's simple face were broken only by a blindfold; the lines of his slender wrists, by chains.

"Tyr'agar," someone said.

Valedan did not turn, choosing to present his back to Ser Anton di'Guivera. In the South, the act was not the insult it would have been in the North; a man's back represented vulnerability, where there were no Tyran or Toran to guard it, and exposing vulnerability indicated trust.

"Ser Anton."

"Have you come to say good-bye?"

Valedan's silence was his reply. But the silence was not, in the end, honest. "Moonlight," he said softly, and then, "yes."

He heard silence, and then retreating footsteps, and this time he did turn. "Ser Anton, a moment please."

The old man's face was visible in the magelights that girded the courtyard's walls. "Some things are best done in private."

"And you would judge me for my weakness?"

Ser Anton smiled. "I have yet to see it."

"Then stay." He paused. "This has been my home. But I will not return to it."

Ser Anton nodded. He stayed, his hand inches away from the hilt of his sword. Valedan did not point out that here, beside the fountain, in the isolation of the Arannan Halls, vigilance of that nature was not required. Because it would have been untrue. But it had been true, once.

It was those days that he said farewell to now. Had he realized how much he would miss them, it would have made no difference; he had chosen a course of action based in part on desperation, and although in the North the word of a desperate man, given under duress, was not counted as a word by men of honor, in the South it was different.

"Kai Leonne," Ser Anton said, after some time had passed in a silence broken by the trickle of water and thought.

Valedan nodded.

"When we leave, our roles will change."

"How?"

"You have studied under my tutelage these past few months. That will cease."

The water really was lovely as the splintered magelights broke across its moving surface. "Because I've learned all you have to teach?"

Ser Anton had the grace to smile—slightly—at Valedan's mock arrogance. "I am constantly learning; all men are, who still live. Therefore to teach all I can would be a work in progress, a never-ending journey.

"But no, and you know why."

"I cannot be seen as a student, even to you."

"Indeed. You must be subordinate to none—for you will, in the end, be beholden to many. Were your power assured, it would not be a necessary to . . . abandon studies that I feel have been fruitful."

Valedan nodded. "Have I learned enough?"

"In the end, the Lord will judge."

"It is not the Lord's judgment that I have asked for, Ser Anton, but rather the judgment of one of the few men I can . . . trust."

"In my opinion, kai Leonne, you are at least Andaro's equal, and he has studied many years."

"But?"

"But," Ser Anton said, gracing him again with a rare smile, "I have seen the General di'Marente fight, and if in the end your future is to be decided man to man in that fight, and that fight alone—as I said, the Lord will judge. You have the advantage and the disadvantage of youth; he has the advantage of experience. But age has robbed him of very little. He is at the height of his power, and yours remains untested."

Valedan nodded quietly. "Thank you, Ser Anton."

Ser Anton lifted a brow; a question.

"You admire the General."

"I admire his skill."

Valedan's turn to smile. "I am not yet so easily offended. You admire the man."

Ser Anton turned to the fountain again. "I do not admire some of his choices . . . but yes, since you ask me to be blunt. Ser Alesso di'Marente is a man of the Lord; there is no weakness in him."

27th of Scaral 427 AA
The Tor Leonne

"The Tyr'agnate of Callesta," the former General said quietly, "will attempt to carry the battle to Raverra. He is well aware of the cost of waging war within his own domain."

"And our information?"

"It is accurate, as far as it goes. The Northern armies—to an extent that will remain unknown until the troops are called to move—will support Leonne in his attempt to take the Tor."

"That is hardly likely to make the Leonne cause more popular," Sendari di'Marano said, fingers pausing a moment in the drape of his beard as he contemplated the map. He had become familiar with the symbols and codes that Alesso used when marking the maps of the Terreans, of the Dominion, and of the Empire.

"Agreed," Alesso replied, without looking up. "However, the addition of Ser Anton to the Leonne forces may prove . . . costly." He lifted brush and lowered it again, deliberate now, his eye unwavering. "And I believe that we labor under the disadvantage of having made the Voyani our enemies for the duration of this war."

"That is not always a disadvantage."

"We have never had all four aligned against us, old friend."

"The four can barely keep from killing each other, and while I can acknowledge in theory the threat they pose—four querulous old women and the undisciplined boys who follow them are a threat only to the serafs in the villages that will be *behind* our lines."

Alesso's smile was brief and sharp. But his hand did not falter as he continued to draw a thin, dark line.

Sendari waited until the line was done, and then said, "I was sent by Cortano to tell you that the men are waiting."

Alesso nodded. "My horse?"

"Ready."

"Good. The serafs?"

"Those who are fit to travel with the cavalry have been seconded."

"Good. Yourself?"

"I have . . . very little. I leave my wives in the Tor Leonne," he added quietly. "They are . . . afraid for my daughter."

"They should be," the General replied, straightening and setting the brush aside. He clapped. "I will be but a moment."

Men—free, all—rushed in to fill the silence left after the contact of two palms. Alesso spoke curtly, and they disappeared; he stretched his shoulders in their absence, and for just a moment, Sendari could see the creases sun had made in brow and the corners of sharp, dark eyes.

An entire building on the flat of the Tor Leonne had been taken over, the view of the Lake lost to anyone of nonmilitary persuasion; it housed nothing but tables—tables in the Northern style—and maps in an endless progression. Men would come and go, and in their passage details would be added, roads altered, bridges removed; all under Alesso's watchful eyes. The mapmakers labored with total concentration; error here was death—and not a fast one—in the very near future.

But there was little chance of error.

Alesso chose his subordinates, as always, with care.

Sendari di'Marano had learned to read the maps made

at his friend's command. He did not have the same fascination with them; the colored lines against paper were just that; they could not convey the truth of the desert, the rise of mountains, the depth of the valleys—or their lushness, their life—in any way that spoke of accuracy.

But they could be used to plan battles and death.

"The Sword's Edge has made perfectly clear that the Widan are not to be as ill-used as they were in the previous Tyr's campaign."

"Indeed," Alesso di'Alesso said, the freedom of movement over. He lifted a sealed scroll—and perhaps, Sendari thought, that was what was so alien about this map room, this map building: the paper, the consignment of words to parchment. It was very . . . Northern. As was breaking the seal, opening the parchment, reading the words as if they were more significant than things spoken, words passed between men.

The General—the Tyr, Sendari thought, correcting himself—crossed the room, navigating the space between tables with care. He found the map he sought—Averda, and the Averdan valleys, and bent over this map a moment, his brows drawing together. Then he nodded to himself, lifted a brush, and drew a trailing mark across the heavy parchment. "I think that should we require use of magery, we have our . . . allies . . . to rely on. However," he added, forestalling Sendari's words, although he had no need to look up to ascertain that they were indeed about to follow, "I believe that we can avoid the Tiagra entirely in this campaign. Our goal is not the North; it is consolidation of our control over the South."

Sendari nodded absently; Alesso had said as much several times, to no one's satisfaction. He had been—would continue to be—vague until he reached the army. That was his way. Generals would be made in the battles that came out of the struggle for the Dominion, but they would be appointed and acknowledged by Alesso after the fact. The war itself was *his*.

Which was as it should be; he would only survive if he won. Lord's man.

"Good."

Alesso straightened. Clapped his hands again. This time, when the mapmakers rose, he smiled and addressed the oldest of their number, a slender man with streaked hair and the sallowness of complexion that accompanies lack of sleep. "Ser Martenn, I have been pleased with your work here, and I commend you for your diligence. The reputation that you have garnered for yourself over the years is justified."

The man visibly relaxed, a sure sign that he had slept very, very little. Although it was not technically a lapse of manners, it was a display of weakness. Alesso ignored it; he was indeed well-pleased. "Let us see if those who gather information below the plateau have been one tenth as competent in the gathering as you have been in the rendering. Call for the coded containers; prepare the maps for transport."

"Tyr'agar," Ser Martenn said, bowing with a lopsided fluidity. He was not a graceful man; he would probably never learn to *be* graceful. But he was an expert, a man obsessed by turning things vibrant and real into the lines and flat curves that war makers valued so highly. He turned to his subordinates and began to bark out orders, and they fled to the various corners of the building that had been both their haven and their prison for months. Even during the Festival of the Moon, they had not found the freedom decreed theirs by the Lady—although perhaps there was an element of fear and a desire for safety in that choice, this year.

Freedom had sharp edges.

"Collect what you need—if there is any detail that has managed to escape your preparations, old friend—and meet me at the gates. We ride shortly, and we will be pressed for speed."

Sendari turned. Paused. "It appears," he said softly, although he did not turn to gaze at his friend, "that we will not necessarily ride alone."

"Ser Sendari," the Lord's creature said. He did not bow, which was both annoying and acceptable. The *Kialli* made, of bows, a thing of sarcasm that was still more perfect than the most sincere effort most mortals made.

"Lord Ishavriel. We were not expecting to see you upon the plateau before we left."

The *Kialli* lord shrugged, his wide eyes the color of a perfect, clear night. "There have been delays in my departure."

"How unfortunate."

"Indeed." The *Kialli*'s gaze swept the room, which had become crowded with the simple preparations for departure. "Has any progress been made with the Lambertan Tyr?"

Alesso di'Alesso gave Ishavriel his full attention. His hand, however, did not touch the hilt of his sword. He was confident in his own ability, or perhaps confident in Lord Ishavriel's disgrace.

"That is not your concern. Your duty, if I understand our agreement correctly, is to accompany Anya to the field that is chosen for our final confrontation. Not more, not less."

Ishavriel grew still cool as stone in evening shade.

"You will therefore not question my activities or my decisions in any matter that does not relate to that duty. Ser Sendari?"

Sendari bowed formally. Properly. He had been in private quarters with Alesso for the past several weeks; he felt the edge of the bow in the stiffness of his knees and his back.

When he rose, Lord Ishavriel was gone.

"We are not so unalike," Alesso said softly, "the *Kialli* and I."

"True or no, Alesso, do not speak those words beneath the open sky, do not speak them where they can be caught or taken by breeze or wind. The Radann lost much and gained much at the Festival, and they are watching now."

Alesso nodded, grimly. "They watch," he agreed.

Marakas par el'Sol stood beneath the open sky. The Lady's Lake reflected the clarity of cloudless blue and the merciless glitter of the Lord's most severe face. It was always thus: the Lady reflected the Lord's severity. Hard to know what lay beneath the surface of either.

But upon the surface, hair now streaked with the sun's harshest glare, the line of broad shoulders bent inward as if they bore great weight, he also saw himself. And judged.

"Are you ready?"

He looked up at his companion; very few were the men who did not when that companion was the Radann kai el'Sol, the man in the Dominion, by the Lord's grace, second only to the Tyr'agar—if indeed he was counted second.

The arguments went full circle, for although only the Tyr'agar wore the crown, it was a pale conceit; *both* men were entitled to the use of the sun ascendant, and it was by that crest that they were known.

"I am . . . ready."

The Radann kai el'Sol's gaze fell from his face to the Lake, and rested there a long moment. Seeing, perhaps, his reflection, and the sky behind it. Both men were clean shaven, but Marakas had always chosen to be so—the request of a long-dead wife had the power of oath. Peder kai el'Sol's smooth chin, and the short, sheared brush of his rounded head, were a gift of fire. "You are not required—by the Radann—to perform this service."

Marakas nodded quietly.

"And in truth, we have some need of you here; we march to war at the side of the Tyr'agar, and the war will be a sword dance."

"He does not intend us to survive."

"No. But he cannot survive—not yet—without us."

"If any man could, it would be he. I have never seen a man so much the Lord's in all the time I have paid attention to the politics of the Court."

Peder kai el'Sol raised a single thin brow. "You have rarely paid any attention to the politics of the Court."

"Not so, kai el'Sol. Fredero made certain that I understood who was most easily offended, and why, every time I returned to the plateau."

"And I note that you did not remain."

"No. But I am not a man of the Court."

Peder bowed. It was the brief bow of respect offered between equals; Marakas accepted the graceful gesture in silence. Scant months ago, such an action would have been unthinkable; Peder had considered Marakas to be Fredero's creature, and at that, too soft a creature to be a worthy foe. So went old prejudices, old beliefs; the Lord had burned them away.

What remained was simple steel.

"You are determined to pursue this course?" The kai el'Sol asked, when the breeze had stilled a moment.

Marakas nodded. "I owe a debt of honor, and I am reluctant to leave it unpaid." He turned back to the lake. "The Lady's intervention in the Tor saved these lands from the

Lord of Night. But that was the battle, not the war." He knelt. Peder kai el'Sol chose to stand, hand on the hilt of *Saval*, eyes on his own reflection in the Lady's Lake. The sun had aged him, carving crescents and creases into his skin, in the short time that the nights had been at their longest.

Funny, that. Sunlight glinted off the golden threads of the sun ascendant as he stared at the stranger in the water.

Marakas carefully removed a flat wineskin from his belt. He unstoppered it with care and then, looking first at the reflection and then at the man who cast it—who had become worthy of it—added, "with your permission, kai el'Sol?"

The kai el'Sol's lips turned up in a wry smile. But he nodded.

As the skin grew round with the Lady's water, Marakas par el'Sol said softly, "None of us foresaw the man you would become; the Lord owns you, kai el'Sol, and it . . . has become a privilege to serve under you."

"Does the Lord own me?" Peder responded softly. "Was not the Lord that we fought for a Lord who desired power and only power, obedience to power, and only power? Was the fitness to rule not decided by that power and the judicious exercise of its sword?"

Marakas' eyes widened, although he did not look up from the now full skin. Instead, he gazed at the brightest of the wavering reflections across moving water. The golden rays of sun ascendant. Men had killed and died for that crest; would kill and die again, just for the honor of wearing it—no matter how long or how short the wearing might be.

"Marakas?"

Marakas closed his eyes. "I thought the question might be rhetorical."

"I am not a man of many words. I do not waste a question when I desire no answer to it."

"My answer is not an answer that I feel will please you."

"There is very little in the coming war that will please me, par el'Sol," Peder kai el'Sol replied. "But it is bitter indeed to know that Fredero kai el'Sol may have been the better man, in every possible way, to fight this battle."

At that, Marakas looked up, almost snapping to attention. "He chose you," the par el'Sol said.

"I planned his death."

"Of course. But he knew. He *chose* his death; he made use of it. He saw the war coming; he did not feel that he had the skills necessary to fight it. And that is the truth. He said as much."

"And Fredero kai el'Sol—Fredero par di'Lamberto—did not stoop to lie. But he undervalued himself."

"No. He understood himself well."

Peder was silent.

"You have not yet added the fourth par el'Sol."

"No."

"And you will not?"

"No."

Marakas nodded. "Then let me answer the question that I believe you have asked. The Lord is concerned with power. But also with honor. It is why the Lambertans have prospered in all that they have chosen to do, even in the face of a weak Tyr and his foolish war."

They both knew that Marakas spoke not of Alesso di'-Alesso, but of the previous kai Leonne.

"It has been the way of the Radann to value power; it is why the Lord of Night once attempted to subvert the Radann first. Or so I believe," Marakas added. "And that is why we were given the five." His hand did not stray to the sword that he spoke of indirectly. But he noted that the kai el'Sol's did.

"Yes. But we have four now."

"Would you seek the fifth?"

Peder kai el'Sol's grip on *Saval* was as tight as his momentary smile. "I will ride with the Tyr'agar and the first and second armies. But I will ride in search of *Balagar*."

15th of Scaral 427 AA
Terrean of Mancorvo

Mareo di'Lamberto stared at the sheathed sword that rested, in a position of honor, in the heart of his chambers. It was not a wise place to put such a sword, for it caught the attention of every man who entered through the sliding screens.

Thankfully, they were few; only the most trusted of his

Tyran, the most faithful of his servants, the most obedient of his serafs, were allowed to lay hand upon those screens and set foot across the threshold.

So only they might see the magnificent simplicity of the scabbard; only they might see the Radann kai el'Sol's crest, stylized by the scabbard's maker, spread thinly from tip to mouth in embedded gold. He wondered if they would understand what he understood as he stared at the sword: That this was the legendary *Balagar*.

He had not drawn the sword. His own sword, called, simply, *Warcry*, had been drawn and blooded countless times in service to Mancorvo, the lands Lamberto both claimed and ruled. It had never failed him, and he was hesitant to pull a blade whose fame—illusory or no, he could not say—was so much the greater.

As if his blade were a jealous wife.

He felt the gaze of Jevri el'Sol upon him every time he passed the closed screens; felt the weight of his stare, his impossible and perfect reproach, as reward for his hesitancy. He had never been a meek man.

But to wield this sword had been his brother's desire, his brother's goal, and his brother's life. Mancorvo, mountains and grasslands and the bitter edge of the desert ring, had been Mareo's, and they had both achieved what they desired.

Fredero was dead.

Mareo's son, beloved kai, was also dead.

And in between these deaths, the death of the clan Leonne.

He heard the shifting tracks of wooden tongue in wooden groove, and he turned in time to see the delicate, pale hands of a young seraf gently pull aside the doors. She stopped when they were just far enough from the adjoining wall that a woman of grace and delicacy might find entrance; she herself remained, a kneeling shadow beyond the screens after the Serra Donna en'Lamberto entered.

"Na'donna," he said softly, as she came to kneel by his side. "Have you come with word? Another letter?"

"Only a letter from my cousin's wife," she said softly. "It is of little import, but it is pleasantly worded, and it whiles away the time."

"Have you replied?"

"I find, of late, that I have little of value to add to her observations, and little of worth. She has a sharp eye and a soft voice."

He smiled. "I have heard the same said of my wife."

She did not pretend, as some wives might, to misunderstand his meaning; she bowed her head and quietly accepted the compliment he offered. But she was ill at ease in this room, with this sword; the smile barely touched her lips before it died—and unlike some ghosts, it did not linger.

"Ser Anton follows the kai Leonne."

Mareo di'Lamberto stared, hard, at the sword.

"I believe that will be one of only two surprises, my husband. There is confirmation of other rumors, however. Baredan kai di'Navarre is the kai Leonne's first General."

"His second? His third?"

"He has none. Or rather—he has no Annagarians."

He stiffened; she had expected that hardening of line, and allowed it to fill the quiet room. "There is more?"

"There is," she said apologetically, "almost always more. As you suspected, the Callestans have chosen to support the kai Leonne. Neither Callesta nor Lamberto were—and my cousin's source here is therefore already flawed—approached by the new Tyr, although the other Tyrs seem to be in his keeping."

"I would not necessarily call the source flawed," he said softly. "The . . . invitation . . . when it came, came much after the fact of the death of the former Tyr. What does a Tyr'agar need to establish his hold upon the other Tyrs? Power. Land. What would he be required to offer to men of their station? What would Alesso *di'Marente* need? It comes down to Mancorvo and Averda."

She was silent; she knew why. The harshest of the desert scarcity touched Mancorvo only at the edge of the ring that started on either side of the Sea of Sorrows, and encompassed the heartlands in a thinning band.

"There . . . is . . . more. It has finally been confirmed that the Serra Diora di'Marano—or en'Leonne, as she has so boldly named herself—is no longer upon the plateau in the Tor Leonne."

"She has not returned to her father's kai?"

"Not to my knowledge. The household of Adano kai

di'Marano has fallen silent; the traffic between our serafs has become nonexistent."

He lifted a hand. "I need no more news this afternoon." And rose.

"Then I will displease you, I fear, my husband."

He frowned. "Na'donna?"

She bowed her head a moment, and then, from the folds of her perfect, pale sari, she brought forth a smooth parchment, stained by a dark, dark ink.

"A letter, from a woman who loved her husband very, very much, and who loves her son more. It is . . . a plea." Her hands were shaking slightly. "A plea for the life of her son."

He caught the letter before it fell, and then, placing it aside as if it were of no concern, he caught the face of his wife between his large hands. "Donna," he said softly. The sun and the sword had callused his palms, had hardened his skin—but he could still feel the softness of hers. Lady's mercy, not the Lord's.

"She wrote," his wife said, in a voice so soft even the strains of a samisen would have robbed him of the words, "from the North, and the letter . . . was delivered. I did not see the messenger. But I recognize the hand, and if the words were forced, they were forced by men of skill who have taken the time to understand the minutiae of a worried mother."

Her eyes were filmed. He lifted his head. Saw the shadow of his Serra's seraf, as perfect in form and stillness as a statue might have been.

He spoke a single word, and that outline rose, taking the momentary shape of a woman in a sari; all other details were lost as she obeyed that command—gracefully, quietly, and *quickly*.

"Forgive me, my husband. I—"

"Na'donna." He pulled her very gently into his arms, as he had done the still body of his kai over a decade ago. She had not wept then. He remembered, holding her now, that her eyes had been as still as the surface of a great lake; the fact of the death of her oldest child, her much loved son, had sunk beneath the surface of those eyes like a great, great weight.

He had found strength in her then. He saw it now; wondered if the memories had become so much worse with time, or if something within her had been broken in a way that he had not seen clearly.

But what she had not shared with anyone that day, he did not desire to force her to share now. He waited.

After a moment, she raised her face to his, her expression serene.

"The Serra Alina di'Lamberto . . ."

"What of her?"

"Is said to be traveling with the kai Leonne as we speak, if the dates given are accurate."

"Why the Serra Alina?"

"I cannot say, my husband. It has been . . . many years since the Serra Alina and I last spoke. But she was canny then, and wise."

"She was a sand viper," he said, with some rancor. "She was not a woman, not an example of the Serras of *this* family."

Serra Donna en'Lamberto bowed her head at once. He could not help but notice that in so doing, she had to put distance between them. "He is traveling without the Northern army. He will come in the company of the General, and the Callestan Tyr."

"And the Serra Marlena en'Leonne told you this?"

"Yes," she said faintly. "Because she knows that of all the Tyrs, my husband, the Tyr'agnate Mareo kai di'Lamberto, is a man of honor. And it is her belief that . . . no man of honor . . . could support the man who slaughtered her husband and his family."

"And of the Northern army?"

"She is a sentimental, self-indulgent woman," the Serra Donna said, with just a trace of the harshness of voice that often came with such a severe judgment. "But she is not a complete fool. She has said nothing of the Northern armies at all."

21st of Misteral, 427 AA
Terrean of Raverra

There was no precise moment at which Valedan knew that he was in a different country; no sudden change of terrain, no tug at the patriot's heart that whispered *you have returned.*

There was, of course, a border; it was drawn upon all the maps he had seen in a way that underlined its existence and separated two countries—Dominion and Empire—as effectively as markings could. But if he expected the landscape to conform to the map—and perhaps on some level he had—he was to be disappointed; the trees were the same on either side of the divide; the river, the same, the sounds of the sea in the distance the same.

He was assured that the people would be different, but his last glimpse of the Northerners and his first of the Southerners belied that common wisdom: border outposts, roadside fortifications, and men with armor and swords waited on either side of the undrawn line to speed him on his way, or to offer him what welcome border guards could.

The Northerners chose their weapons; crossbows and bows were readied as the group approached. There was hostility—some—but it was kept in check when Duarte AKalakar excused himself from Valedan's side and rode forward with a sealed scroll.

The scroll itself carried the word of the Kings' law, but had he not possessed it, the ring he wore would have been worth almost as much: Kalakar House ring. The Kalakar's gift.

Ellora was popular on the border for her actions here in the war a dozen years past.

The border gates—meant to stop wagons and horses, but not in the end meant to withstand a serious attack—were opened, and Valedan and his party allowed to pass. The passage took much less time than it would have had Valedan ridden at the head of armies—if indeed the armies were to travel by road.

From the moment he left the City, having excused his mother from attending him to spare both her dignity and his own, he felt that things were shifting beneath his feet; that everything familiar suddenly cast a shadow that implied an altered dimension familiarity had prevented him from seeing. The cobbled stones that he had always known now seemed to echo under the shod hooves of his mount, building to all sides as it was followed by other horses, until he felt that he was in the center of a large, gently sloped bowl, which was occupied on all sides by the unknown—by things, as the Callestan Tyr would say, he could not see for the sunlight in his eyes.

Everything you do now, from the moment you leave this city in the company of the Tyr and the General—your first General, Valedan—until the end of the war, will be a test. In some ways, it will be difficult, in some, simple. In the North there are many ways to fail a test. In the South, in the end, there is only one.

Valedan glanced up as the horse paused, but the Serra Alina was nowhere to be found. Although she had chosen to travel with him, she had chosen to travel as a Serra; she was hidden from view—both the sun's and the men's—by the very traditional box and curtains that usually graced a palanquin. She had servants, of course; serafs were illegal. But free or no, they had been born in the South, and they had come with the Southern nobility to attend them during their tenure in the North. They were free—of course—by law; they could leave and seek their fortune in the streets of the City itself. But they had not seen fit to do so. Valedan understood it; the Ospreys did not. Although these men were returning to the lack of freedom that had been their home, to a place where there were no laws that protected the slave from the owner, they labored under her slight weight in a silence that spoke of anticipation, not fear. Home.

Too much, Valedan had said, during his final audience with Mirialyn ACormaris. *There is too much that I do not understand.*

Understand this, then, the Princess Royale had said, when he had asked her. *Freedom is not like addition or subtraction; it is not like learning to write the letter forms of Weston, or old Weston. It is not like learning to read, or learning to nock bow and aim true.*

It is not a thing that you learn and keep forever; it is not a thing that you learn and can teach. What meaning it has—and it has many, some strong and some pale and weak—is defined, whole and new, by the person who utters the word; who believes in it, who dreams of it.

But who doesn't want to be free?

Do you?

I am free.

You are the son of a slave, Valedan. And your mother? Does she value the freedom?

That's different. She's a hostage.

No, Valedan. You *are the hostage. She came with you. Think.* And then, relenting because he was young—and he had been young, then—she handed him her bow to pull, and said, *But do not think too hard. It is a thought to while away the afternoon hours, when one has those hours; it is not meant to be a lesson.*

But it had been a lesson of sorts, and he expected that were she to test him, he would fail. Still, she had taught him one other thing: persistence.

As they passed the Northern outpost, the Callestans seemed to relax; they became more lively, although they were not obviously more noisy. Perhaps it was simply that their hands left their sword hilts a little more often; that they viewed the trees, the rivers, the sky, and the earth beneath it as something they owned.

Ramiro di'Callesta did.

General Baredan di'Navarre fell back; the Callestan Tyran rode forward; the Ospreys marched in a tighter knot around Valedan. They had become quieter and quieter, and where the Callestan hands strayed to sword hilt less, the Ospreys strayed more; some balance was preserved, but it wasn't a balance Valedan was certain he cared for.

"AKalakar?"

Duarte glanced toward him; glanced back at the road. But he nodded. He was the only member of the Ospreys who did not constantly touch sword hilt.

"Tyr'agar."

Although the Ospreys had made the attempt—several times—to use the appropriate title, they had often failed within the halls of *Avantari.* Valedan wasn't certain whether to be offended or not, because they showed themselves up to the challenge of remembering what his title was the moment they had cleared the last checkpoint. They were not obsequious—they would never be that—but they had become far more proper in the space of a few miles than they had been in his entire previous acquaintance with them. "Do you expect trouble here?"

The Captain of the Ospreys gave a brief smile that was

clipped at the edges. "We're in Annagar. Of course I expect trouble."

"More so than in Essalieyan?"

He nodded.

"Why? In either case, a demon is a demon, and although I am not familiar with the demonic tendency, I would guess that borders decided by mortals are not of particular interest, either as encouragement or discouragement."

"It's not the demons that concern us."

"What is it, then? I ride at the side of the Tyr'agnate; he is clearly marked and his Tyran carry his flag. Whoever attacks us here, attacks him first. And I think there are very few who would attack the clan of Callesta within Averda unless they intended to war. We are therefore unlikely—" Valedan stopped; his brows drew in, although his expression was otherwise untouched.

Duarte raised a hand a half a minute later; the Ospreys drew blades.

There were horses on the road ahead, and they were moving at speed.

Baredan di'Navarre rode ahead, vanishing almost instantly behind the inconvenient bend in the road. Valedan waited a moment. The sound of horses grew louder; the sound of men speaking stopped completely. But the only men who drew swords were his own; the Ospreys. Ser Andaro di'Corsarro and Ser Anton di'Guivera held their hands, waiting for the silence to break.

And when it broke, it broke first from the approaching riders.

Valedan edged his horse forward; the Ospreys—on foot—followed. Auralis AKalakar came back to his captain, and Valedan realized, with some chagrin, that he had not seen Auralis leave the group. And a man the size of Auralis was not easy to miss.

Duarte gestured, his left hand dancing in the air and across his lips, chin, chest. Auralis nodded, lifting his left hand as well, although the dance was slightly different.

Valedan had never seen a series of gestures so complicated, but he knew it for what it was: silent language. The Ospreys possessed a lexicon of movements that, in much, much shorter form, they used to communicate when words were not an acceptable medium. It was not, therefore, a surprise that they had developed a style of speech that did not deprive them of their swords.

"Captain?"

"The riders," Duarte said softly, treating the rise of the second syllable of his rank as the command it was, "are Callestan."

"One of his Tors?"

Duarte's smile was brief and sharp. "No. They're Callestan. And they're his personal men. Tyran," he added.

Valedan frowned.

"They fly the sun rising, with eight distinct rays. Only the Tyr'agnate's clan would dare to fly that flag, and at that, only those directly responsible to him, or directly responsible for him."

"The fact that they fly it now is significant?"

He nodded. "Ramiro di'Callesta does not choose to wear the sun rising, or to fly it, when he ventures North. Nor does he do so often when he travels in the South. In the North, he does not wish to remind those he deals with of his status as foreign dignitary, and in the South—in the South he expects to be known on sight by anyone he cares to deal with."

"I . . . see. And the men who are approaching?"

"At a guess? They carry word; they wish immediate obedience from those they happen to encounter on the road, if they followed the road at all. There is not a Tor that would dare to disgrace his clan by ignoring that flag without near certainty that its use was fraudulent."

"And fraudulent use of such a flag occurs often?"

"Not often," Auralis said. Valedan did not like the look of the smile that transformed his expression. But it was brief.

"I'm not a horseman," The Captain of the Ospreys said quietly, as he signaled his own forward in a small circle around the man they had chosen to protect. "But I'd guess that they've ridden a horse or two into the ground to carry whatever message it is they're delivering."

A cry of dismay, lifted by several voices, echoed back across the road.

Valedan held the reins and pressed his horse forward with a quick, strong tightening of knees; the horse responded instantly.

"Valedan!"

The kai Leonne cursed; the road banked steeply down with very little warning. He had thought the mountains beautiful at a distance; they were both serene and majestic as they broke—or made—the line of the sky conform to their white caps, their stone faces, their treed breadth.

But the foothills through which the path to Callesta ran were not nearly as lovely at a distance as the mountains had been, and the word itself—foothill—failed to describe the height of the rise and the depth of the fall of the lands to either side.

His horse took the sudden shift in height in perfect stride, slowing to descend.

"A good horse," Ser Anton said. "But I think it best to dismount, kai Leonne. There are stones in the middle of the path that are difficult to navigate."

There was no shame in taking either advice or lead from a man of Ser Anton's stature; Valedan was grateful. They made their way down in silence; the Tyr's men were still as trees on a windless, hot day.

"Ser Baredan?" Valedan said, as the General came to stand behind him in the oppressive silence.

"The eight men you see on the road before us are Tyran from the heart of Callesta, the capital of Averda. But what—" He stopped speaking as one of the eight returned to a clearly exhausted horse and unstrapped something from the side of its saddle.

It was a sword.

"Baredan?"

The General closed his eyes and looked away. "I do not know what occurred, but I believe I recognize the sheath and the sword it contains."

Valedan waited.

But Baredan merely dismounted, and urged his horse forward, where he might meet the Tyr'agnate on even ground. Valedan followed his lead, watching carefully, aware that the eyes of the Callestan Tyran were narrowed and reddened. The General left his horse by the roadside near the grass that was abundant in the foothills at this time of year; he walked quietly, his shoulders slightly bowed, toward Ramiro kai di'Callesta, the Tyr'agnate of Averda. The Tyr'agnate was completely silent; he failed to notice the General when the General at last reached his destination. Nor did the General seem surprised or offended.

The Callestan Tyran had gathered around the man who carried the sword from horse to Tyr. Their hands found the hilts of their own swords; their heads, as if pushed by the Lord's hand toward the ground, hung, casting shadows that were at odds with the crisp and perfect discipline the Tyran were famed for.

Ramiro di'Callesta offered them nothing at all. He simply waited for the sword to reach him, and when it did, he stared at it, his hands behind his back.

"When?" he said at last.

"Two days ago."

"Was he alone?"

"No. He was with four of the Tyran. They were engaged in drills within the city itself."

"And the four?"

"There were no survivors."

General Baredan di'Navarre bowed deeply.

"Your son's sword," he said quietly. But quiet or no, the words carried. Valedan heard them clearly and each syllable cut.

"My son's sword," the Tyr replied. He reached out, suddenly, and pulled it free of its sheath. It was unblooded; the flat caught sunlight and made of it silent lightning across the expression on Ramiro di'Callesta's face.

"Who?"

"We cannot say for certain," the oldest of the Tyran replied. But his eyes were dark and his jaw stiff. "But we found this, and this, when we were called." He held out a hand.

The Tyran gave him two flimsy swatches of cloth.

The fabric itself was red, brown, and orange—although how much of that was due to blood and how much dyes, Valedan could not say at this distance. The distinction was important, for across both of these ragged pieces, in miniature, flashed the golden markings that graced the flag of the Callestan Tyr: the sun rising, and shedding, as it did, eight distinct rays.

Ramiro took the cloth in a hand; the hand became a fist. "*Lamberto.*"

CHAPTER THIRTEEN

24th of Misteral, 427 AA
Terrean of Averda, Callesta

They rode in silence through the fields at the outskirts of *Callesta*, the only city in any of the five Terreans named after the family that ruled. Valedan kai di'Leonne would remember two things about the ancestral city of the Callestan Tyrs. The first: that it was green. For as far as the eye could see, life had taken the earth and wrested out of it shoots of green, gold, and white. Delicate blue flowers became obvious as the horses approached, and in the shade of the trees that seemed to crowd together in huddles, mushrooms, moss and other growths that were less amenable to open sun.

It was not that Valedan was not used to a profusion of life; he was. But in his childhood memories, this would have been an obscene display of a land's wealth. In the streets of the Tor Leonne, dust and heat were as common as foliage was here.

The Tyran unfurled the Tyr'agar's banner three days from the capital, although they journeyed in the haste of necessity and grim silence. From a distance, the serafs who toiled in the Averdan fields made their way to the roadsides wherever that banner was visible. The only place in which greenery was not evident was in the strips of empty soil that lay between trees; harvest had come and gone, and if this was the planting season—and Valedan did not understand farming well enough to know—it had not yet borne fruit. He knew enough of farming to understand that the seasons dictated the course of the wars fought between Averda and Mancorvo.

And he knew enough of people to know that the serafs

who came to plant themselves against the dust and wildness of the roadside both feared their Tyr—which was wise—and admired him. They held themselves in the subservient posture, but their backs were straight, and their arms curved in a way that spoke not of abject fear but of respect. They paid him his due.

He rode on.

But Valedan lingered a moment to watch them. They rose only when the banners had passed them by; when the shadows of the riders could no longer be seen against the road.

"What do you watch?"

Three men waited for him in the road; three men and one boy. It was the oldest man who spoke.

Valedan lifted a hand, asking by gesture alone for silence. Words receded, like wave or tide, as the serafs reached for the wide, stiff hats they had removed before they knelt to the passing shadows of the Tyr'agnate of Averda.

Their hands and arms were stiff, their faces stiffer. The oldest of them—skin cracked and folded by sun, rippled like sand dune by wind—held his hat a moment across his chest, the flat weave of dry bamboo against his open palms. His movements were not graceful; they were not even certain and sure.

But there was about the fold of elbow and the steady bend of neck a dignity that Valedan had rarely seen. The younger men, who were broader of shoulder and straighter of back, were more supple. They turned to the field in silence.

But the children were like small children anywhere. Held down by the threats—or arms—of their parents, they were freed from gravity by the passing of the Tyr; they ran into tall grass and wild growth and ran out again, weaving across the empty stretch of road to disappear and reappear beneath the bower of standing trees. They were laughing in the shadows and beneath the face of the open sky, too young to be of value in the fields. Valedan could not remember the last time he had laughed so carelessly beneath the Lord's gaze.

The older women came to herd them away; the older men watched, faces impassive.

Or not impassive. Some of them were crying. Not weeping; that would have been beneath them. But water caught the light as they turned beneath the sun, and the cracks and suppurations of aged skin tunneled that wet glimmer.

Valedan watched until they had retreated from the road, bearing witness as they had done.

"What do I watch?" he said, as he nudged his horse forward.

Ser Anton did not acknowledge the question he had asked; he merely waited. Andaro di'Corsarro looked over his shoulder and back, but he, too, was silent. The third man, Duarte AKalakar did not look back; he looked forward to the dust on the empty road.

Aidan, sitting astride Ser Anton's horse, asked, "What were you looking for?"

"I don't know. When I was a child in my father's harem, his serafs were nothing like village serafs. They produced comfort for my father and his retinue. They served my father's court. But I think there were very, very few among them who would have wept at the passage of the Tyr'agar."

"It is not for the Tyr that they weep," Andaro said quietly.

"Oh, but it is." Ser Anton seldom corrected Andaro outside of the drill circle. The younger man's silence was stiff and sharp. "The dead are dead; they know no pain. It is the living who feel the passage."

"His son?"

"Yes. His kai," Ser Anton added softly. "If indeed Mareo di'Lamberto is responsible for the death, we will never see peace between the Terreans."

"Unfortunate." Duarte's observation was dispassionate. Distant. "The kai Lamberto died twelve years ago, yes?"

"Yes. He was . . . young. Headstrong."

"We killed him."

Ser Anton bowed his head. "Yes."

Duarte nodded. "Is this vengeance?"

"Perhaps," Ser Anton conceded. "Or perhaps it was the only way that Mareo di'Lamberto could release his son to the Winds and come with naked blade to the blocks at which we might fashion oaths.

"He is no fool; he is not flexible, but he is no fool. He

must know that the Terrean of Mancorvo will not stand for long once the Terrean of Averda is taken."

Valedan kai di'Leonne looked at the empty road behind him, and then he looked ahead. "I think the lands will not be so easily taken," he said softly, "if they care enough for the Tyr'agnate that they offer what he will not shed for his own."

"Ramiro di'Callesta has long been considered the most dangerous of the Tyr'agnati. You have witnessed the reason for it today, and you understand its significance."

He was to witness it again and again as they approached *Callesta*. Fewer children were brought to the roadside as the roadside grew crowded, and intermingled among the farming serafs were the clansmen whose lives were inextricably linked with servitude. Although they were not required to perform full obeisance—were, by rank, allowed the privilege of standing while the Tyr rode by—some of them looked so uncomfortable being surrounded by those whose simple posture brought them in touch with the ground, Valedan almost smiled.

But they wore white bands across their foreheads, and those bands, some edged in gold and some in blue, were the colors of mourning outside of the court. *They value family. They value blood. They value loyalty. Remember these things, Valedan. None of The Ten would exist for more than a generation within the Dominion.*

At the echo of her voice, Valedan looked up, but the palanquin that carried the Serra Alina di'Lamberto was nowhere to be seen.

And that was wise. He had detailed the Ospreys—if they could still be called that—to guard her, but it had proved unnecessary. The crest that would have marked her as Lamberto was gone the moment she heard about the death of the kai Callesta. So, too, was all mention of her name. She was a woman; she was guarded. It was enough.

Unfortunately, the Ospreys—he really did have to force Duarte to find a different name for them—were not that simple. Alexis, Fiara, the others—they attracted attention immediately. It was not attention he wished to attract, but he had little choice. Women in the South did not join the armies, such as they were; they did not go to war. They did not become guards.

There was no better way to mark themselves as foreigners. And that, of course, meant Imperial soldiers. The five kingdoms and the free towns meant nothing to the Southerners; only the Empire existed in the space north of the boundaries of Annagar.

It had been delicately suggested—and briefly—that the women be separated from the men. In the Ospreys, there were only a handful after all. But the delicate suggestion was discarded as impractical, regardless of the difficulty their obvious origin would otherwise cause. Kiriel di'Ashaf was arguably the finest of their number, and unarguably the best at dealing with the demonic, and in the end neither Valedan nor Baredan di'Navarre wished to have her hampered by the guise of palanquin and pretty servitude.

So the Ospreys walked to either side of Valedan.

He had intended to wear the sun ascendant into the ancestral city of the Callestan Tyrs. From the hands of the wives of the Imperial hostages, all of whom remained in the City of Averalaan except for Fillipo par di'Callesta, had come the surcoat; the banner had been a gift of the Princess of the blood. The ring, the signet, had also been a gift of the Princess.

But he treasured the long Northern bow more.

It was only the bow he wore now.

The death of the Callestan kai had destroyed the need for pomp and circumstance. A grand entrance would be almost obscenely inappropriate.

It was therefore as a subdued companion, an ally, not a liege lord, that Valedan kai di'Leonne entered the inner walls of the city of Callesta.

And the first view of Callesta struck him like a perfectly aimed blow, and it was the second thing about Averda that scarred him; the second thing that he would never forget.

Among the trees that grew in the streets of the city, across the windbreaks for the farms within the walls, across the walls themselves, and upon carts and the strawmen that were supposed to scare off birds, there were swaths of white cloth, ribbed on either side with bright, sky blue and dark, midnight blue. Upon the scarecrows, the cloth was a shroud; upon the shoulders of the men who labored, living, in the fields, it was a mantle.

And as they progressed, as they passed fields and reached gated houses, they saw those same colors, pinned to fences like a wide, wide canvas, or a tapestry that told the same story. Where there was money, silver speckled midnight-blue and gold-embroidered sky. And where there was rank, a familiar crest broke the white of the background.

The streets were not empty. The silence that reigned as they passed was the more unnatural for the people who came to stand or kneel or prostrate themselves as the Tyr rode on. The horses made more noise than anything else that moved; no one spoke. Even the Ospreys were somber, although how much of that was due to the mood of the city, and how much due to wariness of the Annagarians he could not say.

The city was in mourning.

At the gates of the palace, Ramiro stopped. He gestured, and Baredan di'Navarre rode back. "Tyr'agar," he said quietly, "the Tyr'agnate of Averda apologizes for the poor welcome you have received in his city. It is an oversight that will not be repeated." The words were slow. Quiet.

"We traveled in speed, and without ceremony, as men travel to war," Valedan replied, his voice strong enough to carry, but not strained enough to sound vulgar. "He has offered me the service of his sword, and I have accepted. There is no better welcome."

The breeze carried the murmur of words shorn of edges. Baredan nodded, the movement a very brief dip of chin. Approval.

Valedan said nothing, because nothing else was expected. What could he add to what had been said, wordless, with white and blue, silver and gold? But when Baredan di'Navarre returned to the side of the Tyr'agnate, Valedan kai di'Leonne rode with him. The captain of his personal guard said nothing; Ser Anton remained behind with the Ospreys and Aidan. Ser Andaro di'Corsarro rode with Valedan, as was his right. They rode in a grim silence. Warriors might mourn, but when they rode to war, they did not carry the colors of mourning with them. Only by silence and attention could they offer respect for the fallen—and the men of the Dominion had mastered both.

Ramiro di'Callesta watched in silence from the back of his horse. *Bloodhame* hung at his side, sheathed and unnoticed. The sword that rested in one hand, across the saddle and either of his upper thighs, was his son's.

The Tyran who flanked him on either side dismounted and ran to help with the gates. Fillipo par di'Callesta rode up until their horses were within inches of each other. He spoke; Ramiro nodded. The words did not filter back. The gates opened. The path was lined with two things: flowers that sat in the shadows of tall, cultivated trees, and men.

Of the flowers, Valedan could name few, but Alina had begun to teach him what she could in the vain hope that he would not embarrass himself in the High Court with his very Northern ignorance. It seemed odd that men who dedicated their lives to combat and killing could also dedicate so much time to the nicety of garden, of quiet music, of verse. Perhaps there was a commonality in all of these things that escaped him.

He hoped that it did not escape him for long; the flowers themselves were beautiful; they hinted at wilderness without giving way to it. He dismounted; cerdan approached his horse and led it away.

The Tyr'agnate of Averda dismounted as well, as if Valedan's action was a signal. When Ramiro's feet touched ground, Ser Baredan di'Navarre joined him, followed closely by Fillipo par di'Callesta.

When they dismounted, they turned almost as one to look to Valedan. The Tyr'agnate knelt first and bowed his head. His movements were stiff and heavy. But if grief robbed him of fluidity and grace, it did not rob him of dignity; his expression as he raised his face was remote. Serene.

"Welcome, Tyr'agar, to this unworthy city."

"Any city, Tyr'agnate, that is home to the Dominion's most feared clansmen could not be unworthy of any visitor allowed entrance through its gates, be he the Tyr'agar, the Radann kai el'Sol, or the Lord himself."

The Tyr'agnate said, "You honor us. The gardens are in disarray and no preparations have been made for the visit of such an exalted guest. Your father, I fear, would not have been so gracious a visitor."

"I am not my father," the young Tyr'agar replied firmly. "I do not visit in time of peace."

"No," Ramiro di'Callesta said gravely, rising. "But neither did your father."

"My father was a man who appreciated finery, but he was not my equal with the sword."

"No, Tyr'agar, he was not. I must attend to my wife. I do not believe that they have interred my son's remains."

Valedan nodded quietly. "Tyr'agnate."

Ramiro waited.

"I did not know your kai. But if you will it, I will honor him in my fashion."

The man who ruled the breadth of Averda nodded quietly. He turned and began to walk slowly toward the heart of the palace grounds, waiting until Valedan had drawn abreast. Then, in a much quieter voice, he said, "The dead seem to care little for the honors the living bestow upon them. But the living are moved in their fashion. The Serra Amara en'Callesta was exceedingly fond of the kai Callesta. I believe she will find comfort in your presence. Let me speak a moment with her, in the privacy of the harem."

Valedan bowed and fell back, aware of the honor that had been granted him. Few were the men who spoke openly of their wives; fewer who spoke of them to men of rank.

The palanquin, curtains drawn against the intrusion of vision, waited in near-isolation between the Ospreys and the Callestan Tyran. Valedan moved slowly, but he moved toward it.

Baredan di'Navarre stopped him quietly. "Tyr'agar," he said.

"General."

"It is best to wait. Serafs will come for her when the Tyr'agnate informs his wife that she is present."

"Does she know?" he asked the general.

"That the kai Callesta is dead? Almost certainly. How? No more than you or I."

"Does she know that Lambertan colors were found?"

"More than colors," the General said softly. "Two of the Lambertan Tyran were also there. They were not alive; the kai Callesta and his guards did not die easily."

"I am wondering what welcome there will be for her in the harem of the kai Callesta's mother."

"She will know what to do," the General replied quietly. "It is beneath your station to express open concern for a woman who is not your wife or your sister, Tyr'agar."

"And it is above your station, General, to criticize me in my chosen concerns."

Baredan di'Navarre bowed low.

"The General is right," the Serra said softly, from behind closed curtains—a reminder, and perhaps a necessary one, that all words spoken beneath an open sky were witnessed.

"Perhaps. But I have my own reasons, Serra, for what I do. Nothing is trivial now. The war starts here. With your permission?" He reached out with both hands; curved his fingers and palms around the rough, raw silk that was sturdy enough to survive a long journey, but expensive enough to suggest the wealth of the occupant's father or husband.

"Of course, Tyr'agar." Her words were very distant, very stiff.

The curtains parted. "Serra Alina di'Lamberto," he said, speaking as stiffly as she had. "Ser Carelo kai di'Callesta was ambushed within the city of Callesta. He rode with four of his father's Tyran. The exact numbers of the ambushers are not known, but two men who have been identified as Lambertan Tyran were present where the kai Callesta's body was found.

"With the permission of the Tyr'agnate—and assuming that the bodies are still present—I would like you to identify them."

Baredan di'Navarre's intake of breath was unnaturally sharp.

The Serra Alina's frown was more so, but briefer. Both passed before anyone but Valedan noticed that they existed at all. "They are said to be Tyran?"

"Indeed." Valedan knew full well that it had been a decade since she had last seen the Tyran of Lamberto—but a handful of years measured against the strength of her memory meant nothing.

"If Ramiro di'Callesta grants permission, I will do as you

ask. But, Tyr'agar," she added, lowering her voice, "I will not lie."

"Not even if it serves my purpose?"

"Not even then. In something of this import . . . I am hampered by my heritage."

"Your heritage?"

Baredan di'Navarre's laugh was a rough, harsh bark—but it was genuine. "She speaks," he said, "of Lambertan blood." He stared openly at the woman in the palanquin as if seeing her for the first time.

And she, being Serra and in the South, failed to notice his sudden lack of manners.

The shadows across the grass were sharp and harsh as the Callestan Tyr crossed the grounds that he had, at the side of his wife, spent years designing. They moved as he moved, although they were unhindered by the simple boundaries of the elements that had suddenly become unfamiliar: the short, twisting branches of the cherry trees past their season, the deep, deep red of the dwarf maples, the tall, wide trunks of the Northern trees that his wife so loved, their long switches trailing groundward at the foot of the large pond. Lilies also floated there, but the falling leaves of the weeping willows destroyed the simple perfection of their white faces.

He saw all this as a stranger. It had become, for this solitary journey, a landscape that he had never walked before. And he walked it alone. Not even his brother had been given permission to attend him as he made this final trek across the lands that were inextricably linked with Callesta.

But his brother had been wise enough not to ask.

His Tyran were less cautious; the loss of the kai Callesta had made them foolish. It had been a long time since Ramiro di'Callesta had been forced to publicly—and curtly—correct them. If he had ever done so before.

They acknowledged the circumstance, however, with grace; they merely obeyed the harsh, sharp sting of his command as if it had been spoken in the careful, modulated tones a man of power was accustomed to—expected to—use.

He did not raise his face to sunlight; he was a man and

he was wary; he chose not to expose his expression to the Lord's full scrutiny. He walked alone for a reason.

Bloodhame was sheathed, but he carried a naked blade in his sword hand. The sword, curved and clean-edged, was heavier than any he had attempted to carry since the day he had first taken *Bloodhame* as his own.

In the South it was acknowledged that light blades were good for sport, but heavy blades were good for duty.

The sword in Ramiro di'Callesta's hand would never be drawn again by Carelo kai di'Callesta. The Tyr'agnate felt a curious detachment as the weight of steel brought his arm to its full length. Ser Carelo kai di'Callesta had been a difficult son. Rebellious. Wild. Only barely intelligent enough not to race headlong into the crudest of political traps.

Loved by his mother, he was her secret worry; the boy who might not become man enough to live up to the legacy of her husband.

His par, the second son, had been as different from the open day of Carelo as a boy might be who might one day be a man. Alfredo was dark-haired, fair-skinned—his mother's son in looks—but where Carelo was aggressive and impetuous, Alfredo was cautious, observant. He made few mistakes; but when challenged by his father, said—coolly—that he did not need to repeat his brother's errors to analyze them.

Carelo snorted. His father could hear the sound as clearly as if it had just been uttered, as if months had not come between the memory and the event.

You can analyze them to death, Alfredo—but you'll never learn *anything from them.*

Oh? And if experience is the only teacher, why are there so many dead would-be swordsmen? Why does our father spend so much money on arms masters?

It's not arms masters or even experience that I speak of, Carelo had said, leaning across the low table in a way that made his mother comment on the amount of time he spent with his cerdan. *If you want to lead men, you have to* lead. *You have to swallow the Lord's fire and let it singe you every now and then because without fire, there's no light.*

There are some fires that burn without illuminating, Alfredo replied. *But it doesn't matter either way. I don't have that fire. I don't want it. I don't* need *it. You will lead, Callesta will follow, and I—who pay attention—will stand behind you and guard your back against the openings you leave for your enemies.*

Serra Amara's face had creased in the way he best loved; with genuine pleasure at the cleverness of her son. The corners of her eyes were cracked by sun and wind, and the fullness of lips bracketed in the same way, but when she smiled, when her smile was for a single moment both unguarded and radiant, a window opened between the woman she was now and the girl she had once been before age had transformed them both.

You watch over your brother, she had said. It was not clear to whom she spoke, perhaps not even to her, although she was a woman who loved words that held multiple meanings.

With my life, they had replied, one with heat and one with an irony that did not deprive the words of meaning. They had looked at each other, then, and Carelo had laughed out loud; Alfredo had smiled.

It had been a perfect moment; it was perfect still, in memory. But memory was an imitation of life, a ghost of something already past.

Wind had guttered flame.

The Tyr'agnate's grip on the sword was so tight it was painful. That pain, however, would end soon; he could feel the tingling in curved fingers that preceded numbness.

He reached the end of the gardens, reached the steps that led to the private courtyard his wives used at the height of the day. There was a fountain at its center, and around it, in the shade provided by carefully cultivated trees and the height of the building itself, were low, flat platforms.

They were empty. His footsteps echoed in a stillness deprived of even the dance of leaves. He had walked the edge of the Sea of Sorrows in his youth, and he could not mistake this palace for that desert, but no other experience had prepared him so well for this walk.

He crossed the courtyard and hesitated in front of the golden rails, the brass chimes, the Callestan crest with the artistic embellishments he allowed his wives to use across the heavy drape of raw silk. It took only a moment before he realized what was missing, and he thanked his wife in silence for the foresight that led to the absence of Tyran.

Ramiro di'Callesta was not a man who spoke to the Lord or the Lady; he was not a man who made a habit of useless gesture and he knew, from long experience, that the gods, *if* they existed at all, had more amusing things to do than listen to the pleas of a person who walked the edge between strength and death.

He bowed his head in silence. He counted, each number like the lash of a whip across open skin. The line of his shoulders was bowed; he corrected this oversight in posture.

Amara.

Carelo.

He pushed aside the hanging and entered the harem.

She was waiting for him.

His wives—the rest of his wives—were nowhere in sight. Although he could see their hands in evidence in every distinguished element in the room—the arrangement of pillows across the mats, the complementary colors of the three fans that rested, in perfect harmony, against the wall, the types of fruit that had been chosen and the way they were carefully washed and arranged in a single, wide bowl—they had fled the heart of the harem, no doubt at the order of the Serra.

He carried the sword to her, but he could not release it; his knuckles were white.

She stood; she did not assume the subservient posture, and he did not expect it, not here.

"When?"

She did not meet his eyes. Her hands, clasped loosely before her, gave her the appearance of a woman of the North. Her hair, the single feature of which she had been so proud, was no longer the color of unsullied night; here and there, streaked as if at the touch of a ghost, he could see the glitter of pale silver.

He knew whose ghost moved her.

It was the Callestan Tyr who bowed.

"I always thought," she said softly, "that he would be his own death. I thought that he would rebel in a way that you—or Callesta—would not tolerate. I spent hours with his wife, planning against such a day." Her fingers danced against the backs of her hands as if skin were an instrument.

She stared at the expanse of wall across which lay a single, simple painting, an imitation of the sky at dawn or dusk, when neither Lord nor Lady could claim dominion over Annagar.

"He seemed so much like you. You always walked the same edge with your father. Did you know—did you know that your mother spoke to me about your safety and the way your impetuousness threatened my future?"

"No."

"I thought her very foolish," she said, and she laughed, and the laugh itself was a terrible sound, both harsh and weak. "Until the moment I spoke to our kai's wife. He was so very headstrong."

"Amara—" He reached for her.

But she was not yet capable of seeking shelter. She shied away from his hand.

From the hand that did not carry his son's sword.

"Alfredo has not moved."

Ramiro bowed his head. The weight of the moment was unbearable.

And he bore it. That ability, in the end, defined him.

"Where is he?"

"He is with the Radann."

"Amara."

She looked away from the illusion of freedom from the whim of gods. "Was he worth it?"

The question was sharp. Pointed. He had expected comfort from her, but accusation seemed natural when it finally came. He heard pain, guilt, rage, sorrow; he did not hear strength.

He could not afford to hear no strength. "You must judge him, as you judge all things, for yourself. Judge for me, as you have done; be my guide."

"He is here?"

"He is here, Amara. He waits in the courtyard of the pale moon, with Baredan di'Navarre and Ser Anton di'Guivera."

A flicker of light danced across the surface of her eyes. "So, that was true."

"Yes." It was his turn to seek comfort in illusion. "The Northern armies will follow."

"We know."

Silence again. Silence had often been a comfort, and perhaps it would be again, but now it was merely a tarpaulin across the unsaid.

"We received word," she said quietly. "I . . . received a letter."

"A letter?"

"From the Serra Donna en'Lamberto."

He waited as patiently as a man in the Hells can. When his wife did not continue, he said simply, "She does not frequently write to the Serra Amara en'Callesta."

"No. And she did not mention the Northern army. But she did speak, in passing, of the rough ways of the men to the South, and of the importance of both oath and family to her husband."

Ramiro di'Callesta closed his eyes.

"She wrote of the death of her son. She asked me—"

"Amara?"

"She spoke freely. She asked me to become her, for a moment. She asked if I thought I would be strong enough to forgive those who brought about the death of my son, if I had suffered such a loss."

"Did you reply?"

"Yes."

"What did you say, Amara?"

"I told her that, for the sake of the Terrean, I would hope that I might forgive what no woman would naturally forgive. I told her that I was not a strong woman—and I am not a strong woman, Ramiro—but that, in the end, the decision to forgive or avenge was in neither of our hands; she and I are merely wives.

"It is our husbands who decide our fate, and the fate of the Terreans themselves." She looked at him then, dry eyed, terrible in the way the edge of a sword is terrible when it is inches from your throat.

He understood what she did not say; how could he not? They were kindred spirits; their rage and their loss was almost identical.

But he was not a man who made commitment lightly. "Where is Carelo?"

"In the temple of stone," she said. "It has been four days, but the Radann have—have done what they can to preserve our son against the hour of your return."

"I must tend to him, Amara."

She nodded. "I will join you there."

"Amara, I will not play the game of rank or status here. Not today. You have been, since I was younger than Carelo, my strength, my grace. If there has been a day since the death of my father that I have required strength and grace, it is this one.

"Join me, if you can, but when you join me, be *with* me; do not wear your anger as armor against me. I am not your enemy. If I have failed you, speak plainly. If I have failed our son—"

She raised a hand to ward off the only weapon he had ever used against her: his words. But he was still a warrior, still a man of the Lord, and he sensed a weakness in her that had not been there moments before, an opening that he might exploit.

He was a ruthless man in his fashion.

"Yes, I have failed our son," he said, the words intense, and no less finely honed for the fact that they were the truth. "I went North. I followed Baredan di'Navarre in his fool's quest. I lingered there, to watch games. I negotiated with the three Commanders who once shed much Averdan blood, solely to return South with a boy who is untried and untested.

"Was it worth my son? *No.*" With his free hand, he reached for her shoulder, and this time she stood for his touch. "But my son is gone. What is left? What is left us?"

She said nothing at all. But the silence was different.

"The bodies of the others?"

"They are with the Radann."

"And are you satisfied with the answers they offer?"

She looked at him, then. Her eyes were not as dry as he had thought them when he had seen her profile. "The Tyran have conducted the investigation. I am your wife, I am Serra Amara the Gentle."

"You offered them no guidance."

"No."

He lifted his hand and very gently cupped her chin—her stiff, tense jaw—in his hand. "I have been in the North overlong," he said softly. "This *is* my home, and I am defined by it, as I define it. But I curse the foolishness that deprives my men of your wisdom in my absence."

"Bless it instead," she said quietly. She closed her eyes and then raised her chin slightly; straightened out the line of her shoulders, the graceful line of her back. The only hesitation she showed at all was brief, but it was marked; she froze a moment before she made a decision about the veil that lay carefully folded upon the pillows.

In the end she chose to wear it, but it was a close thing. That, more than anything, told Ramiro di'Callesta that his wife was almost ready for war, for she trusted herself to show no weakness in the Lord's sight unless that weakness served her purpose.

CHAPTER FOURTEEN

When the Tyr'agnate of Averda returned to the courtyard in which his guests had been left to wait, he was transformed. The dust of the road still clung to him if one knew how to look, but his attire itself was fresh and pale; like the men who wore headbands or armbands, he had marked himself with the colors of grief.

It was Southern, to mark oneself externally so that outsiders might understand that you felt an emotion you were forbidden, by etiquette and the rules of strength, to show. The front panels of his loose shirt were white; the sleeves a pale blue, the cuffs of his wrists, dark midnight. So, too, were the pants; his sash was gold, but a gold distinct from the brightness of sun. He wore *Bloodhame* openly, but that was not remarkable. What was, to Valedan, was the fact that he carried his son's naked blade in one hand.

The Tyran fell into the most subservient stance he had ever seen them adopt in the presence of their Tyr. Each man touched one knee to ground; their sword hands went to their hilts and rested there; their free hands fell to thigh, their chins to chest.

Baredan di'Navarre chose to remain on his feet, but he bowed, and he sustained that bow for a full minute. Ser Anton di'Guivera did the same.

Valedan chose to follow their lead. In the North, he thought, grief was different. He could remember clearly the Imperial reaction to the news of the deaths of their hostages, and no man or woman in the North that he had seen had lost their eldest child. Were they weak for their displays?

No.

They were human.

He raised his face as Ramiro stood, tense and unmoving

beneath the face of the Lord. The Tyr'agnate's eyes were narrowed, his lips only slightly thinned. He did not seem to see the Tyran who waited, like perfect statues or perfect weapons, before him.

But he did turn when a woman joined him.

She, too, wore the colors that spoke of loss and death in the Dominion, but she also hid her face behind the opacity of a veil that fell from the height of her Annagarian hair to her silk-draped elbows. When she reached her husband—for it was clear to Valedan that this woman was no other than the famed Serra Amara the Gentle—he turned to her and held out an arm; she took it, as if it were all of her strength. But some strength remained her, for she carried the sheath to the blade Ramiro kai di'Callesta wielded.

To Valedan's eyes, to his inexperienced eyes, it was not clear who derived more strength from the union of their arms. His father and his mother had never derived strength of any sort from each other.

Or perhaps that was unfair; perhaps what he remembered of his life as a child did not contain the subtle understanding of gesture, or the intricacy of a dependency that was not profoundly unbalancing. He was not surprised, however, that the Tyr'agnate did not speak until this woman was at his side. She had become, although her face was veiled and her manner exquisitely Southern, a woman to rival the Serra Alina di'Lamberto.

A danger, but a fine one.

It was not Southern custom, but he forgot Southern custom for a moment, and he bowed. When he rose, her veiled faced was turned toward him; he could see the line of her chin and cheek, the width of her eyes, but he could discern no exactness of expression that might convey her thoughts or her intent.

"Tyr'agar," the Tyr'agnate of Callesta said, speaking across the bent heads of his men, "It is my pleasure to present to you the Serra Amara en'Callesta."

The Serra Amara en'Callesta removed her hand from the haven of her husband's. She did not choose to lift her veil, but she did choose to prostrate herself in the slender shadow her husband cast.

"It is your pleasure," Ser Valedan kai di'Leonne said, bowing again, "but it is my honor. Much has been said of the Serra Amara, and I see that much of it is true. If it would not offend you, Tyr'agnate, I would be honored if you would feel comfortable enough in my presence that you would give your Serra permission to speak as freely as she might otherwise choose."

"Of course," Ramiro di'Callesta replied lightly as if the request was a normal request beneath the open sky, between two men. "Serra Amara?" He offered his wife his hand, and she accepted with perfect fluidity of motion, although clearly she was not a young girl, with a girl's easy grace.

"If I am to speak freely, let me speak plainly and beg for your forgiveness and your compassion. Callesta has seldom had so important a visitor, and the city itself is ill-prepared to accept you in the fashion you merit. Please, accept a mother's grief as excuse for what must clearly be inexcusable; accept a wife's promise that in future, all honor that accrues to you will be rendered onto you in a fashion that befits both your family and my husband's."

"A mother must care for her sons," Valedan replied. "And a wife, the children of her husband. Only a fool or a weak man would seek to elevate the simple fact of his presence over the loss you have suffered."

Again, the veil protected her expression—but her eyes, he thought, had rounded at the corners. He had surprised her. He was almost ashamed of the momentary satisfaction that gave him, and turned to her husband, who waited quietly, his expression unmarred by surprise, weariness, or grief. "If you would not take my presence as interference, I would pay my respects to your kai."

"The respect of the respectworthy is never unwelcome, kai Leonne." He spoke quietly, but not so quietly that the words would not stretch the distance, and fill the silence, between his men and the men who served Valedan. This was not unexpected. The informality of his tone, the use of the correct but informal title, were. Were it not for the circumstance, such a lack of obvious respect for the differences between their ranks might have been seen as insult.

It could have been, had the tone been different.

As it was, it was a claim. Of familiarity, certainly.

Valedan kai di'Leonne bowed. When he rose, he nodded

to Ser Anton and Ser Andaro; they joined him in silence. "Wait for me," he said quietly.

Baredan di'Navarre was there in an instant, by presence alone imploring him to think better of his next action before it was too late. Valedan's smile was turned inward, a hidden jest. He walked to the palanquin which contained the Serra Alina, and as the Tyr'agnate had done with the Serra Amara, he offered her his hand.

Her expression was flawless, perfect, unadorned by the disapproval he was certain she felt.

"Join me," he said, taking care to speak loudly enough to be overheard. He had learned subtlety at the feet of the woman he now faced; he was certain that the standing guards could barely overhear what was said. Barely was enough; she could not now refuse his request without demeaning the rank that she so valued.

She was, of course, aware of this. He had chosen the difficult route of request rather than command. This was Northern. He had, by making the request something that she could not refuse without damaging his reputation, turned Northern respect into a Southern gesture.

She did not speak a word; she came out of the awkward confines of the palanquin smoothing the wrinkles from silk that had been creased by her journey while she unbent. When she reached her full height, she folded herself to the ground, the soft and tended grass in direct contact with her knees, and bent there until her forehead touched the cool greenery.

The emerald of her sari's edge matched the blue green shade beneath her hands. She wore a single ring, but several strands of gold encircled her throat and wrists. She wore sandals that were meant for palanquin or mat; she was a Serra, not a seraf, and not expected to walk far. At any other time, she would have been prepared for any encounter. But the Tyr'agnate's kai had died, and she did not wear white; did not wear the blues of the sky, the gold of the sun, the pale silver of the moon. Had she been in the North, she would have; the death of a Tyr's son demanded garments of mourning from the daughter of Tyr, although as he was the son of her brother's enemy, she could—barely—survive the breach of etiquette unscathed. At least in the eyes of the men.

The Serras?

The Serras seldom acknowledged the wars their husbands chose to make. They maintained the polite fiction that in all things, matters of war were the games of men, and that women endured in silence the loss and the gain by which they—fathers, husbands, brothers, and sons—measured themselves.

She could not now maintain this polite fiction, and in these circumstances, such a fiction was crucial.

The obeisance was her criticism, and he endured it for as long as he felt necessary. Then he bid her rise and gather her fans, waiting until she was ready before he crossed the courtyard to join the Tyr'agnate.

The Tyr'agnate gave the Tyran permission to rise—but not by word; he simply stepped aside and led his honored guest toward the finely appointed temple that lay within Callestan walls. They rose when his back was toward them, and they followed in silence. Ser Anton di'Guivera and Ser Andaro di'Corsarro joined the Tyran, keeping just enough of a distance to preserve the separate identities of the two groups.

They were not friends, although the journey from the heart of Essalieyan to the heart of Callesta had given ample opportunity for familiarity to grow. But the Tyran had witnessed the pledge of allegiance that both Ser Anton and Ser Andaro had offered the young Tyr'agar, and the memory was a scar. A battle scar, something to be worn openly with pride, even if it could not otherwise to acknowledged.

They *knew* the mettle of the Northerner's allies. And if they did not trust them—and in the Dominion, trust was a child's game—they wasted little time on active suspicion.

The Serra Amara en'Callesta and the Serra Alina di'Lamberto followed between the men who ruled and the men who served. Valedan had introduced the Serra Alina very carefully. It was known that Mareo di'Lamberto had, with some glee and anger, surrendered an unmarriageable sister to the Northern Empire, and that there was little love lost between them.

But the weight of her name on this day was costly.

The Serra Amara en'Callesta had greeted her with a cold, perfect grace; her manner was flawless, impeccable, and utterly devoid of pleasure. The Serra Alina di'Lamberto was wise, Valedan thought; she—in a manner of speaking—bared her throat, forsaking pride in much the same fashion that the Serra Amara had forsaken warmth. She did not acknowledge the Lambertan part in the young kai's death in any other way, but the humility of her posture was enough—for now. The Serra Alina di'Lamberto had come as part of the entourage of the Tyr'agar, and to demand abasement and obeisance from any member of the Tyr'agar's handpicked retinue required either a certainty of power or a willful, reckless madness.

The Serra Amara had neither, or chose to display neither.

But she walked at her husband's side to the Radann's temple, woman or no, for these last steps of their life with their son. She was bringing her oldest son his father, and her husband his kai.

For just a moment, a window, a small arrow slit, appeared between the forces that had shaped Valedan's childhood and the forces that now, vast as mountains, governed his adult life, and with a sharp clarity of vision that he seldom attained Valedan saw the Serra and the Tyr'agnate clearly. He wondered if anyone else could see the echoes of the very first time she had presented her son to her husband in this, the last one.

The temple was small. Wide, long slits in the curved stone exterior let sunlight and skylight pour through to temple floor, but the light was stark and pure.

Gone were the great glass panoramas of the Northern cathedrals; gone the tapestries and the long hangings that were suspended from sweeping heights to stone floor. There would be no choirs here, no voices raised in morningtide and eventide to fill those heights with that tapestry of voices, high and low, that spoke of the glory of the Northern gods.

What does the Lord value?

Men of power.

But why? Why is it that we suffer with so few gods, when the Northerners breed such a pack of them, such a frenzy of beliefs, that there's practically a god to blame for stubbed toes and hangnails?

Kneeling before the temple stairs, the Serra Alina di'-Lamberto could barely believe that she had uttered those words.

Frenzy of beliefs?

But she knew who had uttered the rest, and because that memory was cherished—when so few of her memories were—she held on to the belief that even her perfect Southern manners could be reduced to so weak a veneer that they might crack in places when pressed, stretched, challenged with such infinite care as the Princess Mirialyn ACormaris had taken.

Is that not what you call it? You are a woman, but it doesn't matter to the Essalieyanese; they throw themselves at your feet because you are descended from the descendants of your so-called gods.

They are not my *gods, but my grandparents,* Mirialyn ACormaris had said. *And perhaps the frenzy of belief we have resides in that truth.*

That the gods are your grandparents?

Mirialyn's laughter was rarely evoked, but she had chosen to laugh then. *You speak well for a Southern-bred Serra; you speak with an edge in your voice.*

All women know how to wield words.

Not so, Serra Alina. In my experience, what the Serras know how to wield best is their silence; it is their lack of words that cuts.

Is it not this way in the North, ACormaris? We each make weapons out of the things we can.

Or tools.

She knew that Mirialyn ACormaris was a woman of import; that she was the only blood relative of the King Cormalyn. But she was also cunning and observant in a way that many of the Northerners were not; she knew how to hoard both words and the infelicity of expression which gave away all thought, all emotion. Yet on that day, the sea winds squalling against a gray, gray sky, she had opened up that hoard and offered it to perhaps the only Southern Serra who would appreciate them.

But the gods—let me answer that question. There is a frenzy of belief in the gods because they are connected to us, and we to them, in birth, in life, and in death; they are like the parents—stern, cruel, abusive, or loving—that inform our lives in the Empire. Even after our death we are not free of their influence. Mandaros waits.

Mandaros is the god of Judgment?

Indeed. She did not seem at all surprised that Alina knew who the Northern gods were; but she had never shown surprise when Alina revealed knowledge about anything Northern, with the single exception of dance.

And it was that fact that had first been so intoxicating. This Northern stranger, with her exotic, pale hair, her pale skin, the odd hazel of her eyes, expected intelligence and knowledge from her as a matter of course. She did not dissemble. She did not ask the Serra she spoke with to dissemble. Or to smile or to defer or to bow and scrape. In no public circumstance had the Princess Mirialyn ACormaris been encumbered by the social need to hide her achievements or her abilities; in no public circumstance did she expect the Serra Alina to do so—but she did not comment or deride when the Serra chose, for reasons of her own, to fall into the display of perfect, implacable, Southern manners.

Intoxicating.

Especially to think about that freedom—utter, exquisite, rare—while she knelt, as custom dictated, beyond the open doors of the Temple of the Sun, looking in at the sparse decor from a distance that was equal parts intellectual, emotional, and geographical. Women did not enter that temple. Women did not touch the stones that graced the floor; women did not cast shadows in the light that streamed through stark, simple windows.

And women did not speak their thoughts freely.

Nor do men, in the South, she reminded herself. But they walked in freedom beneath the Lord's roof.

She raised her head as some of these men—Valedan among them—crossed the threshold, and lowered her head again when she was joined on the kneeling ground by the Serra Amara en'Callesta and the serafs who waited, like shadows in unpredictable light, upon her.

I thought I would never come back. You said it was my choice; it would always be my choice.

She bowed her head again.

The Princess of the blood had spoken truth, but it was her truth, Northern truth. Serra Alina di'Lamberto, unmarried, unmarriageable, was marked by the South; by a desire for both dry heat and the silence and serenity of quiet shadows in the face of the Lord's heat. She yearned, too, for the strains of a samisen handled by a master; longed for the vision of the cherry trees in full blossom at the heights of the orchard in Amar, the city that had been her home before she had been cast off to the North by her brother's loss and fury. Those blossoms she had gathered in childhood, and again in her youth, and they had meant different things each time she had done so. She wondered what they would mean today, tomorrow, next month, should she be allowed to walk in that orchard again.

The North had freed her, and the North would never be able to free her.

The Tyrs passed beneath the lintel of open doors, into the rays of slanted light cast by simple, curved stone. Valedan was younger than Ramiro di'Callesta; the shape of his face and the slender rise of his cheekbones was distinctive enough that the two could not be mistaken for blood. But Valedan gave way to the older man, the way a son might for a father.

He was canny, Alina thought. Canny? She felt something akin to shame; was glad for the moment that the Southern women did not speak before the Temple of the Lord. There was, in Valedan's quiet deference, a sincerity that she herself did not possess. And she had seldom regretted it as much as she did at this moment.

She watched.

Light paled the faces of the two men; the different shades of color, the features that spoke of Leonne and Callesta, were lost to white; to a ghostly glow that passed, as they did, into memory. Fillipo par di'Callesta walked behind them, beside Ser Anton di'Guivera; the swordmaster drew his sword as he passed through the stone entrance.

There was a collective hush of breath behind him. Even Fillipo, a match in every way for his kai, paused to stare at the sight of sunlight against silver sheen. He was the Captain of the Tyran; had he desired it, he could have spoken against such a display.

But he honored it instead; he bowed to Ser Anton di'Guivera. "Thank you," he said.

Ser Anton bowed in return, the bow deeper and longer.

"It is all," he said, "that I have to offer. I am of a simple clan; I have coin, but coin is not of value to *men*. I can make oaths," he continued quietly, "but any oath of value that I have sworn, I have sworn to the clan Leonne while its last member breathes; I would not offer a lesser oath in the face of Callesta's loss."

Serra Amara the Gentle stiffened. The sole Lambertan present did not raise her head or turn to the side to see if she had broken with prescribed tradition to look full at the face of Ser Anton di'Guivera. But she heard the rustle of undrawn veil across shoulders.

"You honor us."

"As I can," Ser Anton said. "Come. You are the Captain of the Callestan Tyran."

Ser Fillipo nodded and followed his brother into the slanted light. Ser Anton did not sheathe his sword, but he carried it easily at his side as he joined the younger man.

Ser Andaro di'Corsarro fell back, behind the ranks of the Callestan Tyran. Although it was his right to accompany the Tyr'agar—and indeed, his duty—he, too, gave way to the protocol of loss and grief that could only, in this way, be acknowledged.

After all, men expected to lose things of value in a war. Sons, brothers, fathers; these were the price they paid to *be* the Lord's men. The Lord was not kind.

He did not acknowledge the loss. He only acknowledged victory.

There would be no tears shed today. Serra Alina was certain of it. But when the Lord's time passed, when the Lady reigned—then, in her dark cool shade, they might be free.

A body lay against stone in the heart of the temple. In robes of white, edged only in the azure of the clearest, highest sky, four men stood at the corners of the bier across which the kai Callesta's body had been laid. They wore the sun in gold, and when the Tyr'agnate entered the room, they drew swords as one man and held them skyward, their expressions as open as the surface of the stone upon which the body lay.

Their precision was perfect.

The kai Callesta's arms had been arranged so that they

crossed the breadth of white silk that was not quite shroud. The gash across his forehead had been cleaned and tended, but it was visible, and it was ugly.

Had he survived the taking of that wound, the scar would have served him well. No one trusted an unscarred man. Lack of scarring spoke of three things: cowardice, youth, or inexperience. But the wounds that produced scars often produced other things as well. Death.

The Tyr'agnate stepped forward; Valedan stayed his ground. In the light and shadow of sun and stone, Ramiro di'Callesta bowed.

"Tyr'agnate." The oldest of the Radann returned his bow twofold. The tip of his sword touched the ground and remained against stone as he rose.

But the Tyr'agnate's gaze had moved on to rest a brief moment upon the face of his dead son—and the back of his living one. Alfredo par di'Callesta stood as close to the altar as a man could without lying upon it, his back to them all. He had not chosen to turn to face his father when his father approached.

He could offer—although it would have been fiction, and a fiction that relied entirely on the generosity of the listener at that—the excuse that he had not known whose footsteps resonated above in the meager height of the ceilings; the Radann's brief greeting removed that excuse. But the boy did not turn.

The Tyr'agnate of Averda considered his options briefly. But only briefly. "Alfredo," he said quietly.

The line of his younger son's shoulders stiffened, straightening slowly as if by force of will. But he did not turn to acknowledge the Tyr.

Ramiro felt the spark of a kindling anger. He chose—with care—not to fan it. In a different circumstance, there would have been no anger to fan. And in a still different circumstance, the anger would have been vast as chasms in the Tiagra.

"Ser Alfredo," he said, raising his voice. "A guest of import has accompanied me in order to pay his respects to Ser Carelo kai di'Callesta."

The shoulders stiffened further. The boy's hands, shaking, were bunching into fists. Ramiro wondered how awkward things were going to become. Alfredo had always been the more careful, the more cautious, the more observant of his two sons. He had also been the less tractable. Where the oldest was fire and fury, he was also capable of the tactical retreat when it was expedient. On one or two occasions it had saved his life. The youngest only seldom extended himself, but when he did—when he did, all who knew him understood the weight of the decision. He had chosen to stand and die.

How had two such difficult sons managed to survive their youth?

His eyes grazed the wound on his dead child's face and he grimaced as if the wound were his. And it was; the son had all the need for it that the dead have of anything. *Do not force this, Alfredo. You are all the son I have left; do not disgrace yourself.*

But offering such a warning was in itself a disgrace, for it implied that such a warning was necessary. He waited. His son did not turn.

"Tyr'agnate," the young kai Leonne said, completely unexpectedly, "it is my desire—if it is your will—to see the bodies of the Lambertans before I pay my final respects to your son."

Alfredo continued to face the altar.

Or my sons, Ramiro thought, his anger deepening. He missed his wife. "Tyr'agar," he replied, bowing and holding that bow for long enough to acknowledge his son's dangerous refusal to recognize the presence of a Tyr. "I, too, wish to see my son's enemies."

Valedan kai di'Leonne said nothing at all. But the look that he cast—briefly—at the back of the par di'Callesta was a strange one.

One of the Radann bowed to the Tyr'agnate; he left his position and returned with another, younger man. The young man bowed as well, the movements slightly awkward.

Ramiro wanted, with a fierce clarity of desire, to be in the heart of his harem, where the Lord had no purchase and no dominion; where there were women with perfect grace and a silence that elegantly answered all questions, be they lazy or furious, peaceful or tormented.

Carelo.

Not yet. Not yet, but soon. If, he thought, there would

ever be peace at the harem's heart again. To have peace, he would have to win forgiveness from his lovely wife for his absence from Callesta, when with his presence, the kai Callesta—her beloved son—might still be holding a sword.

To have peace, he would have to forgive himself.

And that was as close as he was willing to come to a night thought in the heat of day, when the Lord waited for a sign—any sign—of weakness.

"Tyr'agnate?" The Radann's neutral voice was less awkward than his bow.

Ramiro nodded, and the man turned toward a more modest set of doors that led into the interior of the temple. He gestured briefly, and servitors—clad predominantly in white, hastened to open them.

"Tyr'agnate," Valedan kai di'Leonne said, before Ramiro could follow the younger Radann's lead. Ramiro turned to see that Valedan kai di'Leonne had dropped into as full a bow as the difference in their ranks allowed.

All eyes were upon them, the Tyr'agar and the Tyr'agnate; the sun through the open windows watched the shadows they cast. "Tyr'agar."

"With your permission, I would like to have the bodies removed from the temple."

I am weary, Ramiro thought. The words the boy spoke made no sense. He struggled with them a moment, but the political edge that informed all of his observations had been blunted and dulled. "As you wish," he said.

The Radann framed by the open door waited. "Tyr'agnate."

"You are sworn to the Lord, not to Callesta," the Tyr said softly. "But Callesta has jurisdiction over the bodies of its enemies. I commend you for your actions in preserving my son's body against my arrival.

"If it pleases you, accommodate the request of the Tyr'agar."

"The Tyr'agar?" The Radann's eyes narrowed in obvious confusion and then widened in equally obvious shock, both of which clearly placed his station of birth. In theory, one abandoned one's responsibilities and duties to blood when one entered the service of the Lord—but blood was strong in clansmen and it did not surrender to simple words and weak will so easily.

"The Tyr'agar, Ser Valedan kai di'Leonne."

While the Radann digested this information—and it took a while for the full significance of all of the words to strike home—Ramiro di'Callesta turned to inspect the play of light across the open ground in which the Radann trained, fought, and occasionally died. There were no stains across stone, but there were boundaries marked in silver and gold in the shape of swords with curved blades turned away from the center of the space.

It was not, of course, a Northern circle. The rules of Northern circles had no place among the Radann. But it was the simplest measure of a man in the Dominion.

Had he been allowed, he might have challenged someone—anyone—to stand with him for the Lord's Judgment. It had been many, many years since he had done so; it was not a challenge to undertake lightly.

But it was better than the challenge he faced now.

He had not thought to be so affected by the sight of his son's body. He was a practical man. He had known, the moment the Tyran had wordlessly handed him Carelo's sword, that Carelo was dead; no other fate would have parted him from that weapon. But to know it, no matter how deeply, and to *see* it, were apparently two separate experiences. Had he known how vast the gulf between knowledge and reality could be, he would have entered the temple alone and dismissed the Radann before he turned to gaze upon the face of his child.

Upon the empty hands that lay across his chest. A kai without a sword. A body without a soul. Both, in the end, meant death.

Aie, he remembered when that weapon had first come to his kai's hands.

Carelo had been quiet and proud; he had been wary. But the sword . . . the sword had been his pride.

"Wear it," Ramiro said, "and understand what it is that you carry. When you unsheathe that blade, you will have no place in my harem; you will have no home with your mother and my wives."

Carelo, face free of expression, had nodded. A moment later, the words that his father had so carefully chosen sank roots; Ramiro could recall the pride that caused the boy's expression to flutter like a startled bird before coming to rest again in lines of gravity and dignity that were vastly too old for his face.

When. Not if.

The Radann had struggled to fall to one knee. In matters of precedence, the line between Tyrs and Radann could be hazy if the Radann so chose, but the line between Tyr'agar and Radann—never. The only man who was not required to offer full obeisance was the kai el'Sol.

This particular, extremely awkward near grovel would have been amusing in other circumstances. As it was, it merely worked to the Callestan advantage by giving Ramiro the few moments he needed.

And as if aware of that, as if aware of the reason for the Callestan Tyr's oblique humiliation of the young Radann, the kai Leonne waited a long, long while before acknowledging the kneeling man. Of course, had he been the Tyr'agar Markaso kai di'Leonne, he would merely have had the man killed for his gross and offensive ignorance. The father, weak and self-indulgent, was very unlike the son. Not so Ramiro and Carelo. Youth and experience separated them; that was all.

Had been all.

Fathers. Sons.

"Kai Callesta?" Valedan's voice. Quiet—as quiet as Serra Amara's voice might have been had she stood behind him at a moment like this. "The Radann are bringing the bodies to the front of the temple for our inspection."

Ramiro nodded. "Why the front of the temple, kai Leonne?"

Valedan's smile was a glimmer of eye, a quirk at the corner of lip that did not otherwise destroy the gravity—the proper, the respectful, gravity—of his expression. "I am not married," he replied. "But I have seen enough of women to know that they are frail in times of loss; they require the strength of their husbands. The Serra Amara en'Callesta has waited for you for months now; I would not keep her from your side for longer than necessary."

Ramiro kai di'Callesta nodded genially, but he met the Tyr'agar's eyes for a second longer than protocol demanded, and he saw in the boy—and it grieved him—a man that his son would never have become, no matter how much wisdom and experience he had gathered.

Mercy was a Northern concept.

White silk folded slightly as he lifted a sword arm.

But he did not return the sword to his kai. When he did, he wished no witnesses. He knew, now, that witnesses would weaken him.

"Tyr'agar," he said, raising his voice. "You are wise."

Valedan said nothing, but his glance strayed again to the back of Alfredo par di'Callesta; the boy had not moved. This time, when the kai Leonne's face offered the inexplicable expression that it had when he had first seen Alfredo, and had first chosen to ignore the gracelessness of grief, Ramiro recognized the look.

He did not understand it, but he recognized it.

Envy.

The men came.

They wore white; they wore azure; they wore gold. And above these three things, embroidered across a sash, the Callestan crest: The sword, the sun, and between them, the falcon, across an azure sky. She had seen the full Callestan regalia seldom; she knew that this was a reduction of the finery that the Callestans chose to wear when they traveled in a manner that demanded the respect of other Tyrs.

But that fact that this simplified emblem lay across the shoulders and chest of the Radann told her much about the relationship that Ramiro had with even these unallied men of the Lord.

It surprised her.

Had she been in Lamberto, it would not have; Mareo kai di'Lamberto was a man the Radann had always respected. But Ramiro, slippery, smooth, diplomatic—Ramiro, called traitor, or worse, because of his trade dealings with the Empire, by those who would never forget their losses at the hands of that same Empire—would not have been a man she would have guessed was held in high esteem by the Radann.

As the Radann approached, she lowered her gaze.

But not in time to avoid the sight of the bodies they carried. Although she had seen death in many forms throughout her life, there was still something about the slackness of body, the peculiar fluidity of limb and joint, that was wrong. Neck and head lolled at angles, arms flowed over the rails of the stretcher the Radann struggled with. They had chosen to treat the dead with as little respect as possible; had they taken care to arrange the bodies, to lay them out at rest as the dead were laid when they intersected, again, with the living, they would not have found their burden so cumbersome.

She readied herself for the stench of carrion, but in vain; the wind, unlike the Radann, carried nothing.

But perhaps that was unfair; although the Radann approached from some hidden exit, some egress meant for the use of lesser servitors, the Tyr'agar and the Tyr'agnate emerged from the temple's depths.

Ramiro di'Callesta crossed the path, a moving shadow against the subtle pattern of uneven stone. He came to stand before his kneeling wife, a sword in one hand, a sword against hip, his expression hidden from the Serra Alina because she wisely chose not to interfere by looking up.

"Amara," he said. Just that.

The Serra Amara rose, her hand in the hand that did not carry a weapon. Her serafs remained against stone.

"Serra Alina," another voice said, and this time she did look up; she met Valedan's gaze. "Rise," he said quietly. "Rise and fullfil the first of the duties you have undertaken." His tone was perfect. He offered her a hand; she took it. Was surprised at how steady his hand was; her own was shaking.

"Tyr'agar." She looked beyond him to where the bodies lay in their unceremonious pile of arms and legs and lolling, slack faces.

"Yes."

Was this where she had thought to come, when she had chosen to accompany Valedan to the South? Was this the homecoming that she had foreseen?

Mirialyn ACormaris' voice deserted her. She heard the howl of the wind, and realized that, had she how to listen, she would have heard it from the moment she had traveled across the border, secure in the confinement of a palanquin whose curtains could be drawn in such a way that they kept nothing out, yet allowed nothing unwanted in.

She inclined her head. Drew breath. She was Lambertan now; that was all that was required. Her gown was green, the color of life that seemed so obscene in this place. But it was also embroidered with gold, and that color was the desert's. Men died and killed for it, always, and it slipped through their fingers like water through a tightly cupped palm.

She began to walk toward the bodies; at some point, Valedan's hand fell away.

Only when she reached them did she feel the lack of support. But she was used to this.

There was memory here, unlooked for. She accepted it.

Who are these men?

The first deaths.

Lambertans.

They are not Lambertan, Brother.

But they are, Alina. They are the people who have given their life in my service; they protect our honor and our lands. The lowest of serafs, the highest of Tyrs—in the end, this is what is left us.

Look, look well.

Memory was such a tricky game.

Why did they die?

They were killed, he said, *in the service of the Lord.*

But we serve the Lord.

He had laughed. Her perfect brother, the pride of their father and mother, the pride of their people.

The Lord cares little for service, and he plays no favorites. They proved themselves worthy of his regard because they did not die like cattle. That is all.

Thus had she first seen the regard of the Lord, and she had vowed that day that she would serve the Lady, if she chose to serve at all.

The bodies were not whole. The wounds that had killed these men no longer wept, but if bodies told stories, the black gashes across chest and throat were the verbs, the nouns, the formality of language.

It was a familiar language. She stared at them for a long time as the cadences of memory gave that language meaning.

"Serra Alina?"

She was aware that the Terrean of Averda and the Terrean of Mancorvo were separated by a profoundly bitter history. Aware as well that if they could not forsake that history, the war that was coming would sweep across them like fire across dry brush.

The flames of that fire were orange and gold, and the winds carried the sparks to every corner of her awareness, as if awareness were geography.

"Tyr'agar," she replied, finding voice because to do otherwise was to tender disrespect in front of men whose respect was necessary. Almost against her will, she bent. The folds of silk brushed the awkward bend of knee and elbow as she reached out to brush face with the tips of her fingers.

The face was cold. Geography indeed. A place.

She could return from it if she chose. But she was not certain where that return would bring her.

It is the first death you will see, Alina; it is not the last. The last death you are certain of seeing is always your own.

But this was wrong. *Mareo,* she thought. It was the first time in years that she had pronounced his name without bitterness or anger, and she felt the loss keenly. *Mareo, what have you done? You could not have fallen so low as this.*

The Lord, he said, *is not concerned with honor.*

Ser Mareo, Fredero par di'Lamberto had cut in, curtly, *enough. The Lord is concerned with honor; he is not concerned with life. Life is not the prize that he grants to those who adhere to his rule. There is more to life than merely living.*

Ai, Fredero, ai. So you have said, and if you say it, who will forsake us all for the Radann, I must believe it.

Fredero was dead.

These bodies brought that fact home bitterly, painfully. The difference between knowledge and loss was profound.

She turned to the boy king who stood at her side, waiting, and she steeled herself to meet his gaze.

He lifted a brow in question.

"Yes," she said. "These men were my brother's men. They were bound by oath to serve the Tyr'agnate of Mancorvo until their death."

He nodded, as if he expected no less, but his eyes did not leave her face; they absorbed the expression that she could not keep from her lips or the corners of her eyes. "Valedan—"

"Thank you, Serra Alina. Thank you. You have done enough. I am . . . in your debt."

She became aware, when he at last looked away, that his were not the only eyes upon her. The Serra Amara en'Callesta's face was carved from the same material as her dead son's sword.

She did not demand Alina's death, although it would not have surprised the Serra Alina to hear her do so. But her hand did not leave her husband's. It was a rare man who was willing to humble himself by such an overt display of affection. Serra Amara was a wife of such a caliber that Alina was almost shocked that she clung to that contact in so public a circumstance—but perhaps that was part of Callesta's strength.

She did not demean Serra Amara's loss by bowing or kneeling or begging for forgiveness; there was only one way to make that plea that would give it strength and truth, and the Serra Alina di'Lamberto was not yet prepared to see the last death her brother had spoken of so many years past.

"Ser Ramiro kai di'Callesta," Valedan said, in the loudest voice anyone had used since they had arrived before the Radann's temple.

Almost grateful, Alina let her attention be caught and held.

"Tyr'agar," Ramiro di'Callesta replied.

Valedan met the Tyr'agnate's gaze without blinking, but his hand—his hand moved to his swordbelt. Before anyone could react, he had unfastened the buckle that held it in place. The scabbard, weapon enclosed, fell to stone, clattering loudly as if from a great height.

She did not understand.

But she heard the intake of Ser Anton di'Guivera's breath. "Tyr'agar," the swordmaster said.

Valedan lifted a hand; his gaze did not waver. "This weapon has no name," he said, "and no history that any man speaks of. I have worn it, I have wielded it, I have attempted to honor it, but it is what it is: a swordsmith's fine work, a thing of metal."

Baredan di'Navarre's voice joined Ser Anton's. "Tyr'agar—"

Again, Valedan lifted a hand. Again, an older, more experienced voice fell silent.

The sun was hot.

"I am not your kai," Valedan continued. "I am not your son, and I will never be that. I will never be Callestan, and I will never live the life of a Callestan clansman—and I have seen, today, that that is a profound loss. I will regret it."

The Serra Amara's fingers tightened.

"And I regret the loss of the kai I did not meet. Let me honor him in my own fashion."

The Serra Alina di'Lamberto understood, then. Understood what Ser Anton and Ser Baredan di'Navarre had understood immediately. She lifted a hand, as they had lifted voice, but let the hand fall away.

"We ride to war. We declare it. At the end of the battle, on whatever field it is fought, I will wield the Sun Sword." His tone allowed for no possibility of failure, although without Lamberto, Alina knew that victory was not possible.

"But if you will it, the sword I draw to declare our war beneath the Lord's gaze and before the Lord's men will not be so insignificant a weapon as the one I wore on my journey home."

Ramiro di'Callesta looked at the blade in his hand; it was the first time he had looked away from the kai Leonne.

He spoke a word, but that word was deprived of sound.

"I will carry that sword against your enemies, kai Callesta; I will carry it against mine. They will be one and the same."

"And what of my living son?"

"When battle is done, I will give to your living son the sword that is his due, now that he must take the place of his brother. I will give him a sword with a history of war; a sword that has ushered in a battle that will define the Dominion as certainly as the first battle fought by the first Leonne did."

"And will you seek justice for us?" the Serra Amara said, speaking for the first time. "Will you forsake your victory for the sake of my dead son?"

"Serra Amara," Valedan replied, "I give you my oath that I will stop at nothing to avenge your loss. I will find your son's killers—not the weapon, but the hands behind it—and I will not rest until they are dead."

She fell to white silk then; rested against stone; her serafs did not dare to approach to slide the mats between her knees and the ground. But she did not face Valedan; she faced the man whose hand she held. Her fingers were white as bone, her arm a line that connected them, be she in the subservient posture and he proudly standing.

"Husband," she said, in a voice that barely carried, that broke between syllables. "As you love me, give the Tyr'agar my son's sword."

"This sword cannot just be given," he replied, eyes not on his wife, but on the Tyr'agar. "It is of Callesta; it is wielded by Callestans. It is the sword the kai carries." He lifted his hand, his free hand, and said, in a voice that was painfully gentle, "Serra Amara."

She released it, although her hand shook as she did.

Lifting his hand, lifting the sword by the hilt, Ramiro di'Callesta faced Valedan kai di'Leonne. He cut the mound of his palm; it bled freely.

Nothing was red in this garden. The fall of blood from a living man seemed shocking as it spread in shaky circles beneath the feet of the Callestan Tyr, splashing his wife's sari.

Valedan walked toward the kai Callesta. When he reached him, he held out his hand; the kai Callesta passed the burden of his son's sword to a stranger.

That stranger brought the edge of a blade that had tasted Callestan blood across his own hand; it, too, bled.

They faced each other in front of men who had become utterly, completely silent, as if wind had stolen all movement, all ability to move. Not even the rise and fall of chest could be discerned. History was being written here, in the only indelible ink.

Although wisdom counseled against the act, the act itself had such raw power it could not be judged.

"*Callesta*," Valedan said softly. He locked hands with the Tyr'agnate, bringing wound to wound and blood to blood.

There was no oath in the Dominion that was greater than this. Serra Alina di'Lamberto had never seen it sworn. Wind bore the word of men. Wood bore the cut of swords. But men? Almost never.

"There is more," the Tyr'agnate's voice was the fire's voice.

"I will face it," the Tyr'agar replied.

"You will," Ramiro di'Callesta said evenly. "You have my blood, and I yours. *Callesta*," he cried. And he drew *Bloodhame*.

Valedan bowed. "Tyr'agnate," he said quietly, "if your kai's sword had a name, let me know it now."

The Tyr'agnate responded, "When we are at last upon the field of battle, and the enemy is arrayed before us, I will tell you what the sword is called."

Sea of Sorrows

CHAPTER FIFTEEN

2nd of Misteral, 427 AA
Sea of Sorrows

The desert was not what Jewel had expected. She had heard tales, carried by her most traveled of merchants—or their guards—and she knew that it was a place that was barren of water, and therefore, of life. She had expected to see that lack of life, to know it on some instinctive level, the way one knows a corpse from a man who sleeps.

But in the wiry, short scrub that skirted the desert heart, she saw a type of life she also recognized on an instinctive level, and when she walked across the scrub and the cracked ground, she thought not of death, or even the absence of life, but of a life that is furtive, hidden, impossible—even in these barrens—to destroy.

"Jewel."

"Hmmmm?"

"You were smiling. I haven't seen you smile with that ease since Alea's death."

The smile broke, wave against seawall.

He surprised her. After a moment, he spoke. "I am sorry. I forget that your moods are only fragile when there is some element of joy in them."

She shrugged, everything about the movement brusque. "There's not a lot to be happy about."

"There never is."

"Avandar—"

"No. There never is. All of mortality is defined by its moments of loss and crisis."

"That's not true."

"Is it not?" He stared into the vista that had caught her attention, and she knew he was seeing something completely different; he always did. "The height of man's greatest achievement lies buried somewhere within its greatest wastelands. And yet in the act of losing what they built, of surrendering the ability to stand, shoulder to shoulder, with the gods and those whose lives have never been measured by time, they achieved a greatness they have never since known."

She would have snorted, but the intensity of the feeling behind his words silenced her. It was genuine. She did not want to know more about it; stepped back, although that did not diminish her understanding. Her arm ached. Her mouth was too dry. "Acts of sacrifice have always existed."

"Do you glory in them?"

"No." She looked at rippling air, heat above sand. "Yes."

"Thank you."

"But there has to be more. More than that."

He laughed.

"What?"

"You have made it not only your business, but your existence, to disprove that. What do you enjoy? What do you love? How do you choose to live your life?"

"Avandar—"

He lifted a hand.

She felt its shadow as a momentary coolness against her skin. She stepped back. Back again, her heels reaching tentatively for the ground behind her, as if she knew that she was standing close to the mouth of a great abyss. Too close.

He said softly, "I know."

She felt his absence, his sudden absence beneath skin, behind thought, as if it were a presence.

"But you cannot stand within the shadows of your early life forever."

"I'm part of the governing Council of Terafin. I'm heir—" and she had never said this so rashly, so *loudly,* "to the Terafin throne. I have the ear of Kings. I am hardly standing in the shadows of my early life."

"No?" He reached out again, fingertips to face, and she shied. "Leave it, Jewel. You have left almost all else."

She didn't look at him. After a moment spent gathering breath, spent straightening the lines of her face, she said,

"We don't talk about our past. When you join my den, that's the only rule: the past *is* the past."

"I was not speaking of my past," he replied. "And I have never been a member of your den." Permeating the spoken words was a very strong distaste at the idea that he might come to her for protection. For aid.

"Can't you understand," she snapped, "that I might feel the same way?" She turned, the robes cumbersome, the boots heavy as she lengthened her stride and left him standing in the morning air, the memories he had invoked driving her.

She sought shelter among the women and their loud and cumbersome children. In their efforts, some brusque and short, she saw her own: they understood that these children *were* Arkosa, and they fed, clothed, and protected them. It was no different from her den, in its way, birth and age notwithstanding.

Tamara of Arkosa met her, interposing her substantial girth between Jewel and the children. She was not otherwise unfriendly, but a warning had been wordlessly given, and Jewel accepted it with equanimity. She understood it.

"Will the children go into the desert?"

The older woman looked faintly scandalized. Except for the faintly part. "Into the *desert*?"

Jewel laughed and held out one hand, palm up, in surrender. "I wouldn't have asked—but they're still here."

"We don't take most of the men, or the women either. The Lord knows no mercy in the heart of the desert. We expect that. But the Lady forgets all mercy as well." She relaxed, the line of her shoulders gradually dropping two inches as her hands found her hips. She did not, however, move.

"Is that why it's called the Desert of Sorrows?"

"It is called the Desert of Sorrows," Tamara said curtly, "by clansmen. And maybe by Northern merchants." She sniffed, her shoulders rising again as they followed the line of her chin. She was possessed of the Voyani gestures of expression, and they were many; they animated the speaker even when words failed to leave their lips.

"And the Voyani call it?"

"The Sea of Sorrows."

"It doesn't look a whole lot like any sea I've ever seen. From a distance it doesn't look like there's much in the way of water."

"Sea can have many meanings. In Torra, everything can." She shrugged. "We don't talk to outsiders much, and you're an outsider. An outsider who looks a little like the rest of us—or would if you weren't so pale."

"At home, I'm not considered pale."

"At home, you're not considered the offspring of deserters."

Jewel was quiet. For about five seconds. Then she lifted her head and met Tamara's gaze. Her own didn't waver. "I don't consider myself to be the offspring of deserters." Each word was measured, level.

"They'd hardly teach you about the *Voyanne,* would they?" Tamara lifted a brow. "They'd hardly teach you the old vows, the old ways, the old words. Because then they'd have to explain why they weren't following any of them."

"As much as any parent feels a need to explain their choices and their lives to any child."

Tamara's brows lifted a moment in surprise, and then she offered Jewel the most generous of her laughs. Rooted in her experience, it was low and deep, both with age and a resonant pleasure. "You've never put a foot on the *Voyanne.* But if I had to guess, Jewel of Terafin, you've walked roads that are harder and longer. None of us have forgotten how you came. Some of us resent the fact that you're just as human as we are, you're the child of deserters, but you've got the Lady's favor."

Her eyes narrowed. "I tell them you've got the Lady's geas, which isn't the same. May our enemies be your enemies if we cannot be family."

"Your enemies," Jewel said softly, "*are* mine."

"Good. Petrie! Stop that now or I'll lengthen both your ears!"

One of the children jumped two feet and nearly dropped his bowl. Jewel felt some sympathy for him; she jumped as well.

"You have to watch them," Tamara said, with a faint hint of smugness. "Even when you can't keep your eyes on them. What were we saying? Ah, yes. The sea. Let me tell you something. I remember the first time I saw the sea. It was while we wandered along the coast of Oerta. The storms there are harsh at the wrong time of year, and it's hard to find good roads. The Oertan Tyrs are not . . . friendly. We had been traveling for days." Her voice fell. The lines of her face shifted. Her expression was like a mask—and masks would never have the same meaning for Jewel ATerafin that they had once had. The stillness was unusual; it captured her age. In the glare of the sun—and the sun had risen—the cracks and folds of skin hid no shadows as she narrowed her eyes.

"For days. We reached the sea. I was a child, understand. Evallen's mother was Matriarch. The children are fed first—you know this. We had been fed, but the Arkosans had almost nothing to feed us. We had no time to stop and forage." She was quiet for a moment. "Although it was tried.

"A village along the coast was friendly to us; the headman's wife was particularly beloved of the Lady, and she aided us as she could. We hoped to reach her, to arrange for the supplies we needed.

"Or they did. I was young. I remember knowing that I was thirsty, hungry, that my feet were blistered, my clothing chafed. The rivers running inland were being watched by the Tyr's men; they were the obvious place to find or catch us. We caught water, when it fell, but it didn't fall often enough; it was dry, at that time. I remember that. I knew that my aunts and uncles smelled terrible, that they were always angry.

"When we saw the sea, it was so . . . so big. There was so much *water*."

Jewel cringed. "Oh, no."

Tamara's laugh was soft. "Oh, yes. The wagons had stopped; the Voyani had built themselves shelters in a small valley beneath the road's line, but near the sand and stone. They were all angry, all of the time. I ran to the water. I started to drink."

"You must have been sick."

"All over. All over everything. I can laugh about it now—but then? I couldn't believe that there could be so much water, and none of it could be for *drinking*.

"I realized then that I hated the sea. It was malicious. It

was salty, terrible. It offered life and gave death in return if you couldn't keep it on the outside.

"The desert was at least an honest death." Her brow creased a moment. "Another child had run down to the water with me. He had been sick; he was weak and fragile. The water that he drank, he threw up—but he couldn't stop throwing up. He burned with a terrible fever for three days, and it only stopped when he died."

Jewel could think of nothing to say.

"People let their children play in the sea. We don't let ours play in the desert." The older woman looked very tired. "I started this because I thought it would be funny—a story about how ignorant I was about your sea. Sometimes a funny story can put a person at ease."

They were silent as their shadows shortened. At last, Jewel asked, "Is that why you call it a sea?"

"No. Here. I think Donatella has finished with the children—let's find some shade, wagon-side, away from prying ears." She gestured with her shoulder, sliding her hands from her hips so she could catch her thumbs in the top of her sash. Like many women her age, she could not bear idle hands; she had to perch and unperch them almost continually if she was on her feet.

Jewel made to follow her, but before she had gone ten feet, she was cut off by a tall man wearing a lot of attitude more easily than he did his leathers and his sword.

Tamara's shoulders came up and back more sharply than they had all through her conversation with Jewel. The hands folded themselves across chest in a way that left elbows tight against upper body. It was clear that Tamara was not comfortable with this man.

Clear, as well, that he was Arkosan. Family. Jewel stopped her hand from straying to her dagger. She watched, but said nothing.

"Ona Tamara," the young man said. He didn't speak with a sneer; he spoke instead with an obvious desire to be polite. To be, Jewel thought, approved of.

"Nicu," his aunt replied, the two syllables so clipped it was a wonder she didn't cut her tongue saying them.

The young man darkened; Jewel winced. There was history here, and she wasn't sure she wanted to know what it was.

"Has Elena finished feeding the children?"

"Yes."

"Just now?"

"Yes."

His pause was awkward. "Funny. Andreas tells me that he didn't see her feeding the children this morning."

Two heartbeats worth of silence followed, enough time to kill a man with a readied dagger. The old woman didn't draw anything sharper than her tongue. "Does the Matriarch know you're telling your men to watch the Daughter instead of the periphery?"

He flushed. "He was walking by."

"Walking by for long enough to watch the entire meal? No—don't answer that. Andreas is just young and stupid enough to walk in circles for hours staring at his toes. But *you* should know better. In spite of your betrayal, you've been given the responsibility of—"

"Don't tell me my duties!"

"Someone has to tell you—you're no good at remembering them on your own!"

"I didn't come here to talk about *my* work. I came here to talk to Elena."

"When you knew she wasn't here."

He flushed. "But you know where she is."

Tamara laughed in his face. The laugh was no more friendly than any of his words had been. "And if I did—*if*—why would I tell you? You don't own her, Nicu. Nobody does. Not even Margret."

"I never said—"

"You've never had to. If you could think of other people once while the Lord watched, you'd know where she was. Now go, before I get angry."

He looked as if he might press his point. Jewel couldn't actually see Tamara's expression, but her tone of voice made it clear that there was no way she could be forced to back down. He turned, after glancing at Jewel, and he left them both.

Only when the dust of his passing had settled did Tamara of Arkosa let go of rigidity. The shadows across ground had shifted; the sky had become a clear, deep azure, a frame for the Lord's gaze.

"He'll hurt us yet," she muttered. "No one can cause as much damage as family, if they've a mind to it."

"I wouldn't know," Jewel said softly. "All of mine died when I was young enough that they wouldn't have tried."

For perhaps the first time, Tamara of Arkosa turned to Jewel with an unguarded expression of horror. She reined it in as quickly as Jewel would have expected of any Voyani woman, but the Voyani were free with their emotions; it hung in the lines and contours of her face for what seemed a very, very long time.

When she had been a child, Jewel confused pity and sympathy. Not now. But her pride allowed her to ignore what was written there so clearly.

"You've . . . you've done well," Tamara said lamely, and after some time. "Without family."

Jewel lifted her hand; she had never thought of her skin as pale until she had traveled with the Voyani, but it looked pale to her now, and gold adorned it, simply. Significantly. "Not without family," she said softly. "But maybe you understand why blood is less important to me than it is to the rest of you."

Tamara nodded. "Come," she said. "At this speed, I'll be feeding the children again before I've said another word."

"There are stories," she said quietly. "We tell them among ourselves when we come to the desert's fringe. You see those plants? The wiry short plants with the deep blue flowers? They grow only here. The old aunts will pick them and press them between their palms."

Jewel nodded; she had seen Donatella do just that.

"They're called serpent scales."

"Serpent scales."

Tamara laughed. "To an outsider, it must seem strange."

"Well, either that or you have some unusual serpents. I mean—small blue flowers?"

The older woman shrugged. "Many things were supposed to be buried beneath the desert sands. One of those things was said to be the great serpents. This—" she lifted her arm in a wide sweep that included everything across the horizon, "was not always desert. There were trees here that are seen nowhere but in the Deepings."

Jewel felt like a gong must feel when it's been hit hard

by a clapper. *Stone Deepings*, she thought. *Green Deepings.* She knew her maps; she knew that the vast expanse of forest—still considered impenetrable by even the most foolhardy of explorers—had always merely been the Deepings. Men had made a foothold in the Sangarin forests in the West, but those men also spoke with dogs and lived in a state of graceful savagery.

She looked out to the sands again, seeing them for the first time not as wastelands, but as something essential, elemental, itself.

"Tamara, do the Arkosans travel in the Green Deepings?"

Tamara's eyes narrowed. "No," she said at last, after studying Jewel's face for minutes, searching for some expression that might ease her—and judging from her own, failing to find it. "We do not travel in the Green Deepings. Only the cursed, the blessed, or the mad enter them willingly. Or at all."

"Is that what this is," Jewel asked softly, as if she had not heard the answer at all. "Deepings? Sand Deepings?"

Tamara said again, "Only the mad, ATerafin." She turned to look at the sand, as if seeing it through Jewel's eyes; it was clear from her shudder that she didn't like whatever it was she thought she saw.

She rose.

As if that movement were the end of an elaborate ritual, Jewel's attention snapped into focus; she rose as well. "Tamara—"

But the old woman shook her head. "I can't stay. I have work. But . . . you are clearly blessed, and cursed, by the Lady. What I can't tell you, it is my fear you will learn.

"We call it a sea for two reasons. The first is that it is deadly, no matter what it contains, unless you can rise above it. The second, that what it contains is deadly. In the old stories, there were beasts that slumbered in the ocean depths; they ate sailors, destroyed ships, made rubbish out of nets and long spears." She nodded curtly. Turned to leave.

"Tamara!"

Stopped. "What?"

"This doesn't make the desert seem any more welcoming."

Tamara laughed. "It's not. The difference is simple. It's easy to forget the old stories about the desert when you're in it. You're too worried about simple things like surviving the sun, the open sky, the wind. Predators have to wait in line."

"Then," Jewel said quietly, "I'll argue against the old adage. In this case, I'll risk the monster I *don't* know." She looked toward the North and East. "We really don't have much time."

The women rose at dawn to perform the ablutions that the Lady required; they escaped their wagons—and their children—at dusk to do the same.

Margret of Arkosa joined them at both of these daily offerings; her shadow seemed, to Jewel's eye, longer than the shadows of her cousin or her aunts, and closer to the ground. She wore what the others wore; the bloused shirt, the vest, the wide sash with its multiple concealing folds. She wore pants and thick leather boots, and her hair was tied back—but, like Jewel's, strands always escaped to plague vision and dignity.

She did not speak.

When her lips opened at all, they moved in the torturous, stiff way that Jewel—at a distance—recognized as ritual speech. The aunts gathered around Margret. Jewel recognized them: Donatella, Tamara, Catia. They were joined by Elena, and it was only in this gathering of older women that she seemed both young and subdued. She stood, or knelt, in the shadows Margret cast. Her lips didn't move.

During the ceremony, Margret held wooden bowl, stone bowl, clay bowl. Into the first, she poured water, and into the second, wine. Into the third, she poured air—literally—and while she poured this last, she made her plea.

At least it seemed a plea to Jewel; the signs were there in the curve of shoulder and bent head, the movement of arms—hands kept below the height of shoulder. Her knees did not move once she had bent them to dirt; she remained bowed until the bowls had been emptied, and the liquid in them—precious, now, at the edge of so much wasteland—given to earth.

At the end of each of these offerings, Margret would rise and leave the rest of the women. They watched her. They watched, and Jewel looked away because there was something so intensely personal about their concern and their fear that she felt awkward being a witness to it.

But not as awkward as she felt knowing that they were right to be so afraid.

3rd of Misteral, 427 AA
Sea of Sorrows

Another day passed.

The Serra Diora di'Marano, bereft of wagon, had been given a sturdy tent—a tent, Jewel thought, that had been made decades past, but had weathered sun, wind, and sand with the same ferocious tenacity the Voyani did. She did not know where the tent had come from; no one seemed to, although many of the men asked. If the women asked, they were furtive in their curiosity.

Just as well.

The sun's heat was fierce; the fear of discovery, fiercer. But the caravan—men, women, children—did not move.

Avandar was frustrated. Having spent well over a decade as the cause of such a state, Jewel was familiar with all of its nuances; the slight compression of lips, the narrowing of eyes, the intermittent movement of the muscle just above his jaw on either side of his face. He did not pace, but he wasn't precisely still.

The Arianni lord was. He could sit in sunlight and make a patch of hard dirt look like a throne. Dirt clung to him, but it clung differently than it did to anyone else; it seemed raiment rather than filth. He did not speak. If he had questions, he kept them to himself. He was like a very beautiful, ornamental piece of rock.

There were times when that would have bothered Jewel; now wasn't one of them. If he wasn't happy, he wasn't obviously miserable; he was one less thing to worry about. The stag had vanished into sparse vegetation, but Jewel *knew* that when the Voyani finally left—or perhaps when she did—he would return. The magic that bound man into stag, and kept mortality at bay was a magic that defied simple geography.

That left Avandar, the Voyani, and the troubling inertia in the encampment.

Jewel's right arm ached. The mark that lay against it, like a brand made of jeweled paint rather than scar tissue, was throbbing in time with the muscles of Avandar's temple. He was too close to where she stood, and she wanted distance, no matter how illusory distance actually was.

It was there in abundance, but unfortunately it wasn't the geographical kind. The Voyani had themselves descended into a silence that had none of the grace of the Lord Celleriant's, and even less ease, if that were possible. The younger men were either sullen or angry; the women irritable or fearful; the older men wisely chose to find the children's playful games extraordinarily amusing.

Kallandras of Senniel College, much like Celleriant, seemed unperturbed by the waiting. He did not look over his shoulder to see if, among the straggly greenery at desert's edge, the Tyr's men lurked. He carried his lute, and he often played it, singing so quietly Jewel could not make out the words unless she stood beside him.

Beside him was one of two safe places to be.

"ATerafin," he said as she approached. His bow was slight, but there was nothing perfunctory about it.

"Do you know what's happening here?"

A brow rose; his fingers rested against his lute's strings as if they were skin. "I believe," he said at last, "that the Matriarch is waiting."

"For what? An invitation?" The words were sharp, but they were *quiet*.

A small frown marred the bard's expression. "ATerafin." He spoke her name in the tone of voice he reserved for the children. "Understand that Margret of Arkosa has the responsibility not of a single den, but of the equivalent of a House. As I recall," he added, his gaze glancing off her profile as she turned away, "you did not leap at the chance to have such a responsibility for yourself. She is younger than you are, Jewel; she is from a harsher place. Examine your own fears and reluctance as if she were your least forgiving mirror."

" 'Gret?"

Margret of the Arkosan Voyani sat on the slender, hard

bench in her mother's wagon. The boy at the wagon's door lingered a moment to one side of the door's frame—the safe side. She waited in silence for him to leave.

" 'Gret?" He called again.

He had never been particularly bright where she was concerned, she thought unkindly. Just well-loved and beautiful. She was in the mood for neither tonight. Because she had been neither, in her own estimation, and was unlikely to ever become them.

No, that was unfair. She had been neither—which was not his fault—and in one day, in one encounter, she had come *this* close to stumbling on the knife's edge and speaking openly of the terrible secret that the Matriarchs barely discussed among themselves. And why?

Because, like any child, she was angry that her mother preferred another. The Serra Diora di'Marano. Her brother. The Arkosans. Always, always, always someone else.

Enough, Margret, she told herself fiercely. *This is beneath you. She had the whole of Arkosa to consider. She didn't have time for kindness.*

Or love? But she loved Adam.

Everyone *loves Adam.*

" 'Gret?"

She retreated from silence for the sake of expedience. "Go away."

Still, he lingered. She put both hands on the lowered table flat, palm down; the sound of her flesh slapping wood was dissonant. He retreated slightly, the movement almost imperceptible. But his fingers curved around the frame to stop Margret from closing the door—or rather, from closing the door without breaking them.

"Is it true that the Havallan Matriarch gave you an order?"

Her hands curled into fists. That was their familiar shape, these days. "You weren't there?"

"No. I was with the children."

"The children were there." She lifted her head, straightening out the line of her shoulders.

"They were there," he said softly, "at the beginning of your argument. But you—when you—why did you kick her instrument, 'Gret?"

Margret said coldly, "I would have thought that would be painfully obvious."

"I didn't ask why you wanted to. I asked why you did it."

"Because I wanted to," she replied, with no satisfaction at all. There was, about Adam, something special. And to tell him something that would drive him away—something with more substance than *get out* or *leave*—was never easy. But she seldom lied to Adam.

Because, damn him, he was selectively perceptive, and a lie was worse than a humiliating truth. He was her blood, her truest blood.

So she said nothing. He waited until he realized that's all she would say, and then he gracefully filled the silence. She could not ever remember being that graceful, that untemperamental. No wonder her mother had loved him best. No wonder they all did.

"I took the children away."

"You—"

"I knew Elena was there. I thought she'd be able to—" He stopped. No loss; they both knew where the rest of that sentence was going anyway. "Did Yollana tell you what to do in front of everyone?"

"Yes."

"Is it—is it true that you obeyed her?"

If he had been a sister, Margret thought idly, because it was easier than reliving the most humbling, the most humiliating, event in her adult life, he would have been a Matriarch that Arkosans would have killed each other to serve. Mother had loved him best, yes.

She should have hated him for that. Some days, she did. But she could not hold on to hatred or anger in the face of who *he* was. Because, in truth, Margret loved him best as well, and she had enough to hate herself for.

She nodded.

"Good."

It was not what she expected. She turned to him fully, sitting while he stood, the open door between them, the moonlight at his back. "Wh-what did you say?"

"I said, good."

"I heard what you said."

"Why 'good,' when everyone else is wondering what's wrong with you?"

"Yes," she snapped, wincing, "that why."

"Because you knew that it would weaken you, and you've always been afraid of weakness. But you listened anyway, which means that you thought she was right.

"You have to choose between what other people think is the right thing, and what you think is the right thing."

"Adam—it *did* weaken me. And if I'm weak—"

"No." He stepped into the frame, like a picture in a fine domo. She wanted more light then. The Lady's time was coming, it was strong; it took away the lines of his face.

"No?"

"It didn't weaken you. Your temper did. Momma used to say, 'ride your temper, don't let it ride you.' "

"I know what she used to say."

"Now I know why it's true. I don't understand why you hate that Serra so much. I think—if I were you—I wouldn't."

"You say that because she's beautiful."

"She *is* beautiful." His concession was devoid of warmth. He might have been talking about a flower, a bird, a horse. "But she is hard as steel. I think—I think once she might have been different. I don't know. But don't tell me I'm defending her because you think I love her. I don't know that anyone smart would.

"I say it because I heard her singing."

"You said you left with the children."

"I *did* leave with the children, 'Gret. I left with them, but I could hear her voice as clearly as if she sat in front of me, and it was—it was so personal—she might have been singing for me alone. I'm sure we all heard it that way.

"The children were weeping."

"The adults were weeping as well." Margret's voice was quiet, hushed. "She sang with the Lady's voice. And I—I have nothing of the Lady's." She slouched into her dagger's hilt, straightened enough to dislodge it from its awkward position.

"You have Arkosa."

"After what I did, I'm lucky to have that." She wanted to tell him the truth. She *hated* that she could not tell him the whole truth. Hated that men were trusted, but only so far, only ever so far, when Adam was a man—or a boy who was on the edge of adulthood—who could be trusted with *everything*.

"It's not luck, 'Gret. You're the only person who *can* do it. We all know that. You're Evallen's daughter. The only person here who doesn't trust that is you."

"Adam, you're lying."

He was quiet for a moment.

"You are such a terrible liar, you should know better than to try." But she loved him for the attempt.

"Anyone who *counts* knows it. Elena knows it. Even Yollana knows it. The others will learn."

"It's not just a matter of trust," the Arkosan Matriarch said quietly. "But you'll know the truth soon enough. When we go to the desert, when we go to where we must go, you'll come with us."

That shut him up for at least a minute.

"C-come with you?"

"Yes. You're my brother, the Matriarch's brother, and you've proved yourself worthy of that, even if you have such a pathetic Matriarch for a sister."

"You're not pathetic, Margret. You're just human." He smiled; she felt something lodge in her throat, and she *hated* that. "Don't be like her."

"Like who?"

"Like the Serra. She's—her song—she's so lonely, Margret. She's so isolated."

"Adam—"

"You *have* family. You have us. Don't try to be what you're not."

Her laugh was low and shaky. "That's exactly what I'm trying to do. I'm trying to be the Matriarch of Arkosa."

The desert heat was miles away, as was the desert night—but here, at its periphery, heat and cold seeped in along the boundaries that separated the Voyani from scrub, bush, and caravan and the endless ridges of sand, the unfettered howl of wind. Even at a distance, the sound of waiting death unnerved those who understood the nuance of its language.

At night, that nuance was chill and death, but it was a chill replete with life—for in all but the harshest of deserts, the Lady had some purchase. Night plants blossomed with their heavy succulence; small desert mice, the large-eared, tiny foxes, the scaled lizards with serpent's tongues—these found food and society beneath the face of the majestic moon.

When the Arkosan Voyani at last set foot upon the part of the *Voyanne* that led into the desert's heart, they would take their cue from these diminutive desert siblings; they would seek the darkness when the Lady's face was full and bright and clear, but before the lands were too cold, and travel least during the height of the Lord's dominion.

The desert was his.

The life in the desert was hers.

As always, it flourished in her time, and at her whim.

They knew it, the Arkosans. The lone Havallan. The strangers who, with the Matriarch's grudging permission, had made the encampment their home. During the day, the Arkosans mingled as freely as they were allowed with the outsiders, but during the night, when the air took a chilly edge, they retreated.

Some sought shelter, where shelter existed; men and women, children tucked between them or to either side, cuddled in that particular human warmth that could, by dint of affection and the insularity of flesh, deny the cold that waited, an hour at a time, until the dawn gave way to heat.

The night fell on a caravan that had not changed in two days. The shadows cast by wagons, the shadows cast by the fire in the growing twilight, the places at which the children sat—these had become fixed in place.

And being fixed in any place made the Voyani restless—regardless of which family they were born to. The *Voyanne* made its demands. Yollana of the Havalla Voyani, left to her own devices as much by her desire as by her host's, was an uneasy exception to this rule; she was an uneasy exception to most of the rules that, invisible as unshed blood, bound the Voyani to their own.

Kallandras, foreign by appearance, by experience, stood beside the log she had made her uncomfortable home. The Serra Teresa di'Marano sat at her feet, as if to pay court to her. None of the Voyani approached her.

But she was approached, as if she had answers to offer to those who had the power or the audacity to demand them. Jewel ATerafin was circumspect; the man who in theory served her was both more and less so.

The two that were touched by the Lady's darkness did not approach at all, but the Havallan Matriarch was no less aware of their presence; how could she not be? The white-haired, pale-skinned man—if such a word could refer to him—was piercing in his beauty and his obvious disdain. The children did not speak when his shadow crossed their path; the Arkosans fell silent until he had passed, and after he was gone, their words were made of awkward pauses and gaps. Their gestures were more eloquent: they warded themselves against the Lady's dark face.

But the stag, the great horned beast that neither ate nor slept, was worse. He wore animal form the way a god might. He did not speak—but not even Yollana would have said that speech was beyond him. There was an intelligence about his eyes, a disturbing direct gaze that animals did not possess, which spoke of either wisdom or knowledge; possibly both.

These two were the shadows that the woman who called herself ATerafin—although her family's blood was once bound to the *Voyanne*, Yollana was certain of it—cast; they were present when she was present.

Yollana gestured imperiously, as she did all else, to Kallandras. With impeccable tolerance, he chose to understand the gesture, and offered her the few logs of dry wood that remained by the fire's side.

Flame was lapping its way through chill; she could feel the warmth of what appeared, to the naked eye, a meager fire. With the help of the foreign bard, she knelt awkwardly before that meager fire, and murmured a few words. Someone familiar with old Torra would know that she offered the fire thanks. But no one familiar with Yollana would guess that if they did not know the tongue, and old Torra was taught to very, very few. *The old things,* she thought bitterly, as she gave the log to the fire and the fire accepted it. *If we could just leave the old things behind. I would have a daughter who speaks to me. My people might build homes for themselves if they chose; they might continue to follow the open road. My grandchildren might have a chance to be children.*

She had never missed youth for her own children. She

had been driven by the necessity of raising leaders; of raising a daughter who could defend Havallans beneath the shadows she was certain were lengthening. Yollana had more than a touch of the old gift—*a curse*—and she knew how deep the darkness would get before it abated.

If it ever abated.

What she did not know, what she had never known, was whether or not she would be there to face it. She turned from the unnatural warmth of such a small fire and looked into the heart of the Arkosan camp, where the wagon of the Matriarch, occupied now, was guarded by two heavily dressed men. This was her nightmare: Evallen's fate. Evallen's departure.

Leaving her daughter behind, as Margret had been left, to face the coming of the Enemy they did not name, devoid of experience, devoid of fire, devoid of Heart.

She turned back to the fire. There was something, in the end, about fire's warmth that was compelling, even if it was magically induced. She spoke again to the wood beneath the flame; implored it—if entreaties and her tone of voice could coexist at all—to resist the flame.

"What is she waiting for?" a stranger's voice asked.

Yollana continued with her slow approbation of wood and the thing that consumed it, but she knew two things: that she should not have heard that voice in this inner circle of Voyani heartwood, and that only a man with knowledge of ways long dead could have made himself so heard.

And *that* drove the night chill home as if it were a blade. She gestured to Kallandras again; he offered her his arm. When she took it, her hand was shaking, and she didn't bother to expend the effort to stop it. She also chose to stay within the lee of the circle her fire, invisibly, created.

With a gesture, she opened her ears; the noises of the night came rushing in. Better, she thought, to stoke vanity; better to pretend that the option of discussion was hers and hers alone. And that might have been true had she been another woman.

"Who are you?" she demanded, speaking to Avandar.

"I am the *domicis* of Jewel ATerafin of House Terafin."

The old woman spit.

"Matriarch," the young woman in question said. She

bowed, smartly, her unruly hair shuffling onto and off of her forehead. "He does serve me, in his fashion."

"So you believe."

Jewel ATerafin shrugged. "I have more than belief, but I don't have any pressing need to convince you of anything. He asked a question that's reasonable. The Tyr's men *must* be searching for us. They *are* searching for us," she added, her eyes widening slightly, and taking, for just a moment, the appearance of flat, dark glass.

That appearance . . . she had seen that look take over and transform an expression completely before—but only on the face of one other woman, and her eyes were violet.

Lady, it was a cold night.

Yollana looked back to the fire. "I know," she said flatly.

"You . . . know?"

"They've been searching for days. We . . . they suspect that we have at least three things they desire."

"Who is *we*?"

Yollana snorted. "Don't waste breath and heat asking questions you know won't get answers. It irritates the elderly."

The younger woman was clearly not a ruler—but she was an authority, judging by the compressed line of her lips. Her so-called servant raised a brow in the direction of his mistress, but she did not condescend to notice it. "Very well, Matriarch. What three things?"

The old woman snorted again, and turned her back. "You lose intelligence when you leave the *Voyanne*, girl, gifted or no. *Think*."

The domicis shrugged when the young woman glared at him. It was a sudden glare, an instant swiveling of head and narrowing of eye. Under different circumstances, Yollana would have found it amusing.

"Never mind," Jewel said, after a moment had passed and her expression had rippled and changed yet again. "If you know we're being hunted, why aren't we moving?"

"It may have escaped your notice, but I am not the Matriarch of Arkosa."

"It may," the younger woman snapped, "have escaped yours as well, given the events of the last half-week."

Silence, as always, was profoundly less giving than what

occurred when it was broken. There were a hundred ways to interpret a silence, perhaps a thousand.

They waited.

Yollana let the moment stretch, and broke it with a dry, dry chuckle. She reached into her pocket for her pipe and looked, piercing now, at the self-titled servant, this *domicis* of the North. But she spoke to the mistress. "You're wasted where you are, girl; you have what it takes to walk the *Voyanne* with a straight back."

"You'll pardon me if my life's ambition is not to be hunted like a rat in the desert."

Again, the corners of the old woman's lips shifted in what might have been the start of a smile. But the smile dimmed as she contemplated fire, seeing—as did all young gazers at fire—her fears and her desires flickering in a dance within the heart of flame. "Young Margret—let these words never leave my fire—erred in judgment, and she is being judged as harshly as only a new Matriarch can be; she lives with her mistake.

"But her people are nervous. The desert waits. She—if I am not mistaken—will not take them into the heart of our oldest secrets without a sign."

"A . . . sign."

"A sign. The Lady is watching. It is the Lady who judges now."

"You didn't even blink."

Avandar Gallais stared out at the stretch of sand that contained the harshest leg of the *Voyanne*: its beginning and—in story, in legend, in weary dream—its end. Jewel did not recognize the expression on his face, but she could pretend that, in the blue-gray of dawn light, she couldn't see it.

It didn't matter; she could feel it keenly. Her arm, when she looked at its momentarily exposed skin, was glittering like jeweled metal. Or scale. She didn't like it.

"No more do I," he said.

"Please stop that."

"Why, ATerafin?"

"You know why."

"It makes you uncomfortable?" His smile was thin. "So

does the decision you offered The Terafin before we left to travel South."

"That decision was my choice," she said evenly. "And I'll thank you not to compare them."

"And had you been given the choice, would you have made it? Or would you have argued with me, and perished?"

"I guess we'll never know."

"I would guess you already do. There is no doubt at all in my mind."

"And there ever is?" She turned to leave, and he caught her upper arm. She had always realized he was not a small man, but the evidence of palm against cloth, the way his fingers closed like a brace around the whole of her arm, was itself like the mark against her skin.

"Let me offer you advice, ATerafin, which you will no doubt accept with your usual grace and intelligence."

Sarcasm was comfortable; she accepted it. But she noticed that he did not release her.

"What has happened has happened. Accept it. Use it as the tool that it could be; become adept with it."

"Use—" She looked at the arm he held.

His voice changed; became something that was transfixing, compelling in a way that his voice had never been. *Yes. Just like this. Use it. Work with it. It will not go away.* She could not ignore it. But she was Jewel; she tried anyway.

What had Rymark ATerafin said so long ago it was almost a different lifetime? *You cannot always be the girl who says "No". You are no longer a child.* As if, she thought, childhood was as simple as that. As if her childhood had been a time of innocence, devoid of the violence and threats of violence that lurked beneath a more polished, civilized surface in a great House.

"Jewel," Avandar said softly. Speaking her name now, putting breath into the two syllables.

No, there had been deaths. There had been violence. Theft. Starvation. She remembered clearly, in the heat of the desert, its most stark contrast: Winter, snow up to her knees, Carver and Angel chattering at her back. She had stopped in front of a snow mound in the early morning streets. There were no footprints across it; the blanket was white and perfect.

It had been a shroud. Winter came one year in ten to Averalaan. It was always deadly.

Angel and Carver had almost knocked her over because they'd been walking with their heads down, faces to ground, to avoid the worst of the wind in the open streets. "What the Hells—"

"Jay?"

And she'd shaken her head. "Go around it."

"What? Go around what?"

She'd gestured to the small mound, the small drift of snow.

"Why?"

Teller had come, then, the youngest, the newest of her den. He was pale with cold, except for his nose, which was red. Eyes the color of ice with reflection, he had said simply, *Someone died here.*

And it was true. Beneath the snow, a boy, younger than any of hers. Unwanted. Or lost. It really didn't matter now. "Don't just stand there gaping. *Move* or we'll join him."

"Jay—"

If it hadn't been Teller, she'd have busted him in the jaw, cold hands or no. She held her temper. Held it the way one holds a large, angry dog, jaw bristling with teeth. "*What?*"

"Are we going to leave him?"

"Leave who?"

He had pointed to the snowdrift.

"Yes," she snapped. "He's dead, Teller, doesn't make a difference to him whether he's buried beneath snow, ice, or dirt. He's *dead.*"

He had looked at her then. She knew—at a remove of too many years—that it was the first time she had realized just how important he would become to her, if he survived. "If it doesn't matter, why wouldn't you walk across him? When we move off the road, the snow's worse." More words than he'd spoken since she'd found him kneeling beside a body between litter piles in Karben's alley.

She frowned. "All right, Teller, it *does* matter. But not enough to die for."

"Does anything?"

"Matter enough to die for?"

"Yeah."

"Yes," she said, the word unequivocal, lightning to the rod of *his* words, a perfect moment of electric clarity that was both blinding and illuminating in its intensity. "You. Angel. Carver. Arann. Fisher. Lefty. Duster. Jester. Finch."

"And to kill for?" another voice said.

She turned in the here and now to see across the years; Duster had shaken off cold, had stood, shoulders in a straight, perfect line, hands on her hips, eyes narrowed; Duster, her killer, *hers*.

She looked at her friend, at her most stalwart defender, her guardian, her assassin. And beside her, ghostly but more substantial, stepped Kiriel di'Ashaf. Except that Kiriel, in armor, hair pulled back in a Northern warrior's braid, was standing beneath the tended pink of cherry blossoms, looking vaguely uncomfortable and out of place among so much that was delicate and ephemeral, although she was delicate of feature in her fashion.

Yes, she said softly, to that memory, to her own.

But to Avandar, Jewel said, "They're in the South. Kiriel. Valedan. The Ospreys."

He raised a brow.

She felt his curiosity, and she realized that he could not delve into memory, into the things that she could see that were not otherwise seen. *I am learning*, she thought.

And she *knew* she would learn more.

Why not? Why not, Jay? This is the only person you've ever met who can't be killed; the only person who will never be your responsibility.

Because. She looked at her arm, and then said, "We'll be leaving in the afternoon tomorrow."

He let her go when she turned away.

When the children were finally left behind the sloping crest of sandy dune, they would take much with them: the last shock of vegetation, with its muted color; the wagons that had been the emergency home of the most important caravan the Arkosans boasted; the aunts, the uncles, and the distant cousins. These things would disappear anyway, as the trek into the Sea of Sorrows progressed.

But they would also take their excitement, their profound lack of fear, their joy at sudden, innocuous things: the stone with crystal flecks; the sandbird's empty nest, bits of smooth, lavender shell cracked but whole within curved strands of dry grass; dry wood; the lingering succulent's blossom that had somehow missed the fact that night had passed and had continued its bloom until the edges of dawn had been burned away.

That had caused excitement among not only the children, although it was their huddle, their press of "me first!" bodies, that had drawn the attention of the Voyani men and women whose duty it was to guard and herd them, but among the adults as well.

The adults—Stavos and his wife Caitla had been on duty at the time—made a path past the shoulders of children by the simple expedient of a firm grip that was never overbearing, never abusive. He guided them out of their argument by joining them. Although his back was twice the size of the largest child—perhaps three times the width—he did not look out of place among them.

The game of me-first was transformed in that instant by the equally youthful desire to expose the intensity of excitement to someone who had the ability to offer approbation in return. It was unalloyed; they were young. The older children who could be easily separated from their parents had long since vanished down the *Voyanne* that only the Arkosans could clearly see.

That huddle of backs, the slight dip of chin, the way soft dark hair fell to shoulders as heads cocked first to one side and then the other, cast a shadow across the momentary warmth of Jewel's observations. It was lessened when Stavos spoke, his warm, deep voice wrapped around Torra, not the Northern tongue her father had spoken when she had come to him—or he to her—in just this way. There was such a certainty behind the words that she felt safety radiate outward, as light from lamp, and she wanted to stand a moment just as the children did.

Stupid, really. She hadn't wanted to be a child for a very, very long time; her own childhood had ended so abruptly.

But before she could castigate herself too harshly, his words fell away and he, like the children, stared at whatever it was that had excited them.

"Caitla?" he said in a hushed voice—the voice of a man who had seen something that was so like a dream, he was afraid the sound of his voice would take it away. She came to stand beside him, making room for herself between his left side and the children pressed there. Then she reached out to grip his shoulder; a simple ring caught the light. Held it until she moved.

She moved quickly.

Margret came. Margret, subdued in all ways since her encounter with the Serra of the High Court, strode across the scrub and brush in the dawn air. The older woman followed behind, and Jewel could see, as the dawn's light grew stronger and brighter, that her cheeks were wet.

"A sign, Matriarch," she said, her voice broken by the tears that ran, unhindered, down her cheeks. "A sign."

Stavos rose as Margret approached. He began to shuffle the children away, but they hesitated, and Margret lifted a hand to stop him. "Is there danger?" she asked.

He shook his head: no.

She let them stay. Watching them, that would remain with Jewel as one of her strongest early memories of Margret: she let the children stay; perhaps drew comfort from their presence.

In the great houses of the Northern Empire, children were seldom seen. Skill, not blood, defined the lines of the ten great Houses who ruled beneath the Twin Kings. But even had children been present in abundance, she could not conceive of the ruler who would have allowed them to crowd underfoot this way—not when people were watching. Not when an event of indeterminate significance had occurred.

But Margret? She smiled at the children; she touched the tallest boy's shoulder, stooping slightly to do so. She asked them what they had found, although she could see it plainly in the growing light: a night blossom, thick-leaved and pale, that should never have waited—could not naturally wait—for day.

For her.

Caitla had fallen to one knee behind the Matriarch's back. To Jewel's surprise, so did her bear of a husband, his knee against the packed, dry dirt, his shadow long against the ground.

Elena came, with no one to guide her. She was joined in ones and twos by the rest of the small encampment. Words, broken by the distance imposed by whisper—for Jewel was an outsider—were passed from person to person; Jewel could see clearly when they had been informed of what had been found, for their heads snapped up, their eyes widened; they stood rigid a moment and then they bowed as if all strings had been cut; as if relief had finally given them permission to relax.

There were tears on the faces of the Arkosans who formed a circle at Margret's back.

A sign. The Lady has given us a sign.

CHAPTER SIXTEEN

5th of Misteral, 427 AA
Sea of Sorrows

The men went out with Tamara and Donatella. They returned with large, covered jugs on the backs of beasts that, while they moved on four legs, were completely outside of the realm of Jewel's experience. Avandar recognized them at once, and with distaste.

"As you dislike horses, ATerafin, I will offer you a warning. Stay away from these. They are at best foul-tempered and ill-humored."

"And at worst?" As the wind changed direction, she grimaced.

His smile was brief. "The same. They will happily remove your hand from your wrist and spit it out. They can probably snap your arm with a good blow from the side of their heads. They can certainly snap ribs with a back kick."

"They can't be that bad, or they wouldn't be here."

"They are that bad," he said, "but for people without the power to control their environment, they are *also* necessary."

"That would be us?"

"Indeed."

Whether Avandar's description was true or not—and he had no reason to lie about something so trivial—the Voyani who handled these large-eyed, hunchbacked beasts were in high spirits.

But not so high and not so sweet as the Matriarch's young brother. "Nicu!" Adam shouted. "'Lena!"

Elena stepped back from her supervision of the straps across camel back; Nicu appeared from between a group of men who were transferring the precious contents of jug and jar into the more supple folds of animal skins.

"Carmello," he said in passing, "you make sure you take the wineskins from the men and empty them."

"But—"

"Now. You know what happens."

"But we all know—"

"Now." He didn't wait to see if they complied; he had already slid between them to catch up with Elena.

They disappeared, and then Elena returned, weaving her way with ease and grace through the thick of working bodies. The women had opened the back of a small wagon and were now struggling with dense folds of cotton and raw silk.

"Jewel," she called. "You'll see it anyway—you can't miss it—but come." She held out a hand.

Jewel took it without pause.

The Matriarch's wagon was undergoing repairs. The body of the wagon—its massive, hardwood frame—was supported across the thick backs of workhorses that made the camels look rickety, and rested perhaps a foot higher than it normally did. Stained wood bore the signs of the elements—chips and cracks in the surface of the walls, rust speckles across the hinges of shutters that were obviously made by different craftsmen than the body of the wagon itself.

Margret and Nicu were already struggling with one of the great wheels and a large wrench. Elena released Jewel's hand and ran to help them, muttering—if something as loud as that could be a mutter—about thick-headed, idiot cousins who didn't have the sense to wait for help. Two of the wagons wheels now lay against the scrub like beached fish. The third was in the process—with luck—of joining them.

Even in the dry air, they were sweating, and as the breeze passed her face, Jewel could taste the pungent scent of sweat and effort.

Jewel privately thought that the timing for repairs was extremely poor; the wagon would not be going with them into the Sea of Sorrows, and mobility for the rest of the Arkosan caravan—once they had fled the habitable, easily searched, regions of Raverra—would be necessary.

Adam appeared from the doorway of the wagon. "Is this what you're looking for?" he shouted down.

Margret looked up briefly. "No, not *that* oil! The other one!"

" 'Gret, there are a *hundred* other ones!"

"The one that smells like it would kill you to drink!"

"They all smell like that!"

She snorted and shoved her hair out of her eyes in a gesture that was so familiar it took Jewel a few moments to realize why: it was akin to her own.

Elena said something that didn't carry as far as Jewel's ears; Nicu threw back his head and laughed.

The two women looked at each other, almost startled by the sound of mirth, and then they joined him; they stood, these three, laughing as the sun passed slowly overhead. She thought them all beautiful, the way people in their prime are; they were full of energy, even affection, for each other.

Jewel smiled as well. Their laughter had that effect. Although she was an outsider, it welcomed, rather than excluded; it proved that in the harshest and bitterest of climes, friendship flourished.

But she wondered, watching these three, how much that friendship would be tested, if it had not already been tested. Knew, the moment that thought passed into the echo of memory, that it had. For a moment, no more, she could see the scars across a back that lay beneath the surface of heavy cloth—Nicu's back.

Margret laughed again, and she realized that she liked the sound of that laughter, perhaps because it was so rare.

"Hey, you!" Elena shouted. "Jewel!"

Jewel's gaze slid from the Matriarch to her cousin.

"Don't stand there sweating for no reason—help us!"

"I—I can get help if you need it—"

"Help with your own hands."

"They're not very strong."

It was Margret who laughed, the sound halfway between mirth and derision. "They're strong enough. You walked through the Lady's fire to reach us. You—if rumor and story is true—faced the Lady down to save her Lake."

"That's not as hard as pulling a wheel from a wagon. Trust me. I've traveled with a merchant caravan a time or two, and I've been 'helpful.' And most of them are still speaking about it."

"This is no merchant caravan. This is no task for a merchant. Lend us your hands here, Jewel ATerafin, and I'll count myself in your debt." Her voice had lost humor and gained intensity; it was worse for the exchange.

But she spoke the truth.

"Voyani debt is not undertaken lightly."

"So I've heard." The Matriarch moved to make room for the member of House Terafin.

"Neither is accepting that debt."

At that, the Matriarch smiled. "You've got good sources, whoever they are."

"I don't understand what you want."

"No," she said softly. "You don't. Most Arkosans outside of this caravan don't understand it either. Yollana might. I don't know. Each of the Voyani families make their crossings in their own ways, and while it's not forbidden to watch it—if you're here—it *is* forbidden to speak of it." She picked up the wrench.

"And you want my help?"

"Yes," Elena answered softly.

"Why?"

"Because," it was Nicu who answered, drawing his arms across his chest. The petulance that she associated with him had left his face; he was an attractive man with shoulders that were broader and stronger than they seemed. "It's a binding."

"Binding?" She hesitated.

Elena laughed; the laugh was not without barb.

"Adam! Have you found it yet?"

"Maybe!"

Margret snorted. She turned to Elena and said, "You tell her. We're never going to get off the sand if I don't help Adam." She accepted the hand that Nicu offered, pushing herself through the open doorway and into the depths of her home.

"Elena?"

"I don't know why she asked you to help," the Matriarch's heir began.

It was Jewel's turn to snort. She did. "You brought me here."

Elena shrugged. Had the grace to look embarrassed. "True enough."

"You don't want to answer the question."

"I—I don't know how to answer it. This part—" she said indicating the wheel with a lift of her right shoulder, "this part isn't all that important. It's just hard work."

"That's why they let me help," Nicu added. But again, there was a lack of petulance in the words that made them easy on the ears. He was, Jewel thought, happy. Excited. She was surprised at just how young he looked—although she shouldn't have been; she knew from personal experience that struggling with the weather could age a person damn fast. "Come on; once Margret finds her witches' brew, she's going to get serious. Let's get the last two wheels off before then."

Jewel rolled up her sleeves. Elena frowned. "Get out of that habit, Jay," she said, using the name as if the other words that might apply—stranger, outsider, ni'Voyani—had been considered and barely tossed aside. "Once we enter the Sea, you'll be asked to do work, but you'll suffer if you roll up your sleeves to do it."

Jewel nodded. Let her sleeves fall again.

When Margret and her brother came out of the wagon, the third wheel—which was much heavier than the Terafin's merchant wagon wheels in Jewel's admittedly subjective recall—had been grounded; the fourth stubbornly clung to the axle until Margret pushed Elena out of the way and bent her own shoulders to the task.

Between Margret, Nicu, and Jewel, the wheel came off the wagon's side and after teetering a moment in protest, was laid to rest against the ground with the other three.

Adam peered out of the elevated door. "Was that the last one?"

Margret apparently didn't have the energy for sarcasm, although in her position Jewel would have been greatly tempted to employ it, given her expression. The Matriarch nodded.

"I'll tell Stavos."

She nodded again. He leaped out of the upper room, landed, and took two steps—then he hesitated and turned his head toward them. "Will you wait for me?"

"I have to get started. But," she added, as he opened his mouth in what was clearly the start of a protest, "it'll take a while."

"It doesn't take that long!"

"It didn't take Momma that long. It'll take *me* a while." She rolled up her sleeve.

Jewel shot Elena a look; Elena smiled cheerfully. "You want to tell her she's being a fool, go right ahead. It's her skin."

And I hadn't noticed it was particularly thick.

The Matriarch was intent on her work now, and her work—to Jewel's untrained eye—seemed to involve a large, cylindrical jar, her left hand, a paintbrush that had obviously seen better days, and the walls of the wagon itself.

"Do you need help?"

Margret paused for just a moment. Then, without a word, she handed Jewel the jar and the brush. "What will you offer Arkosa?"

The phrase had the feel and weight that words gathered when they had been said once a year for generations. Had they been said flippantly or angrily, Jewel's reply would have been different.

She bowed to the Matriarch, the gesture reflecting the unusual gravity of the other woman's tone. "I have so little of value to offer Arkosa," she replied, following the cadence of Margret's voice with words that were far less practiced, less bent to the form of ritual.

But she knew what to offer. She *knew*. Keeping the grimace off her face, she bent and lowered the jar carefully to earth. Rising, she held out her left hand, palm up. "But what I have, take; use what you must in the defense of Arkosa."

"What do you offer Arkosa?" Margret said again. Her gaze was level.

"Water," she replied. "Water of life, of my life."

The shape of Margret's eyes changed significantly. "You understand what you offer." No question in the words.

Jewel nodded.

"But your family forsook the *Voyanne*."

It was, Jewel knew, one of the deepest insults one Voyani could offer another—and it was usually offered on the open road between squabbling Voyani families—although squabble was probably the wrong word for something that claimed so many lives, year round.

"There are many ways of forsaking a thing; many ways of deserting. Perhaps, Matriarch of Arkosa, if what you say is true, and my family did forsake the open road, the *Voyanne* did not forsake my family."

It was Elena who spoke. "Well answered," she said softly.

"I've had to learn to be good with words."

"It's not your words we want."

"I know. But heritage betrays me. With the Voyani, you get words no matter what."

Margret's laugh filled the silence that Jewel's observation had left. "Give us your words, Jewel of Terafin. Give us your blood. We will take whatever you offer, no matter how meager. You came to us in the fires."

"And she'll leave us that way as well," Elena said softly.

Both Jewel and Margret turned to look at her.

"'Lena?"

Jewel said nothing. Although she had never seen her own face when she was possessed by the peculiar certainty of a vision that masquerades as instinct or knowledge, she knew the look immediately when it adorned another's.

She did not want to ask. She was completely certain that she didn't want to know. But the gift had never been kind.

"A visitor will come from a long way off to die. With you. And his death will burn," Elena said, her wide eyes fixed on a spot that was both farther and closer to her than Jewel, Margret, or Nicu could ever be. "It will take you away from us when we need you the most."

Jewel? Avandar's voice.

Go away.

I assume that means you're fine.

She didn't answer.

Jewel reached out to touch Elena.

Elena looked up and the moment was lost. The words, and the memory, were not—but Jewel was used to swallowing memory whole; if it ate at her from the inside, it would have company. "I think," she said evenly, wondering if *this* was what the subjects of her own visions felt like, "that's enough. The Matriarch is waiting, and the Arkosans cannot leave until the Matriarch is ready. They have waited—we have waited—

counting on the scant shadows the Lady provides across this open plain, for too many days as it is."

Elena shook herself. She pulled her hand—slowly—from Jewel's. "Yes. You're right." But she did not meet Jewel's eyes. Which meant, no doubt, that there had been more.

Why not just hear it out?

Because there's not a damn thing I can do about it. Knowledge settled around her like chilly Northern water. She pulled it close enough that she didn't have to inspect it, wondering why Elena had had such a vision when she herself hadn't.

The Matriarch climbed back into the recesses of the wagon, and when she returned, she carried a wide, deep bowl. It had been carved, with care, from a dark, heavy wood; its lip was a relief of symbols that might once have been language. Although the Voyani spoke Torra as fluently as low clansmen, they did not use that language for their rituals. Nor did they use symbols such as the one that lay, in relief, at the bowl's center. At first glance it looked like the full moon or the naked sun, but across its face were markings that she had never seen.

"What is it?"

The old moon, a voice said, whispering so quietly in her ear she almost bent to catch the words. Avandar. Avandar's voice. The sun was getting awfully chilly in these parts.

"We call it the Lady's secret face, although," Margret said, with a flash of a smile, "as you're looking at it now, it can't be all that secret. It can't be invoked except by blood. And we cannot leave without invoking it."

"Do you ever use your own?"

"My blood? I would use my blood in a heartbeart," Margret replied with unusual earnestness, "but it's forbidden."

"Voyani blood cannot be used?"

"The blood of the Matriarch cannot be offered," the Matriarch replied. "Not here, although it . . . will be, later."

"Is it bloodline dependent?"

"No, although the blood of my brother could not be used with great success, and the blood of my heir with less."

Jewel asked, "And the blood of a stranger?"

"If willingly offered, and willingly accepted, it is the strongest," she replied.

"Isn't that ironic? The Voyani are almost legendary for their dislike of outsiders."

"We don't kill them all," Margret countered, shrugging. "Maybe this is why—they have a use."

"Maybe. You ask questions like a merchant who is fully aware of the value of what he sells."

"I *am* a merchant; if someone wants something I have to offer, no matter how highly I prize it—or how little—I know it has value." She tried hard not to wince when Margret drew a large dagger. She didn't bother to suppress the reaction when the dagger's edge bit her; it did not cut the fleshy palm that she'd offered; it hit vein.

"Yours is not the only blood we will spill." The Matriarch's heir spoke as she watched Margret cut not hand, but the vein that led to it. She had the grace to wince.

"Perhaps not," the voice that Jewel least wanted to hear said. "Although that *can* be arranged."

Avandar Gallais reached for Jewel's wrist. Her right wrist.

He was *furious*.

His face was expressionless, his voice about as warm as desert night. But his eyes were like the flat of a steel blade; they reflected the light.

Jewel wasn't sure what was worse: the throbbing pain in a wrist that presented the possibility of severe blood loss, or the throbbing pain in the other wrist, where the mark on her arm—his gift—had begun to burn. Avandar no longer surprised her, but when she glanced from his face to the face of her Voyani companions, she realized that that complacency was a gift of long acquaintance.

The three had formed a tight knot, and the dagger that had been used to cut her wrist was now held out as a weapon. Held warily.

She watched her blood fall across the cracked leather of her favorite boots; it was absorbed by the faded stain, but not quickly enough to prevent its spill into the hard sand that settled beneath tenacious, wiry scrub.

Red dust rose in its wake, as if her sacrifice had allowed a ghost or a spirit trapped beneath the hard earth to take form and shape, to vie for freedom beneath the unforgiving glare of the Lord.

Although she felt the heat of Avandar's anger—and his

anger had never *felt* heated from the outside—more clearly than she felt the sun, she looked up at the glinting steel of Margret's dagger.

It had come out of the sheath very quietly.

"Matriarch?"

They both turned at the word.

"Give me the bowl."

There was a moment of total silence which was followed almost seamlessly by a moment of total panic, and although neither was broken by words, the flurry of sudden activity spoke clearly enough. The bowl flew toward the small rain of blood in Elena's shaking hands.

Avandar's anger, if anything, grew deeper.

"There's no point in being pissed off," Jewel heard herself say, although in truth the pain in her wrist was now unpleasant. "It was *my* choice."

"If a two-year-old accepts the poison offered it in the form of sugar, should I then blame the child?"

"If casting blame makes you feel better, go ahead." *Really* unpleasant. "But I forbid you to—"

"To what?"

She looked up; met Elena's panicked face. "Is this supposed to happen?" The blood in the bowl was moving. Writhing.

"I—I don't know. The only person who's seen it is Margret, and she—"

"No." Margret's ashen pallor was answer enough. It wasn't the answer Jewel was hoping for, but it would have to do. "What is it doing?"

"If I had to guess," Avandar snapped, "the *it* that you so quaintly refer to is doing two things."

"What?"

"It's attempting to reject your offering."

"But—"

"And it's spilling enough power into the surrounding countryside that anyone with power of their own now knows *exactly* where we are." He lowered his voice with obvious effort. "Jewel," he said, through his teeth, "you are bound to *me*. I apologize if that was not made clear to you. What you do here—with the Voyani—is offer another binding. You are trapped on either side by power that you neither comprehend nor control."

The bowl's contents burst into flame; the flame was white. Elena bit her lip, but she did not let go of the bowl.

He was silent for a moment. When he spoke again, his voice was its normal frigid self. "It appears that the Voyani no longer comprehend what it is that they seek to summon. In my youth, you would have been considered very brave. By the foolish.

"Come."

She was having difficulty breathing. Oddly enough, that made it easier to listen to him. She didn't even raise her customary elbow when he enfolded her, from behind, in the questionable shelter of his arms and chest.

She was surprised at how cool, how blessedly cool, that chest was.

"Where are we going to—"

"Hush."

"But—"

He was silent a moment, and then he chuckled; the chest at Jewel's back seemed to lose some essential rigidity. "They must finish what they have started; the offering has been made. If you somehow survive it, we can assume that it was accepted." He caught her as she stumbled. Or rather, fell; she hadn't actually moved her feet. "Accepted with grace? Unlikely. But if you do not leave this site before dusk, it is likely that you will never leave it."

"Domicis!"

Jewel felt, rather than saw, the movement of Avandar's chin as it rested just above her hair. "Matriarch?"

"What—what has happened here?"

He was silent.

Avandar.

She felt, rather than saw, his surprise. Her eyes were closed, although it took her a moment to identify the cause of the pale gray and red that obscured all vision.

ATerafin.

Tell them.

He was silent.

All right, you stubborn sonofa—

ATerafin.

This is *going to be hard. All right, tell* me *and let her listen. I want to know what's happening, too.*

You won't be awake for the explanation.

Try me.

She felt a glimmer of mixed annoyance and amusement, both of which were almost dwarfed by a vast and endless anger. But that anger was not for or at her, and it was not—although it had been momentarily aimed at—for Margret.

"When the Voyani fled their ancestral home— No, do not raise the dagger, and raise no alarm; I reveal enough about myself in this speaking that I am not a threat to you." There was a silence. It stretched. Jewel listened for the sound of a weapon being sheathed; it didn't happen.

But after a moment, Avandar chose to resume his explanation.

"When your ancestors chose to embark upon the *Voyanne* that dominates your lives to this day, they were watched. There were bloodlines within the homelands that were notable and therefore noted, and although the cities themselves were . . . destroyed . . . in a fashion, it was the bloodlines that represented the greatest of threats to the Lord of Night who is not otherwise named.

"He bound the cities with magic—in the magicks he understood and wielded. His work was fine, and long, and deadly. But it was not . . . complete."

She heard the rustle of cloth. "Matriarch, I will offer you this warning. If you attack me, you will die. If you order your people to attack me, they will die." It was the worst kind of threat, uttered in the matter-of-fact tone reserved for observations about simple statements of fact. Like the price of butter. Or the price of bread.

"You're sure of yourself, stranger." Elena's voice.

He did not dignify bravado with response. Jewel was pretty sure that no one expected him to.

You are certain you wish me to continue? There may be consequences. Deaths.

She, too, did not dignify the ridiculous with a response.

"The Lord is a creature who understands power. He understands it in minutiae; he understands it when it is grand and glorious and sweeps whole continents into the sea by the ferocity of its ambition. He understands the desire to preserve what one controls; this is at the heart of rulership, when the ruler is not mad. But he does not understand—and did not—the power that comes from a willing sacrifice.

He cannot clearly understand the power that abjures power, or denies power.

"But he desires that understanding. It is a weakness in both offense and defense to so lack what motivates so much of humanity. I digress.

"When the Matriarchs chose to follow their course, they were forced to abandon their homes."

" 'Gret." Elena's voice. Hushed. Tight.

"Stranger—"

"No one can hear a word I say, and while I speak, no one can hear your response. Shall I stop?"

No one answered.

"They gathered those they could trust about them and they convinced them, by means unknown, that the Lord was coming to war against the Cities. And then they explained that the Cities themselves were covered in a fine veil of magic by which people of power or consequence were watched. Anyone caught outside of the vast array of defenses the Cities offered was prey for the kin.

"They knew the truth of this. However, it was not a punishment meted out *to* the rulers within the cities, for the Lords of these lands had power, and the kin could not be guaranteed to defeat them. Therefore, should they travel in the wake of a power, they might be safe.

"But what they did not understand—what was made clear—was that while they could leave, they could not leave in safety without the Matriarch, and if *she* left, the enemy would be alerted.

"In the end, a minor member of each family stepped forward and offered his blood as the binding by which the spell might be defeated. It was woven—this blood, this integral part of identity—into the magicks cast by the Matriarch, that those watching might see only the identity of the man whose blood was offered, and not the identity of the women whose blood carried that power. It is an old spell and it is not without its debt—on either side. It requires an element of trust."

Silence. Neither Elena nor Margret broke it.

Adam did. Jewel heard his voice at Avandar's back, although as Avandar did not seem even remotely surprised at the interruption, she guessed that the domicis has been aware of his presence.

"We have completed this ceremony every year since the *Voyanne* beckoned, and if there were deaths, if the minions of the Lord were hunting us, it isn't recorded."

"Indeed. I would say that you have diminished significantly in power over the years, to a point which makes this ruse, this binding, unnecessary."

"Then your anger—"

"Jewel ATerafin is bound to *me*. And my power has not diminished at all with the passage of time. If they are looking for me, they will find me. And they will see that I am moving into the heart of the territories mankind once held against them at a crucial time in their war.

"Then," he added softly, "they will come."

Silence.

"Margret—can we—"

"No," Avandar said, before she could answer. "Had the blood reached sand, touching nothing of yours, you could have found a different sacrifice. As it is, her blood is already bound to the Matriarch's line; the bowl is blooded. The wagons are waiting.

"And, I, too, must prepare."

"Who hunts you, stranger?"

He laughed. "It would be more germane, young man, to ask who *doesn't*."

• • •

5th of Misteral, 427 AA
Shining Court

For the better part of one week, the child had cried. She had cried upon waking, cried when going to sleep, and screamed within sleep's fold; she had wept when she was taken—briefly—to the human Court and worse still, wept when Anya came for her.

It had been hard, then, to preserve her life.

But Lord Isladar had faced a similar challenge with an earlier ward. True, Kiriel—even as a small child—had been more robust; the simple howl of Northern wind did not pierce or freeze her skin; the raging fire of Falloran's breath did not burn it. But in the eyes of the kinlords, such simple immunities were taken for granted. They went unnoticed by all save the old woman he had procured to raise his ward.

To build into her the necessary human weaknesses.

This time, he thought he might forgo the interference of another parent. Kiriel had been his first child, and he had learned much in her rearing.

This, this second child, this unlooked-for gift, had come out of the hands of madness into his arms and his tower; he could not conceive of a role for her, should he manage to preserve her. And it had been almost an eternity since Lord Isladar of the *Kialli* had done anything spontaneous; not even reveling in the sensation of the elemental wind had been unpremeditated.

He watched the child.

She slept.

Falloran, he thought. *Will you serve one without even the faintest trace of blood or power?* Perhaps. Perhaps not. While she slept, he watched over her, thinking that the line of her cheek and her upturned nose, in the shadows of a Tower with shuttered windows and the muted glow of lamp against smooth stone, was familiar.

Above her head, the carved symbols of elemental flower that had been invoked to protect his first child were glowing faintly. It took no art to see the light they cast; he had enchanted them for her comfort. She was the third person to sleep in this bed. The first, Kiriel's mother; the second, Kiriel herself. The third? He did not desire that the third should meet the fate he had planned for either the first or the second. Strange, that.

Perhaps it was because the child was so inherently valueless. She had no glimmer of mortal talent and her eyes were as brown as the eyes of the most base of Southern clansmen; not even flecks of gold that hinted at a mysterious ancestry made them interesting or appealing. She was trapped in the span of her years, and unaware of the nature of that trap, she would die confined by them.

And yet . . . his hand hovered above the knotted strands of her too-fine hair, his thumb above the fluttering shell of closed lid.

He felt the intruder at the foot of the Tower door.

It destroyed the fragile moment. In the air, shimmering like horizon in the desert heat, a sigil formed. He had cast this sigil, enforced it, displayed it, when it was new; he had left it when the Tower emptied of both its occupants. But he was almost surprised to see it, whole, his name emblazoned across air a menace with no subtlety.

How was it that the kinlords could be driven by things ancient and things powerful—that the scars of a world that no longer existed could exert such influence and control when the recent, the mere decade, could be so easily forgotten?

He smiled. Rose, and bent with infinite care. His fingers brushed the cheeks of sleeping child. He did not analyze the action; he merely enacted it until he was satisfied, his back bent beneath the confinement of a single piece of stone.

Then, when he was certain she would not wake, he rose. Wondering, as he did, why he had not chosen to deprive her of the memories of parents he was certain—given Anya's comments—were dead. Certainly, at any other time, he would have.

But at any other time, he would have had a plan.

There was an eternity to question. But first, there was an unwelcome interruption to be dealt with.

The kinlord was tall.

He had gathered his shadow around him like a mantle; from a distance—the distance provided by winding stone stairs—that power could be seen as it spilled into ground, seeped into air, announcing the presence of the lord who now held it.

It was not, however, meant as a threat; merely as a statement. The kinlord looked up as Isladar drew near. He did not otherwise shift position.

"Lord Isladar."

"Lord Telakar." Isladar offered no similar display of power. It was not needed. The Tower was his.

Silence stretched; Telakar smiled. "I hear that you have another mortal in your keep. Is this one mongrel as well?"

"You know full well that she is simply a stray human."

Telakar nodded. "I had heard," he said softly, "that she was chosen by the mad mage."

"You are reckless, Telakar; Anya a'Cooper has sharp ears, and she is sensitive."

"She is mortal," he said, his shrug more dismissive than

the momentary current of excitement detectable in the words themselves.

"Yes. And if you wait long enough, she will no longer be a threat. Although . . . that was not always the case with mortals, was it?"

The silence that followed was composed of lack of speech, lack of breath, and the sudden, frozen stillness of shadow. Lord Telakar fell to one knee, slowly, groping for the form of respect between liege and lord that had been used when the *Kialli* were yet alive.

"Lord Isladar." Power such as Telakar possessed was not easily shed; he made no move to release it.

Which was wise. Shedding such gathered shadow often presaged the laying of the foundation for a major spell, and no lord chose that undertaking in the dominion of another unless he was certain that he might prevail.

Against Isladar, the inscrutable, the least predictable of the *Kialli*, there was no certainty.

"Lord Telakar." Isladar inclined his head. He accepted the humbling gesture without comment; they were both aware that, had he desired it, the gesture itself would have been superfluous. Lord Isladar did not desire public displays of power—except as it suited a specific purpose—but rather, its certainty. Among the *Kialli*, there was not a lord who had chosen to bind more of his servitors than Isladar.

Or rather, not a lord who had bound more and survived.

Yet this one, he had chosen not to leash.

He was not entirely certain why. Telakar was *Kialli*, and possessed of the same ambition, the same goals. He sought power. There was no question of trust; he could not be trusted.

They both understood this; it was part of ancient ritual, the dance of the powerful.

He waited patiently while Telakar rose, shedding subservience with grace.

"I did not expect to see you here."

"In truth, I did not expect to be here. The . . . task that you set seemed of interest, but it is not yet exciting, and it is by no means finished."

"Observation seldom is." Isladar's smile was both rare and genuine.

Telakar's frown was no less genuine, but perhaps not as rare as the smile it answered. "Lord Isladar?"

"You were always so impatient. If I could have taught you one thing—if I could teach it now—it would be patience. Very little is boring in the end. Anticipation, with care, can last millennia."

"I was not more impatient than Etridian is now, and he is one of the Lord's Commanders, a part of His Fist."

"For now," Isladar replied. "But he has failed twice."

"He failed against your mongrel."

"Yes. And so, too, would you."

Telakar was predictable. He bristled, but he did not demur. He understood that it was not in Isladar's nature to boast.

"But he failed against the mortals as well. I do not believe his tenure will survive the war. Come, we have had this argument before, and it was not interesting then. And you must admit that Kiriel, when she was present, made things vastly more amusing in the Northern Wastes."

"You came to report something of interest?"

"Perhaps. Ishavriel is canny. It is difficult to observe him without his knowledge, and it requires . . . a greater distance than I had anticipated."

Isladar did not nod; he merely listened.

"He seems, at this distance, to have taken an interest in one of the Voyani men."

"That is not generally where power resides among the Voyani."

"No. But it is where power once resided, and perhaps he seeks to invoke that."

"Perhaps. Or perhaps it is where weakness resides; it is vastly easier to manipulate the weak—but it is less satisfying. Come; you did not return to the Northern Wastes that you so despise to give me that."

"No." He was silent for a moment; shadows shifted around the contours of his perfect, youthful cheeks, lending his face not a sullen air, but a pensive one. "I have not journeyed often to the lands of men since my return. I know that we are forbidden to mention them among the mortals at Court—but Isladar, I remember them so clearly."

"You were young, then."

"Yes, and you—and the others—were old. Do you not remember the cities? Do you not remember the buildings they wove out of glass and magic and desire, out of gold and silver and common clays? In my day, they decorated their walls with their weak; you could smell the dead as you approached."

Isladar watched the expression mute the edges of Telakar's *Kialli* face; for just a moment, as the kinlord spoke, he could see what had been there before the sundering. It was beautiful in a way that Kiriel, or her human nurse, could never understand.

"You were scarred," he said softly, when Telakar's voice trailed into the past.

"I . . . I was scarred," he said; he did not deny what another lord would never have admitted. "But I traveled the desert they called the Sea of Sorrows, and I felt our Master's ancient touch across all of the sands. There are no cities. There are no ruins."

"And yet they gather."

"Yes, they gather. At the desert's edge. For what bastard ceremony, I do not understand. Nor, I feel, does Ishavriel, although he seeks to use it."

"Telakar, at the risk of being offensive, *think*."

"I—"

"They have gathered for generations, and human memory is a weak, pathetic thing; it has no viscera, no fire. If there was truly nothing left, do you think they would stand at the desert's edge, exposed to the men who hunt them?"

"I am no expert in human behavior."

"Then be expert in mine, kinlord. Would I send you on such an errand, to such a place, without cause? I am not—I have never been—without mercy."

"Perhaps not—when it serves your purpose. The quality of your mercy has yet to be tested."

"By you; it has been tested by many."

Telakar was silent for a long moment. His lips thinned and then relaxed; he closed his eyes briefly. Light and shadow played against the perfect sheen of his closed lids.

"My apologies, Lord Isladar. I am distracted. It is not of Ishavriel that I came to speak."

"No?"

"No. In the end, he chooses to dally with a mortal man,

in the cover of night or shadow. He does not declare himself; he does not seek to use his power. Not yet.

"But there was a man who was old when the cities were built; old when they warred, older when they fell. He was one of the gifted, and he . . . survived much. He is known to us, and he still lives, although I do not understand how."

"Continue."

"I am not privy to the discussions of the Lord's Fist, but I believe that Lord Etridian was given the responsibility of either making an alliance with this man, or destroying him."

Isladar's smile was perfect; sharp, cold, brief. "He was indeed."

"I see no servants of Etridian there, and I can only assume this means he failed. His servants are not of a caliber to practice subtlety; if they were there, I would know." Telakar's smile was less brief, although it, too, was a perfect *Kialli* expression. "The Warlord is with the Voyani."

"You are certain of this?"

"Yes."

"How?"

"An hour ago . . . his sigil hovered in the air above the Voyani encampment like a disembodied ghost. They—the humans—are not sensitive to the dispersal of such magic, but it was there. Both Ishavriel and I were forced to retreat—hastily—to avoid detection.

"But . . . the power ebbed. It is detectable now, but it is . . . strange."

"Strange?"

"It is . . . it is undeniably his power. But it is . . . distorted, contaminated. I have not chosen to approach more closely to determine how."

"Wise," Isladar replied, as if wisdom and Telakar were not always found together. "But he is with our ancient enemies."

"Yes. I do not believe they were aware of his nature."

"And now?"

Telakar shrugged. "They are human."

"You speak as if their nature excuses your ignorance."

The kinlord flushed. But he wisely chose to refrain from response.

Isladar gestured a window into being in the Tower wall;

it was large, the sill the size of two men, the height, perhaps three. It seemed to defy the existence of stairs as it opened into the winter courtyard of the Shining Palace.

Ice touched them both as Lord Isladar of the *Kialli* raised his face to the keening death the elemental air promised to all who spoke its wild tongue. Telakar gathered his shadow close; he had learned the elemental arts, but he was not entirely comfortable with the surrender required to barter with the wilderness.

Yet he was moved at the sound of Isladar's voice contorted by air; there was harmony between what could be easily modulated and what in the end could be coaxed, coddled, and only barely controlled.

Isladar was aware of him, as he was aware of Northern air and the sudden shock of ice that traveled the length of the Tower stairs. It was given no egress into the room the child slept in, but Falloran, at the foot of the Tower, was growling in fury, a literal storm of fire about his brow.

Telakar, he thought, appreciated beauty in a way that the kinlords in the Hells had almost forgotten.

Perhaps that was why, in the end, he did not choose to bind him to, and by, blood. He had been a foolish youth, inasmuch as any of the *Kialli* could be said to be young; of all of the Sundered, Telakar was not one that Isladar would have predicted would cling to the bitter identity of memory. But he had, finding comfort in the pain of those who had Chosen the Hells. As the *Kialli* themselves had done, and perhaps with as clear an understanding of what it meant to choose.

But he had not forgotten beauty in other guises, other forms. So many of the *Kialli* had been subverted by the starvation of necessity; their sensuality and sensibilities had become inextricably linked with things of the Hells.

Even Isladar. Even he.

But there was in Telakar a feckless youth that spoke to the kinlord of life, in a way that extinguishing the merely mortal could not.

The winds demanded his attention; he found a momentary oblivion in the struggle to be worthy of the element. An old battle. But the wind recognized the cadence of his voice, and in the end, the battle was disappointing in its brevity. It carried his request, howling, the distance between death by cold and death by heat negligible, beneath contempt.

"I am pleased, Telakar. But you have not disclosed everything."

The silence was uncomfortable, but it was short; Telakar was only half a fool. He found his knees again, and gained them. "Lord."

"Tell me."

"I believe that someone enspelled by Queen Arianne travels with the Voyani."

"Interesting. Is he enchanted to appear as one of the Voyani?"

"He is . . . not. In truth, I would have assumed he is one of the Voyani, but . . . he is far too quiet, he does not interact with them."

"That does not mark him as Arianne's."

"No." He hesitated; the shadow within him gathered against the possible contempt his response might engender. "He travels with a mount, but he does not seek to ride it. It is antlered; one of the Arianni beasts. I am not an expert. I was . . . considered young to ride in the host. But I would say—"

"You would say too much," Lord Isladar replied, no contempt at all in the perfect winter of his expression. "And you assume that this stranger is in control of this mount?"

"I . . . do not know. I had not considered otherwise. I mark this stranger as Arianne's only because there is something about his appearance that my magic glances off. He is defended. I know the Warlord; I know the Matriarch. I recognize the power—when it is used, and it is used sparingly, of the mortal-born talents. His power is none of those things. He barely acknowledges the existence of the others. He wears no armor; he wields no weapon."

"Strange."

"But when he speaks at all, he speaks to the Warlord, or his consort."

Isladar turned at the sibilance of the last syllable. "Consort?"

"The Warlord has marked a woman of the Voyani."

"Of the Voyani? You are certain?"

Telakar shrugged. "She looks like one of the Voyani, if perhaps a bit pale. She is not tall, has no power, wields no weapon. From her voice, I would say she has a human temper; it is easily frayed."

"What does she look like?"

Telakar shrugged.

"Lord Telakar . . ."

With an imperceptible frown, the *Kialli* lord gestured, lifting his hands in the laziest and most minimal of foci. The shadows that he had so carefully hoarded were diminished as he used their edges as the raw material for an obsidian sculpture. It lacked color, and perhaps the finest of definitions, but the likeness was exact.

Jewel ATerafin.

He did not ask about Kiriel di'Ashaf. Had she been present, she would have been the first person Telakar mentioned.

Kiriel. You have lost your anchor. The fact that that anchor now traveled with two of the powers of the ancient world was less of a concern, for the moment. She was traversing the Sea of Sorrows, and in it lay the greater part of the warding magicks set by *Allasakar* himself. And if they did not devour her, they would almost certainly change her. That was the nature of mortality: change.

And death.

Even Kiriel's?

Perhaps. Perhaps even that.

"Will you send me back?"

"You would do well," Isladar said softly, "to be less transparent."

"Am I so obvious?"

"Yes. But as I said, I am not without mercy. I will not detain you in the Northern Wastes. Travel South again, to the deserts that are left of the lands you lingered in. Be my eyes, and my ears, and intervene if you deem it appropriate."

Telakar raised a perfect brow. "Intervene, Lord?"

"Indeed."

"But—"

"I send you South with only a request: inform me of all that passes between the Voyani, and the Warlord."

Telakar bowed.

When he rose, Lord Isladar was gone.

CHAPTER SEVENTEEN

At the edge of the Sea of Sorrows, she sorrowed.

Although Adam, Elena, and Nicu were to stand guard while she worked, they were at a remove; the work itself separated Margret from all that she had ever known, by becoming, in its intensity and isolation, everything she did know. It was the first step, the first step along the *Voyanne* that only Matriarchs walked.

The brush was drying. She paused a moment to stare at the pattern she had created. It was a shadow, she thought, of the work of other women, reaching backward in a line from daughter to mother, daughter to mother, but linked, always, by Arkosa's demands, Arkosa's needs.

But if it was a shadow, it *must be* a shadow cast by the true form. She had thought—had she always been so naïve?—that when the day came to take up brush, she would wear the slumbering Heart of Arkosa, and she would simply know her way through the silent words that were among the Voyani's strongest ritual incantations.

It had not started out that way.

Instead, it had started as all things in Margret's life started: with uncertainty in a time that demanded its opposite. Nothing came easily to Margret.

Her hands shook. She focused on the sharp curve of a trailing symbol. As if that could excuse her life. As if she needed excusing.

She had stood as she knew Elena must now be standing, fingers looped in the folds of her sash, head cocked to one side as she listened for the sounds of life that followed in the wake of the sun's absence. Lamps had been lit, and clothing brought; she knew that she had at most an hour before her fingers would feel the imperative of the Lady's Night. In the desert, neither Lord nor Lady had compassion for the weak or the foolish; they were winnowed. The strong survived.

She had to think about that.

The survival of the strong.

Mother.

There was no one in Margret's life who had been stronger than her mother. For all of her life—*all* of it—Evallen of Arkosa had defined strength for the Arkosan Voyani. They had lived by her whim, died by it, fought for it. They had trusted that her whim was more than self-indulgence, more than temper; that it was guided by the Lady's will.

So had Margret.

Oh, her hands, she hated that they shook. The brush was sticky with drying blood, she worked so slowly. But although she had seen these runes drawn for fifteen years, although she had traced their form in sand and earth under her mother's tutelage—and her mother's unfortunate temper—she had never truly understood what the painting of them would mean.

She cursed loudly. She reached for the lamps and drew them close, snarling at Adam when he dared to approach the wagon to offer his aid in steadying them. She had four symbols to lay down; she had completed only two.

The outer circle was the easiest. The inner circle was fairly simple, too, although the brush was not suited to a steady line. But what lay between the inner and outer circles—the words of the Lady, the words of Arkosa, the words of *home* and *homeland* that were never, ever uttered—these were hard.

They had been passed from mother to daughter. And the passage, in her writing, was complete. It was over. Evallen was truly gone.

Was grief always like this? Was she always to discover, with every task, this sensation of loss, this closing of doors? Was she to see, not her mother's presence in all of the things she had ruled so successfully in her life, but rather, the implacable fact of her absence?

It had been years since her mother had allowed her to be a child; childhood had been that space of years reserved for Adam's use, and Adam's alone. But the early years in which her mother's lap had still had space for her, and her mother's ear, sympathy, were inextricably linked to the meaning of comfort.

She had felt so safe in her mother's lap.

Now, shorn of safety the way foolish clansmen were shorn of their gold, she labored, the runes within the circle complete, the circle closing as they were finished.

She had never liked endings. She had never liked beginnings. She had desired the stability of the immutable, although she knew that not even the dead were unchanging.

The brush started at the midpoint of the circle and swept down in a bold, vertical line. There must be no hesitation in that stroke, nor in the three that followed.

She offered none, but she moved very slowly, feeling the resistance of the wood as it absorbed what she laid down: a trail of a stranger's blood. She drew the next line, a slender crescent that bisected the line at a quarter height, a shallow bowl. It was followed by a circle at the line's midpoint, and another, mirror stroke of that crescent, reversed, at the three-quarter mark.

The third symbol was complete.

She moved around the wagon until she reached the place she judged appropriate for the last of the four: the place in front of which she would stand during their journey—visible to all eyes, should any falter and require the strength of the presence of the Matriarch beneath the harsh spokes of the Lord's fiercest glare.

And they must see her. They must see this.

Without intent, she drew the last outer circle much larger than the previous three. She found it harder to keep the lines even as the size increased, and she struggled with the inner circle as penance for her choice in the outer.

But the runes and the symbols seemed at home in less confined space; they came quickly, easily, compared to the other three; their curves were much smoother, their points more pronounced. Her memory, as the night fell, had sharpened, until it was like a blade, and the forms were almost as she remembered seeing them under her mother's driven brush.

She did not have to think about spacing, about leaving enough room, or perhaps of leaving too much; they fit the space given by the two circumferences. The relief she had felt when the heat of the day had finally broken was gone;

in the passage of thirty minutes, she found herself yearning for warmth. These were the contradictions of the desert, but they suited her life.

She did not want to finish. Hands shaking now, breath visible, she did not want to write the final word. For a moment, trapped beneath open sky, trapped by open road, she felt as if she was on the verge of understanding *something*; the words that were beneath her hands seemed familiar somehow. As if she only had to concentrate, and the familiar feel of this language on her tongue would return; she might speak and give the words a life she knew they had not had since the *Voyanne* had opened to swallow the children of Arkosa.

She *did* concentrate. Her lips were quivering now; she reached for the night clothing she had forgotten to don. She had not dressed for the desert because—until this act was complete—she could not afford to surrender to it.

But she surrendered now. Her lips moved over the words that were written—as all significant words were surely written in the history of Man—in blood. She lifted her hands, as if too exhort them to feel what she felt: kinship. She was aware, for the first time, that the words here had once been spoken; that they had had a meaning that was written in blood in an entirely different manner than it had been today. It had been a way of speaking of great things. Birth, love, revenge, betrayal, death, grief, loss. It had been not only the language of the coldly arcane, of the premeditated, of the murderous—it had been a language by which an entire people had lived.

Great people.

Proud people.

Arkosa.

There were no shadows in the words. Not even the protective shadows the Lady created in the fiercest of the Lord's glares. There was, she thought, as the words came to her tongue, fierce light—brilliant, warm, a passionate display of revealed color that blended and combined into the visual nuances of a life she seldom scrutinized. All this, contained by the shape of words; words had never seemed so strong, so profoundly personal, as now, when they came from someone she had never met, and never would.

But having never met them, she felt the continuity that

came with ceremony, with tradition; she felt, as she spoke the words that she did not recognize and that she would never forget, her mother's presence, and her grandmother's presence, and beyond those shadows, the shadows of other women, standing as she stood, year in and year out, defining their lives by this act, this action, these words.

She wanted to sing them. She wanted to shout them.

She would never be certain if she had done either.

"Caitla, sleep."

The older woman snorted. Her lips moved over the syllables of something curt enough to border on a curse, but she didn't give voice to it; she had, as her husband did, a bear's voice, no matter how quietly she tried to speak, and cursing one's husband loudly on a night like this one invited the Lady's darkest attention.

"Caitla—"

She shuffled through a diminished set of words, and found a couple of curt, but perfectly serviceable ones. "You sleep."

He drew a deep breath. Loudly. Expelled it. "Caitla,' he said wearily "It's been two hours. If there was going to be a sign, we would have been informed by now. It's late. Sign or no, we'll know in the morning. If the Matriarch is alive, we'll continue." He called her Matriarch. Not Margret.

Not little 'Gret. They distanced themselves, all of them, from the child they had helped raise. From the girl they had promised to follow. Why?

Would it ease their loss, if indeed she was to be lost? No. Did anyone believe it would? Aie, that she couldn't be so certain of. People were stupid. "You sleep," she repeated, speaking slowly. "I'm going to wait for Margret."

"Caitla, this is foolish."

"So? You're not sleeping."

Stavos tilted his head to the side, and forced a smile into the corners of his eyes. "I don't sleep well without you."

She snorted again. "I don't care if you lie to me—but come up with something that shows you think I'm *smart*. Not even the children would believe that."

He was silent for a moment, and then he laughed. *That* would wake up anyone insensitive enough to be sleeping. He reached for his wife, and she chose not to move out of the way. It was cold, after all, and it wasn't going to get any warmer.

"They do fail," she said softly.

"I've never seen a failure."

"You weren't part of the Matriarch's caravan until I was foolish enough to marry you."

He laughed. In spite of herself, she felt the corner of her lips tugged upward by the sound. The sky was merciless and beautiful as it stared down on them.

"Evallen was the Matriarch."

"She wasn't always the Matriarch."

"She *was* the oldest daughter, Caitla."

"Aye, she was that. All right, all right. Maybe it's enough. But . . . her mother wasn't the oldest. Her mother was the middle girl, middle of three. We'd been winnowed by raiding, that year. Old story. There were rumors that the Heart of Arkosa had not yet found its way back to the bloodline."

"Why is it that women always cling to the worst possible piece of news?"

"Someone has to."

"Why?"

"Because in the end, if the worst possible happens, the body has to be moved. The ceremonies have to be performed. The Arkosans—those who work—have to be informed. And who will see to that, hmmm? The men? Ever?"

"The men are capable. But that's almost beside the point. Worrying won't change what has to be done. Whether or not you fret here, in the cold, or play under the blankets with your husband, the night will go as it goes, the morning come as it comes. You're old enough to be prepared for anything. You don't need this." He caught her face in his hands; both—face and hands—were lined and cracked by time and sun and wind.

She had never thought to miss the sun or the wind, but in the bitter chill of unusually still night, she did. "Stavos, don't you care at all?"

He nodded.

"Don't you worry?"

"You worry enough for ten of us, never mind two. But no, I don't worry. Margret has too much of her mother's temper, and maybe not enough of her mother's vision—but she has a will and a spirit that even Evallen was missing. Evallen was loved by few, Margret among them. But Margret is loved by many. She was never allowed to be a child; she will not be a child now."

"That's more than you've said all night."

"You made me say it." He smiled. "I'm afraid of what waits in the desert. I'm surprised that she asked us to accompany her. But tonight? One hour, two hours, three—it won't be enough to kill her."

"She won't be able to work after an hour has passed."

"She must be working," he said. "Or it would be over, and we'd be asleep. Caitla—" A light flickered yards away. "Do *none* of the women in this camp sleep?"

"Some of us try to—but who could sleep through a voice like yours?" Tamara, Evallen's sister, crossed the cold, cold sands. She wore three obvious layers of pale robe, and possibly a fourth wound loose round the skin; the fabric dyes were all pale enough the night leached them of color.

Caitla shrugged herself free of her husband's arm and met Tamara halfway; the two women hugged fiercely, clinging to each other.

And as they did, as they created this artificial, human pocket of warmth within sight of the Sea of Sorrows, the night sky vanished.

Light stretched across the width of the encampment, twisting and dancing from horizon to horizon for as far as the eyes could see.

Granted, the eyes weren't what they used to be. But they didn't have to be; although the flash of silver and gold, the brilliance of blue and the dance of fire heart—red, orange, white, and yellow—were like no other display she had ever seen as they cascaded like liquid across frozen, open sky, she could not see them clearly for long.

The tears were fierce and painful.

"Aye, you see, you see, Caitla?" Her husband's voice, quiet now, although it should have been a roar, his lips were so close to her ear—and when had he come up on her, like that? Why hadn't she noticed? "You see? You've never seen a sight so perfect, a sign so marked, and you'll miss it all because you've worried so badly the relief is killing you."

She did what any self-respecting Voyani wife would have done: she hit him. Or she tried; her sight was poor and he was damn fast. But he laughed, and she heard the younger man trapped within him; she smiled, and she felt—for a moment, the younger girl within herself.

Nicu sat across from Elena in a wind shelter that had proved mercifully unnecessary. To preserve oil, they had guttered the lamp whose light had let them find their footing, and their blankets, in the darkness; they had donned outer layers of fabric as the chill grew less and less bearable.

They had offered each other few words, and for once, Nicu seemed content to hear none; they were uninterrupted by Elena's duties to the children, to Margret, to the older women, and they were also uninterrupted by the men of whom Nicu was so boundlessly jealous.

They had even worked together, throughout the day, by Margret's side. Neither Nicu nor Elena had ever been present when the wagons were prepared; neither Elena nor Nicu had been crucial to the pilgrimage—and those that were not crucial were not present. The voyage to the Sea of Sorrows was one that was undertaken by Margret when her mother deemed it necessary, and it was that first voyage that had driven the fine edge of the wedge between the three inseparable cousins.

But tomorrow—tomorrow it would be removed.

Margret was Matriarch. Elena was Daughter. No room for Nicu in that, but for tonight he didn't mind. He was the man who would protect them both with the men under his command.

Without thinking, he reached out for Elena's hand—and then tensed as her head shot up and she met his eyes. But she did not withdraw; she did not make excuses.

Instead, she said, "Thank you for this afternoon." And her hand curled tightly around his for a moment before letting him go.

He was so surprised, he forgot to cling. He just stared at her. She was probably used to it by now.

She met his gaze, held it. In the end, it was he who looked away.

" 'Lena—"

"It's been hard," she continued, as if he hadn't spoken or looked away. "On Margret. On us. I thought we'd never be able to work like that after the—after . . ."

He lifted a hand. It was easy. Here, in this darkness, he felt only the lingering warmth of her hand, the sweet surprise of her words.

He wanted the moment to last forever. He thought, if he knew what to do, what to say, it might, and the fear crept into the moment, heightening it. He had never been good with words.

As if she could hear the words he couldn't use, she said, "It was hard on me. I'm sorry, Nicu. But—tomorrow, we have a chance to really put everything bad behind us. We have something to prove—not because we're too young, but because it's *now*, and the Lord of Night has shown his hand. The Lord of Night." Her eyes widened as she stared at a point just past his shoulder. "He's here," she said softly. "Understand what that could mean for all of us."

He didn't want to ask her what it could mean, although he had no idea what she was talking about. She had never loved stupid men, and he felt . . . stupid. "This must be something only Matriarchs know." The voice was harsher than the words.

She caught the hand she had released in both of hers. "It is something anyone who walks the *Voyanne* should know. What do we vow?" Her voice was both softer and more pointed than the voice she used in open sunlight. He listened because she held his hand and he did not want her to let go.

But he had no answer to give her. He thought the scent of sweat and cinnamon lay across her skin; that the sand and dust in her hair was like a crown. He loved that she was strong enough to do the work of men and quick enough, intemperate enough, to do the work of women.

"Nicu, are you even listening to a word I'm saying?"

In the darkness, there was no blush. "Yes."

"How am I supposed to be able to tell?"

"I'm not interrupting?"

She laughed; the sound was brief, but it was genuine. "I count that as a point. Yours. Pay attention."

"Yes, 'Lena."

"We left Arkosa for the *Voyanne* partly as penance and

partly to serve as the sentries that walked old roads. Remember?"

He did remember some of it. His mother had spoken of these tales when he was a boy, before he had developed a man's impatience with being coddled and treated like a child.

"Of the penance, we do not speak. Speak it now, Nicu. Tell me why we were forced from our homes."

He shook his head.

"Nicu, if I ask anything else of you in the next three days, and you ignore it, *but* you answer this question now, I'll forgive you. Understand?"

"Yes."

"Tell me."

"We— 'Lena, why does it matter? We're not whatever we were then."

"We're Arkosan," she said softly. And then, before he could continue, added, "And that's not true. Of all of us, Margret must be what the first Matriarch was. It's a burden—because the rest of us remember so little."

"Why do I have to answer when you already know?"

"Because I want to know that you know."

"I don't want to play this game."

"—and if you don't know, I want to tell you." Her hands did not let his escape.

"Why? It's all a story, right?"

"You know it's not, Nicu. We lost *Arkosa* because the lords of that city chose to ally themselves with the Lord of Night."

"That's not true!"

"It is not true that *all* of them served," she said softly. "But I . . . believe it *is* true. We were not, then, his mortal enemies. And although in the end we became so, we must have done great harm."

"Elena—"

"There were more than four Cities at the Fall. But only four Families survived, bloodlines and memory intact."

"And what are the clansmen?"

She spit, the reflexive reaction to such a question. "Who knows? The servants of greatness. The slaves." She shrugged. "I cannot speak for the men of the clans. I can barely speak for the Voyani. We left to wander the open road. We left to bear witness, to stand watch. I'm sure of it. And the time has come for the sentries to finally, *finally*, stand their ground, take up arms, be counted. Make a difference."

He was completely silent. Shocked. He no longer felt the warmth of her hands; they were ice or stone around his. After a long pause, he said, "And what then?" because he could think of nothing else to say.

"What then? Then," her voice was quieter now, calmer, but no less frightening, "we go *home*. But there is no home for those who cannot stand against our enemies. Do you understand?"

"Yes."

"Truly understand?"

" 'Lena, what else can I say? Yes, I understand."

Her grip tightened and then relaxed. "Good. I'm trusting you, Nicu. With my heart . . ."

"Elena . . ."

". . . and with hers."

He didn't ask what she meant. He was stupid, but not that stupid. But he felt it: anger, inadequacy. He struggled to shut them out.

And the Lady, whose desert night was so merciless, and whose geas was so terrible, offered Nicu her mercy. She washed the sky in the most pale of iridescent light. It struck Elena's face, like spokes of sunlight too weak to destroy the darkness, and he saw her forehead and her cheeks, the bones heightened by the contrast of light and shadow.

Her eyes widened, first in surprise and fear, and then in sudden comprehension. A comprehension that he did not share. She rose, the lines around lips and eyes deepening as she gave her best smile, the brightest of her multiple expressions.

"She did it! Look, Nicu—look at the sky. Margret—she did it!" There were tears, unshed, that made her face that most lovely of things: vulnerable.

Avandar was still not speaking to anyone.

His silence was not, in general, something to complain about—at home, his silence was taken as assent. Well, either that or absence. Few of Jewel's den wielded silence as a weapon, but she had learned what the quality of a silence meant in service to The Terafin.

The man who had been domicis, and who might claim that he still was, had retreated to the edge of the encampment, and she had, out of force of habit—not to mention the particular exhaustion that came with bloodletting—chosen to join him.

On the outskirts of camp, all manner of strangeness lay in wait—and it said something about her life that she could take such strangeness in stride. She was not, however, immune to it. Never that.

She felt the shadow before she saw it; the complicated darkness of tines, with their unnaturally sharp points, left marks across things that the eye couldn't clearly see. Other shadows. Other light. Her hand. Even thinking about them made her palm hurt—a reminder of what she had accepted when she had saved his life.

The stag who had once been a man, and who would never be a simple animal, came to stand beside her. He was a short arm's length to the side, but he was careful, when he chose to approach, to walk deliberately, to make *some* noise, and to stay at that distance. As if, she thought, it was she who was the wild animal, she who would be easily startled or frightened.

He dipped his antlers.

"I named Celleriant 'Killer,' " she said softly. "Because I told him his name was too pretty. I lied. It sounds too much like celery." Her smile was rueful. "But on reflection, Killer sounds too . . . sounds too much like a name I would have chosen for an eleven-year-old boy who was desperate and starving in the streets of the twenty-fifth holding. I thought I could use it. I use names like that every day. Carver. Teller. Angel.

"But he *isn't* those things. Not desperate, not eleven. Not a part of that city, that life. *I* can't even use it." She lifted a hand to touch tines. Felt a surprisingly gentle warmth emanating from the nubbled surface beneath her palm. "These are the trivial things I think about. I want to ask you what *she* thought about." Jewel raised her left wrist; around it, braided and knotted, a bracelet she had made of a keepsake: the Winter Queen's hair. These strands caught light, and the light wasn't bright; they caught her eyes as well, demanding attention she was both reluctant and eager to give. "I want to ask, but I don't want to know."

He did not answer. She suspected that he never would.

"I was worried about Celleriant. But it occurs to me that I never even asked you your name."

He said nothing. She met his eyes, because that was the only easy way to speak to him. They were large, round, unblinking—as different from her own as eyes could be that still saw.

"Did you know Avandar?"

The stag's gaze was unblinking.

"Is that a yes, a no, or a none-of-your-business?"

Yes. She felt, rather than heard, amusement. *I knew Viandaran.*

She loved the sound of his voice, even though she couldn't hear it. She wondered why she felt so differently about Avandar's. Maybe because she knew too much about his past. "Did he know you?"

The massive antlers swayed a moment, side to side.

"Were you the Winter King in your time?"

He became absolutely still. Absolutely. She thought that the antler beneath her hand had been transformed into stone by the simple question.

"I'm sorry. I won't ask that again. I . . . met the Winter King." She lapsed into an awkward silence as her gaze strayed toward the horizon and back. "But—"

The cold was broken by the clarity of distant amusement; she realized that this man thought of her as a child. "I'm sorry. I have to ask—but I can't force you to answer. Did it change you?"

Very, very carefully, he bowed his great head and slid the side of the nearest antler across her upturned cheek.

She had the grace to blush. "I mean—I meant—did it change who you were, not what you look like. Are. Never mind, it was a stupid question."

He nodded. But he stood by her side in the darkness.

She could see Celleriant against the barren horizon, a shadow with pale hair. The Arianni lord did not speak. He did not join them. He stood, staring into the night sky, as if counting stars.

It seemed to Jewel, as she stared at his profile, that there were two men trapped within it; the one, a stranger, much as Kallandras was a stranger, caught in the midst of the Voyani ceremonies, the other—the other someone who belonged in the lee of the Winter Queen.

"He would have killed me without even noticing who I was," she said quietly.

She turned, lifting her gaze deliberately, carrying it across the landscape and dropping it upon Avandar's turned back, aware that he was aware of her. "Avandar would have killed me. He probably would have enjoyed it less. If he noticed at all.

"I'd like to think you would have been different. But I can't."

"Because you are wise."

"And you," she said, without turning in the direction of the familiar voice, "are eavesdropping."

"Guilty as charged, ATerafin. Am I to be banished or forgiven?"

"Forgiven, and you knew that or you wouldn't have announced yourself." She smiled as Kallandras of Senniel College took his place beside her. She was wrapped in blankets, except for the hand that rested against the stag; he was dressed as Celleriant was dressed.

"Have you come to watch the lights?"

"Lights?"

She frowned. "I'm not sure why I just said that."

"Ah. Perhaps you see more clearly than I." The irony in his tone was not lost on her. "With your permission, I would like to speak with Lord Celleriant."

"You don't need my permission."

"No. But he does."

"Pardon?"

"He does. He is trapped here; he has little understanding of humanity, of the minutiae of mortal existence. I know that he is part of the Wild Hunt, the Winter Hunt, and as such is worthy of both fear and wrath—but you must understand, who might never see it, that he is also part of the Summer Court. The world once revolved around its seasons to a much greater extent than you can know now. He is of that time."

"Evayne told you this."

"Evayne," he said softly, "has forced me to bear witness to much in my life."

"If he needs it, yes, you have it. But—"

"But?" Light, light word.

She shook her head. As if that were release or dismissal, he left her. She watched the Northern bard traverse the cracked, cold ground that separated her from Celleriant.

The Arianni lord stirred and lifted his gaze from the solitary sky, dropping it, slowly, to the waiting bard. She could not see his expression; she could not see Kallandras' face at all. But she had a sudden fleeting impression that these two were somehow kin, that they shared some secret or some pain that she had never shared—and with the Mother's blessing, never would.

It came to her, in the darkness of this lonely night, that Kallandras would—as Celleriant, as Avandar, as the stag whose warmth was so compelling in the chill night air—kill her with just as little regret if it served his purpose or his cause.

But the stag said, in that voice she found so compelling, *No. That was true, I think, of all of us, but I would not kill you now.*

No?

No. You are, as you suspect, weak. Avandar is correct in that regard; were you born in the time that birthed him, or the time that birthed me, you would have perished. Or so it appeared; you are far too straightforward; you say too much. But . . . .

But?

He was amused again, but there was about the amusement an undercurrent of rue. *But even in my day, or his, no one held the road against the Winter Queen who did not have, or did not understand, power.*

She was silent.

His amusement deepened. *You don't find this a comfort.*

I find the sound of your voice a comfort. I don't know why. But no—I don't find your words comforting. You didn't expect me to.

No.

I'm cold.

I know. He stepped toward her. *I never grow cold. I was . . . changed . . . for the Winter, and it is the Winter I serve. Sit with me, and you will feel the cold only when you desire it.*

Thank you, she told him, but she was silent, waiting.

Waiting, face upturned.

Because there were some things you didn't watch from a position of comfort.

The lights that took the sky scattered the simpler light shed by stars; it was grand and glorious, a thing of sweeping breadth, of scintillating color. There, green, an emerald the mines could never contain or never release; beyond it, an opalescent white and black; there the pale gold of dream's fire.

But she was aware that no matter how beautiful these fires, no matter how compelling, how breathtaking, no matter how significant—and they were significant, and she *knew*, the instant she saw them, what they signified—they were cold as ice, or colder; they were above life and the painful loyalties that life, in and of itself, commanded.

Lord Ishavriel saw the same lights, although their truth was no revelation; it was vaguely comforting.

He had been forced to retreat well beyond the limits of the tiny Voyani encampment in the late afternoon when he had sensed the presence of binding magic. At the time, the retreat had been an act of caution, no more; he was now grateful for the warning of the earlier spell, although he was frustrated in all attempts to pinpoint its source.

But the warding done in the afternoon was not a spell that could be cast without power or blood. He could taste the miasma of the combination in the air as it lingered. The wind mocked him.

There *was* no power within these pathetic mortals; he would have bet much on it. It wounded his pride to be proved wrong, although he had not, in the end, advanced his belief in a way that could be used against him.

The boy he had been toying with was nowhere to be found, and this, too, was annoying; the Voyani were clearly about to embark upon their voyage into the desert, and he required time to reaffirm the undercurrent of his influence. He had assumed, when the Voyani took their hasty leave of the Tor Leonne, that the trek into the vast deserts would begin immediately—and judging by the reaction of the Voyani themselves, this was not without cause. But he had been forced to linger, like any pathetic creature, in the fringes of the scrub, waiting, biding his time.

The problem with mortality, with the dealings of the merely mortal, was always time. Time became an issue. And those whose province was—no matter how distasteful—the mortal realm, were likewise trapped. Ishavriel, whose sense of awareness was in every way superior to those he now watched, was aware of its passage in excruciating detail; the lengthening of shadows cast by ugly, minimal plants, the slow movement of sun—and moon—across the barren sky, the aging of plants, the death of small insects, the movement of water beneath the plain.

But those were preferable to this: the cleansing fires.

The Lord, he thought, for the first time in centuries, *was wise. These creatures are not entirely denuded; they have some spark that might, in the end, be a threat.*

That spark was above them all.

He thought the lights would dim and fade quickly. But they remained, raiment to night sky and pale, prickly stars, until he understood that his task was not so easy as he had first assumed. He felt not anger but a strange elation.

For it had been millennia since he had seen a fire dance of this length, this brilliance, this duration.

Indeed, the Lord was wise, he thought, as he summoned the winds and ordered them, in as much as they could be ordered, to carry him away from the interference of the Voyani magicks. *For the desert itself was not the only guardian he set against the coming of his ancient enemies.*

There was a risk. The old powers slumbered uneasily, their dreams and nightmares the totality of their world, and one who would waken the sleeper—if he could—had to be strong indeed to withstand the force of that awakening.

Lord Ishavriel was *Kialli*; he was drawn to wild power because in its raw form, it had a beauty that the precise order of the gods and their creations could never contain.

Lord Telakar was also *Kialli*. But when the lights reigned in the skies, he watched, forgetting all other duties, all other obligations. While the shadows swallowed Isladar's rival, the light swallowed his servant; they were bound by the magic they had witnessed, in ways that defined them.

Telakar could *feel* the power. If he reached out with the

merest tendril of his own, he knew he would have to fight it, or be consumed—and he was not completely certain that he would win such a battle.

It had been years since he had felt such uncertainty. Years, and the decision that defined his existence lay between that time and this.

The world unfolding before him was not the world he had been summoned to; not the world he had returned to serve. He watched it, fascinated, entranced.

The desert had been such a bitter blow. He had traversed it, edge to edge, searching; denying by action the despair, the bitterness, of loss. But his search availed nothing; the sand left no markers by which to find even the grave of the strangest beauty that had come, not from the wilderness, not from the gods, not from the Firstborn—but from the most fragile of their thinking creations.

They are lost, he was told.

And he had come to believe it, in so short a time—because if they were not lost, these scions of inexplicable power, they would surely rule.

He repented of his lack of faith now. But with joy, with an exultant glory that in the end made a gleeful, a youthful, mockery of repentance. It was here. He felt it: the power of the Cities of Man.

It did not occur to him, until after the lights had at last bled from the sky, to wonder if Lord Isladar already knew what he had discovered this night.

In the darkness that followed the lights, two women sat alone. Two men stood waiting in the cold beyond the periphery of their vision; beyond their awareness. They waited, these two; they had become good at waiting, although for different reasons. The women were not interrupted for a long time, perhaps for the better, perhaps not; privacy and isolation are two sides of the same coin.

Serra Diora di'Marano saw, in the lights, not the glow of foreign magery, not the rim of the Sea of Sorrows, but the end, in truth, of the Festival of the Moon. And not the Festival that had passed in the Tor Leonne scant days ago, but a Festival that she had visited, time and again, in the halls of memory.

She felt, in the ice of a desert wind blowing across the

lifeless sands, the warmth of her father's arms, the feel of his shoulders beneath her thighs when she, four years old and far too small, had been borne aloft that she might be those few precious feet closer to heaven.

There was no heaven in the South, but in the North, the heavens were promised to those who had led a life she could not conceive of, did not understand—but desired, as only the naïve could desire a thing.

She could say good-bye a hundred times. She regretted none of them. But in the lights, in the deceptions and the honesties that came with night, she remembered only who she had been.

She knew—who better?—that all safety, even her own, even then, was illusory. That the world of a child was simply the world seen through the narrowest of slits, the vantage chosen so that the blood that flowed, flowed above or beneath their field of vision. She knew that the protection promised made of promises both a mockery and a fervent prayer.

She knew. She could hear the sound of her son's death; a simple sound. No screaming, no struggle.

The lights across the sky, the gift of the mages to the festival witnessed by a four-year-old girl, the life her father had chosen afterward, the death he had given . . . they came, and they went, and in the darkness, the Serra Diora di'Marano placed her hands in her lap, and bowed her perfect head, and not even the ice she felt as she breathed could force her to break that perfect posture.

She was alone.

She was waiting.

She knew how to wait. She had been raised to wait upon the whim of others forever. Here, at desert's edge, she found herself.

Margret of Arkosa was alone.

The warmth of the song of Arkosa had deserted her. She had held onto it for as long as she could—and then, when she understood what the silence entailed, held it longer, held it by the edge of a throat that was raw with the effort of making sound, rough with the demands of breath, of breathing in the desert night.

She had passed beyond thought; beyond intent. The night

was not the Lady's; it was simply darkness, the vast emptiness that existed when she closed her eyes and faced the responsibility of Arkosa . . . alone. Natural, then, to want to fill it. Natural, to grab at anything that passed between one's fingers, to pull it in, to swallow it.

But in the end, she could hold onto *nothing*.

Evallen had taught her that.

The song failed her.

Bereft of Arkosa, but not the responsibility of it, she sat, alone, her knees beneath her chin, her arms wrapped around her shins, her body shuddering with a terrible exhaustion. She was dimly aware that someone was waiting, but she did not want to call him.

She could not afford to ask for help.

Because she knew who he was, and she knew that the darkness that waited was something she would die before she asked him to face.

But Adam came to her anyway.

She sat shivering with cold and shuddering with the fear of failure, with the absolute certainty that her mother, with these words, was gone from the wagon that had been their truest home—home, that forbidden, laughable word, *how could she desire it*?—and he drew from hands that were now too numb to hold them, the wide brush and the slender brush that were used in the painting of the Matriarch's wagon. She murmured something, but he didn't choose to hear it, and although she should have smacked him, she was tired enough that she let *him* take the brushes that should have gone to Elena to clean and store away.

In truth, she wasn't certain where Elena was. She was dimly aware—if she concentrated—that Elena had backed away from the wagons to let her work in peace; that Nicu had trailed after her cousin like clingy shadow. She would have to talk to him about that, but he had been so helpful in the afternoon, they had worked so well together, that she could almost forget anything bad had happened between them.

And she wanted to let go of that past completely.

Which left her with Adam.

He brought her a blanket and a hat, and then when she sat in the darkness staring at them numbly, he brought her a soft, soft cloth and in silence, he wiped her cheeks. It was a good idea. The night air was cold. The ghost of her breath hung in clouds before her face, and between those clouds, Adam's hands were callused but gentle in a way that almost defined strength.

She lifted a hand, caught his, although her grip was no stronger than a baby's. She had often taken comfort from his youth, from the fact that he was so unlike the other Voyani men; the wild, earnest son of Evallen of Arkosa. She did not wish to lose that.

But he said nothing. Instead, he turned away from where she sat, in self-imposed exile, and handed her a deep bowl. Food. It was warm, but it would cool quickly.

Scent rose in stillness; cinnamon, nutmeg, milk, and the wild oats that the Voyani prized so highly as a sign of the Lady's favor. She held it between her hands, breathing deeply, and thinking of the desert nights during which she had held such a bowl at her mother's side. The daughter of the Matriarch. The daughter.

She did not want to be fed. She did not want to be fed by her baby brother. She did not want to be outside, alone, at wagon's side, waiting for the gray between night and day during which she would finally begin this first terrible voyage.

But she could not speak to deny any of these fates. When she groped for words, she would find them, but she would find the wrong ones, and they would say nothing of what she meant. That was the Arkosan way.

"Where's—where's 'Lena?" Her hands were stiff; her fingers sore; the space between the blades of her shoulders uncomfortably rigid.

He shrugged. After a moment, he spoke. "With Nicu, I think."

She nodded. "It's cold."

He looked right at her. "Yes. It's cold."

"Did you eat?"

He nodded. "You eat."

Silence. She groped for words, struggled with a spoon instead. Eating was surprisingly difficult, given how hungry she was.

Adam stood, aware of the awkwardness of the words she offered—and the words she withheld.

I am just like my mother, she thought bitterly. All the things withheld. All the pain given expression only by anger. But Adam was impervious to things withheld; he suspected no cruelty, no emotional manipulation; he accepted things as they were, now, and did not look often to the past or the future. And he was happy.

Why have I never been able to be you? You never cared what Momma thought, and she thought of nothing but you; I always cared, and she gave me a stranger with the Heart of Arkosa.

Matriarch's daughter, she heard the ghost of her mother say. A Matriarch's daughter shouldn't be so needy. Adam only has to be strong enough to bear the burden of you—and you won't be much of a burden. You have to be strong enough to bear the burden of the others.

Why? Why can't they bear their own burdens?

Her cheek remembered her mother's angry reply.

Adam waited, quietly, looking at symbols that were black in the darkness, but still discernible. He lifted a hand. His fingers hovered above painted wood, but they offered no indignity to her crude symbols; he knew that the price for touching them was high.

"You can't stay here," she told him, the spoon now ice between her lips. "It's my vigil. It's my watch. You have to join the others."

He said nothing. The moon moved.

"Adam—it's the Matriarch's duty. No sleep tonight, no sleep for me. Just the Lady at her darkest and coldest." She laughed, but the laugh was a movement of air, and a quiet, uncomfortable silence followed. "Do you remember the stories?"

He nodded.

"Do you think they're true?"

He shrugged. Raised his face to the night sky. Lowered it. She wondered what had passed between his silent profile and the Lady's icy bright silver. Silver, she thought; the color of so many ills. Coin. Steel. Age.

This was her vigil. This, the blood of strangers, the cold of the desert night. In stories, in the stories of the old lineage, women died waiting for the Lady's favor or permission. They were unmourned, passed by, their rule given over to their sisters—or cousins. There was no mercy granted to the women who would be Matriarch. Not here. Not at the edge of the Sea of Sorrows.

"Adam?"

He nodded.

"Did Momma ever tell you about the City?"

He turned to her then, his eyes wide and unblinking, the darkness in them kin to the night sky above. "You were the Matriarch's daughter. Not me."

Answer enough.

"Did she tell you what she had to do? Did she tell you anything at all?"

" 'Gret," he said, more softly, "maybe it's better not to speak. The Lady listens."

He was right. She insulted her mother's memory by even suggesting that her mother might have confided in anyone else. Ever. But she added, "She didn't tell you anything?"

His smile was brief. "You never, ever give up. Had I been a girl, had I been the oldest, I would have stepped aside for you. You *are* Momma's daughter."

"You can't stay."

When he spoke, though, his words were not the ones she'd expected. His face was in profile, his fingers, shaking slightly, still hovered above what she had labored for hours on: the sigils of Arkosa.

"She's really gone, isn't she?"

Margret set the spoon down. She looked, truly looked, at her brother's face, and she saw the tears that he had wiped from hers glistening in the moonlight the Lady cast across his own dark skin.

She nodded. She couldn't speak. He didn't expect her to. She couldn't reach out to touch him either.

But when he opened his arms, she opened hers, and they clung a moment, offering and asking for comfort in the mixed way that children do.

Evallen's children.

"You can't stay," she told him later.

"I know."

The moon moved. She was aware of its shift in position. "You can't stay."

"I know, 'Gret."

She tightened her arms, the movement brief and fierce. "You can't stay."

He laughed. "Say a thing three times and it's true?"

"Or dream it. Or do it. Adam—" She let him go. He let her go. The inside of her arms and the front of her chest felt the cold as a sudden shock when he stepped back. All of life was like that. You could get too used to the warmth and it left you unprepared.

But without warmth, what was the point?

"You know what happens if I don't pass this test."

He rose. "I know. It's weird, 'Gret. You aren't old enough or mean enough to be Matriarch."

"I'll work on the mean."

He laughed. "And time will take care of the old. 'Gret—"

"Go *away*, Adam."

"I'll see you in the morning."

"You'll be sleeping in the morning. I'll probably see you first and throw you off the bedroll."

He laughed again. She wanted him to go on laughing. She loved the sound. But if she were honest, she'd probably love any sound that wasn't her own voice.

And that would be bad.

She watched him leave—no rules against that—thinking that he wasn't as young as he used to be. Wondering how the years would twist him, how the wind would scour him with its voice of sand.

How the wind would scour her.

All the voices were silent; even the sound of his steps died into stillness. She was alone.

And it was *so cold.*

Ramdan approached. He placed a cloak, a heavy rough cloak, colors mercifully hidden in the night, around her shoulders; it was warm. She wondered if it had come from his own shoulders, but she did not ask—she never asked. His role was to serve; hers was to accept. They had taken a fierce pride in their ability to live up to the expectations that the Serra Teresa had of them. The Serra's flight from her own duties could not deprive them of that pride.

The light had died; the stillness and the darkness reigned. The Serra listened for a long, long time, her hands frozen to her lap, her body absorbing the warmth of the body of this most trusted seraf.

He walked away; she heard his steps retreat. But she knew he would not leave. She had not yet retired for the evening; he could not retire before her. He was, she thought idly, old now. He had a handful of years left before he was too bent, too tired, to perform as perfectly as he did this night—or any other.

But she did not rise; did not grant him the mercy of her sleep. Not tonight. She simply watched the black sky in a numb silence until he came again.

He brought her samisen. She knew she should not play it; knew that she should not have brought it here, where the air was so dry, the sun so hot, the night so cold. The strings had already shown a tendency to lose the truth of their notes, and she spent much time coaxing them into tune. She knew that she would not take this instrument into the desert with her. She would send it North, with the handful of men who now waited the Matriarch's command to return to the children.

She hesitated for just a moment, and then, fingers aching with bitter cold, she began to play.

Not since she was three years old, a child in the shadow of her accomplished aunt, had she struggled with the movement of her fingers. The cold made them stiff and slow.

She almost gave up; the sound of the mistimed notes was unpleasant. But this, too, was her farewell, and she understood that what she did not take from this moment of privacy, she would not have again.

She tried three different songs, but the cold had numbed her hands sufficiently that she could not play them. She chose, at last, simplicity.

A cradle song.

The sun has gone down, has gone down, my child . . .

Margret heard the music.

As she struggled to hold on to wakefulness, she was offered the blessed, the familiar, comfort of sleep; the promise of as watchful an eye as the Lady allowed.

She did not recognize the voice—if the voice was not a phantasm born of exhaustion and cold—but it was as beautiful as the lights had been, perhaps more so because it was a thing outside of herself; she could be aware of it, could listen passively, could find the places in the pause between word and note into which she could fit her own memories.

She did not want the song to end, although she knew how it ended. And in the end, she did not hear the last attenuated note.

CHAPTER EIGHTEEN

6th of Misteral, 427 AA
Sea of Sorrows

For someone who had grown up in a city ringed with the white beaches of the Empire, the desert was only nominally composed of sand; it stretched out in a cracked, dusted layer as far as the eye could see; it had none of the soft give that rock and wave had forced upon the shores of the ocean.

The horizon was blurred and indistinct although the sky was clear. The shadows cast against the foot of the desert were long and slender, no matter the shape of the caster; Jewel noted these things in passing, aware as always of contrasts.

The Sea of Sorrows waited.

"Jewel?"

"Hmmm?"

Avandar's frown was brief. Familiar.

"Sorry. I wasn't listening."

She adjusted the heavy cloth that ringed her face in two pieces, one hanging from forehead to just past her brows and the other, from either side of the long cowl that came to the edge of cheekbones, to cover nose and mouth. She had been told that it was necessary to protect the face from the sudden gusts of wind that, in the Sea of Sorrows, were broken by nothing: no buildings, no shelter, no trees, few hills. Dry open tunnels, the corpses of riverbeds in which water and all its forms of life had once run, were occasionally used by the Voyani as shelter—but only when the storms themselves were composed of wind and sand. They spoke of those storms, in this place, the way people of a certain age spoke of demons in the hundred holdings.

Demons. The hundred holdings. Home. She was likely to see only one of these things in the desert.

"Jewel," Avandar said again.

And rain?

When it rained, when the storms were strong beyond the harbor, the squalls unpredictable and sudden, men died in any sea. Even this one.

Her fingers were itching, as was her chin; she felt uncomfortably caged by her clothing. But she was willing to acknowledge the practical. She forced her hands to her sides. Were it not for her height—which the addition of sturdy boots and funny headgear did nothing to change—she would have looked like any of the other Voyani; the differences between gender were lost to fabric in almost every case. Where the woman in question was tall—like Elena—she could stand beside the men and be counted one of them; the women wore long daggers or swords just as easily as the men.

The exception proved the rule: the Serra Diora di'Marano wore desert robes with an ease and a grace of movement that Jewel was certain she would retain even if she were robbed of mobility by something as cumbersome as a broken limb. She was followed by a perfect, silent shadow, dressed in the same desert robes; he was taller than she, but slender and graceful as well. His presence underscored the differences between the life of his mistress and the life of the Arkosans among whom she found herself, and if she did not acknowledge him in any obvious way, his presence was accusation enough.

Kallandras of Senniel College was the only man present who had elected to reveal his face to the clear sight of the Lord. The roots of his hair had, over the course of five days, become pale as sun on water; he looked like he was molting. The dyes he had used to give himself the appearance of a lowborn Southern clansman were no longer necessary, and the visible transition between the deceptive and the natural did not seem to trouble him at all.

He bowed, and bowed low, when the Serra Diora approached. She, in her turn, offered him the obeisance that a highborn clanswoman might, when she was in a tightly packed room and was not given the space in which to kneel or sit with grace.

But she spoke; he listened. After a moment, he turned from her, and two men, dressed in the shirt and pants of the more forgiving road, appeared. Kallandras spoke at length; the men returned words that were much shorter; their lips hardly moved. The bard smiled, spoke again, matching their brevity. Something about the discussion was familiar, although it took Jewel a moment to realize that they were, in fact, negotiating.

At the edge of the Sea of Sorrows, the Voyani were haggling. It seemed fitting.

In the end, they agreed to whatever it was he offered; no money appeared to change hands, but the Serra Diora, standing apart from the argument until its close, took from her robes a long case. She handed it to the men without even a trace of hesitation, and they carried it away with them.

In ones and twos, the men and women dressed for the open road that would lead to life, rather than the dry, hard barrens of the Sea of Sorrows, were taken by it—or perhaps returned to it. The wagons had already been winnowed to a handful—two, to be precise—but the Arkosan guard was not willing to leave until the Matriarch did, even though it became clear they were going in opposite directions.

All this, Jewel noticed in a series of broken glances. Her attention came back, time and again, to the piercing clarity of sky.

"Where is the Matriarch?"

No one had an answer.

The dawn had come quickly, invoking colors that demanded attention from the newly wakened. Ice gave way to a lovely, cool warmth.

"Enjoy it," Avandar said quietly. "It will not last. That is the key to the desert. Nothing lasts."

"And nothing changes," she said.

"And nothing changes." He stared out at the Sea of Sorrows for a long time. "That is the essence of eternity."

"Sounds like it gets pretty boring."

"It wears on one," he replied softly.

"Only if one was born mortal," another voice said.

Avandar did not so much as raise a brow—or at least not on the side of his face that Jewel could see; his profile had not shifted at all.

Lord Celleriant had moved, in complete silence, to stand beside him.

"Or if one has a tremendous capacity to perform the same act over and over again with minute variations and somehow find it compelling."

"Celleriant," Jewel said softly, "do you *know* how to make noise?"

He stepped around Avandar and turned to face her fully—and she wondered, for perhaps the first time, if his near invisibility was an act of mercy. He was beautiful, enough so that the act of absorbing the impression he made distracted her from simple things. Breath. Breathing. His skin was perfect; he had weathered the days beneath the open sky with a slight contempt for the elements, and they had passed him by; there was no hint of sun or wind across the perfect ivory of his skin.

"I . . . know how to be heard," he said, reminding her that she had asked a question.

She flushed. Recovered quickly. "You aren't wearing desert robes."

He shrugged. "If you command it, I will wear them—but they are not necessary. It is only heat."

"Avandar—"

"The Warlord does not require the robes; he wears them because he is lazy and he does not wish to be marked as different."

"Thank you, Lord Celleriant," Avandar said dryly. "Had they brought robes for him, I would have counseled their use. They did not—and I would counsel against their request."

"Why?"

"It's the desert," he said, speaking softly again, but with just the hint of an edge to the words. "The only contingencies the Voyani allow for are those that involve life or death. I do not believe that Tamara or Elena think Celleriant requires protection from the Lord, and to waste the time and effort to clothe him—at perhaps the expense of someone else who is not immediately obvious—would be impolitic."

Jewel nodded.

She might have said more, but the passing clouds distracted her; they cast a very dark shadow against the ground, and that shadow seemed to grow.

And she had seen no clouds in the perfectly crisp morning sky. She glanced up, her face turned toward the answer to the question she had asked much earlier.

The Matriarch was *here*.

Or rather, there, in the sky above, separated from the hard, harsh ground by fifteen feet of air. She stood at the bow of what appeared to be a squat, overbalanced ship. And that ship, rudderless, rested in the currents of the sky, the upward curve of its smooth, rounded belly exposed to those below.

She had seen it before. But it had borne wheels that had made it mundane; the home of the Arkosan Matriarch.

Lord Celleriant said, "So." No more.

Avandar said nothing. But around them, in ones and twos, the Arkosans found their knees, found their silences, found their gestures—used so rarely it should have taken them more time—of respect and obeisance.

The Matriarch.

The Matriarch has come.

She saw the flash of steel as, men and women, they drew blades. Some drew daggers, some drew swords, some drew the knives that they used for simple tasks like eating and separating plants from their longer roots. They exposed their skin to sun and sky, and then they exposed more: the blood that bound them to Arkosa, that made them Arkosan.

Jewel was impressed.

Very few of the men—or women—blanched or hesitated. Jewel had cut herself a time or two, and she vastly preferred to do it by accident in a kitchen than to do it deliberately, as a signature to an oath or a vow.

She did not do it now.

Nor did Avandar, nor Celleriant.

She wondered, idly, what would have happened had she chosen to join the Arkosans.

I would have stopped you, Avandar replied, in the silence hallowed by blood and the implacable faith of the Arkosans as they offered this Matriarch, for the first time, the price of passage into the Sea of Sorrows. *As I have always attempted to stop you from impulses which endanger your life.*

This is the heart of Arkosa, he continued, his voice an uncomfortable intrusion. *There is power invoked by the Matriarch, and power accepted and offered by her kin. The Voyani were always capable of blood magic. But today . . . today it is strong.*

Watch, Jewel. The Havallan Matriarch lifts neither head nor hand.

It was true. Yollana stood, legs stiff, hands gripping the gnarled tops of two walking canes. No one offered her aid, but Jewel didn't blame them; even at a distance, Yollana's expression said clearly, *don't touch*.

And don't approach, don't speak to, don't look at as well. Yollana never seemed friendly—Jewel suspected it was impossible for a Matriarch *to* seem friendly. She bore witness, this old woman, a grim, terrible witness to the birth of a new Matriarch.

Yes, a birth.

Watching the lines of the older woman's sun-cracked, windburned face, Jewel understood then that the flight of the wagon was critical, but it was not the end; Yollana of Havalla watched like a midwife waiting for a newborn babe to draw breath and prove that it is viable outside of the mother who has been its nurture and sustenance.

"Arkosa!" Margret shouted, in a voice that filled the flat lands. She gestured, and a man joined her at the prow of this strange ship: her brother.

She gestured, her hands spread wide, like the pinions of a bird who, in triumph, has taken its first flight. The ship began to descend, its shadow growing smaller and darker as it approached the sand. But it did not land. Instead, it stopped three feet aboveground.

"Rise. We've little time to waste—the Sea of Sorrows is waiting."

They rose at her command, and the silence of respect and obedience gave way at once—as if being shed—to both jubilation and the no-nonsense pragmatism of people who have known what their work will be, and have been waiting only the word of their overseer to start it. They had robed themselves for the desert, and as Margret brought the ship to ground—or as close to ground as it would come—the Arkosans began to appear with the large, clay jugs that housed water. Among the Voyani present, there was no liquid stronger than water in any abundance; in the desert, wine was for the Lady, and the Lady alone.

A plank was placed between ground and floating wagon, and the jugs were cajoled, by muscle and timing, up that precarious walkway.

Gripping the rail of the ship, Margret vaulted easily over its side. She landed on her feet, bending into her knees to absorb impact. Adam joined her, but he landed with an obvious relief that made one or two of the older women smile.

They joined the line of men and women who worked with such speed and efficiency, and in scant minutes, the wagon housed the water that the journey would require. But not the food.

Margret smiled. 'Lena!"

Elena, daughter in waiting, grunted from beneath the last of the heavy containers. The sound passed for a yes.

"Is your wagon ready?"

She nodded again, but she didn't look happy about it.

Margret's smile was not calculated to comfort. "Then bring it to bear, cousin. We travel together."

"I understand," Elena said, grunting between syllables as she set the jug between her feet, "why you used to swear you'd never ride when you didn't have to."

"You can thank me for my generosity."

"Exactly what generosity are you talking about?"

"That information," her cousin replied with mock sweetness. "You got it for free. Now get moving! We're wasting the dawn!"

The Matriarch's Daughter, her red hair confined by the heavy folds of desert hood, her natural flamboyance restrained by the gravity—and the practicality—of the moment, returned in a much less flashy way than the Matriarch had. She stood at the prow of the body of a smaller wagon, one that had also been designed for this strange flight; the underside of the cab was smooth and rounded, like a squat, ugly boat; the axles along which large wheels normally rested had been somehow folded into that surface, and subsumed by it.

But although this airship flew, it flew close to the ground;

the shadow it cast was not distorted by distance. It was not heralded; it provoked no letting of blood, no fervent whisper of vows. It was practical, or as practical as a magic of this nature could be.

I wonder, Jewel thought, as she watched Elena's unusually stiff expression, *if she hates heights half as much as I do.*

And then, because she was a merchant, *What would it cost to get a mage to do this back home?*

"More," Avandar replied, as if reading her thoughts—and he probably was—"than you could possibly pay. There is a reason that magic is used sparingly."

"The mages created the glowstone lamps," she snapped. "And they maintain the wells in the hundred holdings."

"Indeed. But the glowstones are empowered in such a way that they catch the light of day and extend it when the light is gone. It is . . . something that occurs, at times, in nature. These flights—in the heart of the Sea of Sorrows—are vastly more costly."

"Could it be done?"

"Oh, yes. But not in a way that would be cost-effective. The Ten could afford it, if they wished to grandstand. *And* if they received the appropriate permits and writs to allow for such a public display of magic. Remember where we are, Jewel. And remember that the Voyani do not choose to travel on the *Voyanne* in this fashion when they are anywhere else but here."

"Why here?"

His smile was slightly grim. Or, Jewel amended, grimmer than usual; he had the slightest and least friendly of smiles to begin with. "You have never traveled in the open desert," he said.

"He speaks truth."

Jewel jumped about two feet into the air; she would have gone higher, but the clothing she found so uncomfortable acted as ballast. When she landed, she turned to face Yollana of the Havalla Voyani. The old woman had moved quickly and quietly, an ability that Jewel would have bet against. With her own money.

"But even so, he does not understand the *Voyanne.*"

"Does anyone?" Avandar questioned softly.

"Not really." The old woman shrugged. "But the closest one comes to understanding is to walk it." She lifted a hobbled foot, and Jewel wondered, seeing momentary pain contort the muscles of Yollana's face in a passing ripple, if that foot would ever recover. "And you don't walk in the air."

"Does Havalla have its own custom?"

"Do you mean, does Havalla have such a ship, does the Matriarch of Havalla make such a flight?"

Jewel didn't answer.

After a stretched silence, the old woman cracked a smile. "Wise, this young one," she said to Avandar.

Avandar shrugged. "Wise enough not to press the question, but not wise enough not to ask it."

"Take what age offers, and wait for the rest."

"If she survives."

"If." The old woman laughed. "Havalla has its own custom," she said, her voice cracking. "And its own time. And I won't be insulted that you asked, although you must know—stranger or distant bearer of Voyani blood—that the Matriarchs do not speak of their rituals to anyone but their heirs and their chosen."

Jewel nodded. "But you go with us."

"If I did not go with you, I would be far, far away before the rituals commenced. There is a saying, taught me by that pretty, pretty bard of yours." She nodded in the direction of the only unhooded man in the group. "It comes from the Western Kingdoms, so he says, but it could come with ease from the Southern clans. No country is at peace when it harbors more than one man who remembers the weight of the crown upon his brow."

"You have the advantage of not being men."

The woman's laugh was a dry, brief bark. "And that is why I am here, daughter of deserters. But that is not so great an advantage. People are people; even these, the handpicked of the Arkosans."

"Are they?"

"Are they?"

"Handpicked."

"They are the closest of the blood relatives. There is no tie stronger."

"I've seen how some families work. There are certainly ties that are just as binding."

"Spoken like a Northerner."

With not a little pride, Jewel lifted her hand; against skin that had darkened with sun, the glint of gold was both heavy and profoundly comforting. "Yes. A governing member of one of The Ten. Chosen by merit, and not by an accident of birth."

"Let me offer you Voyani wisdom, child. Among people of power, there are no accidents. What works in the cold lands of the North works in the North; in the South, both leading the way into the desert and escaping it, there is only the *Voyanne*. You will understand its harshness better at the end of this journey. If you survive it."

"And you, Yollana?"

The old woman's smile was gone. Her face was like the sand that stretched before them as far as the eye could see. "This is not the first time that I have traveled with a caravan that is not my own. We are not a people who naturally hoard information or emotion. We speak as we think, and we care openly and fiercely. We are not afraid of weakness.

"But I do not speak of what I have seen when the Voyani return to the desert. Ask me why I tell you this, when the blood of deserters runs in your veins. Ask me, Jewel of this Northern House that binds you with gold and power."

"Why are you telling me this?" The question was not perfunctory; it was punctuated by a deeply felt curiosity.

"Because you have eyes that see, and you will walk roads that are harsher than the *Voyanne* before you are allowed to rest. If you are allowed to rest at all."

Jewel felt the chill of shadow cross her face, although the sun was high and the sky was clear. An old woman could cast just such a shadow, if she were born to the sight. "Hardship is not usually reason enough for the Voyani to be so open with strangers."

"No," Yollana agreed, as amiably as Jewel had yet seen her. But she did not offer further words.

When the sun completely crested the horizon, the Voyani were gone. The evidence of their passing had already been taken by wind.

One *Kialli* lord had preceded them into the cracked, barren plains; one followed. Both spoke with the voice of the desert when they chose to speak, and they entered the heat of dry sand and scouring wind without even a trace of the fear that shadowed every mortal.

Their pasts were here, beneath the sands, not above them.

Lord Ishavriel offered no obeisance to the sand itself; he made no concession to the heat or the wind. No more did he choose to acknowledge the ice and the snow of the Northern Wastes; the ability to support life was only of marginal interest to those who existed above it.

He had traversed the width of the desert, and he had, with delicacy and determination, found the lattice of his Lord's magic where it lay, like a net or a cage, around the dormant shadows of what had once been the only significant cities mankind had ever built.

But he had been unable to touch them. They lay just outside the periphery of his power. In the desert, as in the North, he practiced little caution; they were wastelands, they guaranteed privacy. He had exerted considerable power in his efforts. He was unaccustomed to futility in such exertions, but he was *Kialli*; he accepted the truth when he faced it.

The light of Voyani magic echoed with the grandeur and the mystery of the Cities themselves, and he understood that these hobbled people, these diminished, bent fugitives had something that made their hidden life inconceivable to one of the *Kialli*: control of the Cities.

The taste of blood magic still lingered in the open air.

He did not recognize the signature of the power that blood invoked; neither the blood, nor the aura that burned itself into vision sensitive to power, were familiar, although something familiar did linger beneath the surface of the magicks used; a potent power. He had faced the ancestors of the Arkosan Voyani long ago, when the vast stretch of the Sea of Sorrows had been the most viable, the most beautiful, of the Southern lands. No human remembered what he remembered, as he hovered above the sand, arms outstretched, palms turned toward ground.

The stretch of valleys, remembered now only by the empty riverbeds, once housed trees that were vast and ancient as anything found in the heart of the Deepings; they cast long shadows, spoke with the wind's voice when they chose to speak at all. As a child, before the rise of man, he had walked in those forests, and years had passed as he watched the saplings lift themselves from their beds of dirt, straining for the supremacy of sky and sun.

Here, in the heart of these lands, he had first called earth, and the earth, rich with the worms and the insects, the roots of those great trees its only restraint, rose at the first hint of his song. The earth was the youngest of the wild elements; of the four, in its vast deepness, the most tame, the most approachable.

They were strong, these memories, rich with scent and texture; he could feel the runneled curves of ancient bark beneath his palms, and remembered that he had anchored himself against the trees the first time he had called. Hesitancy?

Yes.

Curse Isladar.

He fell, the descent only barely slow enough to be controlled; he released the wind, and it fled. His feet struck the harsh, hard ground. Nothing marked the earth now; nothing differentiated this land from the lands a hundred miles to the South.

He placed his palm down, as if in supplication, against the barren ground.

Memory, here. It lay across the present like a translucent shroud, and because he was *Kialli*, he could see the ghost of his youthful hand against the damp mosses of forest floor, fingers splayed wide in the exact position of the present.

Memory. The moist tang of new-turned earth, the heavy scent neither cloying nor bitter; the fullness of greenery in its varying shades, some brilliant, some subdued, none clashing; the sense, here, of the type of cool found only where warmth presided. Life.

The dark earth had opened then. It . . . welcomed him. He had treasured that welcome; had bowed before it, humbled, as the roots of trees were exposed in all their protected intricacy; as the backs of worms, wet and glistening with the half-light of bower and sunlight, left a trail like the scrawl of written language in the soil.

Why not the wild earth, Brother?

Because he had expected this truth, this present. He

treasured few memories, although he hoarded them all, and he did not want proof, if it were needed, that memory and existence were in no way the same.

He placed the flat of his open palms against the harsh and broken ground that did not resemble his valued past, and the slumbering earth woke; he felt its movement, its slow, cumbersome musculature constricting as it protected the reserves of liquid that rested well below a surface exposed to sun. Its voice was the voice he remembered from that day, sheltered by the bowers of leaves, and he felt something that lived below memory's surface; it was sharper, sweeter, and far, far more bitter than he had expected.

The earth remembered as well.

He had scant seconds to find the air again before the ground beneath his feet shattered and the heart of the elemental earth lashed out.

Rejection.

The earth raged against him; he was no longer a creature of its nature. He spoke with a voice that he had not used since that first day, but although it was, to his own ears, a perfect mimicry of youth, it was not youth.

He could force what he desired from the body of the world, but he knew, now, that he would never be welcomed; he would never again be gifted with intimacy. He could bargain, or threaten, or—in other circumstances—cajole in a dim and impersonal way.

And so?

Fingers curved in toward the center of palms. He was *Kialli*. He had survived losses far more significant than this. If force was required, he would use it; over the passage of time, he had perfected that art.

You will give me what I seek, he told the earth.

And the earth answered, *You will take it. It is not the same.*

Is it not? In the end, I will have what I require, and I will walk away. There is nothing I desire that you can keep from me. Not here, where your power is weakest.

For now, the earth said. *For now. But there is no weakness where life resides.*

I serve my Lord. My Lord paid your price.

* * *

Telakar felt it.

He had never been a gifted elemental mage. He had been born after the wild voices had stilled sufficiently that only the patient, or the sensitive, might stoop to listen to their muted tongue for long enough to learn the cadences of their particularly cumbersome language.

He could call fire; he could send messages into the forge of the wind and be certain that the substance of his meaning would be preserved and conveyed. But he could never speak with the confidence, with the conviction, with the force required to compell the earth to shelter any living creature.

But had he, he would never have the power to force the earth to surrender what it had been made to hold within its heart. The grip of earth was strong.

And the Lord's binding, bought by the required magery of the old compacts, was shifting. Once, no such compact had existed. Once, the Cities of Man had dominated these lands.

The winds were the voice of a heat that belonged to another era. The sands beneath *Kialli* feet cracked and fissured, like the sudden exposure of veins.

Surely, he thought, *the Lord would not expend so great a power now. Not against so trivial an enemy.*

But it was unmistakable—to his ears—as he listened.

The beast roared.

The serpent had been awakened.

Avandar frowned.

His frowns were like geography; over the years in Terafin, Jewel had learned to use the topography of the corners of his lips as a map by which she might better navigate her behavior. It was harder, however, to gauge the details of an expression when the frown was more felt than seen; she cursed the existence of sand, wind, and sun.

And felt a moment's amusement.

It was gone the instant the slender shadow crossed her path and halted there, bounded on either side by the reflection of sun across sand.

"Viandaran," Lord Celleriant said. In the day and a half since they had entered the desert, only Celleriant seemed unchanged. Jewel would have said he had shrugged off the heat, but that would have implied that he felt it at all. She wanted to strangle him, but found the heat difficult enough that the extra effort probably wouldn't have been worth it. Probably.

Avandar nodded. "I felt it."

"Do you know what it was?"

The domicis' frown returned. "No. It is . . . distant. I believe—although I am not an elementalist of note—the wild earth has been invoked."

"Could you not hear its outrage?"

"No. But if you could, and you could understand what it signified, that would be of interest."

Celleriant shrugged. "To you?"

"To the woman you now serve."

He was silent for the space of four heartbeats. It wasn't possible for Arianni skin to pale, Jewel thought—but had it been, he would have been white as sun-bleached bone when all flesh has been stripped from it by desperate carrion.

"Celleriant?" she almost whispered.

And was rewarded by his full attention. "The old earth is stronger here than I would have guessed possible." He lifted an arm, swept it across the breadth of dry horizon, cracked dirt, steady, unbroken sunlight. If he had paled because he had been reminded of his service to her, and of the loss it implied, he said nothing. Nor did she.

"Not even in the Deepings is its voice so strong, and the Deepings hoard the most ancient of living things in its heart. But the earth has been forced to surrender something it valued. I do not yet know what."

"You speak with the earth?"

His smile was bitter. "I listen," he said quietly. "I am sensitive to its song."

"What's happened?"

"I do not know. But if I were to guess, I would say that the *Kialli* are in the desert, somewhere, and that they have invoked what has not been invoked since before the Fall of Man."

"The Fall of Man?"

Lord Celleriant looked to Avandar.

Avandar was absolutely silent.

The Arianni lord shrugged. "If you wish it, I shall travel toward the breach. I may be able to answer your questions more precisely when I arrive."

"No. If there's a really big danger, I think it's better to face it here—because if there's a really big danger, it's aimed at the Voyani."

His gaze turned skyward; flickered off the underside of the wagons that were, in the brilliance of sky, low, squat guides, or guardians. "Yes," he said softly. "At the wanderers."

But two days passed in the heat of the sun and the terrible sameness of cracked sand, and no danger arrived, no dream came to haunt her, no portents leaped out of her mouth before she could catch the words she spoke and drag them back.

Two *whole* days. A person could learn to relax in the space of two days. Even here, in this unbearable heat. The desert became a place in which there was privacy, and if the privacy was an act of nature—who would want to disturb it?—she accepted its gift nonetheless.

But she missed the children. She missed the meals at which they were shepherded, guided, coddled, fed.

CHAPTER NINETEEN

12th of Misteral, 427 AA
Sea of Sorrows

The only good thing about the Serra, Elena reflected sourly, was the effect she had on the men. It wasn't so much their posture, cleanliness, or manners—never a strong point among the Voyani of any family except Elsarre—although these traits did improve drastically. It was their squabbling. It had become almost nonexistent. The Serra had, by simply becoming utterly still and utterly silent, made clear how little she enjoyed the flashes of uncontrolled temper the men were wont to show, and they had either taken such bursts elsewhere—thereby belying the meaning of the word uncontrolled—or forsaken them entirely.

The Serra herself did nothing at all to encourage the Arkosans, although from time to time she did acknowledge them—therefore, this shift in behavior came for free. Her clothing hid almost everything from view; not even the perfect midnight of her hair could be seen beneath the folds of rough cloth and twine. But hidden or no, she was known; the Arkosans—the handful that traveled with the Matriarch, handpicked all—came to offer her their company, their food and their water; they came to stand guard against sunlight by offering to create shadows in which she might rest.

It was not an effect, short of temper and the threat of a good dagger, that Elena herself could have hoped to have, and Elena, of the Arkosans in the Matriarch's van, was—had been—best loved. And given that it seemed highly unlikely that the Serra would condescend to have sex—with anyone, come to think—the fact that they behaved well at all was mystifying. Either that, or they were completely stupid, which given men and sex, was also a distinct possibility.

"Is something wrong, 'Lena?"

She started, and then smoothed the frown from where it had lodged in the corner of her lips, aware of the new lines that would be there when she was finally free of the desert. Of the Sea of Sorrows. "No, Nicu. I was just thinking about how far we have to go."

He raised a brow. "You know how far we have to go?"

Her shrug was a good indication of her annoyance. She was inclined to be friendly, but although she appreciated constancy in almost any circumstance, Nicu was perhaps the one man in the Arkosan encampment she'd happily cede to the Serra's courtly ice. "I know we'll know when we're close." *Careful, careful, Elena.* She missed the children. Nicu's help at their feeding had calmed his temper, eased his jealousy, given him the camaraderie of shared purpose.

She had hoped it would be enough. So much for hope.

"Margret told you that?"

"More or less."

It was Nicu's turn to look annoyed. "*I'm* in charge of the men here," he snapped. "I'm in charge of the safety of the Matriarch. If she tells anyone that—"

"It shouldn't be the next in line?"

He took a step back, but his lips compressed. "No," he snapped. "Not unless she wants you to be the first in line." His hands were curved into the fists Elena least liked.

"Nicu—"

"Why is it always the women? Why aren't the men ever important?"

"The men *are* important."

"The men are important as fodder for clan warfare," he snapped. "The men are important as muscle. The men are there to lift clay urns and wood and wheels from wagons that they'll never helm." He glanced up, the narrow curve of his eyes an act of hostility, and jabbed at the sky that contained Margret's wagon.

"Adam is in the second wagon," she said quietly.

"Only because you're too cowardly to helm it yourself."

Her hand itched a moment with the desire to redden his

cheek. "Maybe," she said, the effort of saying one word where many would do extreme. "But the men—"

"The men serve the Matriarch."

"Nicu, we all serve the Matriarch."

"The men are sent to die at her convenience."

"That is *not* true. You of all people should know—"

"I *do* know, 'Lena. It wasn't your back she scarred."

A hundred words slammed into each other as she snapped her jaw shut on them. "Nicu," she said flatly, "that's the wind talking." She turned, but she stopped herself from walking away—just as she had stopped herself from speaking—by dint of will.

By desire, truth be known, to preserve the fading memories of the great affection that she had had for him when they had both been young. Because she knew if she started to walk, he would try to stop her; would grab either her arm or her shoulder—and she wasn't certain that if he touched her, she could stop herself from lashing out. Verbally. Physically.

If she tried very, very hard, she could see the boy in this man, and it was the boy she had loved.

"Don't you ever think about it, 'Lena?" He was standing within the bounds of space she considered her own. She swallowed. Let him be.

"Think about it?"

"Think about what we used to have. It's here," he added, his arm swinging out in a wide arc. "Here, or there, or there—the sands contain it. The secrets of the Matriarchs. The blood of Arkosa.

"But *I* have that blood. You have it. He has it," he added, jabbing at a random figure who was standing close to where the Serra Diora knelt, beneath the cover of canvas. She squinted. It was Andreas, the youngest of Nicu's men.

She shrugged. "So?"

"Do you think, in that place, do you think, in *Arkosa*—"

"Nicu, *enough!*"

"Am I not even to say the name? There is *no one listening*. This is our place. The clans don't come here. The end of the *Voyanne* lies in the sands."

Elena swallowed. "I don't know who told you that—"

"Listen to the stories we were told as children. Everything about our lives tells me that. This," he said, beating the left side of his chest with the flat of curved fingers, "tells me. We lived. *Lived.* We had more power than the clansmen dream of. And in those cities, do you think the Matriarch slapped our hands when we—"

"Yes?" She could not keep the desert night from the word; she had almost lost the desire to try.

"The women didn't rule," he told her.

"No. *That's* why there are no cities."

"That's what we've been told."

"And you don't believe it? Is that it? You can say that to *me*? You? The only person in Arkosa who has *ever* carried a weapon forged by the Lord's servants—"

He slapped her.

Without thinking, she slapped him back.

In the wake of those two very personal acts of violence, violence was forsaken; the echoes of the sound of flesh against flesh died into a barren, silent stillness.

Just as suddenly as it had come, the anger slid, like liquid, between the clenched fingers of Nicu's hands. His eyes widened, as if he could see himself mirrored in her unblinking stare. " 'Lena—"

Wearily, angrily, she said, "it comes to this, time and again. Nicu, we *all* serve the Matriarch. Even Margret. Especially Margret."

"She is the Matriarch."

She saw him clearly, as child. "You think that means she gets to make all the rules?"

"Doesn't it?"

"No. The rules were made for her. She walks the thin road, the *Voyanne* at its harshest, and she does it for us. Can't you see that?"

He caught her arms—the movement a movement she hated. "I try," he told her. "I try because it's important to you. Elena—"

"Don't, Nicu."

But he bent his head toward her, covering the distance between their heights. His lips pressed against hers; she felt the line of his teeth behind them, and tried to take a step back; the hard, cracked dirt pressed up against the heel of her boot. He circled her shoulder blades with his arms.

She pushed him; he held on. His tongue slid between her

open lips and she controlled a very visceral urge to bite it and be free. But she became completely, utterly still. She gave him nothing.

After a moment, he pulled back, his eyes unblinking, bright. " 'Lena—"

"Nicu, don't ever do that again."

For a moment his grip tightened, and then he released her. "I—"

"Not now, Nicu."

"We should talk—"

"Not now." She had to leave him. She had to leave him because it was either that or kill him, one way or the other.

But she heard him shout her name, and she cringed with each syllable.

There was something pathetic about sexual desire. Lord Ishavriel was not above vanity; he desired a work that was worthy of his intellectual endeavor. This? Were it not for the difficulty posed by the City itself, any of the lesser demons—*any*—could have competently extracted, from the young man, all that needed to be extracted.

He waited, as patiently as any lord waited, for the woman to free herself from an embrace that was clearly unwelcome. The depth of her revulsion amused him, although it was a pale thing compared to the emotions evoked in the Hells.

The heat of the passing day and the cool of the coming night meant nothing to him, but he paused a moment at the glory of the cloudless, untainted sky, the clarity of the sky's color. Here, in the heat, one could truly believe the sky was ablaze.

He watched the motion of sun toward horizon, lost in the awareness of the beauty of its fall, his memory taking the ephemeral and giving it a very personal, very singular immortality. The mortals were forgotten; the Northern Wastes distanced. In his youth he had watched every species of flower lay itself open, petal by petal, leaf by leaf, in its march from bud to death. He had not had the patience to watch all of the trees grow, although those older had. He had thought, in his impatience to grasp the rougher, cruder forms of power, that one tree looked much like another in its unfurling.

He reviewed this thought, this memory. Clearly, he had been young, in perhaps as feckless a way as the man and the woman who stood, separated by their inability to speak a simple sentence. But immortality gave one a chance to mature.

He had played games with youthful mortals in his youth; they were pleasant memories. But to play them now diminished the significance of everything that had passed between that youth and this maturity.

The air, caught between the heat of day and the ice of night, was beginning its lazy movement; he could feel it against his upturned cheek.

It was not the sensation he remembered. And he was *Kialli;* memory was all that he was. No humiliation, no defeat, no loss, could deprive him of his past. Nothing could make him turn a blind eye to what he had been. But he had a capacity for anger that was matched only by a capacity for the desire for vengeance. He *knew* what had been lost now.

His form was fluid; all demonic flesh was, in some sense. It responded to magic and will, to power and the demands of power. It served the same role that garments once had. Perhaps, when he had been alive, his contempt for the merely sexual would have been informed by some recognition of the desire.

But now the touch of wind was distant; the touch of a palm, distant; the feeling of velvet, silk, heat, and the chill that comes with the anticipation of heat—distant except in memory. Everything displaced by the simple expedience of an eternity of choice.

Isladar.

The *Kialli* had awakened. Perhaps—just perhaps—Lord Isladar had done them the favor of pointing out what they did not suspect of themselves: that they slept at all.

How did that serve his plans? What *were* his plans? Not dominion, and not power.

What else was there?

Treacherous, traitorous, the answer came quietly, like the desert night had: *in the Hells, nothing. But we are not in the Hells.*

He drew breath. Was surprised at just how much of a difference there was between the cold, cold winter of the Northern Wastes and the dry of desert sand. The one, bracing, the other a prelude to the hush before the desert life—such as it was—peered out into darkness. There was a scent here of succulents, of the rare plants and flowers that cowered around the surface of the desert's few natural rocks. There were no people in either environment save those who were wary visitors: the much-cozened human courtiers of the Shining Court, in their furs and silks, to the North, and the Voyani, armed with water, with tenting, with the burden of each other's company in the South. That was all. As visitors, they would come and they would depart, leaving no roots, and little trace of their origin or their intent.

Like jackals, Lord Ishavriel thought, the *Kialli* were sent from barren land to barren land, errand runners for the Lord.

He stood a long moment, the sky turning above him, before he realized that both the woman and the man had departed, and his errand was still undone.

Isladar.

He returned to the safety of desert, brooding now, twisted in the words and the images that contained memories, defining them, redefining them. He took care, as he left the encampment, to shroud his passage; there were those with vision who knew how to look, and those with instinct whose response was more visceral, more dependable.

The night had not fallen. The sky was still a blaze of crimson, gold, burnt orange, the colors deep and almost crystal in their clarity. Breath—not his own—hung in the air, like a thin imitation of cloud.

The serpent was resting.

You hunger, he told the creature.

The creature stirred. The scales of its long neck reflected the sunset, breaking it with the lines of overlapping curves.

Soon.

Kallandras had been listening to the awkward shuffling of a young Voyani man for ten minutes. He could not see him clearly for all of those ten; the unannounced stranger had chosen to stand between the gap in two of the large family tents, shoving his hands in and out of his sash and rearranging his footing for most of that time. He was wise enough, however, to believe that he knew his audience; he did not speak a word out loud until he was ready to approach.

"Uh . . . Uh, Kallandras . . . uh . . ."

Kallandras of Senniel College smiled; the smile was genuine, and he kept it to himself, smoothing all lines from the corners of mouth and eyes as he turned to face the young man who stood just outside the circle a campfire's light would trace across the ground. Although he was not a child by Voyani standards, he was not—quite—adult. Youth clung to him in many ways, some more obvious, some less. He had not yet reached his full height, his chest and his shoulders were slender although it was clear his frame was large, and his expression was devoid of the guarded caution that spoke of long, or bitter, experience. He was an earnest young man.

He invoked the same protective streak in many of his people that the children did. No wonder Adam of the Arkosa Voyani was so loved and watched over; he was willing to express himself in a way that made him seem vulnerable—and as they did all things both fleeting and beautiful, his people treasured his youth.

"Adam of Arkosa," the Northern bard said, bowing. "Does the Matriarch require my presence?"

"The Matriarch? Oh—" His skin was the same darkened bronze that typified the Voyani who lived upon the open road, but he still had the capacity to darken. "No," he said hastily. "No, Margret didn't send me." He took a step forward, squared his shoulders, and stepped more firmly into the clearing.

"What brings you here?"

"I—I—well—"

The bard waited patiently. It was his nature to speculate; to guess at what might be said, what might be asked, and what effect he might have by offering any of a handful of answers. But it was also his nature to know when to wait, and to wait with a semblance of patience that was never inattentive.

In all of his projections of the boy's motivation, the truth played little part.

"I—well—you aren't using your—your instrument and I—I wondered if you'd mind if—if I borrowed it."

For the first time in many years, Kallandras was truly

surprised. Surprise did not deprive him of words, but it momentarily robbed him of expression; the lines of his face slid into a studied, cautious neutrality. "You wish to borrow my lute?"

Silence. Adam was young, but not completely stupid. If he had not understood the fact that his request was significant, he would not have struggled for so long to find the courage to make the request. But having found the courage, he now understood that the request was more than significant; it was personal.

The Voyani were very, very careful about accruing personal debt.

"I have not said no, Adam, but I confess I am curious."

Adam's skin darkened further.

Kallandras held his lute's case carefully. "Understand that you are borrowing a friend," he said softly and without artifice. He rarely spoke so simply and with such direct meaning; he was ruefully aware that although he could be immune to Adam's deceptively youthful aura if he chose to, his first inclination was not to make that choice.

"You brought your lute with you."

"Yes."

"But the desert heat—"

"Yes. But it was . . . specially made; it resists the ill effects of most weather. I have never been in more than a squall at sea; I would not test her against a gale if I were given a choice. But I believe that even if *I* did not survive a sea storm, she would.

"I am not worried that you might damage her; short of fire or deliberate malice—neither of which you wield in any quantity—she will be safe in your hands." He paused. "Do you play?"

"N–no."

Kallandras looked not at Adam, but at the lute that sat safely in a battered case. He wondered briefly—and for no reason at all—if any bard's case was ever anything other than battered; it didn't matter as long as the song of the lute itself was preserved.

"Yes," he said.

"Y–yes?"

"Yes, you may borrow Salla." He placed emphasis on the name for the boy's sake. Or perhaps not; he was vaguely aware that in his youth, he would not have been especially concerned if he had broken or lost any instrument—even this one. That had changed.

He wondered what that young man might have said to him, had he met the man he had become—not quite assassin, and not quite bard. Wondered, and knew. The young were not forgiving.

Adam still hesitated, and Kallandras quietly opened the lid of the case. The hinges needed oiling; the case seemed to speak in quiet creaks as he removed Salla. Almost reflexively, he ran his fingers over the strings. He was curious. "Do you know how to hold her?"

"Yes. Uh . . . no."

The bard's smile deepened. "Come here," he said, as if speaking to a much younger child. "Do not pull the strings; never lift her, or any instrument, by the strings; they'll only lose their tune and make that much more work for their player. Put your hands here, beneath the bowl, and here, upon the neck."

Adam did as bid, staring at the smooth surface of the lute. His hands were shaking. "If you don't think it's—"

"If I did not trust you, Adam of Arkosa, Matriarch's brother, I would not place my instrument in your hands."

The boy laughed. "I—I'm not sure *I* trust me." He laughed again; the words were framed on either side by the sweet sound of vulnerability, mingled with the confidence the boy showed in being willing to express it.

Kallandras noted, however, that in spite of his misgivings, Adam took what he had asked for.

And accrued the debt.

Where are you going, Adam? Where will you learn to play Salla?

The Serra Diora di'Marano had not spoken more than five words in a row since she had sung to the Arkosans. The heat and the anger that she allowed—*allowed*—to overtake all sense and caution had evaporated with the song; she remained in the wake of fading notes, exposed, vulnerable.

She hated what she heard in her own voice when she spoke. She hated it, but she had been raised by a merciless woman to *be* merciless in her judgment. She could not pretend that she did not hear what was there.

The moon was high. The Lady's face was bright. The Serra Diora di'Marano had fled the Tor Leonne with so little, she had no propitiations to offer in the Lady's name. But she bowed her head beneath a canopy that was quickly becoming redundant, and she prayed in silence, in stillness, in the perfect repose and grace that was as natural to a harem Serra as breath or life. And perhaps more necessary.

She had learned never to ask the Lady for anything that was too important to her. So, in prayer, the repose was more important than content; the form more important than the ritual itself.

But when she saw Ramdan rise, she realized that she must have observed more than form, for she had been so absorbed in the perfect line of lowered chin, straight back, and arms curved up to hold fan, that she had not heard the stranger approach.

She was understandably wary of strangers, and in a place such as this, wariness was as natural as breathing and only slightly less necessary. But she had perfected the art of deference, and she used it as a defense, bowing her head almost into her lap to avoid meeting the eyes of whoever passed by.

Sadly, the stranger's footsteps approached and stopped. She waited for a full minute; after this, deference segued easily into the awkward. There were few crimes that a Serra could commit—or perhaps a Serra of the Serra Diora's rank—that were worse than public awkwardness. Having discovered just how little satisfaction was to be gained in losing control of oneself, she placed her hands in a lap made of rough cotton and bent knees, and composed herself.

She was surprised to see the young man. From the heavy fall of his feet, she had expected her visitor to be one of the men who had the responsibility of guarding the Matriarch and her companions. They were not, she discovered, cerdan; rules of propriety did not govern their speech or their actions when they were in the presence of the women they were to protect. They regularly exchanged harsh words, blows, and insults; they regularly chose to relieve themselves—checking only for the direction of the wind, and not for any who might be discomfited by the spectacle.

She would have been forced to offer her life in compensation for such poor behavior on the part of her own cerdan had she been at Court with men such as these.

Yet they were fascinating because they were so unschooled, so unfettered by a need to be polite, to be mannered, and she felt that if she could both ignore their excesses and observe them at a careful—critical—distance, she might learn something about men.

This was too close a distance, but this boy was not those men. It was not clear in the way he walked—for his steps were far too heavy for his size to justify—but it was evident in the way he did all else; he failed to meet her eyes, he curled his shoulders inward, he made his height as insignificant as possible.

As if, she thought, he were a child.

He wore the heavy boots and heavy, undyed robes of the desert traveler; he wore the sword. His skin was sun-dark, the shape of his eyes wide and pleasant. But his face was devoid of beard. He reminded the Serra of someone, although it was not obvious who. A question, she thought, for later. She had time, in this place.

He bowed.

The bow was not graceful in execution—but as it was so unnecessary among the Voyani, as either courtesy or obeisance, there *was* a grace inherent in its offer. She was pained by it, and surprised at the pain.

She could not, of course, bid the boy rise; that was not her function, not her place. But again, the rule against the socially awkward put her in a position that she would seldom have been in had she been in the Tor Leonne—for it was clear to her that he intended to remain in his awkward physical fold until she gave him permission to do otherwise.

She hesitated, and then with great care opened the sections of her fan, and raised it to cover half her face. She chose her words with the same attention she paid the fan.

But she was surprised by the words she had chosen when she at last spoke. "I have little water to offer," she said softly, "but what I have is yours if you choose to accept it."

He rose at once. If she had expected his face to crease in naïve or youthful smile, she had misjudged him. He was a boy, but he was not a child.

He was also unoffended by her expectation, if he was

aware of it at all—and meeting those eyes, the Serra thought that there was little in the end that he was not aware of when he chose to pay attention.

"I have water," he said, indicating a slight bulge in his robe. "All the Voyani carry water with them; two days' worth in an emergency.

"But water is not a simple act of hospitality when we enter the Sea of Sorrows, and . . . it is not expected." He did smile, then, and she was surprised by the smile. It cut her.

It reminded her of her dead.

How? How, when he was everything that her dead were not? He was male, Voyani, rough and unpolished; his voice was unschooled in the arts that might keep its tone pleasant to the ear, his movements ungraceful and self-indulgent. But his smile . . .

She had been afraid of seeing Ruatha in the faces of the Voyani, for Ruatha had been her wildling, her impulsive, ever-angry, fiercely loyal wife. But this boy did not have that; he had instead the unfettered sweetness of Deirdre.

Not here.

"I . . . I noticed that you did not bring your samisen." He bowed again, and she recognized that bow; it was an attempt to hide his expression as he spoke. "I—forgive me, Serra, but I listen to the music that you make whenever I can. The children listen."

"You—you watch the children?"

He rose again, pleased. "Yes. I and Uncle Stavos are sometimes given the responsibility. We are almost the only men." The last sentence was said with the youthful pride she would expect from a boy his age.

Things were so different, here. So very different.

"I do not always understand the duties of the Voyani. In the harem, the wives are responsible for feeding and tending to the children—but it is not a privilege that is accorded to those with wisdom or power; it is merely a responsibility."

His eyes widened subtly, his mouth opened. But that was all of the shock he allowed himself to express.

"I understand the honor that is done you by the responsibility you are given," she added gravely. "And I am impressed by it. Perhaps if feeding the children was the responsibility of those who held power, we would be a different people. I—if I may be so bold, I do not know your name."

He flushed again. Fumbled a moment with words until a few came out. "I'm—I'm Adam. Of Arkosa. You might know my sister." His skin darkened. "I mean, well, it doesn't matter."

She realized, as he stuttered, dropping syllables in an awkward pattern that had the cadence of language—but only barely—that he had not offered her his name because he had expected her to know it; he was a boy who was used to *being* known by the people he met within this encampment. But having discovered that he was not known did not give rise to anger or resentment; he was simply, sweetly, embarrassed.

"I'm Adam," he said again. "I'm—I'm Margret's brother."

She had never seen such open embarrassment before. Not outside of the harem's heart.

Her eyes fell to her hands, her adorned hands. In the deepening night, the ghosts of old rings returned to bind her fingers; the ghosts of old songs were carried by the movement of a blessedly cool breeze.

She wondered if her son would have grown up to be just another clansmen, bent to the rules of conquest and death in the High Court.

It was the first time she had wondered.

As if awkward silence was something he too bore the responsibility of avoiding, he said, again, "You didn't bring your instrument."

She lowered her face into the wall of her fan. When it rose again, it was smooth and devoid of any unpleasing expression. "No," she said softly. "I left it in the care of the Arkosans."

"Why?"

"Because the care of Arkosans is kinder than the care of the dry desert heat. It is wood," she added, although it was obvious. "It . . . suffered in the passage to the desert's edge; it would not weather the journey well."

He was silent for a long moment, and then his fourteen-year-old eyes looked up and met hers across the stretched pleats of ivory silk fan. "And will you, Serra, without it?"

* * *

She was absolutely silent. Not even the folds of her sari ventured the sound of cloth against cloth that came with the rise and fall of lungs; they were as still as she was. Her lungs forgot the movement of air, her lips the forms with which words were made. But her hand remembered the position that held her fan before her face like a wall or a door. It had slipped; it had slipped enough that she could not look away from his face. He was younger than she by only two years, but she felt, as his question died at the hands of her unnatural—and yes, very awkward—stiffness, that he was as young as the harem children in any great clansman's domicile.

The winds that had so scarred the Voyani had failed to touch him. The sun that had destroyed so much of her life had failed to mark his. For a moment she felt a cold, dark anger rise and she lifted her head so that she might more easily see his face.

But the anger dissipated.

Had he not lost his mother? Had he not risked sister and family in an attempt to save the city from the harsh and terrible alliances made by its reigning Tyr?

For just a moment, in the rising cold of anger, she saw something else rise as well. And it made her lower her head again. If she could have, she would have sent the boy away. Of all the dangers she had conceived of facing on this terrible voyage, there were two that had never even been considered. His kindness, in the face of so much loss, and her lack of kindness in the face of the same. She had grace and perfect, elegant manners, but nothing in her offered what this boy offered so recklessly—not to herself, and not to anyone else.

"Adam—"

"But I—"

She waited for him to finish. He didn't. It came to her that he was waiting for *her,* and she almost shook her head at the strangeness, the utter strangeness of this conversation, this boy, this place. *Do women rule your life so completely*, she wanted to ask, *that you must wait on* their *words as if their words have such public value?*

But the answer was obvious.

She felt a pang of envy for those women, watching this boy. And a pang of something darker. She could not speak through it, and for a moment, bowed her head once again to recover.

Free from the anchor of her gaze, he said, "I—I brought you this. I know—I know it's not yours, but I thought—you sing so perfectly and you play so perfectly—and it *has* strings . . ."

She looked up again, although she was almost afraid to. Her vision had blurred; her eyes were filmed. She did not understand *why*. Could not. He was a simple Voyani boy. And she was . . .

Shocked.

She lowered her fan with almost unseemly haste, because her hands were suddenly nerveless and she could not be seen to do anything so clumsy as drop it. Ramdan came to her rescue, retrieving that fan from her hand and stepping back into the distance again.

It was Adam's turn to be discomfited. She wondered why, although she knew it had something to do with Ramdan's presence. Did the Voyani truly feel that Ramdan, a seraf, was held against his will? Did they feel that he was treated, in this singular position of honor, as a lesser being, something to be ranked with a dog, but beneath a horse, in a clansman's spectrum of values?

And yet they served a Matriarch, and died at her whim.

She did not thank the seraf; to thank him was to dismiss him and she wanted his constancy. But she was not surprised when he stepped back, to the periphery of acceptable seraf distance, and waited there, hands behind his back.

Only when he was at a distance did Adam approach.

"Do you know what this is?" she asked him softly.

"I know it's not what you're used to," he replied, lamely. "I know it's Northern."

"I play a Northern instrument. Not . . . this one."

"I thought—"

She had never thought to carry this rounded bowl in the flat of her lap. Had never thought to see this lute in any hands but her master's. "How did you come by this?" She asked him, not because she desired to know, but because it gave her an excuse not to touch those strings. She felt an odd fear as her hands hovered above them, and she could not easily name it.

Unnamed fears were always the worst; they had longevity because they were fostered best by ignorance. But so, too, was wonder. This lute had a history that had roots in a time that she knew by story, by conversation, by painting or tapestry: the world into which she had not yet been born. To touch it, to play it, was to make herself some part of that continuity.

But she did not pluck the strings.

It was not that she was unfamiliar with the instrument; she was not. As a pampered daughter of an adoring father—an indulgent father who had gained in rank and power with the passing of years—she had run fingers over every instrument known to man, dismissing some as too robust or too loud for a Serra of the High Court, but committing time and emotion to others.

She had always had a fondness for stringed instruments. But this instrument had a voice that she knew as well as she knew her own; it had never sung for her.

No. That wasn't true. It had offered her its music time and again, but always in the hands of the Northern bard from Senniel College, that mythical residence that produced men who could speak with the voice—the terrible, the relentless voice—of the wind.

She closed her eyes.

Freed from the tyranny of sight, she could hear the rise and fall of reverberating notes that began in her earliest memories.

Kallandras.

What did she remember of the night she had first met him? Vision faded. In the gray-black cocoon of unhurried repose, the decade had robbed her of images. She was an intelligent woman; she could reconstruct what must have been seen by her four-year-old eyes with the precision of an architect—but she could not imbue those images with color or life. A fleeting smile was frozen in time, bleached of anything but the rawest of attributes by memory, her truest impression of Lissa, her favorite of all her father's wives.

However, when she entered the darkness, she shed the need for sight; she was left with the only sensation that scarred her memory. Sound. The first time she had heard this lute, during the festivities of the Festival of the Moon, she had not seen it. Nor had she seen the man who wielded it, deriving strength from the music he both accompanied and invoked. But she had heard his voice, and while the other wives spoke of his face or his form, his exquisite manners, the honor bestowed upon him—and he, a *foreigner*—by the simple fact of his command performance in the presence of Tyrs, she had thought of the quality of his voice.

It was devoid of emotion, of anger or bitterness or avarice, of love or pain or hope. It was the *only* voice she had heard that contained such mystery, such complete privacy. And the prologue to the story that voice told was the strains of the instrument that sat, silent, in her lap.

He had not carried his lute when he had come to the harem the night that Lissa en'Marano lay bleeding to death, the child she carried inside dead, but still able to hurt her. He had not played the lute when he had finally lifted the veil from his voice and had sung—if such a wild, terrible thing could be called song—with the Lady's darkest voice: he had summoned the wind.

He had saved Lissa's life by forcing a recalcitrant healer to heal her. Not more, not less.

And Lissa?

She had chosen to leave the harem—and Diora—forsaking everything she had been given in return for the love of a man who had initially refused to be polluted by the act of healing a concubine. Would loss have been less painful had Lissa been left to die rather than deliberately choosing to abandon them?

Yes.

But would she change the outcome, had she the choice? Could she silence the bard before he spoke with the Lady's power, and allow Lissa to die the death that her own mother had died over sixteen years past?

She remembered the voices and sounds of the women, her mothers in the harem of her father. Pain, terror, fear, and bitter, bitter anger. All of this trapped beneath the surface of inadequate words, the surface of well-trained voice. Only the Serra Teresa had blended resignation into that terrifying mix of raw emotion; only her voice seemed to bespeak, to force, calm.

Of course, the adult thought, as she spoke to the memories of the child. *She has the voice.*

But knowledge of that gift did not—could not—destroy the power of that memory.

Could she listen to those voices again and feel no pain, no desire to ease pain? Could she listen to those voices as they faced the inevitable, and accepted the death of a woman they all loved?

Her hands touched the strings that faced her; her fingers slid over them, resting with enough force to test tension. No sound escaped. She could hear Lissa's voice clearly. Alana's. Illana's.

The past was made of voices such as these.

Where were you, Kallandras?

She plucked the first note; listened to the reverberations of string die in the stillness. This was *Salla.* Of all instruments, this was his—the man whose voice had been a haven, an oasis, a thing free of the strain and terror, the incomprehensible passion, of the rest of the speaking world.

Where were you the night of—

She plucked another, and another, slowly shifting the position of both bowl and neck as they rested in her lap. The music caught her, as it always did; it spoke for her, freeing her from the delicate cage of words, a Serra's words.

But because she was cursed, the music turned, again and again, to the night she could not give the substance of word. Or confession.

Her eyes snapped open because she needed reality, she needed the here and the now that voice and sound alone could never provide.

Across from her, one knee in the dirt, was Adam. His expression was unguarded, his forehead creased, his brows drawn slightly in. She was familiar with the look, although it took her a moment to recognize it because she had not expected to see it on any Voyani face.

She had deliberately invoked such a feeling in the past, without remorse and without pride. It served her purpose in her father's—or her husband's—court. But she found that she did not want a pity that she had not, through artifice, requested. Not from a child.

Not from a child.

* * *

Kallandras stood beneath the growing depths of night-blue sky. The brightest of stars were gathering light and strength; the palest had yet to make themselves seen. The air had gone from pleasant to cool, but it was not yet cold enough to kill the unwary, or the unfortunate.

It would be, in scant hours.

His curiosity had led him here, and he watched as Adam approached the Serra Diora. Watched as Salla left his youthful hands and entered the Serra's, his clumsiness giving way to her grace as if such a surrender were inevitable.

She plucked a single string. The sound, the perfect note, grew softer, louder, softer, until it was swallowed by the intensity of her silence. In the gathering shadow, a lamp was lit. It surprised him, because the lamp was not Voyani in origin; the Voyani carried torches into the Sea of Sorrows, and they lit fires, but not fires as contained as this.

But the lamp was carried by seraf hands. It was set down, a few feet from the Serra's bent lap, where it might cast long shadows in the muted illumination of orange-and-yellow light. She did not speak. Without the subtle nuance of her voice, even Kallandras found it difficult to gauge her thoughts; she existed in the perfect privacy imposed, within and without, upon the Serras of the High Court.

But the boy across from her had known no such life, and when Kallandras saw his expression, he winced. Still, there was no danger here that he could avert by intrusion; he had his answer.

He said, "I've never been alone in my life."

She did not understand why he was speaking. The words were clearly an overture, but an overture to a conversation whose existence made no sense.

He said, "Even after my mother's death—when Margret told the rest of us about it—people came to *me*. Because I'm the one they thought she loved."

The night was cold. She was cold. She could no longer separate the sensations. If she waited long enough, it would become so cold he would have to leave. Nights spent at desert's edge had not prepared her for the desert. The day itself, its terrible heat a dangerous burden, could not prepare her for the night. The lamp, she thought, as she deflected his words with her impenetrable silence, would outlast them both if it was allowed to burn.

It was a waste of light and perhaps heat; she could not feel any warmth the flame gave.

The lute was silent. Her hands rested beneath its curved bowl.

"You wouldn't need the instrument if you could speak without it."

Against all reason, she was drawn into conversation with a boy who was in all ways a stranger. "I can speak without it, but I find I have nothing to say."

He stared at the lamplight, at the lute, at the man who stood paces away, waiting her word or her gesture. "No one spoke to Margret. One of my aunts slapped her. Because she knew that my mother had died, and she told no one. They expect her to be able to bear *any* burden, though. Because in the end, she'll have to."

"Why are you telling me this? Surely this is a Voyani matter."

He smiled. In the shadows, she could see the contours of his cheeks. "Maybe because I can't tell Margret," he said. "And maybe it's because I couldn't say this to any Arkosan."

"And so?"

He did not meet her gaze, although it was a moment before she realized that her gaze was fixed upon him. Night had fallen everywhere; it had descended within her. The boldness of anger and fear and exhaustion took root there. The Lady's hand was *so* cold as it rested upon her brow.

"There are some words that need to be said. Don't you believe that?"

"No."

"Oh." He shuffled slightly from foot to foot, his body beginning the shuddering dance of the cold. "I believe it. Why else would we have been given words when animals weren't? We were meant to use them."

"Animals were not granted words," she replied, letting the night into her voice to expel it, "because if they were, we would only feel guilty when we led them to the slaughter."

He was not so easily put off. "Why? We lead our own to slaughter every day without blinking."

"Not you. You don't."

She thought he would ask. If she could. She braced herself for the question.

But he was what he seemed to be: a gentle man who had not yet escaped the periphery of childhood completely. He did not ask.

Silence settled across the sleeping Voyani encampment, broken by the crackle of scant flame. The Arkosans had chosen to camp between the folded walls of a riverbed that had long since surrendered water and life to the Lord. The worst of the wind—and the wind was there—passed above where their tents were huddled. The wagons had been brought as close to the ground as they would come for their desert sojourn. Donatella had told her that they would touch the ground again only when they returned; to touch ground here, in the desert, was considered an ill omen.

She sat with her knees against that ground, and understood why.

Lady. The night was so cold she looked for no mercy.

"She would talk," he continued, as if there had been no pause, no break. "She would have talked to anyone brave enough to go to her."

"Adam." She lifted the lute from her lap. Held it out.

He stared at it blankly. "Yes?"

"You are shivering. It is cold. I have no words to offer you."

"I didn't mean the words for *me*," he said, and she could not tell if the flush along his skin was due to cold or embarrassment. Little enough of his face was now exposed.

"You must have spoken with her. You must have offered to let her speak."

He snorted. It was the first confident sound he had made, and it changed the texture of his voice, adding a touch of age, like a fine patina, to the depth of his youth. "To Margret, *I* am my mother's baby. I am her baby brother. Like all of the Voyani women, she wants to protect the children from pain and suffering. She wants us to be fed, to be clothed, and to be put behind the lines of war when those lines are drawn. In sand," he said, looking at his feet as they hopped against the ground. "Or across fertile ground.

"I am the only person she could not speak to. Because to speak to me of pain means she would have to tell me—

honestly, and not the way the Onas tell the children in their keep—that pain exists." His gaze became distant again. "That loneliness waits for us when we stop being small enough for the lap."

"Do you miss your mother?"

"Yes." Just that. A matter-of-fact word. She heard what lay beneath its surface: loss. But stronger than that, a fierce, desperate pride. In her. About her.

"I killed mine."

He stepped forward, and then stepped back, both movements wider than his awkward, stuttering attempts to keep warm. "Serra?"

"Yes?"

"I won't take the lute back. I won't ask you what you meant. But—"

"But?"

"No one went to Margret, and no one will."

She nodded.

"No one went to you."

And froze.

"I believe there are words that need to be said because they're too horrible, too angry, to swallow, to keep here," he continued, touching his chest with one shaking hand while retreating from the anger that she had displayed in that single curt sentence. "And I meant it. But I also believe that there are words that need to be shared."

She clutched the lute, lifting it from her lap as if to throw it at his retreating chest, for he backed away from her the way one backs away from a wild, terrified creature, a creature who has wandered by circumstance into the lands of men, and seeks only a way out.

But the lute fell. She watched as he left; watched until she could no longer see his form between the cluttered ground of tents and shadows and distant fire.

"You are not a child," she said softly, but in a voice that would carry no matter how far away he had chosen to run. To herself, quietly, she added, *Your sister deprives herself of a strength by refusing to see all that you are; she is a fool.*

She was surprised, as she slowly rose, to feel the bitter twinge of envy. To hear again, in the faltering sweetness of a stranger's voice, some echo, some shadow, of a dead wife's.

"Ramdan," she said, because she had to say something, "I am . . . tired. It is time that we retire."

The seraf nodded quietly. She had walked past him, had bent again to ground, for the flat of the tent did not allow easy access to those standing, when she froze.

She looked back at the man who waited, who always waited, his form perfect, his expression neutral.

And she wondered what words he kept to himself. Wondered if he, like the boy, felt that there were some words that must be spoken. Wondered what he would say, should she ask him what they were.

She was weary enough that she wanted to ask, but she knew that by asking such a question she would forever change the geography of the life upon which they stood, and she needed the constancy of that ground beneath her.

But she was aware, as she slid into the heavy silks meant for sleep, that her inability to change the way she spoke with this seraf was not, in the end, unlike Margret's inability to see her brother as a support.

More than that, she chose to leave until morning.

CHAPTER TWENTY

Heart or no, Margret of Arkosa knew they were almost at their destination. A day's journey, maybe two, and they would be above it, their footsteps tracing a thin trail in the desert that would be wiped clear by wind, sand, and time as it always was.

A day's journey, two, and she would stand in the same spot where her mother, her mother's mother, and all of the mothers who had come before in a tenuous but unbroken line, had stood for the first time. There, she would have to perform her first true obeisance, offer herself for the first real judgment.

Beneath the deck, the dry hollow of a winding riverbed sheltered her people; the wind's voice was unkind this night, and she had chosen to shelter in the wadi.

Wait. She was not good at waiting.

You'll have to learn. Her mother's voice. Evallen's voice.

Is there anything I don't have to learn?

Manners.

Her mother's voice was so clear it was almost a comfort. She wondered what she would hear of it when she finally stood upon the soil of Arkosa itself. Wondered what she might hear when—if, a nagging doubt said—she entered. She could not know. Although she had accompanied her mother on this journey a handful of times, she had never seen what waited—what truly waited—at journey's end. No one had. Only the Matriarch walked into the desert marked as Arkosan. Only the Matriarch knew where the grave of the City lay.

Or only the Matriarch had.

This time, a stranger held the Heart of Arkosa around her perfect, pale neck. And this time, she thought bitterly, when she retraced her mother's steps, a stranger would accompany her and be accorded the honor that she, living daughter of a Matriarch, had never been accorded.

She would enter Arkosa.

"Matriarch?"

She looked down from her perch in front of the cabin. There, in the faded colors of sunset, stood the Serra Teresa di'Marano, her face obscured by the layers of cloth the Voyani wore to protect themselves from wind and sun. But her voice and her posture—like those of her arrogant, icy niece's—were unmistakable.

"Serra," she said curtly. "You should be inside."

"And you, if I am not mistaken."

"The Matriarch doesn't sleep," Margret said, offering a slight smile, "until the rest of the Arkosans are in bed."

"Then comfort yourself, Matriarch; for those not abed are not Arkosans, and therefore not your burden."

Margret shrugged. "And why are you here?"

The silence was just long enough. The Serra Teresa smiled almost grimly and nodded. "I am here at the behest of Yollana of the Havalla Voyani. She . . . wishes to set . . . Havallan protections around the perimeter of the encampment."

Margret frowned, leaning forward into the hands that gripped the half-height rail. "Why? I mean, why now?"

"She did not say. And I have learned not to second-guess a Voyani Matriarch."

"She couldn't come herself?"

"Not easily. The air is cold; she . . . has had trouble walking."

"Which means she's basically crawling or being carried."

The Serra said nothing. "What kind of protection?"

"I don't know, Matriarch. I am not sure she would answer me if I asked. But you? If you asked, she would answer."

But Margret frowned. "Why now?" she repeated, but to herself. She was aware that Yollana was reputed to have the strength of blood not seen in Matriarchs for generations; that she was gifted with true sight and true vision.

She took a breath. Exhaled it; watched the cloud hang in the still air. "Yes," she said. "Tell her yes, and with thanks, my thanks, for the effort. Tell her that I know it is not the custom for the Havallans and the Arkosans to work together in such a fashion—but it is time. The Lord is watching."

"Well?" the old woman's voice was a crackling, sharp bite of sound.

"As you guessed, Matriarch. She accepted your offer with as much grace as I have seen her accept anything."

"Meaning," the old woman said with a bark of a laugh, and an exhalation of pipe smoke, "she didn't spit."

The Serra's smile was genuine, almost rueful. She failed to comment, but said instead, "She wanted to know why you chose this evening to begin such protections."

"What did you say?"

"That I didn't know."

"Aie, Teresa, you play a game." The old woman spit loose, dry bits of leaf from her mouth along with the words.

"Perhaps," the Serra said quietly. "And perhaps I pay a debt to Evallen of Arkosa. Her daughter has instinct. Let her use it. Let her make a judgment here, when a mistake will not be so costly."

"You trust me," the old woman said quietly.

"In this, yes."

"But not in everything?"

"No more than you would trust me, old friend." She bowed. "What must I gather?"

"In the tunnel? Nothing. I have everything I need. Sleep, if you can."

The Serra nodded quietly, but she did not move.

"What is it?"

"Were you truly given no other vision, Yollana? Was your vision entirely made of the images of the servants of the Lord?"

"Not entirely, no," Yollana answered. The cracks of age were smoothed out of her voice; the ice of night replaced them. "We are almost there, and I can tell you now that no Matriarch of Havalla has ever set foot upon that soil. I am . . . not entirely certain . . . that I will be welcome.

"I saw glimpses, Teresa. Of things ancient, things Arkosan. I will not speak of them."

The Serra nodded quietly. "And nothing of the Voyani? Nothing of Margret, or her heir? Nothing of the fate of those who follow?"

The old woman, canny old woman, looked across the ashes of the incense she had burned. She did not answer, and that was answer enough.

Because she knew what the Serra would hear.

Margret did not walk on the ground. She did not sleep there. It had been her intent to find company among her kin, but she found, to her great surprise, that she was drawn to the heights, and even when the wagon—if she could call something squat and rounded that had been stripped of wheels a wagon—was brought close to ground, she had no desire to leave it. Huddled between the great clay jugs that became lighter with each passing day, she found a place for herself that defied the cold night howl of wind.

There was no room to live within the living space she had known for much of her life; all of that space had been given over to the simple fact of Arkosa's survival. In the night, she would lift her hands and run callused palms against the rough surface of baked clay, which was as close as she would come to touching the water, aside from drinking it. She used the sand to bathe, as she had been taught by Evallen of Arkosa many years ago.

Blankets were wedged beneath her back, blankets around her feet, and blankets beneath the curve of her folded arms. In the dark, she would remove her boots and the mask that protected her from sunlight and sand-laden wind, and she would lie, eyes open, staring at the shadows above until the wind's voice became simple noise, akin to heartbeat or breath. Sometimes that took minutes.

Sometimes it took hours.

And sometimes it did not happen.

Listen to the wind, her mother once told her. *While the others fear it or shun it, listen to its voice.*

But it speaks of death.

Yes. And only death. But sometimes knowing which death you face is your best—or only—chance of avoiding it.

She had been silent then. Evallen had never been a patient teacher, and when Margret was slow to understand a lesson, her mother's tongue would grow increasingly sharp.

What if, she had said, weighing the cost of asking the question with the need she felt for the answer, *the death you hear is not your own?*

What if? It will almost never *be your own. Did I raise such a stupid daughter? You are Arkosa. When you hear the wind speak about the death of your family, you act quickly. Arkosa is all that you are.*

No, she thought, unwinding herself from her uncomfortable, cramped makeshift bed. *It is not all that I am. It is all that you were.*

She rose. She had time to grab her boots; time to fumble with the mask that would provide little protection against the night's chill.

The air, she thought. *Something in the air.*

Something other than the ice that made the walls of her throat close and touch. She could see the breath that hung in clouds before her face; her mother had once called it the smoke from a human fire. She ordered the wagon to rise, and it obeyed, leaving the corpse of a riverbed rapidly beneath it.

The winds were strong. She braced herself; felt it through four layers of cloth. Something in the air.

Lady.

"Matriarch."

She knew the voice instantly. Echoes of its song still reverberated in a place that had encased certain memories in Northern glass, preserving them whole for inspection days, months, years after they had passed into history—no matter how much she might otherwise want to bury them.

She had no way of answering, which was just as well.

"Matriarch." Then, **"Margret."**

She turned in the direction of the voice; the ship turned with her, so much a part of her she need utter no command. Beneath her, in a darkness no longer interrupted by torches or the single central fire they had been able to carry wood for, she saw by starlight; by the interrupted face of the moon.

The Serra Diora stood before her tent, one hand outstretched. Although she was as heavily clothed—and masked—as Margret, there was something about the curve of her arm, the lift of her shoulder, the tilt of her chin, that would never, ever be natural to an Arkosan.

"I am sorry to wake you," she said.

Margret frowned.

". . . if indeed you slept at all."

And smiled, the corners of her lips turning up almost reflexively.

"But the Heart of Arkosa is burning."

The moment she heard the words, she felt their truth. She hesitated—or thought she did—but the wagon itself had already begun its descent, negotiating the still air above the peaked tops of small tents to the steady rhythm of her mumbled curses. The wagon was not meant to fly so close to her people.

There was no space to bring it to ground, had she desired to; there was space to stop, to cast a moon shadow, above the sleeping members of her family. Adam's tent. Ona Tamara's. Stavos.

She stopped above the Serra's.

"I can't land," she said, aware of the flat, thin quality of her voice in comparison to the voice that had brought her here.

"I . . . see that. It is not necessary." The Serra hesitated, staring at the underside of the wagon; it was within reach of her arm if she raised it.

"Can you climb?"

"I don't know," the Serra replied. "It was not one of the skills that was valued by my husband's clan."

Margret chuckled.

The Serra turned to look over her shoulder at the tent whose flaps were motionless in the wind shelter of the riverbed. Hard to imagine that water had once coursed between the runnels in hard-baked earth.

Hard, but not impossible.

Margret shrugged; she lost sight of the Serra as she rummaged in the darkness, with hands growing quickly numb, for the familiar rough feel of heavy twine. Rope. She held it in her hands, tugged it, felt it abrade skin.

She knew she was not the most perceptive of people. Any emotion that was not obvious, any struggle that was not offered openly for her inspection, any conflict that did not cause conflict for her had never been much of a concern. Subtleties escaped her; they had never been as relevant to her life as wielding a weapon, maintaining a wagon, feeding the children.

Her mother had had the sense to point out that some of these nuances, some of these problems, *would* be Margret's, given time to fester. So Margret had grudgingly learned to recognize all of the variations of anger. Because anger, unchecked, undetected, led to death, and it would be her job to either prevent death among the Arkosans, or to selectively cause the ones that couldn't be prevented.

But she wasn't naturally gifted. She had learned the intricacies of anger only when she fully accepted that anger was a weakness she possessed; that when she gave anger free rein, she did things that her mother later regretted. Evallen, in turn, made sure that Margret *really* regretted what she'd done. You could do many things as the daughter of the Matriarch, but you did not embarrass your mother with impunity.

Once she could accept that anger was a flaw and not a right—and she could only barely accept it, and there were whole weeks where the acceptance made no sense—the rest had been simple. The weakness that she despised in others she accepted as simple reflection. And she understood herself.

Fear had been harder. Anger was easy to accept and to own. It might be a liability, but it was also a weapon, a shield, in certain circumstances an act of strength. But fear? She loathed it. To admit to fear in any public way was an act of humiliation and surrender.

Of course. When your people are afraid, they look to you. Her mother's voice. Following those words, she could feel the dim ghost of her mother's swift, open palm. *But if you can't name your own fears, if you can't understand what they force you to, you'll be a piss-poor Matriarch. And no daughter of* mine *is going to fail as a Matriarch, is that understood?*

Later, cheeks stinging, she had stormed out of her mother's wagon, ignoring Evallen's hoarse voice, her angry invective. No one else paid any attention to it either; they were inured to the sound of her irritation.

But Adam often followed her.

She doesn't mean it.

Doesn't mean it?

Doesn't mean any of it. She tells you to pay attention to fear. Pay attention to hers.

Hers? Margret's laugh was bitter; she felt a trace of it between clenched teeth, although it had been a few years.

Three. Adam had been so young then. So young. *What fears does she have? There's nothing she can't do. Nothing she's afraid of.*

He had stood at her back, shuffling in that awkward way that she hated as he tried to choose between caution and honesty (or cowardice and courage). *She's afraid of you,* he said at last.

Of me? Then why is it my *face that bears the handprints?*

She doesn't know how to tell you she's afraid. She's afraid you'll be more afraid than you already are. He paused. *So this is how she speaks.*

Then let her speak to someone else.

He shrugged. *She doesn't like to waste her words. You're the only person important enough to make her this crazy.*

Adam was patient.

She's hit you.

She hits everyone. It's not the same. Perhaps patience wasn't the right word. It didn't occur to him, most times, to *be* impatient. He lived in a world that she could barely see. Sometimes that world was a world of people who looked like the ones she knew, but had nothing else in common with them. Sometimes it was stranger than that. He had a profound sense of wonder, a sense of the other that was only invoked in Margret when Evallen taught her the ceremonies of the Matriarchs, and sometimes not even then; Margret was practical by nature.

When she walked the *Voyanne,* both of her feet were on the ground; when she traveled in the Matriarch's wagon, she knew which way the wheels were turning.

There is no other Arkosan she'd choose for this, he said.

Margret snorted, but with less force. *Ask her that now.*

Why? I know what she'll say.

Elena.

He laughed. *Maybe. Mostly she doesn't want to let go. She doesn't want you to suffer.*

Margret had laughed. And laughed.

It's true, 'Gret. She knows what you'll suffer, and she wants to make sure you're tough enough that it doesn't hurt you.

Hurt me???

Hurt you, he said, looking away, looking toward the wagon in which Evallen of Arkosa was now quiet—more due to the slammed door than anything else. *She wants to protect you, or to teach you how to protect yourself, from all the things that hurt* her *when she became Matriarch.*

Adam was quiet. He was gentle. He was sometimes hesitant. He did not have the force of personality that either Margret or Evallen possessed. But he was strong in his fashion, and his words, given quietly, reached her ears where shouting and screaming failed.

You can see it, he told her.

She said nothing.

You can see it now. Fear. What it does. What it makes you do. What you don't want to see when you do it. She's not a good teacher. She is a good Matriarch. I wish . . . I wish for both of your sakes that she was a better mother.

All this returned to her. This and more.

Because as she stood at the prow of this awkward, unlikely ship in the deadly chill of desert night, the moon was crisp and clear as new steel; the stars, just as clear and just as harsh, just as cold. The Arkosans lay, wrapped like infants or gifts in the layers of cloth that would protect them—most of them—from the worst of the night. There was no one, not even Adam, who could give her insight; who could open a window into her sensibilities from the vantage of theirs. The only other person who was awake was the Serra, and there was nothing of Arkosa about her except for the pendant placed in her hands by Evallen, the Matriarch of Arkosa.

But she understood, from the single backward glance the Serra gave her tent, understood from the moment of complete stillness that preceded the graceful lift of her arms, that she had *hesitated;* that she had teetered on the edge of a decision, that she had, for a moment, felt either unease or fear before she chose to make it. And when her hands caught the heavy, rough twine, when they slid and her breath suddenly ceased because she could not—would not—express so trivial a pain, Margret understood why she had looked back.

And what she had decided.

The Serra Diora di'Marano, without the aid of her seraf, struggled in her heavy, unflattering robes, extended her slender arms, and pulled her slight weight, hand over hand, up the side of a wagon.

She expected no help. Margret had expected to offer none; had expected to feel a vicious vindication as the woman who had always been spared a life of honest labor was finally forced to—quite literally—pull her own weight.

But she had not been forced to it; she had chosen. Margret watched. She said, and it surprised her, "Wrap the rope around your foot; you can stop a slide that way."

The Serra said nothing; Margret wasn't certain she had heard her. She waited. Hand over hand, breath now less deliberate, she approached the rail, approached Margret.

Margret reached out first with one hand, and then both, and as the Serra reached her, she offered what she had never offered a clansman.

She helped the Serra up, onto the almost nonexistent deck of her ship, her wagon. She waited, as silently as an Arkosan could wait, while the Serra caught her breath; felt a momentary pang of contempt as, in the silver light of the moon, the Serra first examined the palms of her hands for any sign of damage before she sagged slightly with relief.

She was shaking, although Margret expected that this had more to do with physical effort than cold or fear. But she forced herself to be still. And when she spoke, she spoke with the same cool distance that informed all her words.

"Accept my apologies, Matriarch. And my thanks for your intervention."

Margret bristled; it was the tone of voice. But she said nothing as the Serra reached into the heavy layers of cloth that hid her and kept her as warm as one could be kept when exposed to this night.

The Heart of Arkosa shone in her hand when she withdrew it. Margret forgot to bristle; she forgot to be irritated at the somber, stately tone of the Serra's superior voice. She saw only the Heart, heard only the pace of its erratic beating.

She took a step forward, and forced herself to stop. Her mouth was dry, but the urgency that the sight of the Heart invoked left no room for the bitter anger that she still felt toward her mother. "Is it—what does it feel like?"

"Feel like?"

"Is it warm?"

"It's uncomfortably hot to the touch, but it doesn't . . .

seem to leave a mark." And she glanced down, although no skin was exposed for her inspection.

Margret did not have time to despise her vanity. Much. "Does it—does it speak to you?"

"Speak to me?"

"The Heart," she said urgently, swallowing the words that she wanted to add. *Just pretend,* she told herself, *that you're speaking to a child.* And then, unbidden, *It's not like she's much older than Adam.*

The Serra hesitated. It was not as obvious a hesitation as she had shown before she caught the rope Margret had thrown her; it was punctuated by no backward glances. But it was there.

"Well?"

And it continued for some minutes. But the Serra chose, with a directness that was informed by her grace and delicacy, to speak. "I do not understand you, Margret of Arkosa. I do not understand your anger."

It was not what she expected to hear. "My—my anger?"

The Serra nodded.

Nonplussed, Margret felt her fingertips reaching for her palms in a reflexive curl. "And what am I supposed to be angry at?"

"Supposed to be? I cannot say. But it is your anger at your mother that I find confusing. She understood all of the facts laid out before her; she chose a course based on those facts. If there was folly, she paid. If there was mere necessity, she paid as well. She chose the price."

It was damn cold out. "You're right," Margret said, each word brittle. "I *am* angry."

"I know."

"And you're being unusually direct about your accusations."

"Yes. It goes against everything I have been taught."

"What a surprise," Margret snapped back, hating the Serra's dignity. Hating her. "A clansman is taught to be dishonest."

"To be dishonest with people who have power over my life—and my death—when the words that are most truthful will be least pleasing, yes. Honesty may be highly prized among the Voyani, but even Evallen came to the Tor

Leonne in the guise of seraf, and remained hidden among the Radann."

"Honesty among outsiders is irrelevant."

Diora's laughter was unguarded. Musical, Margret thought, surprised that anything that seemed so lovely could also sound so bitter. "In my life, in the life of the High Court, there are nothing *but* outsiders. You are not of the clans, but in the end, you feel no more foreign."

"Except for my anger. With my mother."

The laughter was gone. "Except for your anger."

"You want to know why I'm angry? You really want to know?" She turned. Caught railing that for most of the rest of her life had seemed like pointless decoration; she had never ridden the skies with her mother.

Diora nodded quietly.

"In the end, as far as I can tell, my mother died just so *you* could leave the gilded cage."

The words did not seem to surprise the Serra. But then again, so little did. Margret resented her composure. Wondered why she resented it. Wondered if wondering was a good thing.

"She died so that I might fly to a different one."

"What do you mean?"

"The Sun Sword."

"The Sun Sword." Margret bowed her head, as if in surrender. "The Lord of Night."

"The Lord."

They were both silent for a long time. At last, Margret said, "And the Lord is more important than Arkosa."

"I . . . think that enmity of the Lord is the foundation of the *Voyanne*."

"Would you give up everything you valued and everything you knew to defeat him?" Margret leaned into the railing; felt it tucked against her elbows through layers of heavy cloth.

"Yes."

The silence was long. And it was broken by the Serra. "But in honesty, had I known then what I know now, I would give you a different answer. Had I seen the end of the world in the Lord's hands, but been promised the life of my—*my*—family for another ten years, I would give you a different answer. I would take those ten years. I would treasure them. I would face whatever death He offered almost gratefully. If I could, I would never choose Evallen's path, no matter what it meant for the rest of the world. No matter what it meant for my family, in the end, or for me.

"I admire the strength Evallen of Arkosa showed. I admire the dedication that brought her to the Tor Leonne. I cannot conceive of feeling anger for her in your situation."

"Is that why you asked me?"

"Why you are so angry? No. I had other reasons."

"Oh?"

"The Heart did speak to me."

Margret felt a flash of envy someplace deep within her, like the strike of a well aimed dagger. The momentary calm of a conversation she could never have foreseen eluded her as she struggled for breath. Found it.

"Margret, in the end I am merely a way station; you are the heart of Arkosa in any way that matters."

She *hated* the grace. Hated that in her anger she could still, somehow, appreciate it. "What did it say?" The words were gruff, but they were spoken.

"I . . . I'm not certain."

"What do you mean, not certain? Riddles? Prophecy? My mother was damn good at that."

She froze for a moment, and she looked so natural in the ice of desert night, Margret wondered what she would look like if set in the Northern Winter.

"Serra?"

"Your pardon, Matriarch. I meant simply that while the Heart speaks, it speaks in a language I do not understand. It is not Torra, although I hear some of the cadence of Torra in it."

Margret closed her eyes. How many times in her life had she been told her destiny was unique? How many times had she rebelled against a future in which she had had no choice? When had it gone from being something she dreaded to something she valued?

"I think," the Serra continued after a pause, "that you should hear what it says."

"You can repeat it?"

"Yes."

Margret gestured. The wagon rose out of the tunnel, like a bird that appears too fat for its wings. "Not yet," she said, hands on the rail. "Not so close to the ground that the words can be heard."

"If it is important that the words not be heard, the Lady will guard them."

Margret snorted. "Save it," she said, "for them." She nodded to the ground that was receding. "They need it. Matriarchs learn early that we make our own luck."

"So, too," the Serra said softly, "do the Serras." She folded her arms across her chest; above the enclosed walls of the small tunnel, the wind was bitter. Sharp, knife's edge. *Lady's knife,* she thought. It could kill, but it had no color, no scent that was not borrowed, no taste, no true texture. Nothing at all but sound. And the sound was enough; it spoke to her, through her, beyond. Wind's voice. Wind.

She wondered what the cold would do to her skin. Wondered when the corners of her lips and eyes would bear the same lines that seemed to scar Margret's face with their intricate network. Wondered, last, what it would be like to *be* Margret, to live a life assured of one's fate, regardless of beauty, of grace, of physical demeanor; to age into one's power, rather than away from it as the Serras did, groping for each passing second and clinging to the youth that was, day by day, destroyed by sun and wind. It looked, to the Serra Diora, very much like freedom.

And she was wise enough to be suspicious of freedom, although she desired it. She was wise enough to be suspicious of any desire that she did not fully understand or fully control.

"Here," Margret said, her movements masculine, truncated, decisive. Ruatha might have moved that way, had she been born to freedom. "Here, we can talk. What did the Heart say?"

Why did the living make her think so much of the dead?

She composed herself as she drew breath; took comfort, took strength, from the concentration she required to speak to Margret, and Margret alone. She had become bold with the voice as she waited on the periphery of the desert so feared by the Voyani.

"Serra?"

The Serra Diora, lost in the robes of the desert walkers, nodded. She lifted a hand to her throat, and touched the chain that nested there, against her ivory skin. Lift only enough that she might touch the Heart, not that she might expose it to the night sky, the watching s.

It was beneath the night sky that she had lost her life.

The Heart was warm beneath her fingertips; warm against her skin. For just a moment, she wanted to pull it out, to cup it between her palms, to absorb all it had to offer. She was that cold. But she was used to suffering physical pain and indignity with dignity; it defined her. She began to listen to the Heart itself.

Was it called a heart for a reason? It did not beat. It did not pump blood. It could not be pierced—and stilled—by steel, wood, or time. But it could speak. It could contain the darkest of memories, the most insidious of whispers. It had, she was certain, borne witness to evils that had scarred and shaped both the Heart itself and the women around whose neck it rested.

Who better to understand the scarred heart, the swallowed darkness? She let its voice be heard as if she were its kin. Sound came at first like the faintest of breezes through the artful wilderness of the Tor Leonne's tallest trees, a ripple of life against life, a small cascade of quiet. But it grew; it grew as both the sense of word and the sensation of it at the tips of her fingers.

Margret was impatient. Envious. Silent.

The Serra Diora began to speak, her voice retrieving the sounds of an old tongue, cobbling them together, syllable by syllable, her cadence exact as she groped for the subtle space that existed between words, the pause that divided syllabic noise into language, aware that as she watched Margret's face, the effort was pure self-indulgence. Pause or no, she spoke in a way that the other woman understood.

And she knew, the moment she saw the changing shape of the older woman's mouth, the rounding of the corners of her eyes, the lengthening of her jawline, that she should have come in haste.

Margret whipped around, as if spun roughly in place by unseen hands. Her gaze fell upon the darkness in the South; she lifted her head and whispered. Invocation? Plea?

The former. The ship lurched beneath their feet. Serra Diora stumbled and righted herself; the Matriarch did not appear to notice the instability of the narrow wooden planking. The ship moved away from the tenting beneath it and began a steep descent.

"Matriarch!" Diora said, reaching out with only her voice. "What is it saying?"

"Zahar Serpensan."

"What is that?"

"Serpent's tears," she said hoarsely. She was almost immobile. Her hands were rigid, like claws or clumsy weapons. "Wake them, help me wake them." But if she was immobile, her voice was not; it shook, like plates of earth. She fumbled at her waist for something that she no longer carried.

She was terrified.

The Serra Diora responded at once. She spoke to the wind with the wind's voice, bringing her curse to bear.

"Ona Teresa," she said, invoking command with all the urgency one born to wield voice could force into the containment of words. **"Kallandras, come. I call you: Wake."**

Before she could draw breath, before she could speak again, his voice returned in the ice and the cold. **"I am awake, Serra Diora. I have been watching. What news do you carry with such urgency?"**

"Serpent's Tears."

Only silence answered, and after a second, the sounds of footsteps.

She woke to the sound of screaming. Sleep that ended this way was not rare; it was a part of her nocturnal life; the screams were her own.

Avandar was not there; in his absence, light was absent; there was no flickering shadow, no orange of fire contained in glass; she was confined in a small, dark space. When she bolted upward, the rough, scented weave of tenting pressed against her face, like a hand.

She drew her dagger, her limbs shaking, clumsy; she accidentally cut her palm, drawing beads of blood from beneath the thin surface of skin that were dark enough to be seen when the rising tent flap let the light in.

"Jewel."

She hated the darkness. Her hand became a fist, smearing blood, hiding it. Then she nodded.

"Kitchen?" he said softly.

He had never asked. It was Teller, or Finch, or sometimes Angel, who could judge the intensity of the dream, and who would lead her, still sweating, still caught in its mesh, into the relative safety of the place she had always chosen to gather her den in. To Avandar, the kitchen was a place for servants, not masters; he had always disapproved of her choice of council halls, her place of doing business.

And yet he had asked that, who had never asked that, here.

She was awake now. Thunder was in her ears, and it wasn't the simple heartbeat that usually resided there, pounding, after the nightmares had relinquished her to the waking world, the way a bored cat might a mouse.

"We—we don't have time for the kitchen," she said, shaking. Thinking that, even among the Voyani, she had spent so much time on the edges of the place where children were fed. Grateful for the fact that the children were gone; that she had not had to see their bodies carried by rushing water through the narrow, hard enclosure of the dry tunnels in which the tents were pitched.

Avandar lifted his head.

"Thunder," he said quietly.

"And rain," Jewel snapped, rolling her way out of silks and heavy blankets into a very cold night. *"Celleriant!"*

Elena woke. She could not have said what woke her, but her body was moving before her mind understood that she was, indeed awake. Power there. Lady's power or Lord's—in the desert, it didn't matter. Everything led to death.

She came out of the wagon that she so reluctantly occupied, into the first mist of rain.

In the night, no one was pale, no one dark. But the warmth of sleep drained from her. Against her skin she felt the first touch of water; the drop was heavy.

Serpent's tears, she thought. She could not find her voice; the walls of her throat were closing, like some vast, impenetrable doors. What was important? What was important now?

The Matriarch. The Matriarch alone.

No, not only the Matriarch.

She murmured the commands that might invoke flight, and the wagon lurched off the uneven ground like a drunk bird. "*Margret!*"

It was not the Arianni lord who answered Jewel's rough summons.

Kallandras of Senniel College came out from the jumbled chaos of huddled tents as if he had run across them from peak to peak, unperturbed by either his own weight or the darkness. His hair was bound, and beneath the loose drape of desert robes, he wore black. The glint of his weaponry caught the torches that had been lit—they were few—and reflected them in bright red and orange; other than that, he had no color.

He paused before Jewel. "ATerafin."

"I—" Thunder. Thunder, here, and a clap of something too inimical to be light. She shouted over the rumbled, broken syllables of the storm's voice, "Call the wind, Kallandras. Break the storm, or weaken it."

Thunder.

Water.

He lifted a hand; she saw—*saw*—the wind twisting around his finger, his wrist, his arm, like the trunk of a great snake. But he did not speak.

Instead, he met her gaze for a full ten seconds, and then he bowed. Bowed, lifting his arm.

Any other man, she thought—even Avandar, especially Avandar—would have asked her how she knew what she knew. Not about the future; anyone with a brain knew that. But about his ability to speak with the wind, the air; about his ability to take the fight to the heart of the storm that raged well above the earth.

Any other powerful person would have wondered if she had crossed the line between being an ally and becoming a threat. She had become adept, over the years, at hoarding knowledge for just that reason.

But never in an emergency; never in a situation in which the cost would be writ in lives. Other people's lives.

It is a skill you must *learn.*

She did not choose to argue with Avandar because she did not have the time. "Don't lecture me!" she shouted. "*Move!*"

"Move?"

"We've got to get these people out of the tunnels or we'll lose them!"

"Does it matter, Jewel?"

She turned then, and before she could think, before she could become aware of what her hand was doing, it left a mark across his cheek. It stung her. He did not appear to have felt it, although she could see the whitening of his skin.

He held her wrist.

"Never ask me that," she said, as evenly as she could. "Never ask me that again."

He raised a brow, and his lips thinned, curved in a distinct smile. "At your command, ATerafin."

Before she could reply—had she the words to reply with—Celleriant chose to grace them with his presence. He knelt; his braid fell across his shoulder as his forehead bowed almost to earth. "Lady," he said quietly.

"Didn't I tell you not to call me that?"

He said nothing.

"You feel the storm."

He nodded.

"Get up, Celleriant. If you have to prostrate yourself, now is *not* the time."

He lifted his face then, and she took a step back. She had not realized, until she saw his expression, that he had been living like an animal in a cage until this moment.

And it was the storm that spoke to him.

"Yes," he said softly, with something that might have been menace had it deigned to acknowledge her at all. "This storm is no mortal storm; something living coils within its heart."

"Can you speak to it?"

He laughed. Something that beautiful should never have been so cold.

What did you expect? Didn't he come to you from the host of the Winter Queen?

"Celleriant?"

"Yes, I can speak to it," he said. Thunder. "But I fear that my voice is not the only voice it will hear."

"Then *make* yours louder," she insisted urgently. "Celleriant, you were ordered to serve me, to follow my wishes and my commands."

He nodded.

"The lives of these people are of value to me. I want them safe."

He turned to Avandar. "Viandaran, you chose a path that we could not have foreseen when you chose to offer service to this one. Is she as she appears?"

"She is that. More, certainly, but not less."

The Arianni lord had eyes that were round, she thought, and beautiful—but it was only after he drew his sword that she realized why he seemed so strange: he was happy.

Joyful.

"Will you not join me, Warlord?"

A wind had risen in the depths of the tunnels, taking his hair; it streamed back from his perfect face in strands of snow and ice, curling, as it did, around the edge of his blade. The braid, Jewel thought inanely, had come undone.

She felt Avandar's answer before she heard it.

It was not simple; could not be conveyed in any words that she had yet heard him use. Ferocity of desire was rarely expressed in words, and his deprived her of words as she stood before him. His hands clenched; he drew his shoulders back, forgot breath; he raised his chin and looked into the clarity of a night sky that—as yet—held no answers to the questions raised by the nightmare of vision.

She felt fire.

She opened her eyes—when had she closed them? Had she?—and saw that he, too, carried a blade. But where Celleriant's was blue and white, silver and ice, his was—of all things—gold and light.

He raised the blade.

And then, with the thin, thin edge of a smile, he lowered it. "No," he said quietly. "I will not join you."

He sheathed the sword; she heard the rasp of metal against metal. But she could not see where the sword went when the sound ended.

"As you wish," the Arianni lord replied. But the bitter disappointment lingered a moment in the shape of his brows, the turn of his lips.

"Celleriant," Jewel said.

He turned, almost unwillingly, to face her. "Lady?"

"Are all your desires so simple?"

"Simple, Lady?"

"So unalloyed. So absolute."

He laughed. "They would hardly be *desires* if they were muddied. Such a battle as this vanished from the mortal realm when the gods forsook it. And such a battle as this, we did not fight alone. There are glories," he said softly, "That must be shared. Warlord—I will ask again."

"And the answer," Kallandras of Senniel College said softly, "will be the same. Can you not hear it in his words? He has chosen his duties; he has accepted the responsibility of his choice." He lifted a hand. Smiled. "As have I. Come, Lord Celleriant. If you wish a comrade, you will find no other."

"You?" The Arianni lord said, only barely able to contain his scorn.

Kallandras was impervious to it. His hand shed light.

Shed enough light that the Voyani response to its presence could be heard in a widening circle beyond them, in the earthy and very real language of the South.

"You—you—" Lord Celleriant's eyes were gratifyingly wide. Jewel felt—knew—that she was being childish. But it was more than that; without the look of wild, cold arrogance that almost always informed his features he seemed almost approachable.

"Yes," the bard replied.

"Upon your finger—that is one of the five—"

He nodded again. "Myrddion's work."

Celleriant turned, to Avandar, to Jewel. His eyes still retained the width brought by surprise, by shock. But he smiled again. "It is true," he said, sounding pleased.

"True?"

"The time is almost upon us. Perhaps my Lady—perhaps the Winter Queen—was not so angered as she seemed when she sent me to you.

"The End of Days approaches. Legends wake. The princes of the Firstborn must surely be preparing for their final ride. Who among us would have turned away from the opportunity to walk the lands in freedom at such a time?"

"You are not free." Avandar Gallais was once again himself; no hint of conflict, no hint of desire, troubled his expression.

"No," Celleriant replied, although he did not turn his gaze back to Avandar. "I serve the mortal. But I do not walk the hidden ways; I do not ride with the host; I do not turn at the Lady's whim, and the Lady's whim alone. I watch the turning, instead, of sun and moon; I feel the change of day, from ice to fire and back. I see the passage of time across the faces of everyone around me; I saw it in the turn of leaves at desert's edge; I see it in the drift of the stars above.

"What happens at the End of Days will happen, I think, in *this* world, in this diminished, mortal world. But so, too, did the greatest of our wars, the most ferocious of our battles. *These* are the lands that gods walked, and we walked in their wake."

"Don't," Jewel said, before she could stop herself.

He looked up immediately, sensitive to her, to her commands. "Lady?"

"Don't speak of gods walking."

He shrugged. "Lady?"

But he had spoken. She felt it as a twisting of muscle and sinew, a certainty in the pit of her stomach that was as strong there as any fear she had ever faced had been. It did not leave her.

Jewel?

She lost sight of Avandar; lost sight of Kallandras, of Celleriant. She lost sight of the tunnels, of the perfect clarity of desert night, of the clouds of breath that hung a moment from each of their lips before the growing breeze swept all trace of it away.

But she did not lose sight of the shape and shadow of night; it condensed, losing the pinpoints of light, the shades that gave it texture and color as it stretched from horizon to heaven, shrinking inward until it encompassed the center of her vision.

And on the growing edges: the broken spires of the Isle of *Aramarelas,* under siege by winged beasts who spoke with majesty in voices of flame. Fire. The towers were burning. The cathedrals were being destroyed. She could hear the terrible silence that presages screaming as the city drew its collective breath. She could see, beneath the feet of a passing god, the refuse that she would think of, at any other time, as bodies. She was dimly aware that there were other creatures around the heart of Night; dimly aware that they might attempt to stand beside, or before, the darkness that came toward the city of Essalieyan.

And she?

Upon the field of battle. Her hand around, of all things, a pole that felt suspiciously unlike a weapon's haft. Surrounded by the dead, by the dying.

Jewel!

Avandar's voice.

She closed her eyes, but not before she realized that she could not tell if his voice were a part of her vision, or simply an escape hatch from the worst of it: the destruction she *knew* was to follow.

Her knees refused to hold her. His arms did what her knees could not. She felt his voice by her ear. "Jewel." No question.

She could not weep, or scream, or even speak.

Celleriant watched her face closely, his expression slightly perplexed.

She shook her head, to clear it—to give him back the joy and lucidity of purpose. "Go."

Released, he turned again to Kallandras. "Come, mortal. Come. The storm's voice is almost upon us."

No, Jewel thought, *not almost.*

The rain began to fall.

CHAPTER TWENTY-ONE

Rain.

The Serra Diora di'Marano had never lived in the desert; had never lived confined by it. Confined by other things, she had seldom stood beneath the exposed face of an angry sky in the depths of such a bitter cold. She thought the water must freeze, but no—it was warm where it touched her exposed skin.

Her skin.

She raised her eyes to the Matriarch's face; ice lay against her cheeks, and against the sheen of her rounded eyes. Black edged her face until she raised her hands and shoved her hair back.

She said, "It doesn't rain at night."

Just that.

The two women turned toward the sky. Diora thought it strange that one could so be far from the ground and yet still be no closer to the Lady's face or the glittering pinpoints of light that she cast.

"Hold on," the Matriarch said. "Hold tight. We—"

From out of the clear—the *clear*—of the night sky, shadows unfurled. And spread. And spread.

"Matriarch?" Diora whispered, the sound anchored by her gift where any other whisper would have been buffeted from lips by the roar of the wind.

Margret did not move. Could not speak. She raised a finger; it shook.

"Matriarch!"

The wind *roared*. Diora stood, transfixed by what she heard. She knew the wind's voice; she had listened a thousand times as it howled past her, laden sometimes with water and sometimes with dry, arid heat; she had tried, as child, and then as bereaved and isolated widow, to grab words from its folds, to isolate voices, anything at all that sounded as if it had once known life.

She would never do that again. Lady, have mercy in this darkness, this storm—should she see the sun again, she would never struggle to find the words the wind carried.

She heard them now, and if she could not understand the language, she could recognize its cadence.

Had she not repeated it, precisely and accurately, at the behest of the Arkosan Matriarch? But there had been no anger in her repetition. No grief, no hatred, no fury, and no desire; she had stripped the syllables of anything but sound, the comfortable neutrality of air across lip and teeth.

Had she been able, she would have done the same to this voice. She could not; she was transfixed by what she heard contained by words.

Across the darkened sky, the shadow had ceased to spread; had in fact taken form in its deadly flight: the form of great pinions, of moving arches. Wings.

She almost forgot—did forget—to hang on to the rails, but the rocking of the boat was reminder enough. She stumbled, banged her knee; caught the rail with her left hand and the crook of her right elbow, and clung to her footing with an appalling lack of grace.

She lost sight of the Arkosan Matriarch.

Her back was exposed a moment as she struggled to find her feet while the surface of the slight deck shifted, inclining toward ground in a dangerous spiral.

But the exposure was not as terrifying as what she saw beneath her. The Voyani encampment was alive. She could not differentiate between young and old, man and woman, they moved so quickly—but their voices told her what her less capable vision could not. They understood that the storm—and it had suddenly become a storm—meant death. The Voyani accepted no death with grace.

All this she caught in a glimpse, wheeling as the boat wheeled.

But she caught one other thing as well: among the men and women who ran back and forth, was one who did not; he stood tall, remote; he was deliberate as he searched.

At a distance, with no voice to guide her, she did not recognize him until she had passed beyond his vision, and he hers.

Ramdan.

He did not speak; she could not imagine what he would say to anyone who was not the Serra Diora or the Serra Teresa di'Marano. She wondered if any of the Voyani would care enough about his life that they would save him in spite of his silence. His silence and the servitude that they resented or despised.

The ship listed; she heard the Matriarch's guttural cursing. She had never thought to take joy from such base indulgence, but she felt her heart twist in an unaccustomed relief.

"Matriarch!"

"Blind the Lord!" The Matriarch cursed, speaking into the wind and the water. She groped her way to where Diora clung to the rails, threw her arms around her waist, and struggled a moment. "I've tied you to the rail; if you need freedom, cut the twine!"

Diora nodded.

"We're going to try to draw the attention of the—of the storm."

The Serra nodded again. "How much attention do we want?"

"All of it."

"Now?"

"Now."

Diora lifted her face; water streamed down her cheeks, traveling the length of exposed throat, settling into folds of rough fabric more quickly than it could be absorbed. Serpent's tears. Warmer than her skin. She felt the rope cut her waist as the ship careened in the sky; she let that rope take the brunt of her weight while Margret brought the boat to bear, as if it were an unbroken horse, and she only barely capable of riding.

The Serra Diora di'Marano lifted her arms, palms upturned toward the part of the night sky that knew no moonlight, no starlight. For just a moment she stood, listening to the storm, to the people below who, in frenzy, sought to avoid the floods that would follow.

She sang.

She sang and the storm turned.

* * *

Two people looked up from the ground the moment her voice joined the thunder.

"Teresa!"

One looked down again almost as quickly.

Na'dio. She could not clearly see where the voice had come from, but she knew that her almost-daughter was no longer among the rain-drenched Voyani.

Water matted the Serra's hair to her forehead, her clothing to her skin. Everything was heavy, weighted by storm, necessity, duty. She shifted her arm's weight as Yollana stumbled, sliding against ground that had already become treacherously slick. There had been lamps, but the glass hoods that were so precious were not proof against the howling wind; flames had guttered, glass shattered. Warm light was lost to the water; the cold light of moon and star was lost to the . . . storm.

Life, she thought, would follow.

A hand was on her chin, its grip too tight. She followed that grip to see Yollana's grim expression. To see her lips moving over words that were so quiet even her natural talent could not catch them. Not without effort.

She made the effort. Grace served her well; she was limber, she was able to balance the weight of the older woman and the responsibility of safe passage over terrain she could no longer clearly see.

The rain that had started suddenly had gone from heavy drops to torrent in the minutes it took the encampment to struggle from sleep into panic. The tent that had housed the Matriarch of Havalla had been swept away; it was not easy to anchor it in ground as dry as the tunnel had been.

It was not easy to find footing. Not easy to find a way out of the tunnel itself; the water swept fingers away from what had once been a challenging incline. They had pikes for climbing; the water that poured down from everywhere above them made climbing impossible.

The Serra Teresa found a place to stand and turned her full attention to the Havallan Matriarch.

"Tell Margret to flee." Yollana commanded.

"I—"

"I will not tell you how to do it. I will allow no others to ask how it was done. I ask no questions. I have never asked questions. I have trusted you as I trust only Havallans from the moment we first met. Do as I ask. Tell her. She has her responsibility."

She waited for less than the space of an uneven breath.

"Yollana," she said, "if I do not survive, and you do, keep my daughter safe."

"I promise nothing, Teresa. Not now. The Lord of Night has come, and I am already bound by promises older than either of us."

"Promise, then, that you will do all you can do short of breaking those oaths. Your word, Yollana."

"For what it's worth?"

"I value it."

"Then you've grown addled with age. You've blunted your edge, girl."

"A club is blunt, Matriarch, but your people still use them when swords are too dear."

The water had risen, Teresa thought. How much, it was hard to say; the water flowed swiftly through the tunnel creating peaks and vortexes that made measurement difficult. She waited.

"Done, Serra. Done. But tell Margret. Tell her—she's a fool, that girl. She'll ride the storm."

The Serra hesitated a moment longer, and then she nodded. But it was not Margret she bespoke, not directly; she had blunted her edge, as Yollana said, but she had not lost it entirely, and she was unwilling to expose the secret of decades to a woman who could neither control tongue nor temper.

The water came.

Jewel watched as the ground, hard and cracked, refused to absorb it. Avandar caught her roughly by the chin—as if he realized that he had to make the source of the threat as clear as possible—and turned her face up, toward the top of the tunnel walls, the edges of the vast, exposed plain from which they had taken refuge.

She saw a waterfall that stretched as far as the eyes could see. Given the night and her vision, that was thankfully not that great a distance.

Water *poured* into the tunnel. Jewel was pretty good with numbers. At the rate the water was rising . . . she could suddenly understand why the Voyani were terrified, and it didn't have much to do with freezing to death.

The rain didn't look like it was going to stop any time soon.

It may, Avandar said, in that uncomfortable, intrusive inner voice.

She looked up, squinting in pain as the unnatural rain hit her face, sliding into her eyes and her mouth.

"Avandar!"

No answer. She cursed him then, cursed roundly.

Avandar.

Jewel.

We need to get out of here. How do we get up through that?

She didn't like the quality of his silence. Even here, it was oppressive. *Avandar?*

There . . . is no certain way. It would be best if the storm was called away.

And we talk to the storm how? she snapped back. But the words, which would have been sharp and sarcastic when spoken out loud, carried far more of the fear she felt than she wanted to show; she felt silent.

We don't, he replied, as if he couldn't hear it, as if it were possible not to. *They do.*

Kallandras raised face to sky. He did not look down, but said, "Lord Celleriant, I fear you will lose your battle if you hesitate."

The Arianni lord spun at once. "What?" Water did not cling to his face or his hair; his clothing carried it, but the weight did not encumber him.

"Can you not hear her? Someone is challenging the creature whose wings are the storm's heart. And . . . it hears her. I am certain of it."

She heard two things: The voice of her aunt, and the voice of the storm. The storm held sway. The wind was wild, savage; she had been forced to cling to the wagon with fingers, with arms, with the crook of her feet when it was necessary.

It was when she was trying to find purchase against the

cabin wall that she found her first comfort: the symbols painted there in russet strokes were glowing faintly.

"Matriarch!"

The comfort was short-lived.

The storm had arrived. It hovered a hundred feet to her left, its wings the span of the horizon that she could clearly see in the downpour. Water did not dare to strike it; it rose above the element the way the Lord's face rose above the Dominion. Black, sleek, it unfolded a slender neck, a serpent's neck.

She saw its face, saw the first glimmering of color; an eye. Blue, she thought. Blue as the clearest of skies—as if it had swallowed all clarity, all sign of day, had subsumed it, and only this glint remained.

That and the white of teeth, the red of tongue.

"Matriarch!"

"Here!" The voice came, thin and reedy compared to the majesty of what they now faced.

Had visibility become so poor? She tried to look, but she could not turn her face away from the Serpent her power had summoned.

"We have its attention!" she shouted. "Should we not flee?"

"We've got more than its attention!" the Matriarch shouted back.

The neck elongated. Drew back. Snakes did that, before striking.

The Serra reached into the drenched folds of her Voyani robes. The rope around her waist saved her life and bruised her terribly when she let go of the rail with her right hand. But those bruises were rewarded when her hand gripped the haft of the dagger given her by Evallen of the Arkosa Voyani a lifetime ago, in the civilized danger of the Tor Leonne. What had the Arkosans called it?

Lumina Arden.

She drew it from its sheath; felt a warmth in her palm that had nothing to do with fire or flame. It spread. The blade shed light like a topaz caught in the sun's full glare as she exposed it to the storm. The edge glittered, she thought, like diamond.

The last time she had used this dagger, she had killed the Matriarch of Arkosa. Evallen.

She waited, hoarding the only power she had: her voice, the gift and curse that had informed the whole of her life.

She must be in the eye of the storm; she felt calm. There were words she had never spoken building behind the soft walls of her lips; when the serpent arrived, she would say them and be free.

And as she watched the serpent's head snake back, as she watched its descent, she wondered what the world would be like if all killings, all deaths, were acts of mercy.

Wondered if all deaths weren't, in the end.

But if they were, she was to be denied mercy.

The jaws of the Serpent—and it was a Serpent—were taller, when extended, than she. Its breath was the storm, the gale; its voice the wind. She saw teeth, saw tongue, saw darkness and felt—

the snap of rope. Not jaw.

She cried out, wordless; she struggled to maintain her grip on a rail that had never been intended to support such weight.

The head of the great beast sheared air as if air were a textured, heavy cloth. She felt the heat of its breath, saw the light of one great eye, saw the iridescence of scale as it reflected the sudden bright red of Arkosan wards. She heard something—someone—scream or curse. In Torra. The Matriarch.

But she also saw that while she lived she had power, no matter how insignificant it seemed. She had thought to speak to death, but death eluded her; she accepted the other form of conversation battle offered. Lifting her right hand, her palm now fitted around the hilt of the dagger she had kept wrapped close in sash and silk since the Festival of the Sun, she lunged.

Scale gave way to blade almost too cleanly. Blood spilled across the deck, thinned instantly by rain. She might not have known she struck, but her sleeves clung to blood in a way the deck couldn't. The creature roared.

Once again, she was transfixed by the storm's voice, by its promise of death. Or perhaps not; she could move. She could move now. If her hands weren't so cold and the rail weren't so slippery. Her legs sagged as the beast pulled back, pulled up.

"*Diora!*"

Her name. It sounded like her name, but her name shorn of affection, of title. There was only one woman who could use it so roughly.

"*Diora, damn you!*"

She said clearly, the words for the Matriarch and the Matriarch alone, "You wanted to capture its attention."

There was no silence in this thunder, but the Matriarch's voice was lost to the storm. For a moment. When it returned, it offered a strangled, angry—and yes, terrified—laugh.

She thought it would be the last thing she heard. She could not find the twine that the Matriarch had used to bind her to the wagon's upper side. She held the rail with her left hand, and the knife with her right, and the ship careened, weaving in and around the snapping jaws of an enraged creature of the storm.

She could not hold on forever. She was surprised she had held on this long.

Something—someone—caught her hand.

It was not, could not be, the Matriarch. She looked up. Saw nothing. Felt the hand that encircled hers. Her right hand.

"Let go. Let go, Serra Diora."

It was not a request. Her fingers obeyed almost before she understood the words wrapped around the power of bardic voice.

She had been prepared for death—but it was a different death—or perhaps preparation and calm were simply illusion. Regardless, her body struggled against the death that approached; she lost resignation as easily as she had lost anything she had ever cared to hold.

But she did not cry out; the words that she had trapped remained where they were. She flailed a moment, wet robes flapping like injured, soiled wings.

It seemed that struggle might count for something; she passed from storm into silence, and the silence was so sudden, so all encompassing, it was overpowering. The wind did not brush her cheek; the rain did not strike her skin, her eyes. Suspended a moment, she looked up; saw the clouds in turmoil above. And below?

The eye of the storm passed; she fell through it into the maelstrom.

The ground approached. At least she thought it was ground; it was marginally less dark than the clouds above, and there were no points of light in it, no glimmer of silver moon beyond the edge of raven wings.

It was only when the ground receded again, only when the storm somehow found a way to cradle her, to succor her, that she understood whose voice she had heard, whose command she had, without thought, obeyed. *Kallandras.* Who else had the power to speak with such force the wind itself obeyed? She danced a moment in air; found grace in the icy blast of night wind. Gained composure.

"Are you safe?"

"Yes . . ."

"First blood is yours. My companion is profoundly upset. Take the Matriarch to safety," he said. **"Her ship fights the wind, and it cannot face wind and Serpent both. Without Margret, Arkosa will fall."**

"And you?"

The only answer was the movement of wind past her ears, but that was answer enough. The wind found the deck of the Arkosan wagon. It was not the first time that she had been grateful for the wind's voice—but remembering that first time, she wondered what the price of this one would be.

"Diora!"

She spoke through rain and wind. "Matriarch—we must flee."

"We can't flee—"

"We have led the Serpent from the tunnels; the water falls, but—but the wind shunts it away while the Arkosans escape." She had lied with certainty in the past. She had lied as gracefully as she had wielded fan, worn silk, adorned the court of powerful men. But the hesitation was profound, present. She did not understand it.

She could not hear the Matriarch's reply, but the ship circled around the Serpent's head. Diora had sheathed her dagger, had planted it firmly in the water-drenched sash at her waist. She found purchase upon the ship with aching arms, aching hands.

"Matriarch," she tried again, "Why do you think they've

attacked? Why do you think the Serpent pursues? If they destroy you, they have destroyed Arkosa. The war starts now!"

The boat froze a moment. Had it been a bird, it would have plummeted; the magic of the Arkosans was stronger, Diora thought, than any of the clans had realized.

"Na'dio!" Her aunt's voice. **"Preserve the Matriarch! Leave now!"**

It was not a request. It was a command.

But her Ona Teresa was not Kallandras of Senniel College; she spoke with power but not with the wind's own voice. Diora heard the command in the shockingly graceless words, and she deflected it, with effort. She understood the nature of the command, but also understood that to use her voice against the Matriarch here was to lose all possibility of—

Of what?

She grimaced; rain followed the line of the foreign expression. She hated the cold. In the morning—should they see morning again—she would be thankful for the heat, and that thankfulness would be both genuine and ephemeral.

As almost all gratitude was, in the end.

"Matriarch!" She used enough power to make herself heard, no more.

"And am I to watch while they die?" Margret shouted back.

"How will your death serve a purpose? How will it serve *any* purpose but His?"

The boat listed. Diora stumbled, but that did not stem the flow of her words; she had learned to use what power she had in the most adverse of circumstances, and words were the only power she now possessed.

"Na'dio."

She wanted to parry her aunt's voice. Wanted to waste power, effort, and time to say, *Leave me alone*.

Because she understood the discussion she had begun with Margret of Arkosa.

She understood why, by the Lady's grace, she had to be the one to start it, to finish it. She understood why Kallandras had ordered the wind to bring her not to the safety of the earth, but back to the storm and the battle. Suddenly, she understood, and she desired as much distance between comprehension and herself as possible.

But she had been the good wife, the good daughter, the *good Serra* for so much of her life there was no way to gain that distance. She understood.

And so, too, did the Matriarch of Arkosa.

Her laughter was terrible. But it was short.

"That's what you did."

She could not speak.

"That's what *you* did. You watched while your own were murdered."

"No. Worse." She found words. "I listened." She raised her face. She controlled her expression; she controlled the shaking of her hands. She did not, however, fold her knees. She could not, with grace. To do so, she would have to let go of the rail in the storm.

And the storm would sweep her aside like so much dust, so much flotsam.

Would that be so very terrible? She was *so* tired.

"You want me to watch my people die. You want me to fail them. As you failed yours."

The words would not come. For a moment, they simply would not come. When she found them again, it was a struggle to make them heard. Anger could do that to a voice. Or pain.

She was not the Matriarch of Arkosa. She was not the woman whom everyone else called Margret. A Serra of the High Court, she had spent a life beneath the shade of bower or fan while the Lord's glare passed her by. But when she spoke again, when she found the power to force words past the thickness in her throat, she was no longer certain for whom they were intended.

"No. I want you to *live* with the responsibility you so clearly desire. I want you to understand that living is *hard*. Dying is easy. Death is easy compared to this."

At that moment, she loved the rain. Because the storm was loud, she could hear the scream of the Serpent more clearly than she could hear the screams of the dying. Because the rain fell in heavy drops across every exposed inch of skin, she could let her tears fall with it, certain of privacy.

But it hurt her throat, to contain the emotion beneath the veil of words. Her hands were shaking. She wondered—

as the boat careened wildly, as the Serpent's *breath* seemed to turn the rain into small, hard pellets—if she would be able to hold on.

And she almost didn't care what the answer was.

The boat faltered again, the perfect expression for the mind of the woman who was its rudder.

"You're the Matriarch of all of Arkosa, not just this handful of men and women. You're the mother to the Family."

"Shut up! I know who I am!"

"Then live with the guilt, Matriarch. This is not the first time you will feel it. Not the last. Do what must be done."

"They trust me! How can I—" And then she fell silent.

Diora could not know what passed through her thoughts in that absence of words. Did not care to guess. She waited, her hands numb, her throat numb, her memories terrible, even now.

"All of Arkosa," she said again, into the storm. She felt the warmth of the Heart spread from the hollow between her breasts; it was like a fire across dry brush. *"Past and present. Remember the vows of the first Matriarch. Remember."*

"They're *not* my vows!"

"No? Have we not journeyed all this way so that you can make those vows and become what your mother was? We have no more time, Matriarch. Leave this battle, or leave the title."

The Serpent roared.

And so did Margret of Arkosa. Diora heard both. She held on. Held tight as the ship began to lurch, slowly, awkwardly, away from the storm.

She thought, given the speed of their retreat, that the storm should follow with ease, but they left it behind.

She composed herself. She let the tears dry as the rain suddenly—and completely—disappeared, as the moon's face, lambent, full, silver, resumed its dominance of the clear, cold night.

The winds no longer howled; they no longer attempted to pry fingers and hands from the slick surface of wooden railing. But the Serra Diora held on, held tight, a moment longer. Her head was bowed. Her eyes closed.

Composure, she thought. *Composure, composure, compo-*

sure. In the darkness between lid and vision, she remembered all the elements of a life that existed in perfect grace. She fought her way back to that state as she had done so many, many times.

And in that struggle, a single face came to her, a single name—and it was not one of hers, but it made the struggle harder.

Adam.

"So," the Matriarch said quietly, bitterly. "This is your life."

The Serra was quiet. The silence extended until she realized that Margret expected her to say something. "You should . . . find something . . . drier to wear," she said at last. She had not opened her eyes.

"There is nothing drier." Pause. "My mother would have said that."

"Your mother?"

"That it would be just stupid enough of me to die of cold after having survived everything else the Lord could throw at me. Yours?"

"My?"

"Mother."

"I . . . don't know what my mother would have said. According to my father, I killed her." She half-expected the Matriarch to assume some murderous inclination on her part.

"Oh." Another pause. The voice drew closer. "Childbirth?"

And was almost shamed by the expectation. "Yes. Childbirth." She looked out at the storm that was now a distant wonder. The boat had stopped. "He was said to have loved my mother."

"He must have. I've heard men lose wives to infants—they speak with rage and sorrow only when the love was there to lose."

"He was more indulgent than most clansmen would permit themselves to be."

"Until he destroyed your life."

"Until he destroyed my life. But we were speaking of parents, of what parents would say. He . . ." Such a struggle for words. Ona Teresa would have been appalled. Silently, gracefully, coolly appalled.

Or would she? It was the Serra Teresa di'Marano who now traveled clothed as Voyani, her face exposed to sunlight and wind, her life in the hands of rough strangers. "He . . . would have said nothing at all about clothing, or cold, or water. I am not certain he would have noticed them now. If he had been here, he might have told me, 'Look upon the Serpent, Na'dio. Look well. Very few could have passed through the storm of its breath and survived. Learn from the things which have not killed you. Marvel at them.' " She bowed her head.

"My father . . ." Margret said quietly. "I hardly remember him. My father was the gentle one. I don't know what he would have said." Her voice was closer. "I can't imagine him here, in the midst of so much conflict. I know what my mother would have said, would have done. If she were here now, she'd slap me for taking so long to clear out." She was closer. Diora looked up and saw the wreathed mist of breath pass her lips and hang there, cloud surface thinning. "Will they die?"

"I do not know."

"Neither do I." Margret bowed her head a moment. "I'm sorry," she said quietly. "I have no idea what your life is like. You knew they were going to die, didn't you?"

"Yes."

"How? How could you have been so certain?"

"Someone came," Diora said quietly. "During the Festival of the Moon. She spoke to me while—while the others slept. I don't know if their sleep was natural. It doesn't seem to matter now. She spoke, and I heard truth in every word—but she didn't speak of their deaths. Just of . . . of what I would have to suffer . . . to make them mean anything at all." She looked down at her hands; she could see the long gashes that wood had made in her palms. An hour ago, she would have been horrified. An hour from now, she would be horrified again. But between the beginning and the end of that interval, she wanted to see herself as just another person, not a weapon in the war.

And she despised the weakness, she who had let Margret show none.

"She," the Matriarch said, after a long pause.

"A stranger."

"Did she wear blue, and carry her soul in her hands?"

"I do not know what she carried in her hands, Matriarch, but she carried something in her voice. I have often thought about her, in the shallows of evening, between the Lord and the Lady's time—and I think that whatever choices I made, they were not so terrible as the ones she has had to.

"But I hate her anyway."

The Matriarch's laugh was rich and low; it was not a stilted or forced sound, but rather something that came as naturally as breathing. Diora felt it travel the length of her spine. "That's the first time I've ever heard you say anything I could completely agree with—in words I'd even use."

Lightning illuminated her expression as Diora looked up; it robbed her of shadow and distance.

Both women looked to the East. "The rain . . ." the Serra said.

"Yes. It's slowed. Maybe stopped." She frowned. "I wish Adam were here. My eyes aren't a tenth as good as his. That lightning—"

Flashed across the sky, denying night, the moon, the stars. It was hard to look upon.

Just as the wings of the Serpent were unnaturally dark, the lightning was unnaturally bright; the one did not alleviate the other, but seemed, at this remove, to be a part of it, a counter to it. Diora was not surprised when the lightning struck again, but this time she saw its heart: a single, slender man.

The Serpent roared.

She stood, again mesmerized by what she heard in its voice, until the wind answered, the lightning replied.

No, she thought, there was more than a single man who stood in the wild folds of storm-laden wind, but the second man took to shadow and did not announce his presence; she saw him on the edge of a pinion before the wind carried him away from the glittering teeth of the Serpent's snapping jaws.

"Serra?"

Kallandras. She did not call his name.

"Serra Diora? What do you see?"

Without thinking, Diora lifted her hand to her throat, to the invisible chain that hung round it, chafing skin. "Kallandras," she said softly. "Kallandras and another of the companions who travel with the Northerner."

The torrential downpour became, in minutes, simple rain. But the minutes had been too long; the tide of the water was such that it was an effort to stand. The tunnel walls were not smooth; they offered purchase to hands strengthened by the toil of the *Voyanne*. But the water carried small pebbles, hand-sized rocks, and heavy stones within its rolling currents. It swept up tents and silks, adding to its carelessly gathered hoard.

Where rock or tent collided with a hand clinging to a tunnel wall, something had to give.

Jewel heard the shouts and cries of men and women she could barely distinguish as they floundered, wet robes clinging to skin. Those desert robes did them no good now; they were heavy. That was all.

Avandar!

He did not seem to feel the current, but that was artifice; Jewel could see the binding magics that held his feet firmly against the ground; that forced the water—and all it carried—to give him wide and careful berth.

She heard a name, each of two syllables attenuated until it was almost impossible to distinguish the sound from a scream.

The rain had come out of nowhere.

And she *knew* that that was impossible. There should have been warning.

Why? Why should there have been warning? Storms came, suddenly, in the North and she had never questioned them.

Her gift replied, wordless.

But it didn't matter. The current caught something large that floated just beneath the reach of her left arm. Without thinking, she reached out for it, and was pulled half off her feet by the weight.

She braced herself as the weight pulled itself up, clutching at her hand, her arm.

She managed to grip rock with fingers that were white as bone—but her hands were too cold and her grip too tenuous. She saw a face rise out of the current, eyes wide, mouth open to swallow air—

And a hand slid from her grasp and into the water.

Avandar! Help!

He did not look in her direction, but she knew he'd heard: He lifted an arm. She saw the light that bound him to earth—orange light—give way to green, an intense, deep green that even emeralds couldn't boast.

Avandar—

The earth moved. It moved once, like the sudden slap of a giant's hand, breaking and buckling beneath the water as the ground reared up, and up, a living slab.

The water slowed in its deadly rush, but Jewel saw small rivulets push their way around the thin slab of stone.

The water pouring down the tunnel's walls from the barren flats above had slowed; if they could climb up to the heights, they could probably be quit of the currents. But the walls themselves were high, and the Voyani ladders had been swept away by the currents.

She didn't pause for thought. Deeper than thought was instinct. She *knew* that the wall wouldn't last.

So did he.

Kallandras did not speak.

He heard the Serpent's roar; if death had a texture, if it cast a shadow, if it informed the whole of a creature, it was this one. Pinions flexed, changed shape, gathered and extended as the creature sought the height of safer skies.

But neither he nor Lord Celleriant confused flight with flight; the creature sought a better vantage point, not escape. This was no simple mortal combat; there was no posturing now, no obvious ritual, no rules simpler than this: Death ended the conflict. Its death, or theirs.

And are you not mortal now? the wind whispered.

Yes, he replied. *I am a mortal in thrall to the majesty of the wild elements.*

The wind was pleased; its breath was momentarily warm. Kallandras understood the value of flattery. Understood it well enough that he never attempted it if he could not lace sweet words with truth.

Here, suspended between the air above and beneath him, while the wind chose to serve as a buffer between himself and the storm, he drew his weapons. He had never understood why mages who had the vast arsenal of the elemental and the mystical arcana at their command chose—as the *Kialli* or the *Arianni* did—to draw weapon when they faced their peers.

But he understood it now. The hafts of either blade fit into the contours of his hands as if they were teeth in the contours of a jaw; they were the most natural extension of himself.

The wind whispered a complaint; it was sensitive to the nature of the blades, and was disinclined to accept with grace any other power of import. The steady, quiet whisper of its voice lulled; Kallandras dropped ten feet just before the Serpent's claws struck. They missed.

Its tail did not.

Clearly the Serpent had the advantage of terrain. Kallandras was *Kovaschaii*, a disgraced member of the Lady's dark brotherhood. He had been trained to fight in the dark, to fight in the water, to fight in the brightest of light. He had been tested in the billowing smoke of open—and dangerous—fire; he had been required to fight upon building's edge, to maneuver through dense forest, to balance on the rocky outcroppings of mountain in the thinnest of air.

But his training had not encompassed this.

To his surprise—and little surprised him—he had to stop himself from attempting to gain his footing. He had fought in places where footing was not required, but the viscosity of the medium—the Southern ocean—was different; his instincts did not recognize the storm-laden skies as water.

The wind roared. He looked down at his chest as Celleriant's lightning illuminated sky, Serpent, and warrior; the fabric was dark with blood.

It had been years since he had taken such a wound. Many years.

Memory was a dangerous ally. Necessary, but treacherous. Stripped of the context of earth, stripped of the companions he accompanied along the *Voyanne*, stripped of Salla, the lute that anchored him when all else failed, he was left with his earliest memories of combat.

In the Labyrinths.

The voices of his brothers were stronger, for a moment, than the voices of the storm, the dialogue of wind and lightning.

They were always present, of course; that was the Lady's

gift to her faithful, her curse to those who had—as Kallandras—deliberately chosen to break faith and vow. But they had become, over time, like sun, like wind, like rain: a part of the elemental landscape. As such, they invoked a sense of both awe and distance.

The distance was gone. The wound was open.

He was wise enough to change his grip on the haft of either weapon; both had tasted his blood once. Once was enough.

He wondered, briefly, what they would do if he received a mortal wound.

Mortality did not frighten him. In the wilds of the storm, nothing did. The only thing he had ever feared in his life was desertion, and he had learned to live through that fear. To accept the isolation that he had once feared.

He heard his brothers' voices.

They did not speak to him. They were not, he thought, aware of his presence in any but the most minimal way, although should any one of them desire it, they might find him.

No, he thought.

Lightning strobed sky in a brief, terrible flash. He leaped into the wind, remembering.

CHAPTER TWENTY-TWO

Emerald light.

Avandar frowned. The light intensified, and Jewel noticed as it did that it was changing color; a pale, golden light had seeped across the edges of pure green until the power signature he wove looked like a complex tapestry.

The ground shuddered again, rising and falling as if it struggled for breath.

As the water rushed down the tunnel, ground appeared in its wake; the plains surrendered less and less to the tunnels, and the men and women who had been carried into wall and pulled along ground struggled to find their feet.

She recognized one.

"Tamara!"

Thunder broke the word in three places. She tried again. Lost the word to cold. A third time, and the bedraggled woman in question looked up.

"Gather here! Gather around the—around my—around him!" She pointed to Avandar, who had not moved since the storm had started.

Age had tempered the older woman, but it had not taken the edge off her instinct; she obeyed at once, words coming out of her mouth in a rapid, high bark.

"Yollana," the Serra said, looking up.

Yollana of the Havalla Voyani did not answer. The Serra had wedged herself between two large outcroppings of hard rock; she was bleeding in four places from the rocks that had struck her face and shoulder. But she had not been swept away by the current, and neither had the most precious of all her burdens.

But that burden did not stir when she spoke the name again.

My apologies, Matriarch, she thought. She put force behind the next word she spoke. **"Wake. Now."**

The old woman struggled to the surface of consciousness. When Teresa was certain that it would not release her—or she it—she cautiously eased the tension required to brace herself in this awkward place.

Her arms were shaking.

Her legs were only slightly better. "We must go," she said, "to the woman who came in the Fires of the Arkosan Matriarch. We must go now."

Yollana nodded. "The water?"

"It is—it has stopped, for now."

Jewel realized, when she saw a man lurching toward her cradling his arm against his chest, that the sharp bend in the tunnel was probably as dangerous as the water itself when you were rushing toward it in the river's current.

She lifted an arm, pointed to Avandar, spoke briefly in Torra. The man shook his head in denial and came toward her, his gait awkward. She could see the gash in his forehead.

"Stavos?"

He nodded. "Stavos," he replied. "You must help."

"Your wife?"

"She is—she is with Tamara. It is not my wife who needs help."

"Be quick, Stavos. What do you mean?"

"I left them when I saw—I saw—" He turned and pointed back the way he'd come. "The current is strong; the tunnels slope. He went down. I tried to reach him."

"Who?" She frowned as two syllables resolved themselves into both a name and a request.

"Adam."

Adam? Adam. Matriarch's brother. A boy who had not quite crossed the awkward threshold into adulthood.

"Go to Avandar," she said. "No—do as I order. Go to Avandar, and stay with him. Bring your wife and Tamara. *Do not* leave his side again."

"The Matriarch's brother," he said again, a terrible edge to the words.

"I give you my word," she said, lifting her head and

tossing wet curls to either side of her face, "I'll bring him back. *Go.*"

He went.

But not before he had seen, hurtling through the water as if water itself were insignificant, the great, horned beast who remained, always, on the periphery of the Voyani encampment.

Memory:

You will never have to fight alone.

"Joakken, stop."

The blade stilled.

"Kallatin, pay attention or you will never complete the first circle; you will never gain the knowledge required to join your brothers outside of the Labyrinth."

He was bleeding. Cloth had split neatly from elbow to wrist as if the binding that held the seam together had come undone. Accompanying that, a fine line, a mirror in flesh, his own.

He said nothing.

The oldest master present was expressionless for the space of five heartbeats. His eyes were cataract blue, his skin lined by sun and wind; he seemed, at a distance, helpless with age. Distance was deceiving.

He rose. Crossed the floor that separated him from the two combatants, the one newly come from the vows and the joining, the other a man who had served the Lady's will for five years. "Joakken," he said again, and the older man bowed and stepped aside.

Kallandras turned the wound away from the old man's line of vision. The gesture was not lost upon the master; little was. "You hesitated, Kallatin."

He nodded.

"This is natural," the master said quietly. "Many of our brothers do not see the sense of fighting among themselves."

He nodded again.

"But in you, this hesitation is stronger than I have ever seen it."

He had already exposed one weakness, and although the gash was long and shallow, it was reminder enough. He waited patiently for the old man to expand upon—or discard—what he said. The old man also waited.

With swords, Kallandras did not appear to be the most skilled of brothers; not for his age, and not for his weight or height. But no one bested him in games of waiting.

"Very well," the master said at last, into the silence. "There are other ways of teaching what must be taught."

He drew his weapon. The watchers drew breath. They were subtle; the only person who was aware of the break in the natural rhythm of breathing was Kallandras himself, born to listen.

"Leave," the master said, and the others, masters or no, bowed, acquiesced.

The two men stood beneath the rounded height of one of several training rooms.

"Your weapon, Kallatin."

"Master." He did not hesitate.

"Good. You remember how to wield it."

"Master."

"We will fight to first blood." He lifted his sword arm, but he did not move. "You have been here for long enough, Kallatin. The Lady accepted the sacrifice of your name; none here will gainsay her wisdom."

But, Kallandras thought, resigned.

There was a glimmer of a smile around the network of lines in the corner of the master's mouth. "But," he said, nodding, "you have yet to complete the full circle; you have yet to be deemed fit to leave the confines of the Labyrinth to follow the Lady's will."

It was true.

"Do you wish to leave the Labyrinth, Kallatin?"

He looked down at the torchlight caught in the polished sheen of steel.

"You are, it is said, a poor swordsman for your age."

"Yes, Master."

"Yes? Yes, you are a poor swordsman?"

Kallandras nodded.

Before the motion was finished, two swords had shifted position with the simple motion of wrist; steel spoke. Where there had been torch fire, there was now the odd blue of an older man's eyes.

The student had not even seen the master move.

"How poor?" The Master asked, lowering his sword. He turned away from Kallandras; turned toward the empty arch between this particular training room and the rooms beyond it. "Before you were accepted by the Lady, before she took your name, you were one of our most promising students."

"And now," Kallandras said, stung in spite of himself, "I am one of your worst."

The old man's sword cut air, cut distance, filling the space around Kallandras. Like the music of some ancient barbarian tribe, the sound of clashing metal beat out a rhythmic time as he moved and the student moved with him, anticipating all blows.

There was music in the movement, in the dance—and it was a dance—of youth and wisdom, strength and experience, elder brother and younger brother, sword and sword. Kallandras heard it as clearly as he heard the song in the spoken word, the mortal voice.

He moved, circling and in turn being circled; his sword becoming an extension of his hand. Twice he transferred it, right to left, left to right, waiting for the moment when his master would draw the second blade, would join the fight in earnest.

He did not. They fought, each with a single weapon, beneath the rough, rounded ceiling of the Labyrinth's largest room, exchanging the fleeting knell of steel tempered in the forges of Melesnea.

The music stopped.

"The Steel Curtain," the master said, with a severity entirely devoid of humor, "cannot be drawn by a poor swordsman."

Kallandras looked down, not at hand or blade, but to the floor itself. There, in the swirl of dust, he could see where his feet had been, could see the pattern traced there.

"First blood," the master said quietly.

And to Kallandras' great surprise, the old man lifted his blade and opened the mound of his own palm with its edge. It was not a shallow cut.

"We are done, Kallatin. For today, we are done. Tomorrow, return. There is much to learn."

* * *

The wind roared. The Serpent roared. Above both of these, Lord Celleriant raised the standard of the Green Deepings. If air was not his element, he had mastered it well enough to both survive and ascend; he moved with an ease that spoke of experience. There were no false attempts to gain footing in an ether that would not offer it; no hesitations.

But as lightning answered the blurred strike of sword, the lash of supple tail and faintly iridescent claw, Kallandras saw that there was blood.

Thunder. Lightning.

The rain began to fall again.

She looked up and cursed, but swearing was almost as natural as drawing breath; it didn't cost her much time.

Jewel gripped antlers and allowed herself to be thrown up and onto the back of the great beast. She had always hated riding; she expected this to be no different. Or perhaps she had hoped it would be no different.

But it was. The chill and the cold deserted her the moment her legs touched the stag's fur; her hands lost their shuddering, twitchy numbness, her feet and fingers their painful ache.

It did not occur to her, until he leaped clear of the water in one great stride, that she had not spoken a word; had not given him directions or orders. She reached for the lowest of his tines, and then pulled her hands back; she had no fear whatsoever of falling.

The rain fell hard, harder. She saw the water begin to pour into the tunnel again, and cried out in dismay.

But the stag seemed to run across it, or above it, as if it were uneven, dry ground.

I was the mount of the Winter Queen. This is simply water; no more. Do you think the Queen searched for bridges when she led her Hunt? Do you think she crossed no mountains, no lakes, leaped no chasms? The roads walked by the Winter Queen are treacherous, even for such as she.

What will you hunt, Lady?

In the full richness of his words, there was a hint of dark humor.

She kicked him with both heels.

But she answered. *The boy. Find the boy.*

* * *

The Serpent retreated into the heart of the storm, drawing it with him. Below their aerial battleground, the Voyani encampment fell, once again, beneath the shadows of its wings.

He grew to dread the lessons.

The master's palm had not healed by the following day, and although the master made no allusion to it, the bandage that kept the wound free from infection was plainly visible.

The master bowed to the student. "Well met," he said softly. "We will fight to first blood. Any time we meet in this room, or in this arena, it is only the letting of blood that will end our lesson. You are not a fool, Kallatin. You understand."

He did not understand anything beneath the veneer of words, but he heard it all: the regret, the momentary affection, the disapproval, and the growing sense of unease.

He turned to the wall, reached into the bright light beneath the curve of a large lamp, and lifted a weapon. Light curved round the circumference of a slender pole, glinted off the flats of the two small blades at either end.

Kallandras lifted both hands and caught the shaft of the pole arm; it was too heavy, too cold, to be fashioned of wood.

He had time for no more; the master had set his staff in motion; twin blades traced the circumference of a circle in the air before him. Kallandras waited. The circle would shift, the perimeter becoming a weapon, not the bright outer circle of a shield.

There were few ways of breaching such a circle, but defense was not as difficult.

Or not as difficult when one faced another novice.

He leaped and heard the grating rasp of the circle's edge against stone. Felt the blade whistle through his hair at the same time.

Felt the hard, metal rod clip his side with bruising force.

The Serpent was not a simple beast; not a creature like the wolves of the North, the great cats of the South. It had size, reach, a choice of six attacks: jaw, spiked tail, and the great, curved tines of its claws. It could turn in the currents of the storm the way Kallandras had leaped that day beneath the safety of the Labyrinth's ancient stone.

He found purchase in the jutting ledge beneath the ceiling's rise. He had thrown the weapon with as much force as he could; he caught it as it fell.

The old man stood in the room's center. "Well done," he said. "Joakken is not my equal."

From the heights, Kallandras nodded.

"He is not, in my opinion, yours."

But from a man like the master there was little safety in distance. He did not reply.

"Last week," the master continued, "you met Arkady in the Chamber of Fire."

Kallandras, again, offered only silence.

"Arkady is not Joakken's equal."

Silence.

"Does it not occur to you that both of these brothers have injured you in their time?"

"Yes, Master."

"They do not have your compunction; they are not crippled by your sense of allegiance. They follow *our* instructions."

"Yes, Master."

"You fight well enough against me. Not well enough, however, to wound me. Not well enough to end these sessions. I am an old man; I am not as strong as I was in my youth in these halls.

"Will you tell me why you will not fight?"

"I . . . do fight."

For the first time, the master snorted. "Go, Kallatin. We will meet again in three days."

He lifted the pole arm, calmly, and dragged it across his thigh. It was a deeper cut than the cut he had given himself the previous day. "It will take three days," he said softly, "before I will be sufficiently recovered."

The master had limped out of the room, passing beneath the great arch that led to the rooms occupied by both the masters and the oldest of the Lady's ceremonies.

When he was alone, when he heard no shuffling, awkward step, no slightly labored breath—both wrong, both terribly wrong—he released the ledge and let himself fall, near-silent, to the stone below.

He crossed the ground hesitantly, and stood a moment before the small pool of blood in the room's center.

The Arianni lord was bleeding from multiple wounds. The wind was too wild for the blood to fall; it streamed across cloth and skin, changing the color of both.

Kallandras looked up, looked across; he felt the cold. Serpent's breath.

Serpent's tears.

And his own?

She could not see the boy.

She could not clearly see beyond the tines of the antlers she held, the rain fell so heavily.

Jewel.

She nodded, but for once didn't open her mouth. She had swallowed enough water to last a week; she didn't feel like collecting any more.

I do not sense your prey.

She felt the cold then. It spread from the inside out, reaching from heart to fingertips.

What do you mean?

His silence was answer enough.

But she didn't want his silence. And she didn't like his words. And she couldn't ignore them; couldn't just plug her ears and walk away. *What do you mean, damn it?*

You are no fool, rider. But if you will hide behind ignorance, hide a little while longer.

She held her breath. It was a habit left over from youth, when staying *very* quiet meant attracting as little attention as possible. Attention and trouble were almost the same word, back then—if trouble didn't notice her, it might go away.

She exhaled.

Jewel, the stag said again, its voice strangely hollow. *Do not offer me blood. Do not offer me* anything *if you do not understand its power.*

What?

Look at your hands.

I'll fall off.

She could feel his snort. *You will not fall if I choose to carry you.*

He spoke with such certainty, she believed him. But she only let go with the right. Brought it toward her face in the heavy rains. *I can't see anything.*

No, he said quietly. *I had forgotten. You have much to learn, Jewel. Much. Look ahead.*

Something had been trapped at a bend in the river; it had gathered stones, and the heavy fabric of weathered Voyani tenting about it, like a shroud.

Jewel threw herself off the stag's back.

No!

And the water crashed into her legs like the hand of an angry god. She had never understood why the sailors feared the water so—but understanding came to her then, and it would never leave her.

Just as the tents and the rocks had, she stumbled into the body by the bend, carried by current.

He was at her side, and just ahead of her, cursing loudly in a voice that sounded almost human. Before she could tumble, before she could meet the water head on, he had grabbed her robes in his teeth. *Hold on, you stupid, stupid child!*

Her feet left the ground and came back down as she flailed against constraint. If she spoke at all, the words were patina, no more; she was terrified.

Always terrified. Death did that to her.

Her knees had struck something soft and yielding, something heavy and unencumbered by the stiffness of struggle. She knew what it was. Floating, shoved against the rough, hard dirt, he was easy to grab, hard to hold on to. She had caught sleeve and tent; discarded the tent in a fury. *Help me!*

Water raged. She raged back.

High above them both, above them all, oblivious as the rain itself to their struggle, Lord Celleriant pressed the battle, calling for aid that could not come. His brother's.

Three days. Kallandras practiced in the hall; it was empty when the master was not present. He knew reflex was not honed in isolation, knew also that simple repetition did not grant him what he would not take from experience. But he found the weight of steel in his hands a comfort; found that exhaustion gained through physical exertion allowed him both sleep and a false sense of peace.

He practiced with simple swords. Not the Lady's swords, but the Southern swords of the clansmen. He had been born into a world where such a sword defined strength and survival.

Kallatin?

He did not stop. He did not answer. He let the imperative of an arc of steel carry him from one move to the next.

Kallatin?

He knew that Arkady was well aware of his attention, although he did not choose to acknowledge him.

Kallatin!

But Arkady was persistent in a way that defied manners and the careful unspoken agreements that allowed men to both share thoughts and have privacy.

Arkady. What. Do. You. Want.

Where are you?

Don't be . . . so . . . lazy.

Fine, make me work.

Arkady's voice was fine and smooth—when he spoke. But when he was forced to use the inner voice, when he was forced to use the power that had been granted the boys who survived the Lady's harshest tests, his voice was different. Louder, more awkward, the voice of a brash young man. It was not a voice that Kallandras would have liked, had he heard it while he lived in the domicile of his father's family.

But it was a voice he could not help but like now. He shrugged. Put the blade up. Ran, as quickly and lightly as possible, up the side of the wall. Momentum carried him halfway up, and gravity brought him down—but he used the gravity and the wall to choose the style and place of his landing.

Kallatin, Arkady said again, serious now.

When we were told that we would never have to fight alone, Kallandras said at last, *I envisioned something . . . different.*

I don't understand you. Mikka is worried sick, in case you hadn't noticed. And the master—

But he had noticed, of course. He noticed it all; all emotions, all nuances. Fear was strongest; it paralyzed him. Pain was second.

Had he the choice between a brother's pain and his own, his own, visceral and real, was more bearable.

Tell them, Kal.

No. If they don't know—

They don't know because you can keep it from them. I don't know how. I can't keep anything from anyone. Not in here.

Arkady— He sheathed the sword. Surveyed the room. Saw narrow, broken trails of training dust spread from the center of the room's heart to the walls that surrounded it in five evenly spaced points, following the path he had run, walked, landed.

He was not satisfied.

Arkady, you noticed. You understood.

It's not the same.

It should be.

Should doesn't matter. It's not. Tell them, Kal. Tell them, or—

Or you will?

Or someone will die. No threat in the words. Just fear. For him.

He rose with the warm air, fell with the cold. This time, he avoided the Serpent's tail for long enough to deliver a shallow wound along its left flank, a trailing cut that looked like a signature.

Funny, that a creature of such size could move with such grace, such elegance. Such speed. Kallandras leaped, sprang from foothold to foothold, while the elemental air he had summoned taunted the Serpent and struggled for supremacy, pulling the clouds this way and that, as if they were ropes in a child's rough game.

The Serpent was not young enough to be distracted by such a ploy, and not weak enough to lose control over what it had taken.

The ring that had been taken from the earth of an ancient, dead city began to burn Kallandras' finger.

He felt the Serpent's claw.

He remembered.

* * *

Three days.

Shadows masked his face as he passed beneath the archway into the training room. He noted that dust had been laid down across the floor in a spiral pattern instead of the fine, near invisible blanket to which he had become accustomed. Without a word, he stepped over the spiral lines, touching stone with the supple bottoms of soft leather shoes.

He bowed to the man who stood, still as that stone, and as imperturbable, in the center of the vast room. His master returned the bow stiffly and stepped aside.

There was a small, three-legged brazier behind his back. The air above its rounded mouth was still; no fire burned within or beneath its smooth, simple surface.

"Today," the master said quietly, "we will learn something new. Come."

Kallandras did not hesitate. He wanted to. He was young. He was not well versed in all of the mysteries of the brotherhood. And the master's voice told him *nothing*.

He had thought, before this, that he had met men expert at hiding themselves behind their voices and words; that they had returned no emotion, no hint of the thought that lay beneath what they said. And it had been true, in a fashion. But this . . .

Seeing his first corpse had been almost the same; some essential element had fled the body, and he found a sudden, sharp understanding of what the element was by its absence, by the nature of its absence.

Arkady!

For a moment, all breath, all movement, deserted him. He listened, and just as the master's voice returned nothing, so, too, did his brother's. His hands were shaking as his fear grew too suddenly to be easily controlled. Or controlled at all.

Arkady!

Kallatin? The most familiar of all his brothers' voices came, joining and enjoining the chaos of his fear. He struggled for calm, for quiet, and found it less easily than he had the ledge beneath the curvature of ceiling.

Kallatin, what's wrong? Where are you?

He is with me. The master's voice was as friendly as enemy steel. Arkady was no fool. He fell silent at once.

Kallandras let him go, secure in the knowledge that he was alive, that he could be reached; the winds had not taken him.

"You are . . . strong," the master said quietly. "Strong enough that you have failed the first test. Or perhaps I have failed it. The brother who brought you to us was guided by the Lady."

"The Lady guides the dead," the student replied. It was not wise.

Smile's ghost touched the master's lips and vanished. "Indeed. If you are lucky, you will not discover to where. Not today." He lifted his hands, bringing his open palms parallel with the surface of the floor.

The lamps that lined walls guttered. In the darkness, nothing moved.

The master spoke, disturbing air with the flattest of syllables. "Your weapons," he said.

Kallandras' reply was the simple action of curling his palms around their hilts.

"Choose them wisely. You will have no chance to choose another."

"Your weapon, Master?"

"Is not relevant."

Kallandras unsheathed his blades as he inhaled. He was not certain which movement made more noise. "When a challenge is issued among brothers—"

"This is not a challenge, Kallatin. This is merely a lesson." His voice was the voice the dead might have used, if they spoke at all.

But they reminded Kallandras of a brother's first lesson in the artificial night of the Labyrinth. He was not yet certain how they chose their students; not certain of whether or not it was an annual occurrence, or something that happened entirely at the Lady's whim. But he did know that it was not uncommon for all of the young men so chosen to die before they were given a chance to come before the Lady. He bowed.

It helped him hide the sudden stiffening of his features that spoke, clearly, of anger.

Orange light, pale heart of gold at its center, was the

master's reply. Fire fell from his palms in graceful, brief arabesques—a prelude to the brilliance of their unexpected dance. For they touched the floor and rose, a wall, an unexpected mystery.

Behind the translucent slender flames, the master was pale as fine ivory. Or perhaps paler. He had not moved but he had become harder and harder to see. The flames that had curled in a leisurely splendor from hand to floor neither grew nor dwindled—but instead of casting light, they seemed to leach it from the room.

He saw a glimmer of it across the unusual pattern the dust made along the floor before he lost the ability to see anything but the flame itself.

"You know how to listen. None of the brothers I have taught have had half the skill you've shown in the past few months. Listen carefully, Kallatin. That is the only gift that will save you."

The stag was not so graceful, not so fleet of foot, so easy to startle, as his form suggested. As Jewel raged, so, too, did he, but in a different way. He could not release her or she would vanish, as the boy had; he could not force her to relinquish the burden that she had chosen to carry.

He had faced death in the Hunt; had faced the Arianni before it. He had commanded kingdoms, long dust, when he had last walked the mortal realms as a man.

She *knew* this.

And what was she? Scion of a great House, a young woman on the verge of more power than she had dreamed possible when she had been—

When she had been the age of the boy who was slipping from beneath her fingers into the water's grasp.

Between them, if they could not pull one boy to safety, they weren't worth the titles they might have carried, might one day carry. What did they matter?

She had to think. She could not think.

Could not do anything else.

Let go of me, she told the stag, trying to take the wildness out of the words. *Let go of me. Grab the boy. Do it.*

There was anger, hesitation, and acceptance in the space of time it would have taken to nod.

She felt the anchor leave her collar, braced herself

against the ground over which the water flowed, and leaped, up, hands flailing and bleeding—she felt it now—as she reached for his antlers, the scruff of his neck, anything that would hold her.

He wasn't there.

She cursed. Cursed and concentrated, turning her body against the tide; moving out of the way of rocks that she *knew* were coming. It was cold in the water. The cold would kill her.

But the failure would be a worse death.

She could move. She could think. She could react. She did these things, all of these things, her muscles crying out against cold, against the things she could not quite avoid.

Jewel!

Avandar's voice. Distant, distinct.

I'm fine, she shot back, the verbal equivalent of a slap.

She heard his curse; it was brief and elegant, as unlike the stag's as a voice could be, and still be inside her head. The rock that struck the side of her face would leave a bruise that lasted a week. The rock that struck her knee and her thigh on its way around the bend did less damage. She managed to avoid the large rock. Hard to move, to gauge the speed of movement.

No more, she thought, no more rain.

And then she saw him, coming up across the water, something awkwardly draped across his back. She would have called him by name, but she had no name to give him.

You will never survive for long enough to name me, he said, with an anger that was much like Avandar's, but wilder. *We have the boy. Climb, now. Viandaran has cast a magic that is difficult to maintain, here in the stronghold of shadow. If we do not reach him—*

Don't. She caught the antlers he bowed in her direction. Scrambled up the side of his neck; almost sat on the heavy, limp body across his back.

The stag was as good as his word, perhaps better; although the body was not tied in place, although it was strewn across fur and sinew at an awkward angle, she knew it would not fall off.

She held on, felt warmth again, felt movement.

Wait, she said, pressing her knees into the sides of the stag almost instinctively. *Wait.*

For what?

I don't know. But wait.

And then she saw the shadow cross her path where no shadow should have been cast, and she looked up. The underside of a great wagon loomed above, welcome as all other things the sky produced could not be. The glow of firelight danced across its walls, but the wood did not burn.

A ladder rolled down from its side, its rungs wild in their dance against wood. Above it, clothed head to food in wet, wet silk, knelt a single woman. "Aie, stranger!" she shouted.

Jewel looked up; she could not see the face of Elena, but she knew the voice. "I have Adam!" she cried back, but her voice broke between the last two syllables. "Send a rope down. Take him—I'll search for the others."

But the woman shook her head. "No!" she shouted back. "We have the others."

"All of them?"

There was a pause. It was brief. "Yes. All. You are bid to return, at once, to your servant."

The use of power was costly.

Even to Avandar. Especially to Avandar.

She knew it before the stag carried them back to where he stood before a wall of stone. She could see, now, where lines of green and gold ran through gray; could see how they were strengthened by him, how they held the water back while the Arkosans struggled, broken and wet, to the ground around his feet. Some clutched bags, some tents, but most came empty-handed.

Among them were the Serra Teresa and Yollana of the Havalla Voyani. She noted them; they were the outsiders. The ones who were here on sufferance, or for a greater purpose, but who did not share blood and history with the Arkosans; of course she noticed them.

She slid off the back of the stag; the ground around Avandar was merely muddy. Water sluiced past, slapping the air and the ground as it thudded into the walls of the tunnel to either side.

"Serra," Jewel said, voice a rush of breath. "Where is the Serra Diora?"

The old woman answered. "With the Matriarch. Safe."

"And your seraf?"

Silence.

Teresa lifted her head, turned her piercing gaze to the storm whose water raged on all sides. She mouthed a word. A single word. Jewel could not hear it.

Could not hear it, but knew.

She hated magic. She hated mages.

She reached for the antlers of the stag, and it lifted its head. *No,* he said, almost gently. *No.*

We must—

I will go. I will search for him. His eyes met hers, large and unblinking, darker than night. *Do you understand, Jewel of Terafin, that I was once Winter King?*

She nodded. Nodded, and then shook her head, No.

No, he said, *is the more truthful answer. I do not understand how a child could stand against the host of the Winter Queen, and wrest from her anything that she claimed. Had she better understood how vulnerable you have made yourself, you would have stood for seconds. Perhaps less.*

Patience. If he can be found, I will find him, and I will return him to you.

He leaped, lightly, back into the storm, and she noticed, as he ran, that the water did not so much as dampen the fur made silver-gray by night sky.

CHAPTER TWENTY-THREE

Although he had never been in the middle of an elemental storm before, Kallandras knew it from its natural counterpart almost instantly. It had a voice that was deafening, wordless; it destroyed the nuances of other sounds. Like: the flexing of great muscles. The movement of leathery wings folding and opening as they gathered wind beneath their pinions. The movement of air over tongue and teeth as the creature inhaled—or exhaled—in a rhythm of muscle and motion.

Lightning flashed and lingered; Lord Celleriant's signal. White air. Black Serpent. Red blood.

Come.

Kallandras called the wind.

The master was wrong.

It was not his ability to listen that saved him; it was his ability to *speak.* To *command.* He had displayed it very, very rarely—it was a threat, and he knew it was exactly that to his brothers, no matter how much they might say otherwise.

Use the voice on an enemy and it was a thing to admire, like any other weapon. But like any other weapon, turn it upon a brother, expose a brother's weakness, and it was a betrayal.

He forced himself to listen. To be calm. Heard the soft click of multiple objects across stone. They stopped. Became much slower. He had heard no unsheathing of weapon.

Listen, he thought. He could hear—or perhaps feel—the beat of his heart; the pulse kept perfect time near the base of his throat. He could hear the rise and fall of chest as air entered his lungs, and left it.

Only his.

What came out of the shadows was not a brother.

Was not the master.

What? What is it?

He had been forced to hold his breath before; he knew that any other brother would be capable of doing the same.

But although the sounds of something striking the rough stone floor were quiet, they were too rhythmic to be the product of *Kovaschaii* stealth. Whatever it was that hunted in the darkness did so with confidence.

He leaped away, taking care to make no noise. The steps ceased; the almost hypnotically musical clicking stilled.

When it resumed, he learned two things: that his opponent had some method of tracking him in the darkness, and that it had nothing to do with sound.

He *moved.*

Felt the fabric of his shirt split and grow wet. The cut was so clean it took a moment for pain to follow—but there was no doubt that it would; the cut was deep.

First blood. He turned to look at the ring of flame. The master had said that the contests were over at the shedding of first blood. But the darkness remained unbroken.

The silence did not.

His opponent made a visceral sound in the back of an unseen throat. Had Kallandras been any other *Kovaschaii,* he would have heard a simple growl. But he was not; he was the brother who had lost his family because of his gift. He heard more.

Anticipation. Pleasure. Laughter.

The fear that had almost taken root had no further chance to grow. In its place, but stronger, was anger.

He had heard every lecture about the stupidity of temper the masters could offer, both singly and jointly; he had seen examples made of students who could not learn from anything but personal experience—*the folly and privilege of youth,* his master had said—that demonstrated clearly the ways in which it made one vulnerable.

Such lessons were dim and quiet compared to the immediacy of fury. He had never understood the brothers who, exposed to such wisdom, had chosen folly in its place; he understood it now.

He *shouted.*

The force of the wordless cry left a silence that spread outward from Kallandras like the concentric circles that mark the passage of a stone through still water.

The silence did not last; it was broken by a roar that might have been twin to his own. But it was devoid of amusement. Of condescension. The vicious satisfaction this fact gave him was costly; the roar had been almost deafening, and he did not appreciate this fact until the creature was almost upon him.

He bled again; he bled freely.

Underestimate your opponents at your peril.

Claws and a lack of obvious language had lulled him into an assumption about the intelligence of his attacker. It was not a mistake he had ever repeated.

The rain, he thought. The rain had stopped. Disoriented, he looked down to see a river wending its way across the barrens, carrying rocks and sand in currents that slammed into the walls of a once dry tunnel.

Light drew his attention back to the sky. Against it, within its stark and unforgiving glare, stood Lord Celleriant. He was suspended in the silent sky yards away. Kallandras watched dispassionately until he saw the power of the Green Deepings waver. Serpent's foreclaws were gathered close to its chest, taut with tension; its tail was beneath its hind legs, coiled and waiting. Its mighty head rose with a snapping curve of neck, its jaws widened, it inhaled.

He *spoke.* **"Hold."**

The rawness of anger, the unharnessed power of fury, was given its only expression in the single soft syllable. All motion in the room was his, but he could not be certain how long the stillness would last.

He ran. His stride grew longer, faster; he gathered his shoulders, holding his blades at his sides as he took advantage of momentum to break gravity's hold. He spun, somersaulting in air as he felt the sluggish passage of claws beneath him.

His own movements were not bound by compulsion; there was nothing slow about them. He brought his blades down and crossed them in front of each other in a brief passage through flesh.

In the darkness, sound was a sensation. The only sound the creature made was in the involuntary response of scale to blade. Kallandras heard something strike the ground; it was followed by another, heavier, noise.

Silence was once again broken only by the sound of his breath. He waited five beats before he turned toward the lightless flame and bowed. "Master."

The flame was extinguished.

He did not reply; instead he wiped the edge of his blades against his sash and sheathed them. He dropped to his knees, straightened his back, bowed his chin toward his injured chest and sat, waiting with the patience of a student of the Labyrinth.

Light returned, like slow dawn, to the round chamber. He saw it first along the walls as torches released the illumination they had withdrawn; saw it next in the shadows their meager light cast. His eyes became accustomed, again, to the minute differences in the gray and black, the color of stone and night.

The master was no longer standing within the ring of fire, although Kallandras had seen no evidence of his departure. He approached, walking slowly and carefully between the lines drawn across stone.

"Well done, Kallatin. You may retire to the healer. And you may tell Arkady that if he does not practice *silence* for the next three days, I will deal with him personally." He bowed. And then he stopped.

"That is not a test that any other member of your year could pass." He walked toward the arch that was now visible. "There was some debate about your survival. You did not disappoint me."

But Kallandras waited. He knew, from the tone of his master's voice, that the lesson was far from over.

And that it could end in the blink of an eye.

"If we were different men," the master said, his robed back toward his student as he turned toward the arch, "it would be simplicity itself to train you. I would merely tell you that any man who could defeat you would be executed, and I would return you to the testing grounds in search of those upon whom you place a particular value."

The student waited.

"But we are not those men, not yet; the Lady has given

no such commands, and indeed they would be difficult to follow. Therefore it is up to us to make our own choices, to offer ourselves—as we age and become less efficient—in the Lady's service in other ways.

"It *is* my duty to the Lady to train you, Kallatin. To see that your potential, profound and untapped, does not go to waste." He reached into his robes, and drew a dagger.

Kallandras was on his feet, was in motion, his own weapons drawn, the moment that blade breached its sheath. But he was too slow, far too slow.

The wound the master offered himself was to wrist; blood flowed.

"The lesson, this day, is over. There will be one other, Kallatin. One final lesson. You have earned that much with your performance today. Fail, and you will survive, but I will not. Succeed, and you may decide how deep a cut you offer, how much of an injury I retain."

"Master—" Kallandras took a step forward, and the old man lifted a palm—and more—in denial.

Do not. You are too weak as it is. I will not accept any aid you offer.

For a moment, Kallandras stood suspended above the barren grounds, the wind whispering in his ear, the voice of the Serpent a deafening howl of rage. He had been born to *listen.* He had been born to *hear.*

He heard.

Lord Celleriant of the Green Deepings spoke a single word as he raised a faltering sword; a single word as he swung it in an arc that ended with scale, with flesh. It was not a fatal blow; it was simply the first half of an exchange.

But that almost didn't matter.

"Lady!"

The Serpent's blow carried him out of the reach of claw or fang; the tail struck again.

The Lord of the Green Deepings tumbled like a broken acrobat through the air. The black beast roared in angry satisfaction and turned its long neck toward the lesser threat: the brother of the *Kovaschaii.*

It was a mistake; Kallandras felt a momentary ferocity, a savage joy, as he saw Celleriant rise. It did not last.

Gifted and cursed, as the Serra Teresa and the Serra

Diora had been gifted and cursed in this barren land, this Southern continent in which suspicion and hostility governed the actions of even the wisest of men, he had found peace, lost it, and found a semblance of it again.

Decades of experience were shorn by the storm, by the cry that a stranger uttered; he stood facing certain death—not his own, but Celleriant's. Not his own, but a man who, unselfconsciously, evoked the Lady's name with a ferocity, a longing, a terrible desire that spoke to Kallandras so painfully because it was a part of what lay beneath the surface of the life he had built.

"Celleriant!" he yelled. Distant.

The Arianni lord did not turn.

He shouted again, to foe, not friend.

"Hold!"

But the Serpent was too ancient a power, the storm's voice too strong a shield; the great beast turned, in his element, his long neck rising into the roiling, dark clouds as he inhaled.

He spoke to the wind. *Take me there, quickly.*

The wind refused him. He had forgotten how jealous the elements could be.

He asked Arkady to leave him, and Arkady complied. But only physically. His anxiety—unvoiced—could not be contained; it accompanied Kallandras in lieu of his brother, joining the anxiety he himself felt.

All of his training, all of his practices, all of the exercises that had come so close to claiming his life, were poor preparation for what lay ahead. But they were all he had.

The master had given himself one week to recover. One week. In that time, Kallandras labored in solitude.

No other master was allowed to intervene, and as one said, a week in the hands of the Lady herself might—*might*—be preparation enough, but there was no certainty.

He trained in the darkness.

He trained in glaring light.

He practiced in the confines of the high walls and narrow corridors of the Labyrinth's most treacherous maze. He was aware that his brothers observed him, some with curiosity, some with concern, and some with a fear that they kept almost entirely to themselves; he felt the unease, but he could not clearly discern its cause.

He was not, however a fool; he could guess.

He had imagined—in the earliest months of the joining—that he might be placed in a position where he came to the rescue of his brothers. Had, in the youthful arrogance of daydream, imagined himself a hero, a desperate hero; had imagined that at great cost and great risk he might emerge victorious, brother by his side, their blood—for of course any threat to a brother must be a terrible opponent who offered the most deadly of challenge—mingling in the way their thoughts and emotions already did.

The truth, as always, was less romantic, more terrifying.

He was not certain he was the student the master assumed he was capable of being, and all failure led to death.

His voice could not touch the Serpent; it spoke with storm's voice. He had learned to abhor futility—although it was only Evayne a'Nolan who had convinced him that such a thing could exist—and with an ease that spoke of practice, changed strategy.

He spoke to the wind.

"Take me to him."

He was prepared for the wind's outrage. He was prepared for the way the sky lost the solidity of elemental current and opened up to drop him toward the barrens below. It was a risk, with the wind.

His own death was not an ending he feared.

The master had seen that clearly. Had exploited it mercilessly—just as the *Kovaschaii* were taught to exploit all weakness when the circumstance and the task demanded it.

Lord Celleriant cried out again, a snarl of rage, a sound that the *Kovaschaii* would have been incapable of making. But wordless or no, Kallandras heard the frustration and the horror of standing alone against an enemy worthy of . . . his brothers. His Lady.

They were gone, part of the life he had been judged unfit to live. He served a mortal who had been foolish and arrogant enough to stand in the Lady's path; his enemy.

Mirrors were held up in the strangest of places, but when they shattered, the shards still cut.

The wind stopped him from reaching the ground. The

wind struggled against the geas he placed upon it. But he had been careful, this time; he had summoned what he believed he needed, no more.

He met his master at the end of a week.

In a circular room he had come to dread, he knelt against stone now completely clean of training dust, brazier, or any adornment save a short, squat candle whose tallow had trickled down the side, fixing it to floor. The flame was not high; it was not bright. It was meant, as these candles often were, to mark the passage of time, no more.

His back was straight. His hands rested lightly, palm down, in the lap his bent legs made.

There was little ceremony in the master's arrival. He did not announce himself; there was no need. Kallandras was instantly aware of his presence. It was not so much the sounds of motion, for there were very, very few. It was the sudden hush of his brothers' voices, the dimming of their daily conversation, their arguments, their affirmations.

Even those who hunted in the Lady's name allowed themselves to bear some small witness to this event; it had become significant. One of the masters had chosen a form of suicide in an attempt to better serve the brotherhood. Some understood it. Some decried it. All accepted that it was his choice to make.

The master joined Kallandras upon the floor, kneeling. He did not wear the robes of a master; he wore what Kallandras wore; stark, simple clothing rather than the voluminous folds of cloth that were meant for ceremony. He bowed his head to his chest and then raised it. Only his arms moved as he drew the weapons of his choice: the Lady's swords. He laid them across his lap and then raised his face.

Kallandras unsheathed his own weapons. The urge to speak was profound. But he could not speak when the master did not.

Instead, he waited, watching the flame's steady progress through wick, tallow, time.

When it flickered, his hands tensed.

When it guttered, he was four feet above the curved, crossing arcs of his master's weapons.

In his months here, in this room and elsewhere, his focus

had been on defense. He did not forget it now, but for the first time, he looked for the opening that would decisively—and quickly—end the combat.

Aware, as he did, that he was not his master's equal; that he could not be certain that the blow he did land would be the blow he desired. He had seen brothers misjudge their strength, their aim, or their opponents in such contests, and the results had been terrifying.

The stilling of voices.

Their voices, brothers all.

But the risk of death was better than its certainty.

He accepted that. The risk. The certainty. He felt a curious freedom as the decision seemed to spread, like some fine intoxicant, through his muscles, as he relaxed into the knowledge that *nothing* he could do here could be worse than what the master had already promised himself.

He heard Arkady's voice, and although he did not allow himself to listen to the words too closely, he understood their meaning.

You will never have to fight alone.

Was this battlefield really so different from that earlier one? He found the footing he had been uncertain of. He found his weapons. He accepted wind, rain, roar, the terrain his opponent had chosen.

There were differences. He did not face the master, but he faced a creature whose age and experience made him dangerous, worthy. He did not fight to wound—he fought to kill. But he felt the same urgency, and he accepted it for what it was.

He heard, in the Lord of the Green Deepings, isolated and banished, everything that he could not, could never, say. He understood that Celleriant was Arianni, and even if the Lady never accepted his return, to Winter Court or the Court of High Summer, that fact would remain unchanged.

But more. In the instant that he heard Celleriant's voice, his own voices, the living ghosts of a past that could never be retrieved except this way, in memory, were almost silenced by its intensity.

If the Arianni lord never understood what it was that Kallandras desired, it didn't matter. He brought himself above the back of the beast. The wings swept him from the back of the summoned wind; he tumbled, stepping off the shelf of air pressure that arranged itself beneath his moving feet.

Controlled his plummet.

Folded, spun, landed.

The master met him on the way down.

Kallandras was close enough to a wall that he aborted the maneuver and managed to alter his momentum—but not enough so he landed on his feet. He rolled away, his arm shaking with the force of the glancing impact when blade had met blade.

But he held his own.

The Serpent roared.

His back was slick with rain, with blood. The blades Kallandras wielded against him were clean. He wondered what the demon blades took when they pierced flesh, but he did not ask; they had, after all, made their mark on him before taking the shape in which they would serve.

Instead, he leaped a moment before tail struck; he trusted the wind to catch him, trusted that a glancing contact between his foot and the elemental air, a tensing of calf and extension of ankle, would be enough to carry him just beyond the range of that death.

He did not expect the lightning.

He should have. Although the abilities of the masters were never discussed—save in whispers that could be kept entirely outside of the joining—Kallandras had seen him summon the absence of light; had seen him disappear while standing still.

He *moved.*

The lightning struck not him, but his hand; he felt its heat as an awful chill as his arm shuddered uncontrollably. One of two swords clattered noisily against stone. He did not pause to pick it up. To pause in this storm was death.

He saw the spark of steel moving too quickly against stone. Understood that the blow struck—had he not rolled clear—would have been fatal.

Did that change the nature of the fight?

The goal?

Did that change the resolve which had brought him here, to this master, and this fight?

No.

But it would.

He stepped aside from that memory, stepped into the present, wondering at the caprice of fate. He shed that young man, that fight, stepping into his skin, into the imperative of *this* one.

"Celleriant!" he called.

The Arianni lord's sword responded to the flash of lightning, severing it at its root. The act was profoundly, distantly beautiful.

"Mordanant!" the Lord Celleriant called back. "Come. Join me!"

He heard the invitation because he was a bard, born to voice.

But he responded because in the end, he could never entirely escape that young man. He had nothing, nothing at all, to lose.

The Lord Celleriant spared him a glance; his brows rose in something akin to shock, although his features could not express surprise openly. For a moment Kallandras thought he might reject the aid he had asked for—but the rejection did not come. He raised his swords.

And saw that the edge of the Arianni's blade had been chipped and scarred by its egress through scale.

He understood, then, what it meant. Understood what could be lost here, in the strike of a sword, the end of a weapon's arc.

A brother.

This was his truth: He was not afraid to die. But truth or no, fear or no, his body struggled against death; his instincts fought it at every turn. Give in to instinct and movement came before thought the way breath came without it.

He gave in to instinct.

He let the fear go. Of killing. Of dying.

He was aware of the ground beneath his feet, the walls around him, the ledges above, and the open arch at his back. All these would shift, moving as he moved.

He moved.

He did not admire the master's skill; that was the task of an observer, a witness. He did not fear it. He gauged it, and if he did so well enough, he would win.

He heard his brothers' voices. Heard what they did not say. And he heard something he had heard only once, had feared even as he had been stricken by it.

The Lady's voice.

The Lady's voice, the Lady's words, the Lady's quiet attention. He could not understand them. He could not understand what she desired, if she desired anything from him at all.

But he would not forget it. God's voice. A god's voice.

And he understood, as his blades, crossed, bore the brunt of a tail lash and he was driven back into the currents.

His hands were slick with blood. He barely noticed it, although the weapons' grips were not the grips fashioned by *Kovaschaii* hands; not the grips of the blades he had held in visceral memory.

"Celleriant!" he cried, because he knew no other name by which to call him, although he was suddenly certain that there was another.

There is, a voice said, quiet and calm, but loud and sudden as thunder. *There is another name. I offer it, I offer it to you, who are Kallandras of Senniel, no matter how much you have claimed the identity as lie or mask; you who are Kallatin of the Kovaschaii, and who, were, before that—*

He listened, now, and he understood that he heard what underlay the storm's voice, the richness of chaos, the cacophony of natural and unnatural sound: a god's voice.

A god.

But although he listened, the name that was spoken next never came.

He had given it, with his blessing and the whole of his desire, to the Lady, and she had taken it.

The memories came; the memories, the combat, the swords and the shattering of swords.

He saw, in the now of his adult vision, the master's broken blade. Saw that shattered steel had flown from hand to wrist, to the inside of arm; saw that the blood was the old man's. Saw that muscles were severed, that the loss of that blood would be severe.

Had he won?

Yes.

Then, and now.

You have served, god said, in a voice he did not recognize. *You have served me, and mine, with only the fear of loss to sustain you. You have lived the life of outcast. You have learned to stand alone.*

But it is time, Kallandras of Senniel, to stand beside a comrade. Time to fight shoulder to shoulder instead of alone in the shadows.

Time has worn the edges from you. Take them back now. Be broken, be remade. This conflict will consume you; fight, then, with everything you possess.

I have.

Yes, but you have not had enough. God's voice.

He was no youth, to be humbled by god. By any god he had not chosen.

The air bore him. The wind whispered in giddy fascination. The Serpent roared. Celleriant's blade rose.

It would fall.

He saw that; it would fall and it would shatter. He knew what that would mean, although he had never seen it happen. He had sung of it, as had most of the Northern bards, in their little classrooms, beneath the acoustics of Seahaven on the Isle.

Yes, the voice said. *The blade will shatter.*

The name came.

He took it, drew breath in the sudden absence of a god's voice.

"Allele! No!"

The blade froze.

He had seconds. He used them to launch himself at the Serpent's jaws, his blades inferior to the steel of the Green Deepings, but his skill inferior to none.

The lord of the Green Deepings turned, wild, wide-eyed. Vulnerable, in that instant, as Kallandras passed over his upturned face.

He tightened his grip on the wind; the wind bore him. The ring upon his hand burned flesh, reminding him—if he needed reminder—that all things alive feel pain. He could not breathe, did not require breath. He felt the claws of the Serpent pass through his flesh, but he had aimed himself, he had chosen the price he was willing to pay; the wind would not allow a simple attack to change his trajectory.

He bled.

Saw the great eyes of the beast as they grew, large and dark, the perfect targets for the weapons he carried. They reflected nothing, not his hands, not his arms, not the smooth surface of steel. He took them both; felt the membranes give way as his knees lost cloth and skin to the rough ridges between them.

The creature *roared.* What it had seen, it would see no more. Its head snapped back, snapped forward; its tail lashed out; its claws struck.

Ribs shattered. Forearm snapped. But Kallandras held the weapons by which his early life had been defined. Had they changed? In the darkness it was hard to see them, but they felt . . . lighter. Different.

Kallandras fell.

He did not call the wind; he wore it.

But he felt the cold; the ice of desert night; the chill of shock.

It was a long way down.

Avandar of the Guild of the Domicis lifted his face into the rain. His chin rose slowly as he brought his arms, in concert, to his sides. Beside him, Jewel of House Terafin stood, silent, the face of her ring of office cupped inward, in clenched fist. She stared up, into the sky, and saw the first glimmer of moonlight that signaled storm's end.

But the water in the tunnels was a thunderous motion of sound. Rain could stop now; it didn't matter. If they could not climb—and they could not, here—they would perish.

The Serra Teresa was singing softly. The storm did not carry her song from the ears of her captive audience; Jewel thought, as she listened to the quiet, peaceful Torra in which the song was couched, that nothing could.

The Arkosans huddled around her, ringed her, pulled sodden cloth around themselves. As if her song was warmth, they held out their hands, turned their faces toward her, exposing the vulnerability of fear, anxiety, grief; her words turned these gently, inexorably, away.

Only Yollana seemed immune to the effect of her song; she sat in a stony silence, waiting.

The song faltered once.

The earth rose to fill the gap left between notes, the break in melody; it rumbled like the sound that comes from flat palms across the surface of a great skin drum, a slow beat, an accompaniment to the song itself.

Jewel watched the stone wall that kept the water at bay slowly collapse as green filaments left the cracks they had mortared.

Avandar bowed his head.

She felt the movement more clearly than she saw it: the lowering of chin, the clenching of jaw. As if the power that radiated out from him were a part of his body, he strained at the earth. It answered. It rose. And rose again, a hill with a flat plateau birthed whole from the hard, wet ground.

Ascent slowed; song hushed; there was utter silence.

The rain had stopped.

Someone pointed; someone spoke in hushed Torra. To the south, in the sky, the Matriarch's ship was slowly wending its way toward where her people stood.

A long way down.

He seemed to fall forever. The element was silent as he sank into the folds of its mantle. He was silent.

He should speak.

He knew he should speak. The wound he had taken had not touched throat or lip; had not impeded the ability. But his hand burned. The past had stripped him of wisdom, or perhaps reminded him of how thin a veneer wisdom could be.

He closed his eyes, felt the wind rush past his lashes, carrying water away from his eyes. And then even the wind's voice was silent.

A hand touched his shoulder. He bowed his head; his grip on both of his weapons tightened; hands shook with the involuntary effort. He was clinging; he knew it.

But the hand on his shoulder did not leave it.

The sky was silent. The moon was bright. The Lady's face was half in shadow, but she wore a clear veil of stars. He opened his mouth, but he had no words to offer, and after a moment, he closed it again.

"I do not know your name," the man behind him said. "You know mine."

Kallandras nodded. He felt the cold as if cold were all that he now knew. "My apologies, Lord Celleriant. I—"

"And what have you to offer apology for?"

"What any man does, who takes something of value that belongs to another, when he has not been given that right."

"Were you not?"

The voice of the Arianni lord was painfully, starkly beautiful. Kallandras could not reply. It had been many, many years since words fled his grasp.

"I called my brother."

"I . . . heard."

"I was mad with battle. I was . . . fey." There was a smile in the depths of that voice. "You intervened."

"I chose to join you when you took to the skies."

The hand on his shoulder shifted; the Arianni lord turned Kallandras around.

He said, "I have sheathed the sword, but I fear it will be some time before it is . . . mended. There are smiths who might be called, if the time and the price were right. I did not realize what we faced. I thought it merely a scion of elder days, a hint of the former glory of our enemies." His smile was a slight twist at the corner of his lips, and in the night sky, Kallandras could not be certain how shadowed it was. "I was wrong. Such a mistake is often costly."

His eyes were the gray of flashing steel, his hair the crisp white of Northern snow.

He said again, "I do not know your name."

"Kallandras," the bard replied, voice flat. "Kallandras of Senniel College."

A pale brow rose.

"I have no other."

With infinite care, Lord Celleriant's hand brushed Kallandras' still cheek, pushing wet hair to one side of his face. There, beneath the left ear, his fingers stopped, tracing a circle around a mark that ordinary men could not see.

"You speak truth. Do you remember what you were named?"

"No. I gifted my name to the Lady, and all memory of its beginning, all knowledge of its end, resides now with her."

"They do not know." Lord Celleriant lifted a hand, and a cold blue light settled in the cup his curled palm made.

"No."

"May I?" The light blossomed, spreading its tendrils in a slow curl around each of his fingers. He reached out, brought his hand toward Kallandras' chest.

"No."

The hand closed before it made contact. The light guttered. "So," the Arianni lord said, "you are still bound by your vows."

"No more—and no less—than you are by yours."

"I would not care if you could discern the existence of my kin, of my Queen, through touch alone."

"We made different vows."

"If you desire it, I will call you Kallandras of Senniel College."

"It is not a lie," the bard whispered.

"No. No more is Lord Celleriant. We wear our titles. We bear them. But there is more."

Kallandras bowed his head. He was weary. The elemental wind had hollowed him, harrowed him, as it always did. He felt the emptiness, vast and untraversable, between himself and the world that he had once known and valued.

The silence grew.

"I am in your debt," the Arianni lord said at last, eyes narrowed.

Yes, Kallandras thought. *In my debt.*

But when the pale-haired lord withdrew his hand, Kallandras felt something within snap. He spoke, and the word was a shock.

"Kallatin," he said. "I was Kallatin."

The lord did not smile; there was no triumph to be found in the gravity of his expression. "I am Allele."

There is no debt between brothers.

No more was said; they drifted down by the grace of Lord Celleriant's power. But they did not land upon the plateau that had saved the Voyani.

They landed a mile away, upon the dry, cold soil of the undisturbed desert.

The storm was gone. From her perch by the open windows of the odd ship's cabin, Margret watched it die. The clouds that had surrounded the Serpent now shrouded it; she could see them flail and struggle as its wings beat. She could not see what had injured it, but when she looked toward her silent companion, the Serra said quietly, "It's over."

Just that.

The lightning died with the storm; the absence of thunderous roar made the silence seem unnaturally loud. The moon was still. The stars were bright.

The open sky, as always, watched—but what the Lady saw, she kept to herself.

"We can return." The Serra was subdued. She had taken the blankets Margret had offered in hands that were shaking with cold, and had wrapped them about her shoulders without speaking a word. Her face was turned toward the frosted sill of open window, but her eyes were focusing on nothing Margret could see.

Silent, Margret complied; she brought the ship to bear, and as it cornered smoothly, turning without effort into the night sky, she found that she missed the rhythmic bump of wheel against ground, the slight discomfort that gave movement its texture, that told her body there *was* movement.

"Look." The Serra lifted a slender arm. Pointed, turning the injured palm of her hand in such a way that the wound was not visible.

Beneath them, upon a plateau that rose above either side of what had once been the tunnel, the Arkosan Voyani gathered. Margret breathed once, deeply, when she saw the other wagon; it had been brought to ground and seemed to await the arrival of its sister.

"Ready to go back?"

The Serra looked away from the sky. "If I said no, Matriarch, would it make a difference?" Lifting the injured hand, she examined it in the silver light shed by moon.

"You don't want to go back?"

"I . . . do not know. I used to dream of flight, when I was young. But it wasn't like this." She turned back to the sky. "When we land, we will enter the world again. We will worry about tents, and food, and shelter. We will worry about what we have lost, what we might lose.

"I will look at my hand. I will have to decide how best

to hide the injury, and if it scars, how best to hide the scar. I have value, but it is based upon ephemeral things.

"If you fight, you bear scars. But it does not change what you are. You are the Matriarch of Arkosa. What I am . . ." She turned back to Margret and smiled. The smile was perfect. Perfect.

And cold, as the night was cold; distant as the Lady's face was distant.

"Do you ever smile when you're happy?"

"I don't know." She withdrew, although nothing about her visibly changed. "You are wise, Matriarch; I think that your people are waiting. It is best not to worry them further."

12th of Misteral, 427 AA
Sea of Sorrows

In the distance, she watched as the storm broke. The wind was as natural as wind in these lands could be; fierce and cold, an unwelcome rejoinder to the sheets of water that had drenched the barrens.

She raised a hand only once; the other, concealed in the billowing folds of a blue that was dark as the sky, gripped a simple shard of crystal, rounded and made smooth at the behest of the Oracle many, many years past. But the man who stood in shadow beside her raised a hand as well, a gesture of both command and denial, and she lowered hers at once; it curled into a fist at her side.

Watch, he said. *Bear witness.*

She watched. She was not young; she would never be young again. She had learned to take the ice into her, had learned to see through the shadows that she had accepted when she had first chosen to walk the Winter Road, in the arrogance of anger and youth. She could be dispassionate now; she could watch the most horrible of deaths without blinking, without turning away.

Turning away was an act of mercy that she had learned she could not grant herself. Better to accept the crime. Better to understand, in the end, all that she had to answer for.

But it was not easy to watch Kallandras fall.

Daughter, he said.

She, who hated few words, hated that one; she did not answer.

Think. You have seen beyond this time. Do you think he is fated to fall here? This is merely the beginning of a legend. His, and his companion's. Watch.

Her lips thinned, jaw tightened. Almost against her will, she dragged the soul shard from its place before her heart, and her gaze pierced the clouds that roiled within. She watched.

And saw that another had joined Kallandras in his swan's dive. But where Kallandras' fall was awkward and ungainly, where his limbs splayed out as if to somehow catch and hold wind, this other diver was in his element; his body, long and thin, sped toward the surface of the cracked, dry earth.

They met, scant yards above it.

She saw them touch; saw them slow.

Saw the expression upon the face of the Lord Celleriant of the Green Deepings.

"You . . . you interfered," she said softly.

"Did I?"

"I have met Lord Celleriant of the Green Deepings in the Court of the Arianni."

"Indeed."

"I have seen that expression on his face only once."

He said nothing.

"What did you do?"

"I? Nothing." He lifted an arm; a small trail of blue fire followed, tracing the length of the limb from finger to shoulder. "It is not given to me to act. You know this."

"He would not risk so much for a mortal." Flat words. They were true, but they were false; she had seen the event unfold through the orb, and nothing false could pass through its harsh lens.

"You must judge, of course; you are mortal. But I am weary."

"Why did you summon me here?"

He smiled. She did not see it, but she sensed it. "Because it is not yet time for the piece to come off the board," he said. "And I could not be certain that things would unfold as they did."

"And how have they unfolded?"

"I am weary," he repeated quietly. The words thinned. The voice became almost an echo of itself. "But I will tell you this: the Arianni have come into play. They are not the last of the pieces, but they are the first of the old ones. Summer has come to the High Court. Perhaps, in isolation, some of that season has touched the Lord Celleriant.

"You are strong, Daughter. The bard is the strongest of your companions. But he has had to fight alone for long enough. He has chosen. He will pay the price." He turned.

"You have work to do, Evayne, in this place, if my memory does not fail me."

His memory never failed.

"What work?"

"It is not . . . bad. You are not required, tonight, to take life, or to watch it pass beyond you. But you *are* required. There is much to be done in this time."

CHAPTER TWENTY-FOUR

The Matriarch and the Serra chose to stand before the cabin's door, rather than behind it. The moon was bright; they would be visible well before Margret brought the ship to within a ladder's easy reach of her people.

The Serra had, of course, been right. The moment the ship began its return flight to the Arkosans, triumph—and it was an odd and bitter triumph to begin with—faded. Responsibility was left in its wake. She was the Matriarch of Arkosa. She had brought her people into the desert. They had to survive the journey.

Two of the water jugs had cracked in flight, but the cracks were closer to the neck than the base, and all of the water that was going to be lost had been. Elena's ship—and it could be seen, in the heart of the small crowd—seemed to have taken little damage, which meant the food had survived.

The worst threat to the Arkosans would be the effects of the night itself. The Lady showed no mercy.

It was dark and cold, and Margret was certain the edges of drenched desert robes had begun to freeze. She was certain that her own clothing had not done so because of the symbols drawn across the cabin; they glowed, and whenever she passed in front of one, she felt the warmth that radiated from its complicated runes.

Warm or no, they had not served their greater purpose, and she was troubled by the failure. They should have been protection against detection. The enemy should not have been able to breach that spell with such ease. Certainly not with so little warning.

Questions. Too many questions.

This was Matriarch territory, and she was bitterly aware—although that bitterness did not last—that the answers were ahead of her, in the sands beneath the desert, and behind her, in the past, where she might reach for them when needed. *Mother.*

Matriarch.

She took a breath. Things could be worse, Margret, she told herself. They could be so much worse.

The door opened.

The Serra Diora di'Marano stepped out on the small deck. Reached out, gracefully, delicately, to expose her skin to the cold of the night air by gripping the handrail. She seemed so delicate. So perfect.

Margret could not imagine that she could be bowed by so simple a burden as age; that that grace would be leeched from her, year by year, and blemish by blemish. She could not imagine, having seen her in the storm with nothing but a dagger as a weapon, that she could dissemble, could be the protected, unseen harem spirit that women of the clans were groomed to be.

As if aware of Margret's regard, the Serra turned. Her eyes, in the deep blues and grays of midnight light, were unblinking. "Matriarch," she said, and something about the quality of the word put Margret on guard immediately.

"What?"

"They are . . . crying."

Margret's eyes narrowed; she turned, squinting into the darkness. "I can't hear them."

The Serra turned away. "The wind comes across the plateau; it is strong tonight."

Strong. Wind. As they approached the people—*her* people—huddled below, the Matriarch of Arkosa began to count. Her hands moved, her lips mouthed numbers in a simple rhythm that had been part of her life since her earliest memories. One. Two. Three.

Yes, and what comes after three?

Four.

Good! And after that?

Five. Six. Seven.

Yes, yes! I think she's got it, Evallen.

Don't be so excited—you'll turn her into a merchant.

Never mind your mother. What's next?

Eight. Nine. Ten.

To every number, she had attached a face, a name. Her

father's voice fell silent; memory deserted her; her hands froze in the chill night air. She was glad the railing hadn't snapped during the fight; it held her weight. Held her steady.

The ship came as close to ground as the enchantments surrounding it allowed it to come; Margret turned to the cabin to find the rolled rungs of rope and ladder, and stopped in surprise when she saw them in the curved crook of the Serra's arms.

"It is heavy, Matriarch. May I drop it?"

Margret nodded. Watched the slender, delicate Serra, mired in wet desert robes, as she struggled to heave the ladder over the ship's side. She did not offer help; she waited, as if it were natural to have the wife of the former ruler of the Dominion perform the tasks allotted to serafs in the High Court.

Only when the rungs clattered against the underside of the ship did she look away. Back to ground. Back to where her people waited. It should have been easy to crest the rail; should have been easy to catch the ladder's rungs, descend from the short distance that separated her from the ground. But her hands shook, her mouth—in all this rain—was dry.

"Serra," she said, because she needed to say something, "can you get down on your own?"

The Serra hesitated a moment—the hesitation obvious only by the gap between Margret's words and the word that followed. "Yes."

Margret stood, left foot on the top rung, right foot two down; she bowed her forehead into the ship's side and drew breath there as if she were preparing for a dive. She made her way down.

Stavos caught the ladder as it swayed, anchoring it in place. But he did not offer her a hand; he did not welcome her with words, and the moment both of her feet were on the ground, he seemed to melt into shadow.

Margret caught the ladder, unwilling to gaze into the shadows that had swallowed him. She was not Stavos; when the Serra had reached the last of the rungs, she offered her a hand. Felt, as the offer was accepted, the cool, perfect skin of the High Court; and beneath it, the warmth of another living person.

The warmth was brief. The Serra neither withdrew too

quickly, nor too slowly, but she paused before she joined the Arkosans; paused and then dipped in a graceful bow, acknowledging Margret.

Margret waited. She did not wait long; Elena came from between Stavos and his wife, glancing around his shoulder as if she were a child, and not the Matriarch's heir. It was unlike her. So unlike her.

" 'Lena," Margret said, before her cousin had taken two steps. "Where's Adam?"

Consciousness returned to Kallandras. It did not return slowly; it sprang, slapped him forcefully, drove him from the depths of the shadows between sleep and death.

He woke to pain. His side and his arm were on fire. His leg was bruised, but it would support weight, even his own. Especially his own.

The stars were moving above him. The air was cold. The sky was clear, ebony inlaid with points of ice that glittered like diamonds in light. The wind's voice was a serenade, but although he heard it, he did not feel it; a warning there. He lifted his head. Separated the skin of cheek from the warmth of a fabric woven in the court of the Queen, Winter or Summer, that the Arianni served.

His attempt to lift the arm failed; he realized then that it had been tended, bound. So, too, had the ribs. The wounds had been cleaned, the blood staunched, although the injuries were such that they would not be fully healed for some time.

"I . . . thank you . . . for your intervention, Lord Celleriant."

The Arianni lord did not break stride.

When Kallandras realized he had no intention of doing so, he spoke again. "I am capable of bearing my own weight." There was no pride in the voice, no hubris, no need to assert strength or power. He stated what he believed to be fact.

The lord from the Green Deepings was quiet. As if he knew what Kallandras' gift was capable of extracting from something as simple as voice, shorn as it was of the power and grace of battle. But he paused. Let Kallandras slide from the curve of his arms, supporting him beneath the shoulders until both feet were planted against the ground.

He waited a moment.

Kallandras took a step without hesitation, braced for the pain of the ground's impact; he absorbed it without reaction.

"Your people are there." Lord Celleriant lifted an arm, pointing ahead to where the riverbed once stood.

From its depths, the ground had risen; it crested land to either side, and in its center, clearly visible in the moonlight, stood the Arkosans, shielded from the wind on either side by the strange wagons the Matriarch and her heir rode.

He bowed to the Arianni lord, turned, and walked to where the Arkosans were gathered. It was not so far away.

To his surprise, Lord Celleriant fell into step at his side. He carried no shield, no sword, and the rain had finally turned the length of his hair into a damp, long swathe of white. They were both silent, but Kallandras noticed that the rise and fall of their steps was identical; that unless had he been listening carefully, he might have had difficulty judging whether one man or two walked across the sand.

The Arkosans shifted, exposing the man who stood at their heart. Avandar Gallais.

"The wild magic is stirring," Lord Celleriant whispered. He stopped walking. "I have much to consider. But I would ask you now if you understood what I risked."

"Yes," Kallandras replied. "The sword."

Lord Celleriant lifted a perfect, empty hand. "Not now. We have . . . time." And he smiled. "We will either see the world's end or have some hand in its salvation, and we will stand side by side in battles that will make this," he lifted his bright, steel eyes, his wild eyes, to the moon's clear face, "seem simple and trifling."

Kallandras might have replied, but before he could frame the words, he was interrupted by a cry. It was broken at once by a terrible silence.

"I believe," Celleriant said quietly, "that you are needed."

"I?"

"It is the young woman, the one who is fair even for a mortal."

"You recognized her voice?"

"Did you not? I am not your equal in that regard, but I am not without skill." He bowed. "You have chosen to bear some responsibility for her. I do not judge it wise."

"Do you judge it at all?"

"Perhaps. But bear that responsibility now. If I am not mistaken, you will find some comfort in the bearing."

Elena bowed at once, knelt, brought her hands to the wet sand.

Margret froze. Diora had seen such a lack of motion before. In the darkness, she heard Margret bark something in so harsh a voice that the word lost its edges. But not its meaning. Elena rose at once. She lifted a hand to Margret, and then dropped it at once; Diora stood beside the Matriarch, but did not turn to see what her expression was.

She could guess, and in the silence of this night, that was enough.

Her people parted.

Diora hesitated only a moment as Margret moved forward, stride wide, step deliberate. Like a shadow, she followed.

She saw Ona Teresa; saw Yollana of the Havalla Voyani by her side, weight supported by staff and arm. Saw Nicu, the petulant young man whose gaze never left Elena; saw the men who stood—had vowed to stand—to his right and left. She passed Stavos, his wife, and her cousin, Tamara. And then she stopped, as Margret stopped.

Someone was missing.

Or not.

She took a step forward, past where the Matriarch now stood. Knelt before Jewel of House Terafin, the Lady's wayward traveler, and realized that the sound of denial she heard—and felt—was entirely her own. A stranger's. A sound she had no right to make.

She did not speak again. But she reached out for the cold, still face of the Matriarch's brother as if it were a flame, and she a moth.

His head lay in the lap of a stranger; his hair, longer wet than it had ever appeared dry, was strewn across her legs like a blanket. His eyes were closed. Closed.

"Serra." Margret's voice. Harsh; straining beneath the weight of unexpressed pain and anger. But it didn't break. That seemed . . . wrong to her. It seemed so unlike the Arkosan Voyani. Such control, such bitter silence, was a gift, and a curse, of the clans.

Gift? Curse? No. It was simply wisdom. Show your loss

beneath the open sky, and your enemies will know that they have hurt you. They will know how to hurt you in the future, and others will suffer for just that reason: that you have been weak enough to expose that vulnerability at all.

Her hands left Adam's face. She looked up, to Jewel, and then down, to where his hands rested.

She closed her eyes then, because she thought she might have some chance at holding tears—sudden and surprising as the thickness of her throat, the inability to draw breath—back.

Salla lay gripped in his stiff hands.

He saw her look up as he approached, although he made almost no sound as he walked. His legs were stiff, bruised; muscles ached. It had been many years since he had joined a combat so punishing, so demanding. His arm would be useless for weeks, and he would have to take care not to further damage his side. The ribs, however, had not pierced lung.

"Serra Diora."

She did not speak. Did not acknowledge his greeting in any way save this: she looked down. At the boy who lay across the folded legs of Jewel ATerafin.

He looked, as she had, at his face. Saw his closed eyes. Saw his stiff arms.

And then he, too, closed his eyes, but not before he had seen what the boy's hands curled, white-boned, around.

The boy had promised that he would return the lute safely.

It was not comfortable to kneel; he knelt. Physical pain did not linger, and the scars it left he had long since accepted as inevitable. Strange, then, that accruing other scars, as inevitable in nature, could never be so easily accepted.

"Serra Diora." He held out a hand before her shuttered eyes. She had seen much worse than this; would see worse before war's end, should she survive that long.

But he had never been able to read so much in her expression alone; even her voice had become, with time and experience, almost impenetrable. What had the Serra Teresa said? Diora had learned as a child not to cry.

She looked up at him almost blindly. He did not turn away. As he had to the end of his hopes, he bore witness to the end of hers; silent, acknowledging in the full measure of that silence the truth of the loss.

But she surprised him, and he had been trained, in youth, beyond it, to find little surprising. She spoke.

"He brought her to me. To *me.* He knew what she meant to you. But he knew what . . . the music . . . might mean to me. You live in the North, Kallandras; I live in the South. There is a border here," her delicate fingertips brushed the cloth above her heart, "that I have never crossed."

"You have known loss, Serra."

"Yes." The corners of her lips became smooth and full; the use of words seemed to bring back strength and dignity. Odd. "But it is not of love that I speak. No man exists—or woman—who is not touched by love. The border cannot prevent that.

"But this boy, this brother of a Voyani Matriarch, was born in the South, and had—has—a Northern heart. He did not come to you for love of me; he did not come to you for pity's sake. He came . . . for reasons I do not understand. And stayed. And left."

"Do you truly not understand what moved him?"

"Do you?"

His smile was slight; a parry.

"In the North, the gods keep the dead, not the winds, and the dead wait. For us. In the North, where the men are said to be weak, and the blood thin, they have raised champions and armies, and women are—are not—what I have been. Have been proud to be.

"I *hate* these lands. I hate the border." She bowed her head. "But not because of my life. Because of his. Because it is in the South that people who have the grace and strength to be . . ."

"Gentle?"

"Gentle. Yes. As he was. Those people are devoured by the Lady. By the Lord. They are given to wind, to sun. What other man would have done this for a lute?"

"Serra Diora."

She raised her face.

"It was not for the lute; it was for the vow. Accord him a measure of the respect he is due."

He walked to where Jewel sat. She, as the Arkosans, felt no compunction about tears, and although they robbed her face of necessary warmth, she let them fall.

The Arkosans were silent; they had not moved. But they heard the Serra's voice as clearly as they had the day she had offered them the gift of her song. What they could not hear, he heard, for she had dropped the walls behind which she habitually hid.

He did not flinch. Slow and painful death was not enough to force him to flinch. This much he had learned in the youth that seemed closer to him than the present.

Had seemed so, after the battle in the skies. Had seemed more so after the fall. He had stood beside a brother. He had fought, as he might have fought in youth, beside an equal of his own choosing. He had relied on, depended on, a brother to bring him back.

Back?

He had come to the camp to see Salla in a dead boy's hands, and he understood that the past and the present were intertwined in ways that even he, decades later, could not disentangle. Could not understand. Had he been given a choice, he would have turned from the life he led now; he would have walked to the Labyrinths, to the masters who had trained him—of whom only two now survived—and resumed that life.

Or so he would have said.

He knew, now, that he would take Salla with him everywhere he chose to go.

And he knew, now, that should he be forced by the brotherhood to relinquish her, he would hesitate upon the threshold of Melesnea itself. He had not chosen the life of a bard, but like any hostage could, he had come to love his captor.

Boy . . .

Jewel's arms ached. She'd held Adam for so long, any movement hurt; putting him down would be almost as painful as continuing to hold him. She thought about rolling him gently off her lap. Meant to do it.

But he stayed where she had placed him, neck above the crook of her elbow, eyes closed.

The Serra Diora knelt before her; the master bard of Senniel College stood only a little farther away. She had looked at them, and away, at and away, until the movement was as rhythmic as breath.

Jewel.

Go away.

Jewel, it is time. Give him to his family, and come away.

She had never made a habit of listening to Avandar when his advice did not involve the minutiae of politics.

Jewel.

She knew he was right. The cold had entered the base of her spine and traveled up her back and down her legs; she was shuddering with it.

"Matriarch," she said softly, looking past the kneeling woman whose face surrendered tears.

But the Matriarch was frozen. Jewel called her again, and again she failed to move. She shifted the boy; her body protested the slight movement of arm. Shifted him again.

Let me help.

No.

Jewel—

Her breath came out in a huff that looked smokelike, solid. As if she were a winter dragon, and he her hoard, she lifted her chin in defiance.

"Matriarch?"

And thought the better of pride; her arms really were too damn cold to move. Wouldn't be the first time she'd fallen flat on her face.

Margret of Arkosa did not move. Jewel squinted; she stood far enough away that the night robbed her features of distinctive lines, of expression. She looked back to the boy in her shaking arms.

Stopped.

"Avandar!"

Three faces swiveled toward hers, hearing in the name she shouted all the edges that she hadn't put into words.

The woman who had been frozen at the greatest distance found feet, found motion, stumbled between the kneeling Serra and the bard who—as he so often did—bore witness.

"What? What is it?" she said, her voice thin and shaky.

"I—"

She reached for Adam; for his face, his cheeks, his chin; her hands stuttered as they stumbled across features made unfamiliar by stillness. But they came to rest against the side of his throat and stayed there a moment, searching almost desperately for a sign.

There was none.

Jewel *knew* there was none.

But knowing this, she felt her heart beat as hope made her fearful. She reached out and caught Margret's stiff hand. Pulled it away. "Matriarch," she said, putting years of practice at giving orders into use.

Margret did not resist.

"Matriarch."

"Matriarch." Kallandras moved also, quickly and silently approaching her—but from the side, not from behind. He had that much sense.

Margret did not acknowledge him. She looked, instead, to Jewel. Her voice was low and intense; it caught on her words as if they were barbs. "You were sent to us by the Lady," she said. "You came to the heart of the fire. What do you see? What hope do you offer my—my brother?"

"He—he—"

"Yes?" Too quickly.

"Do not bury him yet. Do not mourn him. Help me—help me stand. Help me move him inside."

"But—" She shook her head. "Yes. Yes, at once. Stavos! Elena!"

The tears she had been hoarding blurred her eyes, her dark, narrowed eyes.

From out of nowhere, a question came to Jewel, and she asked it without thought, without control. "Can you do without him, Matriarch? If he lives, can you send him North, into the unknown, and away from the *Voyanne* that you must travel?"

"If he lives, I would send him to the High Courts themselves to serve the clans if that was your price." She drew heat from somewhere, some reserve that the night had not destroyed. Spoke with it. "If he lives, I promise the Lady—"

"The Lady doesn't need your promise, but Adam will."

"*Yes.* Yes, I can send him from the *Voyanne* if that is

all that will save him. He—" Her voice broke again. "He does not breathe, Jewel. He doesn't *breathe*. Can you force the winds to relinquish what is theirs?"

"No." She looked past Margret. Squared her shoulders. Spoke. "I was wondering if we would see you."

Margret's hand was trapped by Jewel's, but she too turned.

"No," was the quiet reply. "You weren't. Well met, Matriarch. Well met, Jewel ATerafin." Evayne a'Nolan, in robes the color of the clear night sky, inclined her head. She took a step forward.

In the wake of cloth that moved to an unfelt, unseen wind, came another man. Jewel recognized him at once, although the last time she'd seen him had been in the healerie of Terafin, a place so different from the desert and the Southern lands that the only thing she could clearly recall of it was the old man who was its heart. The first healer she had met; the man who had saved her den-mate, who had offered her a peaceful place to go within the chaos and turmoil of House politics.

A man as different from the one before her as a man could be who still followed the same tenets. Or, she thought dubiously, professed to.

Kallandras bowed. "Healer Levec," he said softly, speaking in Weston. "You have traveled far from your home."

"I was told," the healer snapped, his voice as brusque as a voice can be without—quite—managing rudeness, "that it was urgent."

"I offered you the choice of accompanying me," his companion said.

The healer snorted. Ran a hand through dense beard. "You could have told me to bring furs."

"We will not, if I judge the situation correctly, remain here long enough to require them."

No one could see her face. The hood hung low and long, and although the hems of sleeve and gown moved almost of their own accord, the cowl's folds seemed frozen in place. But the voice was unmistakable.

"Matriarch."

Margret rose. "What do you want?"

"We have come for your brother."

"You can't have him."

"Margret—"

" 'Gret—"

Jewel had struggled to get her feet out from beneath her thighs without dumping Adam on the cold, frozen sand. Some circulation had returned; she could unfold her knees without cursing or crying out in pain; she could move her arms. She got to her knees and sat over the balls of her heels, Adam on the incline of her lap.

"Matriarch," she said, "you have no cause to love Evayne a'Nolan. But the man by her side is one of the healer-born."

The Matriarch lingered a moment longer in the path between Evayne and her brother, but chose—grudgingly—to give ground.

Evayne swept past her, dragging Levec in her wake. He looked about as happy as Jewel would expect.

But he was the only healer she had ever met who was known across the breadth of the High City for the quality of his temper.

"If you've wasted my time," she heard him mutter—but he saw the expression on the face of the Matriarch, and thought better of the rest of the sentence. He approached Jewel, turned a glare upon both the Serra and Kallandras, which both ignored, and knelt.

"It is *damned* cold." His breath was dragon's breath, like Jewel's. Warm and solid. "ATerafin," he added gruffly. "Your people—"

Her own heart quickened. "My—my people—"

But his attention wavered. Fell. And nothing Jewel could ask would make it rise again; she knew this, and bit her lip.

Finch. Angel. Teller.

His hands, browned with sun, but corded with the muscles of a man who made physical labor his life's work, were gentle as they cupped the face of the boy in her lap. With infinite care, he attempted to pry the lute from Adam's grasp, but he accepted failure there with uncharacteristic grace.

"How old is the boy?"

"I—I don't know."

His frown was immediate, but at least it wasn't followed up with, *you idiot.* Instead, it was followed by something almost as ungraceful: Levec speaking Torra. Jewel had thought he sounded unfriendly in Weston. "You, how old is this boy?"

"Fourteen summers."

"Old."

"Healer, I am the Matriarch of Arkosa—"

"And I am the master of the House of Healing. If you are about to offer me money, magic, or personal fealty for my services, let me make this clear: There is nothing I want from you."

"Can you bring him back?"

"I? No."

The word was cold, gruff, final. But he relented before Jewel had a chance to harry him. "You cannot see him." His voice was soft, so soft, as he cupped Adam's chin. "You cannot see what is he doing. It appears, Evayne, that I owe you an apology."

The seer said nothing.

"I will have to take him with me," the healer continued, as if he hadn't expected a reply. Knowing Levec, he probably didn't give a damn one way or the other.

"You are his family?"

Margret nodded.

"When he wakes, if he is not in a . . . quiet place . . . he will go mad."

"W–what do you mean?"

"He has come late, and sudden, into his power, but his power—his power—"

"Levec." Jewel was surprised to hear her own voice. It was hard as the sand on which she rested. "Tell her."

Although he did not look up from the boy's face, his own had gentled; the lines of it were softer than Jewel had ever seen them. His students decried his harsh use of words, but they were fond of him in their fashion, and for the first time she could see—or could almost see—why.

"He is healer-born."

The Arkosans were silent. They had gathered, closer and closer to their Matriarch, and now they bore witness.

"He—"

"Most come into their power slowly. They become aware of the pain and the injuries, the illnesses and the infections, of others. They are called by it, they are consumed by it. If they cannot be trained, they are often devoured by it.

"You had no sign?"

She shook her head.

"He will find his way back; he is finding it back now. But—he will be without even the rudimentary defenses that others, untrained, have."

"He's not—he's not—"

"Dead? No." He looked at Jewel. "ATerafin, you have held him; give him into my keeping and I will—you have my word—defend him as if he were my own."

She smiled. She had not thought to smile this evening, but it felt good, this turn of lips, this quirk of face. "I would, if I could move. You're right, it's damn cold here."

"May I?"

"Matriarch?"

"Yes. I gave you my word. Yes. But—"

"But?" Levec's voice resumed its deep rumble.

"Where will you take him?"

"To the Houses of Healing."

The distance between the healer and the Matriarch lessened, step by step, until she stood before him. She reached for her brother, and he flinched, drawing the arms that held the boy up to his chest.

But it was a defensive reaction, a bear's reaction; Margret did not seem to be displeased with it; she did not, Jewel thought, deign to acknowledge him at all. She reached out, placed a hand against her brother's chest, and stood in the cold silence, her brows changing the shape of her eyes, her face.

"Will he wake?"

"Yes. Did I not already say so?"

"Will you remain until he wakes?"

A look of unease stole across Levec's face. "It will be hours, Matriarch, before he is conscious. When he is, he will be disoriented."

"Disoriented?"

Levec frowned; the expression deepened.

You're not telling all of the truth, Jewel thought. *And that's not a smart thing to do when you're holding her brother.*

"He will be easily confused and easily frightened."

"And you want to take him away from the only people he trusts?" Elena now, voice sharp as a lash, although

Jewel noted that she stood behind Margret's squared shoulders.

Margret did not remove the hand from her brother's chest. He was still and pale.

"Matriarch," Kallandras of Senniel said, avoiding Levec's glare and Levec's burden as he approached Margret, "It will go ill if he wakes to the company of those he loves."

Margret lowered her face a moment, as if she had expected that answer. "Why?" She did not look up. Jewel could barely hear the word.

"He will have walked a long way in the darkness. He will desire light, life, anything at all that he can cling to. He will be—broken, in some way; unlike himself."

"This is true?"

Levec turned a cold, cold stare upon Kallandras. Margret outwaited him. He nodded.

"But then—"

"The healer-born give something of themselves when they heal, and they take something of their patients. Knowledge. They cannot avoid it. The greater the injury, the more they can take."

She tossed her head impatiently. "You tell me what every child knows. I am not a child. And I am not injured."

"No. But his gift is a gift of touch, of contact. And in order to walk back from the death that he was sent to meet, he will have invoked his power, his full power, for the first time." He looked down at the young boy's face. "He is walking as we speak, Matriarch, and the walk is terrible. Everything about him desires to remain where he is, for he has come to the fastness of the Lord of Judgment, where the winds do not howl, and the mother that he lost is almost—*was* almost—within his grasp."

"That is Northern belief. He is of the South."

Kallandras offered her an elegant lift of shoulder. He did not enter that argument.

"Enough, bard." Levec's voice was ice now. Jewel saw a real threat in the bear's expression, for it had become still; he had taken control of all temper and had begun to hoard it.

Kallandras switched to Weston. "They will owe you a debt of blood, Healer Levec, if you do as you have promised. They will not betray you, or your kind; they will not give up information that could be used to hurt their own. But she will not allow you to leave with her brother if you do not explain yourself.

"And your time—and his—grows short."

"Do not seek to use that famous voice on me," Levec snapped, but the lines of his face fell into the curves and wrinkles of open annoyance again, and he did not seek to interfere further.

Kallandras turned back to Margret. "Adam has not been allowed to stay with his mother. Instead, some terrible force that he does not understand has pulled him back, and struggle as he might, he cannot break free from it. Nothing he can ever do in his life will allow him that grace; he will live."

"You're saying that nothing can kill the healer-born?"

"Nothing natural, short of losing head or heart. And of the heart . . . death is not a given if the healer is powerful enough and well-trained."

Margret's eyes widened; she looked at her brother. She knew better than to smile, Jewel thought. Or perhaps it was just the Voyani habit of doubting all good news. Good was a precursor to loss and tragedy, a way of weakening the defenses.

"If Adam touches you in this state, he will pull from you what he might pull were you injured. He will try to fill the emptiness he feels with whatever it is you can offer.

"But he *knows* you. He trusts you. Are you prepared to pay for that trust by offering him all of the things that by the nature of your responsibilities as the Matriarch of all Arkosa, you *must* keep hidden? You know the price of that. You know what you would be honor bound to do."

"He—"

"And if not you, who? Elena? Stavos? Tamara? Who of you will fill a young boy's mind and heart with all of the shadows that you have felt no need to expose to him before? Yes, he knows you. Yes, you are the only people in the world that he trusts and honors. And yes, in time—in the fullness of his own time—he will come to understand your weaknesses just as well as he understands your strength. But I will tell you now, if you cannot see it for yourself, that should he be thrust from death to that weakness, that darkness, instead of to the comfort he will require to maintain his sanity, he will be scarred forever, and he will cease to trust."

"And this stranger?"

"This stranger has a heart that is capable of traversing the length of the *Voyanne* without bleeding. He will give your brother what you cannot in safety give, for your brother will take everything without expectation. If he sees shadow, he will not feel betrayed because he thought to see light.

"Levec has had experience in this. He may be able to protect himself; to give what he chooses to give and to withhold what must be withheld."

She lifted her head. Turned to Levec. "You may take him. But . . ."

"But?"

"I want him back. We want him back. This is his home."

"If, after his convalescence and his training, that is what he desires, I will arrange his return—but as I am not accustomed to this unsatisfactory form of travel, it would be best if I—"

"When the time is right," Kallandras said, "I will bring him back to the *Voyanne*."

"Thank you." But still she lingered.

"Lady," Levec said, sliding into Weston. They all looked at him, Margret with confusion, and he had the grace to flush. "We must leave."

But she clung, silent, hesitant.

It was the Serra Diora who understood. She had knelt, and she had cried. She rose now, as if those two acts had emptied her of the ability to feel at all. She came to stand at Margret's side, displacing Elena, who had the wisdom not to interrupt her cousin.

"May I?"

Margret turned, the softness of the honest request moving her where the gruff certainty of the healer could not. A frown touched her lips and the lines of her forehead, but did not settle.

Diora did not alter her position. She made no attempt to touch Adam, or to otherwise come between brother and sister; by whim of fate she already bore the responsibility for coming between the mother and daughter, and if she knew herself blameless in that regard, she also understood that pain assigned blame in accordance with the rules of the hidden heart.

She did not lift her face. Instead, she lowered it to stop her chin from visibly trembling. The cold that had descended into her marrow had a stronger voice than she would have thought possible.

Adam.

Adam, I have made peace with your sister, and she with me. Thank you for your gift. Let me take the lute; let me return it to its owner. You have kept your promise. She faltered, continued after a moment. **Even if your promise was never given in words, even if no medallion was cut, and you lifted no sword to make it.**

Come home. You have lost your mother; do not inflict your loss upon your sister; do not leave her alone. You will have the peace denied you in your time. You are needed here.

Come home, Adam. Come quickly.

She rose when she had finished, uncertain how far her voice reached.

She joined Margret, looking to the Matriarch for permission. It was given wordlessly.

Raising her hands, she caught the neck of the lute in one and gently pried his fingers from it. Then she lifted those fingers; the hand came with it; she pressed the palm briefly to cold lips and set it down again, taking care to arrange it against his breast.

Beneath Margret's hand, beneath her stiff and frozen fingers, she felt it: the fluttering start and stop of a beating heart, muffled as it was by wet, cold clothing.

She stopped breathing, as if she could lend what she did not take to her brother in his struggle, and waited. Waited until that beat was strong enough that it could not be an act of her imagination and her desperate desire.

And then she counted three simple beats, lifted her hand, and let him go.

CHAPTER TWENTY-FIVE

But before Evayne left, before she could take a step forward, a hand clutched her robes. The robes drew back, but the grip of almost flawless fingers was sure.

The hood swiveled toward that hand, and from hand it followed the length of arm until eyes met in the darkness.

"Serra Diora." The seer inclined her head. "You are . . . forward."

Diora did not waver; did not falter. Her expression was now as serene an expression as had ever graced the face of the Tyr'agar's wife. She was beautiful, stark as moonlight. Cold as moonlight in this desert. "Forgive me." She spoke in a voice that asked nothing, accepted nothing, that was not her due.

And the seer listened.

"You will leave. I cannot prevent it. And it may be that in the end, I will thank you for your intervention in my life, and in the lives of my companions. But at this moment, beneath this moon, I say to you, stranger, that you owe me a boon, and I will claim it now."

The figure in the robe seemed to flinch. "What boon?" Her voice was distant and cool, but beneath the forced radiance of the Flower of the Dominion, that distance seemed brittle, forced.

"You can see some of what will happen, some of what has happened, if you choose to look."

This woman nodded.

"I wish to know where my seraf is."

Behind her straight back, the perfect line of her shoulders, she heard the sudden murmur of Arkosan voices. Heard Yollana's crisp growl, Ona Teresa's patient reply.

Yes, she thought, *I reveal weakness beneath the open sky, but it* is *the Lady's time, and the risk is mine to take.*

She could clearly see Ramdan standing in the open rain, face turned toward the sky, waiting for her command. Folly, to think of him in this fashion, but she could not help it; Ona Teresa had given the seraf into her care, and she had left him behind because she knew that the Matriarch disliked his servitude.

She had left him behind.

For a moment, it seemed that the seer would refuse the request; the silence was long. But her hand moved; it was swallowed by robes, and when it emerged again, it contained a crystal shard. "*Do not* look, Serra. You have not walked the Oracle's path, and even you might be driven mad by what you see within the depths of this ball."

In the light of the orb, the seer's face was at last revealed. She was a woman, in her thirties, her face pale, the lines of it drawn as if she were in great pain. Her eyes were as dark as moonless night, from pupil to iris; the whites were devoured by shadow.

The Arkosans drew back, tracing a circle in front of their faces with their right hands, and quartering it with their left. Only the Matriarch was unmoved.

She watched, as the Serra watched, her face lit by her proximity to the visible heart of the seer's vision.

Time passed. They watched as the seer's brow shifted marginally; watched as she passed her hand once, twice, and a third time over the surface of the crystal, as if to wipe it clean.

But they did not speak until that crystal, dull surface trapping the hint of roiling clouds, was once again swallowed by the robes she wore.

"Evayne?"

"ATerafin. Well met. I see that . . . you have Yollana of the Havalla Voyani as well. How . . . unusual." The frown lingered as her lips stretched thin. "Forgive me; this is not . . . the time . . . to converse.

"Serra, your seraf is not dead. He is . . . mounted . . . and he is fleeing for his life, but I believe his mount will carry him to the appointed meeting place. Levec."

"Wait!"

But the seer caught the healer's arm and took a quick step forward.

She was gone in an instant; the moon's light struck

ground where a moment before she had forced it to cast shadows.

"Damn her!" Margret spat.

"I think," Yollana said, speaking for the first time, "that there is no damnation she could face that is worse than the one she faces daily. Come, Matriarch. Let us concentrate on what we do know, rather than what we do not."

"What?"

"We're going to freeze to death if we don't find shelter soon. For a start."

The Matriarch frowned at this almost open criticism. Frowned and accepted it; it was true. She shouted for Elena, and Elena appeared at once; they conferred for a second or two, but in the end, there was little to confer about.

They could take to the ships, or they could remain aground, with no tenting, wet clothing, and the rest of the Lady's Night to wait through.

The wagons became a very, very crowded home for the Arkosans. They were not large—a fact driven home by the presence of so many people within them—and those that could withstand the cold with ease were left to their own devices.

Lord Celleriant and Avandar Gallais chose to continue their journey on foot. Jewel had offered to join them, but aside from the dubious entertainment offered the Arkosans when the inevitable argument had ensued, she chose, in the end, to remain with Elena.

Margret, Tamara, Yollana, the Serra Teresa, Stavos and his wife, Caitla, traveled in Margret's ship; Nicu, his two men, Jewel, and Donatella traveled with Elena.

The water jugs, some cracked, were difficult to ignore, and sleep was scant, but that many bodies in an enclosed space produced the heat so necessary to survival.

"It's only one day," Margret told the Arkosans. "One day. If we travel this way, we will arrive more quickly than by foot."

"And how are we going to go home?"

The Matriarch shrugged, deflecting Tamara's well-honed worry with an ease that spoke of too many years' practice.

"Let us hope," she said lightly, "that the ancestors prepared for this, years ago."

"Margret—"

She spread out her hands, weary, the cool, clean air outside an almost irresistible temptation. "Ona Tamara, the food was in 'Lena's ship; the water in mine. We lost tenting and blankets—"

"Which stop us from freezing or burning."

"—but if we must, we can travel like this. As the jugs empty, we can hang them from the sides of the ship, and we'll gain room that way. By the time we're home—"

Her aunt snorted. Turned and smacked her cousin's shoulder sharply. "Don't light that here!"

His great growl filled the small cabinet. "With what? I wanted to make sure it hadn't cracked. That's all. Besides," he added, looking at the contents of his pouch, "the weed is sodden."

Yollana laughed. "If you can stand it, you can have some of mine."

"Yours is dry?"

"Drier than that; that looks like you scraped it off the underside of your boot." She reached into her pouch while Tamara choked back a flood of invective, and brought out a medium-sized jar. The lid unscrewed, tongues scraping grooves as she twisted it. "Come join us, Margret."

"I don't smoke."

The old woman shrugged. "You will." She stuffed her pipe carefully, handed it to Stavos, and took his in turn. When the bowl of both pipes had been filled, she whispered three words and snapped her fingers.

A small fire hung, like a pendant on some invisible chain, between them. Stavos' eyes went wide, but Yollana shrugged. "It won't last," she said, leaning forward. "Best use it now." She exhaled. Leaned back.

"Matriarch," she said, and her voice seemed firmer, "tomorrow."

"Tomorrow?"

"When we arrive, you'll know. You should try this, Margret. It soothes the nerves." Her lips thinned around a transparent stream of smoke.

"I can't afford to be soothed." Margret coughed. Loudly. It was considered poor form—and worse survival instinct—

to openly criticize a Matriarch, even if you were one. She stood instead, seeking the relative peace of the open sky.

The door creaked just loudly enough that she could get out of the way before it hit her.

"It seems," Yollana said, holding an unlit pipe, "that Tamara doesn't approve of my habit."

"And she *told* you this?"

"Eloquently. For an Arkosan."

"It's the night."

Yollana shrugged. "Or her intelligence. We need to speak."

"There are no heartfires here."

Yollana's brows disappeared into her hairline. They fell again. "You don't understand the power of the wards you drew, do you, Matriarch?" She lifted a curved hand. Brought it toward the symbol painted on the side of the ship. It began to glow, and brightly.

Yollana grimaced. "Our ancestors were not friendly."

"Never mind our ancestors; we don't have to look back at the dead to see how we squabble."

"True enough. The squabbles must end, now."

"Between Havalla and Arkosa, they have ended. My word on it."

"And mine."

"Then speak, Yollana. Say what must be said."

The old woman hesitated. Margret found the hesitation profoundly disturbing. "Yollana?"

"We had no warning."

"No."

"We should have."

"Against the storm?"

"Against the creature that brought it, yes. Against an outsider, an intruder, yes. My wards are not as strong as the wards that guide your ships—but they are strong enough. The rain came without warning."

"There are outsiders here."

Yollana spit. "We do not have the luxury of ignorance. Another time, perhaps."

The Arkosan Matriarch raised her face to the moon; held it there, in light too cold, too silver, to offer warmth. A Northern merchant had once said the moon and stars were guides by which sailors swore that they could lead a ship home if one knew how to read them.

She had never learned their language. What guided the Arkosans now was blood and magic. Her heritage, however poorly she understood it.

"What wards?" she asked the question quietly. Honestly.

Yollana sat, heavily, on her legs. "Blood wards," she said. "Of the simplest kind. They are most easily invoked."

The younger woman closed her eyes. She started to frame a question in the darkness, but the answer was obvious, and she hadn't the heart to ask it. "Arkosan blood."

"Yes."

"But you—"

"No. I did not shed it."

"Then there's some chance—"

"No. I am old, Margret. With age comes all manner of infirmity—but wisdom comes as well, with cost. I have been among the Arkosans for long enough."

It was true. Margret knew it was true.

"Help me up, girl. Help me up, help me in."

The unfamiliar weight of a crippled woman tested the reserves of Arkosan strength. But it was easier to help her than to listen to what she had not said.

Someone gave their blood to the servants of the Lord of Night. Someone Arkosan. Someone here.

Because without the blood, Yollana's wards would have blazed with a light that would have been seen for miles beneath the clear sky; for yards beneath the clouds.

She did not ask who.

The simple spell would not give Yollana that answer, and besides, it was an Arkosan affair now.

But after she left Yollana in the Serra Teresa's care, Margret once again sought the night air; the nightmares that drove her into the moonlit sky did not need to wait for sleep.

In the Hells, there was only one price for failure. But the word failure, in the Hells, was judiciously applied: Only the stronger used it, and only when speaking of their inferiors.

The Serpent had been laid to rest. Forsaking the elemental air, the wild wind, the voice of the storm where two elements overlapped, she had landed on the ground not far from where Lord Ishavriel had woken her.

Her blood burned the sands it struck, and it flowed freely. She would be of no further use to him in this battle.

So he watched.

Her great teeth cut the scattered, dry surface of the earth; her claws broke its skin; her tail shattered the small rippled edges wind had made. She roared, as she twisted her back, snapping, snarling at the things she could no longer see.

He was one of them.

Distance would have been the safest course, but at a distance, the spectacle lost visceral impact. He felt the earth riven; he felt the heat of her breath, knew that had she come to nest in a place that boasted life, none would have survived her death.

None would have remembered it.

Ishavriel was *Kialli.*

He stood, the only protrusion upon the flat plain, as she raged. Her claws passed an inch above his head; her tail dug furrows in the sand before his feet. He moved lightly out of her way when she sought to pass through him, partnering the lumbering, frenzied motion of her fear and pain with a series of elegant, silent steps. Twice, he was forced to leap, once over her tail, and once over the wide arc of her snapping jaws.

But he used no magic, summoned no element.

She was dying, but she was still a threat; his magic was not weak enough to pass undetected.

Not yet.

Ishavriel, tender of human souls, had never been a reaver; he had never been a Binder. All of the bindings made or forged in his life upon this plane had been subtle, a patched quilt of emotional manipulation, logic, and gamble.

He did not regret them.

His only regret, in the darkness, was the lack of light; the lack of its play across her moving form; the way night turned her colors—for they were there, a subtle iridescence across the surface of obsidian.

At the last, she grew weary. Her thrashing quieted. She lay across the ground like a creature out of its element.

He was in danger, then.

Even blinded, in the stillness she could sense him.

He knew no pity. If he had once known pity, it was lost with his youth, and not even the memory remained.

But danger or no, something moved him, something foreign. He lifted a hand, laid it against her side.

She was not *Kialli.* She had never served the Lord willingly, although she had served Him in her time, and in His.

You stood against a Lord of the Arianni.

The thought was without envy; although a terrible envy had struck when Lord Celleriant's sword was drawn.

Rest. Rest now.

She lifted her wounded, scarred face; it hovered a hand's span above the earth. He felt her sides expand as she inhaled. She cried out, a roar, a plea, a command.

The earth answered.

He bounded clear as it opened beneath her, like a set of great doors, pulled on either side into a wide, wide chasm. She hovered a moment in the air, and then with a soft whoosh of sound, the air collapsed and the earth reached up to catch her, far far more gently than he had expected.

He had never been a Binder.

He took—as was his right—the weaker and the lesser of the kin, or those who challenged him; he tormented—as was his duty—the fragments of mortal souls who had chosen to abide in the Hells.

This creature was neither of those.

He could not have said why he did what he did next, and he would wonder, later, for he was incapable of forgetting the act.

He reached out with the power that, hallowed by the Hells and purified there, was his by right. He found the shadows that lay across both of her hearts, and he touched them, testing their strength.

The Lord held nothing lightly.

And who better to understand that than one of the *Kialli*?

But this was an old, old binding; Ishavriel was impressed that she had remained in its thrall during the long absence of the Lord; it was a testament—as if one were needed—to the power of the gods.

He touched her wounded side, and when he pulled back, his palms were slick with her blood. The wound still wept; the blood was warm. He knew who she was. Her name had not been spoken since his youth, but he could remember the telling that stretched from one night to another. He recalled it now, while the blood was cooling on his hand. He whispered; exposed the flesh beneath his skin. Blood mingled.

Had she been stronger, he would never have attempted the spell. But he thought she would never be strong again; that she, like the gods, would be buried in memory, and in memory alone would she grace him.

He slid beneath the bindings placed upon her hearts, replacing them with his own. She did not struggle; she accepted the thrall as if she could tell no difference between one master and the other.

He worked as the moon fell, familiarizing himself with the stamp of ownership that had allowed—had forced—her to awaken. But only when the sun crested the horizon did he shrug the old bindings off completely. An act of superstition, perhaps.

Or perhaps an act of desire, for as the night sky faded into the grays and golds, the pinks and blues of dawn, he could see the light play across the entirety of her body, could see what she might have looked like, had she been in her full glory. He held her from her place in the earth's heart for a moment, and that moment stretched.

But he could not afford to let it stretch forever; much was left undone.

He lifted his head, seeking the ships.

He found them, felt them as an extension of himself, and smiled. They moved. They still moved.

And then, a hollow gesture, he released her from his own binding.

He gave her freedom.

The earth reached up to embrace her; she lifted her head. But she had no strength to roar, and if she had, he was not certain what she would have offered him; she had no word for gratitude.

Nor did he, anymore.

He waited until there was no sign left of her passage before he began the last short trek.

Bruises were evident in the sun's light; their dark and purple hearts, tinged yellow or black, adorned Arkosan faces and hands. The passage through the tunnels, at the behest of rushing water, had given hard rock and dirt the opportunity to rub skin from flesh, and most of the blankets that might have been used to cover rents and tears in flowing robes had vanished with the tents.

Had they the luxury of time, they might have attempted to collect their things. No one asked. The Arkosans were accustomed to swift flight; they were accustomed to the loss necessity decreed. They had escaped the grasp of the Lord of Night, and if they had never expected his reach to be so long, they did not dwell on it.

Instead, Donatella, Tamara, and Caitla busied themselves taking inventories of what had, and what had not, been lost, and while they did, they also prepared breakfast. Some false cheer dominated their bustle, but it lasted only as long as the food did, and the Arkosans—and their guests—were hungry. They ate quickly.

Jewel's appetite was blunted; the stag had not returned. She ate sparingly, with an eye to the landscape that the sun had made somehow less threatening. She had searched for tracks, but halfheartedly; she expected to find none.

Avandar ate well. Lord Celleriant did not join her, although he chose to accept the hospitality the Arkosans offered. He took their dried fruit, their dried meat, their water.

She was surprised to see that he, too, had been injured; that his clothing bore the scars of his aerial fight; that his forehead sported a gash that the length of his hair did not fully hide. It made him seem almost human. Mortal.

Of course, Avandar said, *mortality is about death. And the only way the Arianni approach death, the only way they have ever approached it, is in combat.*

Think on that, Jewel.

Kallandras sat beside Yollana. He moved slowly when he moved, and to Jewel's eye, his arms seemed stiff as he brought food to mouth. But although he bore the same wounds that the Lord Celleriant did, although his clothing was perhaps the most spectacularly rent, he seemed younger somehow. When he smiled at Yollana, when he nodded at the occasional comment—too distant for Jewel to actually hear—from the Serra Teresa, the smile seemed genuine in a way that his smiles often did not.

To her eyes, at any rate.

He was charming.

His charm was almost infectious. Elena flirted with him shamelessly, and had he been anyone else, Jewel would have felt embarrassed for him—but he returned the Arkosan's gestures with a laugh that made them seem harmless.

This is what they're like after last night.

Nicu and his two friends ate as well, but Elena's gaiety was clearly unwelcome to the man Jewel understood to be the effective equivalent of Captain of the Chosen in these parts. His expression had fallen into the sullen anger that she associated with his face.

Everything was normal.

Except that neither Margret nor the Serra Diora chose to join them in their meal.

Stavos came late, and he came as errand runner first, taking food—anything he could rescue—from his wife and her cousins and retreating up the ramp of the Matriarch's floating ship.

"Tell her to come down and get it herself!" Tamara snapped, mock-severe. "She spends too much time in the air, not enough time on the ground."

"I always wondered what it meant, to have your head in the clouds," Donatella added, grinning broadly.

Stavos' chuckle was as forced as Kallandras' smile was natural. "She wants to be ready to take the ship up the minute the food is gone." He disappeared and reappeared almost as quickly. "But *I* want food and company."

"Get it in a hurry," the Havallan Matriarch told him. "It appears that we're not to have the advantage of time in the sun to thaw old bones."

She did not eat with her people because she would have had to sit near Nicu, and she could not bear to look at him. Did not want to see his face, and especially did not want to meet his eyes, his wide, brown, perfect eyes.

Because meeting them, she would know.

And she was not prepared to know anything, not this morning. Not now.

Instead, with the Serra Diora for company, she ate in the cabin. She kept the windows open, but they had not been built for light, and the light that did come played across the backs of bruised hands in a very unflattering way.

"You can join them, you know."

"If you wish privacy, Matriarch," the Serra replied, rising immediately—and gracefully, all things considered, damn her anyway. "I will join the others."

"If I wished privacy, I'd have to strangle 'Lena, her mother and Donatella at the very least, and in Matriarch's circles, killing your heir is considered bad luck." She was silent; even chewing made too much noise.

After a moment, the Serra resumed her seat across the thin table. She ate the food Stavos had brought without comment, although she was almost certainly used to better. She drank the water from the jugs as if it had come from the Lady's lake itself.

In the desert, all water is the Lady's gift.

Who had said that? Ah, her father.

"Matriarch?"

"I'm sorry—did I miss something?"

"I—I asked if you were well."

Margret laughed, but the sound came out midway between growl and bark. "As well as anyone can be when they've run from their family, hidden from battle, and lost—"

She stopped. Lifted her hands to her face, her cheeks, aware of how much like an accusation that would sound.

And isn't it? Didn't she force you to abandon your brother, your stupid, stupid brother?

No. She asked me to make a choice, that's all. It was my damn stupid *choice.* "No, dammit, I'm not well. And if you mention that to any of *them,* I'll just settle for strangling you, which on the surface of things wouldn't cause years of hard luck."

"What is wrong, Matriarch?"

"I don't know. My head feels like it's six sizes too big, my eyes hurt when I look at the lights, and the cold is in my bones. I can't feel the sun. I can't feel the warmth." She lifted a hand; it shook. Annoyed, she set it down on the table with a slap.

The Serra Diora's expression didn't change at all, but something about her did, although Margret couldn't have said what for money. "Perhaps we should inform Yollana?"

"No."

"Very well, Matriarch."

"And you could stop calling me that any time now."

The Serra was instantly still, instantly watchful. Maybe, Margret thought, it would have been better if she'd sent her outside.

But then she would be alone with her thoughts, and she didn't actually cherish that notion.

"Serra—"

"If I am not to use the word Matriarch, refrain from the use of the word Serra; we will be two women, in a small cabin, and when we are together, we will claim this space as our own."

Margret almost smiled, and if the smile was tinged with bitterness, it was genuine nonetheless. "Done, then. Done, Diora. I have to ask you—has the Heart spoken to you since last night?"

"No."

"No word at all?"

"None that I am aware of."

"Has it changed color?"

Diora reached into her robes and pulled out a long chain, at the end of which hung the Heart of Arkosa. To Margret's eyes, it was unchanged; clear, crystal, cold. But she could *see* it. She could see it now.

She closed her eyes.

"Why do you ask?"

"I wasn't going to sleep last night. I almost didn't. And no, don't bother to tell me I'm a fool. The others take more pleasure in it, so you might as well save it for them."

Diora's smile was quick, an asymmetric movement of lips.

In spite of herself, Margret smiled back, and realized that she liked this woman's smile. When it was real. When it didn't have that delicate air of the High Court about it.

"When I was asleep, I saw . . . I saw the desert. But it was not the desert we see now. It was a land where the earth was the color of blood; the sands were red. I saw the bones of old buildings, and among them, of creatures too large to be men.

"At a distance, the stones seemed small. Too small. But as I walked toward them, they grew larger, and larger still, and the bones of the dead were like great, open cages. I would not have walked near them at all, but there was a path beneath my feet, and I could not step off it. I had to follow it. But . . ." She looked away, to the open sky, glad—as she was almost never glad—for the light of day. "Do you know where we're going?"

Diora was quiet for a long time. "It is not wise to know Voyani secrets," she said at last.

"No. But sometimes all of life seems unwise. We struggle, endure, and triumph, but in the end we all die. I've always wondered what would happen if we just bowed to the inevitable."

"The same thing that would happen if we do not."

"Is it worth the work?"

"I am not the person of whom you should ask that question, if you desire reassurance."

Margret looked away from the azure sky; it only heightened the darkness of the cabin. "I've often wanted to kill. I've never wanted to die."

Diora's voice was a whisper; it was so soft that Margret failed to catch the words it carried. But she was not so clumsy as to ask again. "You will see almost everything, I think. I don't know why my mother wanted that. You're right, of course; there are some secrets we kill to protect."

"And will you kill me to protect them?"

"I don't know. I hope not. Yollana says we can speak in privacy here. I will tell you what I think you already know. We travel to the grave of the City of Arkosa. It was once called Tor Arkosa."

"And your dreams are of that grave?"

"No. I have traveled, once, to the—to the City. I have seen where it lies. It is nothing like my dream; there is sand, sand, sand." She bowed her head. "In my dream, there is a shadow that lies within its heart, a darkness that is living and breathing. I walked toward it because I had no chance. I woke before it devoured me.

"I don't have true dreams," she added. She hadn't intended to say it. Knew that a Matriarch had to have better control of her tongue.

But she didn't regret it.

"Were you alone?"

"I was. But that's how it has always been, for the long

history of Arkosa. The heir may travel to the foot of the pass, but no farther. No one can, except for the Matriarch." She was silent a moment. "Or perhaps the woman who wears the Heart of Arkosa. I honestly don't know what will happen with you. I thought that you would walk with 'Lena and me until we reached the turning point; that the Heart would then come from your neck to my hand."

"And now?"

"Now I don't know. I am afraid that the City will reject me in front of my people. That you will be the one who must continue." It was hard to say the words. She struggled with each one, made each one a perfect, enunciated sound, each distinct from the last.

"Margret."

Her name freed her from the struggle to speak. She looked up, met large, dark eyes, so like, and so unlike, Nicu's. A small, smooth hand touched the back of hers; the contrast between perfect skin and freckled, windburned knuckles was everything she feared it was—and yet, the certainty that this was not a gesture offered to many was almost enough to stem her resentment.

We all live in cages, she thought. *Why did I hate you so bitterly?*

"You are the Matriarch of Arkosa. Heart or no Heart, you will never be less."

She spoke with such certainty, this perfect, tiny woman, it was almost impossible not to believe what she said was the truth. There were so many things she wanted to ask her, suddenly, so many terrible things.

"Why did you cry for my brother?"

The Serra flinched, but she did not withdraw her hand. She said simply, "He reminded me of one of my wives."

And Margret found no reply.

Again she said, "I don't have true dreams." And then she added softly, "But I feel, in the air, in this place, as if I have two hearts, both beating wildly, and one is getting louder and louder."

"Can you not ignore it?"

Margret frowned. "If I ignore it, we will never come home."

"Home is in—" Silence. After a moment, Diora said, "I do not walk along the Sword's Edge, but my—my father did. He wore the blade and the blood. I watched him for a decade as he toiled to master the Widan's art. I watched him when he thought he had complete privacy.

"And I watched him when he struggled with fatigue. Twice, I believe it came close to killing him. I do not claim understanding of Voyani magic. But I think . . . there must be some commonality between his art and yours; you suffer the signs."

Ah. She stopped her brows from rising; stopped her face from expressing the surprise of sudden knowledge. "I'm an idiot."

Diora laughed.

"I've never—I wasn't a good student. My face wore the print of my mother's hands more often than anyone else in my family. She knew I had no vision. She knew that Elena did—or at least more so than I showed. She taught me to build the heartfires, taught me the wards against darkness. She could not teach me the major wards because I could not follow where she led. I couldn't see the traces of Arkosan power; I could see the crooked claws of her hands, the intense emptiness of her expression. But not the symbols she drew in the air." She rose. "I am not as strong as Evallen was."

"No," Diora told her quietly, releasing her hand. "You are stronger, I think."

"Why? I am fool, yes, and I would give anything I owned if I could believe you—and I want that belief, especially now. Only tell me why you say it."

"Because Yollana believes it. Yollana believes that you are your mother's daughter, and her superior. That you have more power than knowledge.

"That it is *this* voyage, into *this* City, that will be succor or downfall for the Voyani. All of them."

"She—she told you this?"

"Not with words. But it is in her voice whenever she speaks of you. If you cannot trust yourself, trust her."

Margret's snort was as natural as the rolling of her eyes. "Do you trust her?"

"I have less reason to, but . . . yes. Yes, in this. I believe that if she were asked to sacrifice her family in order to win the war she sees coming, she would do it."

"You don't understand the Voyani."

They lapsed into silence; Diora offered no defense against Margret's reflexive criticism.

Margret was *so* tired.

"Margret, if you sleep, I will watch. I will be wakeful."

"Can you gather them? Can you tell them to be ready before the sun reaches here?" She placed the point of her finger against the table, two inches from the shadows cast by the sill.

"Yes."

It was almost the last thing she heard.

CHAPTER TWENTY-SIX

Jewel woke to the sound of screaming.

She was used to this, but—if you could ignore the cramped, small wooden cabin; the knees, legs, and elbows of the various Arkosans as they met her hips, ribs, and legs; and the snoring—there was one significant difference.

The screams were not her own.

She sat up quickly enough to disturb Elena, largely because most of the extra limbs belonged to her, but the disturbance didn't last. Elena was clearly used to sleeping in cramped, impromptu spaces.

It had been many years since Jewel had been accustomed to doing the same. She had thought, even when she first joined House Terafin, that she would never forget the experience, but her body betrayed her; she was used to the privacy and quiet of a large room, and the unfamiliar snoring of strangers was not a melodic lullaby.

In the dark of the cabin, another figure rose as she rose. She could not clearly see who he was; in the height of day, Elena had chosen to close the shutters, to preserve what little of the night's chill she could.

But she knew who it was before he spoke her name.

Kallandras.

"ATerafin."

There were no screams. Save for the snoring, the cabin was silent.

"It's nothing," she told him.

He did not speak, but he did not sleep either.

Neither did she. Her arm throbbed in the dull airless heat. She rubbed it for a long moment, and then stopped. In the shadow, the sigil on her arm glowed faintly.

Avandar.

No answer. She waited a moment, wishing that he had not insisted on traveling by foot.

Avandar?

No answer. She cursed as quietly as she knew how, and shoved her hair out of her eyes; it was matted to her forehead, and her hand came away damp. She wanted a bath, a change of clothing, a real meal. She wanted her kitchen, and not the interior of this ungainly floating ship.

Avandar, damn you, answer me!

He did.

She didn't like the answer.

Where are we?

Her shadow was long and thin, as thin as the shadows cast by great trees. Those trees reached up from thick roots, stretching like a silver-barked limb that ended in a canopy of leaves. Hard to tell what color they were, but nestled among them were small, gold blossoms whose petals carpeted the ground like a gentle snow.

His shadow was taller than hers, broader, but his head was contorted. She looked up at him and took a step back. He was shiny with sunlight. Across his brow, the peak of a great helm rose, and across his shoulders and chest, an expanse of flat, pale steel rippled as he walked. His hair had disappeared; his hands were mailed, his robes—the familiar robes of the domicis were nowhere to be seen.

"Avandar?"

His expression, never friendly, was no warmer than his armor when he turned it upon her. She had to stop herself from taking a step back, from reaching for a dagger. Had to school her expression.

He had taught her that.

He spoke. She did not understand the words, or rather, she did not recognize them. She understood what they meant, and the two—understanding and lack of familiarity, were jarring.

"Did I not order you to remain behind?"

"No."

"An oversight. You will remain with the *Sen.*" He waited for a moment, and when she made no move to leave his side, he frowned. There was nothing about his frustration that reminded her of their life together; it was cold, dark—more threatening than the simple drawing of a weapon.

She did not want to anger this man.

"Go back. *Now.*"

Before she could reply—if she could find the words to frame a reply—the scene shifted.

She was in his dream, of course. Which meant at least one good thing. He was sleeping. That was all she could say for it.

She was dressed, head to toe, in a shimmering, iridescent fabric that she thought was tacky and revolting, although it was certainly more comfortable than the heavy desert robes she'd almost gotten used to. Her hands were covered in gloves made with the same fabric, as was her hair. She wore no House ring.

She bore his mark.

A dour-looking man stood between her and the door to the room she occupied.

And it was a single room, although she had never seen a room so large in her life, not even in House Terafin. There were slaves on the perimeter of the quartered circle; she knew they were slaves, although their presence felt natural.

"Sen Marshal," she heard herself say. It was, and was not, her voice.

Damn you anyway, Avandar; if I have to live in your dream, the least I could do is be with you.

He frowned.

"We will watch the battle."

"I was given no such order."

"You are being given that order now."

He was an older man; his hair was dark with cruel streaks of gray throughout. His chin was narrow, and the thinned length of beard he wore only added to its shape, drawing his face to an uncomfortable point. Had his face been youthful, had he had the softness of youth about his expression, it would have made no difference.

She did not like him.

"May I remind you that I serve the Warlord?"

"The Warlord is not here, and I would see him in his glory." She turned to a slave and bade him open the door.

He did not dare hesitate. She knew, if he did, she would kill him.

She wondered if the Sen would kill him instead. A part of her rebelled; a part was idly curious. The slave she had chosen did not bear her mark; he bore the Warlord's.

"I have my orders."

She shrugged. "And I do not." The slave walked past her in silence and opened the doors. But he did not accompany her as she strode out.

Where she walked, no one but the Sen could, and even he could not do so without an expenditure of power that given the circumstances would be unwise.

Viandaran had designed the balcony for her use. He had bound the air in such a way that it would bear her steps and her weight, no matter where she placed them. The Sen could summon air as he pleased, and struggle for its control. Although neither of these men could speak with the wild air, one of them had learned to master it.

There was a reason the Sen served, after all.

She stepped into the open breeze, let it blow her hair across bare shoulders, perfect patrician neck. From where she stood, she could see the streets, although they seemed a thin and narrow network of regulated veins from this distance. Small or no, it was clear they were deserted. She had never seen them empty before. Not even the slaves who adorned the fronts of buildings were being risked in this war.

But the fires had been lit in the high pyres; they burned now, their golden hearts surrounded by colored auras: orange, green, blue, white, red, violet, gray. She had never seen the fires lit, and gazed at them, not with wonder, but with a slowly growing disquiet that robbed her of motion.

Beneath each fire stood four adepts, their palms the pedestal upon which the fires burned. They would not survive the burning, but they could not be forced to maintain it; they had to choose the sacrifice they would make. She could not conceive of the knowledge that would drive twenty-eight such men to choose the death of the spheres.

She heard his voice; he knew she was there. For just a moment she reached for her own power, because he was almost angry enough to withdraw his, and a fall from this height wouldn't leave much for the healers to gloat over.

But he was distracted; he could not afford the annoyance he felt, and he let it go. Relieved, she took a step forward—

Into a blackened, broken field. All about her feet, the dead lay. But she looked up, looked away, forced her eyes to skirt the horrible manner of their death. She could smell it in the air; she had smelled death before, but not so strongly.

She had never seen a battlefield.

Could not imagine that one could become so grotesque. She had never understood the concept of dignity and the dead; not in her days in the twenty-fifth, when cold and starving, she and her den would force themselves to pick over the bodies of frozen men and women; not in her years at Terafin, although she had come to understand that the living *needed* the respect granted for their loss.

But she understood it now.

And knew herself happier for her ignorance, although it was gone.

The shadow fell.

She heard Avandar's battle cry.

Looked up. Saw him, in his shimmering armor, his helm gone, his face red with blood, white with its loss. He was the man she knew, and had never known. Everything about him was profoundly arrogant. She could not even find voice to call his name, although she knew, and *knew,* that this was a dream.

Over the crest of a ridge that she was certain was not natural, she saw the army come.

He stood against it, almost alone, the City his backdrop, the sky darkening in a way that no one, not even she, could mistake for night.

And at the head of the army, cloaked in shadow, taller than any of those who followed, was a . . . god.

She could not even think, which was good, because some fleeting memory provided her with a name that, even in thought, should not be enunciated.

He was beautiful, beautiful in a way that even the Winter Queen was not. And terrible, terrifying, as she was not. She knew that had he walked the Stone Deepings, she could never have held the road against him; could never have bartered, bargained; she was nothing to this creature, would never be capable of being worthy of even the smallest fragment of his attention.

But Avandar was.

For the god—and the army that followed as if it were raiment—halted his progress and looked.

"Where is your god now, Viandaran?"

Avandar lifted his sword arm, drew his blade. Jewel shielded her eyes from the intensity of its light. Blinded, she could still hear; there were cries, shouts, screams, all cut short. The earth beneath her feet buckled; she struggled to keep her legs beneath her. She did not want to join the dead until she *was* dead.

But when the silence fell, it was Avandar who broke it. "My god is playing with a tenth of your army. If they exist after death, ask them where they are."

"Very good, Viandaran. You have again proved yourself worthy of alliance. Tell the mages of the City that I will overlook their treachery this once."

"The treachery was not ours, Lord of the wastelands. We kept our oaths. You sought to betray them, and succeeded merely in revealing yourself. Tor Carrallon will never serve you again. The men of Tor Carrallon are no one's slaves, be he god or Firstborn."

Her vision cleared slowly. She lowered the hands that she had brought up too late to shield her eyes.

"Ask your slaves if service is better than death. Ask your mages if killing is better than dying."

"Ask them yourself, Allasakar, if you succeed in breaching the defenses of the spheres." His sword rose in an arm that was as steady as the pole that bore the standard upon a field, and she could see, glimmering, barely visible, the magic that swept from the length of its edge. It traveled to the City behind his turned back.

Light filled the sky in a dance that devoured all shadow. It was painful to look at, and cold, as cold as the lights in the Northern skies when the weather hovered at the edge of ice.

But the lights did not remain in the sky for long; they streaked toward the ground like fallen birds of prey, and where they landed, the earth split.

The god gestured; the light avoided him. But to either

side, Jewel could see what had made corpses of the people she now stood among.

Fire. Ice. Water.

Worse.

There was power on this field greater than any power she had seen in *Averalaan Aramarelas.* She prayed that she would never see its like again.

And wondered, as she prayed, who would hear it, and what they would do.

This was the Age of Gods. The Gods walked.

Avandar, I've seen enough. Wake up, damn you, wake up.

But this was his nightmare, and he was—as she so often was—trapped in it to the end. She wondered how much of it was history, how much the fabrication of his fears. Could not imagine, watching this magnificent stranger, that he had any.

The god laughed.

"Have you tired, already, of my brother's gift? You have been elevated, Avandar. You have been granted more than was granted to the Firstborn by simple existence. There is not a creature in my army who could kill you."

She heard a roar of fury.

The god turned his head to the shadows, and the roar became a strangled scream, a sudden silence.

"I could kill you, yes. You have but to move aside and let the army pass through the gates, and I will give you what you desire."

She watched. She watched in horror as the Warlord hesitated for a moment before laying down his sword.

She knew that the City had power. Knew that if the mages could not kill Avandar, they could destroy his ability to act, to function, to think, for a long, long time.

But she knew, as well, that in that single motion of surrender she had witnessed both the betrayal of, and the fall of, Tor Carrallon.

She woke, this time, to the familiar sensation of her own scream; woke to the sound of Kallandras of Senniel, his voice low, intense, impossible to ignore.

"ATerafin, wake."

She said, "Avandar is sleeping."

But he pressed a finger to her lips, brushed the sweat

from her forehead with the cloth of his sleeve, and sang a quiet, quiet song for her ears alone.

In her turn, she reached up and pressed fingertips to his lips, to still the singing. "I'm all right now." She rose, tripped over Elena, mumbled an apology in response to that woman's sleepy curse, and struggled her way toward the terrible, midday sun.

The door opened; light fell across the living; she blocked it, stepping beneath the gaze of the open sky.

She was not surprised when Kallandras joined her. Would have been surprised had he not.

"Do you know where we're going?" she whispered.

"No. But I know that we have passed over the grave of Tor Carrallon."

She started, and his hand was upon her shoulder; it was so gentle she could hardly feel the threat behind the comfort—but it was there. "How much do you know?"

"I? I know what bards know, ATerafin."

"Don't start that with me. I'm not an idiot; I know full well that some bards know more than others."

His smile was rueful.

It didn't fool her.

"All bards learn the earliest of songs." The smile dimmed; his expression grew remote. She could almost see him watching himself in the past, and assessing his lessons, and what he had taken out of them, dispassionately. "The early songs are taught to give us mastery over rhymes and meters in a language that is foreign. Difficult. We vest our emotion in the music itself; attempt to bring the music to a language that has not been spoken in any other way for centuries.

"But there are those in the Order of Knowledge who understand the dead tongues. And there are those among my brethren who feel that the music is lost if the meanings of the words are not retained, and they have labored—some more successfully than others—to give the potency of myth and ancient lore to those who will casually listen.

"But there are almost no lays which dwell upon the fates of the Cities of Man."

"Why were they called that?"

"My understanding? That they were places of power. Places built by the merely mortal that still had the strength to defy a walking god. There was beauty, magery, knowledge in the Cities of Man. I do not think you would have liked them."

"I *know* I wouldn't." She leaned against the railing; the sun didn't feel that hot, and the wind filled her lungs without dragging the scent of every pair of feet and underarms with it. She did not want to go back inside. "Why did the Cities fall?"

"It is not clearly known, except perhaps by the Voyani, and of that, it is not safe to know more, or rather, to speak of it."

Clear warning there. "Were we the *only* people who didn't live forever?"

"There are many, many songs about the tragedy of mortality." He smiled. "But I like Farenzes better."

"He wasn't a bard."

"Very good, ATerafin. No, he was a romantic old man who played at philosophy and had a voice that made a catfight sound pleasant. But he felt that mortality was caused not by the nature of birth itself, but rather by the ability to feel both deeply and broadly. He made a story of it."

"A story?"

"Yes. When the gods made the Firstborn, in the manner of gods, they were pleased. But as the millennia passed, and their children warred without cease, they grew weary—for the gods were fickle as the elements in those days. The nameless god—"

"As opposed to the god we don't name?"

"As opposed to that god, yes. The nameless god then brought forth the mortal races, those who lived and died in such a brief, brilliant burst. And these creatures were strange; they learned simply by living, and yet the oldest of them—a man or a woman who might be ninety, a hundred years—had somehow managed to acquire a wisdom that the Firstborn could not.

"And they realized that all things that know life must know change, and that when those changes are complete—no matter how long they might take—so, too, is the life."

"That's a pretty . . . unromantic story. If you ask me."

"Ah. But the gods loved the strangeness of these creatures, the vividness of their mortality, the desperation of their longing as they burned through their years. They heard mortal voices more clearly than any other voices because they were so sharp, so visceral, so personal.

"There is a reason, after all, why the mortals rule the world, where the gods and the Firstborn no longer dare to walk. Think about it, ATerafin. Those who die, and know almost from birth that death is their goal, envy those who cannot change. But those who live forever envy the newness, the strangeness, the ignorance, and the pain of those whose lives are so easily extinguished.

"The grass is always greener," he added. "No matter who is observing. It is our nature, after all, to desire what we cannot have."

"Why is that?"

"Farenzes never addressed that."

"Good. How old is he?"

He could have pretended to misunderstand the question. He didn't. "I do not know. But there have been stories about the Warlord—in the South—for a long time. There are stories about the Warlord in the North as well, although the name he uses in those stories has far more bitter meaning to those born within the Empire." He was silent, gauging her.

"I really don't want to know this, do I?"

"I don't know."

"I think he wants to die," she said quietly. "I think he wants to die, and he can't."

And then she shook herself, stepped into the waking world, and tried to change the subject, although she knew that Kallandras of Senniel College would betray no confidence. He was famous for his discretion.

"Are you afraid of him, ATerafin?"

"Of Avandar? No. But I don't understand him, and it bothers me."

"He is not of your den."

"No. I don't—I don't know what he is to me," she whispered.

And that probably bothered her most of all.

"Be careful, ATerafin."

The Matriarch of Arkosa woke in shadow, as if from a sudden, vivid dream. A dream with color, sight, sound

These were gone. Her mouth was dry, her eyes closed. She rose, or felt that she rose, for she struggled a moment to straighten her body to its full height. Gave up when she realized that this was not the place in which to do it.

She moved, although she could not have said whether or not she placed one foot in front of the other; movement seemed to have no reward, no obvious consequence.

She stopped the ship.

She was aware of its movement, and she knew that time for flight had ended.

The bowed, wooden top of a wagon that would be her home hovered in the air, too ungainly and awkward in its flight to be a bird, to be a living thing.

She felt sun against her face, but she could not see the light that usually accompanied the sensation of warmth; she thought of gold, of white, of blue; sky's colors.

They meant nothing to her.

But the wind's voice did. Had she feared the wind? Had she ever reviled it? She could not imagine why. In the folds of the wind, in the depths of its wildness, there was freedom.

She heard voices, but they were remote; for a moment she was deaf, blind; her hand had been on the table in a loosely curled fist but she could no longer feel the grain of the wood.

She felt, instead, a peculiar weightlessness, as if it were she, and not the ship, that was suspended in air, touching nothing, untouched by even the wind.

"Margret."

The Serra's voice was clear as a warning bell, clear as a winded horn. She turned in the direction of her name, and saw desert sands that stretched out for miles. In the distance, a distance that was both great and inconsequential, she saw the broken ridges of rocky mountains, their white peaks beautiful as diamonds, but strange and cold.

And she saw that the sands beneath her were the color of rust.

She said, *"We have arrived,"* and felt the words as if they were something physical, tangible, as if they had fallen from her open lips and she could gather and keep them. As if she must.

She descended.

The sand drew closer. She was weighted down by the robes she had chosen to wear, the raiment of desert, the acknowledgment of the Lord's baleful glare. She considered shedding them.

Felt that she could, in safety. The cabin had been almost suffocating in its hoarded shadow, its lack of air. The wind was against her face, and it was blessedly cool.

"Matriarch."

As was the hand that touched her hand.

She frowned. She had had the sense that she was alone; that she had privacy, that rare and precious treasure that she so seldom found.

"Serra?" The Serra Diora stood in front of her, but at a distance, and her face was unblemished, flawless, beautiful.

"You—you should come inside. The ship is descending."

"Inside?" The world returned. She looked at the Serra Diora, and then looked down.

There was nothing at all beneath her feet.

A tiny voice tickled her ear; her own. It told her in no uncertain terms that the fall would kill her.

But she was not afraid of falling, not here. Not *here.* She swallowed. Spoke.

The Serra frowned. "Margret, I'm sorry—but I cannot understand what you say. Speak in Torra."

And Margret replied, "Tor Arkosa," and lifted an open hand in the direction of the sand that stretched in all directions.

"Elena."

The Matriarch's heir was restless, tired, and in a temper that could best be described as foul. It was not the only temper that was on such poor display; Nicu glared at anything that moved, and his mother snapped and fretted in turn. Kallandras was as cool and calm as the longed-for dusk, and when he spoke, tempers stilled—but he spoke seldom, as if preserving his strength for whatever lay ahead.

"Elena."

The Matriarch's cousin frowned. "What?"

"The Matriarch's ship has stopped."

The Voyani woman started to snap, stopped before words left her mouth. She rose and left the cabin, slamming the door in her wake.

They heard her wordless shriek.

She returned scant moments later. "Donatella, Mama," she barked. "We're—we're to land." Her face had lost its pinched, sallow expression, and with it, years; it had taken on the vulnerability of excitement and fear.

The women were relieved because they now had tasks: they busied themselves rummaging through the containers of dry food, selecting what would become the morning meal. As if it would be any different from any other morning meal.

But Nicu, if anything, looked grimmer, the petulance of his expression giving way to something akin to fear. He took over the space vacated by his mother, spreading his shoulders against the cabin's walls.

The ship descended. Diora was afraid to release Margret's hand. Margret spoke to her in the cadences of a language that she both recognized and failed to understand, and Diora knew that she was being asked to join her.

She shook her head.

The whole of Margret's face seem transformed; the lines worn in the corners of her lips and eyes by exposure to sun, wind, and storm grew deeper as she spoke. She smiled.

Diora shook her head again. But the second time, she lifted her hand, as gracefully and certainly as she had ever lifted it, and drew the Heart of Arkosa from the folds of desert cloth. It came as if it were weightless, as if it were already around Margret's neck.

Shaking, Diora lifted her chin, raising the chain that bore the heavy crystal in the same motion.

But it would not come free; it would not rise above the line of her jaw. She felt a brief hope die as she released the chain, and the Heart found its familiar resting place against her skin.

And Margret, Matriarch of Arkosa, who had so resented the separation of Matriarch from the Heart, did not even seem to notice.

"Ona Teresa," she whispered.

"Na'dio?"

"The Matriarch—she is—she is standing on air."

The Serra Teresa did not answer in words, but after a

moment, the cabin door swung wide. There was enough room for another person at Diora's side, but not two.

The Matriarch of Havalla stumbled into the harsh glare of the open sun. She started to reach for Diora's hands, to demand and accept aid. But she dropped her hands as she saw what Diora held: Margret.

"So."

"Matriarch." Diora bowed her head; she did not kneel because in order to do so gracefully, she would have had to release Margret's hand. For the first time—perhaps for the only time—she had cause to be glad of the Voyani lack of refinement, courtesy, manners.

"I understand now, Serra. Evallen was both desperate and wise. You are the bearer of the Heart, no matter what else you have been. You are not Voyani, but you have been accepted by Arkosa.

"Speak of what you see here, and there is not a place in the world that will shelter you from our wrath."

The voice of a woman whose legs could not bear her weight for more than a few moments at a time without support was cold and strong. But she did not wait for a reply—and Diora offered none.

Instead, she turned to Margret and spoke, her harsh, cracked voice like lightning in a storm. Diora did not understand the words, and was grateful for her ignorance.

Margret's reply was the thunder.

"It appears," the Matriarch of Havalla said, switching between this ancient, dead tongue and the living tongue of her people with an ease that spoke of practice, "that if she will not speak Torra, she understands it well. I do not know what passed between you in the storm, but clearly you made your peace; she considers my threat . . . unnecessary." The hint of a smile changed the network of lines, of strong lines, that was her face. "Perhaps insulting would be a better word."

Diora hid behind the delicate smile of the High Court.

"She has no sight. It was Evallen's fear and worry, that lack of vision, that lack of the most obvious sign of our heritage. I wish she had survived to see this, but only her death would have allowed it to happen; it is our curse as Mothers never to see our children take their power—and perhaps it is our blessing as well. Margret has a power that I have never seen."

"A power, Matriarch?"

"You cannot see it. But if I am not mistaken, you can hear it. Listen, Serra, listen well."

She did not need the encouragement. She had heard the voices of powerful men throughout her life; even as a sheltered child, she had quickly learned to recognize power's complicated rhythm. But she had never heard a power like the one that rode Margret's voice, that filled it with such authority.

And the only thing that came close was a bitter childhood memory: Kallandras of Senniel College, speaking with the voice of the wind.

"The City is awake," Yollana continued, almost as if compelled. She did not attempt to keep the awe from her words. "And it has touched Evallen's daughter. If she wore the Heart of Arkosa now, I think there is a great chance we would all be dead. The power of the Cities is not a power that comes easily, or gracefully, to those who must bear it.

"I thought Evallen's choice to give you the Heart was political. I thought it strategic—for I understand your importance in the outcome of the war to come, as Margret, hotheaded and bitter, could not. But now I understand that it was more than that."

"I have been Matriarch for more years now than any living Matriarch. I have made a trek much like Margret's several times in my adult life. I have done what she must do, I have paid the price, I have learned to navigate the winds of the past. But I have never seen what we will see today."

Diora was afraid.

Suddenly, inexplicably, afraid.

"W–what will we see?"

The old woman shook her gray head, pulled her hood up about her face; the sun was almost blinding. "The beginning," she whispered. "The beginning of the end." And to Diora's horror, she bowed her head, and she began to pray.

Had she been a Northerner, the Serra would have had no cause to fear, for the Northerners believed that their gods, benevolent and just, might listen.

But in the South, there was only one situation in which a woman prayed.

Miles away, Ishavriel raised his head.

He had no cause to fear the sun's light, the dry heat, or the cold that would follow. But he was cautious now, in the heart of the desert, for the sands remembered the last time he had walked, on foot, across these lands; he felt the residue of their implacable enmity.

And that should not have been possible. The old earth was dormant. The wildness had gone from these lands.

The mortals had arrived. They had not yet touched the ground, but they were aware of where they were.

He frowned. Knelt, placed his palm against the hot, hot sand.

The ground threw him.

He corrected his position in mid-flight and landed, unharmed, thirty yards away.

Then, leisure forgotten, he began to run. He expended the power necessary to hide himself from the desert's eyes, for he knew, now, that the City would be looking for him.

But he felt almost young as he ran.

It is not possible. They do not have the power.

But if they did? Ah, if they did, and he arrived at the right moment, all that he desired would be his; that and more. The lies he had told the weak Arkosan might become, in the end, a twisting of the truth.

After all, Tor Arkosa was one of the five that had stood against the Lord when the gods shaped these lands.

The ship landed, scudding gently against the surface of the sand.

Margret, weathered hand in Diora's smooth one, had chosen to descend with her people. She spoke to Diora from time to time, although her gaze seemed more and more fixed upon the unchanging sands.

Unfortunately, she spoke in the language of Arkosa. Diora's reply was simple: she held fast; she did not waver.

Yollana blocked the door, waiting. Stavos tried to open it, and she spoke so sharply, even Diora was surprised. She had thought very little in the way of Voyani rudeness could surprise her. She felt a twinge of sympathy for the Arkosan.

"Be prepared, Serra," Yollana snapped.

Diora frowned. Margret, hand still entwined with Diora's, continued her descent when the ship could go no farther. Diora tightened her grip, but was dragged toward the rails. As she had the night of the storm, she felt the hard wood against her abdomen. She braced herself with her free hand almost instinctively.

Which was good.

For although she could not perform the task with grace, or even skill, she was still clinging to Margret when the Matriarch of Arkosa's weight returned in a rush.

She felt her arm extend and stretch so quickly she was afraid it would break.

"Margret!"

But the Matriarch of Arkosa no longer heard her.

She slumped against the side of the ship; her head lolling back.

Yollana rose at once and banged on the door with her cane as if she were required to beat it into submission. The door fell open, as if to avoid her, and Stavos appeared in the door frame.

"Don't stand there gawking like an unshaven boy—be useful!"

CHAPTER TWENTY-SEVEN

Margret woke with a start, which brought her forehead directly into contact with Elena's.

Her cousin's response was longer than hers, but not much prettier.

"It figures," the Matriarch said, rubbing her head with the flats of both palms. "I have to hit the hardest head in all Arkosa."

"The second hardest," 'Lena snapped. "If your aim was better, you'd be the second person in Arkosa to give me a black eye, and the first who didn't look worse because of it." She cursed again—it was something she was undeniably good at—and then sat back on her feet. "You scared me."

"Sorry. What happened?"

'Lena laughed. She shoved the hair that sweat had matted to her forehead out of the way. "We were kind of hoping you could tell us."

"Where—" Margret stopped. Stared at the wagon that rested, slightly atilt, against the hard sand. Her eyes widened.

The wagon was on the ground. Not above it, as it had been for the entire journey into the Sea of Sorrows, but on it, as if it were nesting after an arduous flight.

She paled. Elena's expression lost its tight edge. " 'Gret, it's okay. You did that on purpose. Well, according to Yollana."

"But that means—" She closed her eyes.

" 'Gret?"

"Don't fuss, 'Lena. I can't think with all the noise you're making." She got to her feet and took two steps before she crouched back into a kneeling position. Elena hovered a safe distance away, beneath the makeshift awning that had obviously been put up to protect Margret from the worst of the sun's light.

She found her feet again, this time with an almost grim determination. The heat had dried her robes; it had also dried her lips, and her tongue clung to the roof of her mouth until she made an effort to pry them apart. The wind pulled at the cowl of her robe, kicking sand into her eyes. She didn't remember the wind being this strong, and frowned. "Where are the others?"

"In the lee of my wagon. There's shade there as well."

Sand had crept up the side of the ship; the doors and the windows had been shuttered carefully to protect what lay within. She did not pray, not here; if the winds heard, they'd come in force, and her people could not afford it.

"The winds?"

"They started about fifteen minutes ago. I stayed here; I wasn't certain how safe it would be to move you. Yollana seemed to think—" She fell silent. Silence from Elena was rarely a good thing.

She took a deep breath. "Let's go," she said softly.

They were gathered in the shadows in a rough oval, at the center of which sat Yollana. For a moment it angered her, to see this outsider holding court among her people—but she set the anger aside.

"Margret!" Tamara rose at once, bowl in hand; Donatella was a half step behind, with water.

If Elena's unvoiced concern had been as welcome as wind, they were the gale. She suffered herself to be fussed over by attempting to ignore it.

Jewel ATerafin sat off to one side; her domicis, his face as set and cold as Margret had yet seen it, stood behind her, his back against the wood of Elena's forlorn wagon. Kallandras sat beside the Serra Teresa, and beside him—to Margret's surprise—the wild one; the man who had taken the fight to the Serpent of the skies. Slender and perfect, he made her own people look old and bent, but she was aware that something had changed if he was willing to suffer their company.

The Serra Diora sat on the other side of the Serra Teresa, and although she looked up, her wide, brown eyes meeting and acknowledging Margret's gaze, she did not add her voice to the Arkosan cacophony.

Margret accepted the water. She emptied the cup and handed it back to Donatella; emptied it again, and again returned it to the old woman. But she did not drink a third time, because she was not yet ready to depart; instead, she started toward Yollana.

And came face-to-face with her other cousin. His face was pale and pinched, the circles under his eyes almost as dark as a blow would have made them. His beard had crept up the sides of his cheeks and the underside of his jaw, and his hair was pale with sand dust. Had he not looked so resentful, she might have taken pity on him.

But she did not have time for this sullen Nicu.

"You're awake."

She shrugged.

His arms, hanging at his sides, grew tense; she could see his fingers begin a slow curl into the meat of his palms. Was surprised when he forced them down again. "What happened?"

Shrugged again. "Not sure."

"Is that what you told Elena?"

"Nicu, what I tell Elena is between Elena and me."

He stiffened. "I am the guard, in this place; I am the Matriarch's protector. If it concerns Arkosans—"

"If it concerned Arkosans, I would tell you."

She started to walk, and he moved so that she would have to shove him out of the way. She heard the silence grow at her back, and cursed herself for her temper. She could handle Nicu, had always managed to handle him, but *Lady*, it took time and strength and energy that she did not wish to spend in that fashion. "Nicu."

"Why have we landed? Stavos carried you from your ship, unconscious. What happened? Are we under attack?"

"We landed because this is where we have to be. I can't explain it better than that."

"You've always been good with words."

"Nicu."

He raised his chin. Lifted his shoulders. He was, Margret realized, substantially larger than she. She wondered when that had happened, and why she so seldom noticed it, because it couldn't have been that recent. Her own hand slid to the side she favored for fighting, but she did not grip her dagger. Not yet.

"If you cost me time, and we need it, if you cost me time and the winds grow, you'll regret it."

He held his place for long enough to make a point, and then shook his head, as if waking and realizing that he had wandered into unfriendly territory. He bowed, and it was almost enough.

Almost.

But she was glad that Donatella was behind her, because she could pretend that she didn't know what her expression was.

Before she reached Yollana, Yollana stood, her hands on her cane. She had only one of them; the other must have been swept—like tents and silks—into the tunnels. Margret was surprised that she hadn't noticed the loss earlier.

"Matriarch," Yollana said, before Margret could speak. She did not bow, and she did not kneel, but she raised her hands and pulled the cowl from her hair, exposing the gray of age and wisdom to all who cared to watch. Then she lowered her head slowly and deliberately. It was as genuine a gesture of respect as she had ever seen Yollana offer her mother, Evallen, and of all the things Yollana could have done, it was the most frightening.

But Margret knew how to hide fear, and she hid it now. She bowed her head as well. "Matriarch." All resentment, all annoyance, was destroyed by the older woman's gesture.

"I have taken the liberty of seeing to your provisions," the old woman said, when Margret at last raised her head. "If they are not to your liking, forgive me. Arkosa and Havalla have much in common, but here, at the foot of the *Voyanne*, I fear it is our differences that will define us.

"Your guards are prepared to escort you as far as they must; we found two tents, one in each of the wagons, and we have packed them as well." She lifted her hand; it was curled in a loose fist, around a small glass jar. "This is my gift. I would give you my pipe, but I am old enough to need it.

"Your . . . guard . . . asked me how long you would be absent; I could offer him no answer that satisfied his curiosity."

Anger returned, piercing but brief. "Thank you, Matriarch. Accept my apologies for my cousin. He is never at his best when he is nervous."

"No." The old woman shrugged. "Journey in safety, Margret. When you leave us, you leave the *Voyanne*."

She felt it: a sudden slap across the back of her head that seemed to echo in the inside of her skull. She heard the truth in the words as if truth itself was something that could be grasped and examined. It was as frightening as the gesture of respect had been because both were suddenly too large.

"I have never left the *Voyanne*."

"No."

"But I have been here before, with Evallen."

"You have never been here before, no matter how many times your feet have crossed these sands. This road, this path, *only* a Matriarch can walk. If she walks it beside her daughter, if she walks it beside her ally, it is still *her* path, and hers alone, to choose." And she turned her gaze upon the Serra Diora; it lingered a moment before the old woman nodded, satisfied by whatever it was she could see. Or could not see. "There are rites and there are blessings, Margret. If you would honor me, I would be pleased to offer them. They will, of necessity, be brief; I lost much to the storm, and can offer only the heart of the ceremonies."

"The Heart of Havalla," Margret whispered, "is more than enough for the Heart of Arkosa."

The old woman smiled, and the smile took years from her face—something that Margret would have bet money against a scant few weeks ago. She wondered what made the old woman so happy.

As if she could hear the thought, Yollana said, "If any of my daughters are half as strong as you have been today, not even the winds will be able to keep me from my pride in them."

Margret started to speak, and then stopped, remembering that there was only one condition that had to be met for her daughters to be so tested: the Matriarch of Havalla's death.

But she felt a twinge of pride and pleasure at the praise, even while wondering if she were still such a child that praise alone could mean so much.

* * *

The ceremonies of Havalla were not so different from the ceremonies of Arkosa. From her sash, Yollana took a very small knife and a very shallow bowl. The knife was silver, but the shadows could not prevent it from glinting as if it were under full light. She cut her palm deeply enough that it bled.

The bowl, pale and bright as the blade, caught her blood. She passed the knife to the men and women who had gathered in around her. Her silence demanded silence; she bent before them with the bowl and gathered the blood that fell.

But she did not give the knife to the Serra Diora, Elena, or Nicu.

Only Lord Celleriant hesitated. He glanced up at Yollana, his lips rounded in a smile that was neither friendly nor pleasant, but still beautiful to behold. "Is this wise, old woman?"

Her silence was her reply.

"The Cities of Man were not my cities; I was . . . only barely . . . welcome within them." He held the dagger carefully.

Jewel ATerafin rose as if summoned. "Lord Celleriant."

"I offer truth," he said, looking up. "And caution. If you would have me participate in this ceremony, have me do so with the knowledge of my place in your past."

"The choice isn't mine," she told him. "But if it were, I would take what you willingly offered. Whatever you were, then, there is only one enemy now, and if we cannot stand together against him, we will fall separately."

"Well spoken, Lady." He rose. "But I fear you do not speak with the voice of the Cities."

"Cities don't have voices if they aren't ours."

But Margret said, "Don't be so certain, ATerafin. But even so, I will take what you offer."

He raised a silver brow, met Margret's eyes.

At any other time she would have taken a step back to put distance between herself and what she saw in his.

He placed the knife gently in the cradled cup of his palm.

And grimaced as it burst into flame.

But the flame did not char his skin; it burned with a pale blue light from the tip of the blade to its hilt. He closed his fist around it, grunted, and uncurled his fingers, pulling the blade back as if the separation required great effort.

His blood—for the knife had cut him deeply—was burning brightly. Yollana was still completely silent, but she moved the shallow bowl in shaking hands.

He turned his palm slowly, and she caught the blood that fell from it.

The flames fell with it. Both blood and fire completed the circle of offering; she held the bowl in both hands and made her way to Margret.

Margret could see that the flames continued to burn.

"Take strength from our strength," the older woman said, speaking for the first time. "If you have need of it on the path you must walk, we offer it willingly. You are the door. You are the portal. And you are the key.

"Open the way, Matriarch. Find our past. Return—as no others of us may do—to our home." She bowed her head again, and Margret had the distinct impression that she was supposed to kneel.

But the Voyani were nothing if not practical; there was no way that the Matriarch of Havalla could both kneel and continue to shepherd the contents of this shallow vessel. She held out her hands, and Yollana placed the bowl within them.

And said, "Drink."

The fire still burned, and the bowl was warm to the touch. Margret took a slow, deep breath. It was as much hesitation as she was allowed to show. She stared into the flames that burned; they were no longer a simple blue; there was, within their flickering, dancing tongues, hearts of white and gold.

The fire spoke.

It was all she could do not to take her hands from the bowl.

The way is watched. The enemy is waiting. Use only the old roads. Touch nothing that does not call your name. Take nothing that you cannot control. Offer only that which you can afford to lose; offer nothing that you do not value.

She lifted the vessel in shaking hands; felt the heat of the flames across her brow. But pain did not follow heat; the fire did not burn her. She placed the silver rim of the vessel upon her lower lip and tilted the offering slowly, carefully, toward her face.

She was prepared for flame.

But it did not burn her until she swallowed.

The bowl fell from her hands as her hands rose; she covered her mouth, her cheeks, her eyes, as she fell to her knees. The sand caught her; she could not order the others to keep away.

But someone else could; she heard the command pass through her, swift as a quarrel, and she recognized the voice that had fired it: Kallandras.

She was grateful, in a fashion; she could not speak. Her throat was on fire. She opened her eyes and all she could see was blue and gold.

"Matriarch's daughter."

She stood on the sands, the pale, bleached sands, her feet in her mother's shadow. They were seldom alone, these two. Her eleventh birthday had passed her by, but she was some months from her twelfth; in between these two, her blood had started to flow.

She was no longer considered a child, and among Matriarchs, this was the first of the rites of passage through which she must pass to be called adult. She had journeyed with her mother into the Sea of Sorrows for the very first time, instead of away from it with her uncles. If she had felt special, if she had felt blessed, if she had felt somehow that she had crossed an important, invisible threshold, her mother's irritated formality reminded her that she was still Evallen's daughter, still her child.

"Matriarch."

Her mother's face was lined, her eyes were narrowed. She had, with stiffness, invoked the blessing of the family; they had offered her the respect that her mother withheld. Uncle Stavos had winked, but his expression had been so grave she wasn't certain if it had been her imagination.

"Are you paying attention?"

"Yes."

"What did I just tell you?"

She froze.

Her mother cuffed the side of her head. "I told you nothing. Now *pay attention.*"

"Yes, Mother."

"Good. Why are we traveling at this time?"

Margret had been wondering that; it was the height of

day, the time when the Lord's gaze was at its most merciless. The Voyani did very little when the full weight of his gaze was upon them. Her mother hated guesses, but she also hated silence. Margret hovered between the two evils.

But her mother did not expect an answer. "It is not an act of defiance, although most of the Arkosans think otherwise. We do it because we must.

"This is what we do not say to anyone: When we had a home, it was with the Lord's blessing, and at the Lord's command. We lived in cities that were fashioned from the only law he holds to be absolute: power.

"These lands were once the heart of Annagar, although the Dominion was called by another name, and there was no Tyr'agar. For as far as the eye could see, there was life: plains upon which the ancestors of the Mancorvan horses ran without challenge, forests in which trees that had stood since the beginning sheltered the lives of creatures that exist nowhere but in legend now. There were great lakes, mountains, rivers in abundance. Do you understand? There was no desert here."

Margret looked at the stretch of land that was broken only by cold, distant mountains. The air danced and shimmered as it caught the sun, folding the blue of sky, the gold of sand into the specters of vision.

"We claimed those lands."

"Arkosa?"

"And Havalla, Corrona, Lyserra." Her mother turned and began to walk; Margret had to lengthen her stride to keep up. "There may have been others. I do not know, and if I did, I would not speak of them. It is only here that I may speak, and only to you. But even among the Voyani there are secrets and silences; even the Matriarchs of the other families are not privy to what *Arkosans* know." She stopped for water; handed the waterskin to her daughter and watched, eyes narrowed, as Margret drank. Margret took care to drink as little as possible. The Sea of Sorrows was the only place in which water had more value than blood.

"We had power, then, that not even the clans dream of. We had the luxury of a similar arrogance. And we travel in the Lord's light because we cannot find our way in the night; we cannot find our way by the silver rays of the

Lady's face. The Lady was adjunct to the Lord; it is not to her lands that we travel. Do you understand?"

She nodded. Stopped. Shook her head.

"Speak up, girl."

"N–no."

Evallen frowned. "Too much to be hoped for. The *Voyanne* is the Lady's. The Cities were the Lord's."

"But you said they were home."

"You *were* listening."

She hated her mother's sarcasm. If she had known where she was going, she would have walked ahead. "You taught us that one day we can *go* home."

"I was taught that. And my mother, and her mother, and hers."

"You don't believe it."

Evallen's lips twisted. She stopped walking for a moment. The sun beating down on the peak of her hood cast almost no shadow. "I wish I didn't." But she would say no more.

Margret followed her for a long time, wondering why the word *home* had such value; her life had been spent avoiding the Lord, and the Lord's men, and she had always dreamed—when she thought of home at all—of a land without war, without combat, and without death.

Well, without death for Arkosans, at least.

She looked up; the dance of the air was growing dangerously real; colors that were not variants of sand and sky had begun to appear in the heat folds. Red, green, a lush, vibrant orange, and a subtle shade of gray, the color of rest and shelter.

Yollana's face was still, but her hood rippled and flapped as it spoke to the wind. Margret blinked back the memory. It had been *so* strong, she could still feel her eleven-year-old self lurking beneath the weight of years. She did not see that desert in this one, but she knew they were the same; that they must be the same.

The sun was not yet risen to its height. But it would be within the hour, and she knew that they must cast no shadows when they arrived at the place. She bowed to the Matriarch, and then, bending at one knee, retrieved the fallen bowl.

It gleamed, clean and new, against the sand between her

feet. She touched its surface, and felt no heat, touched no blood.

"An omen." Yollana's voice was smooth and cool. Like, Margret thought, steel. She held out a hand, and Margret passed her the bowl. It disappeared into the folds of her robe.

"Nicu." Margret was almost surprised she could speak. "Ready your men. We leave now." She rose. "Uncle Stavos?"

He rose as well, his expression almost grim. She had hoped that she might see him wink or smile, but years of harsh wind had worn the corners off that expression. "We will wait until you summon us, Matriarch, or until you return."

"Good. Watch over the others."

He nodded. She thought that his eyes were filmed with tears, which was ridiculous—Stavos knew better than to cry in the desert.

Tamara hugged her daughter. The Serra Teresa di'Marano hugged her niece. Donatella hugged Nicu, and then, as if they were his brothers and not his men, Andreas and Carmello.

No one thought to hug Margret.

Jewel watched them leave. She joined the ranks of the Arkosans as they left the side of Elena's ship and flowed around it, pulling the hoods from their shoulders and covering their faces. The wind seemed involved in some sort of dialogue; it came first from one direction and then from another. The sand made her squint, as did the sun's light. Cold was forgotten in the midst of heat, but the sensation of the storm had yet to leave her; she was grateful for the day.

When she could no longer clearly see Margret and her companions, she turned away. She had thought, given the lay of the land, that she would watch them dwindle for a long time, but the heat had already begun to blur the lines of their bodies until it was no longer clear who was who.

She walked back to where Avandar sat, unmoving, by the side of the ship. Had it been a real boat, it would have looked like a beached whale; it was designed to be borne by wheels, not air, and it rested mostly on its flat.

"Avandar," she said, almost gently.

He looked toward her, but he did not speak.

If he had, she thought he might speak in the tongue he had used beneath the mountains, and she wasn't sure she wanted to hear him speak in that language again. Ever.

But she didn't like his silence much.

"Avandar," she said again, keeping her voice as soft as she could. "Who are you?"

He stared at the sand beneath her feet.

"Avandar."

And then, when he did not respond, she closed her eyes. *Avandar.*

Here, too, there was the silence of absence.

He had lived her life for over a decade; he had been an uncomfortable presence, a difficult wisdom, an unknown power.

She had kept as much distance as she could between them, although as domicis, she could in theory trust him with her life—and had.

She crossed that distance carefully, moving across the sand until she stood beside him. She did not touch him, although if she reached out, she could; instead, her eyes found the same patch of sand that caught and held his attention. Wood, softened by layered fabric that had grown damp with sweat, touched both of her shoulder blades.

He had replaced Ellerson, the domicis the Terafin had sent her den on its first day in the manse. Ellerson had been older than her father would have been, had he survived, and a good deal more formal, but she knew, with Ellerson, that what she saw was what he was.

And knew, too, that he cared about her and hers. It had been such a blow to lose him. The years had gentled the loss, but had not removed its shadow.

That was part of the reason for her distance.

Morretz, The Terafin's domicis, a man she also instinctively trusted, disliked Avandar, and mistrusted him. His eyes, the steely cast of his lips, the way he drew his spine to full height whenever Avandar came into view, told the beginning—or middle—of the story, but neither he nor Avandar would disclose the end.

That was another part.

But the last lay buried by sands and time. A *lot* of time.

The past was not a place, but it existed, and with care and attention, a map might be made from start to finish, replete with landmarks, terrain, and roads. If one knew the personal geography behind its making.

Jewel had, in her time, both upheld and decried that geography. She had promised those in her care that if they dwelled in the present she foisted on them, if they met her demands, followed her rough guidance—and it was rough, for she had never been the most patient of people—the past would remain a foreign place, a country in which she could neither speak nor understand the language.

They had accepted her rules because they were desperately hungry. And that hunger had two forms that she recognized. The first, the one that was easiest, she resolved as she could in the streets of the twenty-fifth; she scavenged for food, stealing what she could, buying what she had to. That was one of *her* truths, and a gold ring, a wing in the Terafin Manse, could not eradicate it.

The second hunger was more difficult.

And in appeasing that, she had turned her den into her kin, the only kin that she had claimed after the death of her father.

The past was not a place. The present was not a place, but it was rooted in reality. She had made a geography out of loyalty, trust, and a shaky respect, and she had made it stick; she had made it so real that the past lost its grip to paralyze or terrify in all but the darkest of circumstances.

It was the here and now that she had been best at.

The only past she relied on was her own. Her Oma. Her mother. Her father. Old Rath. Beyond that: Terafin, the Chosen, and her kin—Angel, Carver, Finch, Jester, Arann, Teller.

No, that's not true.

There was Duster. Duster, her killer. Her wild card. Her friend. She had asked no one else for their stories, but Duster's had both fascinated and frightened her, and in the end part of her confidence in the strength of her den was built on the foundations of that story, that past.

What had she said?

I won't judge you. I promised you that. But I need to

know what you are, and to know that, I need to know who you were. No, that's not what I mean. I mean—I mean I need to know where you came from. I need to know why.

Duster had trusted her.

Duster had answered. She had started out so edgy and defiant, the words hard and shiny, her pride in her past and her accomplishments—*death, three killings*—like a light, a beacon.

But beneath steel, there was something else. And after the edge had been ground from her words, after the pride had burned so brightly and exhausted itself so thoroughly, Jewel had found it.

She had never tried that with Avandar.

No, he said.

She jumped.

And you never will.

He was back; he was behind his eyes.

Why?

"Because, ATerafin, you already know what you'll find, and if you find it, you will not be able to accept it. There is nothing of you in it. Nothing at all. But I am . . . touched by your concern."

He pulled himself away from Elena's ship and began to walk off.

"Avandar."

"ATerafin?"

"Did you truly surrender the gates of Carrallon?"

He looked at her for a long time; she felt his gaze as if attention were a responsibility and a burden.

And then he smiled.

She took a step back.

When he turned again, she let him go.

The Serra Teresa had been quiet for most of the day's light. Every so often she would rise and turn in a circle that began and ended with Yollana, her gaze upon the distant horizon.

"Teresa."

"Matriarch?"

"Sit. You make me dizzy."

It wasn't true. Teresa completed her search and resumed her unofficial place by the side of the Havallan Matriarch.

She pushed dark curls away from her neck and stared, almost ruefully, at her hands; they had become darker in the past few weeks than they had ever been. Stranger's hands.

"Yollana, what do we do here?"

The Matriarch reached into her robes for her pipe. Her hands, lined and dark, were as steady as rock. "We wait."

It was not an answer to the question she had asked, but it was answer enough.

The Arkosans had withdrawn; some sought the interior of Elena's wagon, some the makeshift shelter they had erected for Margret.

"How long?"

Yollana settled the pipe in the corner of her mouth after placing leaf around its wide, flat bowl. She searched her robes for a moment and then snorted and passed her hands over the tobacco. Fire, the smallest of sparks, swirled in the wake of her fingertips. Her breath caught those sparks, drew them into the leafbed.

"It varies. I have my own experience to go by, no others. In the Western Kingdoms there is a saying: No country is large enough to contain two heads that have worn the same crown unless one is on a pike."

Teresa smiled.

"It's a good saying, although the Voyani don't invest their titles in symbols; if we had crowns, they would serve a purpose; they would house some part of our power."

"The Crown houses power in direct measure to the power of the man who dares to lift it."

The older woman shrugged. "It doesn't matter. Our lives, our names, are enough. There have never been—to my knowledge—two Matriarchs at the foot of the *Voyanne*. The Voyani do not love the clans, but history has shown that they bear each other no great feelings of fellowship either. I bear the responsibility for some of that truth. If I were Margret, I would have left me with the rest of the Arkosans; I would never have allowed me to travel. Not here."

"No. Evallen would not have allowed it either."

"Indeed. I had respect for Evallen."

"And her daughter?"

"We'll see. But . . . she has surprised me, Teresa. And at her age, that's no small thing." She smoked a while in silence. Teresa thought she had finished speaking, and was almost sorry; her voice, textured and layered with conflicting emotions, was a welcome companion.

But after a moment, she said, "We will not have long to wait. Other Matriarchs have taken days to pass this test; in Havalla, one is given no more than three."

"And if the Matriarch fails?"

"She is no longer Matriarch; she passes the burden down."

Teresa fell silent. She had asked Yollana questions before, but she had chosen each word carefully, aware that answers exposed her to as much danger as a direct threat might have. The Voyani guarded their past a little less carefully than they did their secrets, and there was only one sure way to keep a secret.

Today, Yollana was more forthcoming than she had ever been. "If Margret does not find what she seeks today, she will never find it. The sun is almost at its height. Teresa, don't stand. If she succeeds, we will know."

"But—"

"We will know. What she will do about that knowledge, I cannot say, but we *will* know."

The Serra smiled almost bitterly. She rose. "It is not for Margret that I search," she said simply.

She lifted her voice, her private voice, the voice that, had she been born in any other land, would have been gift, not curse, blessing, not bane.

A mile away, the Serra Diora di'Marano lowered her face. It was a slight movement; she did not cease to walk, to follow the path that the Matriarch followed in the vast, unmarked plain.

But slight or no, it caught Margret's attention. She paused, or perhaps slowed, and turned to the Serra.

"Diora?"

Elena was close enough to hear the unadorned name. Had she been a clanswoman, she would have marked the lack of title as either active insult or act of intimacy, and would have hoarded the knowledge while failing to show that she now had it.

The Voyani, constrained by no such formality, were often

less likely to notice. But Elena's eyes narrowed. The rest of her expression was hidden by desert mask, desert hood.

Margret had no sisters.

Elena, her cousin, filled that role. Cherished it. She had been concerned with the enmity Margret willfully displayed to the Serra Diora; she was concerned, now, with its lack. It was not in Diora's interests to exacerbate that concern.

But she did not correct Margret; that would be worse; that would draw attention to the lapse in the older woman's behavior. Instead, she smiled wanly.

"I am . . . tired," she said, pitching her voice to make it both pleasant and weak. "Forgive me, Matriarch."

Margret's eyes, like her cousin's, were so openly expressive it didn't matter if the rest of her face was obscured.

Diora therefore added, "I worry about Ramdan, that is all." She waited for the name to register, and when it didn't, she found herself adding, "My seraf."

It was Nicu who snorted. His hearing was, sadly, better than Margret's.

Margret turned to him and snapped a reprimand in Torra. Diora failed to hear it; she kept her face as smooth as a mask. That was what a face was, after all, in the High Court. A mask. And that mask was watched carefully, examined daily for cracks.

Nicu's comment and Margret's reprimand seemed to restore a delicate balance to Elena; she became once again absorbed by the pilgrimage.

But Margret tilted the balance again; although she did not stop—could not stop—moving, she reached out briefly and touched Diora's shoulder.

"We'll find him."

Although the Voyani Matriarchs were obligated to bear children, they also took no husband; the fathers of their children existed in a curious limbo. Some Matriarchs chose to bear children in such a way that no father could lay claim to his daughter's blood or title.

In Margret's case, Evallen had been secure enough in her power—and her husband—to risk a more traditional approach. If she had chosen unwisely in her youth, that approach would have been fraught with peril. The Matriarchs ruled the Voyani; that truth was unquestioned.

But in the Dominion, women did not rule, and that, too, was a truth that was unquestioned.

Diora wondered how many fathers of Matriarchs had been put aside; how many had had accidents that, while unexplained, were understood by all. She wondered what it must be like, to be a man who stood so close to power, without ever being able to wield it directly.

And as she did, her gaze passed over Nicu. He did not meet it; he had turned to look—as he so often did—at Elena.

Family, Diora thought.

She turned her attention to the sand, the sun, the wind. To the shadows that were dwindling until they were cast upon the ground by the length of her stride.

The fires still burned within the Matriarch of Arkosa. She had swallowed them, and like a poison, they spread. The heat of the desert, the heat of the sun, the heat of light reflected by pale sand, were nothing in comparison; she did not feel them enough to be forced to acknowledge them.

Her hands tingled. Her legs. As she walked, her feet began to feel the fire's spread until each step she took was a mingling of pain and pleasure. The sensation was strong, sweet; she changed the fall of her foot against sand, lengthening it.

She felt *alive.*

She had faced storm and Serpent, sun and moon; she had accepted the loss of her brother; she had accepted the responsibility laid like a slap across her face. All of these things failed to bow her. She was the Matriarch of Arkosa. She *was* Arkosa.

" 'Gret?"

Her cousin's voice came to her as a hollow, tinny sound. And until she heard it, she did not realize that she was listening to the wind, to the rich fullness of the voice that sent sand scudding across the plain.

"'Lena?"

"You said something."

"No."

"Yes," Nicu said, the sullen weight of his words somehow more substantial than Elena's. "You did."

She frowned.

"Margret."

The Serra Diora's voice was as clear as the wind's. Margret turned at once, drawn to it. "You spoke in the tongue of the Matriarchs." She paused for a moment, and then added quietly, "and your feet are no longer touching the sand."

She looked down; the winds left her.

"I think," she said, as calmly as she could, "we are almost there. Nicu, Elena, set up the tents. From here, we must go on alone."

"We?"

"The Serra and I."

Elena's eyes were as narrow as a blade's edge, but hot where a blade was cold. She would have spoken; Margret knew her well enough to brace herself for angry words even if she couldn't see the mouth they'd come out of.

But Nicu saved her the trouble.

"You're going to take an outsider with you? You're going to take *her* and leave your blood kin behind?"

She didn't trust herself with words. But her nod was as clipped as the words would have been had she said them.

"Matriarch," he said, all ice, "you will not."

Ishavriel heard the words.

Felt them, felt the immediate rage that propelled them. He matched the mortal's sudden fury with his own. How *dare* he? The time was not yet right.

And timing was everything.

At times he could understand Isladar's fascination with mortals and mortality; this was not one of them. Had he been standing beside the Arkosan, he would have cut short a span of years that was already brief enough to be almost beneath notice.

He was not.

He could feel the pulse of the ground beneath his feet. He had come, time and again, to this desert, searching the sands, forcing the old earth to come, at his bidding.

But the earth resisted him here in a way that it could not in the Northern Wastes, the frozen desert. And although he could come close enough to the buried Cities, he could not touch them; could not say with certainty where in the geography of this vast, slumbering body, they lay.

Until today.

Because the Matriarch of Arkosa's pilgrimage was a ritual. That is what they had not seen, could not understand; the magicks that brought them to the City were not the magicks of the Cities of Man; they were hidden, subtle. All language, all invocation, had been subsumed in the trek itself; the symbols to invoke the past were drawn not in blood, not in magery, not in sacrifice. Their outlines, so vast they were not clear to the eye that searched for minutiae, were inscribed entirely by the walk itself, described by the language of movement. With each step, with each retracing of the Voyani path of flight, this mortal brought sentience back to what lay hidden.

He was close. So close.

But he was not the only one.

CHAPTER TWENTY-EIGHT

"I will not?" The night was in her voice. The desert night. She drew herself up to her full height.

Nicu took a step back, and then, as if realizing what that implied, planted his feet apart. Fighting stance. "We have never been allowed to enter the—the homelands."

"We?"

"Arkosans. Any other Arkosans. Not even Elena—"

"Do *not* attempt to speak for me, Nicu. If you indulge in madness, it is entirely your own."

"Easy for you to say," he snapped. His hand fell, but not to the hilt of the sword he wore loosely girded around his hips; he brushed his robes aside, and in its folds another hilt appeared.

Elena closed her eyes. *Nicu.* Opened them. "Nicu—"

"Do not attempt to coddle me."

It was far too late for that.

"You'll be Matriarch if she dies. You'll have your chance. And her daughters—if any man is stupid enough to get her with child—will also have that right. But what of us? What of the sons? What of the men who fight and die to protect Arkosa?"

She closed her eyes again. Sand was in them. Just sand. She lifted her hand to wipe them clear. "Will you speak for the men of Arkosa?" she asked. Her voice was shorn of expression.

"If not me, then who?"

Margret had not spoken a word.

"Let them speak for themselves, Nicu. Let Stavos speak for himself. Let Andreas speak for himself. Let Adam speak for himself, when he returns."

"Adam?" He spat. Water hissed against the ground, in

a voice not unlike a snake's. "A child cannot speak for a man."

She turned to the men who flanked him, left and right. "Does he speak for you?"

They were silent. Their faces were now hidden in the caves of desert hood, desert cowls, but their eyes were both dark and bright. *Three,* she thought.

And three.

She took her place by Margret's side. Her hand fell to her own weapon, but she did not draw it. Were she forced to, she was not certain what would happen. Not one of the Arkosans was Nicu's equal when it came to sword.

And she knew what that sword would do, if it were unleashed.

Nicu, she thought, although she did not speak his name again. Instead, she loosed it silently; she set it free.

But he knew her; he knew her well enough to understand what her silence threatened. The ice left his voice, and she found the heat that replaced it was no less terrible.

"Don't you understand, 'Lena? Don't you see? It is not just our history that lies in this place, it is our *power*. We have wandered like the least of clansmen for centuries. We have starved, we have been taken for slaves, we have existed on the periphery of a land we should have *ruled* because of the whim of the Matriarchs."

"You will destroy Arkosa," she said with absolute, sudden certainty.

"No, no! *I* will save Arkosa. I will save our people!"

"How, Nicu? If our power was here, don't you think we would have taken it? If it could be safely used, if it could be used at all—why would the Cities have fallen?"

She spoke freely of the things which were never, never said, and she was grateful for the first time that she had stepped, in Margret's wake, from the *Voyanne*, for in speaking here, on this barren, ancient ground, she broke no law, divulged no secret.

He was silent a moment. He had not thought of that. She felt him teeter on the edge, and she willed him to fall, to take a step toward them, to come back.

Even though she knew the edge was sharp.

"We abandoned the Cities," he said at last, his voice thick. "And maybe if we hadn't, they would never have fallen. This is the Dominion, 'Lena." He drew himself up, found his center.

She wanted to weep with rage and pain; fear was a distant cousin.

"This is the Dominion of Annagar, and in Annagar, women are not meant to rule." He drew himself up to his full height, which was bad.

And drew the sword, which was infinitely worse.

"I am sorry, Margret," he said, the formality of each syllable clipped and strained, "but you will give *me* the Heart of Arkosa. Now."

They were not too far from the camp. The Serra Diora did not understand what had possessed Nicu, although she could guess; he had been thwarted in his desire. Neither of the men who stood beside him had spoken; she could not gauge their intent from their voices, and she had come to trust her gift. Yes, she thought, gift.

But if she could not listen, she could speak.

"Kallandras, come. There is trouble."

The wind took her words.

But the reply she waited upon came quickly, and in a voice that she had never heard before—and recognized, in spite of that.

"I am afraid that we cannot afford to be interrupted."

From out of the hazy air, a man stepped.

A man who was no man, a man whose voice was death, and delight in death, a servant of the Lord of Night.

He could not hear her. She was certain that he could not. But she was also certain that the Northern bard would hear no word she spoke either, and for the first time, in the height of midday, she knew fear.

It was a clean fear.

"Margret, the stranger is a servant of the Lord of Night."

Margret turned her attention slightly, shifting in place. Whatever this creature's power was, it was contained.

A mile away, Jewel ATerafin looked up. Her eyes widened, her breath stopped.

No one seemed to notice. She struggled to her feet and stumbled away from the ship of the Matriarch's heir.

The air was a haze of heat; the sun was almost above

them, and it cast no shadow, allowed them no relief. But it was not the sun she feared.

"Yollana!"

She stumbled, righted herself, and ran toward the awning beneath which the old woman sat.

"ATerafin?"

"Yollana, there's trouble."

The Matriarch of Havalla lifted her head as if it weighed a great deal. "I know," she said softly.

"We have to go. We may have time. *Kallandras*!"

She did not hear his footsteps, did not hear his movement, although the robes themselves made noise when folds of its heavy fabric rubbed against each other. But he was there, in the sun outside of the awning.

"ATerafin?"

"Good. You're here. How fast can you run in those? Where is Celleriant?"

"I can run, if it is necessary. What have you seen?"

She shook her head. "Not now. You'll know when we get there."

"No." The Havallan Matriarch had found her cane; she used it to rise, and she stood, her legs unsteady in the dry heat.

"Yollana, the Matriarch of Arkosa is in grave danger. If we do not leave now—"

"You must not interfere."

"What?"

"You must not interfere," the old woman said again. "What we can give her, we have given her. You will know—we will all know—when it is time to move."

"I don't know what the Voyani do when they come to the desert. But I'll bet Imperial Crowns—or Annagarian Solarii, if it comes to that, that they don't meet demons every day."

"I wouldn't take that bet," the Matriarch replied, with just the trace of a bitter smile. "But it doesn't matter. If Margret can be bested at the heart of Arkosa, there is not a power here that will save her."

"Matriarch—"

"But there is a power there that will destroy the rest of us. You *will* wait, ATerafin."

"Kallandras?"

"It is not wise to meddle in the affairs of the Voyani, even when they *have* requested it. We will wait."

"Can we wait any closer?"

"ATerafin." Yollana reached out and caught Jewel's forearm in a grip that belied her age and her apparent infirmity. "I have seen what you see. But I have the history of my people with which to unravel its meaning; you have a single life, and at that, a short one. You *must* not interfere. This is a trial that was ordained long before any of us were born. I thought, once, that it would be *my* trial, but I was mistaken.

"It matters not. What unfolds in the desert, unfolds. We must bear it."

Jewel started to speak, drew breath, and held it as she met Yollana's dark, unblinking gaze. She struggled a moment with what she saw there, and then nodded bitterly.

"Tell me one thing."

"Perhaps. This is not a game of barter; there is no give and take on this road. Ask your question."

"What happens if she fails?"

"She fails," the old woman replied.

It didn't take sight to know that she wasn't going to get any more of an answer.

But the old woman was not yet finished; she held Jewel's arm, drew the younger woman close, and turned her palm up to the light. There, with nothing to gentle the light, years of labor were etched into the dry, rough skin of her palms.

"You are not a woman who believes in destiny," she said at last. "But you should be. You, of all people. The road begins to unravel here, where it began. And you have already set foot upon the path that will replace it.

"Walk with care, ATerafin. Walk, if you can, in the light of the Lady's Moon." She turned away.

But not before Jewel had had a chance to see the whole of her face, and the expression that darkened it.

She didn't believe in a destiny that she couldn't make. "What do you think you see there?"

"The Oracle," she replied. "I will not look upon your future again, for it is dark and broken, but I will say this—and I, who should know better than to speak at all. In my youth, the woman we call Evayne came to me. She said that I had been born with a gift of some strength. I knew it; I was young and foolish, and it was a pride, both to me and to my mother.

"She offered me myself; offered me the strength of a vision unfettered by whim and circumstance. You have seen her, ATerafin. Her mark is upon your hand."

In spite of herself, Jewel looked at that hand, as if to read what she did not believe was written in flesh.

"She has command of her vision, for she has drawn it from herself so that she might hold it in her palms."

The soul crystal, Jewel thought.

"I went with her. I walked to the foot of a path that none of my people have walked since the *Voyanne* was first opened to us. And I could not pay the Oracle's price. I understood what I had to gain, but the loss was too great." The old woman sat again, heavily. "Do not be as weak as I, when you are brought before her."

The sun was no longer warm.

There and then, Jewel promised herself she'd be damned before she followed willingly down any path Evayne chose.

As if he could hear her, and perhaps he could—she had never been able to read Kallandras well—the bard of Senniel College said softly, "Make no vow you cannot keep. Evayne a'Nolan is colder than desert night, and far more cruel than the demons she was born to fight."

Demons.

Jewel looked slowly to the South.

Nicu did not acknowledge the arrival of the stranger. He did not move; did not turn; did not look. The men who stood to either side were not as complacent. They turned, quickly, their hands dropping to the hilts of their sword.

Old habits.

He was tall, taller than any man she had seen, save perhaps the pale-haired stranger whom she had suffered to travel among the Arkosans at the behest of Jewel ATerafin. Like that stranger, this one was suffocating in his beauty. Margret's throat was dry, but she did not blame that on the desert; had she been in the heart of the gale, he would have had this effect on her. He radiated power, but it was not the power of the clansmen; it dwarfed that in breadth, in depth. She felt a keen, sharp, piercing desire.

She had never trusted desire.

"This is an unfortunate turn of events." The creature—for Margret could not think of him as a man—smiled. She had seen rabid dogs that looked kinder. "But mortals are known for their impatience, and why would they not be impatient? True patience would consume the full tally of their years."

"Do not interfere," Nicu snapped.

The creature threw back his head and laughed. The length of his hair—for it was dark and unfettered by hood—fell down his shoulders like a gleaming ebony cascade. His voice was rich and thick. She could have listened to him speak forever.

If she had forever.

If she had even a glass full of running sands.

"Would you know of the fate of the Cities were it not for my interference? Would you understand your role in the future if it were not for me? Your complaint is feeble and it comes late. Far too late."

"I do not serve you."

"No, indeed," the creature said smoothly. "You serve your people, and you serve them well."

Margret had heard merchants speak with less sincerity, and for the first time since the stranger arrived, she felt not fear or fascination, but a deep and abiding anger. How *could* Nicu be so stupid? How could a man who shared her blood, her history, her family, be so easily swayed by one such as this?

She felt the fires burning in her fingers, in her feet. She saw them rise, like a veil, before her eyes. But where anger was red, these were blue and white and gold. She looked at the stranger's face and she saw him clearly: he was dead, and he walked.

Abomination.

Servant of the Lord.

His shadows were everywhere; they trailed from the hair that she had admired down the length of the back that faced North, faced away from her. They fell from his shoulders like a great cloak, swirling in folds around his arms, his legs.

She knew that the living could not bear such a cloak; it

would consume them—slowly, yes, where fires were quick, but just as completely as flame.

Nicu was angry, too. "Elena," he said, the last syllable a pitched whine. "Don't make me do this."

Her cousin, her cousin, whose hair was fire, whose heart was heat, broke the simple law of desert travel; she wasted water on him, spitting to the side like an angry cat. "You'll have to kill us. Surely you understood that. You cannot take the Heart from the Matriarch without taking her life as well."

"If she gives it to me, I can bear it."

"Do you understand so little, Nicu? Do you not know what the creature behind you is?"

"Elena—"

She spun in place, her gaze the only weapon she wielded. "Carmello," she said, her voice low and tense, "do you understand what he's saying? Do you understand who you serve?

"Andreas?" Elena's brows, slightly darker than her hair, but still red, still fiery, had drawn together. "Andreas, you can't believe what you're doing is right. Maybe Nicu can. Maybe Carmello. But you? I won't believe it."

Margret felt a pang as she, too, looked toward Andreas. Of all the Arkosans under Nicu's command, Andreas was most like her brother Adam. He was the youngest of Nicu's men, and of them, the most sincere, the most naíve. He believed in the glory of combat; he believed in making a stand, not for reasons of manhood, but because it was the right thing to do.

He met her eyes, and his expression wavered for the first time. "Nicu?" he said, the word a question.

"Will you let her decide for you? Have you understood nothing? The Matriarchs are our masters!"

"Maybe," Elena said, speaking for Margret. "Maybe they are. But we have served willingly. Those who did not wish to walk *this* road have traveled North and made lesser homes in the lands of the demon kings, and we have not hunted them; we have not killed them.

"We are not the danger. We have never been the danger. Did you not understand what happened in the Tor Leonne? Did you not see for yourself what the Tyr'agar would have made of the Lady's Festival?"

Nicu did not reply.

But Andreas did. He stepped forward, toward Margret.

Margret felt the heat rise in her hands, in her face; it was sudden, terrible; it consumed breath. She did not understand it, and because she did not, Andreas died.

Andreas died.

The creature that had come to the desert, to Arkosa, the creature that had tempted her cousin, gestured; swung wide with a long, graceful limb. She had not seen a weapon until that moment; it flickered in air as his hand moved, taking form, substance, strength from the motion itself.

And it passed through Andreas.

He had no time to scream, but he *did* scream, his lips turning the color of blood, his blood, as his chest collapsed forward and onto the sand, leaving his legs behind.

She did not think.

Elena had often accused her of that, of not thinking things through, of reacting when it was dangerous to react.

She cried out as Andreas screamed, and the two sounds were a harmony, a melody, a cacophony.

Fire answered—white, gold, blue. Andreas' cry died in the lap of that flame, and his eyes, before they lost all life, met hers in a dim surprise. His lips moved over syllables that he had no breath to utter, but she saw what could not be heard.

Matriarch.

The shadows of the creature rose in defiance of her flames, and she realized that the flames were no longer contained; she had set them free.

Nicu screamed, a heartbeat after she had fallen silent.

"What have you done?" he cried, not to Margret, but to the creature who was gathering his power beneath the open sky.

The creature did not reply.

"You have something we require, Matriarch." He did not offer her safety in return for the Heart of Arkosa; he did not seek to barter for the lives of her companions. It was a game he did not insult her by attempting to play.

"You will never have it. We made our vows when we set foot upon the *Voyanne*." She lifted her hand, and fire streamed from it.

His eyes widened in surprise when that flame began to

lap at the edges of his power, devouring it. But he laughed. The laughter was louder than the crackle and hiss of flame.

"Serra," Margret said quietly. "'Lena. We must leave."

She caught their hands in hers; they were that close. The sun was overhead; she cast no shadow. She took a step back. Diora came with her.

Elena did not.

She tugged at her cousin's arm; her cousin grunted in pain. The creature's shadow leaped skyward, above the boundary her flame had set. She knew, she *knew,* that she was not his match.

She had made time for flight, no more.

But Elena did not move. *"Elena!"*

Could not move forward.

Margret pulled harder. But she had crossed a barrier that she could not see; the Serra Diora had come with her. Elena had not.

Could not.

No. She had the fire within her. She felt it lessen as the shadows grew. *NO.*

But her cousin understood what she did not, could not. "Let me go, 'Gret."

"No!"

"Leave me."

"No! No, I won't leave you here!"

"Arkosa has its law, and its law cannot be broken. I see that now. Let me go, or the Lord of Night wins, and everything we have ever lost means nothing. 'Gret, let go."

"I won't."

Elena smiled, but the smile was a tight little movement of thin lips; it had none of the generosity for which Elena was known. "I'm sorry, 'Gret. I truly am."

And before Margret could reply, her cousin drew her dagger and stabbed Margret's hand.

Margret cried out in shock, pulling back instinctively. She fell across the sands, and her blood fell with her. Into the ground.

The ground above Arkosa.

Elena turned her back; exposed robes that flowed with the wind. Her dagger glinted in the sun as she faced the demon, her cousin, his man.

Alone.

Margret rose, enraged, terrified. She reached for her own dagger—and felt a hand touch hers.

She looked into the face of the Serra Diora.

"Matriarch."

The word was a slap.

"If he can, your cousin will defend Elena. He loves her, in his fashion. But we must flee, now. Arkosa is waiting."

She hated the Serra.

And she hated Arkosa in equal measure.

But she turned her back on her kin, on a woman who was like a sister to her, and she ran.

Because the sun was in place, and she knew that if she failed to reach the place—*what place?*—in time, she would never reach it.

Elena faced death. She had faced death before. But never like this. She could not look at Nicu. Could not look at Carmello.

And was terrified of facing the demon. It had taken courage to wound her cousin, and she felt that courage desert her. Her hand shook. To still it, she clenched the dagger tight.

The creature walked toward her.

Nicu raised an arm. In his hand, he held the sword.

"Do not be foolish," the creature said, voice soft as the silks of the High Court. "I know this mortal. Is she not the woman that you hoped to make your wife?"

"You will not hurt her."

"Hurt her?" The creature smiled. "No. I will not hurt her. I merely mean to convince her of the truth of your claim. If you refuse me, I will abide by your decision. The Matriarch is not beyond us."

Nicu said tersely, "Elena, come here."

She shook her head; she could not trust her voice.

His brow furrowed. "Elena."

The creature continued to walk. The length of his reach was great. She took a step back; it was a damn small step.

"Do not touch her," Nicu said again, but his voice wavered.

"Do you not desire her? I will not kill her, Nicu. But she is the key to the City, for when the Matriarch fails, it is her blood that will invoke the City's rise. She will aid you."

Nicu wavered. She saw him waver.

She could not bring herself to speak his name. Instead, she clenched the dagger more tightly to her chest.

"Elena, come here. Choose now. Stand beside me, or stand against him alone. I will not ask again."

Lowering her chin, she made her way to Nicu's side.

"Good," he said quietly. He reached out with a hand and touched her cheek; his fingers were gentle.

But she flinched anyway.

He frowned. His hand dropped. He turned away from her, and then turned back, and she could see the fury in his eyes, in the sudden turning of his lips.

Without pause for breath, Elena turned and ran.

There was something flat and hard in the sand. The wind had almost buried it, but the fall of her steps across its surface made her stop. She dug a bit with the toe of her boot, and clearing sand, saw the first hint of stone. It was white as bone in an open grave.

Her lips were dry; her tongue clung to the roof of her mouth. She could not speak, but she did not need to; the Serra stopped as well.

The winds shifted. They howled. Sand flew in all directions. All save one.

The stone.

Margret watched as the wind danced along its surface, falling into worn grooves that had been carved there by a hand far more steady than her own. A veil was being lifted, grain by grain, and as it rose, she saw the circle carved there. It was blank.

Her hand was still bleeding from the cut Elena had made in it. It was a deep cut; no small cut would have had the effect Elena desired.

She touched the blood with her fingers; it was wet. She should bind the wound. Yes. But not yet.

The first symbol had been drawn for her. She drew the second, the inner circle, with her own blood. The ground rumbled beneath her feet. The winds rose. There was not enough blood, and she cursed its lack. Before she could draw her dagger, the Serra Diora offered her a different one.

She took it absently, and looked at its blade only when that blade pierced her skin. It was *Lumina Arden*. She set it aside on the stone, and continued to draw; the line across the circle; the shallow crescents across the line. Then, enclosing the carved circle and the symbol within it, she drew her own mark, start to finish; a larger circle. A containment.

The Serra watched her work in silence. She bent once to retrieve the dagger; Margret heard a tearing sound to the left, but she did not look up. This last part, this last was the hardest, the most intricate of her work: she wrote the name of her family in the space between two circles: Arkosa's, and her own.

The ground was shaking now; it was difficult to keep her hands steady. But she had traced this symbol at the beginning of her journey, with the blood of a stranger; she completed it again with her own.

As she traced the last rune, she rose.

The ground shook, rumbling with a voice that she almost felt she recognized.

The Serra Diora was at her side in an instant; she caught the hand that was slick and sticky with blood. "The blood," she said quietly, "falls too quickly. If you must rest—"

Margret shook her head.

Reached into the folds of her robes, and from them, drew the small jar that Yollana had gifted her with. Diora took it without a word. Opened it.

She did not ask permission to use what lay within. Instead, she touched it; her fingers rose, sticky with unguent whose smell was fresh as new rain on Mancorvan grass. She applied it to the wound. And then, after a moment, she bound the hand.

Margret lifted her waterskin, and waited patiently to retrieve her hand. Then she worked with stiff and aching fingers to remove the stopper that protected her life in the desert. Water.

She lifted it to her lips, drank carefully, and then offered the water to the Serra.

The Serra accepted with grace, and drank—of course—less.

"Are you ready, Serra?"

"Are you, Matriarch?"

Margret's smile was bitter. "No. Not for anything that has happened since we began our travel through this desert. I—I resented my mother's choices. I did not want to bring you here. But I am glad, now, that whatever I face, I do not have to face it alone. Diora—"

The Serra shook her head. "Look," she said softly. "Look at the stone."

But Margret did not need to look; she could feel it. It was glowing brightly. "Take my hand," she said wearily. "We are almost there."

The Serra gently picked up the wounded hand she had so carefully bound.

"Don't let go," Margret whispered.

Diora smiled, and if the smile was less bitter than Margret's, it was genuine; there was nothing of the High Court about it.

Together they stepped into the circle that Margret had traced.

And vanished.

She heard Nicu's angry shout. Knew that she could outrun him if the distance was great enough; that she could outsprint him if given enough of a start.

She clung to that thought as she had not clung to Margret. Clung as if her life depended on it; she was no fool. It did.

But she felt an icy cold take her limbs, retarding movement; felt her knees creak and groan with a dangerous pain. She tried to gain momentum by swinging her shoulders, but they, too, had become stiff.

No, she thought. *No.*

Lord, this is your *land; do not let the servants of your greatest enemy have Dominion here.*

She warded herself against the shadow; drew the circle across her breast in shaking hands. She heard footsteps. Felt the ground shake as they fell.

She saw the haze of the Lord's glare all around her; she did not look back. Whatever was behind her would be upon her soon enough, and she would see it then, in all its dark glory.

She ran.

But she could not run fast enough.

* * *

Margret was on *fire*. The flames that she had contained were contained no longer; they burned. Yollana had been wrong; even if Margret had the blood, she was not welcome in Arkosa without the Heart. She screamed, but the scream was not wordless; as her flesh burned, as her hair curled and died with a sharp, clear crackle, she heard the word she cried out—and the pain was too great for her to be ashamed.

She was her father's daughter, after all.

And she had loved her mother greatly.

She thought she lifted her hands; she could not feel her arms. She felt fire, and the pain that fire caused was indescribable.

She cried out again, but the cry was weaker.

And this time, it was answered.

A cool hand touched hers, and where the hand touched, the fire vanished. She could not feel her own hands, but she knew she had gripped whatever it was that drove the pain away; gripped it tightly.

Heard its intake of breath.

Margret.

Margret.

Margret.

The words drove the pain away. She reached out, as she had not reached out in years, and clung, arms encircling robes, clutching at whatever it was that lay beneath them.

She found her voice as the fires receded. She wept with relief, buried her head in the rough fabric of Voyani robes.

A hand touched her face, brushed the tears away, stroked her head. She felt fingers against flesh.

"Margret."

She recognized the voice. But even recognizing it, she could not stop the tears, could not still the shaking. She had been raised to despise weakness in the face of pain. Tears were something shed in anger, in sorrow; but never in fear.

She did not know why, but the Serra Diora di'Marano held her anyway, spoke her name, over and over again, in a voice heavy with unshed song. The Serra, raised by the clans that despised any tears.

It was dark.

"My eyes—"

"Margret."

"I can't see!"

"Shhhh, Margret. Your eyes are closed. They're closed. You can open them now."

"I can't—"

"You can."

"The fire—"

"Is gone. Margret. The fire is gone. You—you've left it behind." She was pulled gently forward; she had no desire to resist. The Serra's voice was so blessedly cool.

She sat in the darkness, leaning against the shoulder of the Dominion's most beautiful woman. She could not see her, but sight did not diminish beauty; she understood that now. Humbled, terrified, the Matriarch of Arkosa swallowed air and tears and waited.

Fingers touched the lids of her eyes very, very gently. "Can you feel this?"

"Yes."

"Good. Margret, open your eyes. Just a little, but try. If you are truly blind, we must know."

She did not want to open her eyes. Said as much.

"What are you afraid of seeing?" The Serra's voice was so peaceful, so quiet, so unlike the boisterous roughness of every other voice she had grown up hearing.

"I—I don't know."

"I promise you are not blind."

"I don't belong here. Arkosa *knows.*"

"If Arkosa knew, you would not be here. I would be here, alone. And . . . I do not think that I would be welcome at all."

Margret's laugh was shaky. Weak. But it was there. "You would be welcome anywhere. Every one of the Arkosans fell in love with you the day you arrived at our camp. Every one of them listened to you. They knew—they knew what I would say, so they never spoke about it—and for an Arkosan, that's hard. But they're so bad at lying. They wanted to hear you talk. They wanted to hear you sing. They wanted to protect you."

"Maybe," the Serra said. "But they wanted to *follow* you. Where I come from, that is infinitely more valuable."

"Is it?" Darkness. Behind her lids. "You never tried giving them orders. You don't know what they would have done if you had. Even my mother must have trusted you, and she trusted no one."

"No," Diora said, more quickly, the softness peeling away from the words as if it was veneer. "She trusted *us*.

"She died for us."

Margret opened her eyes.

The first thing she saw—the first she wanted to see—was the Serra Diora's face. It was lit from above by a diffuse, golden light that seemed to have no source. Too gentle to be sunlight, too warm to be moonlight, it caught the sheen of her exposed hair as if it were a pliable crown. Her eyes were dark; her lips parted; her chin slightly lowered. Her skin was smooth as Northern glass, but warmer, softer, finer.

"Did you not feel the fire?" she whispered.

"No. But before you say anything else, remember: I did not drink the blood Yollana gathered. That was for you, and only you."

"What does that have to do with anything?"

Her hand was still in Margret's hand. It tightened, and Margret rose unsteadily to her feet. "Look, Margret."

She pushed Margret's shoulders gently but firmly, and Margret had to choose between resisting, or allowing herself to be turned in the opposite direction. She did not resist.

Standing close enough to touch was a living shell of fire; it was blue and white, and for a moment she thought it was a being made of flame.

But she recognized some of the features beneath the flickering tongues. She had seen them before, many times, in the silvered glass her mother valued.

They were, of course, her own.

"I—I don't understand." She looked to Diora, and the Serra smiled.

"If you don't understand, and you are the Matriarch, no one will."

They were silent a moment, watching the fire. But the fire did not move. After a moment, the memory of pain dim enough that she could pretend to ignore it, she said, "does the Heart speak?"

The Serra shook her head.

But she reached to the nape of her neck, gathered the chain that rested against her skin, and pulled it up. It shed the protection of her robes as it came, and she laid it against her breast. "I'm sorry," she said, "but I have tried, and I cannot remove it."

"Then we're not—we're not wherever we have to be."

"I don't think so."

"Can we leave this place?"

"There are doors."

"Good." Margret took a step forward. Stopped. Looked down at the hand that still grasped the Serra's. She could see that her knuckles were white, hers and the Serra's. With a grimace, she forced her fingers to relax. She started to apologize. Stopped when she saw the expression on the Serra's face.

"Thank you," she said instead.

The room was not large. It was circular, and the shell of fire that burned as if waiting stood in its center. Light lay across the ceiling—and it was a ceiling, although it was hard to judge its height—like paint, a layer of perfectly even illumination. If there were markings in it, she could not see them. But she assumed that the ceiling was made of stone, for the walls were, and both were smooth.

Across the floor lay the circle of Arkosa writ large; it was red, the russet color of dried blood. She saw the Serra bend at the knee, and warned, before she could think, "Don't touch it."

The Serra froze. Margret's voice was harsh, but not with anger.

"The doors?" she asked, for she could not discern any break in the curved wall.

The Serra frowned. She lifted the Heart of Arkosa and moved steadily toward the wall, taking care not to disturb the circle—either of the circles—inscribed upon the surface of stone.

The Heart of Arkosa seemed to absorb the light of the ceiling; as the Serra moved, the concentration of light that had appeared so even gathered above her.

"It is here," Diora said quietly. She cupped the large crystal in her palms, and traced the rounded arch of a door; she had to stop because she could not reach the height of its peak, but the shape was clear. The light the crystal shed did not burn the eye; did not leave the marks across vision that the sun's light did—but having followed its movement, Margret remembered its path.

"Can you open it?" she asked, no bitterness in the words.

"No. It's—It has no handle."

"You know what?" Margret came to stand at Diora's side; their robes touched as she placed herself in the center of a door she could not see.

"What?"

"I think I hate magery."

Diora laughed.

Stopped immediately, as if laughter in this place was a profound breach of protocol.

"You might as well laugh," Margret said, frowning. "It can't be any worse than screaming or crying, and I've already laid claim to those noises. Am I at the center of the door?"

"Yes."

"Good." She closed her eyes. Placed both palms against the surface of stone. Pushed.

She had expected something to give beneath the force of her weight; nothing happened. She cursed. Pushed harder.

"Margret"

"What?"

"May I?"

"Why not?" She lifted her right hand; Diora placed her left there. Together, they tried again.

Nothing gave way. They pushed; pushed again. Margret offered a good curse or two. *If I have to shed more of my blood,* she thought grimly, *I'm going to resent it.*

"I don't think this is going to work," she said at last; she didn't bother to keep the frustration out of the words. "But I'll be burned if I—" And then she looked up, as if something had gathered her hair and given it a sharp, hard tug.

The door had not moved, but it had certainly changed.

She could see through it.

"Diora?"

Diora nodded.

"I'm an idiot. Place the Heart against the door. Between our hands."

Diora lifted the Heart in her right hand, crossed her

wrists, and placed it against the surface of what now appeared to be glass.

The glass began to shimmer.

Margret smiled. She took a step forward; felt heat and light and shadow. She turned and reached back through the door.

But her hand touched stone, although she could not see it. "It's safe," she said softly.

The Serra followed. When she had come through the door it became, again, part of a wall. A dead end in a long hall.

The sky was so blue, the sand so white, the wind as strong as she had felt it since the night of the storm.

She ran slower now, stumbling. Sweat fell down her forehead and into her eyes.

She knew that he let her run. She knew that it amused him; that he was a hunter, she his prey; that he had the time and the power to end the chase whenever he desired an end.

But even knowing it, she could not stop. If the only thing that bought her a moment's grace was his pleasure, she was willing to give it to him. The alternative . . .

No. She found strength. She ran.

They walked slowly down the hall, dwarfed by the height of its ceilings, two women in the robes of wanderers. One was fair, and one darkened by years upon the open road; one was tall, the other tiny; one moved with deliberate, heavy steps, and the other could be heard by the shuffling of fabric.

But they walked in step.

Along the halls, carved into the face of the stone, were runes that Margret recognized; she had been taught their shapes by her mother, and if she had never written them so perfectly, so precisely, she knew them anyway. The language of the dead. The ancient vows of her ancestors.

There was no dust on this floor. No sign of the mice or the insects that scrabbled from building to building across the stretch of the Dominion's driest lands. She stopped once or twice to inspect the stone itself; to touch the curves and the peaks of letters that she could not read, as if to absorb their meaning by the intimacy of contact.

But the Serra Diora touched nothing; she stopped when Margret stopped and resumed her walk when Margret had finished.

Had she been 'Lena, she would have cluttered the silence with an endless stream of questions. *Elena.*

She paused for a moment, pressed her forehead into the cool surface of stone. It did not give. This is what she had to be; this stone, that bore the language of the dead, the weight of history.

"Margret," the Serra said.

Margret rose. "I'm sorry. I—"

"The Heart is speaking."

"Can you repeat what it's saying?"

Diora was pale and still. Her eyes were wide, unblinking, but she was not in trance. It took Margret a moment to understand the expression: fear.

The Serra Diora was afraid.

Two weeks ago, Margret would have been gleeful. Two weeks and a lifetime. "Diora?"

"I do not need to repeat it," she replied, in a voice shorn of strength. "I can understand exactly what it's saying."

She thought she had run from the shadow. She had certainly fled its grasp, felt it nip at her heels as if it were a feral dog.

The sky was so clear. If the air weren't so hot, she might be able to see the Arkosan ships; might be able to see Stavos, Caitla, her mother. She had always had good eyes.

The dagger was heavy in her hands, and slick with sweat, in spite of the leather strap she'd wrapped around its hilt when her uncle had first gifted her with it. She clutched it tightly as she staggered.

She could not breathe without pain. Her lips were cracked and bleeding; she had not dared to stop to drink although she needed the water.

Her knee hit the sand as she slid.

Cursing wildly, she struggled to her feet.

The shadow was there.

"Very good," it said softly.

With a ragged cry, she swung the dagger.

The blade shattered in midair. Shards of steel flew across the sleeve of her robes; she felt a sharp pain as they pierced cloth and skin.

"I was never known for my patience," the creature said calmly. "But I forgive your boldness. If you had drawn a real weapon, I would be forced to kill you."

The shimmering heat of desert air resolved itself into a shape. Elena cursed herself silently; the dagger was gone.

It had never been a weapon, not in this fight. She should have understood that.

It had only been her freedom, and she had been too stupid to keep it in reserve against a time of need.

She staggered to the side, but flight deserted her; her legs were weak; her lungs as dry as her lips. She fell. Rolled over, with effort, pushing her weight up on her left arm.

The creature did not touch her. Did not move toward her. She frowned, squinting into the harsh light of day, thinking that her vision had often been better than Margret's or Nicu's.

The creature that stood before her was not the one who had spurred her into wild flight. There were two, she thought bitterly. Of course, there were two.

"Little mortal," the creature said, bending as if from a great height, his beautiful features hidden by shadow from the natural light, "you bear the blood of Tor Arkosa in your veins. Why do you flee when you are so close to home?"

She could not reply.

"Or perhaps you cannot hear it. I am Lord Telakar, and it amuses me to intervene in your affairs."

His hand was almost upon her forehead when he stopped moving; the wind tugged at his hair, but his robes were still. "You cannot trust me," he told her, "but if you are to survive this day, you must. You have little time."

"She has," a voice from behind her said, *"none."*

CHAPTER TWENTY-NINE

Use only the old roads. Touch nothing that does not call your name. Take nothing that you cannot control. Offer only that which you can afford to lose; offer nothing that you do not value.

Yollana's words. Margret paled as she looked at the stone walls across which her fingers had casually trailed. No, not casually. She had found strength in the familiar in this enclosed place. The Voyani were accustomed to the open sky, the unfettered wind, be it sand-laden or no, and she felt their absence keenly.

"Nothing calls my name in this place."

Diora was quiet. At length, she said, "Not yet. But we have not finished walking this hall. I think . . . I think the Heart is warning you. Are you prepared?"

She had cried in the arms of this woman. She could not lie. "No." Not even for the sake of leadership.

Diora smiled. Quiet, genuine, the expression was warm in a way the lights here were not.

"My mother," Margret said, her voice thicker than she would have liked, "did me a great service when she gave the Heart into your keeping. And she was right. I saw the silks and the powders, the combs, the seraf. I heard the title. But I did not see you, and if not for necessity, I would never have learned how to speak your name."

"If a service was done, it was done for me. I have learned much here. I wish . . ." she fell silent.

Margret was afraid. But the Serra did not finish, and at last she turned. "What must I offer? And to who?"

"Trust your ancestors, Margret. You will know." There was no doubt in the Serra's expression; none at all in her voice. "Your ancestors were women like you; they came to this place with questions. They must have received their answers."

What if I don't like the answers? But she walked, the Serra by her side.

The symbols passed, on the left and right, their forms as tall as she. She could appreciate the simplicity of their bold strokes and wondered if she had ever drawn them with such stark certainty. Was positive that she had not.

But she felt, as she walked, that she had drawn them with a living hand; that the act of writing them, in blood, gave them an immediacy that the stone did not suggest, did not convey.

They brought me here. They were good enough.

Their conversation was the simple sound of footsteps, the mingled hush of breath.

They came, at last, to a set of doors. Where the first had been invisible, the second were anything but; they rose to the height of the ceiling, stretching from one wall to the other. They were made not of stone, but of wood, and she was almost glad to see them, because they had been fashioned out of something that had once been alive, had once been rooted in ground, and dependent on sun, on water, on air. If they did not live now, they existed as a part of the history of the living; they had had a beginning, and had they not been felled for such a purpose, would have known an end.

She looked at the symbol that lay across the door; it was red as new blood, and it glistened. Outer circle. Inner circle. The symbol of Arkosa.

And between the opposing crescents, in a language that could not be dead, although it was not one she spoke or wrote at any time other than in the studies of the Matriarch's duty, she could read two things that she recognized.

"Margret?"

Margret lifted a hand; it hovered above the door. She was afraid to touch it; afraid to disturb what lay there. Stone had its function after all. "Serra," she said, her hand above these two lines that had never been part of this symbol. "Was your mother's name Alora?"

"It was."

"Can you read these?"

"I? No. They seem to be in the style of the runes across the walls, but I do not know what they say."

"They're names. This one," she said, lifting her hand, "says Margret, daughter of Evallen."

"And the other?"

"Can't you guess?"

Diora waited quietly.

"Diora, daughter of Alora."

The younger woman closed her eyes. "Do they say nothing of our fathers?"

"No. But the line of Matriarchs is traced from mother to daughter. After all, it's not always easy to say who your father was, but no one doubts who your mother was; it's hard to hide from the birthwives."

"It isn't hard to say that for sons either."

"No."

"Did your brother never mind that you would rule and he would not?"

"You've met Adam. What do you think?"

"I think that Evallen was blessed in both of her children."

Margret smiled. Lifted her hand.

Diora mimicked the movement with her own; they each touched a door at the same moment.

Blood burned in a ring of fire.

As the doors swung open, a voice said, **"Welcome, Daughters, to the Heart of Arkosa."**

What was a heart?

It beat. It bled. Still it, and the body would know no life. But it was hidden, unseen; it hoarded memories and wounds in equal measure.

Neither of the women in question had ever seen a heart, although they had seen the effects of its death; they had never touched a heart, although they had placed their hands close enough to one to know where it lay beneath skin; had traced the lines of pale green, pale blue, that traveled in fine, curving lines, most obvious across parts of the body that were not exposed to the glare of the Lord and harsh screed of wind. And they had listened to its quiet rhythm, the steadiness of its insistent beat, cradled at first in the arms of their living parents, and later in other arms, stealing that moment, that secret, hidden tongue, that could take them back to the safety promised by childhood.

But they knew, as the room unfolded before them in a display of multifoliate light—soft light, yes, but also the light that strikes in storm, the light that destroys shadow, corrupts shade, the light that reveals and the light so bright it blinds the eye just as surely as darkness deprives it—that there was in that promise no safety.

They stood on the threshold, on the surface, and they waited until light resolved itself into shapes they could understand. There were walls that seemed to rise and fall as far as the eye could see; no floor graced the room; no ceiling.

Margret had missed the open sky; she longed for enclosure now. She could not speak. The winds did; roaring from a depth she could not penetrate with something as simple as vision.

She did not move.

Diora did not move.

What do you desire, children of Man? Power? There is power here.

Embedded in the walls they could see were glowing spheres of light, as tall from top to bottom as a man. They had color, but that color shifted constantly. Green, the color of leaves in sunlight, the color of leaves at dusk; the deep green of emerald, the pale green of jade. Blue, the color of open sky, of judgment, the dark of a night in which all longing, all secrets, might be expressed. Gray, the color of cloud, behind which one might shelter from the stare of the Lord, and the gray of the storm, in which one might stand defiant, and one might die, split like tree to the root. Orange now, orange as fruit, as sand in the North, orange as the flowers upon which the butterflies fed. Gold, the color of power. Red, of fire, red of blood, red of lips and the fruit of desert trees.

More. She could not contain it, however much she might have desired containment.

If you have come in search of power, take it.

Margret was silent.

But the Serra was not. If she could not speak—and she was, Margret thought, so still her lips could not be moving—she could sing.

Quietly, hesitantly finding her way into melody, she began. There was no demand in her song; there was no question; no answer. If she had thought to offer comfort, that, too, escaped the range of her voice.

But as each note followed the next, building upon it, Margret recognized the slow birth of song: cradle song.

The heart, the heart is a dangerous place.

She had heard it all her life. Had asked for it, when she was young enough to ask without fear of ridicule. She heard it now, and what was invoked weakly, and wordlessly, touched what she had never seen: her own heart.

Funny, that in this place ruled by women, the voice that carried the song the most strongly in Margret's memory was her father's voice. She could smell him, sweaty and musty with the trailing smoke of pipe. She could feel the walls of his chest, the support of his arms. She could not touch him; he was gone. But the gift that he had given remained.

His heart.

The lights in the room did not change; did not sing what she now sang. They danced, and for just a moment, she thought she could see the hands of men against the surface of glass, chanting. Praying. Struggling.

Not even the Lord of Night could extinguish such a light as this.

She thought of Evallen. Her mother. Wondered if she had seen what Margret now saw, burning and glowing, twisting and dancing, raging like storm, lingering like ember.

A heart, Margret thought. *Just that.*

But this heart was not exposed; it was not known.

She swallowed. She had never feared heights before, although she understood the danger inherent in a fall. But she found the fear she had never acknowledged when she looked down, for there was nothing beyond the tip of her boots.

What do you desire, Daughter?

Yollana had not told her what to ask for. Perhaps Yollana did not know. Havalla and Arkosa were distant kin, but not even close kin were identical.

What did she desire?

Power, yes. The power to succor her people in the shadow cast by her enemy.

But she desired peace as well; she desired safety. She desired—although she could admit this only in silence—love, and the peace and strength that came from its certainty. She desired knowledge, if knowledge could be granted; desired experience because by experience she might better be able to glean folly from bravery.

There was so much she wanted that she stood immobile with the strength of it.

And then her hands moved, as if they belonged to another, and touched the rough edge of a fabric that was suddenly, blessedly real. She knew who had woven the cotton balls into cloth, knew who had cut that cloth, and whose hands had held the needles and thread, from dawn to dusk, until the robes themselves were complete.

These men and women had not known who would wear the robes; they had not known when they would be used; they had known only that Arkosans would find shelter from the desert in their folds, and that had been enough.

She exposed her face to light, and answered the question, although she was no longer certain she could bear the burden of what she asked for.

"I want to know the truth."

Before her feet, ground formed from light. It spread like a crack in dry earth, reaching out in all directions, not a road, but a tree. Around it, the endless fall continued beyond her vision.

And you, Daughter, the voice said, **what do you desire?**

Margret waited. She found it curiously difficult to breathe. She was afraid of what Diora might say, but she could offer no counsel; no advice. They had come here together, traveling not as allies, although they were allies, and not as kin; not as friends, for friendship was a pale word, yet not as lovers, for the intimacy that passed between them was based not in hope for the future, not in love.

They stood together and they stood alone.

The Serra Diora drew breath; she reached for her own hood and exposed her hair, her face, arranging it without thought across her shoulders.

She had learned as a child how painful desire could be, and she had lived her life by shunning its visceral strength; desire did not see clearly.

And yet there were things that she desired.

She had heard what Margret had asked for. She had waited, as she always waited, for Margret was the Arkosan here. And she had failed to be prepared for the question that voice now asked of her.

Failure haunted her. It always had. She schooled her face.

Felt Margret's hand touch her cheek briefly. "Don't," Margret whispered.

She turned, eyes widening slightly; she could not suppress her surprise. The touch lingered against her skin, not hot, not cool; Margret's fingers were surprisingly rough. She lived in the sun and the wind, and dared all.

"Diora, this is the heart of Arkosa."

"There is no safety here. Can you not hear it in the question? The wrong answer will destroy us. The wrong path will lead us only to death."

"You have lived your life in the High Court. Was it different there? Did you not make a home, in spite of the danger of words and impulse? Did you never unsheathe the truth; did you never speak it?"

"I . . . sang it, for you."

"You sang it," Margret countered, her words both gentle and sharp as well-crafted blade. "But you hid behind the mask and veil to do so."

Margret's eyes were dark and still.

Diora's lashes brushed her cheeks. "You are not so different from your brother," she said at last.

"We cannot go forward unless you answer the question."

"I know. But your answer has not destroyed us."

"And yours will?"

"I do not know."

"There is only one way to find out." She held out a hand.

Diora hesitated, but the hand was not withdrawn.

"What do I desire?" She looked up, into the winds, for the winds were howling. "Can you bring the dead to life?"

Howling.

"Can you give the dead peace?"

"The dead are at peace," Margret said softly. "It is the living that are driven. Only the living."

She laughed. "The ones who made this place have passed beyond us; do you think they are at peace? Listen. Listen to the winds."

"The winds carry no words, Serra. What you hear, you have chosen to hear."

"What I hear, I cannot help but hear. I—" words faltered.

"If you desire vengeance, say it. Say it."

She thought she could. But the words did not come.

"Why did you ask for the truth?"

"I don't know."

That was truth. She heard it. "I want to hold my son," she said.

"You—you had a child?"

"One of my wives had a child. He would have killed her in his birthing, but I—I spoke to him."

Daughter, what do you desire of us?

"What do you desire of *us*?" she countered.

But the wind demanded her answer. The light enforced that demand.

"Tell them, Diora."

"I want peace."

"Only the dead have peace."

"Is that a Voyani saying?"

"Yes."

Silence. Here, in the heart of Arkosa, she felt the presence of her wives as strongly as she had felt it since their deaths.

She heard Ruatha's voice, breaking her name by syllable until the name was an expression of pain and horror. She cried out in denial; covered her ears, although she had long since learned that such a gesture was futile.

It was Margret who caught her hands and drew them down to her sides. "Diora, you are one of the strongest people I have ever met."

Strong? She wanted to laugh. Her legs were shaking, and her limbs; her lips were a thin line because she did not trust her words to escape them whole. Her throat burned; she had swallowed fire, that night, and she would never expel it. It consumed her.

"I desire . . . only the strength . . . to do my duty."

And your duty, Daughter?

"To destroy the servants of the Lord of Night."

Thunder struck the sky above her; lightning flashed from the sky beneath. And from that lightning, forked and treacherous, a path formed; it glittered like crystal, sharp and hard.

Two paths. Two different paths.

She started to place her foot upon the one beneath her feet, but Margret had not finished speaking.

"And after you have destroyed them, then what?"

She looked at Margret. "I don't know. I don't care."

"But I do."

"You asked for the truth. That is the only truth I know."

"Then find a different truth. Find another one."

She was so like Ruatha, her wife. And her brother Adam had been so like Deirdre. The roughness of their voices, the darkness of their skin, the strangeness of their uninhibited words, were cosmetic.

She looked away. "Matriarch," she said, struggling for distance, "we must walk."

And because that, too, was truth, Margret released her. But her words stayed with Diora for a long time.

"None? You think too highly of yourself, or too poorly of me."

Elena scrabbled across the ground, choosing her path in that motion. She knew that the creature before her was simply a different death, but instinct had already made the choice, and she followed it blindly. Her blood left a weak trail across the sand; the sun would dry it; the wind would bury it. But she knew a moment's fear: in the North, blood brought predators. She had never thought to fear them in the desert.

She felt the night behind her; it was cold. Too cold.

"Lord Ishavriel. What a pleasant surprise." The creature reached out; she took his hand before she drew another breath.

It, too, was cold. Without effort, he lifted her to her feet. "You will stay here," he told her quietly, although he did not look down at her again.

"Telakar. Do not interfere."

"Interfere? Have you laid claim to these lands? A pity that this was not made clear."

She struggled for breath. Lost it twice.

"Let me make it clear. I have no quarrel with you, but you interfere in my game. Leave, and I will overlook your trespass."

Elena was Voyani. She had traveled the *Voyanne* before she could walk, bundled in the slings in which the Arkosans carried their children. She had taken her first steps, halting and clumsy as all children were, beneath the open sky. She had chosen, as an adult, to tread the path the Matriarchs had first tread; to follow their laws, to live by their mandate.

She had always thought she understood why.

Squaring her shoulders, she raised her head and looked, full and long, upon the two who now spoke. They were her enemies. She had never seen them before, but she knew them. The *Voyanne* had been created to lead the Arkosans away from the games and the subterfuge of creatures such as these.

In the distance, struggling as she had struggled, she saw the man who had once been her cousin. His sword was the brightest of lights, a shard in his hand. The Voyanne was no longer beneath his feet, and no matter where he walked, he would never find it again, for he walked by the side of the Lady's enemies.

"Telakar."

The creature he named smiled. "Will you draw your sword here? Here of all places? Draw it, then."

"I need not waste that power on you. Return to your master."

The creature's face was as beautiful—and giving—as alabaster. Pale, unblemished, he stood at a distance that time had not touched, could not breach. "My master is otherwise occupied." He smiled.

Lord Ishavriel returned that smile, edge for edge.

As one, they drew their weapons.

And the weapons were not of steel, although they glittered as coldly; they were fire, the essence of fire, and they burned red and bright as they clashed.

Neither path was smooth. The semblance of stone bore cracks and gashes, as if the rock had risen at the breaking of earth; the crystal was sharp and difficult to navigate.

Margret laughed, and if the amusement was bitter, it was genuine.

As she met Diora's eyes, she said, "*This* is like my mother."

"Your mother?"

"The heart of Arkosa couldn't be a peaceful, safe place; it couldn't be a haven; no. In the end, it had to be a battleground of tests, tests and more tests, each a failure waiting to happen."

"Did you fail her tests often?"

"All the time."

The Serra hesitated.

"What?"

"I was merely thinking that truth is not always a comfort."

"No. But that's a lot like my mother as well." She paused and inserted a healthy curse as her boots caught in a crack.

"If the path were easy to walk," the Serra said, "you would never trust it."

"And you would?"

"No. But I mistrust this one as well." She looked down at her feet. The crystals were sharp enough that the leather of her boots had been cut and gouged in several places.

She had thought it would be difficult to choose between the branches of the path, for they all seemed to lead nowhere; none strayed as far as the walls. But in the end, the choices were few.

They could choose paths that led away from each other, or they could choose ones that took them no farther apart than an arm's length, and in the end, they chose those.

The room did not seem endless.

The walk was.

When they met the first man on their separate roads, it seemed almost a natural consequence of having journeyed miles into a foreign land.

He was tall; taller than Stavos, perhaps as tall as the cold, pale-haired stranger who had taken to the skies in the folds of the wind to battle the Serpent. He wore armor as if it were silk, wore helm as if it were crown. The visor, however, was raised above a proud, dark face.

Across his chest was a familiar symbol. The outer circle was etched in red, the inner in blue; the crescents were drawn in gold, and the line that bisected them in ebony. Arkosa. Tor Arkosa. But there were no runes between the two circles.

He carried a naked blade, and the shape of the blade was the only thing about the warrior that did not seem foreign. But the length of the steel was lit from within by an unnatural golden light, a light that was matched only by the color of his eyes.

He had demon eyes.

They warded themselves automatically, like nervous girls.

He bowed.

His lips moved, but no sound passed them.

Diora lifted the Heart of Arkosa in a trembling palm. The chain was secure around her neck; it did not budge. Instead, it seemed to gather weight; the stone grew heavy. "Margret."

The Matriarch nodded, but kept an eye on the silent stranger as she lent Diora her strength.

Together they raised the Heart until it rested between them.

". . . she has sent me. She has spoken with the Seven, to no avail; she has spoken with the Sen adepts." He closed golden eyes, and for a moment a terrible loss transformed his features. He gathered himself before he spoke again, but they knew, as they watched him, that the news he spoke had broken something in him. "She did not return from that meeting. I am sorry. I have failed you. But the laws are clear; the god-born may not enter the seat of the Tor. She would not heed my warning."

The last words were bitter.

He knelt. Laid his sword upon the ground.

Before he released it, Margret spoke. "No. I do not accept your death."

He rose again, and his features were utterly changed; his eyes no longer shone gold, and his sword was the color of night. "Accept it, Matriarch. It is long in the past. You desired truth. You will have it. Come. The past waits, and I will lead you to it."

He turned and began to walk.

Margret looked at the ground beneath his feet. "Diora."

"He . . . his voice . . ."

"I know."

The Serra shook her head. "He serves the Lord of Night."

"Yes," Margret said, weakly. "But he serves—or served—Arkosa."

"You cannot say that with certainty. If this is a test—"

"It is no test. Yollana told me to use only the old roads. I think . . . that there are no roads in Arkosa as old as the one he walks."

He turned, as if the dead could still hear conversation. "Margret," he said quietly. Imperiously.

She turned to Diora. "Wait, if you must. But I have no other choice." She began to walk, and Diora caught her elbow.

"I will go where you go, Margret. For as long as our paths cross, I will go where you go."

He led them into a long hall.

Unnatural illumination vanished. Spokes of sunlight streamed between tall columns that had almost certainly been designed to catch and cut their light. Through glass and lead, sun told a story against the stone floor; a story that was punctuated by the near-silent movement of men and women robed in pale silks. Their heads were shaved, their faces shaved; their skin was golden but pale. They did not look up at the passing of the armored man, but instead knelt to ground as he walked by.

Margret knew they were not free.

Each man and woman bore, in the center of their foreheads, the mark of Arkosa.

And Margret bore it now, like a brand, across her memory. She could have asked for so many things in this room, this stronghold, this hidden place. But she had asked for the truth.

He led her, quickly, through these cloisters of light and life, and she was glad to escape them.

Until she arrived at the doors.

He stopped before them. Bowed. His sword had disappeared, but she knew that he contained it somehow; that he could summon it should the need arise.

"The Tor awaits. Sen Margret?"

She nodded grimly. She had never heard the word *Sen* before, but she knew it anyway: It was, of all things, a title.

Something to separate her from the serafs who had fallen to the floor as she passed them by.

And more. It was an old word; it held power.

"Sen Margret, your sister is not welcome."

"The Tor told you that?"

"He was most explicit." The regret was genuine, if unspoken. So, too, was the threat.

"Very well." She turned to Diora. She blinked as she saw that Voyani robes had given way to something resplendent—the silks of the High Court. White and gold adorned her left shoulder; her right was exposed to light as it seldom was. The robes of the Lord's consort. No—that was not quite right. They were the robes of a woman who might one day hope to be the Tor's consort.

But her sister had no such desire. *Sister?* Diora was not her sister. She was the pale, perfect daughter of an unknown Widan; the widow of the man who might have ruled the Tor Leonne, had he survived.

And yet the word *sister* suited her completely. It was, as the word *Sen,* some artifact of the past. It did not denote blood; it did not denote family.

Margret struggled with her knowledge of the Voyani; struggled to contain it in the tide of this other woman's life.

For she had no doubt at all that she was walking in the steps of another woman's life.

Whose?

She shook her head, to clear it.

Flowers trailed from the side of her sister's hair down the length of her cheek and nestled behind her ear; among the blossoms, diamonds and pearls had been arranged, where they might shine or glitter in the sunlight between columns. She wore combs of gold and jade and emerald, and her shoulders, exposed to light, were as pale as cream. But she was no simple consort, no matter how beautiful and demure she appeared. Any one of those combs could kill a man, should she have reason to draw it from the sheath of her hair. Margret could not remember seeing the action, but she knew it was true. Viscerally.

She gave in to memory. To the truth of a distant past. "Return to the Sanctum if I do not leave this room within the hour."

"Sen Margret," she replied serenely.

"Constans, you have your duty."

"Sen Margret."

She thought of threatening him, but there was no point; the Tor was certainly aware of her presence, and the longer it remained on the wrong side of the doors, the more of an insult she would be deemed to have offered. The doors were bound; she could not see through them. Nor did she try. She had once seen magic used within this hall by a man whose name was not written in blood across the sigils and wards that protected the Tor.

The end of the Sen who had attempted such careless invocation had been very, very long. And her name, as his, was not a part of the complicated protections the Tor had chosen to weave.

She did not touch the doors as she approached them; she merely waited. She knew that they would open.

They did.

The Tor sat on the throne of the inner chamber. It was delicate and fine; the work of the Deepings. Thus did the Lords of the forest offer tribute; for it was a living chair, and its roots went deep.

She was used to this sight, and would have paid it little heed—but gathered at his back like a wall were the Seven.

The personal mages of the Tor. His most powerful councillors.

She passed beneath the doors' arch.

"Sen Margret. You were otherwise occupied?"

And knelt at once, although she hated the posture. "Forgive me, *Tyr Sen Ar* Tor. There has been . . . some difficulty." She did not use the most formal of his titles; her own rank did not demand it. Her rank demanded nothing but the use of the unadorned "Tor," but prudence had its own rules. She chose the most significant of the embellishments and used them carefully.

Even though, to some part of her mind, they meant nothing at all.

"Indeed. It is because of that difficulty that you have been summoned."

He did not bid her rise.

She did not. He was not a patient man; he would either decide to kill her, or he would grow bored of so open a display of displeasure. She did not particularly care which he chose, and that was significant.

It was a better death than the one she faced in the Sanctum.

"I regret to inform you that your father's daughter failed in her attempt to destroy me."

She had already placed her full weight upon her knees; there was almost no change in her posture.

"Have a care, Sen Margret. I am aware that the girl was of little value to you, and that she was willful. But your value to me is diminishing. You may rise."

She did not ask about her sibling. She never asked.

"The Lord of the Altar raised the mountains across Tor Haval. He failed to destroy the City, but it is weakened. The Lord of War has, however, breached the defenses of Tor Ellaan. I believe it will fall within the week."

She had heard as much.

"You have been in contact with the Queen."

She did not deny it, although she felt a sharp panic at the questioning.

"Allasakar sent word today. He has informed me that she is preparing to meet his host upon the hidden road. Is this true?"

"I am not in her confidence."

"And you have had no visions? The scribes have sent scant word in the last three weeks, and I dislike the silence."

"Sela Tyr Sen Ar Tor," she said, grazing stone with her forehead. It was cool. "The Voyani have had few visions of relevance to the war since the last one."

"Ah, yes. The betrayal of Allasakar."

She almost spoke then. The words pressed up in a rush behind her lips; she clenched her jaw and swallowed them.

"The Sanctum does not house the only seers in the City. And while the visions of the Sen Voyani are often true, they are often too murky to be of value. Were it not for the alliance, Tor Arkosa would have fallen to the Lord of the Altar. Were it not for the power of Allasakar, Tor Arkosa's gates would have been shattered by the Lion. Were it not for the shadows of the Lord of Night, Tor Haval would lie in ruins now, and the Northern gods would at last have free reign in the heartlands. Is *that* what you hope to accomplish? How long, Sen Margret, do you think any of the gods would suffer us to rule as we have done?"

"We do not rule here by the sufferance of Allasakar," she said, her momentary anger genuine. And then she fell silent. The words felt true.

But they were not.

"My Sen have evaluated the missives of your scribes; they have questioned them carefully. Allasakar has always valued the gifts of the Sanctum—as you are no doubt aware. He has requested our aid in this matter, and we have chosen to comply. Necessity breeds strong alliances. Will the Queen ride with the host upon that path?"

"I have not seen it."

"Do you believe it to be true?"

"It is a possibility."

"The season is Winter?"

"Yes, Sen Tor."

"Very well. Take the Sen of the Sanctum against her."

"P–pardon, Sen Tor?"

"You will take the field against her. Allasakar must be allowed to pass."

She felt panic now. She quelled it.

"Sen Margret, have you seen something that you wish to share with me?"

She swallowed. "Sen Tor—Allasakar has been our ally for the past fifty years, but he is confident that he has almost isolated his enemies. If he scatters the Arianni, there is little that will stand in his way in the South; the Northern gods have retreated beyond the mountain chains. He will—"

"Vision is a tool. Not a leader. You *will* stop Arianne before she interferes. That is all."

She left his room.

Sen Diora, her sister, was waiting for her.

"He did not listen."

She shook her head. "Constans, come."

They walked. When she was certain that she might speak without interference, she said to Constans, "Gather the sacrifices. We will make the offerings and the bindings necessary to begin our work."

"What work, Sen Margret?"

"The Tor has ordered us to take the field against the Winter Queen."

He was silent.

She could almost hear his sudden anticipation, and she wanted to slap him.

She walked. She walked as the Sen Margret, but as words receded and anger ebbed, she could see the harsh track of the *Voyanne* beneath her feet. She could see Diora, and although the clothing and the minute difference of features masked her face, it did not hide her from view. The buildings were so fine they became the towering artifacts of something akin to dream.

As nightmare was akin to dream.

The Tor of the Tor Arkosa was a man who served the interests of Allasakar.

That was not news to her. It was a part of the wisdom and lore of the Matriarchs: the men in power had betrayed mankind by allying themselves with the Lord of Night.

But wisdom was small and crippled; the truth was grander.

And far, far more terrible.

She did not wish to *be* the Sen Margret because that woman, thousands of years ago, could hear the whisper of the dark god's voice across the length and breadth of the City, and it spoke *to* her; it spoke *of* her.

What had the *Serra* Diora said of Constans when she had first heard him speak? *That man is a servant of the Lord of Night.*

Why was it, Margret thought faintly, that she had not heard the same truth in the Sen Margret's voice?

For it was true.

As she approached the Sanctum, the serafs in the streets became sparser. Across from the long, proud stretch of the Sanctum, the tower of the Sen adepts rose without pause; it cast a shadow by which time could be told, as if the whole of the City were simply the face of a sundial that served the adepts' convenience.

She gained the steps that she took only when she had sallied out on official business; the doors at their foot, set in from the steps both for the sake of beauty and the practicality of magical defense, were open and waiting for her.

Constans had traveled ahead at her command; she was left in the company of her sister; her sister almost never left her side.

But there were exceptions to that rule, as the day had proved, and she went straight from that exception to the next without pause. Or perhaps with minuscule pause: she stood outside of the altar room a moment, her hands on the door. It was in this room that Allasakar's voice was strongest; his power greatest. She had chosen the room for two reasons: the first, that it would focus and hone his power; that it would give him access to her when access was desired.

The second, more complicated, was that it had been designed to invoke his attention, and things might be done beyond its walls that might fall beneath his notice if they were otherwise occupied.

And they had often been otherwise occupied, the Lord of the Shadows and the Sen Margret of the Sanctum.

"Sen Margret?"

She shook her head. "It is nothing. Wait for me here."

Within the chamber, she lit the fires.

They burned, but they burned black as she waited. She did not kneel. She did not abase herself. There were no witnesses of note.

The shadows grew dense, grew heavy; she felt the hair on the back of her neck rise, and knew the storm was gathering.

But she was unprepared for it when it unfolded; it unfolded in the shape of a man. The Sen Margret *had* power. She called it now, called it carefully; it permeated every inch of her body, from the base of her heels to the top of her head. She ached with it; it was a dangerous form of containment.

The Avatar of the Lord of Night entered the chambers.

"Sen Margret." His voice was the voice of the multitude, a god's voice in full glory.

"My Lord."

"Have you come bearing word? You have been absent of late, and I have . . . missed you."

"No, my Lord. I have come to ask for your power and

your blessing, for I am sent to clear the hidden way of the Arianni."

He stepped forward, and she waited.

She did not flinch when he touched her face. Instead, she leaned into that caress.

The worst of the memory that unfolded before her next was not the certain knowledge that she had spoken to Allasakar in the course of her stewardship. It was not the fact that the dark god was her ally and a source of her power. It was not the memory of his lips against her forehead, and the scar those lips left, unseen, that would never leave; for if she thought about that moment, she felt a desire that dwarfed all desires save one. It was not even the fact that she was a person of power in a Court with more slaves than she had seen in her life.

It was the deaths of the sacrifices.

From the tone of her words, she had thought to see goats, sheep, even cats.

But four people were brought to her—a baby, a boy, a youth, and a man, and she slaughtered them all in the heart of her sanctum in the City of Arkosa.

For power.

For power's sake.

Sen Constans stood in the mists that had grown up from the floor around him like vines. "How much of the truth can you bear, Matriarch?"

She was too busy retching to answer him.

But the Serra Diora was not. "She can bear as much of the truth as she must. But she will remember everything that you have chosen to show her, and if her duty is to Arkosa, choose carefully."

He did not laugh, but laughter filled the air.

"Well spoken, Daughter. Well spoken, indeed."

It was a woman's voice.

"Sen Constans, you have served your purpose. Leave us now."

He bowed, but even before that gesture had reached the zenith of its respect, he had faded from view.

Beneath the open sky, and above it, a woman stood.

She was older than Margret, and as beautiful as any highborn man's concubine, but she carried her power like a visible mantle.

"And now you know, Margret, daughter of Evallen, and Diora, daughter of Alora. *We* served the Lord of Night."

The Serra Diora was quiet.

"Do you judge us, Daughter?"

"Yes."

Margret rose to her feet. "And I, as well."

"Good. Remember that. We lived in a world of gods. We fought in a world of gods. We did what we deemed necessary to survive. And we learned from our mistakes. Your ancestors were gifted with sight. They saw the fall of the Cities of Man, and they saw the betrayal of Allasakar. But they could not convince the Tors of the truth of their vision.

"Are you ready, Daughter? You have not yet finished walking the path."

Margret drew herself to her full height. Diora thought her beautiful and wild, in a way that this woman—that Diora herself—could never be. "Yes." The word was a curse.

"Sen Margret."

She steeled herself for the inevitable, and turned once again to face her past. Her people's past. She was dressed in finery that made the High Court seem pragmatic, and she was adorned by titles that separated her from the people that she governed. Or killed.

She could not even name the fabric that she wore; it was heavy, but it was smoother than silk, and it caught the light in a way that suggested metal.

"Sen Maris is waiting. He asks you to inspect his work; he will be missed soon."

She nodded. Her hand fell to the hilt of a sword; the edges of the heavy gem at its top cut into her palm. She knew, then, that the fabric she wore seemed metallic because it was; she was armed for battle, here, in the heart of the Sanctum, in her personal stronghold.

The young woman who had been sent for her was dressed in a similar fashion; adorned in the colors of Arkosa, she waited. Margret dismissed her curtly before turning to the Serra—the Sen—Diora.

"Accompany me, Sister."

The Sen Diora nodded. But she walked behind.

Although Margret did not know where she was to go, history did, and the path it followed was not direct. They did not leave the grand chambers in which she was ensconced; instead they passed the pit in the floor that was used to invoke the changing maps of the Southern cradle. It lay dormant now; she wondered idly if it would ever be invoked again. The maps would be almost useless in a span of days; perhaps a month at most.

She lifted a hand, twisted it in the air. The gesture itself was precise, mechanical, and devoid of personal magic. The young woman waited in silence as the fountain in the eastern wall began to bubble. The whole of the wall had been devoted to the fount; it was carved from a single slab of stone that stretched seamlessly from window to door. The sculptor was long dead, but he had been maker-born, and his gift was evident in the subtlety of the dance of shapes that lingered beneath rock; they were human, or they had once been human. A face peered out of the rock, eyes closed; a hand reached out; two bodies entwined as if in play.

Of all the adornments in the room she claimed as her own, this was her favorite, this ghost dance. The waters that surrounded their feet did not touch them, but to her eye, the trapped forms were active only when the water played. They moved now.

She closed her eyes. Concentrated.

"I love this fountain," she said softly.

"That much is clear, Sen Margret. Of the edifices in the Sanctum, not one is better protected against age or malice than this."

"And what other should be? Of all the makers' works that we have gathered, only this bears the madness of the true artisan. It speaks of the dead to the living; it gives truth to the lie that death is the only way in which we might know peace."

She opened her eyes; she was ready.

She knew what would happen, this day. She had been born with the talent of vision, and she had used it as ruthlessly as she had dared, sparing no one. Not even herself.

"Or play?" The younger woman touched her face, her

palms gentle, her eyes for a moment much older than the smooth, pale skin of her features implied.

And should they not be? The eyes had seen much the body had been protected from.

"No, today they do not play." And she walked among the fallen, heard the distant chimera of their laughter, and felt the cold, cold touch of their limbs as she passed *through* them.

There were many ways of traversing the Sanctum, itself a small city within the City of Arkosa. But they were, all of them, magical, and such conveyances could be both watched and tampered with.

And today, she could afford no such witnesses. The worst was almost over, but it was not over yet, and until it was done, discovery was too costly.

She lingered in the waters of the fountain, and then left them and began to walk down the hidden hall, her steps muted beneath the rough ceiling.

"Where is Sen Adoll?

"She has taken the Northern watch."

"The Northern watch? Why?"

"I do not know. She did not explain herself. But at the morning meal, she spent half an hour staring into her empty bowl and weeping. She would take no questions, and when her sister attempted to summon the scribe, she forbid it."

"Forbid it?"

"With prejudice. She . . . fused the door to the wall."

"Then the scribes did not question her."

"No, Sen Margret."

"Did she speak of her vision at all?"

Her sister hesitated. "She did."

"To her sister?"

"Only to her sister. One of the slaves died when she demanded the clearing of the room and he did not move quickly enough."

"And her sister?"

"She accompanied Sen Adoll to the North."

The vision must have been strong. "Was she tainted by the madness?"

Her sister's laugh was brief. Bitter. "You must look at the room when you have finished. I am not a judge of Sen

Adoll, but I confess that I am grateful that your visions are not so shattering, even if they are not so sharp, so clear."

"They are sharp enough."

"Margret—"

"No. Do not weaken, and do not weaken me. If there is time, if there is time, Diora, I will take whatever you offer and be glad of it. But today—"

She had stopped walking. Stopped although every minute was precious, every minute that she delayed brought them closer to discovery and death.

"Sen Margret?"

"Bear witness. Bear witness, Sister, but do not interfere. No matter what you see. No matter what it costs. Promise me this."

"Margret, you frighten me."

"I? I have never frightened you."

"You did not send for a scribe."

"Did I say that I had a vision?" Her voice was so light it had to carry a lie.

The Sen Diora's glare was almost baleful. "When? When did you have this vision? The laws that govern the Sanctum state clearly that a scribe must be summoned if the vision is true."

Margret laughed. "The laws that govern the Sanctum are the laws that govern Tor Arkosa. If I choose to ignore them, and I am powerful enough, they mean nothing."

"If. When, Sen Margret?"

"Three days. Three days. And three days."

"The same vision?"

"At heart, the same. I am prepared. I will not falter. If you falter, remember this: All of Arkosa will perish. We cannot save the Tor—"

"And I would not, given the choice."

"—and we cannot save Tor Arkosa. We cannot win the battle. But we have been betrayed, and we will have justice in the end. Immortality is only one way of ensuring victory through the ages; there are others."

"They are all bad. I want no immortality, Sen Margret. I have borne this life, and I do not want the burden to continue beyond the span of years I am given."

Margret turned and began to walk. Stopped. "Diora—"

"Yes?"

"I do not like the news you have brought. Sen Adoll is the most powerful of our number, and if she is riven by madness, she may speak without being aware of the cost. The Northern watch is too vulnerable to spies."

"Her sister is with her. And her sister understands the cost. Trust her."

"I trust only you."

"As much as you can."

"As much as I can."

She started to walk and hesitated again, and knew herself a coward. It was a weakness she loathed.

We have chosen our path, she thought. *We will be true to it. We will pay the price.*

She did not hesitate again.

The halls in the Sanctum were almost bare; the lights along the ceiling had yet to be laid, and the oaths that she and the Senni Voyani had together sworn had not yet been laid into stone. Nor would it be until the end; until they were ready to abandon their ancient home, they could not afford to have their words committed to anything but memory and heart.

The Tor suspected.

He had closed the gates, as Sen Adoll had foreseen. They were guarded now by the *Kialli,* and even the Sen adepts were loath to test themselves against the lords who watched.

Allasakar was coming to the South.

He had been promised armies with which to invade the Northern Isles. There, he hoped to destroy the handful of gods that remained, and seal his claim upon this world.

But if the gates were guarded, there were older ways still which were not.

She placed her palm against the first door; her sister placed her palm against the second. The door thinned and vanished, allowing them entry into the cavern.

Sen Maris waited. He was the oldest of the Sen adepts, and of the Sen, the most powerful. He wore his age like a crown. She bowed before it, granting survival the respect that it was due.

"It is done, Sen Margret. The vessels are ready."

She walked around the edge of the room, gazing at his work: containments of crystal and magic, clear as purified glass, crouched within the walls. She inspected them carefully. But she did not touch them.

"If you can invoke them, they will rival the seven spheres." He was silent as he met her gaze. "If you think to remove a witness to your crime, I would caution you against it."

"Because I will fail?"

"Perhaps."

"Because you have built your protection into these spheres?"

His smile was thin. "You hear a lie when it is spoken; I will therefore trouble you not to speak it, one way or the other. I have placed much of my power within these orbs, and until they are invoked, that power will remain where it now resides. I would not have done this if I did not believe what you have seen will come to pass in some fashion.

"But this is Tor Arkosa, and it is my home. I will not travel with you, Sen Margret. And because I will not travel with you, my place will be among the seven. If you seek to avoid pursuit, you want the seven to be at the height of their power."

"Indeed." She bowed. "You have my gratitude, Sen Maris, and my promise: Tor Arkosa will fall, but of the league, it will be one of five that rises again."

An expression very similar to pain rippled across his placid features. "Only five."

"There were to have been eight," she told him, although it was unnecessary. "But three of our conspirators have failed."

"And the others?"

She lifted her head. Counted the great glass orbs within the walls. There were seven.

As if she had not heard his question, she walked quietly toward the cavern's center. The ceilings had been carved up into a peak; they were lifeless, dark, shadowed by the poor light. Sen Maris had asked her if she desired illumination in this chamber, and she had quietly demurred.

She did not need light to see by, not here.

The eighth globe was suspended in air. Its glass was so fine, so thin, the layer so clear, she knew a moment of panic. If it failed, if it was as delicate as it appeared—

"It is the finest of my works here," Sen Maris said, almost coldly. He could not read her thoughts. She *knew* this with certainty, although had he desired to do so, he had the power; he was one of perhaps three men who did. But her hesitation, brief though it was, was critical enough; his was a brittle pride.

But a justified one.

"My . . . profound apologies for my lack of grace, Sen Maris. I could not conceive of such creation with my own meager skill, my own lesser ability."

He was only barely mollified. *Now,* she thought, and her knees shook. Her lips were dry, but her expression did not falter at all. She bowed to him, and he gestured.

Light flared briefly around his body, a signature. She had become familiar enough with his work that she recognized the distinctive flavor of his magic.

But not so certainly as she recognized the power that ringed that light, denying it.

She turned to face her son.

CHAPTER THIRTY

"Sen Margret," he said, lifting his sword. His true sword, not the weapon that he adorned his armor with. Her hand had fallen to the hilt of her own jewelry; the ruby beneath her skin was cold and dark.

He was so very, very beautiful. His skin was neither the pale, untouched white of the cloistered Sen, nor the bronzed and darkened sheen of the simple soldier, but some golden color between these two extremes that at once suggested both. His hair was as dark as hers had been in her youth, and his eyes were as wide and expressive as Diora's.

But his mouth was thinner, his lips—and his expression—far less generous.

"Adar—"

"Diora." The word was sharp. "If you move, I will be forced to kill you."

Her son. Her only son.

Her sister did not move again.

"You will allow Sen Maris to leave us," Margret said evenly. "No accusation you make against him will stand in the face of the Tor's need."

"You mistake me, Mother," he said, bowing.

She felt the cold. She knew it would never leave her. Her son had been her pride, the single thing of value to come from his father's line.

"Do I?"

"I have not come to accuse anyone of any crime. Sen Margret, you are the scion of an old and honorable family. You understand the value of that lineage. If you are unwise, you are never unwise enough to threaten what the family has spent so many centuries in building.

"The Tor knows this, of course." He bowed to Sen

Maris, and that bow was genuine. "Sen Ar Maris," he said, choosing the formal title. "You honor my family with your presence."

Sen Maris inclined his head. He was a mage of subtlety and power, and he feared little.

But he was wise enough to understand that fear had value.

"My apologies for my interruption. But the work that you have undertaken on behalf of my family is complicated and delicate. My mother has been . . . busy of late. Her duties to the armies of the Tor have consumed much of her power. I have brought scribes chosen by the Tor himself to aid her in understanding the significance of her visions, that she may better serve her lord.

"But as her duties have been grueling, I am certain that she has not had the time to familiarize herself with the significance of what you have built.

"She is not, after all, an adept." He smiled. "But she has raised no fool. I *am* an adept, and if you will take the time to explain your work to me, I will see that you are fully compensated for it."

He turned his attention to his mother. "Sen Margret," he said coldly, "the Tor's scribes await you in your chambers. They have been ordered to bring you to the Citadel without delay. You will leave your sister in the Sanctum. But have no fear; realizing the importance of *our* family, the Tor has personally chosen the adepts who will guard you against possible harm while you reside within the Citadel."

She knew, of course.

Sen Maris met her gaze. He raised a pale brow, and she almost flinched at what she saw in his eyes. But she nodded.

"Will you claim the Sanctum, Sen Adar?" Sen Maris was quiet. Respectful.

"I will."

"No man has ruled the Sanctum for more than a handful of years."

Her son shrugged. "I merely seek to shepherd it through the difficult absence of my mother."

"You will guide seers with no vision of your own? You are brave, Sen Adar."

"No. I am merely capable. What is this room?" As if it

were the trace of breath upon morning glass, his smile faded.

Sen Maris fingered the length of his beard almost absently. The line of his shoulders shrank; his neck shortened. He seemed to recede into age, to be swallowed by it. Only the robes of the Sen gave lie to the appearance of age, for no other house dared to adopt the silvered emerald hue as their own, and he wore them with the carelessness of long association with power.

"I am afraid that if the Sen Margret is forced to evacuate the Sanctum in all due haste, you will receive little answer to that question."

Eyes that were beautiful at their widest narrowed unpleasantly. "I serve the Tor directly. I am one of the Seven adepts. You will answer the question."

"And who did you kill to take that title?"

"Sen Barres."

He raised a brow. "You are accomplished for your age, Sen Adar. Accomplished enough to judge the truth of my words in whatever fashion you deem suitable." There was a threat in the calm statement.

Sen Adar did not choose to hear it, but he was silent for a moment while he considered his options.

Margret gazed upon him dispassionately. If he attempted to take the Sanctum in anything other than name, the Sanctum would destroy him. He was her son, but he had never understood the delicate balance of power maintained among those who walked the thin edge between madness and vision.

Those of lesser power, of course, could be used when vision was upon them, but they could not invoke that power at will. Unfortunately, those that could invoke it at will could not ignore it at all; they were often overtaken by vision when it was least convenient.

Sen Margret was among the former, but those with greater power tolerated her because they *knew* that she always worked in the best interests of the Sanctum. And they would read her son's lies so easily.

"Very well," her son said at last. Sen Adar. She must think of him as the man he had become, not the boy he had once been. "Sen Margret, you will oblige me by explaining the purpose of this room."

She hesitated, or appeared to hesitate, and he turned to the only obvious weakness she had: her sister. Diora was completely impassive.

The sisters who served the Sen of the Sanctum had been trained from birth to accept death. They had no family; they could bear no children. The only ties they were given were ties to the women they served. Some of the Sen were careless with the lives of their sisters. Sen Adoll in particular had survived five, but of the Sen who served, she was the most powerful, and it was considered both honor and duty to serve her.

But some of the Sen formed attachments to the women who had been raised with none; trusting them, in truth, with everything that they hid even from family.

And Sen Margret did not insult her son's intelligence by pretending that she was not one of those.

She walked, carefully, toward her son, summoning none of her power. He was warded, of course, and although she knew some of his weaknesses, he had long since passed the age where she could easily discern his strengths.

"Of course," she said quietly. She passed him, as if he were still a child, and she a lesson master given charge of his education.

The slight was not lost on him.

"There is no magic within these structures," she said, although she knew he could see that for himself. "But they are the finest containments that could be built discreetly." She passed beneath the first of the crystals. It stood at a height a foot above hers; if her son desired to do so, he could reach out to touch the transparent rounded curve. He was no fool. He kept his hands to himself.

As did she. The crystals drained power when it was offered them, and that power did not return.

"The Sanctum has long been a thorn in the side of the gods," she continued, passing beneath the first as she made her way to the second. "Twice, *Arianni* have come to kill those they could glean information about."

He shrugged.

The *Arianni* were not the only assassins the Sanctum had to fear. "But against the power of Allasakar, their threat is a pale shadow."

"Do not lecture me, Sen Margret. I am aware of your

petition to the Tor, and I am aware of his refusal to hear it. You do not claim to know all of his power. Trust that it is great enough to withstand all enemies."

The old arguments were strong. "The Tor does not claim to have the sight. What we offered him was—"

"Fear. Weakness. Hesitancy. Continue. You have little time."

She had passed the third of the spheres. She stopped a moment beneath it. "Fear is not, in itself, a failing. It is a mine, like any other; work it, and you will have the raw materials that become caution or prudence."

He was angry.

So, too, was she.

"The room, Mother."

"It was meant to be the seat of our power. These globes, in miniature, are replicas of the Seven."

He fell silent then. She continued to walk as the enormity of that claim sank in.

"Sen Maris, is this true?"

"Your mother is not given to empty mimicry. There are seven spheres for a reason."

"And that reason?"

"I believe you must ask the Sen Margret. I might be able to answer that question if I were given leave to study the spheres when they are in use. The spheres, as you can see, are not active."

"And you would provide this power?"

"Not for the Sanctum, no."

"I . . . see." Disappointment came and went, like a passing breeze, across his features. His hands, clenched a moment in fists, relaxed as he turned from Sen Maris. "This is most interesting. Please. Continue, Sen Margret."

She had quickened her pace, passing beneath the fourth sphere and onto the fifth by the time her son caught up with her. He was taller than she, taller than his father. Had he been born with the seer's talent, things might have been different.

But he had not. That past was simply another dream, and she had long since learned that the realm of dream and the realm of nightmare were almost the same.

"The Sanctum is the heart of the City," she said quietly.

"In Tor Arkosa, nothing but the Citadel has stood for longer."

"I am not interested in history."

"No? Very well. But I fear you will be disappointed, Sen Adar. This room was created for the sole purpose of protecting the legacy of Arkosa. Our history is contained within these walls. Men and women whom I have chosen will—would have—become the voices of our age, and their knowledge—what they would be willing to part with—would remain here."

"This is a . . . library?"

"It is that, and more." She had passed the sixth sphere. The seventh waited, and she paused again as her son approached. "Tor Arkosa will fall to Allasakar."

"The city will not be destroyed. The Tor has been offered proof of that. The Sanctum does not hold the only seers within Arkosa."

"Nor has it claimed to."

"It has tried."

She shrugged. It was true. "We believe," she said calmly, "that the city will not be destroyed completely *because* of what we have chosen to accomplish here. In this room. This is the heart of the Sanctum."

"But it has not been invoked."

"No."

"And the power that would be gathered here upon such invocation has not yet been dedicated."

"Such an investiture of power would be seen across the cradle; there is not a City standing that would not feel it. The Tor himself would be forced to act against us, and he will not have the power, or the time."

Her son frowned. "Mother." He chose the word with care, and shaded it to wound. "I am not a fool. If such an invocation would draw the attention of the Tor, how would you have time to gather the information you desire to preserve?"

"I can answer that," Sen Maris interrupted.

"Please do."

"The gathering itself has already begun. You have seen messenger crystal, yes? Some similar substance has been imported here, in quantity. Its use is so common, it would not be noted; even were sufficient quantities gathered, the power contained within them could be inspected, its use discerned; messenger crystal is dedicated.

"But it is also finite. It is created to give a message to one who might otherwise be protected against more refined magicks.

"It is the preservation of that message that requires power." He did not move, as Margret moved, but his words carried in the belled shape of the rounded dome.

"Such a simple task—preservation—would not justify the complexity of the power that could be gathered in seven such spheres."

"Preservation is *not* a simple task," Margret snapped.

He smiled. "These are meant to gather and contain power." It was not a question.

"The power that can be gathered," Sen Maris continued, speaking above such an obvious observation, "cannot be gathered without limitation. These spheres are *not* the Seven. Those were created by Sen of greater nobility than now exist, and they were created in full sight of the Tor. They cannot be invoked without his blessing. They cannot be used against anyone who resides within the City."

"I am aware of their purpose, Sen Maris. Did I not say I was one of the Seven adepts?"

"Indeed. But men of ambition always examine objects of power with a mind to their personal use.

"Do you think that I would create such a repository if any Sen's power could be used to invoke it? I value my existence, Sen Adar. Were my power, my *raw* power, able to activate what Sen Margret designed, I would never have agreed to aid her. She is Arkosan. I would not have survived the completion of the task." He raised a pale brow, and glanced at the woman of whom he spoke.

Her smile was cold. "It is true. I have killed many people in order to preserve what we have built. A Sen of Maris' skill would be a challenge, but not beyond the realm of the possible."

Her son shrugged. "What protections did you build into the spheres? That the offer must be willingly made?"

"No. That would still give the Sanctum too much leeway. Too much power. Arkosa has long existed by the grace of a balance of power that I have no desire to alter. These spheres can only be invoked," he replied, with a sidelong glance at the Sen who had commissioned the work, "by the blood of Sen Margret."

Sen Adar did not look at her. But he lifted his head slightly at the mention of her name. His hand came to his chin, a gesture that had developed in his youth. She wondered if he was aware of the pose he struck. "The Seven cannot be invoked without absorbing—and destroying—the power offered to invoke them."

"The Seven above? No. These were designed to reflect their function in some fashion. When Sen Margret is ready to complete the circle, she will lose whatever she offers in pursuit of that task.

"But you must know that Sen Margret values the Sanctum above all else; if her death brings it immortality in a fashion, if her death ensures its survival . . ." He shrugged. "It was not her first choice."

That was both true and false. It was not what she had asked him for, when she had first approached him years ago. It was not the challenge she had tempted him with, when she had presented this intellectual, this rigorous, task. But it was, in the end, what she had desired.

She had trusted his prudence and his suspicion. He had offered his services in return for a small change in her plans: that it must be her power, the power of her blood, that set the spheres in motion.

"When the power is gathered, is it automatically dedicated, or could it be diverted? Could I use what lay within the spheres?"

Because she had seen the look that now crossed her son's face before, because she had seen that it would be offered her, now, in this room, she did not flinch from it; it did not wound her. It had already caused her all the pain that she could afford to allow.

"I do not believe that the power is automatically dedicated to a specific task. Were you to be present when that power was invoked, I believe you could divert it for your own use."

"You believe?"

"I do not know for certain. If such a repository were so easily built and so easily used, it would be seen across the length and breadth of the Cities of the cradle. They do not now exist."

"It takes a skill that is very rare to contemplate a containment of this nature."

"Indeed," Sen Maris said, with a brittle, but very real pride. "However . . . there is a reason that I will not be present when the power is gathered. If I have built a flawed vessel, if even one of the spheres is not precisely aligned, they will shatter."

"And you could not test this."

The question was beneath contempt. Sen Maris did not answer.

Margret did. "He was not allowed to test what would then be obvious, and undedicated, magic. We were to work in secrecy, if you recall."

Sen Adar shrugged the scorn aside. "Understood, Sen Maris. Is that all?"

"There is one other element of uncertainty involved. I built the containments, but the flavor was not mine; the signature that wards them, the identity that binds them, is the Sen Margret's."

"But . . . she is not a Sen adept."

"She is not a mage of your rank or power. But I have found, to my surprise, that she is not without skill."

She could see her son's open greed, but even that did not destroy the lines around his mouth, his eyes, the familiar contours of his face. She turned away from him and walked into the center of the room.

"How would that power be invoked?"

Sen Maris was silent.

"Sen Maris, I asked you a question."

"Indeed. I am old, but not infirm. I heard it."

When his silence lasted long enough that it was clear he did not intend to answer, Sen Adar made his first misstep. "Your presence here is not known. The Tor has no reason to suspect your . . . disloyalty. It would be unfortunate indeed if I were forced to disclose this information."

"Indeed. Unfortunate. The adept who forces the Tor to acknowledge that any of his *necessary* allies could work against him is unwise. I am an old man; you are a young one. Perhaps it is time to test the Tor's will in—"

"Sen Maris." Sen Margret lifted a hand, slowly turning her palm to expose it to her son's inspection. Everything, among people of power, was done slowly and carefully. "It is almost over. I will answer my son.

"But . . . thank you."

He bowed.

"Do not try anything, Mother. I am aware of your capabilities."

She nodded.

"Tell me what I wish to know."

"The spheres, as you suspect, have not been entirely dedicated. The power that is to reside within them *has* been promised. The bindings around the containments can only be broken with care, and at some risk to the Sen who would attempt to do so."

"You . . . bound . . . his magic?"

She shrugged. Answer enough.

"You were the author of that binding."

She did not answer.

"Mother, you know what I want. Your power will never again serve the family; it will never again serve the Sanctum. But I know my duty."

"And I am to give power to the man who has betrayed me?"

"I have not betrayed the family," he said simply. "Only one woman within its long line."

She had so desperately desired that her vision be fallible. It was a child's hope; a novice's hope. But she had not realized just how visceral that hope was until it died. Had she thought herself beyond pain?

She unsheathed her sword. He was not impressed, and not threatened, by the gesture; the sword was a simple steel artifact, no more. There was no magic upon it, no magic within it. And to summon a true weapon in this circumstance would invite her son to do the same.

She had no illusion; she knew that she could not stand against him in single combat.

She lifted the blade in a steady hand and drew it across her palm, spilling her blood upon the floor in the center of the room.

Her son approached her bent back.

"Do not touch me," she said quietly. "Do not disturb me. What is written in my blood must be written from beginning to end without interruption."

She *felt* the song of his power as he summoned his sword. Saw its glow across the stones; saw the shade of crimson change as golden light transformed it into a wet, ruby red.

She traced the circles of Tor Arkosa upon unyielding floor. Nothing absorbed the blood; nothing disturbed it. Outer circle, inner circle; the two crescents. She had made the cut a deep one; perhaps too deep. It was hard to keep up with the flow of the liquid that ran down her aching hand.

"The symbol of the City. Why the City, Mother? Why not the Sanctum? Why not the family?"

"Because, my son," she whispered, as the line of blood halved the inner circle, "the City will *not* be destroyed. We have made an alliance that is foolish in the extreme, and we will be betrayed by that alliance in ways that you cannot see.

"The Tor is a man of power. He understands everything about holding it; nothing about letting it go. If I had any other choice, I would have chosen a different course.

"But I have been touched by Allasakar. He knows me. He knows what motivates me, inasmuch as a god can ever understand the weakness and folly of mortality. *I* cannot stand against him; that was a part of his binding, and it burns me still with its weight and its imperative.

"But I have vowed that what I cannot do will still be done." She clenched her bleeding hand into a fist. "We are a proud people. But perhaps we have never been proud *enough*. My people will never serve Allasakar again. The cost may be written in blood; it may be written in time. But it is written."

She rose. "I give what I have valued. I give what I have honored."

He waited, his sword ready.

Her blood began to burn.

From the recesses of the ceiling that contained them both, that protected them from the watchful sky, the last sphere descended.

It was in form and substance no different from the spheres within the wall; it was the height of a man from the top of its curved surface to the bottom, a transparent bubble that might have been blown in delicate glass and offered to a spoiled child.

"What is this?" her son asked, the suspicion in his voice tainted by wonder. By a wonder she had not heard there since the death of his father a decade ago. Her pain was not a clean pain; it was complicated, and it clung.

She replied simply, "It is the sphere of invocation."

"Sen Maris?"

He, too, looked up, his gaze following the descent of the sphere. "It was not crafted by me, Sen Adar. It is . . . wholly of your mother's making."

"Impossible."

"Can you not see her signature?"

"My mother does not have the talent."

"The mother was not a clear judge of the character of her son; why should the son assume he has seen everything that his mother is capable of?" He glanced away a moment, as if to give them privacy, although his words continued. "What a parent shows a child is not what she shows the world outside of her family, but it is not all that she is. You have no children, Sen Adar. Or none that you have cared to lay claim to."

Sen Margret turned to her son.

"Is this what you desire?" The question was soft.

He hesitated for a moment, and his hesitation was almost her undoing. But his face closed; his expression became the expression she had seen on the faces of the men who had ruled Tor Arkosa for all of her life.

The sphere came at her call; it descended slowly, as light and ethereal as morning mist in the cradle's magnificent valleys. She reached up with both of her hands, exposing her palms to the delicate touch of its rounded surface. It weighed almost nothing.

Contact.

Beneath her palms, ice and fire blossomed, both living forces. She bore the pain because it was a simpler, cleaner pain. Her power, such as it was, flowered as the crystal began to draw it in.

The surface that had been transparent sparked and shifted. A moment of fear crossed her face as she recalled Sen Maris' words. She did not know if she had crafted well enough, and she stood beneath the matrix as it descended, wondering if it would shatter.

Wondering if that would be a worse death than the one that faced her.

She felt the crystal pulse beneath her hands. Saw clarity give way to cloud, a great, rolling blanket that obscured the rounded curve of ceiling, the unornamented gray of stone. Sparks of light burst from their depths, sparking and crackling as they leaped from surface to surface. *Gold,* she thought. *Silver. Blue.*

She closed her eyes; she could see the scars of their passage on the insides of her lids.

Her eyes snapped open as she heard the crisp slap of her son's leather boots against bare stone. "Do not touch the sphere!" she cried.

He laughed. "I am no fool, Sen Margret. I do not seek to take this task from you. I wish merely to bear witness."

"Stay your ground, Sen Adar!"

Her voice was weak.

The sound of lightning was stronger; the sound of thunder stronger still. Gold gave way to orange; silver to gray, blue to purple; red tinged the clouds that now filled the crystal, twisting and gathered as if to spring.

She staggered beneath the sphere's sudden weight. Bent her arms as it continued to descend, drawn to ground by gravity. She dropped to one knee. The sphere continued to fall, and she braced herself against the ground as it absorbed her strength.

Not yet. Not yet.

The walls danced; the light grew brighter and more dizzying as the colors of the spectrum were birthed in cloud. They struggled against the surface of crystal, gathering strength and speed. She could not contain them. Knew she could not. But bowed by the weight she had undertaken, she did.

She lowered her head; her forehead touched the side of the sphere; it was hot, fevered now. It was almost time.

"Diora!" she cried.

Her sister came.

Her son glanced back, hand on sword, his attention divided between them, Sen and sister, master and servant. But he did not interfere, did not cut her down as she lengthened her stride, as she ran.

She skidded to a halt before the burning circles that contained her Sen, her pale face reflecting the shade and shadow of a magic she had never possessed.

"Margret, what must I do?"

Margret could not answer; her lip bled where teeth pierced it. Her arms shook. Her legs shook.

Diora's hands caught her shoulders; braced her upper arms. It helped, but it was not enough.

"Margret, what must I do?"

Margret could not answer. She did not know. But she looked up, as she knelt, and saw her sister's pale face, and was comforted by what she saw there. She dropped her other knee. Not enough. It was not enough.

And her sister did the unthinkable, the unpredictable: She lifted the skirt of her dress, raised it above the grasping leap of flame's tongue, and came to stand within the inner circle.

"Diora, no—"

She lifted her hands, but not nearly as smoothly as Margret had done; all grace had deserted her simple movements. But she turned her palms up, her fingers already bent, her shoulders locked to take the weight that Margret could no longer bear on her own.

Sen Adar was silent.

Sen Maris was not. "Sen Diora," he said, his voice stern and loud, "You do not know what you do. You *must not* intefere. You have no skill, no gift." Lightning punctuated his words, the rise and fall of syllables.

And she turned to him, this woman who had been deprived of husband, of family, of the ability to bear her own children, begin her own line; light was reflected across the glowing sheen of her skin. "I have what I was born with, Sen Maris. I have what Sen Margret granted me. I will take that risk."

Her hands touched the sphere.

Margret watched in mute horror. She had not seen this. Her son, yes. Sen Maris, yes. But not this.

The sphere's weight was gone in the instant her sister accepted it.

She screamed. She screamed because Diora could not. The sphere could not draw power from her; it had been designed—they had all been designed—for her blood, and hers alone.

But it could draw life; it could draw breath; it could devour sight and hearing, touch, taste, all sensation. She could not stop it; she did not have the strength.

And had she, had she, she would have destroyed a life's work in the process, for to break the sphere was to destroy the dedication for which it was intended.

The scream went on and on, but Diora did not; she was rigid as magic scoured her of all signs of identity.

But she held the sphere.

She held it for long enough.

Lightning burst from its chrysalis, breaching the folds of cloud, the surface of crystal, bathing it with its light. It erupted toward the ceiling in a flurry of bristling, crackling energy, seeking escape, seeking release. The ceiling shattered, and shattering, broke the light; it flew wide, trapped in a pinwheel, strands of energy that spun out from what had been the curvature of dome.

Seven strands.

And each, pale and tenuous, was connected to the sphere held above the burning ground in two pairs of hands, one living, and one dead.

This should have been the moment of her triumph; the moment at which all sacrifice, all loss, was justified.

But she could not see it; her eyes were filmed and watery; her gaze was locked upon Diora's blind eyes.

One by one, the strands of light snaked toward the spheres set in the wall. They touched the surface of crystal, clung there, slowly enveloping each globe in a lattice of light.

"Sen Margret," her son said.

She turned, her forehead grazing her sister's death, her eyes weak with tears, her knees against the ground.

"Enough. You will release the sphere now."

She laughed.

"I warn you, Sen Margret. Your power is gone. You cannot hope to stand against me. I do not desire your death, but if it happens, it will serve a purpose. The Tor will know that I chose his service over my own bloodline."

"And will you kill me, Sen Adar? Will you brave the circle to take what I have made?"

He hesitated, this son, this stranger.

She raised the sphere in both hands. Diora's hands fell

away; she crumpled, a hollow shell, and the fire flared as it devoured what remained of her body.

He had never been a fool.

His eyes widened as she gained her feet. He lifted his sword, spoke a word; his shield appeared across his arm, shimmering opalescence.

But it did not matter; it served no purpose.

She threw the sphere.

He struck at it, and lost his blade; raised his shield, and lost that as well. The sphere descended upon him, its surface parting to swallow him whole.

He screamed.

Not in pain, for she had had enough mercy to spare him that. But she heard his rage give way to fear, his fear to terror, and his cries were not wordless.

The ground broke as he struggled. Gaps opened in the stone; earth rose and fell, like a slow, dark liquid. But the ground beneath her feet remained solid.

The light that was anchored by the sphere flared as it drew his power into the seven, feeding them, invoking them. She waited. Wept, for some part of her wanted to answer his pleas, to offer him a comfort that he would never have offered her.

She wrapped her arms around her body while her eyes slowly dried, and waited.

The silence was a blessing.

"Not my blood, Sen Maris," she said quietly. "But my bloodline."

Sen Maris did not speak. She did not look at him.

Instead, she continued to wait. The sphere collapsed in a rush of motion; clouds again broke the surface of the crystal and fled skyward, denying light. The earth broke at her feet.

"It is time," she told the Sen, "for you to leave. The Tor will know what we have built here. You had best be away when he comes."

"Sen Margret—"

"The scribes are already dead; they were expected, and measures were taken to deal with them. The adepts who accompanied them are dead as well. This is all that remains, and if you are witness to it, you must pay the same price. The spheres will have no choice."

"The Tor Arkosa," he said quietly, "will remember what you have done."

"Yes. Arkosa will remember."

She felt his sudden absence, but she did not look away as the sphere continued to dwindle. She had planned to kill him, but she had no taste for death now.

The fires around her began to bank. She waited. Heat gave way to warmth, and warmth gave way to a chill that she was certain would never leave her. Her eyes cleared; the light receded to the spheres that the walls had been magicked and built to contain.

She looked down. The blood that she had shed was a black mark across stone; the gash from which it had come, deep and painful, was gone.

As was the sphere. What had been the height of a man was now the size of a fist, hard and dense, its edges sharp and clear. Nothing of her son remained within it.

She drew her sword again. Cut her palm, but this time more carefully; she had to be precise. Her hands trembled, but the trembling no longer disturbed her; she waited until it had stilled before she began.

Between the inner and the outer circle, she began to write, in blood, the oath by which Arkosa would be judged in the final reckoning.

We will live as free men, and we will fight as free men; not for power, nor for love, will we again serve the Lord of Night.

She felt his kiss upon her brow, and she wept.

The City will fall, but it will not be destroyed; it will slumber until the Lord of Night comes again. We will claim no lesser Dominion for our own, and when the End of Days is finally come, we will return to Arkosa and claim it again as our home.

So swear the Voyani of Arkosa, and by this blood and these oaths shall we be known.

She gestured; the stone beneath her feet spread across the ground in a narrow bridge. It held her weight as she walked toward the last of her works. She knelt, and placed both hands once more upon what was left of the sphere. It was cool to the touch.

She lifted it; held it against her chest.

And cradled it there, rocking, while the only world she had known ended.

Lord Telakar was not the master of the game. He knew it before he drew his sword, but to draw it *here,* in the heart of these lands, brought him a pleasure that even the Abyss had never brought him. Ishavriel roared, his voice full, loud; Telakar replied in kind.

They traded names as sharp as insults; they traded blows; they danced in the still, hot air, as they might once have danced in air, fire, water. Only the earth impeded their movements, but the earth had not yet been brought into play, and no matter how the battle went, neither lord would invoke it here.

Shadow trailed behind them, a scant cloak. To summon their Lord's power was a risk that at any other time they might have taken.

But a woman born to the bloodline now walked across the thin shallows of the slumbering earth, and the earth itself had been invoked to defy them.

No, he thought, twisting as he moved out of the gale of fire and force, it had been invoked to defy *the* Lord. The earth was deep and slow, but it would recognize them first by the mantle of their master.

Too great a risk.

Too great.

She watched them when she could bear to watch them. She listened to the wailing of the wind, for it moved at the whim of their weapons, and its voice was a dry, high whistle, a warning, a song. But she could not look at them for long; they invoked a dread in her that she could not name.

And something else that she was afraid to.

Her cousin had stopped as she stopped, and because she was aware of his presence, she waited, hands clenched. She had no weapon with which to defy him, but she was not certain he knew it; when his gaze flickered up from the fight, when it found her, it was wary.

She waited for Carmello to join him, but he did not appear. Her cousin was one man; she one woman.

He carried two swords. But he hesitated.

"Elena."

She almost answered. Bit her lip instead. She could barely hear him, after all; the creatures were roaring as they fought, and they spoke with the voice of the Serpent, the storm in the cadence of their wild anger.

But he did not listen to what she heard.

His face fell into the lines that she found most repugnant, that mixture of petulance and anger that belonged on the face of a child. A child, she could chide. A child, she could correct. He was beyond that now. He began to walk toward her, skirting the edge of the fight.

It almost killed him.

Were it not for the sword he carried, were it not for the speed of his reflexes, he would have been cut in two, for Telakar lashed out almost casually, his sword's edge twisting in the air, an afterthought as he launched himself forward.

The red blade struck the bright one.

Her cousin staggered back, across the invisible line the battle had drawn in the sands.

"She is *mine*, mortal. Serve who you will at your peril."

She shrank groundward, holding her place upon these sands, the heat of the sun a bane that did nothing to warm her.

Margret returned to herself slowly; her hands, empty, fell away from her chest. Her eyes were dry, but they were wide. She lifted her face from the stone and saw that the path she had taken was still surrounded, on all sides, by a thunderous sky.

No, not on all sides.

Crystal hedged her in from the right. She looked up.

Met the eyes of the Serra Diora.

In the flashing light of the seven spheres, she saw that Diora held the Heart of Arkosa in cupped palms.

Throw it away, she thought grimly. *Give it back to the void. I will not take it.*

"Daughter," the woman said quietly. "You asked for the truth."

She rose, then, her feet planted as firmly as the twisting, narrow path would allow. Her boots were scored leather, worn and cracked; her robes were the robes of the Arkosan Voyani—harsh and heavy, stained with dust and blood.

She lifted her hands; they were as dark as a life beneath the open sky could make them, and they, like the leathers, were cracked. Strong hands; her own hands. They had never relied upon the labor—or the blood—of slaves.

"Do not call *me* daughter."

"You are the daughter of Tor Arkosa. You bear the blood of the Sen. If you did not, you would never have found the City."

She ignored the woman's words, and turned, lifting her feet with care, to face the Serra.

The Serra's face was white; her hands were white; her hair was black. No combs adorned it, no jewels, no flowers; it had been pulled, braided, and bound with a single long stick. Although she wore the boots and the robes of the open road, she had not been born to walk it.

And Margret had despised her for it, when they had first met.

She had no right to that contempt now. The Serra had undertaken the difficult task of walking the *Voyanne* with a grace that had both confounded and infuriated the Arkosan Matriarch. Both were gone; they were replaced instead by bitter knowledge. In her place, Margret could not have walked the thin, narrow path that had confined *her*. She could not have negotiated the halls and the tame, pretty gardens, the politics of silence, the politics of words that were never clear, never brutal, never direct. Not even had her life depended on it.

"Matriarch." The Serra said the word slowly, her voice turning the syllables into something that sounded like song.

Margret could not speak the word. The taste of ash was in her mouth, bitter and dry. "Did you see it?" she whispered. She hated herself for the hope that flared in the silence the Serra offered.

Hated herself more for the disappointment that followed the Serra's gentle nod.

"How can you stand there, then? How can you stand there with *that* in your hand? Do you not understand what we did?" She turned away. "She—the Sen Margret—planned to kill her son to create the Heart of Arkosa. She had always planned it that way. She knew she was too *valuable* to die in the chambers."

Dioro nodded again, her hands steady beneath the pale

light of the beating Heart. For it was beating. "I understand it now. I understand what it says." And the Serra smiled, her lips a shallow turn, a quirk of mouth, that no Court had produced.

"Look, Margret. Look." She lifted the Heart, and Margret finally understood what she saw: the chain dangled in the air, its links catching light and losing it as it swayed.

CHAPTER THIRTY-ONE

Margret turned to the woman who stood upon ground that had long since vanished, her delicate robes still although the voice of the wind in the cavern was strong. "Why did you show me what you showed me?"

"You asked for the truth."

"And what did you show my mother? What did you show my grandmother? What did they ask for? What—"

Diora's hand was upon her shoulder. She jumped, startled, and turned. The Heart of Arkosa now rested in one pale palm. "They can tell you," she said softly. "They can speak."

"They?"

"The Matriarchs, Margret. Your mother, your mother's mother, her mother before her. The Sen Maris did not lie. This crystal was created to hold memory, to hold the thoughts and experiences of the dead."

Margret glared at the Heart in silence. "Ask them," she said at last, the two words flat as blade's side.

"I do not know if they will answer me."

"Please."

The Serra's gaze was steady. "I am not their daughter," she said quietly. "I do not have the right to question them."

"You bear the Heart of Arkosa. It was given to you willingly. You have walked our road in order to wear it. You bear its weight better than I ever could, and I have never borne it. You *have* that right."

"I walked your road," she replied, "in order to walk mine. I walked the *Voyanne* because I thought it would lead me to the North, where the armies lie waiting. I did not expect to find anything else."

"And have you, Serra?"

She flinched.

And although she did not want to, Margret understood why. She looked away. Felt a terrible pain take the words from her throat.

"Ask them . . . something else, then."

But Diora closed her eyes, and her fingers left Margret's shoulder. Margret felt the absence, and was ashamed. She *hated* shame.

"They saw the fall of the City," Diora said.

"What?"

"You asked me to ask them what they saw when they entered this chamber. It was . . . different. They did not see endless depths and endless heights; they saw a large, large room; they saw the spheres. They—they spoke to their ancestors, as we did when we first met Constans. They saw the fall of the City. The death of their people at the hands of the demons who served Allasakar. They heard . . . they heard his claim."

"His claim?"

"He claimed the City and its inhabitants," the stranger said. Margret had almost forgotten she was there, a witness to the conversation.

"And because he had secured his alliance with his power, he was able to enforce it. The Tor—who had willingly accepted the gift of Allasakar's power, was unable to deny his command; that power turned upon him, and his own was not great enough to defy its master. He fell fighting, and six of the Seven adepts fell by his hand before he could be stopped.

"The Sen Maris was true to his word. When Allasakar came to the gates, he offered his power to the Spheres, invoking them with the aid of other adepts. The Seven . . . could not be easily breached, not even by the power of a god. Allasakar could have defeated one such City, but he would have squandered too much of his power in that defeat; he used subterfuge instead.

"The Sen adepts of the North tower attempted to destroy the Sphere it housed, and were it not for the sacrifice of Sen Adoll—who they did not name, because they did not know her—the sphere would have fallen, and the defense of the City would have been broken."

Margret lifted a hand to her forehead. She was shaking.

She remembered the memories of the woman she loathed. "He kissed her."

Diora frowned.

"He kissed her. The Sen Margret."

"Who kissed her?"

"The Lord of Night."

Diora's eyes widened; it was the first thing that Margret had said that disturbed her. Or that disturbed her enough that she was unable to hide the expression.

"That—that—is not possible."

"I *was* her, Serra. Diora. I was her. I felt what she felt. I asked for the truth—and that *is* the truth."

The Heart was glowing now. Its light was golden. "The Matriarchs say—they say it cannot be true."

But Margret turned to the woman who waited. "That's why she knew we had to leave quickly. We could not stay; we could not wait for Allasakar's armies to arrive."

"We do not speak that name in this room."

"I don't give a rat's ass what you don't do."

She heard Diora's intake of breath. It gave her a brief, and a gleeful, satisfaction.

"She had to leave because if she stayed, if she remained within these walls, she would have suffered the same fate as the Tor. The Lord of Night would have called her name, and she would have come, like the least of his creatures; she would have laid her life at his feet, been his weapon."

"You see deeply, Sen Margret," the woman said.

"Don't call me that!"

"Margret—"

"She used his power." But it was more than that. "She *wanted* to use his power."

"It is because she used his power that she understood his threat."

Margret spat. "I asked for the *truth.*"

The woman fell silent.

"Did she ever stop missing it? Did she ever stop thinking about him?"

"What do you think, Daughter?"

Margret felt the kiss of the Lord of Night upon her brow, cool and graceful. Felt it more clearly than she felt the wound across her hand, her hands upon the sphere. "If no one had ever used his power at all—"

"Does it matter?" the woman replied. "What might have happened has long since passed; the possibilities vanished with the lives they clung to. The men and the women who began this long story have been dust, less than dust, for centuries. What the Sen Margret desired was not a simple thing.

"But what anyone desires is not simple. She weighed her desires, one against the other, and she made *this* choice. For the future. It was the only way she could think of to fight him and succeed."

"Margret," Diora whispered.

Margret chose to ignore her. "Who was she?"

"She was the Sen of the Sanctum. She was much as you see me now."

"And you are alive?"

"No. I am long dead, and my will, my desire, died with me."

"What were you called, when you lived?"

"I was the Sen of the Sanctum. I was the Seer majere. I was the—"

"What was your *name?*"

"Do you not know? Can it be that you do not understand?" She turned slightly, her gaze shifting until it rested to Margret's right. Upon the Serra Diora. "Will you not tell her?"

Margret, too, turned. Met Diora's gaze, her wide, round eyes steady and unblinking. "No," she answered, although she looked at Margret. "I will not tell her."

And Margret knew.

She *knew.*

"Tell me." Her voice was thick; the words sounded heavy and swollen as they left her. She wanted to cling to them, to keep them on the right side of her lips. But something forced them out.

"Her name was Margret. Margret na'Sarasheen."

Margret reached out, the movement completely beyond her control. She caught Diora's arm in her hand and held it too damn tightly. Knew that she did, but she had to; her hands would shake too much otherwise. "And her sister's name was Diora."

Diora nodded.

"Do you know what she did to her sister?"

"She did nothing."

"She killed your parents. She bound your body. She destroyed your ability to have children; denied you the possibility of family. She took you away from everything that I—"

"That you value."

Margret could not speak.

"Margret, she did not do that."

"Then her mother did. Or her father. Someone did."

Diora was silent. After a moment, she said, "What *she* did to *her* sister was not done to me. But had it been, it would still be kinder than the crime my father committed. This other Diora lived in a different time, a different place, but she lived as I have always lived—at the whim of the powerful. And if the Sen Margret was powerful, and if the Sen Margret did all that you accuse her of doing, if she deprived me—or her sister—of those things you value, she did it in a way that caused no pain, no loss. What loss can be felt for something you have never had a chance to love?"

"How can you say that?"

"Because I lost everyone I loved in a single night, and I lose them over and over again without pause. I lose them when I sleep, and nightmare takes me. I lose them when I wake, alone. I lose them when I see something that would have drawn a smile from their faces. I lose them when I watch your children, and I hear them speak a new word or take a new step, and I think of all the things that my child will never do."

"And is that how she felt?"

"I know that she made her choice freely."

"She did not. She was chosen by the Sen, and had she refused, she would have been used as just another sacrifice."

"That isn't the choice I speak of."

"Then what?"

"Her death. I know that the only loss she could not face was yours."

"My loss—no, the loss of the *Sen Margret*—would have been her death," Margret snapped. "The Sanctum killed sisters who failed in their duties. It wasn't a good death."

"Did you see that?"

"No. But I *know* it."

Diora was silent for a moment. She looked at the stone in her hand, at the chain that moved in the slow even dance of a pendulum. "Did the Sen Margret never love her, then?"

It was a terrible thing to ask.

"Margret, answer my question; I have answered yours."

"She has answered your question," the pale woman said. "Inasmuch as she can, she has answered it."

There was a long silence. Margret would have answered the question just to spite this ghost, but she couldn't. And she hated to be so transparent to something that, in the end, wasn't even alive.

"Diora, did all of the Matriarchs of Arkosa come here alone?"

"I think you should ask them. They're *all* here, Margret. The greatest of them, and the least. They have been waiting for you to complete this journey; they have been waiting for you to bear their voices."

"I don't want to touch the Heart."

"I know." The Serra Diora drew herself to her full height. It wasn't impressive. And it was.

"Diora—"

"No, Margret," she said, her tone taking all sting out of the refusal. "I have borne the weight of the Matriarchs for long enough. It is your turn."

She held out the Heart.

Margret swallowed air. "Not here." She began to walk again.

And this time the ground did not branch before her; it did not shift or turn; it spread across air in a wide span of stone, welcoming her at last into the heart of Arkosa.

She paused. Diora hesitated for a moment and then stepped from the sharp, harsh crystal to the flat smooth stone. It was wide enough for both of them, but Diora stumbled as her foot touched the ground. Her boots would have to be replaced; there was no repairing the damage the crystal had done.

Margret caught her elbow, steadying her.

"I hate my mother."

Diora shook her head, but the corners of her lips turned up in a rueful smile.

"I wish she were still alive, so I could tell her how much."

"I have reason to believe that would not be very satisfying."

They walked together. The vast expanse of the room seemed to shrink and dwindle.

"Why did you ask for the truth?"

"I don't know."

The path led to a circle that had been scorched into stone. Within it was another circle and between these two, the oath. She had never spoken it aloud. Until this day, she had not possessed the language with which to do so.

She must have hesitated, for Diora touched her gently. "Must we stand in the circle again?"

Before Margret could frame an answer, Diora lifted her robes and stepped lightly upon the mark of Tor Arkosa. She waited in silence, and Margret knew that she would wait that way forever. If they had forever.

Margret had never been good at waiting.

She stepped into the circle as well, and noticed that she had chosen to stand in such a way that her toes brushed the top of one of the Arkosan crescents. Diora's touched the other.

The Serra lifted her hands, and held out the Heart.

Margret flinched as she raised her own, palm down. She was weak. She hated weakness.

"Diora?"

"Yes?"

"Will you hold the Heart?"

Diora's smile was slow and sweet.

Margret's hands touched the Heart, and as she did, her fingers brushed the Serra's hands; she felt their warmth more strongly than she did the cut of the crystal.

She knew when the fight was over.

Or knew that it would be, soon. Telakar had taken the edge of his opponent's blade across shoulder and chest. She had thought the wounds shallow, for they did not appear to slow him, but perhaps he fought in such a focused frenzy that he could not hear their message.

He bled; she thought he bled. But the sand beneath his

feet was dry and newly cracked with the force of their steps. Blood wrote no message there.

She gathered her strength. Her forearm ached. She looked down; the gashes made by flying metal were shallow, the blood sticky. She drew out a single shard of metal and held it carefully between her fingers.

It caught the light like a sliver of ruby, dark and red, the facets of its cut broken, its beauty destroyed, its essence unchanged.

She was not the Matriarch of Arkosa. She knew that she would never bear that title.

She had been gifted with the visions Margret lacked, and if they were not Evallen's visions, she had learned to trust them with the passage of time.

Blood had always been the key to the Matriarch's power. Even here, in the desert. Especially here, where liquid had a value that was incalculable, no matter where it came from.

She lifted her head. Straightened her shoulders.

She dropped to her knees, reached for the sand, spread her left hand across it, splaying her fingers as wide as they would go. In her right, knuckles white as the bone beneath skin and flesh, she clutched the remnant of her dagger.

But she did not pray.

The Lord was watching, and the Lord sneered at prayer. She had one chance, and that chance involved no show of weakness, no hint of fear. As if she had been born to the High Court, she made of her face a mask behind which she could hide.

"Elena."

His voice. Her cousin's voice. She did not look up.

Not even when she heard Ishavriel's triumphant cry.

She felt the light. It did not change; it hid beneath the surface of flat, smooth gem, pulsing with a familiar beat. But it was warm, not hot, and it was blessedly silent.

She looked up to meet Diora's eyes.

And she met her mother's instead.

Her mother's. Evallen's.

It should have been strange. But it wasn't; she had spent long enough walking in the memories of a dead woman.

"I was going to tell you how much I hated you," she said, no heat in her words.

"I know."

"Mother—"

"I stood where you stand, the Heart of Arkosa around my neck and within my hands. And the first thing I saw was my mother. I told her . . . how much I hated her." She smiled. The expression softened her face in a way that no living smile had ever done. Not in Margret's memory.

No. No, that wasn't true. She had looked that way when Adam was young enough to be carried for long stretches beneath the open sky. When the day had passed, and the night had not yet taken the color and hue of the world and made it gray and silver. She had looked that way, sometimes, when her father had lived, and Evallen had stood within the hollow of his arms, staring out at something neither she nor Adam could see.

Margret had always wanted to be the recipient of that smile.

Instead, she was the recipient of all else. The responsibility. The family. The *Voyanne.*

"You're dead."

"Yes. I am dead."

"Then what is this? How can you talk to me?"

Again, her mother smiled. "I spoke to you, Daughter, long before you came here. In this room. Within the seven spheres. I saw you standing here so clearly. I heard what you *would* say. I saw *so* much. I knew that you would not come alone. There was a power in the spheres that sharpened all vision, all talent; I absorbed it. My vision was not strong before I entered this room, but when I left it as Matriarch, it was greater. I thought that *that* was the ultimate gift of Arkosa: a strengthening of vision. That, and the advice of women who had had to live, as I had lived, ever since the *Voyanne* unfolded before us.

"And I knew—"

"Mother."

She fell silent. The smile left her lips. "You were not born with the gift. Your cousin was. I thought, for years, that I might be forced to make Elena Matriarch after my passing."

Her daughter closed her eyes and looked away, but the

Heart beneath her hands was warm; it took the sting from the words that she had always suspected were true.

"When did you decide not to?"

Her mother hesitated.

Margret swore. "Even dead, you make me angrier than anyone I've ever met. What harm can there be in telling the truth?"

"Don't you know?"

"No."

"Very well, Matriarch. I made my decision when I saw that Elena would set foot off the *Voyanne.*"

All words left Margret in a rush.

"I could not be certain when, or why; I saw it only briefly. But I saw it clearly, and I knew it for truth. I spent many years afraid of death, of what my death would mean."

"Then *why did you walk into it?* Why did you leave us, now? Why did you take the Heart of Arkosa with you?" She had thought that anger had vanished; she had spoken the word hate with such a happy irony.

"Because the seer came to me, and she told me both my future and my fortune."

Evayne.

"Do not judge her, Margret. Of all creatures in this war, of all people twisted and broken by its necessity, its brutality, do not judge her."

"Why?"

"Because I would live any other life, given a choice. I would live no life at all if it prevented me from bearing her burden."

"And her burden is so great? Her duties so terrible?" She could not keep the scorn from her words. "Is that what she told you?"

The Evallen of Arkosa that Margret had known for almost all of her life returned to the calm, gentle stranger who stood on the other side of the Heart. "You'll mind your words, Daughter. I'm not a fool. She told me *nothing* because to share her burden at all might cost her everything she's worked for. What I say is what I saw, the first time I met her.

"And the last time I met her. She knew what I would walk into. She knew how I would die."

"And she let you do it."

"Did you not desert your cousin?"

Margret cried out in denial, in anger, in pain.

And another voice spoke. "Na'eva," a woman said quietly. "You are too harsh. Always, always too harsh."

To her mother's left a figure appeared. Her face was familiar, although Margret was certain she had never seen it before.

"And *you* were always too quick to forgive. You almost failed in Arkosa. You almost failed to offer what was necessary to preserve the *Voyanne.*" Evallen of Arkosa said, almost grimly, "This is *my* mother. We all have our ties, and our burdens, to bear."

The voice that had spoken took shape and form, standing across from Margret as she touched the Heart of Arkosa. Another ghost, Margret thought. Another Matriarch.

The woman was older than her mother; the sun had shaped her face, the winds had cracked her skin. But the wrinkles in the corners of her eyes and mouth were the remnants of years of smiling.

"You look a little like your mother. You certainly have her temper. She didn't get that from me."

"My father," Evallen said softly, "was not a patient man."

Margret did not remember him.

She had always wondered what it would be like to have a grandmother; she was the only child in all of Arkosa guaranteed not to.

But many, many other children, with no such guarantee, had also been born without a mother's mother to ease their passage into the world.

She regretted the loss now.

"There is no loss, Matriarch. Do you not understand what the Heart of Arkosa is?"

The corpse, Margret thought bitterly, of the Sen Margret's son. And her sister. "No."

"Our voices. Our memories. Our lessons. Our stories. It is our knowledge, preserved, as it can be preserved, for you."

"But—"

"She knew, the first Arkosan Matriarch knew, how bitterly lonely a Matriarch can be. She knew that Matriarchs would bear the burden of the *Voyanne* alone. She was a hard woman, and a cold one, but she understood that no people can survive the winter desert for long.

"She gave us the only comfort she could give: the company of those who had learned the price of power."

"Did you? Did you learn the price of power?"

"Some of us more than others. Come, Margret. Walk among us for a time. There will never be another place where our voices will speak to you so clearly, and our shades be so alive as they are here."

But Margret shook her head. "Mother," she said quietly, "you haven't answered my question."

"I have."

"You haven't told me what Evayne said."

"No."

"Tell me."

"It would make no sense to you, Margret. Not until you have led my life. Have you found a father for your children?"

Margret rolled her eyes. "I did not come all the way to the Heart of Arkosa to have this argument again."

"Arkosa needs children."

"Mother!"

"Arkosa needs daughters. Elena's namesake, five generations ago, bore four sons. You are not as young as you once were. You have your duty."

But Margret shook her head slowly. "Mother—"

Her mother was silent.

Other voices spoke in her stead. Some were harsh and some soft; some were grating and some musical. The women who accompanied those voices were tall, thin, large, short, small; they were gracious and graceful and clumsy and ancient; they were young and beautiful, sorrowful and joyful.

She looked at them all as they filled the chamber with their presence in ones and twos, and she felt the Heart of Arkosa beating out a familiar rhythm beneath her palms.

"Mother," she said again, "you know there's no point in talking of children."

They fell silent. As if they were one woman, their voices stilled, and she could see in their faces that the truth of her words had reached out across the generations; that each woman, standing here before her, preserved in the Heart and the memory of Arkosa, had in her time stood within this circle, her palms cupped about this same gem, waiting for word that the *Voyanne* had finally led them back to the fabled homeland.

No. Not fabled.

Among the women present was the first Matriarch.

The Sen Margret made her way through the crowd as if it were, in truth, a crowd and not the artifact of magic, not an illusion sustained by the presence of the seven spheres. She slid deftly between arms and shoulders pressed too tightly together, pushing her way past the older women who did not seem to acknowledge her presence.

"You came here alone," Margret said to her mother, the words almost an accusation.

"Yes. We all traveled alone. That was our duty. That was the law. One or two of us attempted to bring our daughters to this hallowed place, that our daughters might draw strength from the presence of their ancestors. But our daughters were refused entry.

"Only the Matriarchs could enter. And only if they carried the Heart of Arkosa within their hands. The Heart was enchanted . . . in a way that made it sensitive to the bloodline. The Matriarch Raven, daughter of Deverra, lost the Heart to the man who ruled these lands, centuries past. He took it from her before he killed her. But the Heart returned to her daughter. And she was not the first to lose it; not the first to guide her people without the voices it contained. When you have time, or desire, when you are willing to face death, you will know how each of your predecessors fell.

"But I ramble. The Heart returned, ten years later."

"How?"

"We do not know. There are glimpses of memories that do not belong to any of us within the crystal's depths. Do not touch them, Margret. Do not disturb them."

Margret knew a moment of fear, her first among these women. "Those strangers—did the Matriarchs speak to them?"

"The Heart cannot speak, not directly, to anyone who does not carry our blood in their veins."

"You're certain?"

Again they were silent.

Margret frowned. "But the Serra Diora is no Arkosan."

"Perhaps in the past—"

"Mother."

"You may as well tell her, Evallen. It's not likely to harm us."

"If the Matriarch dedicates the gem—and the dedication is complicated, and the act involves many, many things, not the least of which is the waters from the Lady's Lake—we can sometimes speak to strangers. But we cannot speak without the will of the living Matriarch behind it."

"And you were."

Again, she was silent.

"Margret." The Sen Margret spoke. Her voice stilled the others. "You know that that is not why the Serra Diora can hear our voices."

Margret said nothing.

"You know, or you would not ask why they came alone. And by exclusion, why you did not."

"She is not here."

"Who?"

"You know who. The Sen Diora."

"No. I never meant for my sister to be part of the dedication of the seven spheres."

"You were ready to kill everything else."

The stranger flinched. But she accepted Margret's judgment.

"I did not intend for her to be part of the dedication because I knew that I could bear children and that she could not. The dedication was complicated, Margret. The spell was years in the making, and it was a subtle spell. It had to be bound to the bloodline. And Diora's was at an end." She bowed her head.

"But in the end, without the aid of my sister, I would have lacked the strength necessary to make the Heart. I went to the North tower before the arrival of the Lord of Night, and I spoke with Sen Adoll. And on that day, another also traveled to the North tower. I do not know how she knew to be there. Had the Seven been invoked, she would not have been able to pass the walls, no matter how simply she chose to travel."

"Who?"

The Sen Margret raised her face, and her eyes were a blue flash of light.

"Will you seek the truth one more time, Matriarch?"

"Why not?"

She stood upon the battlements at the height of the North tower. It was the tallest of the towers, and the sphere it housed was black as night; nothing moved within it. Margret did not think that such a dark thing could draw light and hold it, but she knew that she was being fanciful; it had been built for that purpose, and if, in its dormancy, it chose shade and shadow, it mattered little.

The guardians of the tower faced outward, their eyes absorbing and examining the smallest movements in the streets below. Their robes were blown this way and that by the play of strong wind, but the wind did not move them; they were adepts; they could walk in the folds of the most violent of storms without harm.

She could not join them, and she found the wind at the heights uncomfortable in its strength. But Sen Maris had ordered the adepts to allow her to pass, and they suffered her presence with no outward acknowledgment. To be ignored by an adept was far safer than to be treated with an obvious display of respect.

She bowed her head, waiting.

She had waited for an hour; she marked the passage of time by the length of the shadows cast by the adept who manned the eastern watch.

Sen Adoll joined her upon the battlements.

Sen Margret smiled when she saw her, but the smile froze across her lips. For Sen Adoll came alone; no sister kept her company; no sister watched over her.

"Sen Adoll," she said faintly. Sen Adoll was without dispute the most capable seer the Sanctum had yet produced. And because of that, she was dangerous. "The wind is strong across the heights."

Sen Adoll nodded gravely.

She was placid. Calm.

Sen Margret could not remember a time when either of these words had described her demeanor accurately. They were words that were used when outsiders were present, but they were heard with an understanding of the context of Sen Adoll's life.

"Daughter," Sen Adoll said quietly.

Sen Margret dropped at once to both knees. Were it not for the presence of the adepts, she would have abased herself completely, but such an abasement would be noted and questioned.

"Rise. Such a posture does not suit the woman who has protected my followers from danger for so long."

She rose at once, gathering her skirts as if they were thoughts that could be put in order.

"Firstborn," she whispered.

"Why have you come to this tower? I am not at home on the heights of such a bastion."

Sen Margret swallowed.

"You did not choose to venture down my path."

"No, Firstborn." She bowed her head.

"Why? You have sent many others to me."

"My gift was not as strong as theirs."

"No?"

"No."

The Oracle's smile was cool and subtle. "Your gifts are many, Daughter. Your sight is weak because you have chosen to hide from it."

Stung, Sen Margret bowed her head.

"And because you have hidden, you have no avenue to seek the answers you desire. You chose the path of the coward, Daughter; you chose to live in fear."

"I chose to live as those without true vision must live; I have a responsibility—"

"You have deserted the responsibility you now attempt to hide behind. If you seek truth, Daughter, offer it first."

"Had I come to the foot of your path, I would offer no less."

"But I am the guest here, and you the host?"

"No, Firstborn. The tower is not my home." Sen Margret studied the woman who wore Sen Adoll's face.

"You avoided the path because you did not wish to expose all that you are to my inspection."

"Firstborn, all that I am, and all that I will ever do, is open to your inspection." She said it without bitterness or rancor.

"Perhaps. But giving something is not the same as having it taken, in this time, or any other. You accept the vulnerability that you cannot avoid with admirable pragmatism—but you avoid vulnerability at all cost when you have the choice." She raised a hand and gestured briefly; furrows formed across her brow as she frowned.

Sen Margret said quietly, "I avoid what you yourself have avoided."

The frown melted into a smile—the cool smile of a teacher who thinks a student has said something precious or clever.

"You misjudge me, Sen Margret. What is, is; what will be is . . . more so. I am vulnerable in ways that you will never understand to someone who chooses to walk my path.

"But you have led those who would travel my path to me, and of those who survived their journey, you have been the protector and guardian. I understand well the ways of the Cities of Man."

Sen Margret fell naturally into silence. She was of the Sanctum.

But she had never seen the Oracle prophesy before. She watched. And even she could not remain impassive when the Oracle reached into her own chest, and drew forth . . . a heart.

"Do not look too deeply."

Had Margret the choice, she would not have looked at all. But her eyes would not obey the command to close; she saw what lay cupped within palms that seemed human, beating. Bleeding.

"You are correct in your surmise," the Oracle said. The pretense of Sen Adoll's voice vanished; she spoke slowly and evenly, her words punctuated and broken by breath. "The hands of your sister changed the nature of your spell in a way that you had not foreseen.

"But the spell itself is true. You will leave the City within the week, when the moon is at its nadir." It was not a command; it was barely an observation.

"You will bear your children. You will begin your line. But the blood of your children alone will not be enough to retrieve all that you have preserved."

The Sen Margret knelt at the feet of the Firstborn. She

reached out to catch the blood that fell from the beating heart; it was red, warm. Like any other blood that she had ever touched.

"My sister had no children."

"No. And she is lost to you. There is nothing of your sister preserved within the Heart of Arkosa but your memories of her. And those memories will not be enough."

The others, then, she thought bitterly. The others. Havalla. Lyserra. Corrona. But three were better than none.

"No, there will be a fourth, and it will be the first. Arkosa. The time is coming, Daughter. There will be a sundering. The world will know a loss that is measured not in lives, for lives are lost as we speak. In the North, a child has been born. He will grow to manhood, and he will carry a sword that the gods have, in ignorance, forged.

"He is the beginning of the end. But he is not the end, not yet."

She did not speak. It had rarely been so difficult for Sen Margret to keep her peace, but she knew that visions could not be interrupted without cost.

"The gods will leave this realm. Some willingly, some by force, but they will leave. And with them leaves the glory of your Cities, the zenith of your power, who are mortal and have chosen to play the games that gods play.

"You understand mortal memory, or you would not have undertaken the work that will destroy your life. But you cannot conceive of how long the path from Arkosa to Arkosa will be." The Oracle smiled. "Yes. Your descendants will walk again through the heart of the City. You have a question, Daughter, and our time is short. You may ask it."

"How? How will the City be reborn if my sister's bloodline is no more?"

"You are mortal, but some part of your being is not. What is taken can return, again and again, seeking answers to questions that birth itself destroys. And that return starts when the gods choose to play a different game. Mandaros will sit in judgment, sifting through the dead who wait.

"She will return. You will know her. The Heart of Arkosa will know her. And when one of your descendants is strong enough to bear the loss of her mothers, two again will walk into the City of Arkosa."

"And on that day?"

"The End of Days begins."

"The End of Days?"

"When the gods die."

She rose. "Gods have already died."

"Gods may kill gods, Sen Margret; that is their covenant; that is their stake in the game that they play. What they kill, they subsume. What they take, they bring a different life to.

"But when the End of Days begins, it is said that mortals will kill gods, and those deaths will be true deaths; there will be no rebirth, and the lands at last will grow wild and unkept. Then, the Firstborn will know age and decay. Then, the gods will know fear and hunger. Then, the mortals will hold the key to the heart of a far greater kingdom than the Cities of Man." The Oracle drew her hands to her chest.

"I do not understand."

"You understood my words."

"Your words, Firstborn, yes. But . . . if you speak of the death of the Firstborn, why do you offer me aid?"

"I am the Oracle," she replied quietly. "I stand at the center of all paths. I speak not of the inevitable, but of the possible. And I fear all things equally."

"And at the End of Days, what will there be?"

"Poverty," the Oracle replied serenely. "Poverty of vision, of power, of beauty. All will dwindle." She bowed. "You have your answer. I have paid my debt. What you tell your children now is your choice."

"If we do not . . . invoke . . . this history, what will happen?"

"Do you not know?"

"No."

"The Lord of Night will rule."

Beauty. Power. Grandeur.

Vision.

The Sen Margret bowed her head. When she raised it, the Oracle was gone.

Margret of Arkosa stood in an empty room. The voices of her mother, and her mother's mother, were stilled. But her hands were upon the Heart of Arkosa, and her fingers brushed the hands of the Serra Diora.

The past and the present existed, inseparable, in this moment. She did not want to lose either. Or to claim either.

"Margret," Diora said, making a question of her name.

Do you understand now, Margret? Her mother's voice. Evallen's voice. *Do you understand why?*

No. Then, grudgingly, *Yes.*

I had to know. I had to see the creatures who served the Lord of Night with my own eyes. And then, when I understood the truth that Evayne a'Nolan had offered me, I had to make a choice. The Heart spoke to me in a voice I had never heard.

And it spoke to me in a voice that I recognized.

If you are here, I did not choose poorly. But if you are here, Daughter, you are faced with a choice that I was too cowardly to make.

If you raise the City, he will come, and it is upon the Arkosans that the force of his fury will fall. Perhaps he will not come in your lifetime. Perhaps he will come in the lifetime of your daughter, or your daughter's daughter; gods do not feel the imperative of time as mortals do. But he will *come.*

Yet if you fail to raise the City, he will war in the North, and if the North falls, we will fail.

"Why do you say that?"

"Margret?"

Because, Margret, when Sen Margret reached out and captured the blood of the Oracle, she blessed the Heart of Arkosa with it. I will tell you what we did not know while we lived. A boy has been born in the North who has not yet grown to manhood, and an ancient weapon is waking as he grows.

That weapon, the gods would destroy, if they knew how to find it. They do not. Nor does the boy.

The Lord of Night does not know him, yet, but he will. And if his attention falls too soon to the North, and that boy dies, the Cities might stand for a generation. Two. They will not stand forever.

"We are too few," she whispered.

Yes.

"Margret?"

"Can you hear my mother's voice?" she whispered.

Diora was silent for a long moment, her expression completely neutral. Margret hated the silence. The Sen Margret had been good at waiting; the Matriarch was not. But she would have to learn, she thought bitterly. If she had the time.

"Yes, Margret. I can hear her."

Margret hovered a moment between panic and relief. Her hands were shaking. "Help me."

Diora's eyes widened slightly.

"Help me," she said again. "Not as sister to Sen, whatever that means—that's gone. I never want that back. I never want—" She looked away. "Help me as you helped me in the storm, Serra."

The Serra's expression was inexplicably gentle. "I did not help you in the storm."

"You did. You forced me to acknowledge my duty, to accept it."

"I knew what your duty was, then."

Margret laughed. "And now?"

"Now? This is Arkosa. You know what you face, and you know, better than I, what you *will* face. There is power here."

"I don't trust myself to wield it." There. It was said. "I *hate* what *she* was. I hate what this city was. Everything I have ever loved about my life does not belong to a place like this."

"Margret."

"How can I rule a place such as this?"

"You will have the Heart."

"It is *not* my heart, Diora. I understand that now. It was *never* my heart."

"And where is your heart, Margret?"

"With my mother. With my mother's people. With my father, and my father's people. With the open sky, be it ruled by sun or moon. If this is home, I don't want it."

Diora gripped the Heart of Arkosa carefully in her right hand; her left, she slid free.

It was cool and soft against Margret's cheek.

"Where is your home, Diora?"

The Serra's gaze was steady as it met hers. "I have no home."

"And you have no desire to find one?"

"Does it matter? I know what I must do. My path does

not end in Arkosa. It travels to Averda, Mancorvo, or Raverra. It ends where it began." She pulled her hand away from Margret's cheek and looked at her palm.

In the Heart's light, Margret saw the gashes wood had made in flesh. Imperfection.

"I do not know what the Cities of Man were. But I know what the Matriarch of Arkosa *is*. Do you despise your ancestors? You have the freedom to choose what of their history you accept, and what you reject.

"Do you dislike what the Cities were? Then change them. Make *this* place your home, and offer it to the people you have chosen to lead."

"I was born to lead them."

"You could have walked away." Diora looked at the ground beneath their feet. Spoke the words, not in the ancient tongue, but in Torra. "We will live as free men, and we will fight as free men; not for power, nor for love, will we again serve the Lord of Night."

"There was more," Margret said weakly.

"That is the heart of the vow. It's a vow you could make, and live by."

"I know." She clutched at the Heart as if she were afraid it would fall. Or as if she were afraid she would drop it.

"Margret." Diora did not move, but her tone alone conveyed the sense of motion; she was closer, somehow. "Not one of the Matriarchs is speaking. Not one."

"So?"

"I have learned something of the Voyani. If they were concerned, they would speak, and speak freely. But their silence can only mean that they do not believe you would turn away from Arkosa, no matter what you have learned today."

Margret looked at the Heart, just the Heart.

"Why do you hesitate?"

"I don't know." She shrugged. "Maybe I'm tired of bleeding." The smile she offered was wan. She looked at the circles beneath their feet, and remembered what she had drawn there, and why. "I hated you so much," she said softly.

"I know."

"When this is over—"

"This will never be over."

"When this part is finished, then. What will you do?"

"Go North."

"And will you find what you're looking for there?"

"I don't know. You found what you sought here, and it was not what you thought you were seeking. Maybe . . . it will be the same with me."

"What will you do?"

"If," Diora replied, glancing at her hand, "If I am still suitable, if the travel beneath the open sky, upon the open road, has not diminished my value, I will find the kai Leonne."

It was the answer Margret expected, but it stung anyway. "And will you marry him? Will you bear his children?"

"If he survives. Yes. Yes, Margret, I will marry him. I will be the crown. I will be the symbol."

"You will be the symbol of the Tyr." Margret spat. "I *hate* it. Diora—you can't be happy—" She stopped. Looked more closely at the Serra's face, at the expression of serenity that had settled around her wide eyes, her perfect lips. "Can you?"

"Happy?" The word was remote. But the Serra's expression was not. "I don't know. I no longer know what happiness is. But—"

"Yes?" She spoke too quickly.

Diora's smile was as still as the woman herself. "I will be grateful for the rest of my life for this journey."

"Why?"

"Because the Heart of Arkosa believes that *I* was once the sister to the Sen Margret." She waited, and when Margret did not speak, she continued. "And I believe it as well, because I want to believe it."

"Why?"

"If *I* once lived and died, it means that *my* dead might live again. I might never meet them. I might never know. But the possibility that they are waiting for me . . ." She bowed her head. Raised it again, her eyes glimmering in the Heart's light. "It is more than I hoped for. When we leave this place, when we finish here, if the sky is waiting and the sun is high, I will listen to the wind. And the wind will be . . . just the wind."

Margret bowed her head. "I want you to stay."

"I know."

Margret had asked for truth. Diora had asked for duty. Margret closed her eyes. She had never been good at farewells.

"Ruatha would have loved you, had she ever met you."

"Ruatha?"

"One of my sister-wives. The least graceful. The most fierce." She lifted her hand again. Three bands lay across her fingers, simple bands that Margret had never really paid much attention to. "Can you hold the Heart a moment?"

Margret nodded.

The Serra Diora hesitated. Then she lifted her pale hands, her perfect hands, scarred or no; they disappeared behind the nape of her neck. She removed a single strand of gold; it was finely crafted, the links interweaving leaves and tiny blossoms.

Her hands shook a moment as she lowered the chain, and then she said, softly, her gaze cast groundward, "I would be honored if you would wear this."

"But—"

"It is not of great value; you might sell it, if you desired, and receive some small compensation for it. But it has significance to me."

Margret paled. "I have nothing to give you in return."

"You have already given me something that no one, no matter how wise, or blessed, no matter how powerful, could have given me." Her hands still trembled as she held the chain. Margret wanted to touch them, to still them, but she held the Heart of Arkosa now. "I wore this chain at the Festival of the Moon. The last true Festival."

"Diora, if it is special to you—"

"It is. I wore it in the cloistered garden of the Tyr'agar's harem. It was not special then, but I wore it because I could carry three rings around its links and no one would be wiser. If I had time, if I had skill, I would craft you a ring like those: a heart of emerald, and beside each, a pearl.

"But I do not have the time. You do not have it." She reached, very carefully, across the Heart of Arkosa; her feet did not move. "You would have hated life in the harem."

She fumbled with the clasp, the Serra who never fumbled with anything. Margret felt the flutter of her fingers beneath wild Voyani hair. "It's too delicate," she mumbled.

"I carried the best of my hopes around this chain that

night. I wanted to change the way the world was, I hoped—" She stopped speaking for a moment.

Margret could see her face so clearly she could not speak.

"And the world changed. It *did* change. I hated the change for months afterward. I hated the Lady, for giving me what I desired."

The Matriarch of Arkosa looked into the eyes of the Serra Diora en'Leonne, and saw the desert in them, the desert at night.

She did not know why, but the words of the cradle song came to her, then—words that she had never understood as a child. "The heart, the heart is a dangerous place."

Diora's eyes were now luminescent. Trails of light swept across her perfect cheeks. Margret could not breathe; in that moment, in this terrible room, the burden of all Matriarchs ever to be born within the cradle of her hands, she realized that she had never in her life seen anything so beautiful as that face, those tears.

But the Serra had not yet finished speaking.

"I do not hate it now. I thought that the world had died when they died. It did. But it was my world, not *the* world. Ruatha would have liked you. You are so much like her.

"I have known you for so short a time. If I could stay . . ." She shook her head. But she did not touch her eyes. "But I cannot stay, and you cannot leave. I do not want the only binding between us to be the Heart of Arkosa. I do not want the only binding to be a binding of women long dead. I must make my stand against the Lord of Night. But it will bring me comfort to know that a sister brings life to the barren lands in order to make that same stand." She straightened then, grace returning to her movements.

"I never thought I would walk in such a dangerous place again."

She lifted her face slowly, and pressed her lips against Margret's rough cheek. Margret returned that brief kiss.

It was funny, how much like blood tears tasted.

CHAPTER THIRTY-TWO

It was over.

It was over with the simple thrust of a blade.

All noise, all thunderous roar, faded; the earth ceased its trembling rumble. Cracked and broken ground at last grew still, and above its newly opened fissures, the two creatures who served the Lord of Night stood.

But Lord Telakar had become the awkward sheath for the Lord Ishavriel's sword. Shadow seeped from the wound, not blood; it was cold in the light of the sun.

Elena had witnessed all nature of combat before. Some had followed the vine's fruit, when the Voyani, restless, gave in to their anger and frustration; some had followed the movement of raiders who had come seeking slaves for the markets of the Tors; some had been the result of the challenge that followed grave insult.

But although she had seen men fight—and die—she had never seen a battle like this. It was not simply the magic, not the fact that the swords burned trails across the air; it was not the shadows that bound the two together. It was more and less than that.

It was a dance; the swords in their flashing weave were like sculptor's tools, wielded with ferocity and precision so that, between these two, they might carve a tableau that was both terrible and beautiful.

The last cut had been made.

The Lord Telakar pulled himself, audibly, from the tongue of the blade. His sword wavered in the air before it fell, its flame banked.

But it made no sound as it struck the ground. Before Elena could move, it vanished.

Lord Telakar's back approached her.

"You still stand? You are more powerful than you once

were, Telakar," Lord Ishavriel said. There was no admiration, no flattery, in the words. "Leave us, or I will send you back to the Abyss."

Telakar did not speak.

If she lifted a hand, Elena could touch his robes. Her hands were still.

Lord Ishavriel turned to her slack-jawed cousin. She could not help it; her gaze followed as well.

There was no petulance in his expression. And no triumph either. He seemed weary. Old. Her breath did not pass her lips. She was numb with a stupid, foolish hope.

But when he met her eyes, she could not bring herself to speak his name.

"Nicu," the creature said, "we must hurry. Our time has been compromised by the actions of our enemies. If we are to gain the Tor Arkosa for your people, we must act now."

Lord Telakar laughed.

"You are too late," he said, his voice thinner and weaker than it had been.

Lord Ishavriel frowned.

"Did you think to offer this mortal the keys to Tor Arkosa?" Telakar coughed. Laughed. Both were bloody sounds. "If the Lord had vision as deep and clear as the Firstborn's, perhaps that would have been a fair offer."

"The Cities were bound to the earth; they were bound at the Lord's whim."

"Oh, indeed. But they were bound because they could not be destroyed. Do you not remember the Cities across the open plain? Can it be that you have forgotten their towers and spires, their brief and painful art, their song, the immediacy of their passion? Can it be, Lord Ishavriel, that you believed that such an offer was within your power to make?"

"Tor Haval, Tor Corrona, Tor Lyserra, Tor Arkosa. Four of the five." He coughed again.

"Telakar," Ishavriel said. He gestured. No sword came to his hand.

"Too late," Telakar said again.

The wind blew across the open plain; it was cool and gentle. A different wind.

Elena looked up, her gaze skirting the blindness offered

by the Lord to the careless. He was right. Somehow, he was right.

"The keys to these Cities were never ours, brother."

"Impossible. Had they the means, would they live like slaves across the length of the Dominion? Had they the power, would they have allowed the Tyrs their rule?"

"The answer must be yes," Telakar replied.

Elena reached out, then; touched the folds of his dark, long robes. She felt a shock of pain, a burning cold, enter the palm of her hand, rendering her arm useless. But her fingers, curved, became claws. She knew how to hold on.

The ground spoke, breaking around the syllables of a word that she had used casually for the whole of her life. Silence deserted her as she replied.

Arkosa.

The Lord Ishavriel's eyes grew wide; had he been a man, she would have seen the whites. But he carried only shadow, a vast expanse of growing night. The flame that limned his blade guttered as he turned in the direction that Margret and the Serra had run.

"This is not possible."

Arkosa.

"Nicu, what is happening?"

Nicu shook his head, his eyes upon Elena. He had his sword; it hung, slack, by his side.

"It *cannot* be possible. We have watched the Sea of Sorrows for as long as we have been summoned to walk the face of this plane. The power does not exist that could accomplish this!"

Telakar's laughter was rich and textured. Listening to it, she heard all the things she herself could not wrap words around. The wound he had taken had taken some part of the darkness with it. She did not trust him.

But she understood a debt when she owed it.

Arkosa.

"Telakar!"

He pulled away from her, or tried.

"Telakar, you *must* leave this place. You cannot survive what is to follow!"

Again he laughed, and the reckless, wild quality of his voice was both sweet and familiar. "What is to follow, little mortal? Do you even know?"

She didn't. But she *knew* that he could not survive it. Not upon this ground. Not so close. She was Tamara's daughter. She paid her debts. She grabbed his cloak with her other hand and pulled, hard.

But he did not move at all; he might have been part of stones that lay buried—that she knew were buried—beneath the earth.

Yollana of the Havalla Voyani rose.

She moved too quickly. Jewel, sitting in an angry, even silence at her side, rose with her, hands braced to catch some part of her weight.

But the single cane was all the support she required for the moment. Her hair was the color of light on water at dusk. Her eyes were Voyani eyes, midnight eyes, but they were sharp and glittering, like new steel.

"Serra Teresa," she said, ignoring Jewel's outstretched arms.

Jewel let them fall. It was petty, but she half-hoped the autocratic old woman would stumble or fall.

Serra Teresa rose at once, as if she were seraf or servant. The arm that she offered, Yollana accepted.

"ATerafin," the old woman added, once she had braced herself against the pull of the ground, "my apologies. But our debt to you is great enough." She lifted a hand and arranged the hood of her robes across her hair. "The wind has changed. It is time."

"Time?"

"Stavos! Tamara! Come. Gather the Arkosans."

Stavos' brows drew together. "Matriarch," he said, forcing due respect into the title, "the ways of Havalla must differ. We are forbidden to follow the Matriarch of Arkosa."

"You were forbidden," the old woman replied, gentling her rough voice. "But Margret will want you. Come."

He hesitated, this bear of a man, and at last looked to his wife for guidance.

His wife nodded.

"But the law—"

"'The absent Matriarch is not as dangerous as the one who sits by your fire,' " Tatia said.

He grimaced.

"Listen to your wife," Yollana added, in grim humor. "The Matriarch of Arkosa is younger than the Matriarch of Havalla, and her heart has not had the chance to develop calluses. Where is Kallandras?"

"I am here, Matriarch."

"Good. Use that sweet voice of yours to talk sense into these people. Or at least use it to make sure they don't get in my way."

He bowed, perfectly and precisely.

"Lord Celleriant?"

The Arianni lord—the only person present unwise enough to stand in the full light of the sun without the obvious protection of Voyani robes—shook his head. His hair danced across the perfect line of his shoulders. "I do not believe my presence would be . . . welcome."

But the Matriarch shook her head. "There is blood between your Queen and the Matriarchs. Come. You're in no shape to draw that pretty weapon. But if you're tempted, take my advice . . . don't try."

He glanced at Kallandras. Kallandras did not speak, but he returned the glance; something passed between them. Jewel frowned.

Tamara had already gone to the Matriarch's wagon to retrieve water.

In their hands, as if it were a living Heart, they held the memories of the women who had guided Arkosa. Fallible, poignant, bitter, furious, terrified, all their voices returned, a maelstrom of sound.

It was not worse than the storm Margret had weathered to walk these halls at all. But it was close. It helped that she stood in the eye of the storm. It helped that the only person she could clearly see was the Serra Diora, whose expression, intent and serene, did not waver.

Light washed across Diora's face, brilliant and blinding, as harsh as the Lord's glare. There was no cloud to soften it, no shade to dim its fire. Her robes slapped against her legs as the winds rose.

But the wind could not dislodge them from the heart of the circle in which they had chosen to stand.

She saw the light change; saw orange glow give way to green; saw green deepen until it was blue, emerald giving way to sapphire, both deep and rich. Red joined them, a red the color of sunset across the clear sky; it did not give way before the gray of dusk, the turning of time.

The seven spheres thrummed at her back, at her side, and beyond Diora's back; she could not clearly see them, but she knew that they now burned.

She looked at the Heart.

Felt its weight grow in their trembling hands. It was no larger than a cupped palm, but women had died under its burden, and she felt as if she knew them all, as if she could contain them.

Become them.

Look, they said, and she listened. It was not a command, but neither was it a request; it teetered on the thin edge between the two.

The Heart was growing.

The golden glow at its center thinned, spreading across the field of her vision, like mist in the morning of the Aver-dan valleys.

Margret had loved the mist as a child, when the care of the wagons, the horses, and the people who depended upon them were not her burden. Not for distance was the mist intended; it hid things from the casual view, from the sight of people who had no desire to approach it.

She had, as a child; she loved the early mornings and the late evenings, when the blanket of fog would roll across the lowlands, like grounded clouds.

Even when she had passed beyond childhood, she had Adam as an excuse to return to its joys, and she would take his small hand and drag him through the undergrowth looking for things made new and interesting because they were now concealed. Trees loomed suddenly out of no-where; bracken and ferns grew around the width of hollow fallen trees; thickets tall as whole forests appeared as they took careful steps across the hidden ground.

The fog had never been golden.

But because it was fog, she approached it, waiting to see what she might find, what might be made new, by the grace of its mystery.

She saw Adam.

Not a boy, not the child who had willingly offered a hand much smaller than her own; not even the boy who found horses so fascinating at a distance, so unnerving up close. He was taller than she by a good six inches; she could meet his eyes only by lifting her chin.

But his hesitant smile was still gentle, and if he stood with an authority that youth had not yet granted him, there was enough about his expression, his unguarded affection, that she could recognize the boy she loved in the man.

But as he grew closer, she saw that he wore a thin circlet across his brow and the mark of Arkosa across his chest; that he carried a sword as easily as he had ever carried water or food at his mother's command; that he held a book in one hand, and a cup in the other.

She knew that she would one day see him this way. That a window had been opened between the now and the then that separated them. A fierce joy tightened her throat as she nodded.

"Sen Margret," he said.

She looked away.

When she found the strength to look up again, he was gone. But the mists continued. She saw the side of a building, a great stone edifice whose height was swallowed by fog. She passed its side until she came upon doors that bore the symbols of Arkosa, and these swung open, silent, as if to beckon her. She saw within that building the light of gold and silver, the gleam of steel, the light of a hundred, a thousand, candles; she heard music carried by voices unaccustomed to song, harsh and beautiful.

Men came out of the doors as she stood. They were silent, or rather, they did not speak; their armor spoke for them, a cacophony of metal against metal, a song and a vow.

They passed to either side of her; they did not speak her name.

She was profoundly grateful.

Yet she felt Adam's presence, as memory, as comfort, as the mists changed again.

And she was happy, for a moment, for she stood at the heights above the Averdan valleys. The Voyani called no place home; that was their law. But if they had, Margret would have tempted the wrath of Tyrs by locking her wagon's wheels here.

But not today.

She recognized the standard of Callesta. It grew upon the ground like a wildflower, brilliant, intimidating. Men surrounded it. Averdans. Cerdan, she thought.

Then, as she looked more carefully at their surcoats, at their horses, she swiftly revised her opinion. Tyran. The Callestan Tyr was on the field.

She had never seen him. She had no desire to see him now.

I have, a familiar voice said. *He is present. There.* The voice fell silent. But, so much like her mother, it did not continue to maintain that silence. In a hush, a woman who had *never* willingly answered her questions said, *He bears* Bloodhame, *Margret. Aiee. We will see deaths, this war.*

We always see deaths in a war, Mother.

Don't be stubborn. Look at the cast of his face.

She looked. And looked away.

But he was not on the field alone. Another standard flew in the wind. The sun, she thought. The sun ascendant. She knew that the fog had a will of its own, but she pushed against it with hers, as if it were solid, a hanging, a curtain that she could grip and force back.

Because only two men in the Dominion could raise that standard: the kai el'Sol and the Tyr'agar.

Margret was raised Voyani. No Voyani woman—no intelligent woman, period—walked fearlessly among so many armed clansmen. She knew she was not truly here, but she found herself holding her breath as she approached the small cluster of men who stood at the height of this hill. Grass, wildflowers, weeds, had been crushed by the heels of men too numerous to count.

But as she could, she ignored them, finding spaces between where they stood to pass through.

She came at last to the standard and paused beneath it. The sun ascendant.

It was not her symbol, but she bowed her head a moment before she passed beyond the ground it marked.

Five men cast their shadows against the bent grass; the feet of many cerdan had passed this way, but not enough to destroy what grew there. The Tyr'agnate stood, arms folded, expression sharp as a blade, and as giving. To his left stood an older man whom she did not recognize.

Age bowed some men, but some it merely hardened.

Again her mother's voice tickled her ear. *Ser Anton,* she whispered.

Ser Anton? Ser Anton di'Guivera?

Yes.

Ser Anton. The Tyr'agnate. And the man to his left? He was of an age with Ramiro di'Callesta, broader of shoulder and chest, and perhaps an inch or two shorter. His hair was dark. But he wore the crest of the Tyr'agar's armies.

Do you not recognize him, Margret?

No. She did, however, recognize the tone of the question. She was torn between annoyance and a crazy gratitude, for *this* was the mother she remembered so well.

Three Generals, she thought. Three men. But she could remember the name of only one: Alesso par di'Marente. And it was not for his prowess in war that she remembered him.

That man is Baredan kai di'Navarre. The Commander of the third army.

And why should she remember him?

He was friend to the Voyani, in his fashion.

The Arkosans? She thought she would know, if that were the case.

If we are to win the war, Margret, in the end there can only be Voyani. We must forgo the bitter rivalry that has always dogged the South, be it among the clans or our own people.

Margret laughed bitterly. *I have to stop the fighting? When you couldn't?*

The Matriarchs have always cooperated when it suited their purpose.

She started to answer, and then remembered the feel of the mask in her hand on the night of the Festival Moon. She bowed her head again.

Baredan di'Navarre, she thought, inscribing the name in memory.

Who is the pale man, Mother?

That man? I do not know him. He stood beside Baredan, but it was clear from the General's posture that they were not friends. And that left only one man.

The youngest by far.

She studied his face. It was slender with youth, and clean shaven, which was rare among men of the South. His eyes were wide, his lashes almost too long. His cheeks were high, and his pale skin was framed by dark hair loosely drawn back in a warrior's knot. He did not speak; the older men did. He listened, intent on their words.

He reminded her of someone in that moment, but she could not think who.

"Kai Leonne?" Ser Anton di'Guivera said.

Kai Leonne. *This* boy was the last of the Leonnes? The surcoat he wore was her answer, for it alone bore the full face of the ascendant sun. Slim shoulders to carry that weight, to bear that claim.

"I think it will be too costly," the boy said at last.

"For who?" The Tyr'agnate's words were clipped.

"For all of us. I understand your desire, Tyr'agnate, but in the end, *all* of these people will be mine, no matter whose banner they now stand beneath."

"The Callestans will willingly bear that cost."

"Will they?"

Ser Anton's expression grew still as the stone cenotaphs in the vaults of the Tors. But he did not speak.

The Tyr'agnate did. "Do you doubt the loyalty of my men?"

"Your men? No. They have chosen to bear their arms in your service, and they bear them proudly. But ask the serafs who toil in the valleys. On either side of this conflict."

She was stunned by the answer, by the enormity of the insult he offered the Tyr'agnate.

This was the man to whom Diora would travel?

He will kill her, she thought, too shocked to be angry. *He will kill them all.*

The Callestan Tyr was absolutely silent.

Remember, Margret, Evallen said, *he was raised in the North.*

He cannot govern here, Margret snapped. *He cannot hope to rule.*

No?

Mother . . .

Is that not what we hope to do in Arkosa? Look at him. Do you think he speaks in ignorance? Do you think he does not understand what he has said? See, his hand falls to his sword.

The gaze of the Tyr'agnate fell to the kai Leonne's sword as well.

"We will have justice, Ser Ramiro."

The Tyr'agnate did not speak.

"But let that justice be seen, let it be understood. Let it begin and end in such a way that it does not continue a war without end."

His voice was quiet. His words were sharp and clear.

The mists began to roll across the well-trod ground. Margret ground her teeth, but she did not fight; the men looked up, beyond her back. She heard the sound of cerdan approaching.

But it didn't matter. She knew who the kai Leonne reminded her of, and she took a bitter comfort from the knowledge.

Adam. Her baby brother.

The wind that carried the sound of their steps changed as she waited, her hands clenched around something hard and sharp. She did not look down.

She knew what she held.

Instead, she lifted her face; she felt the dry voice of the desert give way to the wet, humid air of the ocean. The sea. She heard gulls in the distance, cawing and braying like quarrelsome children. Saw the flash of sun upon water that moved, slowly and steadily, toward a great wall.

Seawall, someone said. She did not recognize the voice, although she knew it as one of her own: the Matriarchs.

The voices of these women, she knew then, would always be with her—while she bore the Heart of Arkosa. It was a comfort, and for a moment she understood the enormity of her mother's sacrifice, for her mother had chosen to live—and die—alone.

Pay attention, her mother snapped.

Above that wall was a large building, and from its heights she could hear, clear and piercing, a distant song. A lone voice. She squinted, but the building stood too close, and the heights were taken by the sheer side of a wall; the figure was beyond her vision.

She saw the Isle that rose out of the waves, its towers tall and fine, their flags bent and wrapped by wind into cloth, rather than symbol; but she knew that she looked upon the city of Averalaan.

Averalaan Aramarelas.

She drew closer to that Isle, and it grew larger, and large still; it clung to the mainland by the thinnest of bridges She had never liked the sea, but she could understand gazing upon this place, why her dislike was not shared b the Northerners.

But it was not enough; the mists that rolled seemed t carry her through a place that was louder than the cras of waves against the distant wall. If she had ever hated th Tor Leonne, with its multitude of scents and odors, its pres of bodies, its small houses one almost on top of the othe she repented; she did not think she could ever walk in place such as this, in streets so full, without panic o paralysis.

You had better learn.

The irritation the words invoked was blessedly—annoyingly—familiar.

The sun's light dimmed; the streets grew gray. The people that crowded their way between the walls of close buildings were armed and armored. They carried swords, an across their backs, the bows of the North, great curve poles of wood that they had somehow thought to turn int deadly weapons.

And at their head rode two men, their visors open, thei faces exposed.

They were beautiful, profoundly beautiful. Margret coul not say why. They were not like the Lord Celleriant, n like the Serra Diora; they were not perfect of feature, perfect of form. They wore regalia that she did not recognize Swords, rods and crowns, eagles, wolves.

But when their gaze turned at last upon her, sh understood.

Their eyes were golden.

She had been raised in the South. She knew that th golden-eyed were demon-spawn.

And knew that what she had known—all of it—mus eventually be proved false, for these men could not be th spawn of the Lord of Night. She had seen the Hunters o the night of the Festival Moon. They had provoked fea anger, and a terrible sense of mortality. But they had no invoked what she felt now: awe, and yet . . . and yet . .

some sense that she might attain, through effort and will, what she admired so instinctively.

One of the two men nodded and smiled. The smile was brief and gentle.

She almost reached out, but something caught her hand; something held it fast.

You will not stand alone in the war, a voice said. It was a familiar voice. Evallen's. *With men such as these as your allies, you will never stand alone.*

They passed away at the head of an army that seemed to go on forever. She looked up, then, to see that the clouds in the sky were dark.

The fog rolled in.

The forest floor was once again beneath her feet. She stepped across a bed of moss, moved her foot so that she might avoid crushing the drooping fronds of a plant she had never seen, its wide leaves splayed outward like a slender hand, its veins white and red. The rich tang of earth, the sharp scent of the trees, told her that this, too, was foreign land—but it was peaceful, silent.

The baying of dogs rose like distant song.

But unlike the singer in the strange building above the sea, the dogs did not choose to remain distant. She heard the snap of twigs and the crush of undergrowth as they approached, and in spite of herself she held her breath.

But a voice called them in a tongue she did not know. She listened carefully. The leader of the pack was larger than any wolf she had ever seen, but its coat was strange: silver-gray with a hint of black flashing around its forefeet and left eye. Its ears were folded back, its teeth exposed; it skidded to a stop, its wild cry descending into throaty growl.

She heard the voice again, a man's voice; it contained both anger and affection. She did not have the time to wonder what the man who had spoken looked like, for he came, ducking under a bare, low-lying branch, his hand comfortable against bark.

He wore green in many shades, although his boots and his belt were brown. His hand was curved around a simple, silver horn.

The dog's growl slid into a whine. But clearly the man

was accustomed to dogs, or at least these; he was implacable.

A young boy appeared from behind the man. He wore brown. He spoke to the man, the man nodded, and he turned his attention to the dogs. They were instantly attentive.

As was she, although with different reason. She found the boy disturbing, but she could not say why. He was obviously son to the man. His hair was the same dark mess, his eyes the same brown, but they were larger, the lashes longer; his jaw was slightly more pronounced, which was unusual in a child of his age.

Two more boys approached her. No, one boy, and one girl. They were dressed in brown, but they wore it as if it did not suit them; they were not born to the colors, she thought.

The boy was fair. His hair was the color of gold, his skin the color of the High Court. His lips were full; his chest slender. It was also heaving as he bent and gripped his knees, struggling for breath.

"Am I the *only* person here who can't keep up with the dogs?"

And she understood his words.

The girl laughed. "Yes." She shrugged her hair out of the hood of her short cloak. Margret had thought the boy fair; next to the girl, he was ruddy. She was slender, and although she wasn't gasping for breath the way the boy did, she seemed delicate and fine. But her eyes were the color of steel.

The boy rose.

And Margret saw that *his* eyes were the color of gold.

"Uncle, you've always said that men don't strike women. But according to Mother, I'm not a man yet." He lifted his arm.

The man laughed. Loudly. He answered, and Margret wished she could understand what he said, for she loved the rough sound of his voice.

I never said you should hold your hand because they were delicate or weak, one of the Matriarchs offered. Not a voice she recognized.

How do you know that?

It is a language that has roots in the Southeast. Now pay attention, Daughter.

The boy frowned. His brow furrowed, and the expression that resulted was incongruously old. But he looked up, and when he saw Margret, his eyes widened.

"I am from Arkosa," she said. She could not have said why.

The girl turned on her heel, then, like a startled deer. They stared at her, this boy and this girl, golden-eyed and steel-eyed. As if she were actually there. As if they were prepared to listen to whatever it was she had to offer them.

But that did not disturb her. The winds did. They had changed again. The pungent scent of strange trees, the tang of wet earth, the smell of sweat, of sweet-sour breath, dissolved. The chill did not. Like desert night, the absence of warmth came suddenly. Unlike desert night, she was unprepared for it.

Gold gave way to ice, ice such as she had never seen. There were no trees, no valleys; the hills, such as they were, were sharp and white. Everything was white.

She squinted against the glare.

But white had shades. Where the hills peaked and trailed frozen water, they cast shadows of gray and pale, pale blue.

There was no movement across this white landscape for as far as the eye could see. Had she thought the desert harsh? It was, but it knew warmth and heat. In this wasteland, there was only cold, and the turning of the day would not change the death it offered. She was certain of it.

The sun was setting.

White gave way to crimson, blue to purple, gray to gray. There was a majesty to the sunset in this place that the desert did not boast, could not possess.

But she was not swayed by its beauty.

For at night, she saw lights in the distance that she had not noticed in the height of sun's rise. She did not want to see them. Could not fail to do so. The air, cold and clear, obscured nothing.

She did not move, but the lights grew closer, and closer still, until she stood at the foot of a mountain. There, midway between foot and crown, she saw the outline of a city in the pale silver of moon. She had missed it, in the day, and as she approached it, unwillingly, she knew why. It was a part of the mountain. She could see no cut stones, no clay, no mortar; no rushes or reeds, no wood. If there was a road that led from the bottom to the heights, she could not see it.

The silence was terrible. She would have babbled to fill it, but she was almost afraid to make noise. The Voyani loved shadow, for it hid them from the sun's light. But she knew better than to seek the shadows here.

The lights had made the edifice above seem small, but this, too, was a lie; the lights occupied only a scant portion of the largest building that jutted from the mountain's great side. She was drawn to them because anything that needed light was less of a danger than things that abjured it.

She climbed, although her feet were still. Momentum was provided by the mists. Her hands were stiff and cold, and she was torn between a desire to release the Heart, and a desire to cling to it, as if it were her only protection. In the end, she clung.

She passed through a large arch, its gates open to the night air. She heard music, and the scattered hush of quiet voices; no song was raised. No banner.

There were men and women within a great hall. Wood burned in a fireplace that stretched from one wall to another, but clearly it offered sparse heat. Furs lined cloth too thick to be silk, breath rose in faint clouds. She did not recognize the first people she saw. She took comfort in the fact that many were fair of skin, their hair burnished bronze, or pale red.

But she paused, once, and instead of fear felt contempt and anger, for she recognized across the chest of one man a small golden sword that trailed rubies.

Sword of Knowledge.

What a surprise.

Feel contempt, if it helps. a woman said. *But remember, it was not the men alone who chose our paths when the Cities ruled.*

She recognized the voice. Sen Margret.

The other Matriarchs were silent.

She passed beyond these halls. The lights dimmed, and the color they provided faded as well. The stone of the floor was smooth and seamless; the arch of the ceilings that towered so high above her she could not see their end in the night, seamless as well. She reached out to touch the surface of one wall; it was warm as ice.

But more unsettling.

No more, she whispered.

Because she knew what she would see. She knew. The halls vanished; the open sky, stars bright as diamonds, remote as the dead and as silent, stared down upon a vast, open courtyard.

In the heart of the courtyard lay a creature the size of three wagons. No, not one. As shadows resolved themselves, she counted two, each with jaws half again the size of Stavos from end to end. She heard the rumble of their lungs; they rested. But their lids—if they had them—did not close; their great, red eyes, looked out on the world, waiting for some sign of movement.

She heard the Sen Margret's rough curse.

And it appeared they did as well, for their heads rose; the spines that lined their backs rose as well, bristling. Their tails lifted, swinging to and fro as they gained their feet.

She knew what a rabbit knew when it gazed at the oncoming jaws of a wolf.

She closed her eyes. Felt the keening of wind as it moved around their teeth, heard the snap of their great jaws as they passed through her. Their breath was the wind across a battleground rich with carrion.

But their roar was worse.

They thrashed in anger, in fury. Fire singed the stone, blackening it as it engulfed her.

She did not burn.

She froze.

And she might have remained frozen but for the unexpected sound that followed: a child's scream. Her heart beat a thousand times in the minute between the roar and the scream as she gazed up, and up, and up.

Against the night sky, two towers rose. The cry came from one, but she could not clearly tell which.

She rose as well. Rose. It was disconcerting.There were no stairs, nothing against which her feet might find purchase. There was the Northern air, the backdrop of sky and stone and snow. She wondered if flight felt like this, and decided that she was glad she'd been born without wings.

The child screamed again, but this time the wail trailed

off into sobs, muffled but not contained. There was a window, tall and slender, from which the sound came. She readied herself.

But she did not leap.

For she could see, clearly, what occurred within.

Light grew, fire trapped by a glass lamp. Its orange glow was soft; it was meant to gentle darkness, not destroy it.

The child was a girl. She was perhaps six, although Margret thought it more likely that she was younger; she was slender in the way that only children can be. Her hair was a profusion of curls and tangles, her eyes were wide and dark, and her skin was bronze with the touch of a sun that the North could not know.

The child clutched blankets around herself, her chin hidden in the top of their folds.

A man came to her as she sat in the center of her bed.

She tried to swallow her tears, and to Margret's surprise, she succeeded. But the effort made her shudder. It was terrible.

For the first time since she had entered these Northern wastes, she desired the strength of form, because she longed to grab the child and run.

But she knew her arms would be no haven, provide no warmth, not here.

"Ariel," the man said quietly. "Why do you cry?"

She looked up at his face, and drew the blankets more tightly around her shoulders.

Margret would have done the same; there was something in the stranger's voice that she did not like.

She looked at him in the light. He was tall and slender—too tall, too slender. His face was pale, his hair pale as well. His arms were long, his hands long, his fingers unblemished.

"The beasts," she whispered.

"They are hundreds of feet beneath us. You have seen their jaws, Ariel. Do you think they could fit through the doors of this tower?"

She didn't answer.

"Come," he said. He held out his arms.

Margret, as a child, would never have willingly entered them, but this girl did, and to Margret's surprise, he held her as carefully, and as gently, as a parent might—although she *knew* he was no parent. The girl's fingers curved 'round his neck, she settled into his chest, and when he lifted her, she looked even smaller than Margret had first thought.

He carried her to the window.

Margret's mouth went dry; she was terrified that he would simply throw the child out.

But he tucked the top of her head beneath his chin instead. His gaze, as it fell upon the beasts in the courtyard below chilled Margret—and she had thought nothing could be colder than this place until she saw his expression.

He took a step out of the window, bending slightly to avoid collision with its curved peak. The child did not demur; her tears had stopped completely.

"Do you remember what I told you?"

"Yes, Lord Isladar."

"Good. No matter what happens, do not let go of me. Do you understand?"

"Yes."

The air held him as he made his way down to the courtyard below.

Margret shouted a dozen curses at his dwindling form. A hundred. But none of them reached his ears.

The beasts snapped, snarled; their flames colored the courtyard in a way not unlike the way the lamp had colored the room.

He landed ten yards from the nearest snapping jaw.

Again, instinct stung her, anxiety answered. *Now,* she thought, *now he will feed the child to the beasts.*

But if that was his intention, he showed no signs of it. He spoke to the great beasts in a voice that was equal to theirs, and she was astonished at the sound of it; it was low and deep, like the rumble of earth, and although she did not understand the language, she felt the command inherent in the words.

So, too, did the beasts.

Significant, she thought, that none of the Matriarchs chose to translate what he said, for she was certain the Sen Margret knew the language.

Yes, that ancient voice whispered. *I know it. But I will not speak it here.*

They growled, but they fell to the ground, their great bellies scraping stone audibly. He waited.

And then, to Margret's astonishment, he approached

them, the child still safe within the shelter of his arms. He bent his head a moment; she was far enough away that she could not hear his words.

But the child gazed upon these humbled creatures for a long time.

She had seen Arkosan children held exactly that way when they were first introduced to horses and other large beasts of burden.

She bowed her head, took in lungfuls of cold, crisp air. And then she heard another voice, and she forgot to breathe.

The beasts were absolutely silent.

The man who held the child was more so. He knelt. She lost sight of the girl as his slender form folded at once into a posture of complete subservience. His hair fell around his shoulders, blanketing stone; his back bent, curving up toward the moon. The small hands that had been clasped around a slender neck vanished as well. He became cloaked in shadow, bathed in moonlight. No sign of the child remained.

But Margret knew she was there.

She had no desire to bow, although if she thought it would have saved her, she would have.

From the height of the second tower, forgotten until this moment, true night descended.

In form and seeming, it was much like the stranger who had carried the child to view the beasts: tall, slender, perfect.

But the form did not contain the power within it easily. Margret watched because she no longer remembered how to look away. She should have been afraid, and she was, but the fear was complicated by too many other emotions, all of which she struggled to leave unnamed.

He would see the child, of course. She could not; she would have said the child had simply ceased to exist if she had not known otherwise.

But she knew that the death the beasts' jaws offered was a better death; cleaner and swifter than the death offered by the Lord of Night.

"Isladar."

The man upon the ground did not move.

"What do you seek to hide?"

"Nothing that exists within the Shining Palace can be hidden from you, Lord. I merely protect it from the elements."

"You may rise."

He unfolded so slowly Margret wondered if he meant to disobey the command. But he rose, and as he did, the child's face was revealed.

There was no question whatsoever that the Lord of Night would kill the child. She had seen it too many times.

No.

She had *never* seen it.

But the memories crowded in upon her, approaching her as any other truth had approached her in the gathering mist. The Sen Margret had seen it many times, as coldly and casually as Margret had witnessed the slaughter of livestock in the valleys. And Margret was tainted, would forever be tainted, by the memories of that woman.

She had offered him children such as these, and she had allowed herself no mercy; she had learned to listen and watch without betraying the slightest emotion.

Had there been none?

The Lord of Night was so terribly beautiful. That was the worst of it. As he descended, as he approached, she saw the lines of darkness that formed his face, his skin; she saw the hair that trailed behind him, around him, like a flowing crown, some raiment too costly for the merely mortal to procure. She reached out involuntarily.

Reached out to touch him as he passed.

And she felt the strands of his hair burn her palm.

Worse, though, was his sudden stillness.

Descent stopped. He turned to her in the light of the moon, and rose to greet her. His eyes were dark and perfect, although they looked like no eyes she had ever seen. They did not pass through her. They looked *at* her.

"What is this?"

He drew closer; she could not prevent it. Reached out to touch her. Her hands were frozen and rigid. She held them cupped before her in the cold of the winter night, and she gazed above them.

"Allasakar," she whispered.

He frowned. The frown cut her sharply.

"What is this?" he said again, and she would have gladly

listened to the roar of the beasts if they were able to drown out his words.

She spoke in a voice that was not her own, but she knew it well. "I have come, at last."

The frown deepened. "I know you," he said.

Some part of her was terrified. Some part of her was bitterly glad. He reached out; she felt his hands as they brushed her cheek. Saw the hint of a smile in the cold, cold line of his lips.

She knew him.

"How have you journeyed this far? How have you waited this long? I am served by lesser mortals, by inferior vessels. I thought that I would never again see a worthy mortal. Come."

She obeyed.

But something held her feet; they would not move.

"Why have you not summoned me? Why have I not heard your voice before this night?"

"I could not summon you. Before this night, I had no voice, my Lord." She flinched, but she did not flinch. "I may not stay. I have come to say good-bye."

His eyes widened and then narrowed. "I release nothing that I have claimed in my time."

"It is not your time," she whispered. "Or mine. They have passed."

She felt the visceral desire of a long dead woman; it was so unlike any that she had felt in her life that she stood apart from it for just a moment.

But the moment was long enough.

Margret, daughter of Evallen, lifted her chin, struggling for control of her voice.

She gazed upon the face of a god for the first time.

She raised her shaking hands. Sen Margret had served him. Sen Margret had loved him. Had loved him in a way that she had never loved another; not her Lord, and not her husband; not her son; not even the Sanctum that had been her life.

But Margret of the Arkosa Voyani *hated* him. His servants had killed her mother, and his servants had killed her cousin.

She raised those hands with a cry of denial greater than any she had uttered: a single word.

The golden mists shattered. The palace of stone and ice disappeared in the swirl of their storm. She cried out again as she was pulled back, pulled hard. Closed her eyes as the world flowed past her, as people she knew and people she would never know spiraled outward in images too numerous to contain.

The god called her name.

Margret.

She *felt* it, visceral and sudden, a terrible need, worse than any desert thirst.

But something else called her name as well. A hundred women. The Matriarchs of Arkosa.

And a single woman. The Serra Diora di'Marano. A hundred voices and one bound her in place, held her fast. Only one voice was silent.

She hated the Sen Margret, and she pitied her.

For the Sen Margret had never had voices such as these with which to deny that call; she had had only her own. Powerful woman. Powerful and terribly alone.

Come, Mother, all my mothers—this is why we were born.

The lights leaped from the spheres. The fires raged in the room outside of the circle of Arkosa. And Margret held the Heart of Arkosa in blistering hands.

CHAPTER THIRTY-THREE

The earth sloughed off the thin layer of dry pale sand, not as snakes shed, who slide whole from the transparency of their casing, and not as animals who have passed through the cold threat of winter, but rather as men might cast off the enemies who have managed, for just a moment, to gain ascendance by virtue of their weight and size.

The winds had no time to grasp at those loose grains; fissures, deep and broad, formed in the ground, swallowing the looser, lighter sand.

Elena saw this from a distance that was no longer safe. She was not aware of how far she had run after she had forced her cousin to release her arm, but she knew, with a certainty that was bred in the bloodline, that this had been a bad idea.

The daughters were always left behind; they were ordered to wait, and they tested their endurance beneath the full glare of the Lord at his most powerful. She had water, she had the robes that had been manufactured year after year by the most august of aunts; she had the scarf behind which she might hide her face, if common sense overcame the visceral pride of being stronger than the Lord.

It did not cover her nose and mouth now.

The hands that had pulled at the back of a demon's robes slackened, but they did not fall away; her grip had been so tight that nerveless fingers still forced the shape of curved fist upon them.

She used that grip to pull herself across a hairline split in the sand, seen because of the sudden fall of loose, pale grains.

Lord Ishavriel turned to Lord Telakar. "You have cost me," he said, the night of his voice diminished somehow. "But perhaps you have done me a service by your interference." He drew his arms across his chest in a gesture that looked like ritual, it was so stilted. "In the Shining City, we will meet again."

But Lord Telakar laughed, his low voice wild enough that it reminded her of the keening of wind. "In the Shining City? I think not, Lord Ishavriel. Gather the Fist, if you will. Alert our Lord, if he needs such a warning. You have games to play in the South, but they are yours.

"Mine are here. Here, with the Cities of Man."

The Lord Ishavriel smiled. "When the Lord at last turns his attention to the South, when the war with the Generals has been won, he will find you, Telakar. If you were not beneath his notice, he would find you now, and he would call you.

"Or do you think that you have somehow escaped the binding?"

Telakar was silent.

The earth was not.

What had been flat plains for as far as the eye could clearly see now looked like slowly crumpling parchment that had yellowed with age. The desert was withering before her eyes; it was being peeled away, a rough, heavy blanket that crumbled with age and decay.

"I am *Kialli*, and I serve the Lord with as much grace as the strongest of his Generals," Lord Telakar said. "In my youth, I was beneath your notice. If I am beneath it now, it is of little consequence to me. Go back, Ishavriel, but I will stay. I will bear witness."

"You are a fool."

He shrugged. She felt the rise and fall of his shoulder beneath her cheek, and she pulled away as if stung.

Her cousin stumbled. For a moment she thought the earth would take him. She teetered between fear and desire. But she did not call his name.

"Do you think to see the Cities of Man rise again?" Ishavriel laughed. "What was interred was mortal; you witness the unearthing of its remains, no more."

"If that is true, why leave?"

Lord Telakar was trembling, but Elena could not tell if it was merely due to the movement of earth, for the earth's trembling matched his. "I have witnessed the unearthing of remains before," he said. Voice low, words imbued with a past that Elena both felt and was ignorant of, he added, "What, after all, is *this?*" and he lifted an arm.

What his sword had not done, his words did: Ishavriel took a step back, eyes wide.

And her cousin turned to him, eyes narrowed, face pale. His hair was as black as shadow beneath the folds of his hood, although he wore sand dust like a fine powder. "Will you leave now?" he cried. She heard the fury that followed betrayal in the way he extended the last word.

Ishavriel's smile was uglier. "There is nothing for me here. Not yet. And if you are wise, little mortal, you will leave as well."

Her cousin was silent, but the silence was a facade; he would have screamed without control if he had had the words at hand to express his rage. Her grip fell away from the demon.

She had seen him this way before, and although the fury was real—and dangerous—it had never evoked fear in her. Not for herself.

The air was dry. Her lips were cracked. Her tongue stuck to the roof of her mouth.

He had *betrayed* her. He had betrayed Arkosa. He had broken the laws upon which the *Voyanne* itself was founded. She struggled to hold on to her anger and her contempt, to raise them, as the clansmen raised the heavy shields they wore when they rode to war.

But hers had been a temper like his; it was not a thing of fire, and not the heated glare of the endless sun, but rather the lightning's strike. It passed with the storm, but sometimes—sometimes it left bodies in its wake when the clouds had blown past.

Nicu, she thought, betraying herself, her resolve. *Nicu, no.*

He raised the sword. With a cry, with an inarticulate cry, he launched himself.

Ishavriel's laughter was louder, for a moment, than the frenzied shudder of earth. She stumbled; fell awkwardly to one knee. She dropped her hands to either side of that leg, to steady herself, to preserve what little balance she could.

Head bowed, she still heard the clash of steel against steel. Not flesh.

"If I had time, if I had the inclination, I would kill you

for that. But it was pathetic. You are not worthy to bear the name Arkosa."

He laughed, and she lifted her head, her palms shifting as the surface of the plain shifted.

She met his gaze, and held it.

"I would do your work for you," he told her quietly, "but you will take more from it than I could. Enjoy yourself, little mortal. I have no doubt if you survive the next hour, that we will meet again."

He was gone.

Where he had stood, the first of the great stone buildings broke free from their casings and reached upward, and upward again, for the blue of clear sky.

She saw it lift itself from the dirt and she understood what it meant.

So, too, did Nicu, her foolish, stupid cousin.

He leaped for its flat, wide surface, for it alone did not seem in danger of answering the earth's rumble by shattering or breaking.

"*Nicu!*" she shouted, pointing.

Behind him, held by claws that were made of gold—but a gold that pulsed and danced—was a glowing sphere that was larger in all ways than he.

He didn't even notice. His eyes were wide as he found her by the combination of her voice and his name. "Elena!" He reached out with a hand that was ten yards too far away.

The earth convulsed.

She stumbled across its broken surface, running toward him, but it was far, far too late: the surface rose, and rose again, in jerky, sharp movements; had she been beneath the building upon which he now stood, it would have been too far above her by the time she reached him.

But she saw the look on his face as it ascended, and the fear of her own death did not destroy the sudden, painful desire to weep.

She did not, however, give in to desire. She reached up and shoved the robe's hood from her face, exposing her wild red hair to the dust-laden wind.

In the changing landscape, she saw other buildings rise, but they were miles away, sharp, rectangular hills in the newly exposed earth.

"*Elena!*"

Reversing course, she turned from her cousin's anguished expression and ran again, vaulting over crevices, staring ahead, always ahead. The earth that the building shed tumbled down like the deadly snows in the mountain passes, and she did not wish to be trapped beneath it.

But there were so many things she didn't want, and in the end, she had had to face almost all of them.

Three buildings. Four. Five. Six.

But they were deadly havens.

She ran away from the City as quickly as she could.

And she only missed her footing once, but once was enough.

Her foot gave way as the earth moved, sliding out from beneath her weight, and her full momentum, before she could change course; both of her hands flew out and slapped sand just before her face did.

Pain did different things to different people; she did not cry out. But she rolled along the flat of the sand, her knee to her chest, her hands gripping the boot that covered her left ankle, her breath a short, forced gasp that came again and again through clenched teeth.

Something grabbed at her robes, something dug itself into the flesh of her back. She struggled a moment and then she was airborne as the land threw her.

But what she struck was not sand, not stone; it was soft and warm. Her hands clutched at air, and then at fur, and she felt arms wrap themselves around her upper body. She opened her eyes, then, and saw antlers.

Antlers.

"My pardon, Serra," a voice said in her ear. The words were stilted, the accent formal. She twisted around to see the Serra Diora's seraf, his aged face cut and bruised, his robes torn. "I have her!" he shouted, and the world began to move.

She had ridden horses before, and she had always been the first to admit that she was a poor rider. At best. But the beast beneath her was no horse. She clutched his sides with her knees, and cried out as a shock of heat and pain traveled up her left leg.

"Do not hold fast," the seraf said roughly. "This creature—you cannot fall from his back if he wishes to carry you."

"But the ground—"

Broke. And broke again. But wherever sheer, flat earth presented itself, it was always to the side, never beneath the hooves, of the great stag.

She looked back.

Margret.

The pain was terrible.

Nicu.

They did not answer her.

But something did.

"Where do you flee to, daughter of Arkosa?"

She looked up; the air was thick with sand and heat. And shadow.

The Lord Telakar fell upon her like an ancient doom; she felt his hands beneath the pit of her arms as she was dragged from the back of the stag.

"Come. You do not wish to miss the moment of your clan's triumph."

She rose, then. Felt the seraf's hands on her leg as he tried to pull her down.

She bit back a scream because she did not wish to share it with a demon.

He rose, and she rose with him as his arms circled her chest and waist. "If you struggle, you will fall," he whispered. "And if you fall, you will die."

She could not see his face.

But she could see the ground fall away as he carried her up, and up, beyond the reach of the bones of the City below. And she could see the stag return for the seraf who had been pulled from its back by his attempt to save her.

They met across the impatient earth, the stag dipping head and antler to catch the fallen man.

"Come. If such as you can know gratitude, you will know it when this is done. I should have seen the hand of the hidden Court in this. Do you know what it is that you rode?"

No. But she could see the stag now; could see that he bounded from foothold to foothold without once staggering or stumbling, as if a path was visible to him, and him alone. And she could see that beyond him the ground quieted, the earth stilled. Only where the City rose was it treacherous.

She could not see Margret. Could not see the Serra

Diora. But she could make out the wagons of Arkosa as they lay fallen against the desert floor, like lost ships.

The seventh building rose.

And in its center there was also a sphere, glowing like captured sun.

"The Seven Spheres," Lord Telakar said, the words tickling her ear, running the length of her spine. "They still burn. You were right, little mortal. Had I stayed my ground, I would have been devoured by their fire, their ice. Did you know?"

He laughed.

Had she feared for his life?

Did he even have one to lose? Such creatures came from the Hells, and to the Hells returned when they were vanquished. Thus went the stories, the songs, and the legends.

"*I* did not know. I was not here, not at *this* City. No wonder the Lord chose to bespeak the old earth; he could not destroy this place without using the full force of his power, and he was at war."

He laughed again, and the sound was terrifying because it was so beautiful.

But the air was cold. In the heat of the sun, it was chill. She heard the wind's howl as it threw her hair back, and she could not stop herself from shaking.

"But he negotiated with his blood, and the old earth accepted it. Never accept the blood of a god in return for service, little human, no matter how fair the exchange seems at the time."

Her teeth made more noise than his voice. Elena had never been fond of heights. The ground surged forward and back; it would not stay still.

"Do you think he asked the ground to bury the Cities at its own convenience? Do you think his blood was offered and accepted carelessly?"

She could not answer.

It didn't matter.

"No," he told her, his voice almost lilting. "You witness the beginning of the end of an age."

She *knew* the words for truth when they were spoken, although she would never have thought to speak them herself.

From the heights, at a distance, she watched the City

rise. An eighth building's broad dome jutted out of the ground, joining the seven, and then, after it, other buildings too numerous to count.

And as she stood in the air at the height of day, she felt fear give ground to wonder, for she had never seen a city so vast as the one that rose now, and she had traveled the length and breadth of the Dominion, following the *Voyanne*.

"This City," Lord Telakar whispered, "stood against the armies of the Lord. What he had planted for his own use was too frail; it was discovered and destroyed before he could use it to break the Spheres. He suffered losses that day that the *Kialli* remember still."

"W–what do you mean?"

"The mortals served the Lord, as did we; they accepted the power he offered, as did we. But they were numerous, and he had chosen only the most powerful among their number to receive his gift. They proved to be short-lived, and they fought his command in a way that the lesser Allasakari could not, breaking the oaths they had been foolish enough to make. Mortals are not what we were, not what we are. Death freed them. Do you understand? Death *freed* them, and saved these edifices, this history."

He gestured, and she cried out, grabbing at the arm that still held her waist.

His laughter was low and rich. "If I wished you to fall, you would fall. Come. The Spheres slumber a moment. Can you feel their power?"

She shook her head.

He laughed again, but a coolness had entered his amusement.

"You are not so accomplished a liar, Arkosan, that you can lie to me. I spent centuries within the walls of these Cities, studying the ways of your ancient kin. My kin chose to watch trees grow; I chose to watch you."

She swallowed air, hating the cold.

"I will ask you again, do you feel the power of the Seven?"

She did. But she did not understand what exactly it was that she felt. It was as if she had two hearts, as if she could separate their mutual rhythm. He was waiting for an answer. She felt the winds buckle beneath her feet, although he did not threaten her.

"I feel . . . a heartbeat."

"Is that all?"

She nodded.

"Where?"

"I don't know." The winds dropped her again, but this time, he removed the arm that she had clung to. "*I don't know.* I'm not the Matriarch. I'm only barely her successor."

He stepped back; she stood above the distant ground, alone, his gaze as compelling as the Lord Ishavriel's had been.

"You can't know what I see, when I see you," he said softly. It was not what she had expected to hear. "I did not see it clearly when I last walked these lands."

She didn't ask. She didn't want to know.

But he spoke anyway. "I see what dies, and I see what cannot die. I see your name."

"My name?"

"Yes." He lifted a hand; trailed the line of her chin with the tips of his fingers.

"Only demons have hidden names."

He laughed. "Is that what you were taught? Only demons? Is that what I am?" He turned away, lifting an arm. "This desert was once the cradle of the lands your petty Tyrs now rule. From those mountains in the South to the heart of the Deepings, lakes lay beneath the fronds of great trees, fed by the rivers that ran toward the distant oceans.

"The Arianni hunted in the wilderness beyond your walls. And there, upon the peaks of those mountains, Verasallion lived above his ancient hoard; in the clearest of nights, when he so cared, he crested the thermals above the Cities, drawing their fire, and responding in kind.

"There," he said, "the spirits of the forests gathered to speak and dance, and many a mortal traveler was lost to the circles they spun of grass and flower, branch and leaf.

"Look. That building there, that large, long crescent, do you see it?"

She nodded. It had broken through the ground slowly, for it was not tall. But it formed one of two arcs that surrounded the base of the first tower to struggle its way to the heights. No building that she had ever seen had its shape, and in the light of sun, it glittered as if it had been painted with liquid gold.

"The Sen adepts dwelled there."

"And the—the other building?"

He laughed. "The other? The other crescent? Do you truly not recognize it?"

She shook her head. A sharp retort made its way to her lips, and she bit it back with effort. She should have been afraid. And she was—but not afraid enough.

"It was the other half of the City's power, the subtle half. If the Sen adepts provided the power that fueled—that still fuels—these Spheres, if they provided the defense that a god at war could not breach without peril, the women who ruled the northern crescent provided the warning by which the adepts planned their battles and made their decisions.

"There are mages now, in the lands of the mortals, who have the power of the least of the adepts, but I have not heard yet of one who has taken up the mantle of the Sanctum. The seers dwelled there; the women who had walked the Oracle's harshest road, and passed her final test." His smile dimmed; his eyes narrowed.

"You do not know what you have lost," he said quietly. "I do, although it was never mine to lose." He lifted his chin, his gaze unwavering as it sought the harshest of the Lord's glares. He did not fear for his vision.

But he looked down again, drawn, compelled, by the City below their feet.

"Ah. Do you see the circle?"

She could not help but see it; it rose last, but although it was thin, its line was unbroken as it circumnavigated the City.

"The walls," he whispered. "They closed them against us. Against *all* of us."

"But—"

"But?"

"But how did they feed the people?"

He shrugged. "We were not witness to the how, but it was clear that those of worth did not starve."

Although she knew it was pointless, she asked anyway. "Those of worth?"

"How is worth defined in the Dominion? Anywhere?"

She said, after a pause, "I don't know. We feed the children first."

"Before the Matriarch, daughter of Arkosa?"

"Before anyone," she replied flatly.

"How unusual. So many of the children die before they reach an age at which they can be useful."

He was smiling as he said it. She turned away, to watch the City unfold, to see history made and remade.

To hide what she suspected could not be hidden: her contempt and her disquiet.

No one spoke.

They had barely started their journey when their steps became punctuated by the trembling of the earth. Stavos drew the circle over his chest and turned to his wife; she was worried. But she did not speak.

Yollana stumbled, but the Serra Teresa prevented her from falling. "Matriarch?"

"We are safe here."

"And if we continue?"

"We will know when to stop, Serra."

Serra Teresa di'Marano was silent. Silence could convey so much in the hands of the right woman. And it could conceal just as much.

Jewel ATerafin stared across the desert, seeing the air move in the twisting dance of heat. There wasn't a cloud in the sky; in Averalaan she would have been able to see for miles. "Are we stopping?"

"No, ATerafin," Yollana replied.

At least two minutes had passed between the question and the answer. Jewel frowned. She hated the heat because it was so deceptive; she longed to pull hood from hair, to feel the open breeze that now blew, cool and sweet, across the barren plain.

"I would not," Avandar told her. And because she expected it, she kept her grimace to herself.

They resumed their walk. The old woman set the pace, Serra by her side; the Arkosans followed. Their shadows had lengthened perceptibly, although it would be a long while before the sun set across the distant horizon.

"ATerafin."

She looked up. Kallandras had approached her so quietly she hadn't noticed his presence at all. She frowned. "What's wrong?"

A pale brow rose and fell. "I do not think the news is bad." He lifted an arm, and she followed the folds of his robe, the curve of his hand.

In the distance, running across the sand so quickly there seemed to be no contact between hooves and ground, was the stag.

"Who is that on his back?"

"I cannot see clearly, but—"

"It is the slave," Lord Celleriant offered.

She jumped at the sound of his voice.

He, too, raised a silver brow.

"Celleriant?"

"Lady?"

"Make *noise* when you walk."

"As you command, Lady."

She would have asked him if he was certain, but it was clear that he was, and besides, the stag was moving so damn fast, she'd be able to see for herself who he carried in a minute or two.

But he didn't wait the minute.

Jewel.

You found him!

Yes. But I found things less pleasing in the desert. The Kialli are here.

Demons, you mean.

No, ATerafin. Kialli *lords.*

"He—the stag—says that there are *Kialli* in the desert."

She was surprised by Avandar's response. He laughed. "They are foolish indeed if they are anywhere near this place."

There is more. One of the Kialli took the Matriarch's cousin.

Elena?

I believe that is what she calls herself.

Took? Took where?

I did not have time to watch and bear witness. The City was rising beneath our feet, and I had given you my word that I would return this man to your keeping, if he lived.

The City?

Tor Arkosa, he said.

* * *

The fires left her. The winds receded. The lights dimmed. But the voices whose silence she half-feared simply hushed; she was aware of their presence.

The Serra Diora was alabaster and ebony; her eyes were unblinking, her expression nonexistent. And her hands were shaking.

"It's over," Margret whispered. Her throat felt raw, as if she had spent an hour screaming.

"Is it?"

"Yes."

Diora looked away. "I heard . . . Margret, did you hear it?"

"I heard a lot," Margret answered wryly.

"Did you hear the earth's voice?"

"I heard the earth breaking, if that's what you mean."

"No . . . I mean the earth's voice."

Margret was silent a moment. "I heard no words," she said. "I heard you. I heard the Matriarchs. What did you hear, Diora? Why have you gone so pale?"

But the Serra shook her head, as if to clear it. Or to deny what she did not wish to speak of.

The seven spheres that lined the room's walls were guttered. The light that had joined them in the room's center now lay entirely contained within the Heart of Arkosa. Margret gazed at it for a long time. She knew that she could carry it now. She could lift it from the Serra's trembling hands, catch the chain that seemed too slender to bear its weight, and place it around her neck.

She knew that when she did, she would have the voices of the Matriarchs, as guidance, as company, and as strident critics all, for the rest of her life.

But she hesitated.

"What is wrong?"

"I—I don't know what we're supposed to do now. I don't even know how we're supposed to leave this room."

The Serra Diora's hands ached. Her arms ached. She felt the slow movement of earth as if the dense, dark soil that both bore life and buried it were a part of her flesh.

She was afraid.

All things had voices.

If she paused for a moment, if she closed her eyes, she could recall them clearly: the lap of water against the stones in the Tor Leonne, the cry of wind, the chittering, high song of birds, or their raucous cries. She could hear the sorrow in the whining of dogs, the amusement in the nickering of horses, the droning hunger in the flight of insects.

But although she had listened for all of her life, she had never heard them speak with words.

The earth's voice was like no voice she had ever heard. Not even the wind's voice had frightened her as much.

But perhaps that was because Kallandras controlled it, and nothing that he controlled could be so wild, so dangerous. She had heard death in his voice before, beneath the pretty skein of his words. But it had never been for her.

Take back your home, child. Take back your world. The oaths that bind the wilderness and the old gods have been sundered, and payment is due.

Speak. I know you listen. I feel your feet upon the surface. Speak now.

She was almost mute with fear. His command was like no command she had ever heard; she could not fight it, had no desire to try.

But her power had fled her; she could not speak.

The earth rumbled beneath her feet.

Who are you?

I am Diora.

What is Diora?

She did not know how to answer the question. She could tell the force beneath her feet that she was a woman, that she was born to Sendari par di'Marano and Alora en'Marano; that she was seventeen; that she was the widow of the man who had once been heir to the vast lands of the Dominion.

She could tell him that she had been alone all her life; that she had had a few brief months in which she had learned not to be alone. That it was the most costly of lessons.

But she knew that those words were too thin and fragile a truth.

What did the earth know of life, after all, but its end? She could hear the echoes of the movement of tree roots through wet soil, could feel the passage of water beneath the surface of dry, hot sand, could almost touch the small flowers that tickled the surface in their brief hold on life.

What is Diora?

Words had often failed her. Silence had failed her. But song had not. The Serra Diora sang. She shed the words that so often contained the gift; they would offer the earth no meaning.

She knew so many songs. The cradle song came first. She sang it as if it were the first sound that she had known—and if it was not, it was the first she remembered clearly, when, as a child, she had been held or carried in the arms of adults who had offered the false promise of safety. And love.

Her rhythm was the rhythm of the falling earth, and between one song and the next, she offered the silence of the grave.

But there were other songs. She sang the lay of the Sun Sword, wordless, emotion carrying her from one note to the next; she sang the song of the first kai Leonne, and his battle with the falling Night.

The earth rumbled. Moved beneath her feet.

She did not offer her silence to what lay there; she had started; she meant to finish.

She sang of the Dominion. She sang of the Radann. And then, sensing that the song itself was not finished, the audience not satisfied, she left behind the songs she had been taught.

The music was wild. Harmonies were unsung. She took each breath as if it were a step across treacherous terrain, offered each note as if it were the last she might be allowed.

Beneath her hands, she felt the warmth of the Heart of Arkosa; it was the only comfort she was allowed to seek, and even that was bitter, because she knew it was almost at an end.

She did not sing of the City.

She sang of sun and wind, of day and night, of the storm that carried the Serpent at its heart. And then, because it was not enough, never enough, she turned at last to her sister-wives, and into the wordless melody, she placed their names. Faida. Deirdre. Ruatha.

And when she sang of them, she sang of Na'dani, her strength failing, and she returned at last to the first song that she had heard, the first song she had sung, the first song she remembered: the cradle song. But this time, she sang it as she had sung it only in the precious hours of night when she had been given the care of her son. That song trailed into the mourning song, the quiet ululation of a woman alone, arms empty, praying in the night to the Lady for a mercy that was almost never shown.

And the earth sighed.

It has been a long time, Daughter, since a mortal offered me their song.

I know you, now. The rivers know you, that have slept beneath my surface. The land will know you as you pass above it. There will be life, yours and mine, within this cradle.

I take your gift, instead of your blood. Bind yourself to the path you have chosen, and when that path has been traveled, when that burden has become, at the last, too heavy, I will carry you.

I will sing.

"Diora." Margret's hushed voice. Thin and weak and easily missed in the wake of the earth's, but more precious for all that.

She looked up.

"Margret," she said quietly, her own voice foreign to her. "Your shadow."

Margret nodded, but absently. "Look, Diora, look." She lifted a hand. One hand; the other held the Heart of Arkosa.

Above them both, the endless azure of the open sky looked down, bearing witness. The Lord's face was blinding, a white-gold sphere that had never waxed or waned. Or failed.

The earth was completely still.

But it was no longer flat; it was no longer the wide stretch of dusty sand that ran from Raverra to the mountains in Oerta.

Great stone edifices rose from the ground around them. Towers taller than any Diora had ever seen stretched up toward the endless sky, as if to claim its ownership. Their faces were carved with symbols, great indentations in stone that seemed to both catch the light and shed it at the same time.

She could not read what was written there; did not try. But Margret's eyes lingered on them, as if to absorb what lay there, newly exposed.

Domed ceilings rose like helms across the heights of the buildings whose roofs were distant enough to be seen; they were simple, but not austere, and they too were adorned, not with symbols but with statues. Had those statues been brightly colored, had they been painted or leaved, she would have mistaken them for people.

But people seldom chose to ride horses from the edges of rooftops.

There was glass here.

Glass had always seemed so fragile, and in the South, glass was worked in such a way that it might provide accents to the austerity of the homes of powerful men. But she could see glass that stretched, unbroken, from wall to wall, glass that stretched from ground to roof, be that roof three times the height of a tall man.

She saw flags, saw hanging signs, saw the perfect curved basins of fountains and wells.

She knew that she could spend the rest of her life exploring this City without discovering all that it contained, for she had never seen a city so vast. But she knew, as well, that she would have this day, this hour, this minute; that she would take only the time she needed to find the road that led from the place she now occupied to the gates the walls must contain.

"The Seven Towers still stand," Margret whispered, in a voice that was almost a stranger's.

"Seven? There are more," Diora said gently.

"There are seven of note. *The* Seven. Can you not see the Spheres that burn at their heights?" Her smile was also a stranger's. "And they did not fail."

"Margret?"

"If they had failed, there would be no City. Look at that sign, Diora—can you see it?"

Diora nodded, although she could see more than one.

"It is wood. Wood, stone, gold. But it looks newly made. And that flag. That banner. Can you not see the brilliance of scarlet, the depth of azure? They still exist. They have not aged." Her smiled broadened.

"And there—that is the artery. That is the street that

leads from one place of import to another, in an unbroken circle." She laughed. "I recognize this street. The one we're on. I know where we are!" She started to move, and then jerked to a stop, her hand still upon the Heart of Arkosa. "Look, look! There's sand there, dirt—but if you cleaned it, if you swept it away, you would see that these roads form the crescents of the symbol."

Those streets wound their way around the base of the closest tower, and from there, past buildings large and small, littered with sand, with stones, with things of the earth that they had clung to in their long captivity.

"Margret," Diora said gently. "Take the Heart. Take it. Wear it. You will be free to move."

Margret hesitated.

But she did not lift the crystal.

It sat between their hands, between their wounded palms.

"I don't—"

"You will have to take it sometime."

"I know."

"Why not now?"

Margret looked up, forgetting the city for a moment. She met the Serra's gaze, and held it. "Don't you know?"

"We will have time," the Serra replied. "We will have time to say our good-byes."

But Margret, daughter of Evallen, shook her head, the smile fading from her lips as sun faded from the sky at the close of day. Her skin was dark; it was lined and creased with sun and wind. Her hair was wild and dusty, her jaw too pronounced. She was not lovely. She was not graceful.

But she was very, very beautiful. "None of them will mean what this means."

"Shall I remind you again of all of the luxuries that power does *not* give you? Or shall I remind you instead of the luxuries that duty does not give me?"

"No. Maybe."

"A servant of the Lord of Night walked these lands. If your cousins survive, you must find them. If they do not, you must find their bodies. Your people are waiting, and I think they are no longer waiting patiently." She frowned a moment, and then laughed.

Lifting her voice, she spoke to the breeze that seemed to come from a quiet, cool place. "**Ona Teresa**," she said.

"Na'dio."

She offered her aunt no other words; nor did her aunt offer questions.

Margret, daughter of Evallen, caught the chain that held the Heart of Arkosa. She lifted it in one hand, and watched the light gold cast in shards across her feet. In silence, she raised it. In silence, she watched as the Heart left the Serra's open palms.

She donned it quietly, and felt all the weight of its burden as she raised her head to meet the eyes of the Flower of the Dominion.

As Matriarch and Serra, they stood.

"It is done," Lord Telakar said. "The City has risen. Is your vision so poor that you cannot see the two who now walk the streets?"

Elena swallowed.

"I see them. They wear the robes of your people, but they have exposed their faces to the sun your people shun. One is fair, the other dark; one walks like a warrior, and the other like a courtesan. But they walk in step, and they walk toward the East Gate.

"Ah," he said. "If you cannot see them, it is of no consequence. You must be able to see the river."

In spite of her fear, she turned to look.

Across a large rent in the surface of the desert, water gushed, as if from a great wound. It was no small river, and as she watched, it seemed to spread from the heart of the City outward to either side, sweeping beneath the walls that denied entry to all else.

"The earth has awakened. I think it will not be long before life returns to the wastelands." His smile faded. "It will not be long before the Matriarch of Arkosa begins to understand the workings of the Seven, and I will, I fear, meet with a poor welcome when she does. I feel their power now. It is . . . exquisite and unpleasant."

He lifted his arms a moment, pointing. He spoke, his words guttural and harsh.

"I cannot stay. But I thank you for your company. It has been a long time since I have had such an opportunity; in the Hells, no one visits who does not intend to stay."

His smile was brief. Cold.

He vanished.

And Elena fell.

But she did not fall for long. The air caught her in its folds, and she felt the arms of the demon around her. "It has been too long."

She closed her eyes, clinging to him in spite of herself, the fear of the imminent death greater than the unknown one.

He laughed. As if he could see every layer of fear she felt. She wasn't surprised that he enjoyed it.

The laughter faded; the arms held.

"Things *have* changed," he told her. "Believe that we were not always what you see now. We must leave. There are those who might interfere in what must unfold, and I have already been injured."

The world vanished.

The last thing she saw was the City of Arkosa.

The last thing she heard, although she could not see him, was the voice of the Northern bard.

"Elena!"

Lord Celleriant touched Kallandras' shoulder.

Kallandras turned his gaze from the empty sky. "We could not afford that," he said quietly. "Not now. The City has barely risen, and it stands empty."

"What they know of the City is not enough to be a threat. Unless it were the Matriarch herself who was taken—and perhaps even then, I cannot say—your enemies will learn little of substance or value."

Kallandras frowned. "You are not concerned."

"No. But my vision is better than yours."

"What did you see that I could not?"

"Who held her," was his quiet reply. But although he had told Kallandras to disregard the open sky, his gaze lingered longest upon the place that had been occupied, in the distance, by the two.

They waited, Arkosans, the Serra and her seraf, the stag, the Arianni lord, the Northern bard, the Northern seer, her quiet companion, and the Havallan Matriarch. Clothed in the robes of the Arkosan Voyani, they weathered the heat of the sun, the touch of its fire, and although they tried to speak among themselves, their words drifted into silence before they could complete a sentence.

What words could they have that would describe what lay before them? They felt no joy; not yet. They felt no fear, although perhaps the awe that they did feel was tinged by it; no wise man walked carelessly into the unknown, and the Voyani who had survived to be Yollana's age, or Stavos', had become, by grace of experiences which had not yet killed them, wise.

They waited.

And waited.

An hour passed. And another. Their shadows had lengthened against the newly exposed earth, the restless ground, but they kept their vigil.

And when the sun had begun to edge its way past the horizon, that vigil was rewarded. The walls of the City shimmered to the West, as if they were liquid stone. Through that curtain of liquid, unharmed, passed two women.

They wore the robes of the desert wanderers, but their faces were exposed, and at a distance of less than a mile, it was clear who they must be. They stopped as they gained the desert beyond the walls, and they gazed out.

The taller of the two lifted an arm and waved.

That was their signal, for in the absence of battle, they had developed no others: Stavos let out a cry of joy and began to run across the sands, arms wide, as if the distance was negligible.

His wife snorted; his cousin laughed. Tamara hesitated, as did Donatella by her side. Six had left the Arkosan encampment, and it became clear, when Stavos was halfway to the Matriarch, that only two would return.

But they joined the slowly moving group.

All save Lord Celleriant and Kallandras.

"Can you hear the City?" Lord Celleriant asked.

"No."

The Arianni lord lifted a platinum brow, but did not otherwise accuse the bard of lying. "There were songs sung in the Cities of Man that rivaled the music of the Arianni. Their bards met our bards in the Summer Court—and in the Winter Court, in their time—and they made a contest of even their art."

"Even? All things are measured." But Kallandras smiled, his eyes upon the distant walls, the ancient towers that jutted above them so perfectly. "Who won?"

Lord Celleriant laughed.

And Kallandras stilled, his eyes drawn from this ancient City to the man at his side, as if the man held the more enduring mystery, the more valuable artifacts.

"Have I amused you?"

"No," the bard replied, measuring the words he spoke. "You have surprised me."

"Oh?"

"I . . . have not heard you laugh."

"Your memory fails you, bard. The night the Serpent flew, I laughed."

"That was not laughter."

"No?"

"No more than the wind's voice, although the wind felt the same joy."

"Joy?" Lord Celleriant fell silent a moment. The laughter that had been so rich and unhindered was gone, a ripple in the surface of face and expression. "Perhaps. These lands are not the lands I walked. This war is not the war I fought. I have lived by the law of the Queen for all of my life, and I find it missing here.

"But it is . . . less unpleasant than I thought it might be. We did not know, not for certain, the fate of the Cities. We were to hold the roads against the passage of the Lord of Night, but we were met by his servants, and the Queen conversed long with their leader—a woman from Tor Arkosa.

"But from this, I believe we can gather two things. That four of the Cities survived.

"And that three of the Matriarchs will now be hunted with care and planning. One City is a threat that the Lord of Night can afford—for some time yet—to ignore; these people are ignorant; they are not what they were. But two such cities? Three? When word reaches our enemy, there will be a race in the Sea of Sorrows, and the *Kialli* will once again hunt there in numbers."

"With difficulty," Kallandras replied. "I have . . . traveled . . . with the Voyani."

"Oh?"

"It is considered unwise to speak of it."

"And yet you speak. To me."

"And yet," Kallandras lifted a hand to his brow, shading it from the sun's dimming light. "There are no people who cross these lands who know them better than the Voyani. If they are hunted in the wilderness, there will be death, but it will not be theirs."

"They will not be hunted by the Arianni, then."

"Even by the Arianni, Celleriant. The world is not the world you left; it is gray and dismal, its magic diminished, its song so silenced only those born with the gift can hear it. But in its muted shades, there are still places of power and knowledge that were never given to those who did not know time so intimately. But I am not certain that the Matriarchs themselves knew what to expect when they undertook this voyage. I do not think that the Matriarch Maria or the Matriarch Elsarre expect that their next voyage into the Sea of Sorrows will be their last.

"And I am not even certain that it *will* be their last. The Voyani families are *not* the same; they guard their secrets, and their secrets—their strengths—are different."

"You know this, and yet live?"

Kallandras lifted a brow. His smile, a slight turn of curved lips, lasted longer than the Arianni lord's laughter. But he did not answer the question. Instead he said, "If you must stay, stay; I must go to greet the Matriarch and the Serra."

He began to walk across the sands, his steps lighter and more certain than any step that had yet forged this path across the new land.

And from a distance, he heard Lord Celleriant's voice. "The mortals won," he said. "On almost all occasions. They had a gift for creation and their voices burned the memory with the immediacy and the tragedy of their brief lives. Why do you think I asked? I remember what I heard, even though it has long since passed.

"There has been a reason, always, for the fascination the dying hold for those who must seek death if they are to meet it at all."

CHAPTER THIRTY-FOUR

Margret spent the night in her wagon for the last time.

She knew that Stavos was worried for her because she had been so quiet when they met. She allowed herself to be bear-hugged, to be kissed, to have her hair pulled and ruffled as if she were no more than a child.

But she had retreated from the questions that rose almost instantly on the lips of her aunt, her aunt's cousin.

She had been grateful for the absolute silence offered by Yollana of Havalla, because that silence muted her people's curiosity by reminding them that they were among outsiders. She would never have thought that, surrounded by creatures out of legend—the great stag, the pale, tall Lord Celleriant—they would have needed that reminder. But the Serpent's storm had broken many barriers the night the rains fell, not just the ones that had divided Margret from Diora.

Night had stripped the land of warmth, as it always did; in the desert there was no room for seasons, no room for the compromise that occurred between night and day wherever life gathered.

She could hear the distant sound of the river that now flowed through the desert—and the City—that she would make her home.

But clearer than that, she could hear the creak of the plank that was the sole method of entry into her wagon's cabin. Without Elena, Nicu, Andreas, or Carmello, the Arkosans had had room enough in Elena's wagon to give Margret the privacy she needed.

She would not have asked for it, but when it was offered by Tamara, she gratefully acquiesced.

Therefore she rose to answer the door. There was no one else to do it for her, no one else to hide behind.

She could not sleep.

She could not; she knew that she had one task left to finish. And she desperately wanted that task to fall to anyone else, anyone but her. Later, perhaps. Later she might delegate such a duty.

She took a breath to steady herself. To remind herself that she must breathe evenly and deeply to remain calm.

Donatella stood, framed in the door, her hands exposed to the night air, palms up. "Matriarch," she whispered.

Margret had hoped for someone else.

"May I come in?"

She should not have had to ask. Margret knew it. She nodded and stepped aside.

Donatella entered the room, closing the door. She put her hands behind her back, and leaned against it.

"Tell me," the older woman whispered.

"Donatella—"

"I know. I know you have said you will explain it all when we take the ships to the City. But I am only a mother, Margret. I am only a worried mother. Tamara is stronger than I; she is willing to wait, although the wait is terrible. Will you show so little mercy? Tell me what happened. Tell me about my son."

"I'm sorry, Donatella. He is dead." She hung her head a moment, as if to hide tears. Was surprised to find truth in the lie of that posture. "I was selfish. I did not wish to speak of it, and I—I did not think of the harm it would do you."

But when she looked up, she saw that Donatella's eyes were dry as stone.

"We were attacked by a servant of the Lord of Night. My cousins—my cousins formed a line between the servant and me, and I fled. Had I remained, things might have been different. Had I remained, we might have lost the Heart—and the City—of Arkosa."

Donatella still did not speak.

"The servant of the Lord of Darkness took your son from you, and my cousin from me. I know—I know that Nicu did not forgive me for publicly lashing him. I wonder, sometimes, that you do." She lifted her hands and examined them unsparingly, as if she could see all of the blood they had ever shed, be it her own or another's. "I would have done anything to save him, Donatella. Believe that. But he was beyond my ability to save."

"You did not see him fall?"

"I did not see him fall, no. And I will search the City from end to end when I have the wagon airborne again. But the City rose beneath their feet—I can't think of any way they could have survived it. I'm sorry, Donatella. I did not expect what happened to happen."

The old woman was still, still as stone. Margret wished her own expression could be. "You are not lying to me, Matriarch?"

"I wish I were," Margret replied evenly. They were both aware of the enormity of the insult in the question. No wonder Donatella had been so quiet in the desert. "Or do you doubt me?"

At that, Donatella's expression shifted; the lines of her forehead gathered above her eyes. "You? Margret, I have never doubted you. I am a mother, but I am not a fool." She looked as if she might ask something else, but she held her peace, held her words.

"Thank you, Matriarch. I will—I will not trouble you more this night." She opened the door and turned to leave.

But another visitor stood in the doorway. The Serra Diora. She made way gravely and gracefully, finding room somehow between the door and the rails across from it. Donatella was not small.

She watched a lonely, bent old woman, her sorrow gathered around her like a blanket, her arms empty, and then turned to Margret; Margret silently held the door open until she had entered the wagon. The night air was cold; it chilled a cabin that contained too few people to generate heat.

When the door was closed, Diora said, "Why did you not tell her the truth?"

"Every word I told her *was* the truth."

"Yes, and she believes none of them. She wants to. Perhaps one day she will. But she does not believe them now. Why did you not tell her what happened?"

"Why? Will you?"

"It is not my place, Margret, and if you are her Matriarch, and you have chosen otherwise, I will abide by your decision. But I do not understand it."

"No?"

"He would have killed you. He would have betrayed you all."

"I know. I was there."

"Why allow his memory to be honored? Why allow his memory to be linked with Elena's? She was as a sister to you, and she never wavered."

"Can I point out that she was the only one who drew blood?"

Diora did not dignify the question with a response.

"Why does it matter to you, Diora? What difference does it make? He's dead."

"Only the living can give a death meaning."

"Don't quote Voyani wisdom at me."

The Serra fell silent. It was an obdurate silence, one that better suited Margret's temper than it did the Serra's.

"Why did you come? To argue? To tell me that I should inflict pain on an old woman who has been as constant as Elena for the whole of her life?"

"You inflict no pain on her that she does not already feel. You might even acknowledge the truth that you have forbidden her to acknowledge."

"Don't even try to tell me that you have her best interests at heart."

"No. I don't. But if you are to rule, is it not best that people understand what the price of betrayal *must* be, no matter how close to you that betrayer once was?"

"No."

"Margret—"

"No. You understand power among the clansmen. It's different. It *has* to be different. Diora—it's not just Donatella. If it were, if it were just her, you might be right. But it's all of us."

"He cost you Elena. Were it not for his—"

"I know that."

Diora fell silent at once.

Margret struggled to rein her voice in. It was too close to breaking. "It's funny. You—you're arguing with me as if you were—as if you were Arkosan. Do you know that?"

"I apologize if it offends."

"Of course it offends. But—" She took a deep breath. Held it. Exhaled. "I loved Nicu," she said quietly. "I grew up with him. We—Elena, Nicu and I—planned to marry when we were adults. We used to fight for space on the same laps. We used to argue over the same food. We used to defend each other, lie for each other, trust each other.

"Those men and women, those Arkosans—they were like parents to us. All of them. This is the beginning of a new life. A new future. Can I start it by telling them that he died as an enemy? That he died because he betrayed everything they believe in?"

"It is the truth."

"It is *one* truth. Maybe if I had been different, he might have been different as well. Maybe if men were allowed to be Matriarchs, maybe if men were allowed to rule, he would have been the leader he desired to be."

"You don't believe that."

"No, I don't. But I don't want to believe it. I want to believe that everything was his own choice. And because of that, I cannot trust my own motivation. I have to allow there is truth in that possibility."

"Why? I have no vested interest in his life, and I can clearly see—"

"Diora." She lifted a weary hand. "Why did you come here tonight?"

Diora bowed her head.

"Diora?"

"I came because you lied to your people."

"What? When?"

"Today. On the sands outside of the walls. You told them that you did not know where Nicu was."

"Why do you accuse me of lying?"

"Because you did lie. You do know."

Margret shrugged. "You came to accuse me of lying?"

"No. I came because I knew that you would take the ship to the City tonight. And I did not want to climb that ladder again."

Margret was absolutely silent for a moment. At last, she said, "I did not even know that I would have the ship to take."

"You do not know your people well enough, then. But I think you did know."

She shrugged. "Does it matter?"

"No. But I know why you go, Margret. Why you must

go. You should have gathered your people. I have watched them, and I have watched you; you take strength from each other when strength is needed. They would understand your decision. They would respect it. They would feel as you feel, measure for measure.

"But when I heard the lie in your voice, I knew that you would deny yourself even that. And I did not want you to go alone."

Margret closed her eyes. She felt the ground wobble slightly beneath her feet, as the earth had in Arkosa. She knew that she should order Diora to leave, knew also that if she did, the Serra would obey. But she allowed herself this one weakness. Because in truth she did not want to face Nicu on her own.

The ship of the Matriarch of Arkosa rose gently in the still of the night, beneath the Lady's fullest face.

The Serra was as silent and pale as the face of the moon. Her eyes were as dark as sky. But she was slender, diminutive, graceful; she was, in her fashion, gentle. Margret did not know how to approach her. She tried to speak, twice, but the words never passed her lips; she felt as awkward as she had the first time she had fallen in love.

And was she?

No. Not in love. Maybe in awe.

"I knew you lied," the Serra said, surprising Margret, "because I could hear it in your voice. It sounded so wrong, coming from you. I have heard lies all my life; they are part of survival in the High Court. Grace—and the illusion of beauty—does not easily accommodate truth; truth is blunt, and often brutal; it is a face that, once exposed, is unavoidable. When we speak a plain truth, we take a risk, always, because the truth lingers in the memory of both the speaker and the listener.

"We save our truths," she added softly. "As if they are valuable only when hidden. We hide our affection; we hide simple things. Love. The loyalty that comes not from duty but from other complicated desires."

She had not once looked up at Margret.

"You could hear a lie that no one else could hear. You know me that well."

The silence held for a moment longer than necessary. Margret understood that this was Diora's hesitation.

"I could hear a lie that no one else could hear, yes—but that truth and your supposition are not the same. I know you no better than the Arkosans among who you've made your life. I have seen things they will not see, but it is not the same.

"If Stavos lied to me, I would hear it. If Elena lied, I would hear it. If the Tyr'agar himself chose to ornament his words with deception, I would know, if I were present."

Margret frowned. "But—" She turned to look at the Serra Diora.

The Serra did not shrink from her inspection, but she turned at last to face the Matriarch of Arkosa, her face as pale, as distant, as the Lady's.

Margret understood, then.

"You are—you are saying—"

"I was born with a gift. And a curse."

"But—"

"I have never walked unarmed among your people. Even when I have set my dagger aside, I have always had a weapon, should I choose to use it."

And understanding was both sudden, like the strike of a knife, and gradual, an unfolding, a retelling of the story of their short days together.

"Your song. That day. The day I . . ." The day she had kicked the samisen from the Serra's lap. The day she had humiliated herself in front of her people.

Diora nodded. "I knew they would listen," she said. "I knew I could tell them my story, without words or with them, and they would feel everything that I could not say outside of the song."

"I never asked you why."

"Why?"

"Why you sang that song. You must know that the only person it saved was me."

"I know," she said softly. "But I think I was wrong, then. The ability to hear and the ability to understand are not the same. Your brother has a different gift, if I understand what was said by the healer."

She did not mention Evayne. Margret did not mention

her. But her shadow hung above them both, as welcome as the storm had been.

"But your brother understood. He came to me, the night of the storm. He stood in the cold, his teeth chattering, his knees shaking, because he pitied me. He thought I was alone."

Before Margret could ask—if she thought to ask at all—the Serra added, "And I was. You do him an injustice, to see him as a child."

"He is a child."

"Yes, but he is more than that. Had he been my brother . . ." her smile was almost rueful. Her expression had opened, as if it were the face of a fan, its pleats painted in delicate colors to suggest a story. "Had he been my brother, I would have been terrified for him, for he shows his weakness easily.

"But I would have loved him for the strength that allows him not to fear that weakness. I miss him."

Margret bowed her head. "I miss him, too. But I know that he'll come back. To me. To us."

"But not to me," the Serra said quietly. "I have a favor to ask of you, Matriarch."

"Matriarch? Why so formal?"

"When one asks a boon, one is always formal. It is easier, if that boon is refused, for all concerned."

Margret laughed. "There is nothing—almost nothing—I would not do for you. Ask."

"May I visit, when the war is over?"

"I would be happier if you simply asked if you could visit, with no conditions imposed."

Diora's smile was sweet, an echo of her brother's smile. It was the only warmth Margret had encountered this evening.

She said, "Almost no one else knows."

"Your gift?"

"My gift."

"Why are you telling me?"

"I am not entirely certain. Because I wanted you to know."

"Why?"

"Because truth *is* valuable. Because trust is valuable.

Maybe it is even necessary." She waited a moment, and then said, "The ship has stopped moving."

Margret knew. She covered her face with her hands, and then let those hands drop. They were heavy, a burden to her. They were also clumsy. Margret struggled with flint in the shadows, trying to coax light into being. She gave up.

Whispered a word. Drew a great circle in the air before her chest.

What flint could not cede her, magic did; her hands tingled in its faint wake. Power had never come so easily before. But she was Voyani; she understood that power had its price, and that the price was not to be paid lightly. When the lamp's wick, soaked with old oil, began to burn, she let the power go.

Felt it, curled like a cat tensed to strike, as it rested against her chest. The Heart of Arkosa was heavy.

She turned and walked the length of the cramped wagon, maneuvering between the large clay jugs that held life beneath their stoppers.

She paused by the table, found room to kneel against the crowded floorboards.

Diora came, wordless as her seraf, and took the lamp from Margret's hands. She held it steadily, and asked no questions. Margret nodded gruffly, and placed her right fingers along the edge of the bench, seeking the three fingerholds carved there.

There were small blades in each of the holes; Margret had not examined their edges in years, and wondered how sharp they were, and how clean. She closed her eyes, and ran her left fingers along the bench's short underside. Found the small knobs recessed into wood, five in all. She placed her fingers against them, and then, when the three blades failed to trigger, pressed them in, one by one, in a sequence that her mother had taught her.

There was a quiet click, but it was the only noise in the cabin.

The Serra Diora set the lamp upon the table and moved away.

The sitting bench farthest from the door creaked as Margret lifted it. It was pale and simple, unadorned by the carvings that the Northern merchants favored. But its purpose was not decorative.

Herbs were placed here; unguents, oils, and powders. Gold was here as well, although not much of it; Evallen had taken most of it when she had left the encampment for the last time. There was a silvered mirror, edges adorned with jade carvings; a bracelet, enamel cracked in three places, but obviously valued in spite of the damage time and the elements had done. She lifted it and smiled.

"My father's morning gift," she told Diora. The smile faded as she set it down again. "I should have known, when she left this, that she didn't think she'd be coming back."

She felt her mother's joy and sorrow, although it was wordless. Since she had returned to her people, the Matriarchs had fallen silent.

It was a mixed blessing.

She picked up and set down many things, as if this uncovering of stray moments of her past was a part of the ritual of opening the bench. Or perhaps some part of the reward.

But in the end, she picked up the one item that had no happy memories associated with it: the sword of Arkosa.

It was not particularly fine. The least of clansmen beggared themselves to buy swords superior to this one for their sons, that their sons might carve a name and a legacy for themselves in service to a Tor or, if very lucky, a Tyr.

But those weapons were meant to last a lifetime; those weapons were meant to take names, to become a part of a living legend.

This sword had nothing of that history, although it *had* history.

It was the executioner's blade, no more, no less. It was not long, it was not heavy. But it was meant to be drawn and raised for only one purpose.

No Matriarch could kill one of her own with a sword that she wore every day. Shedding a kinsman's blood was forbidden, both in spoken law and in the visceral laws that Arkosans lived by, day to day. Oh, it did happen—but Margret could count on one hand the number of times it had resulted in a death.

There was only one sword that was, in theory, allowed to mete out justice. And what woman could kill her own, and wear that reminder, day in, day out?

Only a madwoman, and if the Voyani were passionate, they were not—for the most part—insane.

She closed the bench slowly, and then stood, girding herself with the sword's workmanlike belt. The clasp was dull and tarnished; Evallen had had little use for the sword, but was uncomfortable enough with its presence that she had taken no care for its upkeep.

Margret hoped that the blade was sharp.

She did not want to draw the sword, but she did; she held it out in full view of the fire's face, and she examined its edge carefully.

"What are you doing, Serra?"

Diora looked up; she was rummaging through the piles that lay against the far wall. "I am choosing blankets."

It was not what Margret expected to hear, although it was, in fact, what the Serra was doing.

"Are you almost done?"

"Yes, Matriarch. If you are ready?" She walked back to the table, blankets dangling over either side of her left arm. There were at least two.

"We don't need the lamp." Margret took a breath. Forced it into the recesses of her chest. It was cool, not cold. She sheathed the sword, and walked to the cabin's closed door.

As she touched its surface, she hesitated. "There is a terrible irony in all of this," she said at last.

Diora waited patiently.

"Every time a Matriarch invokes the Heart of Arkosa *in* the heart of Arkosa, she has—since the founding—been forced to—to offer a sacrifice of sorts to the City."

"Margret—"

"I knew of it. I dreaded it. I did not tell Elena. I could not tell Adam." Her hand was shaking; the flat of wood beneath her palm was not steadying enough to prevent that.

"But it only had to be done to close the City. I didn't understand what that meant. I still don't."

"Margret," Diora said softly, "I do not judge your people."

"I know. *I* do. Me." Her eyes were wide when she looked over her shoulder to Diora. "We performed the libations of offering to the Lady: wine, water and blood. But each of those were placed in a furrow in the earth, and we asked for the earth to guard our City from intruders and notice until the time when we could return to claim it.

"And this *is* that time. This time, I have no offering to make, no ceremony to perform. I was so afraid of it, Diora."

She shook her head. "But ceremony or no, blood is still being shed, and it is still the blood of Arkosa."

"It was not . . . not to the Lady that those oblations were offered," Diora said faintly. "And . . . I believe that the offering that was made was not made in vain." But her expression was so neutral Margret knew she would not speak of what she meant.

She opened the door into the coldest night she would ever know.

Let me kill him, Margret. It was hard not to say the words. She meant them, although she was not a killer by nature or vocation. Her life in the Courts had taught her exactly what the value of a life was, and if that had not, her life among the clansmen would have taught her what the value of an enemy's life was.

She knew that she could raise sword and execute this man without remorse, without regret.

But she knew that it was not a gift she could offer.

She shivered as the cold emptied the room of warmth. Margret's back receded through the humble frame of the cabin's door.

Diora followed quietly, drawing the blankets to her chest and clasping her hands beneath their hanging folds.

When she gained the night air, she stopped. The ship did not move, but it was nowhere near the ground; it was above the City. In the light of the moon, the streets below were only barely visible. But the outlines of towers stood, like immovable sentinels, against the night sky, a veil against stars that trailed too near the earth.

All but one.

It was too close to be remote, and it shed light instead of absorbing it.

A great, glowing Sphere stood at its center, contained by obsidian claws.

And beneath it, shuddering, knees curled into his chest for warmth, sat Margret's cousin. His face was hidden by the hanging hem of his hood; his hands had been pulled from the dangling length of sleeve, although she could see the jut of his elbows in the stretch of fabric above them. He did not seem to notice either the ship or the Matriarch; he was lost to the cold and his own misery.

Margret grabbed the rail with one hand; she gestured, with a curt, sharp motion of head, for Diora to do the same. When they were both anchored in this fashion, she brought the ship to the edge of the tower's flat height. And then, slowly and carefully, she crossed between the two. Diora followed, but far less fearlessly. She was grateful for the night because she could not see with her own eyes just how far a fall a misstep would cause.

But she did not misstep.

That, at least, her training made almost impossible.

Margret cleared her throat.

Nicu looked up. In the moon's light, his expression would not have been visible—but in the unnatural light of the Sphere, it was. His relief was profound; it made him look like a four-year-old boy who had been lost for so long he had almost given up any hope of being found.'

Against her will, she felt pity.

For him. For Margret. For Margret who flinched visibly and seemed to shrink back.

"D–did 'Lena s–send you?"

"Elena?"

"S–she was w–with the other c–creature. S–she watched the—the tower rise. I tried t–to catch her, 'Gret. I tried. But s–she was t–too far away. I'm sorry. I'm s–so sorry."

"What other creature?"

"A–after you l–left another creature came. I–I thought y–you would know. H–he must b–be on our side. He fought Ishavriel."

"Another creature?"

Diora had seen men plead for mercy. She had seen men scream. She had seen them struggle, and crawl, and beg. She had felt pity for them, and contempt for their weakness, for their inability to accept with grace the inevitable.

And because she had seen these things, she had thought, until this moment, that she would be immune to Nicu's pain and fear.

But this was worse. He did not even understand what he faced. His ignorance, his pathos, were things she had not expected.

"Nicu," Margret said, her voice so terribly gentle, "what happened to Andreas? What happened to Carmello?"

"Ishavriel k–killed them. I t–told him not to. But he killed them."

"And Elena?"

"S–she disappeared. With the other one. They were standing there—" He pointed with his head; he did not have the strength to lift his arms, to place them in the cold of his sleeves. "And they vanished."

Margret was silent.

"I–its c–cold, 'Gret."

Diora stepped forward with the blankets she had gathered. She had only taken two, but, hands shaking, she passed them to Nicu. He stared at them with a blind gratitude that was almost physically painful to observe, but he did not touch them; his arms were still wrapped around his chest.

She should have thrown them at his feet and let him freeze. She should have turned away with the icy contempt only a Serra can convey. She should have told him that they were here to execute him for his treason, not to save him.

But it was cold, and the words froze before they left her. She felt a burning contempt for this man, this boy, that did nothing to ease the night's chill. And yet.

As gently as she could—and she could be very, very gentle—the Serra Diora walked to his side, and wrapped the blankets around him, tucking them beneath his shaking chin.

She rose and turned away, but there was no relief in that, for she came face-to-face with Margret, and saw that Margret was as frozen as she had been. The sword was in its sheath.

Neither woman spoke.

" 'Gret?"

Margret closed her eyes. She closed her eyes, and her knees, which had locked the moment she'd placed her second foot on the flat of the tower, buckled as if the weight above them was too vast to even contemplate.

She threw her arms around her cousin's neck.

He wept.

And Diora, whose hearing was so acute, became aware, again, of why her gift was a curse.

For Margret was weeping too. "Nicu, Nicu, Nicu."

"I–I'm s–so–sorry. I'm s–sorry. 'Gret—I–I d–didn't know—"

She placed her fingers on his lips. Nothing Diora had seen had prepared her for how gentle the Matriarch was capable of being, and that gentleness did what no amount of anger or strength could do. Although she was aware of the rules of life in the desert, she wept also, but her tears were silent.

"'Lena is still alive," she told him softly.

"W–where? W–where is s–she?"

"I don't know. But I know it. Here."

"H–how?"

"The Heart," Margret said softly, as if to a very young child.

Yes, Nicu was that, at this moment. The years of experience, the complicated lessons and frustrations of adult life, had been stripped away by the night, by failure, by shock. All that he was, the Serra Diora could plainly see: a child. An Arkosan child.

And she knew what value the Arkosans placed, inexplicable and profound, on their children.

She knew, then, that Margret could not kill her cousin.

And knew, as well, as if for a moment she had been burdened with the gift of sight, that she could not afford to fail. This was her test.

And it was as bitter a test, in the end, as Diora's had been. As scarring.

No, she thought. *No. He earned his death. He betrayed Margret. He betrayed Elena. He lied to those who loved him best. This is* not *the same.*

But she heard his gulping breath, his shattered voice, heard his regret and his terrible, terrible faith. Both of these, for Margret. And they were genuine. He did not dissemble; she heard everything that his voice had to offer; nothing was hidden.

It did not occur to him that Margret had come to do anything but save his life.

"D–don't t–tell my mother," he whispered.

"Never. I will never tell Donatella anything. You never told my mother how you got the scar on your left arm."

His laugh was shaky, but it, too, was genuine. "But she b–beat y–you anyway."

"Hush."

The Serra Diora closed her eyes; the few tears that had not yet fallen adorned her cheeks as her lids shut them out. The night was cold; she wrapped her arms around her chest and realized after a moment that she was rocking, empty-armed, in the clear night, the first night of Arkosa.

"Diora," Margret said, gathering her strength as if she had never shed it. "Leave us."

Diora nodded. It would be a relief not to bear witness to what would—what *must*—occur.

She turned toward the waiting ship. She even managed to take a step before she was drawn back to the two cousins who cuddled beneath the light of this captive moon, this glowing orb.

"Margret—"

"Leave us."

She had come in the dark of night because she had not wanted Margret to face her cousin alone, and if her Southern upbringing had in no way prepared her for *this* death the resolve that had brought her here was one she was unwilling to abandon.

" 'Gret—it's c–cold. C–can I g–go home?"

"Hush, Nicu. Yes. Yes, you can go home now."

He struggled a moment; his arms were bound beneath robes and blankets and he did not want to free them. Margret helped him to his feet, and he swayed there, his legs almost useless.

She bore his weight as they turned their back on the Sphere.

Diora began to sing.

She had never thought to sing this song for a man—any man, anywhere—and had she, she would never have imagined that man would be this one.

But the cradle song came to her lips, and she underlay it with the command that was her birthright.

The sun has gone down, has gone down, my dear, Na'nicu, Na'nicu child.

He looked up at the sound of her voice, his face alight with a smile that broke her heart. But broken or no, she had the strength to sing.

The Lady is watching, is watching my love,
Na'nicu, Na'nicu child,
And she knows that the heart that is guarded and scarred is still pierced by the darkest of fear.

To sing him to sleep.

The time it may come, it may come my love,
Na'nicu, Na'nicu my own,
When the veil will fall and separate us,
And I'll bury you when you are grown.
For the heart, the heart is a dangerous place, it is breaking with joy and with fear,
Worse, though, if you'd never been born to us,
Na'nicu, Na'nicu, my dear.

He stumbled as Margret walked, bearing more and more of his weight. She bore it without complaint, without comment, as if it were the most natural thing in the world.

And Nicu's steps grew smaller and smaller under the thrall of Diora's song, until they ceased completely.

"Mama?"

The Serra closed her eyes. **"Sleep, Nicu. Sleep."**

She took the cold away with the force of her command.

And then she walked across the flat of the stone tower, her vision suddenly treacherous. She turned once she'd reached the rails, and gripped wood that should never have been so cold in one shaking hand.

She watched as Margret struggled a moment longer with her cousin. He did not stir.

Margret was weeping openly now as she bore his full weight.

"I don't want this," she whispered, looking up to Diora with all of the anger she had hidden from Nicu. "I *do not* want this."

"You are the Matriarch of Arkosa," Diora replied, as gently as she could. But that was all she said.

The Lady, in the desert, knew no mercy. Her light was bright, and if it allowed shadow, that shadow did not fall upon Nicu's exposed face.

The muscles that creased his forehead, that broke the line of his lips so pitifully, relaxed.

Margret bent down and very gently kissed his right

cheek; she touched his left with her hand. "Nicu," she said softly, so softly that had Diora been any other woman, she would not have heard the words. "Wait for me. Wait for Elena. We will come to you in time, and we will forgive you everything then.

"We never stopped loving you, Nicu."

His lips curved in a smile, child's smile, and not even the line of his beard could invoke the specter of the adult he had become.

Margret struggled a little longer with his weight, and because she carried all of it, she labored. But Diora knew better, now, than to offer help with this last burden.

It was all she would have of him.

Margret made no sound at all as she stopped between the tower and the ship.

With infinite care, she pushed her cousin over the tower's edge.

If the Lady knew no mercy, the Serra Diora did.

He did not wake to cry out.

EPILOGUE

14th of Misteral, 427 AA
Tor Arkosa, Sea of Sorrows

They buried Nicu two days later.

The Matriarch of Arkosa rose in the morning and set out to the City, and when she returned, her ship casting a sharp, harsh shadow across the lands beneath the open sky, she carried his body.

She wept when she carried him from the wagon, but although the plank that led to the ground was wobbly and thin, she desired—and accepted—no help. Stavos waited at the foot of the ramp in silence, his wife by his side; Tamara stood, hand in hand, with Donatella.

Margret did not find Andreas or Carmello, although she found a single sword glinting in the upturned earth near the base of the first tower; the passage of stone and soil had twisted it almost beyond recognition, but she carried it with her when she returned—a reminder of the cost of the war.

As if Nicu were not enough.

Donatella took her son from the arms of the Matriarch, and only when she had gathered his limp and broken body in the cradle of her arms did she finally weep, and her disconsolate cry woke in the others the grief of loss and endless separation; no eye remained dry in the wake of her pain.

She never again questioned Margret about the end of her son, and what Margret knew, she carried with her for a long, long time in the impenetrable silence of a Matriarch.

The Serra Diora and Jewel ATerafin attended the last rites of Nicu of Arkosa; the rest of the strangers did not, although had they desired to do so, they would have been mutely accepted.

It was a far cry between acceptance and welcome. And silent, they knew it: Lord Celleriant who had ridden the winds to battle the Serpent of the storm, Kallandras of Senniel College, who had joined him, Avandar, the domicis that no one—not even his master—fully trusted, and the stag who had fulfilled his promise and returned the seraf Ramdan to his mistress.

The Serra Teresa di'Marano and the Havallan Matriarch likewise chose to absent themselves; they stood beneath the lengthening shadows of the City's walls in the dusk.

Yollana took the last of the tobacco from her small jar and carefully filled the flat bowl of her pipe. She gazed not toward the City, but rather toward the river that ran through it.

"We will see life return to the desert in our lifetimes," she said, the stem of the pipe hovering, untouched, near her cracked lips.

Teresa nodded quietly.

"Will you stay in Tor Arkosa, Teresa?"

"Will you?"

The older woman snorted. It drew a smile from her companion. "Will you take water?"

Yollana shrugged. "Drinking water is no longer in short supply. Yes, I'll take water if it will give you something to do with those pretty hands."

Teresa poured. There was, in the movements of her hands, the grace of a life spent at Court; she spilled nothing and when she placed the bowl at Yollana's feet, it defied the broken ground to stand completely still.

"What will your niece do?"

"She will go North."

Yollana nodded.

"And you?"

"I will go North as well."

The silence fell again; Yollana lit her pipe as she watched the shades of color begin to deepen the sky.

"Matriarch."

Yollana raised a brow, no more. But after a moment, she gestured. "What?"

"Did you know what would happen here?"

"No."

"Ah. Do you know what will follow?"

"You ask too many questions, Serra."

Teresa smiled as well. "Yes. But I am no longer Serra here, and I think it will be my fate to travel with the Matriarch of Havalla for some time yet."

"I will be in your debt."

"Yes."

Yollana raised a brow. "There have always been two ways to discharge unwanted debt. Don't forget it." But the rough words carried no threat.

They turned to look North, beyond the City's curved walls.

"The Lord of Night will know," Teresa said quietly. "If he does not already know, he will be waiting for you. You must travel in haste."

"Aye, I know. I know it. But Havalla is not yet ready to face the test that Arkosa has faced." She grimaced. "Your child will travel North, to meet with the armies of the young kai Leonne."

"Yes."

"That will be the first battle, the first true test. I will travel with her for a time."

Teresa's dark brows rose. "You will not have that time, Matriarch. I am not—"

"You are not Matriarch. Had I known what I know now, my choices would have been no different—I would have lived in greater fear, that is all. I will have to decide what word is carried to Lyserra and Corrona."

Teresa's expression did not change. At all.

Yollana's chuckle was dry as the weed that burned to embers in her pipe. "What did you expect, Teresa? Does Callesta know, intimately, what actions Lamberto takes? No. Men have died to make sure that it remains so. And yet their fates are tied in this war. The Voyani are no different. This has happened too soon," she added quietly. "I do not understand the timing. We are not gathered; our people are scattered across the Terreans of Mancorvo and Averda, waiting word.

"Maria and Elsarre will not be prepared for the journey that Margret has undertaken."

Teresa's silence was forced.

Yollana snorted. "I'm in the mood to talk. Ask; let manners be damned."

"The Lord of Night has returned," the Serra said, hesitation in her manner, but not in the clarity of her voice.

"Yes." The word was short and testy.

"Yollana—even I, who am outsider, have heard the word homeland leave the lips of the Voyani of *all* families before."

Yollana shrugged. "So does the word love. What of it?"

"If there was ever a time to return to such a home as this, would it not be now?"

"Teresa," Yollana said, slapping her leg with a loose fist, "do you think that Margret *knew* what would happen here? Do you think that she even dreamed of this?"

"I . . . do not know. But seeing it, I cannot imagine that such a City could be forgotten."

"Imagine it, girl. What we have thought, what we have hoped for, was so much smaller than this. An enlarging of our lore, a strengthening of our power, an opening of the caches of weapons and spells that were once used *against* the Lord of Night. Do you honestly think that Cities rose out of the lifeless grave in our dreams?

"We *knew* what lay beneath the sands," she added. "I knew. I . . . have heard its voice. Teresa, I do not need to tell you that it is death to speak of this."

"No."

"Good. I owe you this; you will be with me, I think, until the end. Yours or mine. I would grant you the blood, but I do not think you would accept it; it bears other burdens and other responsibilities."

"I am honored that you would consider it."

"No, you're not. You're no one's fool." The old woman's smile was brief and fierce, but it was as affectionate a smile as Teresa had yet seen grace her face. "Where was I? Ah. What I heard. What *I* knew lay buried in the sands. Old chambers. Hidden burial grounds. Ancient artifacts. The lore of the dead; the language, the writings, the songs.

"But this? This is like preparing a body for burial and having it rise, whole and living, before a spade of dirt can be turned. I could not have foreseen this. Not alone," she added softly. She shook her head.

"And are you ready now?"

"I? I least of all." She emptied her pipe carefully. "Least of all.

"I don't know why I endanger your life by speaking to you." She put her pipe away. It seemed that she had finished speaking, but after a long pause, she continued. "Until the war for the Dominion has been fought and decided, I will make no trek into the Sea of Sorrows, and Havalla will remain, interred and silent, beneath the desert sands." She closed her eyes. "I do not know what Margret did to lift the City from its grave."

Opened them again. "I would not wish the passage to the homelands upon my daughters. If it is possible, I will return, and I will do what must be done."

She shivered then.

And the Serra Teresa heard the edge of fear in the words, and was surprised by it; Yollana's rough voice usually gave very little away.

"If you ever meet a woman named Evayne," the Matriarch said quietly, "run away. Run as fast as you can, and listen to nothing she says."

"I have met her, Matriarch," the Serra replied.

"Then you, too, are damned, in your fashion."

But Teresa shook her head. "She saved Adam."

"Sometimes death is a mercy."

15th of Misteral, 427 AA
Averalaan Aramarelas, Houses of Healing

Healer Levec was a busy man.

And being busy made him perpetually grouchy. His brows were a single dark line across the bridge of a square, workman's nose. His brow itself was a set of furrows, and the lines around his eyes and his lips were the subtle scars left by ill humor.

He taught no classes for three days, and for this reason—if no other—his students were grateful to the mysterious stranger who slept in the tower rooms that were forbidden to all but the masters.

But they were damn curious as well; they whispered and placed bets and made suggestions that would have curled the toes of a more prudish man. They had the intelligence not to do it when Levec was in earshot, but they cared nothing for the presence of strangers, no matter how finely attired they happened to be: strangers were Levec's problem, and no matter how rich you were, if you angered Levec, he'd just as soon let you die in the streets as raise a hand to save your worthless life.

Daine, a healer in service to House Terafin, was painfully aware of these things; he'd spent many years as one of Levec's beloved—and much cursed—students. And he knew—as well as any other student could—that the tower rooms were for Levec's personal use. Patients and clients were *not* welcome there.

Finch sidled up to Daine. "Are you *sure* he wanted us all here?"

"With Levec," Daine replied, offering her a rare smile, "it's impossible to make a mistake. He's pretty blunt."

Carver snorted. Angel stood against a wall, hands shoved into his belt, a lock of hair hanging just over the edges of long lashes. He glowered at anyone who happened to come too close—which was easy to do; the hall was crowded.

"These people can't all be students, can they?" Jester asked.

Daine laughed. "They're all students. Not all of them are healer-born, but they're all here to learn the medical arts."

Arann was the only person present who had come in his House uniform; he wasn't given much opportunity to change. Ellerson wore the distinguished uniform of the Terafin wing, and he stood like a patrician's servant, but the occasional snort of suppressed laughter dulled the appearance of dignity.

Only Teller was silent.

"How much longer are we going to have to wait?" Carver looked over his shoulder. It was a habit he'd picked up in the last couple of months. Finch hated it. It made her nervous.

Then again, these days there wasn't much that didn't.

"We wait," Daine replied, with quiet dignity, "until Levec is ready."

"Oh, good. And I suppose our report to The Terafin will wait on Levec as well." Finch grimaced. "Sorry. You didn't deserve that."

Daine had the grace to look pained. "Healers are only

a little less valuable than Makers," he said at last. "And they're not used to being hurried."

"That means yes," Jester added helpfully.

"Well, if it'll take your mind off The Terafin," Carver said, "we were followed."

Finch swore. Loudly. Then she turned and smacked Carver's chest. "Don't *do* that."

Carver shrugged off her blow as if it were entirely ineffectual. "Suit yourself. But we were."

"Carver," Ellerson said, speaking in the voice reserved for wayward students. He used that a lot.

Carver shrugged again.

"Daine, I really don't think we should be here. Teller, help me out please. You *know* what Gabriel is going to say if we're late. Again."

But Teller looked past her, to the foot of the steps.

One by one, they all did.

The city's most infamous curmudgeon stood there, arms folded tightly across his chest in the suddenly silent hall, his brow dovetailing in an exquisite expression of pure annoyance. "*If* you've finished, ATerafin?"

He led them up the stairs. It was obvious to Finch that Daine was shocked, because when Levec stepped aside and lifted his arm in the universal "go that way" gesture, the younger healer froze, staring.

Which did nothing to improve Levec's demeanor. "I see that a life of ease in one of the Ten Houses hasn't improved your wit, boy. Didn't you hear the ATerafin? You're on a short schedule. Move!"

Daine flushed. For a moment, anger transformed his features so thoroughly, Finch wasn't sure that *he* was Daine. She did not like the look.

Levec, however, was immune to it, and that gave Daine time to find his face again. He mumbled an apology which was about as graceless as Levec's curt command, and led the way up the steps, the fall of his feet just a little too heavy.

But Finch, following at the rear, saw the old bear of a healer turn his gaze upon Daine's stiff back; she saw something like anger in his face, but saw more—pity, pride, and regret. She managed to look away before he noticed she was staring instead of walking.

They stopped on the large landing just outside of a set of fine doors, ignoring the steps that continued up to the heights. Levec pushed his way to the front of the gathered crowd and lifted a hand, demanding—and more notably receiving—silence.

"I will offer one warning. My patient is *not* to be touched. You may speak to him, you may answer his questions, you may ask questions of your own—but if you touch him, I'll break your arms. Is that clear?"

Daine frowned. "Healer Levec?" he said, raising his hand.

Levec did not seem to notice anything unusual about the gesture, although Daine was clearly well past the student stage of his life. "Daine?"

"Is—is the patient a student?"

"Very good. Yes. And no."

"But—" His eyes widened. Whatever he'd been about to say, he thought better of it. But he audibly swallowed a question as Levec turned and very gently opened the door.

Finch had never thought about what the rooms of the House's master would look like. She'd seen Alowan's room on a number of occasions, and it was clutter personified—so unlike the healerie he presided over, she'd given up trying to understand how the powerful chose to live.

But these rooms were sparsely furnished; the ceilings were tall enough to be imposing, and the windows were clear but finely crafted. The floor was a dark, dark oak; the beams in the ceiling, exposed to inspection, darker still. There was a door on the far side of the room, and against the wall beside it, a desk that was closed. She suspected, given the brass-plated keyhole, that it was also locked.

But the centerpiece of the room was definitely the bed: it was larger than Jay's from headboard to foot, and wider again by half. Great, thick comforters were carefully arranged across it—they were as simple as the room, but no less expensive. They were undyed cotton; the counterpane—if there was one—was nowhere in sight.

But lost in those comforters was a young man.

His head was propped up by pillows thick as Arann's chest, and his hair, dark and wavy, was spread across those illows in wet locks. He had either been bathed recently, r he'd been sweating a lot—and judging by the look of he rest of him, Finch was willing to bet on the latter.

There was a pitcher beside the bed, on a table that was bviously meant to be reached by an attendant, not a atient.

And that attendant now crossed the room to lift it and our water into a solid, silver mug.

"Adam," Levec said, "these are the people I spoke of." Iis voice was not a voice that was easily gentled, but the dge was off his growl.

Finch frowned. Levec was speaking *Torra*. She took a loser look at the boy; his skin was dark, his eyes dark as ell. He was a Southerner.

Finch, Carver, and Teller spoke Torra; Angel, Arann, nd Jester didn't, although they'd at least picked up the urse words over the years. It would have been hard not o; Jay used them liberally.

The boy in the bed sat up. Levec snapped something that as clearly meant to be a warning, but the word was low nough that it didn't carry.

"Are you Jewel ATerafin's family?"

Finch froze.

The boy repeated the question.

"Do you speak Weston?" she asked softly.

He frowned apologetically. "I speak some—Weston?—f the merchant tongue. But only a little."

Angel stepped forward, and found the bulky form of Iealer Levec in his path, his expression grim. Finch caught p with her den-mate and grabbed his sleeve in a pincer-ght grip. He tried, and failed, to shake her off.

"He said Jewel ATerafin, didn't he?"

She nodded.

"Can't he speak Weston?"

"Not really."

Angel swore. A lot.

Apparently, the boy had also learned the essentials of a ew language: the curse words.

Teller approached the boy quietly and slowly, by-passing evec by the simple expedient of choosing the other side f the bed.

He stopped more than an arm's length from where the

boy now sat, hands raised above the comforters tha
hemmed him in. "Yes," Teller told him in serviceable—
though accented—Torra. "We are her family. How—how
do you know her? Have you seen her recently?"

The boy nodded.

"Was she well?"

"Well?"

"Was she all right? Was she injured? Was she in
trouble?"

"We—we were *all* in trouble," the boy replied. "There
was a rainstorm in the Sea of Sorrows." He winced and
fell silent, turning his face toward Levec's broad back.

"Jewel ATerafin was uninjured," Levec said brusquely.
"When I traveled to the South, I traveled in haste, and
returned in haste. We had little time to converse."

"She pulled me from the tunnels," Adam added quietly.

"Tunnels?" Carver's voice was lower, and sharper, than
Teller's; it demanded attention. "In a sea?"

"The Sea of Sorrows is the name—one of the names—
for the desert. Next time, pay attention to your geography,"
Finch snapped. Carver shrugged.

"Finch, what is he saying?" Angel demanded.

"I think he's saying Jay saved his life."

"When?"

"Angel." She lifted the hand that wasn't hanging on to
him, and turned it, palm out, in front of his face. "We're
trying to find out."

Levec frowned. "How do you know that, boy?" he said,
as if the rest of their conversation hadn't taken place. O
wasn't important enough to pay attention to.

"I heard her."

"You must have been dreaming." Finch could tell, by
the sudden unease in Levec's frown, that he was having
second thoughts about his invitation to the ATerafin den
of Jewel.

"I wasn't dreaming," the boy replied confidently. Quietly. "I couldn't see anything, but I could hear *her*. She
was . . . upset."

"What do you mean, upset?"

"Carver, have a care." Daine, silent until that moment,
joined Finch. He did not touch Angel, but he stood close
enough that he could. If it was necessary.

Finch had never heard Daine speak anything other than
Veston, but it didn't surprise her that he could.

"She thought I was dead. She thought I was dead but—"
Ie shook his head and turned, to Teller. "It didn't matter.
he was *angry*. I think she was shouting at the water. I
eard her. She curses a lot."

In spite of herself, Finch laughed.

"She thinks I'm a child," he added, when Finch's laugh-
er had dwindled. "But . . . she thought you were children
s well. Not now. But then. When she first found you."

"Adam, I think that you have taxed yourself enough for
ne day. It is time that the guests left."

But he didn't want them to leave. Finch saw the sudden
neliness in his face, the sudden fear of isolation.

Teller saw it, too. He made no move to obey Levec, and
eller rarely antagonized anyone.

"She thought about you, I think," Adam told Teller. He
niled hesitantly when he realized that they had no inten-
on of obeying Levec. "She came to us in the Lady's fire.
he helped us save the Lady's waters from the Lord of
ight."

They were all silent then.

"She rides a great horned beast; she walks beside a crea-
ire that even our stories don't mention. She argues with
er—her servant. All the time."

Finch laughed again. "That would be Jay. I mean Jewel."

"She didn't have a great horned beast the last time I
iecked," Carver added.

This time, Ellerson chose to add his voice to the quiet
iscussion. "Where did you meet them?"

"Just outside of the Tor Leonne, during the Festival of
ie Moon."

Ellerson nodded grimly. "Then she made it that far
outh."

Adam frowned. "I think—I hope—she has made it far-
ier. She was traveling with—with the Matriarch of Arkosa.
ut I'm forbidden to speak of where she's going."

"How did you arrive here?"

"I—" This time he turned to look at Levec.

Levec rolled his eyes. Nodded.

"I'm not certain. I heard the Serra Diora speak to me. I
lt my sister's hand on my chest. And I felt Levec carry

me from the cold into this place. But I didn't see wha happened." Tears had started to run from his eyes, but h did not weep.

Angel started to ask questions; Teller took them an made them intelligible, cushioning the harsh, sharp word in translation. Adam answered them as clearly as he could and Teller again conveyed the meaning of words to th least patient member of their den. While they spoke, Finc disentangled her fingers from her den-mate's sleeve, an quietly joined Teller.

He watched them speak to the boy, waiting quietl There was energy, eagerness, anger, and desire in the me and women of House Terafin—who seemed, to Levec, t be little more than children, no matter how old they were– as they surrounded the young Annagarian.

He wondered who would be the first to break his edic Not the pale-haired, sullen one; not the dark-haired ma whose Torra came so easily. Not the young man who at tempted to wedge humor between the seriousness of hi words. The quiet man, perhaps. Or the girl.

He did not like the patriciate. In the city, only those wit the weight of nobility behind them chose to wield thei weight in the Houses of Healing. Or chose to try.

But these?

The streets that had birthed them were at the root o who they had become. And Daine, healer-born and traine had somehow been absorbed by those roots.

Evayne, he thought heavily.

His eyes wandered to the boy. For three days, that bo had lain abed weeping; had grabbed Levec's hands or arm if they came within reach. Were it not for his weakene state, Levec would have had trouble prying himself free He had asked, over and over again, for his sister, or hi aunt, or his cousin, his voice quailing with a piteous terro

Not even Levec was entirely proof against it.

Do you know what this boy could be, Evayne?

Yes. I know it well. But I know what he must become, i he is to reach the potential you see.

I do not play games with the lives of my students.

Then do not take him as a student, Levec. If he is onl healer here, it will be costly in ways you cannot conceive o

He is part of the war. His part will not be clear until some years have passed—but if he is not prepared when the time comes . . .

Adam was weeping again.

And this time, the young woman who seemed to speak for the den reached out and very gently wiped the tears from his face.

He grabbed her hand in his; from a distance, Levec could see how white his knuckles had become.

But she did not flinch, did not turn away. Did not disentangle herself.

Who is he, Evayne?

He is the brother of the last of the Arkosan Matriarchs.

Levec walked to where Finch now sat. "It appears that attentiveness is not taught within the great Houses. Or do you think that your House name will protect you?"

She looked up, startled, and then looked down at the hand that was now captive.

"Adam," he said, as gently as he possibly could.

Adam clung.

"Adam, you know why you must not do this."

He refused to look up; refused to meet Levec's eyes.

But Levec could see the change in his features, a slight widening and narrowing of eyes. Gods, the boy was talented.

He waited a moment longer, and then said, "I will not take her from you, Adam, for more than a few minutes. I am a man of my word. But I need to speak with her."

Adam swallowed. With obvious effort, he let go; the struggle wasn't pretty in a boy of his age.

Finch drew her hand away, but only when she had retreated far enough from the bed that she could turn her back to the boy did she begin to try to massage blood back into her pale fingers.

"Healer Levec?"

"ATerafin. If it comforts you, I believe that Jewel ATerafin has been busy enough surviving that she could not wisely send messages back and forth with her domicis."

"I bet she hasn't even thought about it." She tried, and failed, to keep the bitterness out of the words.

"I would not know. She was holding the boy's body in her arms when I arrived. She was cut and bruised, her cheek was red with dried blood. I don't think she was even aware of her injuries—and no, before you panic, they were *not* life-threatening. At least not her life." He smiled at her expression before he continued.

"She thought he was dead, but she wouldn't let go of him." His face lost its harsh edges as he gazed into the distance of that memory. "She cannot return yet," he added quietly, "but I wished you to know that she is still alive, still fighting in her peculiar way."

"Thank you for that."

"Don't thank me."

Finch held her breath; she heard the give and take of the dialogue that otherwise occupied the room. "Why did you *really* send for us?"

"That boy has a raw power that I have never seen."

She turned to look at Adam, wan and forlorn on the bed, and raised a skeptic's brow. "That doesn't have much to do with us."

"No?" He looked at the hand she was still massaging.

She grimaced. "I wasn't thinking," she said lamely.

"What a surprise."

"What—what do you want from us?"

"I must ask a favor of you."

"Of *us?*"

"Yes. I realize that sounds surprising. But . . . I wish you to take the boy under your wing."

"What?"

"I have seen how Daine has fared in House Terafin, among your den."

"But—but—"

"But?"

"Jay decides who's in, and who's out."

"And that is your answer?"

"Wait—no." She lifted her hand, stared at it a moment. "No, it's not. Look—maybe you don't understand the position *we're* in. The House—it's mobilizing for—for—"

"War?"

Her feet suddenly became very interesting.

"I'm not a fool, ATerafin. The House has been mobilizing, as you call it, for some time, and at least one of its members was foolish enough to injure one of *mine.*" And he looked up, past her face, to where Daine now stood. By

Teller's side. "It is not spoken of, but it is acknowledged. The House will war when The Terafin dies."

"Yes. And that's exactly why we can't take someone in. Not now. It wouldn't be right. He's—he's just a boy."

"And you were just a girl, your Teller just a boy, when you were left to fend for yourselves in the hundred holdings."

"But here, he's safe." She watched as Teller bent over the bed, speaking slowly and softly, hovering just out of reach. "In House Terafin—"

"ATerafin."

She looked up and met his eyes. Before she could look away again, he caught her chin and held it firmly.

"I am willing to trust you with that boy. That should not come as a surprise; I believe that Jewel ATerafin was willing to trust you with the House."

"But—Healer Levec." She swallowed and then raised her chin out of the cup of his fingers, straightening her young shoulders. "People have already died. Some by poison, and some by steel. I'm sure we'll see magic before things are decided one way or the other."

"Yes."

"He's what—fourteen? Fifteen? He doesn't speak Weston, and I don't think he's ever lived in a city—any city—before."

"He hasn't."

"Any other House would be safer."

"It is precisely because House Terafin is not safe that I ask this favor."

"I don't understand."

"You don't have to understand," he said gently. The corners of his lips turned down in a frown. "But he needs to learn what you alone are capable of teaching him, and I believe that it is not only a worthwhile risk, but a necessary one.

"If you do not wish to do this, you have only to leave, and to leave him here. Walk away, Finch ATerafin. Don't look back."

She drew a breath. "It would be better for him."

"Would it? Decide, then."

She turned away from him and walked back to join her den. He watched.

He knew what her answer would be, for Adam caught her hands in his again, and she did not demur, did not draw back. She had, he thought, a foolishly soft heart for a woman upon whom so much rested.

And in spite of himself, he liked her. Liked her den. Even liked the short-tempered, unkempt woman who commanded their loyalty and their very tangled love.

Who is the boy, Evayne?

He is the future ruler of Tor Arkosa. And if he cannot learn to navigate the treacherous waters of politics, magery, and war, he will not survive to become the healer you envision.